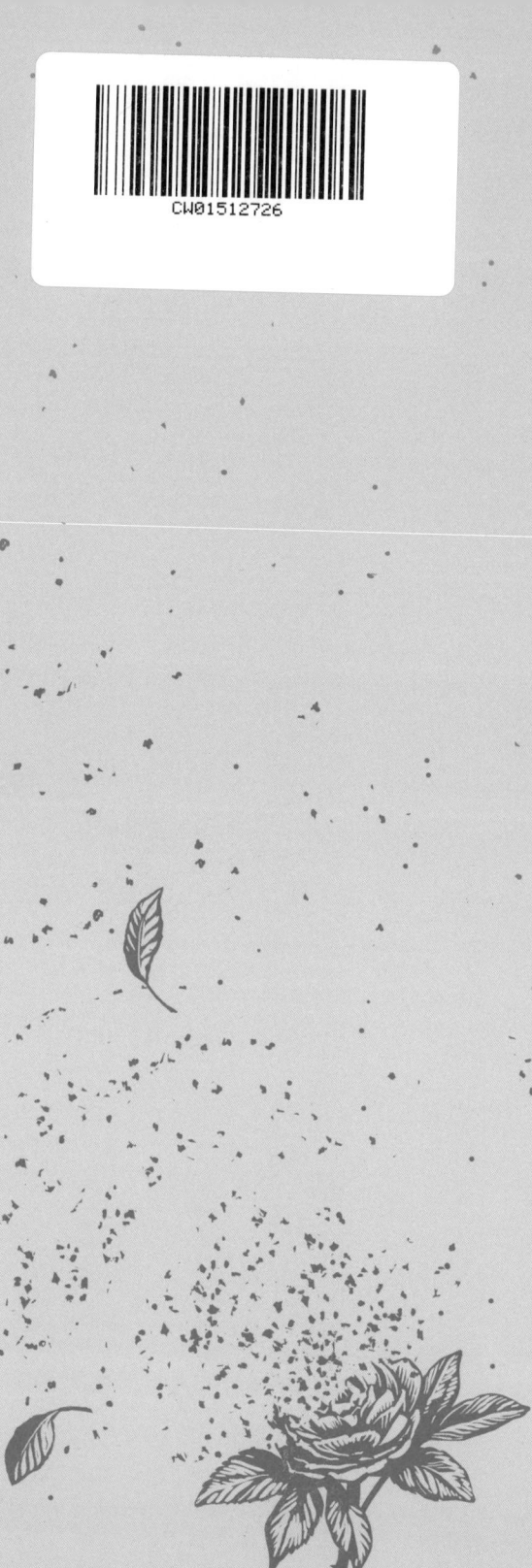

THE BOOK OF DUST

VOLUME THREE

THE ROSE FIELD

Also available from the world of Lyra Silvertongue
in a variety of editions and formats

PHILIP PULLMAN

THE BOOK OF DUST

VOLUME THREE

THE ROSE FIELD

Illustrated by Chris Wormell

DAVID FICKLING BOOKS
in association with
PENGUIN

The Rose Field is first published in Great Britain in 2025
by David Fickling Books, 31 Beaumont Street, Oxford, OX1 2NP,
in association with Penguin Books, One Embassy Gardens,
8 Viaduct Gardens, London SW11 7BW

www.davidficklingbooks.com
www.penguin.co.uk

978–0–241–45869–3 (HARDBACK)
978–0–241–45870–9 (TRADE PAPERBACK)

978–0–241–41404–0 (COLLECTOR'S EDITION)

1 3 5 7 9 10 8 6 4 2

Set in 11/15pt New Baskerville ITC Pro
Typeset by Six Red Marbles UK, Thetford, Norfolk
Printed and bound in Great Britain by Clays Ltd, Elcograf S.p.A.

The authorised representative in the EEA is Penguin Random House Ireland,
Morrison Chambers, 32 Nassau Street, Dublin D02 YH68

A CIP catalogue record for this book is available from the British Library

David Fickling Books Reg. No. 8340307

Penguin Books is part of the Penguin Random House group of companies
whose addresses can be found at global.penguinrandomhouse.com

Papers used by David Fickling Books and Penguin Random House
are from well-managed forests and other responsible sources

To Caradoc King, MDOC.
Sixty years . . .

Entre la rose et moi, je la vois qui s'abrite;
Sur la poudre qui danse, elle glisse et n'irrite
Nul feuillage, mais passe, et se brise partout . . .

Between the rose and me, I see her shelter;
On the dancing dust, she glides without stirring
The leaves, she goes past in a thousand pieces . . .

Paul Valéry, *La Jeune Parque*

Contents

At the end of the previous book, THE SECRET COMMONWEALTH, *Lyra reaches the deserted city, al-Khan al-Azraq, in her search for her dæmon, Pan.*

Under the moon, she goes alone into the ruins.

She'd turned to avoid a broken mass of gleaming marble that had once been a temple. There she found herself at one end of a colonnade, which cast black bars of shadow across the snow-white stone of the path.

And there was a girl sitting on a fallen piece of masonry, a girl of sixteen or so, of North African appearance and shabby dress. She wasn't a phantom: she cast a shadow, as Lyra herself did, and, like her, she had no dæmon. She stood up as soon as she saw Lyra. In the moonlight she looked tense and full of fear.

'You are Miss Silvertongue,' she said.

'Yes,' said Lyra, astonished. 'Who are you?'

'Nur Huda el-Wahabi. Come on, come quickly. We have been waiting for you.'

'We? Who—? You don't mean . . . ?'

But Nur Huda tugged urgently at Lyra's right hand, and they hurried together along the colonnade, towards the heart of the ruins.

And now the final part begins.

PART ONE

1

BEINGS OF ANOTHER KIND

'But who?' said Lyra. 'Who is waiting?'

'Me,' said Nur Huda, 'and my dæmon, Jamal, but they won't—'

'Is he here? Is your dæmon here?'

'Yes, but they won't let him – won't let me . . .'

Lyra stopped. The moonlight shone full in the younger girl's face, glistening on the lip she was biting and on the unshed tears in her eyes. All around them were tumbled columns of marble, statues of long-forgotten queens or gods, some still intact, and walls and arches and colonnades, gleaming brilliantly white where the moon touched them, among jagged shadows of fathomless black where it did not.

'But who are *they*?' said Lyra.

'Just voices. I don't know! It's like a war in here. They fight, and I don't know why, I don't know who they are, and I can't see them. I'm so frightened. Just voices. I can't see them.'

'And they won't let you do what? Take your dæmon away, is that it? They're keeping him prisoner?'

Nur Huda nodded. The movement shook a tear from one eye and she wiped it away with the heel of her hand.

'And how did you know my name?'

'Your dæmon told me. Pan. He said you were coming.'

'Pan? You've *seen* Pan? Where? Is he here?'

Lyra's eagerness was so sudden and passionate that she didn't even notice that she'd seized the girl's arm. Nur Huda pulled away, her eyes wide with alarm.

Lyra let go. 'Oh, I'm sorry, I didn't mean to startle you . . . Only, I've been following him all this way, trying to find him, and if he's not here . . .'

But she'd spoken too quickly, too impatiently. The girl was hungry, and tired, and horribly alone.

She was going to cry, so Lyra hugged her and said, 'Let's sit down. We're both exhausted and frightened. Just tell me everything that happened to you. I won't interrupt, I promise.'

They sat on a crumbled shelf of stone surrounding a basin where a fountain had once played. A trickle of water still fell from the time-smudged mask of a satyr; it must have gushed from his mouth when it was built, and the spring that supplied it was still flowing. Nur Huda turned and scooped up a handful of water and sipped it. Lyra did the same. It was ice-cold and clean, and she drank some more. She had no idea she was so thirsty.

'Where have you come from?' Lyra asked.

'From Baghdad with my family. But we were in a boat and it sank, and when I swam to the shore I found Jamal was gone. I thought he was dead and that meant I was too, and I was very afraid. I was alone for a while. I didn't know what to do. But then Pan found me asleep on a hill and he guarded me and when I woke up he told me about you and we thought Jamal might have come to this place so we came here. Pan was with me so it didn't look as if . . . you know.'

'Jamal is your dæmon?'

'Yes.'

'What did Pan say?'

'He said he was looking for something you'd lost.'

'Did he tell you what that was?'

Nur Huda shook her head. 'He said he was going ahead of you to find it and keep it safe. To the east, where the roses come from, that's what he said. But he told me you would come here soon and I would know you because you had no dæmon, like me . . .' Her voice was unsteady.

'And . . . is Jamal here?'

'No. I don't think so. Something happened. A man came out of the desert and was hiding from a giant bird, and then he saw that Jamal was close by, and snatched him before I could reach him.'

'A man? Was he one of the voices?'

'No. Only a man. He looked like a Scythian, I don't know, maybe Chorasmian—'

Lyra blinked with surprise.

Nur Huda noticed, and went on, 'I don't know. He might not be real anyway. He's only got one eye . . . The bird was hunting him. It was so big, when it flew overhead it darkened the whole sky. I thought maybe the man took Jamal to give him to the bird as a – as a, you know, when you throw something to a wolf to distract it . . .'

'A decoy?'

'I didn't know that word. Yes, that. I don't know, I'm sorry! I'm so frightened . . .'

'And you said it's like a war here . . . What did you mean? Dæmons fighting other dæmons, something like that?'

'I can't tell. Only that sometimes the air is full of screams and anger and crying. Probably not dæmons. There are not many dæmons here, really. Only the voices . . .'

'What do they say? What language do they speak?'

'Many languages. They whisper. Sometimes you think it's insects, maybe crickets, cicadas, and then you hear them say real words . . .'

'When do they speak?'

'You can hear them now.'

Lyra listened. The silence was vast. It was the sort of night when you might hear the planets moving among the stars. She found herself comparing it with the silence in the world of the dead, but that was a closed silence, where nothing was alive, and that world was stale and stuffy, for all its immensity. But the silence in al-Khan al-Azraq was open, and not quite silence either. There were little scratches, little susurrations and clicks and rasps, none of them louder than a pinch of sand dropped on the skin of a snare drum, and they all meant . . . nothing. She remembered a night some years before, in Oxford, when she had thought that everything had a meaning, and had seen how she might understand it. But that was before she'd read Gottfried Brande and Simon Talbot, at a time when Pan was still happy with her.

'You can't hear them?' said Nur Huda.

She spoke tentatively, anxious that Lyra should believe her, and Lyra saw how young the girl was, and how much she'd suffered, and felt how tightly Nur Huda was still gripping her arm.

'Yes, I can a bit, but I don't know what they're saying. Is this the best place to listen to them?'

'It's better in the marketplace. This way.'

They had to clamber over the fallen stones and make their way around the broken walls of a basilica before they came to an open area that did look like a marketplace, a public space to hold meetings: a forum.

The sand underfoot was so fine and white that it might have been newly milled flour. In the centre of the forum there was a plinth where a statue had once stood. The statue itself lay in three pieces beside it, toppled by an earthquake, perhaps: a bearded god whose sightless eyes glared up at the moon. Lyra and Nur Huda sat on his muscular chest. There was nothing moving in the forum, not a sign of life anywhere, and everything around was drenched in moonlight and frozen in stillness.

Lyra gradually became more aware of the scratchy little susurrus, the scraping of insect claws, the clicks and rustlings like dry leaves in a porcelain bowl being stirred by a breeze. The girl's arm pressing against hers, her flesh warm in the cold air, made Lyra realise a little of what their dæmons must be feeling, so bare and vulnerable away from the solid comfort of a human body.

She gathered her breath to say something, but Nur Huda whispered, 'Sssh . . .'

Lyra could hear no difference in the tiny scratchings and scrapes. She strained to hear better, and tried to focus her ears on whatever was there, and then remembered Giorgio Brabandt telling her how to see the secret commonwealth: *You got to look at it sideways*, he'd said. *Out the corner of your eye. So you gotta think about it out the corner of your mind. It's there and it en't, both at the same time.*

Of course. She shouldn't strain at it. She should listen as if she was reading the alethiometer in the old way, as if it didn't mean anything, and as if it did. She relaxed her mind and her eyes and her ears, and let the night flow in and out of her body. A nimbus of perception spread out around her as if her senses themselves were slowly merging with the city of the moon.

And in the clicks and rasps and scratches she began to hear words:

. . . you alone . . . we want you to hear . . . this is not for the girl . . . send her to the fountain . . . this is your task, not hers . . .

Nur Huda heard them as well. She gripped Lyra's arm more tightly and began to say something, but Lyra hushed her and she fell silent. The voices were scratching softly at the silence.

. . . girl . . . Nur Huda . . . you must leave us . . . go to the fountain . . . wait there . . . you will know when we have finished . . .

Nur Huda whispered, 'Should I go?'

'Yes,' Lyra whispered in return. 'Go there now and wait. I'll come and find you soon.'

The girl rose unsteadily and walked away, looking back every few steps as if to make sure Lyra was still there. The floury sand rose up like mist around her feet as she made her way out of the forum, and then settled back infinitely slowly.

Lyra waited till everything was still. Then she said into the dark, 'Who are you? Are you angels?'

. . . *we are beings of another kind* . . .

'Are you part of the secret commonwealth?'

. . . *deeper by far than that* . . . *we come from the gulfs between the good numbers* . . .

'The gulfs between . . . Did I hear you properly?'

No reply.

'Then tell me something else,' she said. 'Tell me what's in the red building in the desert of Karamakan. The building the roses come from.'

. . . *an opening into another world* . . .

Lyra was silent for a moment. The stars wheeled overhead.

'An opening – d'you mean the sort of thing Will used to call a window?'

. . . *a doorway into another world* . . . *that is why they guard it so fiercely* . . .

'The world where the roses come from?'

. . . *they could come from nowhere else* . . .

As simple as that, and she hadn't thought of it. A knife-bearer from Cittàgazze, long ago, must have cut that window in his travels from world to world, and left it open. Her grasp on things was loosening, and she felt giddy, as if she'd lost her sense of up and down, of now and of then, of here and of everywhere.

The voices said something else, but she didn't understand it.

. . . *the alkahest* . . .

'The . . . alphabet? Is that what you said?'

. . . *the alkahest* . . .

'Alkahest? What's that?'

. . . *the destroyer of bonds* . . .

She heard it clearly, and it was impossible to understand. 'What d'you mean? What about this alkahest? What is it?'

. . . *destroy everything* . . .

Lyra was bewildered. It was too much. She dragged herself back to the present task. 'Where is Nur Huda's dæmon? Where is Jamal?'

. . . *in the treasury* . . .

'And where's that?'

. . . *behind you* . . .

Lyra turned to look. The building that had stood there was now a jumbled heap of stones, with a few dry shrubs growing through them.

She said, 'Who is keeping him prisoner?'

. . . *a man who is asleep* . . .

Her eyes had become used to the moonlight; it was almost as clear as day, and she stepped easily over the stones and looked more closely at the place called the treasury. It was the sort of place where snakes might easily hide, and scorpions, and venomous spiders. Oh, there were so many things to be afraid of.

She took a deep breath and pressed her hand to her heart to slow the beating. It didn't work, of course, and she needed both hands to help her clamber over the shattered masonry, so she let her heart do what it wanted and moved on, hand over hand, foot carefully placed before foot. Inside her she carried the new knowledge about the red building in the desert of Karamakan like a precious vessel full to the brim with rare oil. Don't tremble, don't trip . . .

When she'd gone a little way into the rubble she saw a gap in the ground ahead, and realised it was the shaft of a great staircase leading down deep into the ground. In a treasury, where would you put the most valuable thing? In the vaults under the ground. There must be some kind of strongroom down there . . . And how was she going to open it? In the dark? With no tools?

She shrugged. It might not even be possible to reach it. But the steps that led down were not too cluttered with fallen masonry, and the moon was at just the right angle to light the way down, so she had no excuse. Right hand on the wall, left held out for balance, she made her way carefully downwards, aware all the time of the danger of slipping, twisting an ankle, or worse.

Down, and further down, and still the moonlight lit her way. At the foot of the stairway, she had to stop: the passage that led away into the dark was entirely blocked.

But there at the side, out of the shaft of moonlight, was a man lying on his back, asleep. At first she thought he was dead, he was so still, and her veins flooded with ice-water; but he was snoring quietly, and there was his dæmon, a small desert mammal of some inconspicuous kind, clinging to his shoulder in her sleep. His face had been battered and torn in what must have been a furious attack, and his left eye was missing: the socket lay empty and blood-clotted.

His right arm was resting on something at his side, and when she looked more closely she could see what it was: a crudely made cage about the size of a shoebox, nailed together from rough planks, with a heavy steel mesh front. Inside the cage was a dæmon, Nur Huda's dæmon, a little animal like a mouse with large ears and long back legs like those of a kangaroo. He was crouching in the darkest corner, shivering.

'Are you Jamal?' Lyra whispered.

'Yes – where is Nur Huda?' came the reply, so quiet she could hardly hear it.

'She's waiting for us. I'm going to take you back to her. Who is this man?'

'He caught me and nailed this cage up and I can't get out – he was hiding from a big bird – like an eagle – it was going to take me and he fought to get me away from it and then he put me in this cage – I'm frightened. Who are you?'

'Sssh. My name's Lyra. Keep still and don't talk. I don't want to wake him up.'

She had to reach across the man's body to touch the cage, and he stirred and groaned loudly, startling her. She kept as still as she could till he was snoring again, and then moved her hand to the cage, feeling to see if she could lift it away from his grasp.

But it wasn't going to be possible unless she knelt on his chest: there was nowhere else to lean on, and unless she supported her weight somehow she'd overbalance and wake him up anyway. And her left hand was still painful after her fight with the soldiers on the train from Smyrna just two days ago.

She felt as far as she could around the cage. The wood was very dry and splintery, and the steel mesh was far too strong to bend, and stapled deeply into the wood all the way round.

She sat back to think about it.

Jamal whispered, 'Please, can you open it?'

'Sssh.'

She was aware of the moon moving across the sky: the shaft of light was moving too, and unless she got the dæmon out soon she'd have to work in the dark. If only Will . . . If only the subtle knife . . . It would cut through the mesh in a moment.

A thousand things distracted her. The smell of the sleeping man: not just a dirty body and unwashed clothes, but something worse, like gangrene. She saw that his leg was injured as well as his eye; he'd probably die soon. The sound of something much deeper underground, the faintest possible rumble, like rocks grinding together. The stillness of the air, the closeness and clamminess down here in the vault.

A thought struck her like an arrow.

The alethiometer—

The metal of the needle—

The Welsh miners on the North Sea ferry had noticed it. So had Will, a long time before. It was the same colour, the same material, as the subtle knife.

She moved away a little further, back into the shaft of moonlight, and felt in her rucksack for the alethiometer. Its familiar weight sat in her hand so rightly, and she raised it to her cheek and held it there for a few seconds, loving it.

She'd never opened it, never tried to prise it apart, but there must be a way of doing so. The mechanism had been made by a human being, and then put in its gold case, and then the glass had been pressed shut. She could almost hear the *click* as she thought about it. Or else they'd screwed it down. If it had been closed, it could be opened.

Malcolm, the skilled mechanic, would know how to do it. What would he do? She held the body of the instrument in her aching left hand and tried to unscrew the glass as if she was unscrewing the lid of a jar. She'd watched a clockmaker in the Covered Market in Oxford unscrewing a watch glass, gently, firmly, just like that. She tried, but without success. Either it was stuck after centuries of not being moved, or it wasn't screwed at all.

And then came another memory-arrow: it was thinking of Malcolm that brought this one. He'd found a wooden acorn with a message in it, and couldn't open it till he tried unscrewing the wrong way, clockwise.

So she tried that.

And it worked.

The glass turned smoothly as if it had been made the day before, and after three revolutions it came away in her hand. The dial of the alethiometer, with its thirty-six tiny pictures, lay open to the moonlight. Its three black hands were pointing to the camel, the angel, and the walled garden, but the symbols didn't matter for now; it was the silver-grey needle that was important, slender, infinitely sharp, quivering in the air of Madinat al-Qamar as the air of Prague drifted away from it.

'I'm sorry,' she whispered to the heavy golden instrument, so beautiful, her companion for ten years or more, the guide that had led her safely into other worlds and into the world of the dead and then home again.

And with all the delicacy her pain-filled bones and exhausted muscles could manage, she lifted out the needle.

It came away easily from its shaft. There was so little of it – it could have weighed only a little more than a hair – that she was immediately terrified of dropping it. If that happened, she'd never find it again. She held it between the thumb and forefinger of her right hand, and they were damp with sweat and fear, so she laid it carefully on the open palm of her left and wiped her right hand on the fabric of her blouse, though that was wet too. So she rubbed her fingers instead into the dust of the floor, which did work, and then took the needle again.

'Stay at the back and keep still,' she whispered to Jamal.

The little dæmon, who'd been peering through the mesh, darted into the shadow at the back of the cage.

Lyra thought: *I don't know if this will work. But it's all there is.*

Whatever she did would depend on her left hand not giving way. She had to lean on it a little, or not reach the cage at all, but it hurt so much. She leaned over the sleeping man, put her left hand on the top of the cage, and very slowly let it take her weight as she reached over with her right.

Gripping the needle as firmly as she could, she pressed the side of it, just behind the point, to the steel mesh at one edge. The wire was thick and heavy, and it would have needed a bolt-cutter and a strong wrist to make any impression on it; but it parted like a cobweb.

Lyra wanted to shout with triumph, but she'd hardly started. One by one, keeping her mind on everything about the task, she cut through each of the strands of wire until the entire front fell away loose.

'Wait,' she whispered urgently, because Jamal had come to the front of the cage and looked as if he wanted to leap out at once.

But the sleeping man was stirring. He must have felt the cage shift under his hand when the front fell away. He groaned and lifted his arm – and touched Lyra's – and woke at once.

He shouted in fear and seized her wrist. His one eye glittered, open wide.

'Jamal! Run!' Lyra called, and the little dæmon sprang over them both and darted up the staircase like a spark along a fuse.

The man was struggling to sit up, because Lyra had fallen across his body, struggling against horrible pain as she tried to tug her wrist loose from his grip. Without thinking about it she realised she still had the needle in her right hand, and thrust it hard into his arm.

He cried out in anger and shock and flung her off. The stink of the gangrene, if it was that, enveloped her and made her gag – but she kept hold of the needle and pulled it away as the man rolled over and struggled to his feet. He saw the open cage and cried out, and kicked Lyra in the ribs before staggering and almost losing his balance – and then he saw the gold of the alethiometer gleaming in the last shaft of moonlight, and snatched it up and scrambled away up the steps too fast for her to follow.

She lay half stunned, dizzy with pain and exhaustion, winded from the kick to her chest, but with the needle still in her trembling fingers.

The curved glass she'd taken out of the alethiometer reflected a little image of the moon up at her. She scooped it up, seized her rucksack, and scrambled for the stairs, trembling in every limb, tripping, skidding on the sand that had blown down from above, trying not to cry aloud with pain and fear, dizzy with weakness, and came out into the full moonlight of the silent forum.

There was no sign of Nur Huda's dæmon. But there was the man, the Scythian, the Chorasmian, whatever he was, clutching the alethiometer to his chest as he stumbled away—

And then without any warning, in total silence, an immense shadow swept across the forum and submerged the man in darkness. As Lyra clung to the wall, unbelieving, the creature that threw the shadow swooped down on him, snatched him up in giant claws, and in a swirl of dust thrown up by its vast wings, carried him up into the sky. It had taken no more than a couple of seconds.

It was half lion, half eagle, immense and savage, and as its shape passed across the full moon Lyra saw the man struggling in its claws and heard his distant screaming. With him went the alethiometer.

But she had the glass, and the needle, though she could barely hold them. With trembling care she dropped the needle into her breast pocket and the glass into her rucksack.

Nur Huda was sitting with Jamal in her hands, talking softly and urgently, raising him to her lips and her cheeks and her ears, stroking his back, kissing him, cuddling him close.

She jumped up when she saw Lyra. Her face was brilliant with happiness.

'This is Jamal! He's safe!' she said, and Lyra wanted to embrace her and absorb some of that joy; and then Nur Huda, clutching her dæmon close to her heart, threw her other arm around Lyra's neck and kissed her.

In doing so she crushed Lyra's left hand against her. Lyra couldn't help flinching, and Nur Huda drew away in alarm.

'You're hurt! What happened?'

'I . . . I don't know. I can't remember. How will you find your way home?'

'Jamal will find the way. No need to worry about that! With Jamal, I'm always safe. Anyway, my home is where my family is. We'll look for them and that's how we'll find a home. Like you with Pan.'

'Yes . . .'

'When you find him, will you go home?'

'I don't think I've got a home . . . I don't know. Maybe we could look for one.'

'Yes! Look for a home. That's a good idea. But the most important thing is when you find him, you must kiss him and kiss him.'

'*Will* I find him?'

'Of course!'

'And . . . will he find the thing he's looking for?'

'Of course he will. He's very good at looking. He'll find it and everything will be all right. Then you will find a home and marry someone nice. Thank you, Lyra! Thank you!'

And she turned away and began the long walk home, with her little dæmon skipping and leaping beside her. Lyra could hear their voices chattering and laughing together for some time after they vanished from sight beyond the moon-drenched colonnade.

Abdel Ionides, her guide into the desert, was sleeping when Lyra returned to their camp at the edge of the city. Quietly though she moved, he heard her and sat up.

'Miss Silver! Your dæmon was not there?'

'He was there, but he's gone. And there were voices – they spoke about something called the alkahest . . . Have you heard of the alkahest?'

'No. Who said that, anyway?'

'I couldn't see them. Just voices.'

He shrugged and peered at her more closely and said, 'You hurt? What happen?'

'I saw a gigantic bird, like a lion . . .'

'Bird like a lion? What you mean? I think you too tired to speak any sense. Come on, lie down, go to sleep till morning. It will be very cold soon.' He shook out a blanket and laid it on a pile of several others.

She had to. There was no alternative. She felt him gently arranging the blankets over her, and then she was asleep.

She dreamed that Pan came back to her, without a word, at the darkest point of the night, and slipped under the sheepskins and found his old place around her neck.

'It's a window, Pan!' she murmured. 'Like the ones we used to go through with Will! In the red building – a window into another world! The world where the roses come from! That's what it is!'

She heard the dream-Pan whisper, but what he said was a mystery, and in her dream itself, she fell asleep.

2

THE INFIRMARY

Some time before Lyra arrived at the City of the Moon, the director of Oakley Street had had a visitor. The organisation had been officially disbanded, and Glenys Godwin had been ordered to retire and surrender all control of the records, files, offices, property, everything, to the Home Office.

She'd done nothing of the sort. She was determined to keep as much as she could out of the hands of the faction now running the government, and to continue the fight and uphold the principles she'd sworn to support when she joined Oakley Street as a young woman forty years before.

Since their offices had been commandeered, she and her senior team were working temporarily from a large and dingy flat near Battersea Park. No one, she thought, knew where they were; so it was a shock when the doorbell rang in the late morning and her secretary came in to say that an elderly man would like to see her. He'd given his name as Makepeace.

'Did he say anything more than that?'

'No, ma'am. But he said he'd specifically come to see you.'

'Me by name? Not just the director, or the person in charge?'

'He gave your full name.'

'What does he look like, David?'

'Seventies. Quite vigorous, though, I should think. Dusty black suit, rather shabby, but more like a retired craftsman than a vagrant, for example. His dæmon's a cat.'

'Well, I'm curious. Show him in, but stand by next door, won't you?'

She stayed at her desk as the visitor came in. The secretary's summary was accurate, but he hadn't mentioned the air of intellectual force expressed by the man's clear eyes and commanding expression, nor the faint smell of wood-smoke. The man was carrying a small battered attaché case.

'Thank you for seeing me, Mrs Godwin,' he said. His voice was educated, his tone aristocratic. 'I won't take up much of your time.'

'Do sit down, Mr Makepeace. First, how do you know my name? Second, how did you know how to find me?'

'I've been aware of Oakley Street for a long time. I knew Tom Nugent very well, and I agreed with the principles he worked for. I knew your name because he told me before he died that you would succeed him, and I knew how to find you because I've been here before, when it was used as a safe house.'

'But—'

'All you need to know is what I'm going to tell you about these things.'

He opened the attaché case and took out a brown-paper parcel about the size of a large man's fist. He opened it to reveal two flat stones, greenish-black in colour, each with one side shinier and flatter than the other.

'What are those?' said Godwin, picking one of them up and feeling its weight.

'If you have one of these, you can communicate instantaneously with the other, no matter how far they are apart. They work by a process of quantum entanglement, but I haven't got time to tell you how. You'll have to discover how to use them yourself.

They will give you an immediate and powerful advantage over your enemies. *Our* enemies.'

'Where do they come from?'

'From another world.'

He spoke with the same sober dignity as before, his eyes steady and clear, his hands folded calmly in his lap; but . . . another world?

'I see,' she said. 'And how did they come into your possession?'

'Very simply. I saw them in a junk-shop window, and recognised them, and bought them. In the world they come from they're known as resonating lodestones.'

'And this other world . . .'

'You'll remember the Barnard-Stokes hypothesis.'

'I thought the point of that was that each world is completely unreachable from any other.'

'That was a part of the mathematics put in quite late to deceive the authorities into thinking that the many-worlds idea could have no practical application, so it could be examined theoretically without falling into heresy.'

'So if these things have come through, somehow, from their own world, there might be ways for people to do so as well?'

'Yes, but they're difficult and dangerous. Human travel is virtually impossible. But objects do find their way sometimes out of one world and into another. Chance, accident, forgetfulness.'

'Where had you seen things like this before? You said you recognised them.'

'I recognised that they hadn't come from this world. Once you've learned how to see that, it's unmistakable. It's like training your senses, the way a piano tuner learns to recognise harmonies and intervals. I had no idea what they were used for until I met a traveller who had seen them and spoken to the strange people who used them. I've told no one but you, but the time has come for them to be used again.'

All kinds of possibilities flickered across her mind like the figures in a phantasmagoria. He sat calm and steady, returning her gaze.

'What do you do, Mr Makepeace?'

'I used to work at what we once called experimental theology. That term seems to be going out of favour these days, so I like to let it be known that I am an alchemist.' Something changed in his expression. A little glint, a shimmer of complicity, and she knew they understood each other. He closed his briefcase. 'Time is pressing, Mrs Godwin. But I would like a receipt for these things.'

'My secretary will make one out.' She pressed a button and spoke briefly to him, before turning back to Makepeace. 'May I know where you live?'

'In Oxford, in the district they call Jericho. Juxon Street, to be precise.'

The door opened, and her secretary came in with two copies of a typed receipt, which she and Makepeace both signed.

He took his copy and stood up. They shook hands, and she came to the door with him.

'Thank you for bringing me these,' she said. 'And you think I can discover how to use them?'

'I do. And if whoever you're communicating with can find out anything at all about the alkahest, they would be doing something very valuable.'

'The alkahest? What's that?'

'A term from alchemy. Mrs Godwin, your political masters will quite soon find out this address. I think it would be wise to move before they do.'

'I've always liked the sound of Hemel Hempstead,' she said. 'Such a romantic name.'

Another little flicker: he understood. He smiled, and nodded, and left.

'Well, David,' said Glenys Godwin to the secretary. 'Now we've got some work to do.'

*

22

Marcel Delamare, President of the High Council of the Magisterium, didn't often leave the building in Geneva, known as *La Maison Juste*, that held his office. His comfortable apartment in a nearby building overlooking the lake, the cathedral, an occasional visit to a restaurant or a concert, and a walk along the lakeshore for his health; the world he moved in was quiet and well ordered. He hadn't been to the mountains since he was a very young man, when he'd thought that an enthusiasm for climbing would be a useful part of a well-rounded reputation.

So it had been at least twenty-five years since he had trodden the snowy paths above Les Diablerets, and he had never taken the route that led to the phenomenon he was now examining. In fact, said his guide, hardly anyone ever had. If the third man present was familiar with it, he didn't say; he said very little. Colonel Schreiber was completely at home in the mountains, and like other senior officers under the command of what used to be known as the Consistorial Court of Discipline he was used to keeping quiet. His stocky form, his Franz Joseph beard and moustache and bare chin were familiar to all those under his command.

The thing they were looking at stood among densely growing pine trees in a steep valley, and Delamare had never seen anything like it. It looked as if someone had cut a hole in the air.

It was hard to see, and in the pale afternoon light it might easily have been missed by anyone who wasn't looking for it, because the land on the other side – through the hole, so to speak – was very similar to everything around it on *this* side: pine trees, a rocky slope under snow. It was so much the same that anyone walking there might easily have missed it, not least because all their attention would have been focused on keeping their footing on the steep rocky slope under the snow.

'Do they all look like this, Beamish?' he said to the guide.

Hugo Beamish was a lean, grizzled, sunburned man in his forties. 'Yes, they do,' he said. 'All roughly this size, all in isolated places, not easy to get to, not easy to see.'

Delamare found a firmer footing and leaned closer. The edge of the hole in the air was clearly visible when he was close, but not so easy from a little way back. The opening was big enough for an adult man or woman to step through, and irregular in shape: no straight edges or smooth curves, more like something cut freehand and perhaps in a hurry.

'What happens when – Colonel, I wonder if you would oblige – could you go behind it, so to speak, from the side ...' said Delamare, stepping carefully back a step or two.

Colonel Schreiber did as he was asked. Balancing lightly on the snow-covered rocks, he stepped up to the opening from the side and moved behind it. He vanished at once. His dæmon, a porcupine, hadn't gone with him, and was intensely agitated: she whimpered and rattled her quills, scuttling back and forth in front of the opening.

Delamare took a deep breath. The guide had seen this thing before, and leaned on his stick and just watched.

'Colonel? Can you hear me?'

'Yes, I can hear you, but I can't see you. Either of you.'

'Would you come back, please?'

Schreiber appeared as if he'd just stepped out from behind a building, though there was nothing to see but the steep rocky slope, the close-growing snow-covered trees.

'Stand where I am, if you please,' Delamare said, 'and watch as I go through.'

The colonel moved next to him. Delamare was conscious of a feeling something like fear, but deeper and stranger. He stepped up in front of the opening and looked through as he'd done a moment before, and then stepped forward and into the space behind it. His owl-dæmon went with him, but she gripped his shoulder ferociously.

He looked all around. He might have been in his own world, in Switzerland, in a forest above Les Diablerets, on a cold pale day. Everything was almost the same; but something fundamental was different, and he couldn't tell what it was.

It made him uneasy, so he stepped back through to join the other two.

'Very well,' he said. 'Now back to Geneva.'

The following morning, M. Delamare welcomed the guide to a small office not far from the central railway station. They weren't meeting at *La Maison Juste*: the President wanted to keep his visitor away from that building, for various reasons, and this anonymous and undistinguished little place, which was rented in the name of a non-existent firm of accountants, served his purpose well.

Hugo Beamish was unique among Delamare's advisers in that his background lay not in theology, or law, or finance, but in geography. He was English, and the path of his career had traced a convoluted journey from the Hampshire rectory in which he'd been born, through academic work in Cambridge and fieldwork in northern New Denmark and the Siberian Arctic, to the office of the Director of La Maison Juste, who had become the President of the new High Council of the Magisterium. Marcel Delamare had sent him on this unusual and exceptionally confidential mission two years before, seeing in Beamish a man whose diligence and taciturnity were quite out of the ordinary. He was glad to see that his confidence had been justified.

The office they met in was small, but clean and warm; the furniture was anonymous, modern, and functional; the sun was shining outside, coffee was served.

'Now, Beamish,' said the President, 'how many of these things have you discovered?'

'Seventeen,' said the guide. 'In every part of the world. That's to say, seventeen I have personally visited. There are others I've heard about, eight to be precise, but haven't yet seen in person. All my notes, all the map references and so on, are here for you.' He indicated a bundle of five or six bulging cardboard folders, tied together with heavy cord, which lay on the low table between the two chairs.

'Pictures? Photograms?'

'The phenomenon has a strange effect on photogrammic film. I've taken pictures of what is to be seen *through* the opening, and what there is on this side, but the emulsion seems to be disturbed in some way by what happens when light from both sources falls on it. There will be a way of doing it, but I haven't succeeded yet. The pictures I have are in the files, among the other notes.'

'And how are they regarded by the local people, these doorways?'

'If they know about them at all – they often don't – they talk about them with fear and superstition. In some places they're believed to be entrances to the spirit world, something like that, and avoided and shunned. In general, very little is spoken about them – that's what made the search so difficult.'

'And did you go through in every case? Did you explore what was on the other side? I take it you weren't put off by local legends?'

'No, I went through, in each place I found. Again, the details are in the notes. The doorways I found were all in wild places, with only two exceptions, and the landscape on the other side was usually very similar, as it was with the one we saw yesterday – as if the place had been chosen for that very reason. But in every case I had a distinct impression . . .'

He looked troubled.

'Go on,' said Delamare calmly. 'You're reporting something strange, not committing heresy. What were you going to say?'

Beamish cleared his throat and said, 'When I stepped through any of those doorways, I had the distinct impression that I was in a different world. Not like being simply in a different country, or a different climate, a different landscape – more than that. Somewhere not in this world.'

'Did your feeling at that point have a spiritual aspect?'

Beamish hesitated again. He looked troubled, and Delamare said, 'Don't forget, you were doing this on my direct orders. No possible blame can attach to you, whatever you saw, whatever you report.'

'Thank you, sir. A spiritual aspect . . . I don't know how exactly I'd know that . . . It was different in each place. That was another surprising thing. It was as if the doorways on this planet each opened into a different part of the universe altogether. Or . . . into a different universe.'

'I can see how that might be disturbing.' Delamare looked at the visitor appraisingly before standing up. 'You're looking tired, my dear Beamish,' he went on. 'A glass of apricot schnapps will soon restore your vigour.'

He poured some golden liquor into a couple of glasses.

'And did you see any living creatures in those other worlds?'

'In one I could see, in the distance, the buildings of a city, and I could never have imagined . . . The sheer size of the buildings, the shapes . . . In another there were beings, creatures, at work tilling the soil. Not nearby, you understand; each doorway was placed with some care away from settlements or roads. Lonely places, well chosen.'

'These beings or creatures – tell me about them.'

'I looked at them through my field glasses for thirty minutes or so. They were the size of small horses, but six-legged, like intelligent insects. They talked among themselves as they worked the soil. I could hear their voices very distantly.'

'Did they have tools?'

'Yes, small ploughs or harrows, but the machinery seemed to be self-propelled, and self-directing in some way. There was a discussion at one point – one of the ploughs seemed to want to take a different course, and the insect-creatures tried to persuade it not to, but it had its way. They were gradually working their way towards the slope where I was watching, so I thought it best to come back through before they saw me.'

'Did you see any creatures anywhere that might have been human?'

'Once or twice in the distance, on a road. But too far away to see clearly, even with the field glasses.'

Delamare sat back, resting his head on the back of the sofa, and gazed at the ceiling. He had the air of being in deep thought.

After a minute he said, 'Did you anywhere, at any stage in your travels, talk to anyone about this phenomenon? I mean, a serious prolonged discussion?'

'Three times, M. le Président. Once to a Malian scholar in Tombouctou, who told me about such a doorway in the Atlas Mountains. I looked, but I could never find it. Once to some shepherds in Mongolia, who had lost some sheep to what they thought was a raiding party from . . . the other world. They didn't dare pursue and bring back their flock; they were just going to move on and avoid the place in future. And once to a spice trader in Java, who told me about a friend of his who had vanished through one such doorway and never returned.'

'You made notes of all these conversations? Names, addresses, and so on?'

'All in the files.'

'Did anyone in authority question your interest?'

'No, sir. Wherever I went it seemed to be a source of mild and rather sterile curiosity. Something that was out of the ordinary, but not fundamentally useful or interesting.'

'And did you ask how long these things had been known about? Were they spoken of in old traditions, for example?'

'In pre-literate societies, times and dates easily become "In the time of our grandfathers" or "Since before the great fires" or "Older than the forest" – that sort of thing.'

'And are you aware of any of these things that have changed? Grown larger or smaller? Closed altogether?'

'The people who spoke about them seemed to think they had always been the same. Though, as I say, not very many people did speak about them.'

'Thank you very much, Mr Beamish. Leave your notes with me; I'll read them avidly. Let my secretary know where you're staying.

28

I suggest you relax for a while after your travels. Take it easy for a week or two. Where are you staying?'

'At the Hôtel de la Tour.'

'Very good. I shall want to see you again, so don't go too far away, and expect me to be in touch.'

Delamare seemed to have made up his mind swiftly and decisively about something. Beamish, who had become quite fond of his doorways, and would have been happy to talk about them for longer, found himself outside in the quiet Geneva Sunday morning street wondering what he'd done, and whether it had been wise to do it.

Once he could see Beamish walking away down the street, the President pressed a buzzer on his desk. A moment later the door opened, and Colonel Schreiber came in.

'You heard?'

'Every word, M. le Président.'

'Those are the files. Take them when you go. Wait till Beamish has returned to his hotel room, and then have him arrested, and take everything of his out of the room and bring it away. Deal with him painlessly, but finally. I want him to vanish. Then I want you to read these files and bring to me a plan for destroying every one of those openings, wherever they are in the world. I imagine explosives would be the most effective way; try with the one we saw yesterday at Les Diablerets, and let me know the result as soon as you've done it. Let me know – word of mouth only – how small a force you could do it with, and what materials and equipment you'd need. Highest degree of confidentiality. If we need to meet in person, we shall do so here only, and not at *La Maison Juste*.'

The colonel saluted and turned to leave.

Delamare's white owl-dæmon watched him go, and then turned her head back to the President. He was watching her with a complex expression she knew well, and both loved and feared.

'Well?' she said.

'I'm beginning to see what we have to do.'

'Apart from murdering innocent geographers?'
He dismissed that with a wave of his hand.
'Things are coming together,' he said.

Lyra was dreaming of her dæmon, but in the waking world Pantalaimon could smell a river. Or maybe hear it: his senses were extremely sharp, but not necessarily distinct from one another. He existed normally in and out of a state of synaesthesia, which he was quite happy about, especially when he heard a river. Or smelled the reeds and the mud and the fresh water.

He had come a night's journey away from the dead city. He had no idea what this river might be called or where it would lead, but it was moving east as he was, and when he slipped through the reeds on the bank and saw the slow-flowing water under the stars, no wider than the Thames at Westminster, his heart lifted. The guilty sorrow that had come with him as he left Nur Huda at Madinat al-Qamar seemed to fall off like a suit of clothes, and he left it behind on the bank and slipped easily into the stream.

He floated without effort past the poplars on the bank, past a little fishing village with its three or four boats tied up at a jetty, and the fires where people were cooking their evening meal, and their voices that carried quietly over the water.

He floated on. Perhaps this river would flow into a great lake, or even into the Caspian Sea. At some point between where he was and the distant desert of Karamakan there would be mountains, and perhaps he'd perish there, an unmeasurable distance away from that part of himself called Lyra, and she would perish in the same instant.

Luxuriating in this tragic vision, he was startled by a bird that came out of the dark and swept low over his head. He heard the beat of wings and a strangely muffled call and twisted in the water to look up, but it was gone. It couldn't have been an owl, because he wouldn't have heard the sound of its wings; he had the impression of a creature that might have been young, almost clumsy, and full of fear. And maybe not even a bird: the wrong shape, the wrong sort of cry—

And again it swept low above him, and Pan heard something almost human in its call.

He turned towards the bank, swimming quickly, and then from higher above there came a scream – then another – intensely wild, almost unearthly.

The first creature flew low again, and there seemed to be a sob in its voice, more urgent, closer, directed to him.

A warning? A cry for help?

And then more screams from high above, a volley of them, harsh and full of hate – and then something big and heavy hurtled into the first creature and drove it down into the water close by.

Pan's senses flared with confusion, but some things were clear: the second creature was a bird, a massive thing, and it stank of rotten flesh, and the first creature would be drowned if he didn't save it. The struggle threw up the water in all directions, and the raucous gurgling shriek from the huge bird was sickening, so close—

Then a moment when he saw clearly: the bird had seized the smaller creature in its claws, and was trying to snap at it and tear at its head. But it wasn't in its own element. The vast wings were getting waterlogged, while its beak snapped and snapped in the empty air or the water while the creature writhed and twisted to get away. If once that beak closed on it, the victim would be dead.

Pan knew about beaks. The muscles that opened them were much weaker than those that held them shut. If he could get close enough to sink his own teeth into that beak, he might be able to hold the bird underwater long enough to drown it. If he was lucky.

The bird hadn't seen him yet, but if he didn't move at once, he'd lose any surprise he might have. He twisted in a convulsion, driving himself forward. One more twist with all his strength and he was under the water, right in among the turbulence, close enough to feel the thrashing terror of the first creature as it struggled to reach up to the surface and breathe.

Pan felt his face smash against the scaly leg of the huge bird, and snapped his teeth shut on it. At once the bird screamed and let go of the first creature, who twisted up and out of its grip.

Pan coiled away in a tight full turn and then hurled himself directly into the bird's face and tore at it with claws and teeth. Then he writhed away, feinting sideways; the bird turned to follow; and Pan drove forward again, lashing his tail, whipping his spine like a snake, and seized its beak in his own powerful jaws.

But he only had the tip of it. The bird flung itself this way and that, and Pan held on, knowing he had to let go in order to seize it more firmly, and feeling all the strength of the creature in the slamming beat of its great wings. He could sense every pulse of its movement, and just as it raised its wings, just for that fraction of a second when it had no momentum, he let go and surged forward and closed his needle-sharp teeth further up the beak. This time he'd have to keep them there.

But it could still beat its mighty wings, waterlogged though they were, and scrape with its filthy claws, rank with the rotten flesh it had been tearing apart all its life. In its wild thrashing it nearly had Pan under the water, where it could drown him in a minute or less.

But his claws were sharp too. With all his weight hanging from its beak he tore with his claws at every part of the bird he could reach, breast, wings, throat, eyes, and still the creature went on making that obscene gurgling shriek, shaking its head trying to dislodge him, flinging itself – and him – this way and that, half in and half out of the water, on the riverbank and back in the water again, splashing, flapping, twisting.

Pan's jaw was aching with the effort, and he was gagging from the putrid stink of the bird's head so close to his lips and nose, and he'd taken several brutal blows from wings and feet. He was nearly at the end of his strength; and then he felt the bird's power leave it all at once and its body sagged away and drooped down into the water.

He had to tug and twist hard to pull his teeth out of the keratin-covered beak, and feared that he'd be drowned by the enemy he'd killed; but finally the beak came apart in his mouth, and he fell back in the water, sore and shaken, watching the body float away into the darkness, and thought: surely Lyra must have felt this happening.

There was a flutter of smaller wings, and the first creature landed on the bank nearby. With an immense effort Pan pulled himself out of the water and lay panting on the grass.

The moonlight showed him something he'd never seen before. She had wings, but was not a bird; and four legs and claws, like a lion, but was not a lion. She was as big as a domestic cat; her eagle-head and breast and wings were covered in feathers, the rest in fur; and like Pan, she was wounded. A deep scratch had raked along her flanks, and she was bleeding.

'I owe you my life,' she whispered.

English? She was speaking English?

'Get back in the water,' said Pan as soon as he saw her wound. 'Straightaway. You need to get that clean as soon as possible.'

'You too, then,' she said. 'But you're at home in water and I'm not. You'll have to help.'

Her voice was rich and low, her English lightly tinged with an accent that might have been Persian. Between them they managed to flush her wound free of blood and of whatever foulness the bird had left in it, and then Pan did the same for himself. The birds were still there high above, shrieking, but the noise was diminishing, as if they were moving away.

'What are they?' he said.

'*Oghâb-gorgs* from the Tien Shan mountains.'

'But that must be two thousand miles away . . . What are they doing here?'

'Looking for war. My name is Gulya. What is yours? And you are a dæmon. Why are you solitary?'

'I am Pantalaimon, the dæmon of Lyra Silvertongue. I am going to the desert of Karamakan to look for something she has lost. What did you say about those birds?'

'The *oghâb-gorgs* have come to find a war. Possibly they sense a war coming towards them. They can smell flowing blood across five thousand leagues of steppe and desert.'

'I can still hear them. Are they fighting one another?'

'No. My kin are fighting them off. We do not allow such filth anywhere near us.'

Pan lay still and listened to the distant commotion high above. The most raucous cries were quieter now, and the centre of the fight was moving away.

He said, 'Who are your kin? What kind of creature are you?'

'A gryphon. I am no bigger than this because I am under a curse. I am seventy years old, but until I kill the sorcerer who cursed me, I shall never grow to full size.'

'How long do gryphons live?'

'Several hundred years.'

'And how big is full size?'

'Bigger than the largest horse in the world.'

'How do you come to speak English?'

'I speak every language.'

'And your kingdom . . . This is your kingdom, here?'

'Our kingdom extends from the Black Sea to Kamchatka, from Himmaleh to Taymyr. That is the outer kingdom. The inner kingdom is even greater, and includes the sun, the moon, the planets, and the stars.'

'The inner is bigger than the outer?'

'That is the way of all things.'

Pan thought about that. He could see how that might be true.

'Listen,' said Gulya. 'They have fled.'

The sky was silent. On the ground and in the undergrowth

along the river little creatures were beginning to stir, as if they'd been terrified into stillness while the combat was going on above. Then Pan heard something else: the beating of great wings, the rush of air through feathers, and a single long scream of triumph.

Gulya looked up and spread her wings, beating them hard, shaking the last drops of water off them. He saw both her intense pride and her incurable shame, and felt a pulse of admiration for her.

'Wait here,' she said. 'Hold yourself calm, and bow with respect when they land. Say nothing until you're asked.'

Then she sprang up on her lion feet and leaped into the air, circling above the river, catching the faint breeze, her little form climbing higher and disappearing into the dark.

Pan lay on the bank, loosening his muscles as much as he could, taking in his injuries and the particular form of his fatigue. He stretched, flexing his spine, working his jaw, and he wondered what he could say to Gulya's kin, and how much he should conceal.

A few minutes passed. Then he heard voices in the air, and a rush of wind, and then two – three – four immense beasts landed on the grass. Pan could see their great wingtips spread like fingers against the starry sky, their lion feet grasping the soil, their savage eyes glaring red as they sought him out among the shadows. They stood facing him like stone sculptures that had just stepped down from a Persian temple. He didn't have to remember how to behave: he stood because he couldn't help it, and bowed his head because he was overwhelmed.

Last of all came little Gulya, sweeping down between him and the others. She tilted her body up and beat her wings inwards, and hovered a moment before dropping to the grass as lightly as a wren.

'Pantalaimon,' said one of the gryphons; Pan couldn't see which. The voice, coming as it did through an eagle's throat with the power of a lion's chest, seemed to make the ground tremble as much as the air.

Pan bowed his head again, from politeness, but then raised it high and gazed from one to another of the mighty forms.

'I am Pantalaimon,' he said, thinking that he mustn't let Lyra down. He must show all the confidence and presence of her at her best. 'I want to thank you for fighting off those birds, whose name I can't remember. I hope none of you were wounded in the combat.'

'Say less,' said Gulya quietly.

'What has Lyra Silvertongue lost?' asked one of the gryphons.

It wasn't easy to see which of them was speaking, nor whether it was the same speaker as before, nor whether the speaker was male or female, nor whether he or she had some kind of authority over the others.

'Her imagination,' he said.

'Why do you think it is in Karamakan?'

'I have searched all Europe for it in vain. I have spoken to the author of a book that made it flee, and found that he knew nothing. I know that the enemies of the imagination are gathering their forces to invade the desert of Karamakan, and I believe they think that something in that desert nurtures the imagination and allows it to flourish, so they are going to destroy it whatever it is, and wherever they find it. I want to find Lyra's imagination and save it from them, and with its help, with her help, with her, I want to defend the imagination and fight its enemies.'

He worried that he'd said too much, but he could hardly have explained it in fewer words. When he'd finished he stood still, trying to look into those terrifying red eyes, and having to drop his gaze more than once; but he always raised it again, and faced them.

'What is this imagination?' said a different gryphon voice. 'Gulya, what do you know?'

'I believe it is a way of seeing. To see as we do, not as worms do.'

'Is that your understanding, Pantalaimon?' said the first gryphon.

'Yes. My person Lyra Silvertongue saw like that once. She saw everything and everyone in a light of gold. She saw correspondences and analogies and echoes and resemblances, so that nothing existed without a thousand connections to the world, and I saw them with her. For her the world was rich with meaning and alive with delight. Then little by little this way of seeing left her, so I set off to find it and bring it back.'

'Where is she now?'

'I don't know. I hope she is safe. I know she is alive, because otherwise I would be dead. I am her. She is me. We are one being, and we disagreed, and we were very unhappy.'

'How will you travel to Karamakan?'

'As I have travelled so far. Along the surface of the earth.'

'Your enemies are moving faster.'

'Then I must waste no time.'

'Why did you save Gulya? You might easily have left her to the *oghâb-gorgs*, with no dishonour.'

'I beg your pardon, but I don't know how to address you. How should I do that?'

'You say, Your Excellency.'

'Thank you. Well, Your Excellency, to answer your question I shall have to disagree with you. To leave Gulya at the mercy of that creature would have been a matter of great dishonour.'

'But you did not know who she was.'

'I would have saved any creature rather than lose honour.'

This caused the four gryphons to murmur together, to move closer to one another, to bend their heads together. Pan felt a curious combination of emotions: pride, in saying the words he'd just said and finding that he meant them; apprehension, for he had not the slightest idea how the great creatures would react to this little English-speaking dæmon; and love, love for Lyra, love for Nur Huda, love for Gulya. But it wasn't complex, it was simple. These were all one thing.

The gryphons turned to face him again.

'We want to know more about this imagination. It seems to us that it is a matter of concern for every creature in our worlds. You must come with us and explain everything you can to our queen.'

That voice seemed to come from one who hadn't spoken before. It was lighter and more musical, and even sympathetic.

Pan gathered his courage and said, 'But, Your Excellencies, I have a task to do, and I must not step aside from it. I would be honoured to speak to your queen, but if it means losing a single day on my journey, I must respectfully say no.'

This time it was Gulya who replied, and as she spoke she sprang into the air and flew around, beating her wings in rage.

'What do you think you're saying? How dare you be so insolent! I won't have it. If you are invited to visit Her Celestial Majesty Queen Shahrnavāz you do NOT refuse! Now you must apologise and beg to withdraw your refusal. Do so at once!'

And she landed on the grass in front of him, bristling with such fury that she seemed to throw out little darts of it, invisible sparks that scorched the air as they flew and stung him like bees.

It would have been funny, but he was so tired. He wanted to sleep for a thousand years. So he bowed to the little gryphon, and to her companions, and said, 'I beg your pardon, Your Excellencies. I have learned a lesson tonight. I will gladly visit your queen and answer any questions she has. My only questions to you are: how shall I make that journey, and how far is it?'

'Climb on to my back,' said the gryphon who'd spoken last, and she knelt to make it possible.

Pan sprang up, and found her back broad and muscular and warm. He lay between her wings, where the eagle's feathers gave way to the lion's fur, and felt a mighty surge of power and movement as she leaped up into the star-filled sky. He felt utterly safe, and exhilarated, and full of wonder; and a moment later he fell into the deepest sleep of his life.

*

In the garrison town of Küçüklü in the south-east of Anatolia there was a military prison, and the prison had a small infirmary, where captives uncooperative enough to resist torture were sent to reflect on their obstinacy. If they didn't seem inclined to do that, the infirmary was, after all, a convenient place to die.

Some weeks after Sebastian Makepeace's visit to Battersea, in fact on the very night when Lyra was rescuing Nur Huda's dæmon over a hundred miles to the south, a young man lay in the Küçüklü infirmary, half conscious and sweating with pain. He'd been discovered unconscious on the train when it made an unscheduled stop, and he was clearly a criminal; no innocent person, having been shot, would have tried to conceal his wound like that unless he wanted to avoid the attention of the police.

Accordingly, Malcolm Polstead was taken directly to the prison hospital, where if he'd had the slightest sense of responsibility he would have died promptly. He'd lost quite enough blood.

However, he was clearly stubborn as well as criminal, and unusual too, for a man of violence. The prison governor was new to his job, with enough spare intelligence to have cultivated an interest in archaeology, and he was intrigued by the papers discovered in Malcolm's pocket, listing his scholarly credentials. A fellow archaeologist!

He brushed his neat military moustache upwards and sent for the medical orderly at once.

'That fellow Peters, the man who was shot. The Englishman.'

'What about him?' said the orderly. 'Colonel.'

The insolence was only in the timing, but it was there.

'Is he losing a lot of blood?'

'Yeah. Won't be with us long.'

'I want him seen by a specialist. He might need a transfusion. Where's Dr Osman?'

'Gone home.'

'Send for him at once. Then come with me to the infirmary.'

Five minutes later the governor was standing by the only occupied bed of the six in the squalid room, while his canary-dæmon perched on the iron frame. The yellow light sifting through the dust on the feeble bulbs overhead didn't illumine very much, but it was enough to show the dirt on the headboard, the stains on the linen, and the prisoner's blood already coagulating on the floor tiles. The man's face was dreadfully pale, his red-gold hair dark with sweat. His cat-dæmon lay on the pillow beside his head, barely breathing.

'I found the doc,' said the orderly.

'Ah, good, good. Doctor, have you examined this man?

'Of course I have.' Dr Osman was irritated; he had been going to take his wife to the opera, and this delay would make him late. His lemur-dæmon looked sulky.

'Has his wound been dressed?' the governor demanded.

'Yes, yes.'

'Then why is he still bleeding?'

'It's a serious wound. I'd be surprised if he lives to eat his breakfast. Now can I—'

'No. See to this wound at once. Dress it again, and better. And then see about a blood transfusion.'

'A blood transfusion? Here?'

'If he loses any more blood—'

'Impossible. We can't do that. We haven't got the equipment, we haven't got the staff, we haven't got the blood. What's it matter anyway? Who is he?'

'An English archaeologist.'

'Too bad. He shouldn't be travelling here, should he. Looting, no doubt. Serve him right.'

'I want you to arrange for him to be transferred to the Memorial Hospital. Immediately.'

'They won't accept him. You remember we tried before with the murderer who blew his own legs off. Sent back three times, because they wouldn't allow an armed guard on duty with him, and you wouldn't let him go without one. As if he was likely to run away.'

'A very different case. This man is not a criminal, he doesn't need a guard, and I do not want him to die here. Kindly do as I ask. Dress his wound and arrange for him to be taken to the hospital.'

The doctor's dæmon snarled at the governor's, who raised her wings in protest.

'At once,' the governor added. 'And, you,' he added to the orderly, 'clean this floor. Then get him ready for the ambulance.'

Muttering, taking off his coat and gloves, the doctor set about dressing the prisoner's wound. To judge by the look of it, the previous dressing had been put on by the orderly. The governor winced. The orderly fetched a mop and a bucket while the governor gazed down at the prisoner's broad face, the damp curls of his hair like gold coins, and the too-tight prison pyjamas.

'Where are his clothes?'

'In there,' said the orderly, jerking his thumb at a row of steel lockers.

The governor tried to open the only one that was closed, and found that it opened anyway, because the lock was bent out of position. Inside he found a bundle of bloodstained clothes and a rucksack.

'Has anyone checked this rucksack?' he asked.

'Yeah, me. That's where his papers were.'

The governor knew better than to ask what else had been in there; if it was valuable, the orderly would have stolen it already. The rucksack itself was battered, dusty, faded. One of the buckles had been replaced with another that didn't match the remaining two.

'I thought you said the papers were in his pocket.'

'Can't remember.'

The orderly knocked against the bed frame with the handle of his mop, and the prisoner groaned.

'Be careful,' snapped the governor, and bent forward to look more closely. The prisoner was frowning in his sleep. His brow was damp, and his dæmon was twitching and extending her claws, no doubt because of a dream.

The governor emptied the rucksack on to the cleanest-looking bed. It contained nothing but a spare shirt and underclothing, socks, a book in some foreign language, a paper bag containing strips of dried meat, a small flask of some kind of alcoholic liquor, a copy of an English-language magazine called *The Economist*, and that was it. No archaeology.

'He must have another bag, another case, something else . . . Are you sure this was all he had with him?'

'Far as I know.'

The governor turned to the clothes in the locker, and found nothing in the pockets but a handkerchief. The man seemed to have hardly any possessions at all. Of course, anything interesting or valuable would have been taken by the soldiers who found him, or the police who'd brought him to the prison, or the admission staff.

After another look at the prisoner, the governor went back to his office and read through the papers again.

'Martin Peters,' he said aloud. 'Doctor Martin Peters.'

His dæmon said, 'He's in a bad way.'

'Well, we'll have to wait and see. Nothing more we can do now.'

The governor drummed his fingers on the desk, looked at his watch, tidied the Englishman's papers again, strolled to the window, which was one of very few in the administration buildings that had a view of the street, and failed to see an ambulance anywhere in the dense traffic.

'I bet he hasn't contacted the hospital,' said his dæmon.

'But why wouldn't he? I gave him an order.'

'He'd say that medical matters were his concern, not yours.'

The governor sighed. 'Have we ever dealt with a more idle and uncooperative staff? Mulish. Not a single one of them with any—'

The medical orderly opened the door and came in without knocking. 'He's dead,' he said.

'What?'

'Oh, didn't you hear me? I said he's dead.'

'What, Peters? The Englishman?'

'Him in the bed down there.'

'What happened? Did he say anything? Did he wake up?'

'I dunno what happened. Nothing happened. I was finishing off the floor and I suddenly noticed his dæmon was gone. So that's it, innit. He's dead.'

The governor pushed past him angrily and set off at a run. When he reached the staircase he stopped and said, 'Why am I running?'

'Because you think he might not be dead,' said his dæmon.

'Well . . . H'mm.'

It was because the man was an archaeologist, that was all. The governor had been looking forward to some civilised conversation.

He went on downstairs quite carefully. There would be reports to write, forms to fill in, information to seek. It was curious, though, the man's situation. He must have been attacked, but why conceal the wound? He was possibly involved in smuggling antiquities, as the doctor had said so cynically. That was not impossible, if reckless at the present time. And his documents – forged, no doubt.

Pity. The governor would have liked the chance to interrogate the man, because he was convinced that his own method of gentle friendly enquiry was more effective than the robust techniques that were officially approved. He might have prevented, or even solved, a major crime.

The infirmary was even more dismal than before because the afternoon light was fading fast. The man's body lay just as it had done earlier, eyes closed, arms by his sides, head resting on the greasy pillow. The dæmon had gone. What form had she had? The governor tried hard to remember. Cat? Could have been.

He looked under the bed, but only for the sake of form. The floor was newly washed, but patchily, and not rinsed properly. There was nothing else to see.

'What is it? What's the matter?' he said to his dæmon, who was perching on the iron frame at the end of the bed, uttering little soft whimpers of fear.

'Something's wrong,' she said.

'Oh, come on, we've seen a dead body before—'

'His eyes are open.'

They were, and looking at him.

The governor uttered a yelp of terror and leaped backwards, stumbling and then falling back on to the next bed.

'What's the matter?' said the orderly, who had just come in.

It was galling to know that the fool must have seen his undignified sprawl on the bed. The governor struggled up and turned to face him.

'Where's his dæmon, damn you?' he shouted.

The orderly blinked and shrugged. There was the hint of a smirk on his face. 'Told you, she's gone. Vanished, like they do.'

'Look! He's not dead, you shit-brained ape! She must be around! Must be close! Find her! Don't stand there goggling like a frog – damn you, look for her!'

The orderly, as frightened as the governor now, backed away as he'd done, and bent to pick up his fluttering, cackling hen-dæmon.

'I swear it – she en't here – I looked all over—'

'You lying mongrel! Get out and search the whole wing! Now!'

The governor was conscious that the man on the bed, whoever he was, had heard and seen everything. He wasn't dead. And yet he had no dæmon. The ancient fear of the uncanny, older than history, probably even older than language, had the governor's heart in its grip.

The man on the bed was opening his mouth. He wanted to say something, but his throat was parched. The governor looked around quickly, found a dirty cup, and filled it from the shower in the corner. Mastering his fear, and admiring his own resolution in doing so, he helped the Englishman sit up and held the cup to his lips.

'*Merci,*' the man said.

'*Vous êtes Français?*'

The prisoner seemed to consider. '*Non,*' he said. '*Anglais.*'

'That was what I thought,' said the governor, in English. 'And your name?'

The man swallowed more of the water, which was faintly brown and smelled of some strong disinfectant. 'Peters,' he said. 'Martin Peters. Where am I? Who are you?'

'I am the governor of this prison, Mr Peters. Dr Peters. We have examined your papers.'

'Why am I in a prison?'

'There are civil disturbances in the city. It was felt that you would be safer here than in the hospital.'

'Am I a prisoner, then?'

'Never mind that. When I examined you earlier there was no doubt that you were alive. Your dæmon was present. Now she has vanished; my staff and I are puzzled, to say the least.'

'Oh, has she gone? I thought so. Why does my hip hurt so much?'

'You were shot. Don't you remember that?'

'No. The last thing I remember was going down a staircase in an empty house.'

'Where was this house?'

'In Antalya.'

'That's a long way away.'

'Was there a train? Did someone put me on a train?'

He was trying to sit up. The governor, overcoming his reluctance to touch such an unnatural being, put another pillow behind him, first turning it round to put the cleaner surface on top.

'You were found on a train, certainly, but—'

'Why did they bring me to a prison?'

'Please don't concern yourself about that. This is the infirmary. You're having the best of care.'

The wounded man looked around. The governor could see quite well what he thought of the place.

'The best care we can manage to give you,' the governor enlarged. 'These are difficult times.'

'Where are my clothes?'

'We have them safe. They are soaked in blood, of course.'

'I would like to have them, and washed, if possible. Can someone clean them for me?'

'Yes, we shall do that. But—'

'And then I shall leave.'

'It's not as simple as that, I'm afraid. There are procedures to be followed, higher authorities to be consulted, assurances to be sought. Regrettably this is not a hotel, Dr Peters. It is a prison, which however we do try to make civilised and not too unpleasant. While you are here—'

'No, no, wait. If I am a prisoner, I need to know what offence I'm supposed to have committed, and I need to talk to a lawyer. If I can't do that, I shall leave.'

The governor was saddened. Furthermore, he could still not quite believe he was talking to a man who was dead. There was a little hum of fear in his head that wouldn't go away.

'It will all be sorted out without difficulty,' he said in his most soothing voice. 'I guarantee that I and my staff will do everything we can to see you on your way as soon as possible, and in a much improved state of health. I simply cannot allow a man with a wound like yours to risk travelling at this time. A few days' rest, some nourishing food, some dedicated medical care—'

'I'm too weak to argue,' murmured Malcolm.

'And there is the difficulty caused by – by the absence of your, er, your dæmon . . . You know how people . . . And the staff here are frankly very likely to be alarmed . . . They are credulous peasants, most of them. Of course I shall give orders, and they will be obeyed, but . . .'

'Yes, I understand.'

'Has this ever . . . Forgive me, but has such a thing ever happened to you before?'

'It's not an unknown phenomenon. You are wearing a military uniform. You have seen battle, I take it?'

'Well, not recently, but what has that to do with . . .'

Malcolm was fully conscious now. Despite the pain, he was thinking quite clearly.

'You haven't encountered post-traumatic cytokinesis?' he said.

Of course the governor hadn't. 'Oh, so this is a case of . . . I see. That does explain it. Still alarming, of course, to those unused to it . . .'

'My dæmon will return stage by stage. There's really nothing to be alarmed about. In the meantime I would be grateful for a cleaner bed, and for someone medically qualified to attend to my wound.'

'Ah. Well, there I've thought ahead. You seem to have lost so much blood that I thought a transfusion might be necessary. We can't do it here, obviously, so I've sent to the Memorial Hospital for advice and assistance, and they should . . . They might get back to us quite soon.'

'And a cleaner bed?'

'Mm. On thinking about it . . . Let me see what I can do.'

The governor left his prisoner there in the dusty gold half-light and bustled away. Being unable to stay awake, Malcolm closed his eyes and fell asleep.

Asta, his dæmon, had never found it difficult to escape from enclosed spaces. The military prison might as well have been made of mist. While the governor was talking to that part of herself called Malcolm, Asta was stepping silently from shadow to shadow in the heart of Küçüklü. She and Malcolm had discussed this as they lay in the infirmary pretending to sleep, and it was clear to them both that Malcolm wasn't going to be able to move for some time; so the big ginger cat-dæmon pressed herself into the darkness by the door, and as soon as the orderly came in, she slipped past his legs and out of the room. Ten minutes later she had discovered what she wanted to know.

3

Towards Aleppo

When Lyra woke up under the sheepskins it was to find the sun not yet risen, the stars not quite all absorbed back into the sky. The air was very cold. From where she lay she could see the sleeping form of Abdel Ionides, and the camels slumbering on their folded legs, and the outline of the ruins of Madinat al-Qamar stark and still against the horizon.

She'd have liked nothing more than to lie there half asleep, clutching the dream of Pan to her breast, but there were private things she wanted to attend to before Ionides awoke. The cold was piercing, and her hand throbbed unmercifully, but she felt clean and empty and calm, and she knew the secret of the red building.

She wrapped herself up again and watched the dawn take over the sky.

There were no birds to sing in that wilderness; the only sounds that came to her were a subdued occasional snuffle from one of the camels and the quiet breathing of Ionides. The air was still, so there was not even the whisper of sand grains shifting over one another.

She thought again about what had happened in the moon-washed forum, and then deep in the treasury, and afterwards when she spoke to Nur Huda beside the fountain. It felt now as if everything she'd done and said in the City of the Moon had taken place in a state of delirium. She sent her blessings to Nur Huda and her little jerboa-dæmon, to guard her and wish her well on her journey home, and although she felt a helpless little sob from part of herself, knowing that the alethiometer was gone for ever, there was also a curious relief . . . A sob from part of herself? How many parts did she have? Was Pan aware of what she'd done? He was a part of herself too, or she was a part of him. Perhaps he wasn't far away. Perhaps he was waiting in the desert near Aleppo. She, or part of herself, was also feeling a distinct excitement, a tingle of expectation and hope. And there was that dream . . . And the warning, if it was a warning, about something called the alkahest . . . There were so many things to find out!

Dawn was coming, and it came quickly: unlike the gradual reluctant sunrise of the high latitudes, it seemed to arrive between two blinks of an eye. The camels were shifting. Ionides must have heard them, because he turned over and sat up smoothly. Lyra saw his dæmon scamper up the rock beside him and stretch herself in the first rays of the sun.

'You awake, Miss Silver,' he said, not as a question. 'You beat me to it. How was your visit to Madinat al-Qamar? Did you find news of your dæmon, I venture to ask?'

As he spoke he rose to his feet and flicked out his blankets, laying them over the rock, brushing them clear of sand. His voice was as clear as that of an actor on a stage: not loud, just brightly audible.

'No,' she said.

'Ah.'

While he went behind the rock, presumably to empty his bladder, Lyra took off the shirt she'd been wearing and changed it for another, carefully transferring the alethiometer needle from one pocket to the other. Then she tried to tidy her hair. She was aware of how wild she must look, not that she was concerned very much about that; but something had lightened in her. She longed for a shower.

She crouched by the fire, which Ionides had banked against the night, and began to move pieces of wood around, hoping to rouse it into flame.

'Miss Silver! What you doing? This is my job. You employ me to make fires, to cook, all that, not to sit like a pasha watching while you put this one out!'

He bustled her aside and bent to correct her clumsy efforts.

'Look, see this, the flame want to go this way. You draw it, you give it energy, you help it. See this wood?' It was a gnarled and prickly twig with drops of resin oozing through the bark. 'This is your friend. This is your best servant. Like a shepherd has a dog – you have the redthorn. You save two, three pieces at night, you keep them close to hand, you watch till the little baby flames flicker up the height of one fingernail, and then . . .'

Like a candy-seller pulling sugar out of the air he twined and twisted the redthorn in the little flames, and soon he was able to pull them upwards, stretching them, twisting them like yarn, and touching them down on another stick. Before long the fire was blazing securely. Ionides thrust the end of the redthorn in the sand to put it out, and handed it to her before settling the pot on the fire to boil for coffee. Lyra put the charred twig into her pocket.

'When you come back last night,' he said, squatting back on his heels, 'you tell me you see a gigantic bird like a lion, or a lion like a bird. Naturally I think you are briefly out of your mind.'

'You've never seen anything like that?'

'Never. Such things are said to exist, but if at all, only in the mountains of the Elburz.'

'They're not the birds you told me about before? The *oghâb-gorgs*?'

'No, no. Those are mere savages. The kind you describe is very noble, very proud. Some people say they are spirits, some people don't believe in them at all, other people say they do exist, but only in stories. I don't know English word for them. In French they are called *griffon*.'

'Gryphon,' said Lyra. 'Same word in English, almost. I wonder what he was doing in al-Khan al-Azraq.'

'Looking for gold, maybe. They love gold. If anyone steal their gold, they chase them to the end of the earth.'

So the one-eyed man had been taken up into the sky for the sake of the gold of the alethiometer in his hand. But he hadn't had it for more than a few seconds; the gryphon can't have been pursuing him for that. Perhaps he had more gold in his pockets.

'You see any dæmons in there?' Ionides went on.

'Yes. But not mine.'

'You want to try again?'

'No. My dæmon's not there. He was there, but he left.'

'So you had some news, anyway. Where did he go?'

'East. Further east.'

'You know where?'

She said, 'Yes,' but she hesitated, and then wished she hadn't. He was too acute to miss it.

'If you know where, you will want to follow him, no?'

'I know where in general terms. Not exactly. East is a big place.'

'East is a big place,' he repeated, uttering the words without any mockery, but she could see the enjoyment in his eyes.

He adjusted the pot on the fire and passed Lyra a bag of dates. She ate one; it was intensely sweet.

'Aleppo is east,' said Ionides.

'He won't be in Aleppo.'

'We shall be there tomorrow morning. What will you do then?'

'I shall go to Marletto's Café.'

That surprised him. 'You know Marletto's? How you know that place?'

'I know more than you think,' she said, and put another date in her mouth; they'd be nourishing, at least.

'Who you going to see at Marletto's?'

'Depends who's there.'

'And then what?'

He poured some boiling water into the coffee pot and stirred the dark drink briskly with a twig whose end had been split several times to make a rough brush. When the froth reached the rim of the vessel, he added a pinch of something he took from a screw of paper.

'What's that?' Lyra asked.

He held it out. It looked like salt. She took a small pinch and found that it was.

'You didn't notice when I put salt in before?' he said.

'I wasn't capable of noticing anything very much.'

'And now you are?'

'Yes. Why do you put salt in coffee? Most people put sugar.'

'Make the coffee taste better. Plenty sugar in the dates. You want me to make some bread? Very quick. Very nice.'

'No, thank you. The dates and the coffee are fine.'

'Full of nourishment. When you ready, we go. We leave this melancholy place. What kind of dæmons you see in there?'

As he packed everything on the camels' backs she told him a lot of lies about what she'd seen and done in the Blue Hotel. She didn't mention Nur Huda. It felt strange to be lying again, or storytelling, at least; the endless facility she'd had as a child was a marvel to her now. Making it up wasn't hard, but making it convincing was. If Pan were with her, he could have helped by supplying details, prompting, pretending to qualify or correct . . . She wondered, as she spoke, whether that was what he'd meant by imagination.

Ionides listened with close attention. He seemed to find her nonsense both illuminating and probable; but when she was securely on her camel and he on his, he said, 'Miss Silver, you are being satirical.'

'Oh, you don't believe me?'

'Not one word. But your story is very good.'

'Mr Ionides, what is the alkahest?'

'The what?'

She said it again. 'Something told me about it. Have you ever heard the word before?'

'No. Never.'

'It sounds sort of Arabic . . . What do you think the imagination is?'

'Why you ask me?'

'Because you're here. But what do you think the imagination is?'

'You don't think I tell the truth?'

'Not all the time.'

He laughed, and she found herself joining in. Then she said, 'You haven't answered the question.'

'Ah, is very difficult.'

'We have plenty of time.'

'Plenty of time for such a question? How many years you think people talk about this? And you want me to tell just like that, flash bang?'

They had joined the rough road along which they'd come the night before. Ionides turned his camel's head eastwards, and Lyra's followed.

'Well, you could tell me what you think,' she said, 'and I could consider it and then tell you what I think about your answer, and we could keep ourselves amused for hours.'

The morning air was pleasant in her lungs; the sun was warm but not yet hot. The movement of the camel under her felt steadier than it had done at first, so she must be getting used to it. The aches and pains of various kinds were still there, but subdued, and even her broken hand was a little less swollen, a little more mobile. Ionides had noticed.

'You look different, Miss Silver,' he said. They were riding side by side, and it was easy to talk.

'I feel different.'

'Something happen in Madinat al-Qamar, no?'

'That's right.'

'Something real, not imagination?'

'Well, you see, that's interesting already. You mean, if it's imagined, it can't be real? What about the other way round: if it's real, it can't be imagined? They're complete opposites. Is that what you mean?'

'This is your game, Miss Silver, not mine. I am a simple man. I don't know the rules. If something look real, is it real?'

'It depends on—'

'No, it doesn't depend. If it look real in every way, is it real?'

'Yes. I suppose it is. Until you find out it isn't.'

'No, you won't find that. It look real, it taste real, it smell real, the right weight, the right size, everything you can see or feel about it is just like what it should be. Is that real?'

'Yes, then. It must be.'

'Then if somebody say to you, this is not real. You think it's real, it look and feel and weigh like everything it should be, but it's not real. What would you say to that person?'

'I'd want to know why they thought that.'

'You wouldn't believe them ever?'

She had to think about that. What would Gottfried Brande say? The only thing that counted for him was hard evidence that could be expressed in numbers. He'd have no truck with the idea that something unreal could be real. Simon Talbot, on the other hand, thought that the distinction between real and unreal was a cultural construct, entirely dependent on the social and political context, with no permanent validity.

'Wait a minute,' she said. 'I was talking about the difference between real and imagined. You made it into the difference between real and unreal. What happened to the imagination? Where did that go? Do you think that imagined means the same as unreal?'

'I am only a humble guide, Miss Silver. Your questions have a philosophical depth far beyond my ability to understand. Again I say, why you ask me?'

'Because I don't think you're a humble guide at all. I think you're a very clever man, who conceals most of himself from sight. I think you could easily answer those questions, and I really would like to know what you think.'

'Of course you are right,' he said cheerfully. 'I know everything, but is not good for business to say so. I give to a customer my business card, if I had such a thing, it would not say "Abdel Ionides, he know everything". They would look at me and say, "If you know everything, why you dress like a beggar?" Not easy to explain that, Miss Silver.'

'You've done it again.'

'What I do again?'

'Avoided the question. If something is imagined, does that mean it's untrue?'

'All right. You drive me into a corner. You hunt me down like a cat with a mouse, and there is no escape for me. Here you are. This is what I know: without imagination you never see the truth about anything. Without imagination you think you see more truth, but in fact you see less. You know who tell me that?'

'No. Who was it?'

'A holy man from India. He was in prison with me in Baghdad. Very holy man, but not very clever, so he get caught.'

'You were in prison?'

'Many times.'

'What for?'

'In some places, Miss Silver, they put you in prison with no reason. No crime, no trial, no sentence. They don't like your face, in you go. Say you arrive in a city you don't know. You need some money. There is a marketplace. You offer to play a game, backgammon, chess, cards, whatever they like, and you sit down and start playing with some honest citizens, like yourself, but pffft! Along come a policeman. "What you do?" he says. I explain, simple game for innocent amusement with my friends. He doesn't listen, he say is against the law, I have to go before the judge.

The judge say give me some money or I send you to prison. Well, I got no money, and prison is not so bad. Somewhere dry to sleep, something to eat, interesting company. Like the Indian holy man. He tell me that piece of wisdom, so in exchange I show him little game with three cards, so he can get some money to buy food when they let him out, and so we pass the time till they let me out.'

'Did they let him out?'

'I don't know. Maybe I see him again. Maybe not.'

And so they rode on towards Aleppo.

The prison governor at Küçüklü had still not managed to transfer the English archaeologist to the civilian hospital. They didn't want him; they had no beds – the transport situation was difficult – there was a shortage of blood in the transfusion unit – they could not allow the transfer of prisoners without adequate security staff (which was the precise opposite of their objection on a previous occasion), and so on.

So Dr Martin Peters, whose dæmon had vanished, still lay in the grubby and ill-lit prison infirmary, looked after by the same idle and superstitious orderly. When a case of dysentery turned up elsewhere in the prison, and then another, the governor became seriously alarmed.

'The patient Dr Peters,' he said to the orderly. 'He can't stay in there if we have two patients with dysentery.'

'Prisoners.'

'What? What?'

'They en't patients. They're prisoners. So's he.'

'Take him out of the infirmary and put him in a clean cell, and then—'

'Put him in a what?'

'A cell that you have thoroughly disinfected. Put him there, and then move the two infected prisoners to the infirmary.'

'Not allowed to do that, sir. Only military staff can move prisoners.'

'If I tell you to do it, you're not only allowed to do it, you're required to. Don't waste any more time. Get one of the day guards to help you. And do it now, not—'

A peremptory knock, a stamp of boots on the wooden floor, a loud parade-ground voice. 'Sir! Visitor, sir. To see you now, sir.'

The guard who stood there, saluting smartly, was the most soldier-like of all the prison officers, which was why the governor had given him the duty of greeting visitors.

'Well, who is it? Where's he from?'

'Colonel Grigorian, sir. Intelligence Corps. Urgent, sir.'

'Ah. Yes. Well, show him up. And go on, go on, man,' he snapped at the orderly. 'See to that cell at once.'

Rolling his eyes, the orderly followed the guard out, leaving the governor more agitated than he'd been for days. Intelligence Corps? Was he in trouble? Should he have reported the English archaeologist to someone?

The visitor arrived quickly, and saluted the governor, who fumbled a salute in response and cursed himself.

'Colonel Grigorian, ah – welcome,' he said. 'Please do sit down.'

The officer was slim, in his fifties, with very dark eyes and a hawk dæmon. He wore a khaki uniform with an astrakhan cap, a Sam Browne belt and a holstered pistol. The governor didn't recognise his insignia.

'I won't take very long,' said Grigorian. 'The prisoner Peters. Dr Martin Peters. How long has he been here?'

'Oh, er – let me see – I can find out in a moment . . .' The governor started fumbling among his papers, fully aware of how unmilitary he must seem, next to this smartly turned out, fierce, unblinking soldier.

'All right,' said Grigorian, 'never mind now. I'm in a hurry. I want all the papers you have relating to this man. Every single one. You understand?'

'Every single one,' said the governor, nodding.

'Now arrange for him to be taken down to my car. I understand he's wounded. Is that correct? Can he walk?'

'No – shot in the top of the thigh – he'll have to be stretchered, I'm afraid. He—'

'See to it, then, at once. And send whatever possessions he arrived with.'

'Of course. Yes. He's – umm . . . I expect you're aware of post-traumatic cytokinesis?'

'Of course. It's hardly surprising. I shall wait outside with my car.'

He saluted again. The governor knocked some papers on to the floor in his haste to respond, and rang his bell for the orderly. Would the wretched brute have cleaned the stretcher since bringing Peters into the infirmary on it? Perhaps this Grigorian wouldn't notice. And now there'd be no conversations about archaeology. It was all so difficult.

They had to wake Malcolm to get him into his clothes and on to the stretcher, and he was deep in a morphine dream. In the course of the uncomfortable journey down the stairs and into the car, he woke up enough to see what was happening, and when the car began to move away and the yellow light from a street lamp fell across the face of his captor, he understood a little more; but the morphine claimed him back before he could speak. He didn't even notice when Asta leaped up from the floor of the passenger compartment and lay purring on his chest.

Marcel Delamare, the President of the High Council of the Magisterium, had recently returned from a successful and productive visit to London. Successful meant that he had had his way over every item on the agenda, and productive meant that the memorandum of understanding signed by the two sides had a sequestered annexe that was not mentioned in the press release.

Officials were going to clarify the details later, and from what Delamare had seen of the Brytish delegation, there would be little difficulty from them. It had been understood by both sides, and loudly proclaimed in the press, that the discussions expressed the profound and enduring friendship between the kingdom and the Magisterium. To mark the occasion, the President of the High Council was made a Knight of the Order of St Stephen and St Paul, which entitled him to wear a flamboyant gold cross set with pearls and rubies. Having been officially photogrammed doing so, Delamare decided privately to put the ridiculous thing away and never look at it again.

The sequestered annexe, which no one was to know about, said that the two sides had agreed to the deployment of Brytish troops and armaments in the Magisterium's Central Asian venture. Brytish soldiers and Brytish guns would soon be sent (inconspicuously, which meant that stern reporting restrictions applied) to cross the Channel by night and entrain (the War Office loved that sort of jargon) at Calais for Constantinople, where . . . well, where something else was going to happen.

The only people to know about the sequestered annexe were the President and his Private Secretary on the Magisterium side, and the First Minister, the Secretary of State for War, and the Chief of the General Staff on the Brytish. Normally, the information in the annexe would be conveyed to the King at the Private Council, but King Edward the Twelfth was in his late eighties, and no longer had a firm grip of the details of statecraft. It was felt better to spare him the burden of knowing what was being planned in his name; he would not have had a very clear idea of it even in his prime, and these days he was amiably willing to sign any document placed in front of him. His penmanship was shaky, his memory was tenuous, but his courtesy was unfailing.

Meanwhile, the Magisterial diplomatic corps was busy researching the causes of the war its forces would soon be called on to fight. Researching, of course, meant inventing. In this task M. Delamare's officials were greatly helped by the Corporate Relations department of Thuringia Potash, or TP; a private company can hide almost anything under a bland title. What TP meant by Corporate

Relations was, basically, arranging wars and then winning them, but doing so under a different name. TP Corporate Relations could start a war for you, fight it, win it, and all without troubling the courts or interesting the press. It would cost you a fortune.

The chief executive of TPCR, Dr Emil Sundberg, a social scientist by training, joined M. Delamare in his office before the official talks began. The morning sun glowed richly on the mahogany desk, the snowy blotter, and the President's deep black fountain pen.

'A very good morning to you,' said Sundberg, whose chameleon-dæmon was taking her time to replicate the precise maroon of the leather armchair he was about to sit in. 'And many congratulations on your knighthood.'

'I'm deeply honoured, of course,' said Delamare, taking the other armchair.

'Do they give you something to wear? A ribbon, or something?'

'The protocol wouldn't let it be worn in Geneva in any case.'

'No, of course. And were your talks in London productive?'

'Indeed they were. I shall give you a full summary when we meet with our officials later. For the moment I want to hear an outline of what your company proposes.'

'By all means. We strongly suggest that any action we take should be characterised in press releases, briefings and the like, not as war, but as police action, humanitarian in purpose. We have extensive contacts among governments and press agencies, with whom we have developed a powerful culture of discretion and control, and we have an unparalleled record of news curation, widely recognised for its effectiveness. We can plan and execute a swift—'

'Yes, I've read your brochure. I want to hear what it *doesn't* say.'

'I wouldn't want anyone to think,' Sundberg said, having planned and executed a swift change of approach, 'that news curation is our major activity. We have extensive experience in the field of controlled, focused, and robust paramilitary action.

And all of it will be carried out with total discretion. It will appear from nowhere and vanish back to nowhere.'

'Is that what you did during the raid on the Tashbulak station?'

A tiny quiver shook Sundberg's eyelids. 'Precisely,' he said. 'The "men from the mountains", as we succeeded in naming them, attacked suddenly with speed and power, and withdrew into silence. There is nothing to suggest any connection whatever with Thuringia Potash, or with the Magisterium.'

'Then how do you account for these photograms?'

Delamare reached across to the desk and handed the other man a large envelope. As Sundberg took out the pictures inside, his dæmon crawled up to his shoulder and began to turn the silver-grey of his suit. The photograms had been taken through a telescopic lens, and the quality was not high, but they showed with perfect clarity a group of white-robed horsemen riding away from the camera, accompanied by three pick-up trucks with more white-robed men sitting or standing in the back. The rear panel of the nearest truck bore the well-known monogram of TP.

Delamare said, 'These were taken nearby, immediately afterwards.'

'They have been forged, of course,' said Sundberg.

'Let us suppose they haven't. How are you going to explain them?'

'Where have they been seen?'

'In this building. So far, nowhere else. Before long they will appear in newspapers in every country involved in the Tashbulak research, and it will make some difference to the terms of the contract we are going to discuss this morning.'

'I can assure—' Sundberg began, but Delamare cut in with a voice that sliced like a piano wire:

'I repeat: how are you going to answer the charge that Thuringia Potash was involved in the attack?'

'By ignoring it. It's a contemptible amateur attempt to smear the name of a company known throughout the world for its philanthropy as well as its leading pharmaceutical research, which has benefited people with all kinds of medical conditions. It's not worth considering.'

'You and your colleagues had better consider it very carefully before we meet later this morning. Save your meaningless corporate-speak for curating the news, and have a serious answer ready. I do not want to see a picture like this again, do you understand?'

'I completely agree, Monsieur le Président. We shall do exactly that.'

Sundberg was finding it hard to look at Delamare's face. He had never seen eyes quite so intimidating, although the rest of the President's expression was mild and even kindly. His bearing spoke of a comfortable life among luxurious surroundings and agreeable work; his body was solid and slightly plump; his perfectly manicured hands were clasped across his belly; his lightly pomaded dark hair was greying at the temples; his suit of fine dark grey English worsted, his shirt of snowy cotton, his tie of a quietly patterned silk, all proclaimed the successful bureaucrat, the embodiment of worldly experience and power. Only his eyes seemed to belong to a different character altogether, possibly not even to a human being.

'The men from the mountains, for instance,' Delamare went on. 'I want to know who commands them, how you contact them, what you will do when they start acting for themselves.'

'The answer to the last question is that we will dispose of them robustly. They are a rabble, and they have a collective leadership, so they claim, but their most prominent spokesman is called Zafar Sayadov. He is said to come from Azerbaijan, but no one is certain of that. There is also a woman . . .'

'A woman? In charge?'

'Her position is not clear to us, but she is clearly important. She is called Leila Pervani. She was an academic at the University of Alexandria, an experimental theologian of some kind, until she became involved in this movement.'

Delamare made a note. 'How do you contact them?'

'We do that through a network of tradesmen, merchants, camel-drivers, never the same people twice. They are very ingenious, and at times surprisingly disciplined, but fundamentally a rabble, as I say.'

Surprisingly disciplined ... Delamare's view was that no one in Sundberg's position should find anything surprising. The President let two small chains of thought begin to unreel in his mind: one concerned the need to establish his own contacts with the men from the mountains, and the other examined various ways of detaching Thuringia Potash from the coming conflict, when the time was right. They were simply not big enough; their ambitions were limited.

'Thank you,' he said. 'I look forward to meeting your colleagues in an hour or so.'

Delamare stood up and extended his hand, with an expression that was almost genial. Sundberg shook it and left, feeling that he had handled the interview with great skill.

Colonel Schreiber, who had been ordered to arrest and 'disappear' the guide Hugo Beamish, was making a second visit to Les Diablerets, to see what effect explosives had on the opening in the air. He thought it was a mistake to get rid of the guide, who could still have been useful, but after all they had his detailed notes, and the colonel never questioned his orders.

He'd been told to 'destroy' the opening, and the first problem was what Delamare had meant by that. If Schreiber had been going to destroy a *thing*, an object (a wooden case, say) a little less than a metre wide and two metres high, it would take a specific amount of explosive, which could be calculated with the help of various tables of figures from the schools of mining or military ordnance training departments. The colonel had learned all about the process at military college. He could have blown up a *thing* very competently: a wooden thing, a metal thing, a solid thing, a hollow thing; there would be a bang and some smoke, and the thing would be reduced to a mass of smaller pieces in no time.

But a *nothing* was a different problem. You could blow up everything around it, but when the smoke cleared away the nothing might still be there, unaltered.

'The essence of the task, though,' his porcupine-dæmon had said when they were thinking about it, 'is not so much destroying it altogether as making it impossible to go through it. Something that melts the air at the edge and crushes it together – that would work, wouldn't it?'

' "Melts the air",' the colonel scoffed.

'Well, you know what I mean. Thermobaric sort of thing.'

'The trouble is there's only one thing to test it on. That's the real problem.'

There were more problems than that, though. Would it be better to place an explosive charge on *this* side, in this world, or on the other? That was one question. Would an explosion merely enlarge the opening instead of closing it? Or would the noise and the smoke attract the attention of the authorities in that other world, who might investigate and demand reparation, or worse? Or might there be some simple method of closing the damn thing that he had never thought of? His dæmon suggested the analogy of a primitive or savage finding a coat, and wearing it, but having to leave it open because he had never heard of a zip fastener, and thought the rows of little metal teeth were merely decorative.

'Something like that, anyway,' she said.

The colonel had little taste for analogy; that was what dæmons were for, after all, and they rarely said anything useful. Thermobaric, though: there might be something there. An explosion in two stages, the first filling the air with a flammable mist or vapour, and the second igniting *that* – the very process Lyra had used with a bag of flour when she'd rescued the children from Bolvangar all that time ago, but of course Colonel Schreiber knew nothing about that. He was thinking of a device known as the *tonnerre double*, prohibited in warfare between civilised nations because of its abominable effects on the victims – or indeed any nearby creature with lungs. 'Prohibited' merely meant that the armaments manufacturers couldn't sell it openly, but of course research and development continued, and Schreiber's special connections made it easy for him to obtain two examples of the latest and most conveniently sized *tonnerre double* grenades.

He took the squat little canisters out of his rucksack and connected them to a timer that would ensure both detonated at the same moment, and placed one on his side of the opening, tucked down firmly next to it, and the other in a corresponding position in . . . the other world.

'How long?' said his dæmon.

'Ten minutes. Plenty of time to get to that big rock with the tree growing out of it.'

The dæmon remembered that rock, and scuttled ahead over the rocks and the tangled roots, tugging as hard as she could at the invisible bond between her and Schreiber so as to make him hurry.

They got to the rock with five minutes to spare, and settled down on the side away from the opening.

'What do you *think* will happen?' she said.

But as she spoke, she heard someone coming. There was no path, as such, so he – it was a man, whistling – had to do as they'd done, and clamber over the mossy rocks as best he could. The dæmon couldn't help it: her quills shook, and the soft rattle they made sounded to her and to Schreiber unhelpfully loud in the still air.

The whistling stopped, and so did the sound of movement.

They could picture the man looking around, puzzled. He said something to his dæmon, and her dove-voice responded.

After a few moments the man started to move again. They could hear slow footsteps creaking in the patches of snow, the rustle of undergrowth, the little metal click of his steel-tipped alpenstock on rock. Schreiber laid his hand on his dæmon's back, pressing her quills gently down towards her tail.

If the man continued in the same direction at the same pace, he would be very close to the explosive at the moment it went off. And unless they could remove what would be left of his body, it would be found by anyone coming this way, perhaps to look for him, and that in turn would draw their attention to the opening in the air. It was the last thing Delamare would have wanted. But to warn the man would reveal it as well, and leave him alive, which might be even worse.

The porcupine-dæmon shared every quiver of the colonel's thoughts. It was all grotesquely unfortunate.

Then the timer did exactly what it was designed to do, and detonated both grenades. The first explosion made a small noise, not much louder than the sound of hands clapping once. The sounds that came a fraction of a second later were much louder, and included (the dæmon thought) a cry of surprise from the man, itself cut off by the ignition of the cloud of naphtha vapour.

Schreiber and the dæmon waited for the various fragments of rock and tree and human being to fall to the ground, and for the air to clear a little, and then moved cautiously out of the shelter of the big rock and back to where the opening had been.

There was very little left of the man, but the colonel was familiar with that kind of thing. More interesting was what had happened to the opening. In the place where it had been, the smoke from the explosion was twisting in the air, and drifting or seeping out into small shreds of vacancy, twenty or thirty of them, some as big as his hand, others like the holes in a pepper-pot.

The porcupine-dæmon sneezed. Smoke was coming through from the other side too. 'When it's cleared,' she said, and sneezed again, 'there won't be anything to show it was there.'

'Much less, anyway,' said the colonel.

A few little patches of oddness, scraps and tears in the air; nothing like the door-sized weirdness that had been there before. As for the unfortunate passer-by, there was no shortage of scavenging birds or mammals in these forests. In a week or so there would be nothing left to find. There was nothing to worry about after all.

Schreiber gathered up every scrap he could find of the *tonnerre double,* and lifted his rucksack on to his shoulder.

The dæmon said, 'Of course he might have come out of the other world, that man. He might have been going back to it.'

'Serve him right for trespassing then,' said the colonel.

They set off back to Geneva.

'Post-traumatic psycho— what?' said Colonel Grigorian.

'Cyto. Cytokinesis. It's the term for what happens when the living cell splits in two. As if your dæmon vanished for a bit after a traumatic shock. The best I could think of on the spur of the moment,' said Malcolm.

'Well, it's not bad. You seem a bit more lively now. How are you feeling?'

'Painful and weak, but clear-headed. Where are we going, Timur?'

They had been travelling for an hour or so – Malcolm was vague about that – since leaving the prison hospital. As the morphine daze evaporated, he realised firstly that Asta was in the car with them, and secondly that the Colonel Something in the astrakhan cap and the gold shoulder-flash was a man he'd last seen in the offices of the Botanic Garden in Oxford: the historian Timur Ghazarian.

'We're going to Aleppo. I have a friend at the consulate there. At some point we'll have to abandon this car, which I stole. What is your wound?'

'Gunshot in the hip. I think it got worse because I moved too much. I'll have to hope it isn't infected.'

'Who shot you?'

Malcolm told him about the dying director of the research station, about the false nurse, about how he got away from Smyrna.

'But you, Timur . . . Where is Oakley Street?'

They went through the catechism that let one agent recognise another. Ghazarian was word-perfect.

'I was hibernating,' he explained. It was an Oakley Street term for the position of an agent who had retired from active duty, but who was still on a reserve list. 'I don't know how much you've heard, but we're working on Christabel terms now. Oakley Street has been officially disrecognised. You know that expression?'

'It's new to me, but I can guess where it comes from. Christabel, eh?'

'Christabel' was the name of a series of highly secret measures that were to come into operation when Oakley Street was under serious threat. Glenys Godwin must have moved quickly.

'They sent me here to look for you,' Ghazarian said. 'Glenys didn't know you were wounded when she sent me to find you, or she probably wouldn't have done.'

'Then don't tell her.'

Malcolm leaned back in the seat because the pain was becoming difficult again. He closed his eyes. Ghazarian noticed, and eased back a little on the accelerator. The desert road was empty as far as the horizon, and the moon was bright, so he turned off the lights and drove on without them.

Asta lay along Malcolm's shoulder, and they half whispered, half thought together.

'You went to look for him?' Malcolm murmured to her. 'But how did you know he was nearby?'

'I just thought he might be,' said his dæmon.

'H'mm.'

'And what can we do in Aleppo?'

'Look for Lyra.'

'But why would she be there?'

'I just thought she might be.'

'H'mm.'

'Besides,' he said, 'any traveller going further east would have to go through Aleppo.'

'It won't be easy to find her.'

'There are people to talk to. Mustafa Bey, for example. He's a man of business. If we give him something in exchange, he'll deal with us fairly.'

'Then we'll just have to discover something valuable for him.'

She felt something happening in his awareness. 'What is it?' she said.

'Here comes the spangled ring again.'

It might have been a star, or the glimmer of a house light among the distant hills, or a glowing bulb on the car's dashboard, but something had set off the reaction in Malcolm's vision that happened from time to time. The little golden thing shimmered and twisted minutely in the darkness and compelled his attention, just as it always did, no bigger than a point at first but growing steadily as if it was moving towards him.

'I can feel it,' Asta whispered. 'Like something tightening in my head.'

'But not see anything?'

'No. What does it mean this time?'

'Sometimes it doesn't mean anything.'

Ghazarian must have heard them murmuring. He said, 'All right?'

'Yes, thanks, Timur. Just something in my eye.'

'Do you need a handkerchief, or something?'

'No, actually, it's a scintillating scotoma, if you know what that is.'

'Sort of migraine?'

'Yes. Just a visual thing. It lasts about twenty minutes and then fades away.'

'Do you get it often?'

'Half a dozen times a year, I suppose. I'll just sleep for a bit and let it run its course.'

But he was wide awake, and so was Asta. After a minute or so she whispered, 'You should tell Lyra about it.'

'Why?'

'She'd be interested.'

'D'you think we'll ever find her?'

'Bound to. It's not very big, Central Asia. Not many places to hide.'

He grunted. The spangled ring was becoming obstreperous now; this was the central stage, when it took up most of his visual field and made reading, for instance, impossible. He lay back with his eyes closed, the scotoma shimmering snake-like in the dark, Asta tense beside his head.

He shifted slightly to ease the stiffness in his leg. Ghazarian noticed and said, 'I'm going to stop for a minute. I need to empty my bladder.'

He pulled the car in to the side of the road and got out and urinated on to the sand before lighting a cigarette. Malcolm got out too, into the darkness and the wide silence. He held on to the car door and tried leaning to his left and right, and then a little forwards and backwards, and found that every movement hurt.

'What did they give you in the way of medication?' said Ghazarian. His voice was quiet in the open night.

'Morphine. I think I remember an injection. Also a small bottle of tablets made by Thuringia Potash. That company's one of the forces leading into this.'

'You know the new Master of Jordan College is an executive of TP?'

'Really? I knew he was in pharmaceuticals, but that's interesting. Listen . . .'

There was a sound in the sky, or that was where it seemed to be; distant, very high up, and savage: a wild animal screaming. Or more than one.

'What's that?' said Ghazarian.

They both looked up. Against the starry sky there might have been a little flicker of movement – something dark pulsating, or struggling – very small and far off; but that was where the sounds were coming from. The remains of the spangled ring were trembling at the edges of Malcolm's vision, but the central part was clear enough to make out the combat going on high above. It looked like one scrap of darkness fighting another.

'Birds?' Ghazarian said.

'Bigger, I think. Hard to tell. But—'

'They're falling . . .'

The struggle – it was impossible to make out individual birds, if they were birds – was definitely sinking through the sky, almost directly for the two men, it seemed; and the screams of anger and pain were louder.

'They're not birds . . . or are they?' said Malcolm.

'Can't tell. Enormous, though. They're tearing each other to pieces.'

The creatures, whatever they were, scrambled over and over in mid-air, struggling to stay aloft as well as fight, and half succeeding at both. It would have been hard to make out what was happening even in daylight, so quick and so savage were their movements, and all the time they were tumbling lower and soaring up again, tearing and snapping and slashing at each other, and screaming, roaring.

Finally one of the creatures tore itself away and soared up high, or so it seemed; the men couldn't see it any more, and the other creature uttered a howl of triumph or anger and spread its wings wide to glide away, letting the silence return to the sky and the desert.

'Let's move,' said Ghazarian.

Awkwardly, Malcolm got back into the car and lay back panting with the effort and pain. Ghazarian started the engine and pulled away.

Malcolm opened the window and listened as the car gathered speed. Apart from the engine and the tyres on the road, there was nothing to hear but the faint brush of the wind against the sand.

'Timur,' said Malcolm after a mile or so, 'did you ever come across a student called Lyra Silvertongue? A member of St Sophia's.'

'I don't remember the name. And it's not very forgettable. What about her?'

'She used to live at Jordan. She was orphaned and the old Master sort of adopted her. I taught her for a while . . . I think she's travelling to Karamakan and Tashbulak, but I've no idea where she might be now. For the matter of that, where are we?'

'You see that faint light in the sky ahead?'

The moon had set, and dawn was some way off. Malcolm looked where Ghazarian was pointing. 'What is it?'

'It's the lights of Gaziantep. The Syrian border's not far beyond. Somewhere soon – a couple of miles – we'll turn off the main road. Now I think we should move on.'

Malcolm could feel a different freshness in the air that came into the car through the not-quite-shut window.

'I'm surprised there's so little traffic,' he said.

'If we'd come by the other route we'd have faced at least two road blocks. Gaziantep is normally a busy commercial centre, but the authorities are very nervous right now. They don't want anything to hold up the troop trains and convoys.'

'Which forces exactly?'

'Under the command of the Magisterium, nominally, but the alliance includes a number of Brytish troops.'

'*What?*'

'When were you last in touch with Oakley Street?'

'Before that particular deal was announced.'

'It never was announced. It was a secret arrangement between the War Office and Marcel Delamare.'

Malcolm was silent. The world was changing so fast and so thoroughly that he almost felt dizzy until he realised that his head was still affected by the spangled ring.

'This is going to make traitors of us,' he said after a minute.

'I wonder, though. Since the arrangement hasn't been made public, and probably won't be, it might be a defence in law to say that we had no way of knowing who the enemy was, and no reason to expect it would be our own troops.'

'It won't come to court,' said Malcolm. 'The law would be irrelevant. We'd be outlaws, to be shot on sight.'

Ghazarian reached into his jacket and handed Malcolm a smooth flat stone a little smaller than the palm of his hand.

'I nearly forgot,' he said. 'Glenys wanted me to give you this.'

'What is it?'

'I have no idea. You can use it to keep in touch with her. Don't ask me how.'

'Well,' said Malcolm. 'Thanks, I think.'

Sleep was overwhelming him again. He put the stone into an inside pocket and closed his eyes.

4

AT MARLETTO'S CAFÉ

Lyra had never seen a city so elegant, so much at ease with its prosperity, so welcoming to strangers. Tree-shaded streets were lined with cafés and fashionable shops; the men and women, the citizens of this happy place, were smartly dressed in silk suits or floral dresses, and among the gleaming limousines and the yellow taxis, market traders with camels or horses mingled with people from every part of the world, it seemed: curious travellers taking their time to look around, busy merchants or public officials; and everyone with an air of contentment or even outright happiness on this spring morning.

'Is Aleppo always like this?' said Lyra, gazing around.

'Like this in what particular, Miss Silver?' said Ionides, from his camel an arm's length to the left of hers on this busy street.

'Busy, peaceful . . . Everyone seems to have things to do, but they're not in a hurry. And sort of relaxed and confident. Not like Seleukeia, or Constantinople, or Smyrna. There doesn't seem to be that sort of tension here.'

'In Aleppo everyone has good time. Here they make music, they study architecture, they sell books, is a world-famous centre of the cultured and artistic mind. Also they like very much making money.'

'When I was in Constantinople,' she said, 'I heard about some people called the men from the mountains. D'you know—'

His right hand reached for her wrist and gripped it suddenly, wrenching her broken hand with a slam of pain that nearly made her scream.

'What are you doing?' she gasped.

He held it more gently, but didn't let go. 'Lucky for you we are speaking English and not French,' he said with quiet intensity.

'Why? What are you talking about? Please let go.'

'Many more people speak French than English here. You must not use that phrase again, Miss Silver, that expression. I beg your pardon for hurting your hand. In my anxiety to save your life, and mine too, I forgot the wound you sustained. Forgive me, please.'

Lyra moved to take back her hand, and he loosened his own with great gentleness. She had to breathe deeply and regain her balance on the camel, which wasn't easy; while her hand was throbbing so painfully it was hard to think about anything else.

'Will you tell me more when we're out of the crowd?' she said.

'I expect it will be possible at some time. Your hand will remind you of the peril and danger.'

'H'mm,' she said.

After another few minutes Ionides said, 'Very soon, Miss Silver, we shall be outside Marletto's Café. What is your desire, now that I have all but fulfilled our contract?'

'I shall need somewhere to stay. A cheap hotel. Then I shall pay you the rest of your fee.'

'I know the very place. Furthermore, the owner is a friend of mine, and I shall negotiate a price that is even beyond the reach of a great trader like yourself.'

'I want to ask you some more questions,' she said, because she had become used to his presence on their journey, and even to trust him a little. She liked his never-failing fluency, the ironic tone that underlay his flattery, the sense he gave of a wide and well-stocked memory, which he was always prepared to embellish. She'd be sorry to leave him behind, she realised.

'Questions, Miss Silver? Never in my life have I had to answer so many questions, and of such a boundless variety. I am only a humble dragoman, please not to forget.'

'But you always answer with such confidence,' she said as he led them out into a busy square where magnolia trees were in full bloom.

'What else I got?' he said. 'No fortune, no beauty, no family. I am a poor wanderer over the surface of the earth, having to earn a meagre living by doing whatever is useful to travellers more important than myself. No confidence, no living. Look, Miss Silver, on your right: there is Marletto's Café.'

The café was an elegant establishment, with the air of having been transplanted from Saint-Germain-des-Prés or the Piazza San Marco. The tables on the pavement in front were shaded by two great cedar trees, the largest Lyra had ever seen, and the place was busy; waiters in long white aprons moved from table to table with trays nonchalantly held high over their shoulders on the palm of one hand, and the customers sipped their coffees or aperitifs and nibbled their pastries as if the world was a fine place, and they had the freehold of it.

'It looks expensive,' Lyra said.

'Money is not wasted when spent well. The hotel I mentioned is in the street over there – under the palm trees – the Hotel de las Palmas.'

Two minutes more, and she was glad to get off the camel and stretch her back and her legs. The reception area of the hotel was shabby, but clean enough, she thought as she sank back into a large leather armchair and let Ionides deal with the camels and haggle over the price of a room for her. She was tired; it would be easy to lean back, let her head droop, close her eyes.

She had almost done so when Ionides turned away from the owner and came to her with a satisfied smile.

'All settled, Miss Silver. I have agreed a most economical rate, which I can assure you would not be matched by any other hotel in the city. Here is the key of your room. Please take all the time you need. I shall be waiting to escort you to your meeting at the celebrated Marletto's Café.'

Lyra lifted her rucksack and climbed the stairs. She was still surprised every time she slung it over her shoulder – surprised at how light it was. The alethiometer had been nearly everywhere with her for half her life, and it was heavy; how had the young child Lyra carried it so far? And without dropping it or losing it, apart from the time in Will's world when it was stolen from her? And what had she been thinking, to lose it so easily in Madinat al-Qamar?

But of course she had to. Everything had unfolded with the speed of a dream, and just as in a dream, she was helpless. And now, there was no doubt about it, her rucksack was lighter; she couldn't bring herself to use the word burden, but she was certainly free from something.

Her room was like the hotel lobby, modest but clean, and she was perfectly content with it. She changed her clothes without having to decide what to wear, because there was only one other skirt, one other blouse. She noticed that women in this city had the freedom to dress lightly and go unveiled if they chose; in fact, she had seen no more than two women whose faces were covered.

But she'd have to buy something else to wear, and get these things laundered.

She washed herself as well as she could in the little basin with its lukewarm water, and looked in the mirror dispassionately. The bruises on her face were fading, but she was tanned by the sun, and her cheeks and the bridge of her nose not far off from being actually burnt, so she must find some cream or ointment to deal with that. A broad-brimmed hat would help too.

She spread a very little of the rose salve on her nose and lips, her cheekbones and forehead. Then she sat down and thought about Ionides.

He'd been very helpful so far, but could she trust him any further? This part of the world was completely new to her, whereas Ionides was at home with the languages here, and the customs, and the modes of travel. Could she manage without his guidance? She could probably afford it. She still had most of the gold that Farder Coram had given her. Ionides hadn't let her down yet, and besides, she liked him.

The man at Marletto's, this Mustafa Bey whom Bud Schlesinger had recommended. She didn't know what to do. The alethiometer would have helped her decide, of course; even without the books, and without risking the sickness and disorientation of the new method, she'd have gained something from it; her knowledge of the symbols was much greater than it had been, and just to hold it would have given her thoughts something to focus on. And now it was gone.

But she still had the glass, and the needle. If she didn't find something safe to keep them in, though, she might not have them for long. The glass was merely a glass (she supposed), but the needle . . . She took it very carefully out of the pocket it was in, and laid it in the centre of a piece of scrap paper, which she folded over and over till the needle couldn't slip out, and put it in a compartment of her rucksack.

Then she thought of the old gentleman on the train, and the cards he'd given her. She took out the pack and shuffled it and spread the cards face down on the bed beside her. Now what could she do? The alethiometer worked by blending the meanings of three symbols. Should she pick three cards? Or just one? Or what?

She chose one and turned it over. It showed a man behind a barricade trying to defend it from a group of soldiers, against a background of gunfire and bursting shells. She looked at it despondently for a minute or so, and gathered the cards together again.

*

Ionides sprang to his feet as soon as he saw her come downstairs.

'Miss Silver! Now I am your guide and guardian for the journey to Marletto's Café. May I ask if you are hoping to see the well-known and respected Mustafa Bey?'

'How did you know that?'

'It was a guess purely and entirely. A traveller of your consequence would of course wish to pay her respects to such an important gentleman, and Marletto's is where he is to be found. It is as good as a headquarters for his multitude of enterprises.'

He held open the hotel door and walked along beside her with the air of a senior courtier accompanying a princess. He looked no different from the ragged and none-too-clean individual who had first appeared outside her hotel room in Seleukeia, but he bore himself with such confidence and brio that Lyra felt herself to be acting a part too, and enjoying the attention of other passers-by. Most of those who looked at her were disconcerted, of course, by her lack of a dæmon, but she remembered the woman she'd seen in Amsterdam, strolling along magnificently indifferent to the hostile stares of other people, and she remembered Farder Coram's advice too, to bear herself like a queen.

'Mr Ionides,' she said.

'I am all ears,' he declared.

'From now on my name is Tatiana Iorekova. I am a queen of the witches of Novaya Zemlya. You are a magician from Prague, and you are in my service.'

'Ah! I completely understand. This is how I shall present you to Mustafa Bey, no?'

'That's correct.'

'And what is my name?'

'Magister Parathanasius.'

'Parathanasius. A fine name, which I shall strive to deserve. How should I address you, Queen Tatiana?'

'Like that. Say Queen Tatiana, may I present His Excellency Mustafa Bey?'

'Not "Your Majesty"?'

'No. We witches live plainly and without ceremony. Ah! – Wait here.' She had noticed something in the window of a dress shop, and went inside. After a minute she came out with a length of narrow scarlet ribbon.

'That for me or for you?' said Ionides.

She smiled, which surprised him, and it occurred to her that she couldn't remember the last time a smile had come to her face. She tied the ribbon around her head, across the middle of her brow, and let the ends fall in front of her right ear.

Ionides watched critically, and said, 'You permit?'

She nodded, and he adjusted the ribbon slightly.

'There. Very royal. What my name again?'

'Parathanasius. Magister. Like Maestro. Master Parathanasius.'

'From Prague.'

'That's right.'

He looked around. The street was busy; it was a late morning in a prosperous cosmopolitan city, and no one knew they were in the presence of a queen and a magician.

'All right, Queen Tatiana Iorekova,' he said seriously. 'You wanted me to guide you to Aleppo. Here we are, and you will soon pay me forty dollars—'

'Thirty.'

'As you say. When I take you to Mustafa Bey our contract will expire, not so?'

'That's right.'

'And what then? The whole of Asia is open to you. What is your destination? Will you require a guide to accompany you there?'

She had already made her mind up, but there were formalities and customs to observe.

'Master Parathanasius, this is not the right place nor the right time. A queen of the witches does not bargain in the street. When I have concluded my business with Mustafa Bey, you and I shall go to another smaller café and discuss the matters you raise over a glass of tea.'

He nodded slowly. His expression was serious, his clothing ragged and dirty, the scar across his face white against the brown skin and the greying stubble. He looked like a beggar. But he stood upright, his body was lean and tense, and his eyes were alive with complicity and, deep inside, amusement.

'All right, we go to find Mustafa Bey,' he said. 'You come with me, Queen Tatiana, and my magic powers find the way.'

He strode along beside her for all the world as if he really was a magician in the service of a queen. Lyra was pleased with her own bearing too. Like panthers, that was the way Farder Coram had described the way witches bore themselves. She found herself thinking something unexpected: she wanted Abdel Ionides to feel proud of her.

He swept imperiously into the entrance of Marletto's, stopping in mock astonishment only when a white-aproned waiter said a few words in French, sharply, and barred his way.

'*Vous nous prenez pour des MENDIANTS?*' Ionides said in high indignation. '*Écoutez, espèce d'imbécile. Voici sa majesté la reine Tatiana Iorekova, qui gouverne le royaume entier de Novaya Zemlya, et moi qui suis son sorcier particulier, le gardien de ses finances, le président de conseil de ses affaires d'état, le Maître Parathanasius!* Queen Tatiana,' he went on, turning to Lyra and switching in a moment from arrogant to emollient. 'I apologise for the ignorance of this low-born rascal. Please forgive him, because now he knows who you are, he will hasten to bring you everything you desire, and conduct us without delay to a corner of this establishment which is fit to receive us. And,' he added to the waiter, 'take word to His Excellency Mustafa Bey that Queen Tatiana Iorekova will receive him at once.'

The waiter looked from Ionides to Lyra, from Queen Tatiana to Master Parathanasius. Ionides was bursting with angry pride, and Lyra held herself still and faced down the waiter with a gaze that came from the coldest fastnesses of the northern ice. Privately she was delighted.

The waiter bowed nervously and led the way to a corner shaded by a potted palm whose leaves waved delicately in the breeze from a fan on the ceiling. Ionides held out a chair for her while the waiter hastened away.

'When you've presented him to me, you can go,' Lyra said quietly. 'I saw a fountain in the square as we came through. I'll meet you there in about an hour.'

'You don't need interpreter?'

'I'm sure I can manage. Here he comes.'

Mustafa Bey was a large man in a physical sense, and an imposing one. His wealth was visible in the exquisitely cut cream linen suit, the hand-made shoes, the massive gold watch on his wrist, the golden signet ring on his little finger, the immaculately groomed grey hair; his power was manifest in the way he seemed to carry a field of magnetic force around him, compelling attention, demanding respect, knowing with utter certainty that his every wish would be not only fulfilled, but anticipated. His dæmon was a cheetah. If Lyra had not been a queen, she might even have been intimidated.

Ionides inclined his head briefly and said, 'Queen Tatiana, may I present His Excellency Mustafa Bey?'

Lyra extended her right hand. The great merchant bent to kiss it, and Lyra responded with a smile.

'Please join me, Mustafa Bey,' she said. 'I know how busy you are. I would be grateful for a few minutes of your time.'

She indicated a chair, and Mustafa Bey sat down. Ionides was giving an order to the waiter, who hurried away, and then Master Parathanasius bowed deeply to Lyra and withdrew. Mustafa Bey still had not said a word.

'I was advised to consult you,' Queen Tatiana said, 'by a learned scholar in Oxford, Doctor Sebastian Makepeace.'

The merchant's large and profoundly dark eyes widened a fraction of a millimetre. His expression changed from one unreadability to another.

'And there was a friend I last saw in Smyrna,' she went on, 'who said that the one source of all the information I would ever need on my journey was Mustafa Bey, whom I would find in this café. One such recommendation would have been enough to make me come here – two, and I had no choice. Mustafa Bey, I am glad to meet you. Will you take tea with me?'

She could see the waiter hastening to her table with a loaded tray.

'I would be honoured,' said the merchant. His voice was unexpectedly light and gentle.

The tea was poured, the pastries were set out, the waiter bowed and left.

Mustafa Bey was not going to start this conversation. He was a busy man, but he was clearly curious, and Lyra was aware that they were being watched by many eyes that were equally interested. She was glad she had not come to him as a petitioner, having to wait to be seen: this table gave her a little enclave in the middle of his territory, like an embassy, where she could command things, to which she could summon him, from which she could dictate the course of their encounter. It also meant that the initiative belonged to her: she must get on with it.

'As I mentioned, Mustafa Bey,' she said, 'I'm on a journey. I want to travel to the desert of Karamakan, and I would like to ask the advice of someone who knows the Silk Roads as well as anyone alive.'

'My advice would be a single word: Don't.'

'I shall bear that in mind, but I won't take it. I'm determined to go.'

'What do you think you will find there?'

'A red building that contains something of immense value.'

'And what is that? Do you know what is in this red building?'

'Yes, I believe I do.'

'And you still want to go there, and put your life in danger, and risk not being able to return?'

'Yes.'

He sipped the hot tea. Despite his bulk, all his movements were delicate and graceful.

'I have never been to the red building myself,' he said, 'but I know the conditions under which it must be approached. The traveller by land, the dæmon by water. Do you?'

'Yes, I do.'

'And your dæmon?'

'The witches of the Arctic have the power of separation. At the moment, my dæmon is attending to an important piece of business somewhere else.'

He nodded, and set a calming hand on the head of his cheetah-dæmon. 'And what do you need to know about the journey between here and Karamakan?'

'How long does it take for a camel-train to go that far?'

'Six months, more or less.'

'And a traveller alone?'

'Less time, but more danger.'

'Danger from what, Mustafa Bey?'

'Bandits on the ground. And even more from birds in the air. There are no zeppelin routes across these lands for that reason. The birds are immense and ferocious. They command the air almost entirely. Do your people ever fly across Central Asia?'

'Very seldom.'

'With good reason. But, Queen Tatiana, you are not telling me the truth.'

Lyra was aware of a deep soft growl, almost too quiet to hear. It was the merchant's dæmon, whose black-rimmed eyes were staring at her throat.

'In what way?' said Lyra. Her skin was prickling.

'You are not a witch. I have dealt with many witches – please do not interrupt me – and you are not one.'

'Could you tell at once?'

'No. I had to listen to you first. Now I am certain. Your name is Lyra Silvertongue.'

Lyra didn't move, though every nerve was urging her to run out. She felt breathless.

He went on quietly, 'We are being watched. While we sit here together, you are safe. I shall make sure you can leave without being followed, but you must do as I say.'

'How do you know who I am?'

'Your friend in Smyrna – Bud Schlesinger? I thought so. You must realise I have a thousand connections, more, from Morocco to Nippon. Very little happens on the Silk Roads that I do not hear about.'

'You know about the research station at Tashbulak?'

'Yes.'

'Do *you* know what's in the red building?'

'No. You said you think you know. What do you think it is?'

Lyra thought: *If Bud Schlesinger trusts him . . .*

'It's an opening into another world,' she said.

His cheetah-dæmon stood up, her tail slowly swinging. Mustafa Bey whispered a word or two, and she sat down again, her eyes never leaving Lyra's face.

'You know of such places?' he said.

'Yes. I know how they're formed, and I know how to close them. I have been through . . .' she tried to remember how many, but couldn't. 'Several.'

'Each into another world?'

'There are billions of worlds. The door that opens inside the red building leads to the world where the roses come from. The special roses.'

'Well, that I did not know,' he said.

'I don't know it for certain. I want to go there and find out.'

'And what will you do then? If you go through, you will not be able to return.'

Lyra picked up a piece of baklava. She was recovering a little of her composure. 'Mustafa Bey,' she said, 'please tell me what you know. You haven't told me how you know about the red building, or who made it, or how the rose-oil trade is carried on, or what is happening to it now. If you know that no one who enters that building is allowed to return, there must be other things you know.'

He nodded. 'For centuries, for thousands of years,' he said, 'there was a small trade in those roses and their oil in that region. It was like any other trade in precious material. High price, small quantity, important to guard but easy to transport, very specialist market.'

'How did you . . . How did merchants get hold of the material? Surely they didn't go to the red building every time?'

'There is, or there was, a recognised guild of brokers. They would meet agents of the rose-growers and distillers at various centres of exchange, Tashbulak for one. I believe that those brokers made regular journeys into the desert, to the red building, and paid generously for the rose material. There was nothing to indicate that such brokers had any dealings with another world, or indeed were any different from the traders who bought from them, my own agents included.'

'Who bought the rose material? What did they want it for?'

'Ritual purposes? Medicine? Expensive cosmetics? There was no need to enquire more closely. If a customer has the money to buy it, and the commodity is not explosive or poisonous or bulky and heavy, and does not interest those who gather taxes, then trade will soon come into being. Respectable merchants such as myself will of course be happy to help the process work easily and to make a modest profit. For a long, long time the trade went on without change, interruption, increase or decrease. A steady demand, a steady supply. If I thought about it, it would only be to speculate whether the roses might be grown somewhere else and sold more widely, but every attempt I heard about ended in failure, and there seemed no danger of the existing supply drying up, so I concluded that there was little point, given that the market was so small.'

'So you're not interested in the roses themselves, really?'

'I am interested in everything. Money, for example. Have you much money, Queen Tatiana?'

'I have a little gold.'

'Would you lend me a gold coin? I want to show you something.'

Lyra wanted to see this something, so she felt for one of Farder Coram's gold coins and put it on the table.

'You look suspicious, Queen Tatiana, but there is no need to be. Ah! A coin from High Brazil.'

He weighed it briefly on a little set of scales that he produced from his pocket, and made a note. Then, with a quick flick of his fingers, he gestured to a soberly dressed man sitting a few tables away. The man bent to listen, and Mustafa Bey murmured a few words. The man, who was probably a secretary, set off at once to speak to a customer at a table in the corner, who listened and then stood up at once and made for Mustafa Bey.

He bowed and took the chair the merchant indicated. The secretary joined them, with writing materials to hand.

Mustafa Bey indicated the scales and the gold coin. The customer listened closely; they weighed the coin and exchanged a few words; the secretary wrote them down, and the customer and the great merchant both signed the paper. Mustafa Bey put the gold coin in the customer's hand and nodded.

'Er – what have you just done?' said Lyra, watching the customer walk away with her coin.

'I have bought a grove of olive trees. Ali . . .'

Another instruction to the secretary, who went and brought someone else to the table. Polite greetings; a bow of respect from the customer; the secretary gave him the paper to read, and then Mustafa Bey spoke to him for a minute. The man nodded, looked at the paper again, rocked thoughtfully on his chair, closed his eyes and murmured a few words.

Then he opened his eyes and nodded. Another agreement was written out and signed, with gestures and words of mutual respect, and Mustafa Bey sent the secretary away to bring someone else. Meanwhile, the waiter came with fresh tea.

'What have you bought now?' Lyra said.

'A consignment of very fine carpets from Bokhara.'

The same thing happened again. This time Mustafa Bey exchanged the carpets for a fishing boat currently docked at Smyrna, and then he exchanged that for some precious stones from Ceylon, and finally he exchanged those for . . . some gold. Four coins of the size of Lyra's now lay on the table where her one had lain.

'There is your gold coin, or one exactly similar,' said the merchant. 'Please allow me to weigh it to confirm what I say.'

He did that, and then slid the coin across the tablecloth.

'Yours,' he said, and added one more. 'This is the interest your coin earned while it was in my care. The rest is my profit.'

Lyra blew out her cheeks, and then thought that was rather a vulgar thing for a queen to do, and brought her expression back to normal.

'Well,' she said. 'So that's what money can do. And the roses? How do they come into it?'

'It was a small fluctuation in prices that brought them to my attention. I am not the only merchant involved in this trade, you understand, though by some way the biggest. Some of the steady customers began to complain that they were being outbid by strangers, and in turn my agents found that the rose oil was selling in regions further west than previously. There were rumours of adulteration with inferior products. I sent a small team into the desert of Karamakan, and only one man came back. He described the red building and everything he saw inside it in terms so rapturous that I thought he was quoting poetry. He said that the red building had two doors, the one he entered through, and through which he came back, and another through which he could leave, but not return.'

'Really? What did he say?'

'He spoke of rose gardens and meadows rich with colour – incidentally, the roses are a unique colour, did you know that?'

'I've never seen them.'

'Partway between red and yellow, he said, but not orange. Some blend of colour that was impossible to describe, but beautiful, subtle, complex. He told me of an air scented with fragrance, of fields and gardens tended with care and skill, of profound craftsmanship in every homestead, where the growers boil the petals for rosewater and then distil it in simple vessels down to the finest and most exquisite oil – a barrel to make a thimbleful. And then the exchange – a process of ritual and courtesy, attended by hospitality and ancient formulas. Only members of a guild of dealers from the region of Karamakan are allowed to take part in the commerce, and everything they take for exchange is the finest this world can offer. My agent learned that the prosperity brought by the market in rose oil was spread throughout that city, that nation, that people. Everything was harmonious, everyone busy with work they valued and enjoyed, everyone well rewarded. I was happy in my turn to hear of a place where such prosperity existed, where people were glad to live and proud to work. I was eager to help the trade that sustained their wealth and did no damage to mine, and happy to accept their conditions and obey their laws. And now you tell me that the place where the roses grow is another world entirely.'

'But how could your agent know all that, if he couldn't go out of the other door?'

'I do not know. Perhaps he was allowed to look out of it. And now you tell me that he had been looking at another world?'

'If I'm right . . . But please could you keep that to yourself?'

'You have told this idea to no one else?'

'No one. Could I speak to this man, I wonder?'

'His dæmon became sick later, and they both died.'

'Oh, I'm sorry . . . And Mustafa Bey, have you ever heard the term alkahest? The alkahest?'

He shook his head. 'Never. Is that a term of botanical science?'

'I don't think so. I heard it and just wondered what it meant.'

'It is unknown to me.' He sipped the tea. A waiter, watching from some way off, saw this and hastened to refill his cup before withdrawing again. 'Tell me this,' Mustafa Bey went on. 'Why do you want to go to this place? There is no need. I can supply what they produce.'

'In the hope of finding someone I used to know,' she said. She was taken aback by the faintness of her own voice.

The merchant nodded. His expression was serious and preoccupied. His dæmon spoke again, in a rumbling whisper, and he bent his head a little to hear her.

Lyra sipped her tea, which was now cold. This was all so difficult . . . Then she remembered Farder Coram all those years ago in the town of Trollesund, talking to Dr Lanselius, the Consul of the witches, in his neat little parlour. The answer to the question Farder Coram had asked had led them to Iorek Byrnison, and the success of their expedition. She'd followed his example once before, and that had worked too.

'If you were me,' she said now, echoing Coram's words, 'what question would you ask of Mustafa Bey?'

The great merchant looked at her steadily for several seconds. She couldn't read his expression, but she felt he was reading her, and clearly too.

'I would ask him to tell me what he knows about your servant,' he said.

'My – oh, Master Parathanasius, My personal magician, *Mon sorcier particulier*. Why? What do you know about him?'

'He used to be a professor of mathematics at the University of Alexandria.'

'*What?* When?'

'Until about ten years ago. There was a scandal, possibly sexual, possibly financial, possibly political, possibly all of them. The details are unimportant. He had to resign his position. Since then he has had many occupations, including that of spy, but never before, I think, that of personal magician.'

'A spy? For whom?'

'Commercial interests, mainly. He has also worked for various governments, including that of Muscovy. With the authorities in Geneva, however, he has had no dealings of any kind, as far as I have heard.'

'He sounds very well known, for a spy. I thought spies had to be inconspicuous. Practically invisible.'

'There are few people – I think very few indeed – who would be able to tell you this. I can, because I became interested in him. Perhaps one day I shall employ him myself. What name did he use when you engaged him?'

'Abdel Ionides. Is that not his real name?'

'Who knows? The name he used as a professor of mathematics was Rashid Xenakis. He has used many others.'

'Did you recognise him, then, when he introduced us?'

'As soon as he came into the café. When I saw that he was with you, my interest was doubled. The performance he put on for the maître d'hôtel was enjoyable, but too loud. He enjoys playing a part, but he should remember to be an actor, not a star.'

'He's been a very good guide, so far. I employed him to take me to Aleppo, but I'm thinking about suggesting he continues with me to Karamakan. Do you think that might be a bad idea?'

'Does he charge a high rate?'

'We came to a satisfactory agreement about his fee for this part of the journey.'

'He would make an excellent guide, if that was all he did. But if he agrees to do it he will certainly have his own motives for going to Karamakan, and they might not be helpful for you.'

Lyra cast her eyes around the café without moving her head too much. It seemed like what it was: a comfortable, welcoming place with a wealthy, cosmopolitan clientele. If anyone was watching her and Mustafa Bey, she didn't see them.

'Rashid . . . ?' she said quietly.

'Rashid Xenakis.'

'A Greek surname again, and an Arabic first name. Well, Mustafa Bey, you have given me a lot to think about. I'm very grateful to you. But you said something was going wrong with the rose-oil trade.'

'It is. Something is at work, very quietly, very subtly, and things we thought were firm and solid are weakening and giving way.'

'Things like . . . What sort of things?'

'Things we trusted. You will see examples all around if you look. Whether this infection is coming from the east, the west, the north, the south, the air or the water, the earth or the fire beneath it – I don't know. Queen Tatiana, let me put it like this: it would be useful for me if you succeeded in your journey to the red building, because I would be very interested to know what you find in there, and indeed on the journey. Therefore I would like to help you. For example, I can provide you with a safe journey, and a much quicker one than you would manage on your own. There is a new fleet of international buses, extremely comfortable and fast, in which I have an interest. Camel-trains are unrivalled for transporting goods, but believe me, you would be vastly better served by one of my buses, for the first part of your journey at least. In exchange I would like you to do something for me: I have agents and representatives in every city you will visit on the way. Written reports of anything you find out, or hear, or discover, sent to me through those agents en route, would amply repay any help I can give you. They are not hard to find.'

'Mr Ionides will realise what I'm doing. He's too clever for me to do it without being noticed. He'll have to know.'

'I would expect that.'

'And what about the Magisterium?'

'Of course, report what you hear about them.'

'That wasn't what I meant. What's your relationship with them?'

'Polite but distant. We have different concerns.'

Lyra toyed with the baklava and licked her fingers automatically. 'Very well,' she said. 'I agree. Thank you.'

He signalled to his secretary again. The man came at once, carrying a small leather box, which he set down on the table. Mustafa Bey opened the lid to reveal a rosewood writing-case. The secretary waited with hands folded and eyes averted while the great merchant uncapped a fountain pen and wrote a short paragraph in Arabic script, and another paragraph in what looked to Lyra like Cyrillic.

Lyra saw all that with unfocused eyes. She was thinking of Ionides as a professor of mathematics; it was both difficult and easy. Should she ask him?

Finally Mustafa Bey wrote one last paragraph in English, before blotting the paper and handing it to her. She read:

> *The bearer of this letter is Her Majesty Queen Tatiana Iorekova.*
> *She is my personal emissary, and is to be given every courtesy and*
> *assistance wherever these three languages are spoken.*
>
> *Mustafa Bey*

'Thank you,' she said.

He took it back and inked his large signet ring on a pad held out by the secretary before pressing it carefully at the foot of the letter. The ink was blood-red.

'I'll write to you about everything I discover,' she said. 'I really am very grateful.'

He stood up. She extended her hand, and once again he bent to kiss it. As he left her table and returned to his own corner of the café, she could feel the attention receding from her like a tide and following him, and presently when she left, with the ink dried and the letter folded in her pocket, no one took any notice of her at all.

*

The research station where the murdered botanist Dr Hassall had worked stood empty for some weeks. The men from the mountains had swept through it like a cyclone, killing many of the staff, smashing windows, tearing off roofs, scattering scientific equipment and plant specimens, and ransacking every part of the buildings. They hadn't come to steal anything: just destroy it. Laboratories, greenhouses, administration offices, bathrooms, the accommodation block, the kitchen, the common room where people could relax and talk together, the janitor's stores – all torn open, all scattered and smashed. The planting beds outside, the ranks of plants carefully germinated and tended for their potential value in medicine or commerce, were driven over and set ablaze. The distillery and all its equipment where the essence of various plants was distilled into tiny vials of precious oil were broken up and shattered beyond repair.

The men from the mountains, having completed their priest-like task, vanished as swiftly as they had appeared. When people from the nearest village came carefully to see what had happened, they found the bodies of several scientists from Europe and Africa as well as those of their own people, cooks and cleaners and outdoor workers; they buried them all with the respect and care their own customs commanded, and searched through the ruins for anything still usable. Cooking vessels had generally survived, and so had various kinds of tools, and non-perishable kitchen supplies; and items such as these, which had escaped the wrath of the holy purpose, were soon being used in local households or traded in villages and settlements as much as a day's ride away.

One man who came back to the ruined station several times was Chen, the camel-herder who had guided Strauss and Hassall to the red building at the heart of the desert. He had lost most of his animals – the men from the mountains had driven them away, or killed them – and he was reduced to an extremity of destitution he'd never known before. But he was convinced that there was more left in the research station than the men from the mountains had managed to destroy, and he had no fastidious reluctance to search through filth, ash, broken glass, soil, sand, rotten food, or anything else; he set about the job with a will.

He took to sleeping in one of the storerooms that still had a ceiling, and furnished it with torn cushions, soiled blankets, and rolls of horticultural fleece that kept him warm at night. It was more comfortable than any place he had ever known; there was still enough dried food to scavenge, and he was never disturbed. He made sure of that by howling and screaming in the night, and by setting fire to some kind of oil he found in the distillery, so as to illuminate various crude devil-masks he made from scraps of wood and cardboard. Soon the station was known to be haunted, and Chen was master of all he surveyed.

5

NUMBER THEORY

Lyra found Ionides on a bench near the fountain, reading a newspaper in the full sun. It was just past midday, and men in shirtsleeves and women with parasols were strolling comfortably through the square, tempted this way or that by the smell of grilling meat or spices or baking bread, or sitting on the low wall around the fountain to enjoy the coolness of the drifting spray.

Lyra sat down beside Ionides and took off her royal ribbon.

'You not a queen now?' he said.

'No. I'm travelling incognito.'

'And me no more *sorcier*?'

'No. You're in disguise as a poet.'

His gecko-dæmon laughed, a little silvery sound. He folded his newspaper. 'Not the first time,' he said cheerfully.

'Come and walk with me. I want to find somewhere quieter under the shade of some trees, a garden of some kind or a park. I'm sure you could find somewhere like that.'

'This way,' he said. 'The Ambassador of Brazil was a generous man. He give his embassy and garden to the people of Aleppo in memory of his wife. Is very romantic. Lot of trees.'

'What did the Brazilian government have to say about that?'

'He not tell them yet. Too late now.'

The pavements were too crowded to let them talk easily, so Lyra said nothing as Ionides led the way. No doubt the people now coming out of their workplaces for lunch would take a siesta afterwards, unless the desire to make more money was stronger than the desire to lie down in a cool place. Again Lyra was struck by the charm of the city, the pleasure in the faces and voices around her, the straightforward sensuous joy in the fact of having a body in a world that suited it so well. She hadn't felt anything like that since Pan left – in fact, since before that: the last time she'd felt so uncomplicated was on one of those long summer evenings with Dick Orchard by the river, his hands on her body and hers on his, kissing and being kissed while Pan and Dick's pretty vixen-dæmon played nearby. As she and Ionides entered the embassy garden she felt a pang so sharp that she couldn't help a soft murmur of pain and loss.

Ionides stepped a little closer, as if to catch her if she stumbled, but he said nothing. They walked along a gravelled path to a bench under a wide-spreading cedar tree.

She sat, and then he joined her.

'Now, Mr Ionides,' she said, 'I want you to tell me about the good numbers and the spaces between them.'

'Good numbers? Forty is a good number for dollars,' he said. 'And the space between me and forty dollars is very wide.'

'Well, all right, that was a good answer. Let's get that over with first.' She counted out thirty dollars. 'That is what I owe you, and this' – an extra ten – 'is what I'll add to it if you agree to go with me to Karamakan.'

'Same rate as to Aleppo?'

'Certainly, provided we can agree on the distance and the time.'

'All right, Miss Silver, I trust you. We shall count as we go.'

They shook hands. His grip was firm and dry and cool. He folded the money away.

'Now,' she said, 'again. I want to know about the good numbers. Don't try and fool me.'

'How you know if I fool you or not?'

'When you're not telling the truth, your left eyelid flickers. I've noticed it before. Now come on, I want to know.'

'Where you hear about good numbers?'

'In the dead city. In Madinat al-Qamar. There were voices speaking to me, and they said they came from the gulfs between the good numbers. They wouldn't tell me any more than that.'

'You mind if I smoke?'

'Can you smoke and talk at the same time?'

'Yes. Easy.'

'Then I don't mind. What do you know about good numbers?'

He fished a cigarette from a battered packet and struck a match. He blew a thin stream of smoke, watching her with eyes whose lids didn't flicker at all.

'There is so many kind of numbers,' he said. 'There is numbers on the number line, like one and two and minus forty-six and eleven point five. Then there is numbers that go on for ever, like *pi*. Then there is prime numbers. You know prime numbers?'

'Yes.'

'Then there is infinity.'

'Is that a number?'

'No. But this is where we think about it. Then there is imaginary numbers, like square root of minus one.'

Lyra remembered: that laboratory on the very edge of the world, the endless Arctic night, her father explaining something . . . She nodded. 'I know about them,' she said. 'Go on.'

'Question for you, Miss Silver. Square root of minus one. Did it exist before someone think about it?'

'It must have done . . . I think. It was hidden, but it was there.'

'And you think that is the only kind of number that is there but we can't see?'

'No,' she said slowly. 'Probably. There might be others we haven't thought about. Actually there must be.'

'Like maybe good numbers.'

'Ah.'

'Maybe.'

He blew a smoke ring that floated away and wavered and frayed and broke up. It wasn't difficult, Lyra decided, to imagine him in the academic dress of a scholar, giving a lecture on mathematics to a room full of students.

'Is that all?' Lyra said.

'There might be moving numbers,' he said. 'Or Viennese numbers. Or dark numbers, or heavy numbers. Or bad numbers.'

'Those words could mean anything.'

'They could be names for kinds of numbers we haven't discovered yet.'

Something from a physics class stirred in her memory. She tried to see it clearly, but it shimmered for a moment, like a goldfish, and then retreated into the depths.

'You know about fields?' she said. 'I mean fields like the gravitational field or the electromagnetic field. Spaces where some kind of influence works.'

'I know what *field* means. What is it *you* mean?'

'I wondered if the good numbers could describe points in a particular field.'

He didn't say anything for over a minute. His expressions changed rapidly: abstract, troubled, calculating, speculative, amused, mischievous, melancholy. He might have been acting: perhaps none of them meant any more than that he knew she was watching him. Or they might have been true pictures of his thought. His left eyelid didn't flicker, but she'd made that up anyway.

'Well?' she went on. 'Suppose, like numbers we can't see yet and we can't see them because we haven't imagined how they could exist . . . If we didn't know about that particular field we wouldn't have thought it needed particular numbers to describe it. What then?'

'How would we know?' he said.

'We'd have to . . . I suppose we'd need an instrument that didn't exist yet. Or a process.'

'Or just look in different way.'

'What sort of way? What would your friend the Indian holy man say?'

'He would say you are very curious, Miss Silver. Never in all his life he meet someone so curious. He also say we have answer to many things before we know what question is. We just have to find the best way to see it.'

'That makes it sound very easy.'

'No, is not easy, but you can do it. You ask me once about something you call the secret commonwealth. You remember?'

'Yes, I do. You said you'd never heard of it.'

'Yes. Then you explain, and I recognise it.'

'You didn't say so.'

'No, I understand. I know the thing you talk about. What you say just now, about fields – suppose it is a field, your secret commonwealth. Like gravitational field, which is everywhere, and no one knew about it till Mr Lord Newton see an apple fall and wonder why it go down and not up.'

'Wait a minute. The secret commonwealth is a *field* . . .'

'Yes.'

'And that's your different way of looking at it?'

'Yes. It's good, no?'

She laughed. So did he.

'But . . .' she said.

'Another example for you. Like calculating *pi*. You could go on for ever. A hundred digits, a thousand, a million billion, you never come to the end, never exactly right, always an approximation. People take a lifetime and go mad doing it. But like this . . .'

He bent forward and traced a circle in the gravel with his finger, and then drew a line across the middle.

'How long that take? Two seconds? And there it is, perfect picture of *pi*. Of the idea of *pi*. The ratio between *this* line and *that* line. You see it, you understand. Not approximate. Exact.'

'H'mm,' she said. 'Yes. All right.'

'Same thing, different way of seeing it.'

'So if I saw the secret commonwealth as a field instead of . . . however I used to see it . . .'

'Might be clearer.' He looked at her watching him, and yet another expression came into his eyes, as if he were assessing her in some way. 'Nothing is empty,' he said more slowly. 'You can't see nothing in this cup or that box or that room with nothing in it, but they are all full of fields. Of every kind. Some we know about, some we don't, and some we don't even think are fields at all. Consciousness . . .'

But he stopped, as if he'd said too much.

'Consciousness is a field? Is it?' she said.

'Yes.' He looked uneasy.

'The Rusakov field? D'you mean that?'

He found a scrap of smokeweed on his tongue, and worked it to his lips, and spat it out. 'Maybe,' he said. 'It's possible.'

'I'll think about that. It's interesting.'

He pinched out the burning end of his cigarette with finger and thumb. Lyra flinched, but Ionides didn't seem to feel anything.

He said, 'Now another question, Miss Silver. This time something I want to know.'

'What?'

'Where we go. You say Karamakan. Well, by God, that is a damn big place. Full of sand. Where exactly you want to go?'

'A place called Tashbulak, near the edge of a lake called Lop Nor. There was a botanical research station there. Within a few days' journey of that there is a red building in the desert, and that's where I want to go.'

'Why? They don't let you in. They don't let nobody in.'

'How do you know that?'

'Abdel Ionides, he know everything.'

'Oh, of course. Well, I think there's something I have to do when I get inside. I think it's something only I can do. And it's important because it reminds me . . . The atmosphere of it . . . The feeling I get when I think about it . . . Once a long time ago I stood on a mountain in the Arctic and I saw another world opening in the sky. The feeling I had then . . . I think the red building in the desert is like that.'

'So you got something important to do in the red building. I wait outside, guide you back. Same price. No extra charge. Now, Miss Silver, what Mustafa Bey say to you?'

'Many interesting things. He knew who you are.'

'No,' he said calmly. 'He think he know, but he know little bits of things, no more than that. What else he say?'

'He gave me a – a passport, I suppose you could say. And he asked me to send him reports at each stage of the journey.'

'A passport?'

'Or a *laissez-passer*.' She took out the letter and showed him. He read it and whistled quietly.

'Do those other languages say the same thing as the English?' she said.

Ionides nodded. 'The same in all three. You know how valuable this is? Look after this very very close. Very well, Miss Silver, I arrange everything for journey. Now I must make myself look like a real *sorcier particulier* for Queen Tatiana.'

He stood up and bowed before handing her back the letter and sauntering away.

Lyra looked around; the little garden was empty but for a mother and child sitting on the grass some way off. She could see their dæmons playing together, and hear the mother's voice and the child's laughter and the soft purring call of a turtle dove; but the streets and squares beyond the tree-shaded buildings were hushed, as if the city were holding its breath.

Marcel Delamare, in Constantinople on Magisterial business, stood for a carefully timed moment at the spot where Saint Simeon Papadakis had been martyred. His head was bowed, his eyes were closed, his lips were moving in prayer.

Then with a visible sigh he moved on towards the Council Chamber, where the bloodstains were protected by plate glass in low wooden frames. Here he knelt in prayer. Prominent among those who joined him on their knees was a bright-eyed young monk in the robes of a senior sub-deacon. The newly promoted Brother Mercurius was more than usually assiduous in the care and attention he showed to the visitor, but this visitor was more than usually important, and Brother Mercurius's response to the nearness of power was not unlike that of a needle in the presence of a magnet.

Finally Delamare began to stand up, and there was a friendly hand ready to help.

'Don't touch me,' said the President, clearly enough for everyone present to hear, and Brother Mercurius let go with a modest smile of apology.

Delamare went out in the company of a handful of officials, leaving the young sub-deacon not in the least abashed. Had not the Lord Himself said those exact words to St Mary of Magdala?

'This corridor is to be closed,' Delamare said, and the senior official took a note. 'Have the floor taken up and framed in gold and hung in a place of honour in the Chamber. Lay another floor here, tiled this time, and then re-open the corridor. Now show me to the Patriarch's apartment.'

The suite of rooms where the Patriarch had lived was small, modest, even shabby, Delamare noted with approval. It would all be preserved exactly as it was, as a testimony to the sanctity of the late occupant.

But it was not suitable as a place to receive visitors. His offices, on the other hand, where he was shown next, were large, comfortable, and anonymous, as if they'd been designed by an architect specialising in hotels for wealthy business travellers.

'This will do,' said the President to the official who was showing him around. 'Bring my visitors up here as soon as they arrive.'

'I believe I can see their car now, Your Holi . . . Mr Pres . . . Sir,' said the young man, looking down into the courtyard and wishing they'd decided how the President was to be addressed.

'Sir will do,' said Delamare, who on the whole preferred not to make his staff uncomfortable. 'Show them directly up here, and have some refreshments available.'

The young man was not part of Delamare's Geneva staff; he belonged to the Constantinople secretariat, but he was not ordained as most of them were. Delamare liked the look of him. His dæmon was a sparrow, who perched on his shoulder, head cocked, calm and curious.

'By the way,' Delamare said as the young man opened the door, 'what is your name?'

'Felix Murad, sir.'

Delamare nodded, and the door quietly closed.

The President was expecting three guests: that was all the Patriarchate staff knew. This was the first time that most of the clergy there had met him, and his ostensible reason for visiting Constantinople, as well as to pay homage at the place of Saint Simeon's martyrdom, was to attend the consecration of the next Patriarch, who had already been chosen, but whose identity mattered very little.

He had explained that he was expecting these visitors, so the great engine of the Patriarchate smoothly and silently changed gear, and immediately arranged everything to make the visit go well.

Delamare took some papers out of his briefcase and spread them on the desk, and waited. Quite soon there was a knock at the door, and Felix Murad opened it and showed the visitors in.

Delamare stood to greet them. Two men and one woman, in western dress, though they looked Persian or Iraqi; a decade or so younger than Delamare, which put them in their mid to late thirties; one man heavily bearded, the other clean-shaven but deeply pockmarked; the woman slender, apparently delicate and frail until she moved. Then it was clear that she'd had some athletic training, and her grip was powerful, as Delamare discovered.

'Monsieur le Président,' said the bearded man in French, 'I present Doctor Leila Pervani, and this gentleman is Mr Zafar Sayadov. I am Mr Omar Husain.'

Delamare shook their hands, offered them comfortable chairs, and sat with them rather than behind his desk. The staff were well trained; no sooner were the guests seated than Felix Murad knocked again and let in attendants who carried trays with tea, coffee, water, and honey-cakes. While this was going on, Delamare watched the pockmarked Zafar Sayadov quite openly. He was mild-mannered, modestly dressed, slightly balding, about middle height, with a soft handshake, and he looked like a minor civil servant. The bearded man, Husain, seemed much more formidable, and yet Delamare could see that both he and the woman deferred to Sayadov with great care.

When the attendants had gone, and tea and coffee had been poured, Delamare said, 'I am most grateful to you for calling on me. I shall not be in Constantinople for long. So, Monsieur Sayadov, you are the leader of these men from the mountains?'

'That is wrong, Monsieur le Président. We have a collective leadership. I am a representative, not a director.'

'Thank you for clarifying that. And Doctor Pervani? Are you a representative also?'

'That is correct.'

Her voice was low and quiet. Her dæmon was a small desert-brown snake with emerald zigzag markings. Delamare found himself impressed by the beauty of her eyes, but he allowed nothing of that to show in his expression, which remained bland and courteous.

'May I ask what name you yourselves have for your organisation?' he said. 'You are known as "the men from the mountains", but is that a name of your choice?'

'No,' said Leila Pervani, 'because it is inaccurate. Among ourselves we say simply "us" and "we".'

'Of course. Now I'm interested to learn about your relations with Thuringia Potash. Let me tell you why: it is because the Magisterium is in the course of discussing a contract with that company, and because I know that you have had dealings with them. I may say that I am less impressed with them than I am with what I have heard about you. It might be to our mutual advantage to explore ways in which we could deal with one another directly and not through the cumbersome bureaucracy of a large company.'

'"With one another"?' said Sayadov. 'You mean us with the Magisterium, and you with us?'

'That is what I mean, yes.'

'Does TP know you are talking to us?'

'No.'

'So you would deceive them?'

'My principal object is the well-being of my organisation, not the well-being of Thuringia Potash.'

Sayadov nodded. The other two remained inscrutable.

'Please continue,' said Sayadov.

'I am curious to know your overall aim,' said Delamare easily. 'The actions of yours that I know about, those that have been publicised in the west, for example: would you have done those things, or similar things, if Thuringia Potash had not paid you to do them? Did they have an ideological aspect for you, or were they purely commercial transactions?'

This time it was the woman who replied. 'Nothing is pure,' she said, 'not even the thoughts of the angels. We do not lift a finger, M. le Président, without the impulse of a hundred different motives. But yes, we were in agreement with the aims of Thuringia Potash in the actions you mention.'

'What aims do you have, then, in the matter of the building in the Karamakan desert?'

'It is a source of evil,' said Omar Husain. 'So naturally we want to destroy it.'

'And you?' said Sayadov. 'What do you want with that building?'

'We want to control the traffic that goes through it,' said Delamare. 'The trade in rose products. That means first under-standing it, and then gaining control of it, and then if necessary closing it down. We share the view of its nature that M. Husain has just expressed—'

'That it is evil?' said Husain.

'Yes. But we consider that if we destroy it without understanding, we would leave open the possibility of its resurgence in another form. Hence the need to do it in the way we intend.'

'You have gathered a large force already. Why do you need our help?'

'Because you can move swiftly and silently, as a large force cannot. You have shown that you can strike without warning in any spot from Constantinople to the western frontier of Cathay. Because you are skilful and imaginative; your use of those TP vehicles in the Tashbulak affair was very well managed. Thuringia Potash is, to my mind, not at all well governed, whereas it seems to me that however your collective leadership works, it is more effective and much less cumbersome. I am offering you the chance to ally yourselves with an organisation bigger, richer, and much more influential than any commercial enterprise. I think we have a basis for discussion.'

'A basis, possibly,' said Zafar Sayadov. 'But we have clashed with the Magisterium in the past. We would need assurances that persecution of our organisation will cease.'

'Of course. And I need assurances from you. I can tell you that the preparations taking place all over Europe and beyond, the gathering of troops, the making of alliances, the agreements and treaties we have been assiduously working to bring about are part of the necessary diplomatic underpinning of a holy war, with the aim of capturing and destroying this fountain of evil in the Karamakan desert. I would like to announce that the agreement whose skeleton form we are discussing now is very much part of that. But to do so, you understand, I shall have to name you, and it would help to establish a publicly known identity, a brand, one might almost say, by which you can be known to the faithful all over the world. I believe that in one instance at least one branch of your movement has called itself the Brotherhood of the Holy Purpose. I might mention that the body in Geneva which I headed before assuming the Presidency of the new High Council is called the League for the Instauration of the Holy Purpose. I think that a title containing those words would be both accurate and inspiring.'

The three visitors looked at one another. Delamare couldn't read their expressions, but at least they hadn't rejected the idea outright.

Zafar Sayadov turned back to him. 'Let us continue to talk,' he said.

When a date for further talks had been agreed, and after the visitors had gone, Delamare sent for his private secretary.

'A woman who calls herself Leila Pervani,' he said. 'Late thirties, perhaps forty. Average height, or a shade less. Slender and athletic. Black hair. Possibly Persian, possibly Kurdish. Apparently once an academic. Find out everything you can about her.'

6

EAGLE WORKS TERRIER 1500

Timur Ghazarian said, 'This is where we leave the car.'

Malcolm, fully awake but stiff and aching, said, 'Where are we?'

It was early morning. Ghazarian had brought a change of clothes for Malcolm, who now looked like a respectable traveller. They were somewhere in the western outskirts of Aleppo, on a wide road lined with small factories, wholesale furniture distributors, occasional dusty market gardens, and car repair workshops.

'As soon as we see a bus stop we'll put the car out of sight and join the commuters,' Ghazarian said.

They had crossed the frontier with no difficulty. The guards were sufficiently impressed by Ghazarian's uniform and Malcolm's papers to put aside any misgivings. Malcolm thought that the officer in charge seemed preoccupied by some bigger anxiety, and Ghazarian agreed.

'The problem for them is that their senior command has no idea of what side they should be on in case of a conflict with the Magisterium. You can see why that makes them anxious.'

'I can . . . Timur, can you pull in at the next set of gates on the right?'

Ghazarian did so, checking the road ahead and behind. There was no sign that they were being followed; the traffic was already beginning to build up, but it was flowing easily. While the car came to a halt, Malcolm, sorting through his wallet, took out a business card and tucked it into his top pocket.

'My name is George Hanson,' he said.

'As you wish,' said Ghazarian, looking at the building behind the locked gates. 'But why here? Oh, I see. TP . . . Them again?'

The place looked like a medium-sized academic establishment or research institute. The Thuringia Potash sign, a rampant lion barred in red and white, hung over the entrance. There was no sign of activity.

Malcolm stiffly got out of the car and looked around. The gates were padlocked, the gatekeeper's office closed, the car park empty.

'It's early still,' said Ghazarian, who had joined him.

'It's not that. Look at the shrubs, look at the flowers in the planters. You can bet that TP would have a team of gardeners to look after them, but they haven't been watered for a week.'

'Curious.'

'Across the road there – is that a café?'

It was, and it was open. Two men were sitting at one of several tables outside; a waiter came out of the door with a tray. The white-painted building was set back a little way from the road, behind an empty space that had room for half a dozen cars.

'I think I need some breakfast,' said Malcolm.

'I'll wait in the car. Uniforms make people nervous. Don't stay long.'

Malcolm limped across the road and went into the café, watched silently by the men at the table outside. There were no customers inside; the proprietor responded to Malcolm's greeting with a wary nod. Malcolm ordered coffee and pastries and spoke quietly with Asta while he waited.

'Attractive place,' said Malcolm. 'Clean and fresh. This would have been the natural place for TP staff to eat and drink. He'll be missing the trade.'

'I think Timur's right. Better not stay longer than we need.'

When the owner brought the coffee and a plate of limp-looking croissants, Malcolm said, 'That place over the road – Thuringia Potash – how long has it been closed?'

'Two weeks, maybe.'

'D'you happen to know why?'

The proprietor shrugged. 'Just suddenly one day . . . No one has tell me. Why should they?'

'No, of course not. The thing is I'm supposed to have a meeting there this morning. Agreed weeks ago. I'm a representative of an engineering company.'

The proprietor nodded slowly.

'I don't know what to do,' Malcolm went on. 'I think I can see some kind of notice stuck up on the entrance, but I can't get past the gates to read it. I was hoping there might be a contact address or something. I never heard anything about this. I suppose you had a lot of customers from across the road?'

'Yes, many. Every day. Now . . . nothing.'

'And they didn't explain to anyone why they were closing? No warning, nothing like that?'

The man's dæmon, like a large starling, said something quietly on his shoulder. He nodded. 'Some people say they had big project that go wrong. Not suppose to talk, suppose to be secret, but you know, in a café people talk all the time, they tell me things, I overhear . . . They had big project, but no one hear about closing. Big surprise for everyone.'

'What sort of project? I mean, don't tell me if it's a secret, but I've come all this way to talk about this new filter my company's developed, and they'd have had to tell me about what they were doing, obviously. Did you hear anything at all about what this project involved?'

The proprietor looked out through the window at the road, through the glass door at the two customers outside, and behind him towards the kitchen, although he was clearly the only person there. Then he looked at the wallet Malcolm had taken from his pocket.

'For your trouble,' Malcolm said, and laid a couple of notes on the table. 'I'll have to explain to my boss. Anything you can tell me . . .'

'What I hear I don't always understand. One day I hear someone say they were trying to make some kind of drug, some new medicine, something like that, and it didn't work. They spend a lot of money, lot of resources, and they got clever people there, you know, but they couldn't make it work. I don't ask too many questions. I just listen, you know. But not always understand.'

'Well, thank you anyway. That's a great help. At least I've got something I can tell my boss. Do you happen to know if TP has another office or plant in Aleppo?'

'No. This the only one.'

'And they didn't leave anyone there to, I don't know, keep watch, answer enquiries?'

'No. All gone.'

Malcolm finished his coffee and stood up. He shook hands with the proprietor.

'Well, thank you very much,' he said. 'I hope your trade picks up. Maybe some other company will take the place over and bring it to life again. New customers for you.'

'Too late for me. Soon I have to close this café. Go well.'

Malcolm and Asta left. The two men outside ignored them. The road was already busier with the morning traffic; it took longer to cross back.

And when he reached the car, he found Ghazarian in conversation. He was standing by the driver's door, talking to a middle-aged man who looked uncomfortable in his casual clothes, as if he'd much rather be wearing a suit. His dæmon, a dejected-looking woodpecker, sat on his shoulder with her eyes closed.

'Ah, here is my guest,' Ghazarian said as Malcolm approached. 'Mr Hanson, you ready to move on now?'

'Just about. Good morning, sir,' Malcolm said to the other man. 'Are you connected with Thuringia Potash?'

'I was chief accountant. All closed now. You came to see someone?'

'Head of the engineering department. Here's my card.'

He held out the card he'd put in his pocket, which said that he was George Hanson, Sales Executive of Coventry Hydraulics, makers of pumps, filters, and compressors.

The man nodded sadly. 'Too late,' he said.

'What happened?'

'Too much money spent, not enough supervision.'

'They were making some sort of medicine, weren't they? That's what they wanted my filters for, anyway.'

'Biosynthesis. Not my speciality. If you have a filter to stop money leaking away, I would be interested. Anyway . . .' He looked around, and stood a little closer, dropping his voice. 'Anyway, they have a new project, further east. Much further. Very confidential, but something big like that will always leak. Filters or not.'

'Have you heard any details about that?'

The accountant shook his head. 'I should not say anyway. Even if I knew.'

'That size, you say . . . Something very large?'

'No. Said enough.'

'Is there a name connected with it? Someone I can get in touch with?'

Another shake of the head; regretful, but firm. He shrugged and handed back the card.

'Wasted journey,' said Malcolm. 'Well, I've had those before. Nice to talk to you, Mr . . .'

'Nassim.'

They shook hands, and the melancholy Nassim resumed his walk. Malcolm got into the car, and Ghazarian drove them away.

Lyra stayed in the garden of the Brazilian Embassy for some time. She felt as if she was in a state of suspended animation, almost a coma, or a dream; all her energy seemed to have evaporated in the warm air, leaving her with no more weight or will, no more imagination, than a shadow. Her eyes were closing, and it was hard to resist; her head was so heavy, and the garden was empty and silent . . .

She nodded herself half awake, realising that if she fell asleep sitting on the bench, she'd fall off on to the gravel path, so she lay down on the grass beside it, under the shade of the cedar branches above, and found herself playing with Pan. They were very young, because it was long before they were separated, and they were making a dam on the Castle Mill stream, and every time they got a few sticks fixed in place the miller came out and shouted at them, so they summoned an army of beavers and got the dam fixed in a trice. The miller surrendered and his wife came out with a tray of fish and chips and they all sat on the dam to eat and then Pan screamed, so loud and close and so angry that she woke up and found herself struggling there, now, in the embassy garden, with a young man – half familiar – no, she wasn't struggling with him; he was struggling with Pan, her Pan, her old Pan, her dearest Pan, and she woke up fully and hurled herself at the assailant, whose alien hands were all over her dæmon and inside the heart of her own *being* – she was back at Bolvangar inside the cage under the silver guillotine – Pan was clawing at her arms, her shoulder, her hands—

No! It wasn't Pan – how could she ever think that? There was no Pan. It was *Olivier Bonneville* – he was shouting about the alethiometer, his face red, eyes wild, spittle flying. Lyra hit him with both fists and immediately cried out in anguish herself, because her left hand—

Bonneville had one hand around Lyra's neck. She twisted her head this way and that, trying to reach his wrist to sink her teeth into it, while with her right hand she slashed and tore and pummelled at the young man's face, and slammed her knees and feet into his thighs and shins. His hawk-dæmon swept and dived and wheeled close above them and Lyra managed to seize a wing for one anbaric second and wrenched it hard and the dæmon fell fluttering and screaming beside them, so Bonneville let go of her throat and turned to scoop the dæmon up and Lyra kicked him in the back, below the ribs, and he sprawled gasping on to the gravel. The target was still there: she kicked it again, merciless, smashing a foot with all her force right where his kidneys were.

She would have killed him if she could. But he had enough strength to scramble away, and she hadn't enough to follow, so she stood shaking and panting and holding tight to her left hand and watched as the young man dragged himself upright on a cedar branch before stumbling away and out of the garden, his dæmon hanging limp in his hands.

Lyra fell back on the bench in the empty garden and sobbed.

Alice Lonsdale, asleep on a hard bunk in a commandeered and nearly derelict barracks, found herself shaken awake before dawn. She pushed the hand away violently.

'Alice Lonsdale, get up,' said a man's voice.

'Don't you touch me again,' she said, heavy with sleep.

The sheet (dirty) and the blankets (thin) were suddenly snatched away. She was sleeping fully clothed because of the cold. Her dog-dæmon Ben, who had been asleep by her feet, immediately leaped forward to guard her, snarling, and Alice sat up and put her arms around him tightly.

There were two men in the room: she could see them against the dim light from the window. They both carried heavy batons.

'Get up, Alice,' the same voice said. 'Someone needs to talk to you.'

'D'you want to put your coat on?' said the other man, taking it down from the hook behind the door.

'What's happening?' said the girl in the upper bunk, only just awake. 'Alice, who is it?'

''S all right, Sonia. You stay there. Here – have these blankets. I don't suppose I'll be back for a while.'

Alice threw her blankets up and the girl murmured her thanks before pulling them up and turning over.

'Here, put it on,' said the man holding out the coat. 'It's cold out there.'

'Where we going?'

'You'll find out. Come on.'

He pulled at her arm and she snatched it back.

'Let me put my bloody shoes on,' she said.

'Manners,' said the first man.

'Fuck off.'

The sleepers in the other two bunks were awake now, Alice could tell, but none of them dared make a sound. The shoes were not her own, but loose gym shoes with fragile laces. She sat on the bunk and tied them, carefully in case they broke.

She tugged the coat around her shoulders and snatched her arm away from the man who tried to hold it.

'I en't going to run away. Take your hands off.'

They locked the barracks door and marched her along the pitted road between the other buildings. In the faint dawn light she could see that most of them needed repair, and in one the roof had entirely collapsed. The road led up to a high steel fence shutting off the barracks from the woods beyond.

'Where we going?' Alice said, again.

'Inspector Mackenzie.' It was the second man who spoke.

'Who's he?'

'He wants to ask you some questions.'

'Yeah, but who is he? Is that a police rank or what?'

'If he wants you to know, I expect he'll tell you.'

'So you don't know then. What about your boss here? Does he know?'

'He en't my boss.'

'Shut up,' said the other man to Alice. 'One more word and you can go there in handcuffs.'

Not far from the fence they came to a junction. They turned left, parallel to the edge of the woods, where the road was wider and better maintained. The darkness was retreating every minute, as if it was withdrawing from the buildings and sifting into the trees. One building actually had some lights on in the windows. It was made of brick, like the dormitory buildings but bigger and in a better state of repair.

'Is that where Inspector Mackenzie is?' said Alice.

'Yes,' said the second man.

'What's this building called then?'

'I told you to shut up,' said the first man.

'Just asking.'

'You don't need to know,' he said, but by that time they were outside the front door and Alice could read the brass plate beside it. It was new and highly polished, and it said:

BRYTSEC
ORD Corrective Division
Southern Region

'That's not straight,' Alice pointed out.

It had been put up in a hurry: the light was getting clearer every minute, and in any case an anbaric lamp had come on over the door, and Alice could see the scratches on the brass where a screwdriver had slipped.

'Just shut up,' said the first man again as his colleague rang the bell.

'It wouldn't have cost much to get a spirit level. Even I could do it straighter than what that is. And what's BRYTSEC? And ORD?'

'Ask Inspector Mackenzie.'

'I will.'

A key turned in a lock, and the door opened narrowly. The first man showed a pass or a badge, and the door opened fully. The second man urged Alice forward with a hand on her back. She twisted away from the touch.

'Inspector Mackenzie,' said the first man.

The officer at the door nodded. 'Name?'

'Alice Lonsdale. B5. Mind she behaves herself.'

B5 was the dormitory building where Alice slept. The officer ticked something off on a clipboard and said, 'Follow me.'

Alice turned and looked at the two men who'd taken her from the cell, memorising their faces.

'Go on. Follow the officer,' said the second man.

Ben nudged her knee, and she sauntered towards the officer, who was standing at the foot of the stairs tapping his fingers on the clipboard. Alice heard the front door close behind them, and caught Ben's eye. They both thought, *They didn't have the key. It's not locked.*

'Where we going?' said Alice.

'Second floor.'

'Who's Inspector Mackenzie?'

'ORD Special Services.'

'What's ORD?'

'None of your business. Save your breath, and get a move on.'

His dæmon was a crow, and she watched them with a cold eye as they followed him. The stairs were bare concrete, with a wooden handrail on both sides. On the second floor they went along a drably painted corridor under flickering overhead lights, and passed no windows, no pictures, no notice boards; just an endless row of numbered doors, painted the same institutional cream as the walls.

The officer knocked at number 239 and opened the door straightaway.

'Mrs Lonsdale, B5, for you, sir,' he said.

A man's soft voice said, 'Thank you. Show her in.'

When Alice entered the room she found that the inspector was a plump man in his fifties, with brilliantined grey hair, pale blue eyes, and an expression of kindly understanding. His dæmon was a grey Persian cat. Something about him reminded Alice of the librarian at her school, who had been the only member of staff to take an interest in her, but it was an interest she hadn't enjoyed.

'Sit down,' he said as the officer left and closed the door.

There was a single upright wooden chair in front of a light, flimsy desk. The window on the inspector's left showed the steel fence on the other side of the road and the wood beyond, where the first light of dawn was developing into a damp grey. Apart from that, the only lighting was a fluorescent anbaric tube overhead.

Alice sat down. The inspector had been leafing through a file, turning the pages and making an occasional note in pencil. There was nothing else on the desk, no shelves on the wall, not even a filing cabinet. An iron radiator under the window put out a thick oppressive heat, which seemed to intensify the musky kind of cologne the man was wearing.

The inspector went on looking through the file; Alice kept on looking at him. It was a paradoxical face: patience and even friendliness, as her first impression had shown, but there was something pitiless there too. It was the kind of soft face that would take pleasure in watching someone else being very cruel. His white uniform shirt was a little grubby around the cuffs: this was so early in the day that he must either be wearing yesterday's or have worked all night. There was a little redness around his eyes.

Alice took all this in, and then stared at the cat-dæmon, but cats were inscrutable; this one's flat face and half-closed eyes gave nothing away.

Inspector Mackenzie closed the file and laid his pencil down beside it, precisely parallel to the edge. He raised his eyes to look at Alice.

'Do you know a man called Malcolm Polstead?'

Alice was only slightly surprised. 'He's an old friend.'

'Lover?'

'Mind your own business.'

'Known him long?'

'Since we were kids. Twenty years, more or less.'

'Where is he now?'

'Buggered if I know.'

'You might want to watch your tongue. When did you last see him?'

'Early January, far as I remember.'

'When did he go away?'

'Soon after that.'

'He didn't tell you where he was going?'

'Why would he?'

'You're old friends. You see him often?'

'Every few weeks, I suppose.'

'What's he do?'

'He's a scholar. An archaeologist.'

'What, you can do that for a living?'

'If you're good at it.'

'Does he do a lot of travelling?'

'A fair amount.'

'What's that mean?'

'Well, if his job involves digging up old ruins, he's got to go where the ruins are, hasn't he? Why are you asking about him, anyway?'

'Has he got any family? Wife, kids?'

'No. His parents are alive. He sees a lot of them. No brothers or sisters.'

'Does he ever talk about his work?'

'Not to me.'

'What *do* you talk about then?'

'College gossip, mainly.'

'What college is that?'

'His or mine?'

'You're not a scholar, are you?'

'How d'you work that out?'

'You're not bright enough.' The softness in his expression hadn't hardened at all. 'You don't sound like a scholar, you don't look like one. Why would a scholar like him waste his time with a servant? Unless there's sex involved, which you haven't denied.'

'I haven't admitted it either. What law are you holding me under? What gives you the right to ask questions of any kind, never mind indecent personal ones?'

'Which college? You didn't answer that one either.'

'He's a Scholar of Durham College.'

'Where's that? In Durham?'

'In Oxford. You know all this – it must be in that file.'

'What college do you work at then?'

'Jordan.'

'What do they call you? What's the title of your position?'

'Housekeeper.'

'How long have you worked there?'

'Fifteen years, sixteen, I dunno.'

'Let me ask you again about Professor Polstead—'

'He en't a professor. Dr Polstead.'

'When he goes away digging up ruins, does he get in touch with you? Letters, postcards, anything like that?'

A movement outside the window caught Alice's eye, and she turned her head slightly to see a pick-up truck move slowly along the road beside the fence. She recognised the model: it was an old EW Terrier 1500.It slowed to a halt, and then moved on again.

She turned back to the inspector. 'No. He's usually in a jungle or a desert or something. Where's he going to get postcards from?'

'Tell me about his friends. Do you know any of them?'

'A few, I suppose.'

'You ever go out together? Say, to a pub or something like that?'

'Not often.'

'When did you marry Roger Lonsdale?'

'Fifteen years ago.'

That was why she'd recognised the pick-up truck. Rog had one just like it.

'You're not together any more?'

'He died a year after.'

'How? What of?'

'Building accident.'

'Children?'

'No.'

'What's your relationship with a girl called Lyra Belacqua?'

'I used to look after her. She was an orphan.'

'And where is she now?'

'No idea.'

'There's a rumour about her and Dr Polstead. Any truth in that?'

Alice was genuinely startled. She composed herself calmly. 'What sort of rumour? What you talking about?' she said.

'You haven't heard?'

'No. You going to tell me?'

'Improper conduct between a teacher and a pupil.'

'I never heard anything so stupid in all my life.'

'Where is she now then?'

'I told you. No idea.'

'She went away about the same time as him, didn't she?'

'I can't remember.'

'Two close friends of yours go away together and you can't remember when?'

'Who said they went together?'

'Didn't they?'

'No.'

'Who went first?'

'I think she did.'

'So he was following her?'

'No! You're trying to make things look—'

'I'm not trying to make anything look anything. I'm just trying to establish the truth.'

'You want to tell a lot of lies.'

The inspector looked reproachful. The cat-dæmon, dozing on the desk beside her, half opened her eyes and looked at Alice directly.

The man licked a finger and turned over a few pages in his file. He read for a minute and turned another page.

'How long ago was it when he was teaching her privately?'

'I don't remember. About four years ago.'

'So she would have been about fifteen?'

'Sixteen.'

'And you don't remember anything about that time? Did she confide in you?'

Alice felt a low growl coming from Ben, who was lying at her feet. She reached down and laid her hand on his neck. He knew what she meant, and stopped growling, but of course the inspector had heard, and seen.

'There were things we talked about, and things we didn't,' Alice said. She was pleased that her voice was steady. 'She knew I couldn't understand her schoolwork or what she learned at college, so we talked about other things.'

'Did she tell you about anything connected with Malcolm Polstead?'

'No.'

'Nothing at all?'

'Nothing at all.'

'Not even why they suddenly stopped these private lessons she was having?'

'She'd probably learned all she needed to about that subject. I don't know. You're not getting anywhere with this, and you never will.'

'So you don't know why she might have been crying on her own after one of these . . . teaching sessions?'

'What?'

'And why your friend Malcolm Polstead was seen adjusting his clothing after leaving the room that day?'

'Where'd you get this bloody rubbish from?'

'A member of the college staff.'

'Who?'

'I'm not at liberty to disclose their name. You don't know any more about that incident?'

'There never was any *incident*. You made it up. I wouldn't like to have your mind.'

Another lick of the inspector's finger; another few pages turned; another minute of silence as he read.

'Do you know a girl called Pauline Simms?' he said, looking directly at Alice.

'Yes.'

'Who is she?'

'She works at the Trout. That's Mr and Mrs Polstead's pub. Malcolm's parents.'

'How old is she?'

'About seventeen, I suppose.'

'You aware of any connection between her and Dr Polstead?'

'Well, they know each other, obviously. That's his home.'

'I meant any sexual connection.'

Alice knew that Pauline had a crush on Malcolm. So did he.

'Ridiculous,' she said.

'You're aware that she's pregnant?'

'Never heard of it, and I don't believe it.'

'Course there's nothing illegal about that, she's above the age of consent. But what with that and the business with Lyra—'

'There wasn't any *business with Lyra*. How can you sit there lying like this? Have you spoken to Pauline?'

'Indeed we have.'

'And what did she say?'

'She said the father of her child was Malcolm Polstead.'

Alice took a deep breath. 'I've known Pauline since she was a kid,' she said. 'I can't imagine why she'd say that, because it isn't true. So you must have made it up, you bastards, you and your squalid lying colleagues. You'll never get me to incriminate Pauline, or Lyra, or Malcolm Polstead.'

'I can see it's difficult for you to admit you might be wrong. But there are witnesses. And what with Lyra and now with Pauline, you see, it does say something about his taste for girls much younger than he is.'

'Bloody garbage.'

'How did Pauline come to get a job at the Trout?'

'I got her the job.'

'You introduced her to him?'

'No,' and Alice put as much contempt into the single syllable as she could. 'I introduced her to Mrs Polstead. Malcolm's mother. She's the cook and she needed help in the kitchen, and I told her about Pauline, and she got the job. That's it. That's all.'

The inspector made a note, and then closed the file and looked up. His expression was calm, even a little satisfied, but his pale eyes were bright. He ran the little pink point of his tongue around his lips.

'You finished?' said Alice. 'Can I go now?'

'In a minute. You know, you're in a difficult position, Alice.'

'Mrs Lonsdale to you.'

'I haven't even begun asking about your own . . . irregularities.'

'Nothing's stopping you.'

'Apart from taste.'

'What's that supposed to mean?'

'My appetite for the sordid is limited, and so is my time. But we'll have another talk before long, Alice, me and you—'

'What's Brytsec?'

'Brytish Security. As you can see from this uniform.'

'I thought you were ORD. Why don't you make your mind up?'

'The ORD is a division of Brytsec.'

'What's it stand for anyway?'

'The Office of Right Duty.'

He gestured towards the epaulettes on his shoulders and the badge on his lapel. He was leaning back in his chair, trying to give an impression of effortless domination.

Alice said, 'Well, first I can't read those things from here, and second you must be some new gang, because I never heard the name before.'

'We used to be known as the Consistorial Court of Discipline. I expect you've heard of that.'

'Bunch of swaggering bullies. That explains it. If these questions you've been asking are the best you can do, you need someone a lot brighter in charge. You finished with me now? Can I go back to my nice warm cell?'

The inspector's cat-dæmon rose to her feet and stretched her back languorously. Ben, lying at Alice's feet, growled in response, and the cat glared at him and hissed.

Instantly Ben sprang at her. Alice knew that would happen, and was ready: as the cat leaped away she reached forward, seized the front of the desk and flung it upwards with all her strength. The inspector was too slow to pull himself upright, and he fell back with the desk on top of him and the chair in pieces underneath.

Before he could even cry out in surprise Alice and Ben were out in the corridor and running for the stairs. Those wooden handrails: there were some just like them in her school, and she knew just how to descend in a hurry, diving forward while sliding her hands halfway down and then gripping tight and swinging her legs down and on to the floor at the foot of the flight. She'd got detention for doing that at school, and here she was in detention again, but not for long. She swung down the lower flight in the same way and ran for the door.

Somewhere behind them a bell began to ring. Someone was shouting, but no one on the ground floor seemed to be responding, and then they reached the door and—

Yes! It was still unlocked.

They flung themselves outside. Only a few yards away the pick-up truck stood, with two men unloading paving stones from the back, and Alice didn't hesitate. She knew how to drive these things: Roger had taught her, and she'd delivered building materials for him many times during their short marriage, pretending to grumble, secretly happy.

She threw open the driver's door. Ben sprang in and scrambled out of the way for her to follow, and she slammed the door shut before the men behind could even begin to protest. She flicked the little truck into gear, and the anbaric motor responded at once and shot away from the workmen, with paving stones tumbling from the back.

'Hey!' came a shout.

'Where we going?' said Ben, lurching from side to side as Alice swung the truck round a bend in the road.

'Out, soon as we see a gate,' she said.

'*There's* one!'

'Where?'

'In the fence. There on the right – into the woods.'

'Get down on the floor,' she said, and turned the truck off the road and over the grass verge directly towards the metal gate across the path.

She held the wheel in her left hand and flung her right arm up over her face. The tough little truck smashed into the gate with a scream of metal and a crash of glass, and stopped suddenly as the engine whined and the wheels spun. Alice was flung forward on to the steering wheel, but her arm took most of the force, and she threw the truck into reverse, backed away from the obstruction, and slammed it forward again. This time it burst through.

A muddy, overgrown path stretched ahead. She pressed her foot down hard, and with Ben gripping the seat in his teeth to avoid being flung out, the Terrier 1500 bashed its way through the branches and the brambles, swaying and jolting and bumping, deeper and deeper into the wood.

7

THE ORANGE TREE

M alcolm was sitting in the dappled sunlight under an orange
tree in the garden of a villa in a northern suburb of Aleppo,
reading the papers in a file headed *Tashbulak C/108/OS91*, and
from time to time turning over a flat stone on the table beside
him. The stone told him nothing at all.

He'd already had something to eat and some proper attention
to his wound, and he felt a lot better. The villa was rented by the
Brytish Embassy from its owner, a Syrian diamond merchant,
and was often used to put up visitors or newly arrived staff before
they could find a place of their own. Timur Ghazarian had taken
Malcolm there and arranged it all with the embassy officials;
the economic attaché would be coming to see him later that
afternoon, and would no doubt have some interesting questions
to answer.

So Malcolm sat in his long chair under the orange tree, with
the sunshine golden on the pages of his file and the leaves rustling
quietly overhead, and considered what he might say to the attaché.
Part of the problem was that the task Oakley Street had sent him
there to do wasn't economic so much as philosophical, and the
diplomatic service hadn't yet seen fit to appoint any officers to

the post of philosophical attaché; Malcolm would have to do the best he could.

He'd been trying to make notes as he went along, but the paper in the file was annoyingly shiny and his pencil slid over it without leaving much of a mark. He felt strange, passive, calm, almost indifferent. It was a long time since he'd felt like simply sitting still; perhaps you needed a special gift to do it without restlessness; or perhaps it was something to do with the oceanic feeling of wide unforced attention he found himself paying to the garden, the distant sounds of traffic, the light playing on his chair. No doubt it was partly due to the medication they'd given him.

He put the file back on the little rosewood table beside him, and picked up the stone again. It was a long oval in shape, about the length of his palm and as thick as the tip of his little finger, a dull greenish-black with no iridescence; it was smooth as if with long wear, the edges worn down thinner than the centre. It was very hard; he'd tested it with his pocket knife, and hadn't made a mark. It felt a little heavier than it looked.

Because one surface was not at all shiny, but a smooth and inviting matt, the idea occurred to him to try the pencil on it. It worked beautifully; he'd forgotten the pleasure of using a sharp pencil on a surface that resisted the line without impeding it. He remembered who had pointed this out to him first: it was Mr Palmer the Art teacher at his elementary school, who'd shown him how much more satisfactory it was to draw with a sharp pencil on paper with a slight tooth than with a blunt one on paper that was glazed like porcelain. 'Feel it,' he'd said. 'Educate your fingers as well as your brain.'

So Malcolm was perfectly at home in the world of the senses. And when he touched the stone with his pencil-point, sharpened only a few minutes before, he recognised the coming together of the right tool and the right material with a little sigh of satisfaction. But why had Glenys Godwin sent it to him? Timur Ghazarian had known nothing more about it. Malcolm drew a curved line, and then on impulse added a series of zigzag markings along it like the scintillating scotoma, his personal aurora, the spangled ring.

When he'd done that he wrote his name underneath, and then he had the shock of his life.

The spangled ring gently vanished as if sinking into the surface of the stone. Then his name disappeared in the same way, and some new words appeared in a handwriting he recognised:

Polstead? Is that you? GG

Glenys Godwin . . .

This was impossible. He blinked and shook his head, as if he was trying to wake up from a daydream; but there were the words, and that was the way she signed her initials.

Chief? he wrote.

Yes. Where are you?

Aleppo. Villa Edessa. Where is Oakley Street?

Oakley Street is in Hemel Hempstead.

That made him pause. Then he wrote *So romantic.*

The answer came at once: *There worketh a spell.*

And he replied *Which is lord of thy utterance, Christabel.*

Good. Tell me what the Magisterium's doing.

Malcolm wrote down everything he'd observed, including what he'd seen at the Thuringia Potash building, which took some time. As he wrote, the words a sentence or two before faded into the stone, leaving room to write more.

Finally he wrote *And what in the world is this stone? Can anyone else read it?*

I have an identical one – there are two of them. It's a resonating lodestone. They only communicate with each other. Now why won't you obey orders? What the hell are you doing in Aleppo?

Recovering from being shot in the hip. I'm going further east.

'Sir, Mr Polstead, sir, there is a visitor to see you.'

It was the servant who looked after the place. His leather slippers made no noise on the flagstones.

'Who is it, Ali?'

'He would not give a name, sir. He looks not respectable. If you like I will stay nearby while you talk.'

'Thank you. No need to stay nearby. I'll call if I need to.'

'Sir.'

The servant withdrew. Malcolm wrote *Visitor. More later* and laid the stone upside down on the papers beside him, and then on second thoughts laid a piece of paper on top of the stone.

He looked up as the visitor arrived. Ali showed him into the garden and withdrew without a word.

'I am Abdel Ionides, dragoman, interpreter, guide, factotum,' the visitor said. 'And I hope that you are Mr Polstead.'

'I am Malcolm Polstead. Good morning. What can I do for you, Mr Ionides? Please, do sit down.'

Malcolm indicated another chair. Ionides was intriguing: his clothes were shabby and tattered, almost those of a beggar, but his bearing was easy and confident, and his heavily scarred face expressed a quick and subtle intelligence.

He moved the chair a little into the shade and sat down.

'I heard your name,' he said, 'from a young man who is determined to kill you. But there is something strange here, because he referred to you as Mr Matthew Polstead. And from another source I heard your name as Mr Malcolm Polstead, and now you yourself say Malcolm. Which is the correct name, sir? Is there another English gentleman with a similar name?'

'Malcolm is correct. And your young man must be Olivier Bonneville.'

'Indeed, sir.'

'Where is he now? Do you know?'

'No. I last saw him near one of the dead cities to the west of Aleppo.'

'The one called al-Khan al-Azraq?'

'It has other names, but that is the one, yes. I had a brief conversation with him in which I learned your name, incorrectly as it now seems, and I persuaded him not to kill the person I was guiding towards Aleppo. He might be still in the desert, or he might have arrived in this city; I don't know.'

'How did you find out where I was?'

'It was not difficult.'

'Why did he want to kill the person you were guiding?'

'In order to get hold of something she had. He is an arrogant young man full of passionate desire for vengeance, which he calls justice.'

'Yes, I believe that. And you came here just to warn me about him?'

'No, not only, Mr Polstead. I came also to ask you about a particular problem. It concerns the Rusakov field and its associated particle. Dust, of course.'

Asta opened her eyes. She had been lying on a flagstone in the sun, seemingly fast asleep, but now her red-gold fur was anbaric with attention, and Ionides's gecko-dæmon reacted in a similar way: she ran from his shoulder down his arm and then sprang from his hand to the table. Asta leaped up to join her there, and they touched noses cautiously.

'Why do you think I can tell you anything about that?' said Malcolm. 'It's a matter of physics, and I'm an historian.'

'I know you were involved in the transfer of some documents and papers concerning the Rusakov matters.'

'Involved in the transfer . . .' Malcolm had to smile. 'You could put it like that. In fact, I stole them, but that was a very long time ago. I've never been professionally involved with that field of research. What's your connection with it?'

'Until ten years ago, I was a professor of mathematics at the University of Alexandria, and I was closely involved in the study of the Rusakov field. My colleagues and I made some discoveries that came to the notice of the authorities, and we were commanded to stop. But we continued, and the institute I directed was forcibly closed. My enemies in the university administration concocted a scandal, entirely false, and made it impossible for me to continue in any academic field. Since then I have lived as a dragoman, guiding, translating, arranging things for my clients. Sometimes a beggar, sometimes a thief. The world forces us into these roles, and we have to play them as well as we can.'

'Tell me about your discoveries about the Rusakov field.'

'Thought experiments only, for the last ten years. At Alexandria, I was studying variations in the field strength. The gravitational field, the anbaromagnetic field, they vary with distance. We all know that. This field, the Rusakov field, seemed to be indifferent to distance. There was a minimum strength that remained the same no matter how far from the source—'

'The source? What's the source, in this case?'

'This is where the danger begins. This is where it becomes forbidden. The Rusakov field is related closely to human consciousness. When it varies, it does so not because of distance but because of the attention of a human observer. The equations are hard to follow, but the implication is that the Rusakov field permeates everything in the universe. There is consciousness everywhere. Not all the same kind of consciousness in every part, but something it would be hard to call anything else. And that was what the authorities objected to.'

'Of course they would. But in this case, which authorities do you mean?'

'The university, the civil government, and the religious powers. Only the police were not interested. A matter of experimental theology, of philosophy? They can't investigate that when they have thieves and murderers to catch.

'So now we come to roses. And the imagination.'

Malcolm saw how this beggar-academic was enjoying the process of telling his story, like an actor in front of an attentive audience. Asta and the gecko-dæmon were side by side on the little table, listening, and Malcolm thought: *Where is the Dust in this garden? It must be surrounding all of them, swirling with currents of understanding and expectation.*

'Tashbulak,' said Malcolm. 'Karamakan. A red building, fiercely guarded.'

'You know about it. You been there?'

'No. But I'm going there. Tell me about roses and the imagination.'

'The oil they make from their special roses, you know about its power? You know what it can reveal?'

'Yes, I do.'

'You know Thuringia Potash?'

'They seem to be involved in these matters, but I don't know very much about how.'

'They have been trying to synthesise this oil for two years now.'

'Ah,' said Malcolm. 'So that's it.'

'They have been using all their resources, pharmaceutical laboratories, every kind of expertise and research, and a great deal of money – and they can't do it. It refuses to allow them to do it. There is a molecule in the original rose oil that has different properties according to how they analyse it. They do it one way – such-and-such a result. So they think, that is how to make it! And they synthesise it exactly, and with no result. Just ordinary rose oil. So they analyse it a different way – different result – they try that – still nothing. They try another – same thing. As if it knows what they're doing and play trick on them.'

'As if it . . . Wait a minute. You mean like the photon that seems to know which slit to go through?'

'Yes. Very like that. Whatever you try, it's the wrong way. There must be a right way, because the oil exists, but you can never synthesise it. This is the point I get to when I was working on it theoretically. I could have saved TP some time, but I was happy to see them waste their resources.'

'How do you know this? If you've got no academic position, how can you follow—'

'I know many people, many things. Now we talk about imagination.'

'Go on then.'

'Tomorrow the President of the High Council of the Magisterium is going to make a big speech in Constantinople. Here is the text.'

He reached into an inside pocket of his shabby linen jacket and drew out a folded stack of several closely typed pages. Malcolm took it, more puzzled than he'd been for months. He unfolded the sheets and read the heading:

Sur L'Imagination
Doctrine fausse, séduisante et dangereuse

'He's making war on the imagination now?' he said.

'This is the first time he make it clear. Full, clear, passionate. Mad.'

'How did you get this?'

'I was involved in the transfer.'

'You stole it.'

'Of course.'

'May I keep this to read?'

'If it's in your hands, it's dangerous for you and not so dangerous for me. Yes, keep it. Now I have one more thing to tell you, which is why I tell you these other things first, or else you would not hear them with the clarity they deserve. I believe you know my employer.'

'What? Who is your employer?'

'I have been guiding her here from Seleukeia. Her name is Miss Lyra Silvertongue.'

Malcolm felt a rush of emotion along every nerve in his body. He didn't move.

'Where is she now?' he said, polite, urbane.

'At Hotel de las Palmas, Zakkum Street. I can guide you there in twenty minutes.'

In fact, it took thirty, because Malcolm could go no faster than his leg would let him. Ionides was solicitous, at one point disappearing for a few moments into a bazaar and reappearing with a walking stick for Malcolm to lean on. He refused to accept any money for it.

They found the Hotel de las Palmas in a state of confusion and panic. The receptionist, a middle-aged woman with a yapping terrier-dæmon, clearly had no idea what had happened or why, and the guests – some half dressed, having been interrupted during a siesta, or something else that required little in the way of clothing – were variously angry, frightened, embarrassed, resentful, shocked, and anxious to placate any authority that needed placating, while demanding apologies from everyone that didn't.

They milled around the lobby, shouting, pleading, explaining, apologising, accusing, and sobbing. Malcolm and Ionides watched from the doorway, and as soon as someone who might be the concierge appeared, Malcolm stopped him with a firm hand.

'What's the reason for all this?'

'Police raid, sir. Nothing to matter. All finish, all over. No reason to alarm . . .' He stood on a chair and clapped his hands. '*Messieurs-Dames! S'il vous plaît!* Excuse me, ladies and gentlemen! Listen, please! The emergency is all finished! Please go back to your rooms, or carry on whatever your business! The police have gone – no need to concern – do not disquiet yourselves . . .'

He was trembling and sweating, and he kept trying to smooth down his hair, which was already flat and dank across his head. He went on talking, while Malcolm and Ionides looked at each other and nodded.

Ionides eased himself past a plump man with a small moustache who was jabbing a forefinger into the desk top as he protested in fast and furious French about his luggage. The receptionist spread her hands, baffled, frightened, and Ionides leaned forward and spoke quietly in Greek.

While he was doing that, Malcolm turned to the concierge, who was trying to climb down from his chair, and offered him a hand.

'Thank you – *merci, monsieur* – yes, ladies and gentlemen, everything is safe and fine – Monsieur?' Malcolm's hand was holding a five-dollar bill, and the concierge deftly vanished it into a pocket. 'At your service entirely, sir. How can I help?'

'You mentioned the police. Were they looking for someone in particular?'

'I don't know, sir. They don't explain. They might not have been police. I had to call them something when I explain just now, and the word *police* people recognise, you understand.'

'There was a young Englishwoman staying here alone. Was she here when the police came?'

'I don't think so, monsieur. The middle of the day, she is probably elsewhere. When they left they had no one with them. Let me ask Madame Galatas . . .'

He turned to the receptionist, but Ionides was already moving away from the desk, shaking his head.

'Not here,' he said.

'Where did you last see her? Was it here?'

'Brazilian Embassy garden. Not far. You walk all right?'

Olivier Bonneville, full of pain, bitter, burning with subdued rage, carried his wounded dæmon to a house not far from the embassy and opened the front door.

A young woman he had previously ignored was sitting behind a desk in the entrance hall. She watched him come in, watched him slouch towards the staircase, watched him set his foot on the first step, and then she said, 'Hey.'

'What do you want?' he said.

'He wants you in there,' she said, jerking her thumb over her shoulder. 'Right now.'

'I'm busy.'

'You're in trouble. That beats being busy.'

He turned away from the staircase, glowering. From this angle she could see the scratches on his face, the dust and dirt on his clothes, the torn knee of his trousers. She had no sympathy: the boy was a thug, a spoilt brat, and if someone had taught him a lesson, it was about time.

'What's he want?' he said.

'Nothing to do with me.'

Her expression was cold and hostile. She knew precisely why he'd ignored her in the past: it was because she wasn't pretty. He paid enough attention to that blonde in the consular department.

He shrugged, which made him wince, and then she saw the broken wing of his dæmon, who lay limp and dull-eyed in his arms. She was shocked enough to feel a moment's pity, but he moved past and the moment was gone. She heard him knock and heard the man's snapped reply. The boy opened the door reluctantly and went inside, and then, hearing nothing more, she went back to her magazine.

Bonneville faced the man behind the desk with a look of defiance, or so he thought. The man was Father Gerhardt, the Magisterial Nuncio, and there was someone with him: a woman of forty or so, maybe Persian, in western clothes, with a heavy gold chain around her neck, and eyes darker and larger than he had ever seen in anyone not famous for being beautiful; for she was certainly beautiful, and to the best of his knowledge not famous. Anyway, he had never seen her before, and her presence made him feel even more wretched than he did already.

The nuncio, a lean and sour-faced man, said, 'Where have you been?'

The woman looked at Bonneville with frank curiosity. He avoided her eyes and said shortly, 'I found the girl.'

'And? What happened?'

'She . . . I think she must have been deranged.'

'I said *what happened*?'

'We fought.'

Bonneville had seldom been so uncomfortable. He could even see, after a flickering glance, a smile playing around the woman's lips. He looked down at the carpet.

'And the outcome? Stand up straight.'

The pain in Bonneville's kidneys, where the bitch had kicked him, was almost crippling. He tried to stand up, but had to take it slowly, with a deep breath. His dæmon lolled in his arms.

'What happened to her?' said the woman, indicating the wounded hawk-dæmon. Her voice was low, her tone concerned. Perhaps that smile had been sympathetic. With every second that went by, Bonneville felt worse.

'The girl injured her,' he said sullenly.

'Where did this happen?' said Father Gerhardt. 'Quickly, now.'

'In the garden of the Brazilian Embassy.'

The woman raised her eyebrows towards the nuncio.

'In effect a public park,' he explained, and to Bonneville: 'Is she there still?'

'Probably not.'

'Speak up, boy!'

'I said probably not,' Bonneville snarled. 'But I hurt her too. She might not have gone far. And I can tell you something else.'

'Well?'

'There is a man who has been guiding her. His name is Abdel Ionides. I saw him after I – after she attacked me. But he is not a guide. He knows too much – about the roses, and other things. You should arrest him – he will tell you a great deal about her and where she is going, everything.'

'Abdel Ionides?' said the nuncio, reaching for a pen. 'Describe him.'

Bonneville did, with some accuracy. The nuncio wrote it all down.

Then the woman spoke. 'The young woman. Was her dæmon with her?'

It was disconcerting, having to face her when she was so beautiful.

'Who is this woman?' Bonneville said to the nuncio.

'Someone of more importance than you. Go and clean yourself up and wait in your room.'

The woman looked at Bonneville and said, 'Dr Leila Pervani.'

He nodded and said, 'Olivier Bonneville. And no, her dæmon was not with her.' To Father Gerhardt he said, 'What are you going to do?'

'Find them both and deal with them, as you failed to do. Now get out.'

Bonneville knew, as he painfully climbed the staircase under the eyes of the smirking receptionist, that he should never have tackled Lyra on his own. When the girl had kicked him in the kidney it had taken all the strength out of him in one horrible moment. But that was nothing compared to the feeling of her hand wrenching his dæmon's wing: as if she had reached inside his own chest and snapped a rib. That a *girl* should do this! And now that he should be humiliated beyond measure in front of a woman whom, five minutes before, he had never heard of. That would never happen again.

8

THE POWERS OF THE AIR

Father Gerhardt ignored Dr Leila Pervani, which was all right with her because she was intrigued to see him at work. As soon as Bonneville left the room the nuncio lifted the telephone, turned the handle hard, and spoke rapidly to someone whose harsh voice said the one word '*Jawohl*' in response.

Father Gerhardt stood up swiftly, took a small pistol from a drawer and dropped it in a pocket of his cassock, and glanced at the woman in a calculating way before shaking his head.

He swept out of the office and through the hall, ignoring the receptionist, who was used to that, but who watched with interest as Mademoiselle Pervani came out more slowly after him. The woman's clothes were expensive, and she moved elegantly without making any noise on the stone floor. She smiled at the receptionist and began to climb the staircase; the scent she wore lingered faintly after she'd gone past, something woody and spicy and almost intoxicating. The receptionist wished she had the nerve to ask the woman what it was.

In the courtyard the men of the Magisterial guard were climbing into the back of an adapted prison van painted in desert camouflage – unnecessarily, since it had never been used outside the city – under the supervision of a sergeant and Father Gerhardt. The nuncio's rasping voice said loudly, 'Take them alive. You understand – alive.'

He climbed in next to the driver. One of the men swung the gate open, and the van moved out into the street.

Leila Pervani knocked softly on the door of Olivier Bonneville's room and waited. Finally his voice came: 'Who's that?'

'I want to talk to you,' she said.

'Wait.'

Movements inside the room, and then the door opened. He looked out, flushed, scowling, in his shirtsleeves.

'May I come in?' she said.

She had the ability to make everything about herself soft, gentle, agreeable. He had no power to resist. He stood aside, and as soon as she entered, she uttered a little gasp of sympathy at the sight of his hawk-dæmon perching on the back of a chair, one wing stretched out, broken.

Her own dæmon, a sand-coloured snake with emerald markings, hissed in her sleeve. She held her arm out towards the chair, and the dæmon flowed out and on to the seat, from where, she knew, he would talk very quietly with the wounded hawk.

'Are *you* hurt?' she said to Bonneville.

'Yes,' he said shortly. 'I told you.'

She could see he was mortified by everything that had happened, including her interest in it.

'May I sit down?' she said.

He shrugged. There was nowhere to sit but the bed. She sat on the end, and after a moment he sat down carefully on the floor with his back against the wall. His face was stiff with pain.

'Olivier, is it? I'm Leila. I'm so sorry about your dæmon. These things cure themselves, but it'll be painful for you both for a while. I was interested to hear what you said about that man, what was his name? Ionides. How did you meet him?'

144

'He was following me. Out in the desert, near some ruins, I cornered him and asked him what the hell he was doing. He told me some yarn about treasure. Well, I wasn't interested. The only thing I want is something that girl stole from me. He's some kind of guide, interpreter, pretends to be, anyway, but really he's just a thief. He fooled that girl, but he couldn't fool me.'

'He's working for her, you say?'

'She wouldn't have got this far otherwise. She's lost her dæmon. I suppose she's looking for him.'

'What did she steal from you?'

'My father's alethiometer. There's a man involved too. Polstead, Matthew or Malcolm, I don't know.'

'Is the man Ionides after the alethiometer as well?'

'He's had plenty of chances to take it, so probably not. He wants this treasure he was talking about. Somewhere in the desert, way off to the east. Almost Cathay.'

'Why is he going with the girl when he could move more quickly by himself?'

'He needs her. There's something only she can do before they can get to the treasure.'

'And what is this treasure?'

'No idea. As I said, I'm not interested.'

She nodded. She looked at his wounded dæmon, all sympathy, all kindness. As hard as Bonneville looked he could see no deception there, but the habit of mistrust was lifelong.

'You know,' she said, 'I was talking to Marcel Delamare the other day.'

'Where?'

'In Constantinople. At the Patriarch's palace.'

Bonneville knew that Delamare was there. So far she might be telling the truth.

'He told me about you,' she went on. 'He said you were the best alethiometrist he'd ever known. He admires you very much.'

'Maybe he did once. But he treated me like a servant. Do this, do that. Look for this. Don't look at that. I wasn't going to be his tame oracle. I had my own purposes.'

'Quite right. But now you're back with the Magisterium?'

'On my own terms. They have facilities I wouldn't be able to use otherwise.'

Leila Pervani remembered the scene in the nuncio's office. If 'on his own terms' meant being sent to his room like a naughty schoolboy . . . But Bonneville was humiliated and hurt and angry and nearly crippled with pride. She reached out for her serpent-dæmon, who hissed a farewell to the hawk and slipped up into her sleeve.

'Thank you, Olivier,' she said. 'I'm grateful. I hope we can talk again soon. There are things each of us could learn from the other, and your knowledge is unique. Lie flat now. Let your back heal.'

She smiled. He looked away, and she left.

'There she is,' said Ionides. 'On that bench.'

He and Malcolm had just turned in to the Brazilian Embassy garden. The afternoon was heavy with heat and thick with insect sounds, and the garden was nearly deserted; an elderly couple were feeding some sparrows from a paper bag, and a young woman lay asleep in the dappled shade on the bench Ionides was pointing to.

'But that's not Lyra!' said Malcolm.

So thin, with short dark ragged hair—

'Yes, it is!' said Asta, and leaped across the grass to her side.

Malcolm followed with all the clumsy speed his wound allowed. He'd noticed the astonishment with which Ionides saw that he and his dæmon could separate, and the moment of swift calculation that followed.

Asta was already standing on the arm of the bench, near Lyra's head, and purring. Seeing that Lyra was deeply asleep, Malcolm tried to kneel beside the bench to wake her gently; but it hurt so much he had to give up, and pushed himself upright again. Lyra was so still she might have been dead, and of course with no dæmon . . . He'd never seen her before without Pantalaimon.

He realised that if she woke up while he was standing just there the sun would be in her eyes, and moved round to a spot where it would be in his face rather than hers.

He leaned on the back of the bench and said quietly, 'Lyra! Can you hear me? Lyra, wake up.'

Ionides had withdrawn a little way to keep watch. Malcolm leaned down a little closer.

'Lyra, wake up! We're going to have to move away from here. Don't be startled. Wake up gently now.'

Still no response. She was frowning in her sleep, hot, drawn. He could never have imagined her looking so unhappy. He reached down and laid his hand on her shoulder: the first time he had ever touched her.

'Lyra—'

She cried out, twisted away, leaped up like a wild animal about to flee.

'Miss Silver,' said Ionides calmly, and she turned, bewildered, and then looked back to Malcolm.

'Lyra, it's all right, you're safe,' he said.

'Malcolm?'

He nodded. She looked at the bench, where Asta was watching.

'Malcolm, is that really you?'

Her voice was a little hoarse, a little strained, a little thick with sleep. Malcolm's hand still held the memory of her shoulder: how fragile! He wanted to enfold her in his arms, but knew nothing like that would ever happen.

'Yes, it's really me,' he managed to say. 'Thanks to Mr Ionides, who brought me here. Come with us. We'll go somewhere safe.'

'How did you – where did you . . .'

'Did you find Pan?' he said. 'Is he anywhere near?'

'No – oh, my rucksack: I must take that . . .'

It lay on the grass beside the bench. She picked it up and swung it over her shoulder.

'The hotel,' she said. 'There were police there, or something . . .'

'Left anything there?' said Malcolm.

'I've got everything I need. What are you doing here? How did you get here?'

She was still only just awake. She looked exhausted. She was wearing a floral skirt that was far from clean, and she could hardly keep her balance, and she was blinking and trying to open her eyes fully in the sun. And the hair – she looked like a stranger – and she'd hurt her hand – 'Show me your hand,' said Malcolm.

She held it out, trembling, and he took it on his palm. The bruise was floridly coloured, and her first and middle finger were bent out of alignment.

'That's broken,' he said, and she nodded.

'Mr Malcolm,' said Ionides. 'Listen.'

He listened, and so did Lyra. The sound of a siren was coming from three or four streets away.

'It's coming this way,' Ionides said.

'The young man with the alethiometer,' said Lyra.

'He was here?' said Malcolm.

She nodded. 'I had to fight him, and I hurt his dæmon,' she said. 'He must've . . .'

'We must go, *now*,' said Ionides.

'Is there another gate?' said Malcolm.

'That way, but they keep it locked.'

'Come on. Lyra, can you run?'

'You're limping,' she said. 'Can *you*?'

'Just hurry.'

She followed where Ionides was leading, along the gravel path and then left round the side of the house. Ionides was waiting for them to catch up.

'You got a plan?' he said to Malcolm.

'I've got two. Is this still an embassy?'

'No.'

'In that case, I've got one. Where's that gate?'

'That way—'

The siren was rapidly getting louder, and then there came the sound of another, from a different direction.

Shadows flickered over them as they struggled to hurry to the gate. For a moment Malcolm thought it was his private aurora, the spangled ring, but it wasn't: as the first car turned into the gate behind them, with the noise of an air-cooled engine straining in a low gear and the siren suddenly increasing in volume, the shadows vanished and the garden blazed with sunlight again.

'Something's happening,' said Lyra, looking all around. 'Something else . . .'

She, Malcolm, and Ionides were still on the path, a hundred yards or so from the group of trees that shaded the other gate. The camouflaged van slammed to a halt, spraying gravel to left and right, siren still blaring, and then from behind them, out of the trees, came another, this one marked with the word POLIS.

Malcolm crouched to whisper to Asta: 'Whatever happens, whatever it takes, *stay with her.*'

He and Ionides moved closer to Lyra, one on each side, and she took a short stick out of her rucksack. Malcolm transferred the cane to his left hand and took a small pistol from his pocket with the right. Ionides seemed to be holding a knife.

The sirens were both still screaming, one ahead of them and one behind, making the air of the garden shudder and ring to the point of hallucination. Men with guns were leaping from the back of the first van and running to spread out in a line, all aiming at the three of them, and then more shadows sped over them: it was like being dashed with cool water.

Some of the armed men looked up and stumbled backwards. One fell over. Two others turned and fled.

The man in command of the first van gave an order to the driver, and the siren stopped. A moment later the other did too, and then they could all hear something else, like gigantic wings, windmill-sized, beating the air.

Malcolm hadn't taken his eyes off the soldiers. He was calculating: sergeant first, pull Lyra behind him, that tall man second, but those *shadows* – his very sight was flickering – and if it wasn't the scotoma, it had the same effect on him: a revelation, a new way of seeing, the opening of windows into a different vision of the world—

The combat in the sky during the night of the desert? Had those creatures come here too? He looked up, but the light was too dazzling.

A shout from Ionides: Malcolm and Lyra both looked, and saw him being wrestled to the ground by three soldiers, with a grey-faced man in a clerical robe directing them.

Before they could move to help him, one soldier braver than the rest fired upwards, and at once a vast creature swooped low and seized him and bore him screaming into the sky – then *dropped* him from high above treetop height, still screaming until he hit the ground—

Lyra hid her face in Malcolm's shoulder.

More shadows – a well-loved voice crying Lyra's name – she turned her face up and shouted: 'Pan! Oh, Pan! Here! Here I am!'

Her right hand shaded her eyes – she was gazing into the sky, into the flashing shadows, into the bare sun—

A crash of gunshots, human cries, a screaming roar from the sky—

Ionides struggled, but they had pinioned his arms. A soldier clubbed him from behind. Malcolm struck at the soldier with his cane, slashing him across the head so that he fell and scrambled up and ran away. Another two held on to Ionides and dragged him towards the truck. Lyra was pulling at Malcolm's arm, face turned to the sky, shouting something he couldn't make out, and then he pulled away to reach Ionides, if he could, and tug him to safety. But before he could, something whose power was greater than anything he'd ever known seized him by the shoulder, lifted him off the ground, and with vast beating wings bore him higher and higher above the garden, above the buildings, above the city. Lyra was shouting: 'Malcolm! Malcolm!' but she was on the ground, and Asta – Asta was down there with her – just as he'd told her, staying close to Lyra.

In the battering whirlwind of sensations and feelings, the pain, the shock, the fear for Asta and for Lyra, Malcolm found himself still capable of thinking clearly; and what he thought was that these creatures who had swept him into the sky, whatever name they had for themselves, whatever name they were given by poets, were of the same order of beings as the fairy of the Thames and the old giant of the riverbed, and that he'd had dealings with them before, and that he'd survived, and so had Lyra.

PART TWO

9

Gold, and Gold

L yra ran, of course. There was nothing else she could have
done. The embassy garden was long and narrow, with
the embassy building facing part of one of the long sides. The
commotion, the struggle and the panic and the terrifying swoop
of the gryphon were enough to distract the nuncio's guard from
the slender figure of a girl running for the trees; and luckily the
trees were thickly planted – more of an untended shrubbery; so
it wasn't hard for Lyra to conceal herself among the hibiscus and
jasmine and listen to the shouts, the revving of tinny engines, and
the occasional gunshot.

There was someone beside her.

She gasped, stifling the sound at once, and saw only an
arm's length away something red-gold, the size of an unusually
large cat—

'Asta! No – *is* it Asta? Is it you?'

She whispered breathlessly; she'd have been breathless whether
she'd been running or not. The dæmon sat calmly and spoke
softly in return.

'Yes. Asta. That creature took Malcolm before I could do
anything. What was it? Have you seen one before?'

'A gryphon, I think. I saw one take away a man a few nights ago. As if he weighed nothing. I don't know anything about them at all. Oh, this is horrible. I don't know – I keep saying that – I don't know what to do, now. Was that Mr Ionides with Malcolm?'

'Yes. He came to see us, Malcolm and me, just a few hours ago – we were staying in an embassy villa – he came to tell Malcolm about you, and other things, and we set off right away to find you.'

'And now they've arrested him,' said Lyra, and nearly sobbed.

'The gryphon you saw earlier – why did he take the man away?'

'I think he must have stolen something – all they care about, the gryphons, is gold, apparently, and the man had – he snatched my alethiometer – it must have shone in the moonlight. Oh, this is unbearable . . .'

And then she did cry a little.

Asta moved closer. 'And Pan?' she said. 'You haven't found him yet?'

'No. And now I probably never will.'

'I heard his voice. Didn't you? Just now – from the sky – from above – I heard him calling your name.'

'What? Really? I thought I did too, but—'

'I think he was with those gryphons.'

'Those? I only saw one, and only for a second. How many were there?'

'A dozen. Maybe more.'

Lyra felt dizzy. She tried to listen, as if Pan might still be calling, but heard nothing that sounded even vaguely like his voice. And now this: it was too much to take in. The sound of the police car engines was diminishing among the normal city noise; the turtle doves were still purring in the garden, as if nothing had happened; cicadas shrilled among the leaves overhead.

'Do you think the police were looking for you?' said Asta.

'They might have been. They took Mr Ionides, and they must have known he was guiding me . . . Asta, till things are safer, shall we pretend that you're my dæmon? Pan did that for a girl he'd met who'd lost her dæmon – they pretended – I found her in the dead city and she told me about it . . .'

'Good idea. It would be safer for both of us. We need to tell each other everything that's happened. Now let's be practical. Have you got any money?'

'Yes, I have. Thanks to Farder Coram. Oh, Malcolm knew him, didn't he?'

'Yes, he did.'

'And we need to rescue Mr Ionides.'

'You call him Mister? Why?'

'Respect. He's very important.'

'From what I've seen and heard of him, I agree. Have they all gone now, the police or whatever they were?'

Lyra stood up carefully and looked around. The garden was just as it had been when she arrived; only the gravel path was a little disturbed where the vehicles had skidded to a halt. The gryphons seemed to have come and gone in a moment. The mother and child had left, but an elderly couple were strolling slowly arm in arm, and a man in Arab dress was sitting down on the bench and opening a newspaper.

'I think we could try now,' said Lyra.

'What will your name be?'

'Ah. Well, for the moment I'm Queen Tatiana Iorekova of Novaya Zemlya. That was Farder Coram's idea too. I've got a document to prove it, signed and sealed by Mustafa Bey, no less. What about you?'

'I've never had to do this before . . . Something beginning with A.'

'Atalanta.'

'Too long. Make it Afra. Can you feel if Pan's in danger?' said Afra-Asta.

'I used to think I probably could, because I'd be afraid. But I'm afraid almost all the time since he left. Are you afraid for Malcolm?'

'No, strangely enough. But I don't think he's in danger.'

'Not even . . .' Lyra looked up involuntarily.

'No. I think the gryphons took him for some other reason than to harm him. And if I was right and I did hear Pan, they must be looking after him too.'

'Let's hope so, said Lyra.

With the dæmon padding elegantly beside her, Queen Tatiana Iorekova stepped out of the bushes and on to the shaded lawn. Together they moved through the garden, easy and confident, the glass of courage and the mould of calm.

The gryphon who had seized Malcolm in his claws soared high above the city, gripping him so tightly by the shoulders that Malcolm thought he might faint with pain before he fell a thousand feet to the earth below. On the whole he'd rather be unconscious at that point anyway, he thought, but then the gryphon probably wasn't going to let go, so he might as well put the pain out of his mind and take in what information he could.

First, this creature wasn't alone. Ahead and to each side there were six others at least, and possibly more behind.

Second, he had definitely heard a voice calling his name, and though it wasn't impossible that these creatures could speak, the voice sounded as if it came from someone small.

Third, they weren't going to fly a long way. They were making for a range of hills, a long low plateau, to the south-east of the city, and Malcolm saw some of the other gryphons stop beating their wings and start to glide, losing height as they made for the nearest slope.

Soon the one who was carrying him began to do the same. The powerful rise-and-fall ceased, and that was a relief to Malcolm's shoulders; instead they sailed steadily downwards to sweep up again as the foothills of the plateau began to rise below, and then the great wings beat again, this time to slow their forward movement and prepare to land.

The ground seemed to come up with alarming speed, but the gryphon had calculated perfectly, hovering for a few seconds a foot or so above the ground for Malcolm to drop before flying a few feet further on and landing himself. Why *him*self? Malcolm had no idea, but the great creature seemed to him male rather than female. Others – perhaps a dozen or so altogether – were already standing nearby, easing their wings, or stretching out their lion legs and flexing their muscles.

Again Malcolm had to remind himself: he'd seen strange things before. He wasn't hallucinating. As if to confirm that it was true, a little spot of light began to sparkle and flutter in the corner of his vision. He welcomed it and sat down on a rock to steady himself.

And then that voice again – 'Malcolm! Malcolm!' – and bounding towards him over the rough grass was a dæmon – Pantalaimon! – his warm brown fur and white throat and chest very clear in the level afternoon light.

'Pan! Is that you?'

'Yes – me – is Lyra with you?'

'No. She – I'd just found her in that garden – but when these – what are they?'

'Gryphons—'

'When they came down she ran towards some trees – Asta was with her.'

'Then we're lucky to be separators already.'

'That occurred to me too.'

'You're bleeding—'

Malcolm felt his shoulder. The gryphon's claws had penetrated his skin in more than one place, but not deeply; it was still the wound in his hip that troubled him most.

'But, Pan, what do you know about . . . ?'

He spread his hands wide, looking all around, shrugging in wonderment. The great creatures were talking, some of them, their eagle-throats and lion-chests uttering deep harsh growls that rose and fell in every way like human speech. The vivid sunlight shining on their feathers brought out a thousand different colours, from the blackest purple to the most dazzling snowy-white and every kind of rainbow-glint in between. Soon Malcolm's private aurora was winding and shimmering as if part of this gryphon-blaze had come loose to make its own way through the air.

Pan could see that Malcolm was preoccupied by something interior. He sat still close by and said nothing, and presently the little gryphon Gulya flew down beside him.

He held up a paw: hush. Gulya was gazing at Malcolm, whose eyes were closed, and who was sitting upright facing the sun, his gold-red hair glowing in the clear light. The battered old canvas rucksack lay on the grass beside him. Pan could see something he'd never noticed before: a scatter of freckles over Malcolm's nose and cheeks, and a sheen of gold where the stubble was growing around his jaw.

Gulya leaned forward and whispered, 'Come with me.'

Pan followed as Gulya led him towards the largest gryphon. He'd been with them now for long enough to know the proper form of behaviour, and the names of the most important among them.

'My greetings to you, Prince Keshvād. I am here for you to command.'

The gryphon prince was gazing at Malcolm, as Gulya had done. 'Who is that man?' said the prince.

'His name is Malcolm. He is a learned man, a great scholar, a famous craftsman. He can dispute with philosophers and work with wood and metal. And glass,' Pan added recklessly.

'What is he doing now?'

'He is seeing a vision, great prince.'

'A vision of gold?'

'Very likely, great prince.'

'He is not the human you were looking for. Why did my servant pick him up and not her?'

'As far as I could see, great prince, my Lyra escaped from a band of soldiers and fled among some trees. Perhaps your servant couldn't reach her. And this man – well, yes, he does look as if he's made of gold. But he is a human being, a man like many others. He is a great friend to me and to Lyra, and he will be glad to pay his respects to you and your nation.'

'He has no dæmon.'

'His dæmon fled with my Lyra. This sometimes happens.'

'Her Majesty my mother Queen Shahrnavāz will want to see him. We shall fly him to Damāvand today and tonight. You will come too.'

Pan remembered what happened the only time he tried to argue with a gryphon's decision: Gulya had had to save his life. These creatures were intensely proud and passionate. He wasn't going to try it again. He bowed his head to Prince Keshvād and moved away to speak quietly with Gulya.

'Why will the Queen want to meet Malcolm?' he said.

'He is treasure.'

'Treasure? You mean – well, what do you mean?'

'He is gold. Didn't you know that? Look at him. He has the scent of gold.'

Pan felt a little lurch of dismay. They *believed* that. He said, 'But what will she do with him?'

'Keep him in her treasury.'

'I must tell him about this—'

'It will make no difference. He will be her treasure.'

'He'll be a prisoner!'

'He will be treated with honour and respect. He will be the most valuable being the Queen has ever received into her treasury.'

'But she can't just . . . How does she know about him anyway?'

'We have always known this man was coming.'

Pan felt as if his head was spinning. 'And . . . how far away is Damāvand?'

'Very far. South of the Caspian Sea. Sacred mountain.'

Pantalaimon felt nothing but despair. He rocked back and forth without knowing he was doing it; a little keening sound came from his throat.

'Leave me,' he said to Gulya when he found his voice again. 'I want to speak to Malcolm.'

Gulya seemed unaware that Pan or Malcolm would regard his fate as anything but a great honour. As she flew away, Pan tore at the grass in rage, but only for a moment, because Malcolm was sitting up and looking around.

Pan bounded over and leaped on to the rock beside him. 'Awake now?'

'I wasn't asleep. I was watching something.'

'Well, listen, because we're in trouble. The gryphons have a queen, who is all-powerful. And they're going to take you to her, because she wants to put you in her treasury, because you're made of gold. Or you have the scent of gold, or something. Don't laugh whatever you do. They're so proud, so impulsive, so passionate. They won't be denied. I'll make them take me too, to speak for you. I think the best thing to do would be for you to be just as proud, just as touchy, to make demands. Behave like a prince yourself – they understand that sort of thing.'

'Gold? Made of *gold*?'

'Your hair, your skin. You don't understand how much it hypnotises them.'

Malcolm wiped his hand over his head and blew out his cheeks.

'But what about Lyra?' he said.

'If she's got Asta with her . . .'

'I'm happier to know that, I must say.'

'We'll have to stay together. I'll be – I don't know – your servant or something.'

Malcolm didn't seem very pleased at the idea.

'What were you doing in Aleppo anyway?' Pan went on.

'Looking for Lyra. What else? Oh, spying too, investigating things like Thuringia Potash. We'd only just got there. But mainly looking for Lyra.'

Pan glanced around. There was a purposeful order to the way the gryphons were moving; it looked as if they were going to set off quite soon.

He called: 'Gulya! Gulya!'

The little gryphon heard and flew to his side at once.

'Here is what we're going to do,' Pan said. 'I shall go with Malcolm at all times. We must have a comfortable flight and human food. Fruit, bread, cooked meat at least. You must all treat Malcolm with the utmost respect. And me too because I'm his servant.'

'But—'

'That is what will happen, Gulya. If Queen Shahrnavāz learns that we have been badly treated, what punishment will she order for you?'

'No, no, Pan, please don't do that. Of course you will be well looked after, very well looked after, I promise.'

'What did you mean just now when you said you had always known this man was coming?'

'He is the man of gold. We know it from always. He is part of the future that lived in the past.'

'That's correct,' said Malcolm. 'Now tell me, do your people speak in words alone or in pictures as well?'

Pan was puzzled, but Gulya seemed to understand.

'We understand both,' she said, 'but when we have something eternal to say, we use pictures.'

'How can you—' Pan began, but stopped at once when Malcolm gave him a warning glance.

'Tell your companions, your fellow gryphons,' Malcolm said, 'that I am not only gold of flesh but gold of knowledge, and that I have true gold of that kind to give to you all, which I shall do when I speak to Her Majesty Queen Shahrnavāz. That's why I have come among you. Furthermore, my attendant Pantalaimon must be free to remain with me or to go anywhere he needs at all times.'

'Yes,' said Gulya. 'And you are a philosopher and a craftsman? An artificer?'

'My companion has told you that?'

'Yes.'

'My companion always speaks the truth,' said Malcolm.

His tone was calm and steady, and conveyed an impression of powerful authority.

Gulya bowed her head. 'I shall return when we are ready to leave,' she said, and flew away.

Malcolm turned to Pan. 'You told them I was a philosopher? And a craftsman?'

'Well . . . You are, aren't you?'

Malcolm just looked at him. Pan felt like curling up in shame, but he recovered after a few moments and said, 'What did you mean by speaking in pictures? She knew what you meant, but I don't.'

'I wanted to know whether they had a metaphorical under-standing as well as a literal one.'

'And . . . what did she mean about something eternal, having something eternal to say?'

'The same thing. Something eternal – something outside time. Language uses time, all kinds of time, but pictures only have the present. Clearly the gryphons understand the difference. I wonder if they make pictures themselves, physical things, or have any craft or art at all. I'm curious about the way they apprehend things.'

'When you say *apprehend*, do you mean – like the language thing – seeing in pictures? Ideas in pictures, I mean, like the alethiometer?'

'Yes . . . Did Lyra have it with her when she left?'

'Oh, she'd never leave that behind. It's been everywhere with us. Look, I think we're going to ride on Prince Keshvād's back.'

Malcolm stood up and slung the rucksack over his shoulder. Prince Keshvād was circling in the air above them. Most of the others were already aloft, but two were circling with Prince Keshvād, like guards or attendants.

Prince Keshvād glided down and landed close by, and then (Malcolm found himself thinking in the language of heraldry) lay couchant, in the attitude of the Sphinx, so Malcolm and Pan could climb up on his back. It was so broad and deep that there was plenty of room to lie and make themselves comfortable, just where the lion fur ended and the eagle feathers began; and then the immense wings spread wide and high, and the two travellers felt beneath them the working of the gryphon's mighty frame and the beating of his muscles as they soared up into the sky and east towards the summit of Mount Damāvand, a thousand miles away.

Despite her boast about the document signed by Mustafa Bey, Lyra felt uneasy about the thought of using it so soon, and so close to the great merchant himself. It would be useful several hundred miles away; in Aleppo it would merely be embarrassing.

Well, she would have to be cunning. Before anything else, she and Asta had to find out where Ionides had been taken, and then think of how to get him out. Before the night in al-Khan al-Azraq she would have reached for the alethiometer automatically, but now . . . For a moment the Myriorama came to mind, but she didn't know it well enough, and there wasn't time to learn it as well as use it, even if . . .

'Those soldiers,' she said to Asta, 'they must have been some kind of authority . . . If not police, then . . . Did you see any sign on the van? Any word or symbol, anything at all?'

'Yes, actually. In among the camouflage colours on the driver's door there was a little crest, something like that. I thought it was strange to see it there, because I half recognised it. It was a picture of a little lamp, a Roman sort of lamp, with a flame at the tip. Like when Malcolm was at school, there was a thing called the League of St Alexander—'

'The Office of Right Duty!'

'Is that what they call it now?'

'Yes, I think so. There were some officers on the ferry from King's Lynn, when I was escaping. Same badge . . . Well, that's who they are, then. That's interesting.'

'Did they try and arrest you on the ferry?'

'They would have done, but I fooled them. I don't think I could try the same trick here though.'

They came to the gate, and stopped to look out along the street. It was the hottest part of the afternoon, but the traffic was moving briskly, and there were still throngs of people on the pavements.

'There's a policeman at the crossing,' said Asta.

She had jumped up on the stone gatepost so as to see. Lyra moved closer.

The man wasn't directing traffic, just keeping an eye on everything around. Before she felt too nervous to do it, Lyra set off quickly to speak to him, aware of Asta leaping down and keeping pace.

The officer had a pistol on one hip, a baton on the other, handcuffs on his belt, and some kind of anbaric apparatus clipped to his shoulder-strap. His dæmon, a German shepherd dog, rose to her feet and growled quietly as Lyra came near.

'Excuse me, sir,' she said in English.

'What you want?' he replied haltingly.

'I need to report something, sir, but I need the Office of Right Duty, not the police. It's not a crime exactly, but I think it's something they're probably interested in.'

'Office of what?'

'I think that's what they're called. Office of Right Duty. There were a couple of their vans in the garden back there a few minutes ago and I tried to catch them up but they left too quick—'

'What you want me to do?'

'I just need to know where their main office is, so I can report it, sir.'

'Where you come from?'

'Gibraltar, sir.'

'Where's that? – Oh, never mind. I think what you mean is the *Bureau d'Obligation Correcte*.'

'That sounds like it, sir. Thank you. D'you know where their headquarters is, sir?'

'What this thing you want to report?'

'It's not a thing, more of a person really. Someone I saw looked like a man I heard they were looking for.'

'What his name? Where you see him?'

'I think there's a reward for it, and if I tell you . . .'

'I share it with you. Fifty-fifty.'

Asta was talking quietly into the ear of the dog-dæmon, who turned to the policeman with his tail between his legs, and said something in Arabic. The young man looked down, and then back at Lyra, his callow features trying to show something like respect.

'The clock tower,' he said. 'Bab al-Faraj. You know that? Huh?'

Lyra nodded, though she didn't.

'You go along that street across there, with the café on the corner, well you go along there till you can see the clock tower. There's a little street on the left called Hâsbeiyâ Street. There is the palace of the nuncio. *Le Bureau*, that's where it is.'

'Hâsbeiyâ,' said Lyra, and he nodded. 'Thank you very much, monsieur le gendarme.'

He saluted briefly and was clearly glad to see Lyra and Asta move away.

'What did you say to his dæmon?' Lyra asked.

'I said you were the daughter of the mighty Prince Edward of Windsor.'

'Well, it seemed to work. I'll have to live up to it.' They crossed the road and set off in the direction he'd indicated. 'The nuncio's palace, did he say? What's a nuncio?'

'Sort of ambassador of the Magisterium. That would make sense. What are we going to do there?'

'We'll think of something.'

No more than ten minutes later, they were there.

'Not much of a palace,' Lyra said.

Hâsbeiyâ Street was a quiet semi-commercial place, with apartment blocks set between office buildings and small workshops, and there was nothing to show that an important official of the Magisterium lived and worked there but a brass plate on a large dull respectable-looking house. The lettering was too small to read from across the street.

'It must be that,' said Asta. 'Have we thought of anything yet?'

'Yes. We won't go in that way. Let's look in here first.'

The only shop in the street was a narrow shabby place that sold household goods: buckets, dusters, brushes and small tools and so on. Asta followed Lyra inside. The proprietor put down his newspaper with a faint sigh while Lyra paid for a broom, a small blue tablecloth, a packet of safety pins and a brush and dustpan. The shopkeeper picked up his newspaper again and they left.

'I think I saw a narrow alley opposite the palace. We'll go down there for a moment,' Lyra said, and Asta scouted ahead and told her it was clear.

'You know, you could talk to me and we could plan things together,' said Malcolm's dæmon.

'I'm sorry. You're right. I've been on my own for so long it's hard to remember . . .'

There was another reason too. If Asta had been her own dæmon, and they were talking quietly together, she would have been sitting on Lyra's shoulder; but the great prohibition against touching seemed even more absolute when Malcolm was involved. But Lyra didn't think either of them would mention that.

Once out of sight of the street, which wasn't very busy anyway, Lyra unfolded the tablecloth and tore it in two. She put the larger part on like a headscarf and fastened it with a safety pin. Then she tore the rest of the tablecloth into two smaller pieces and crumpled them up in the dustpan, and dirtied her face a little with dust from the brick wall.

'My rucksack . . .' she said.

Asta replied 'The dustbins. If they're full, better not leave it near them, because it might be time for the collectors to come. But if they're empty—'

'Good idea!'

The first bin had a layer at the bottom of what looked like the contents of a few waste-paper baskets.

'That'll do,' Lyra said, and felt inside the rucksack for her Pequeno, her little stick, and put it in her belt. Then she retrieved the alethiometer needle and dropped the rucksack in the bin.

'Now you're going to be a housemaid, are you?'

'We are both going to be a housemaid.'

'We can't go in the front door, then . . . Wait! Listen!'

The unmistakable sound of an air-cooled engine came from the street. A vehicle was just leaving the building across the road, and gathering speed as it moved away.

Asta darted to the corner and looked across, and then turned back. 'That's it,' she said. 'One of those vans like the ones in the garden. Maybe the same one.'

Lyra joined her, peering out cautiously.

'See the main building? There's an archway at the side. It came out of there.'

'Then that's our way in,' said Lyra.

'Just like that?'

'Exactly like that.'

They crossed the street and went under the archway into the courtyard. As they did, a door opened in the main building and a soldier of some kind came out. He had a sergeant's stripes on his sleeve. Lyra bowed her head low and shook out one of the 'dusters' before slipping past the sergeant and in at the same door.

She was remembering the advice of Anita Schlesinger, about the actress who could make herself invisible, and now she, Lyra, was doing the reverse, just as the witches did, just as Will could do, and Asta saw at once and joined in perfectly. The sergeant saw a house-maid shaking a duster, and took no more notice.

Once inside the door Lyra moved purposefully – heavily but purposefully – along the corridor and stopped at a corner. This part of the building was like the service area of a hotel: shabby, functional, not a showplace. The floor was covered in rough matting, which at least was silent to walk on.

The building around them was quiet too, but not silent; there were people there; work was going on. Lyra thought: *if it was Pan beside me now, we'd know exactly what to do.* No need to say anything. Perfect understanding. But Asta was doing everything right, and it was comforting to have her quick and intelligent company. As they hesitated at the end of the corridor, Malcolm's dæmon whispered, 'Someone coming.'

They heard the sound of conversation before they could make out any words. One voice dominated, a middle-aged man's, snapping impatiently, occasionally answered by a younger voice, soothing, apologising, reassuring. The voices came from round the corner of the corridor, and somehow below, as well; and then a door opened and the speakers came out.

Lyra was already kneeling and making herself busy with the brush and dustpan. She didn't look at the men. Asta was doing what a housemaid's dæmon would have done, making herself humbly useful, but she was ready to flee, or fight, or simply to look for another spot that needed cleaning. The voices moved away. They were speaking Arabic. Another door opened and closed and the voices vanished.

'Did you understand what they were saying?' Asta whispered.

'No. Did you?'

'The older man was asking about a light that was on when it should have been switched off.'

'Odd. He sounded important. They came up from downstairs – a basement or something. Let's go and look.'

'Lyra—' Asta began, but stopped herself. 'I mean Tatiana.'

'What?'

'I'm not even going to say take care. There, I haven't said it.'

A door opened in the corridor behind them, the one they'd come in through. Lyra bent to brush away some non-existent dirt from the edge of the floor as two more men, the sergeant from the courtyard and a private, came past and took no notice. The soldier was questioning the sergeant about something, in Italian this time, and the sergeant merely grunted. They went past Lyra and Asta without seeming to notice them, though the terrier-dæmon of the private turned to look briefly before they turned the corner and went through the distant door as the others had done.

Lyra and Asta shared a glance, and understood each other at once. Any observant person would see something odd about the pairing of this girl and this dæmon. It might pass without notice in a busy street or marketplace, but it wouldn't take long in a setting like this to realise that the two of them were not one being. And that might be fatal. Anita Schlesinger was right: don't attract attention.

'We can't just turn and go,' said Lyra. 'Let's look downstairs.'

She took up her cleaning things and moved housemaidishly round the corner, looking for the door through which the first two men must have come. It was only a few feet away on the right. Broom under her left arm, brush and dustpan on the floor, she reached for the door handle. A moment later they were through, and found themselves at the top of a staircase.

A single anbaric bulb on the wall showed peeling paintwork, stained and scraped and scratched. A smell of damp and mould hung in the air.

'We're in the right place,' Lyra whispered.

They went down the fifteen wooden steps to the floor below. Another dim bulb showed doors along both sides of the corridor, each with a small shutter like a letter box at eye-level. There were five doors altogether, and beside each one there was a light switch. The floor was bare concrete, and Lyra couldn't hear a sound.

She looked closely at the first door, examining the handle and the shutter-box. While she was doing that, Asta moved to listen outside each of the other doors. Lyra tried the handle: it was fixed, which meant there probably wasn't a handle on the inside, and that the lock was accessible only from the corridor.

Asta came back and whispered, 'They're all empty except the last one on the right. There's a man sleeping in there. But how—'

'I can open it. You'll have to keep guard.'

She went to the last door and put down her cleaning things, very quietly, and tapped on the little shutter. The plywood cover was designed to slide in a groove, but it was stuck.

'Mr Ionides,' she whispered at the shutter. 'My personal sorcerer. Are you in there?'

No reply, no sound at all. Then came a murmur: 'Miss Silver? That you?'

'Yes. I'm going to open the door,' she whispered. 'It'll take several minutes. Be quiet, and don't be surprised. Just keep watch.'

She took a much-folded piece of paper from her breast pocket. Her hands were trembling: that wouldn't do. She took several deep breaths and wiped her hands on her dress.

'Asta,' she said, 'the light's very bad here. You'll have to help me see. I'm going to use something very delicate and if I drop it I'll never find it again, don't take your eyes off it.'

She took out the slender silvery needle. Why on earth had she thought this might be possible? But it had to be done.

She bent over to peer closely at the keyhole. There was a steel plate, greatly scratched, around it. Most of the mechanism would be inside the wood of the door; she'd just have to dig away till she got to it.

Another deep breath, and she set to work. It was really only the size of the needle that made it hard to do; the steel and the wood parted like butter. But it was no good just cutting straight in: she had to slice it away, bit by bit, flake by flake, until the lock itself was exposed.

Asta watched, at first astonished, but silently, her cat-eyes taking in the slightest detail.

When the metal of the lock itself was exposed Lyra stood up to ease her back, and folded the needle into the paper before stretching and bending from side to side. Her eyes were stinging, her fingers trembling, and to make things worse, the light was behind her, so her shadow was always blocking her view of what she was trying to do.

'What *is* that?' Asta whispered, meaning the needle.

'I had to . . . sacrifice the alethiometer. But I kept the needle. I'll tell you more—'

Before she could finish there came the sound of a bell, a large bell like that of an oratory, some distance away but resounding through the whole building. It made Lyra start and nearly drop the needle in its paper, but it wasn't an alarm; it rang three times, slowly, and then stopped. Lyra stood quite still, and was about to reach for the needle when the bell rang again, another three strokes. Another pause, and then another three strokes; and a further pause, and then it rang slowly but steadily and continuously.

She blinked, and shook her head. *Carry on*, she thought. This time she knelt instead of bending down. It was just a question of persistence, cut, cut, cut, piece by piece. She let them fall to the floor: there was no point in trying to catch them, and the sound they made was minute.

She stopped to whisper through the door again: 'Mr Ionides! Come to the door if you can hear me.'

But there was no sound of movement, no answering voice.

'You did hear his voice when I did?' she whispered to Asta.

'Absolutely. And that's an Angelus bell. Interesting.'

Lyra didn't know what that meant, and wasn't in the mood to find out. Eyes burning, fingers cramped, knees almost numb, thighs trembling, she worked away at the lock, slicing and chipping, until a pile of wooden splinters and curls of metal lay around her on the floor. The door was still locked fast. She was having to reach deep into the thick oak now, and still there was more to get out, and still time was passing.

The bell stopped.

She looked at Asta, dizzy, blinking away the sweat in her eyes before wiping them with the back of her hand. They both listened, but there was nothing to hear. Surely some guard would come along soon to check the prisoner, to bring him food, to take him away for interrogation?

She shook her head and turned back to the task. Tiny slice after tiny slice, oak, steel, oak; then her sweat-slick fingers lost their grip, and the needle fell to the floor in total silence. She uttered a little gasp, but Asta had been watching closely, and touched the place among the wood-chippings where the needle had fallen. It was invisible. Lyra would never have found it, but Asta lifted it out with her mouth while Lyra stood and stretched and took deep breaths.

'Nearly there,' said Asta, after placing the needle carefully in Lyra's palm.

'I'm worried though. I can't hear anything.'

'I can. He's breathing. He might have been beaten, but he's alive. Another few minutes and you'll be through.'

Every muscle ached. Her eyes stung with the sweat she kept trying to mop away. She bent down and started again.

Asta's ears pricked. She looked back towards the stairs, and Lyra noticed and paused, but she couldn't hear anything.

'Don't rush,' said Asta.

'Easy to say.'

And a minute later she laid bare the deadbolt, the hardened steel bar that slid into the door frame when the key was turned. Once she was through that—

But something was wrong. The needle didn't cut through. It didn't even scratch the surface. A little sob of frustration, disappointment, something, shook Lyra's throat, and she nearly dropped the needle again.

'What is it?' said calm-voiced Asta.

'It's – I think I—' She tried again, with the same result. 'It's not – I don't know what . . .'

She stood back, took a deep breath, closed her eyes and breathed again, trying to force herself to concentrate, even against the pain in every joint, the sweat, the trembling. Such a short way to go! And there was no steel, no diamond, nothing, in any universe, that could resist the edge of the needle. Unless they'd discovered something that did? The broken bones in her left hand throbbed like a pulse.

One more shuddering breath. What would Will have done? What had Farder Coram told her? What did Giorgio Brabandt say?

Then she laughed. Something was funny, if only she could remember it. Asta looked up at her, curious.

'It's not the needle and it's not the lock,' Lyra said. 'It's me.'

Be intent and relaxed, both at the same time. Concentrate calmly. Her mind had to cut, or the needle wouldn't. Think and simultaneously act without thinking.

Easy. One light stroke with the needle, and the deadbolt fell away, and the door hung freely on its hinges.

'Well done,' Asta whispered.

Lyra put the needle away in its folded paper and then pulled gently at the door. It swung heavily, silently, and opened into a room with no light. Only the faintest glimmer from the bulb at the foot of the stairs showed her anything at all, but her eyes were adjusted to the semi-dark, and as she looked into the cell she could make out a narrow bed, and a man's body lying on it.

'Miss Silver? Why you take so long?'

His voice was hoarse and weak. But it was Ionides, and he was alive. In a moment, heedless of every kind of pain, Lyra was kneeling beside him.

'Oh, my sorcerer, what have they done to you?'

'Mr Malcolm, he get away?'

'A gryphon took him – as if it had been looking for him – but you, now, can you move? Can you walk?'

Asta was already close in silent conversation with the little gecko-dæmon, whispering and nudging and licking her, gathering knowledge in the way dæmons could.

'You help me sit up, Miss Silver, maybe I can walk too.'

His throat was damaged as well as his mouth. It clearly hurt him to speak. Lyra stood up and took his left hand with her right. She was a little giddy herself, and she let him take his time to pull himself upright.

As his face became visible in the dim light, she saw how badly he'd been battered. One eye completely closed, blood coming from one of his ears, his nose smashed, broken teeth; a great surge of passionate anger rose in her breast.

'Whoever did this,' she said shakily, 'I will see them dead.'

He swung his legs round and set his feet on the floor, but something else was troubling him.

'Your ribs?' she said.

He nodded, but even that hurt. How on earth would they get him out?

Then two things happened at the same time. The bell began to ring again, and a shadow fell over the bed.

Lyra looked round at once. She saw the figure of a woman in the doorway, and the woman said, 'Who are you, and what are you doing?'

10

ALWAYS LEILA

And she said it in English too.

Her silhouette against the light was slim and tense, just as ready to fight as to flee. Asta flowed down to the floor and came to stand close to Lyra, who stood up slowly, hands by her side.

'What are you doing?' said the woman again.

'You can see what we're doing,' Lyra said in the same quiet tone. 'My name is Tatiana Iorekova, Queen of Novaya Zemlya. This man is my counsellor, and he's been badly beaten and tortured. I am releasing him and we are shortly going to leave. Now tell me who you are.'

'You are no queen. And this man's name is Rashid Xenakis. He is a liar and a confidence trickster, and a thief and a smuggler, and more besides. My name is—'

'Leila?' said Ionides in the half-audible croak they'd made of his voice.

'Always Leila,' she said. 'But what have they done to you, Rashid?'

'They've hurt him badly, and we're going to take him away, and if you try to stop us I'll kill you,' Lyra said. 'You don't think I can? Look at the door. Look at the lock. Then stand out of the way.'

Asta had moved a step closer to the woman and stood watching her, eyes wide, fur bristling, tail slowly swinging.

It was hard to read the woman's expression, because what little light there was came from behind her, but her slender snake-dæmon had extended her neck some way forward and now swayed a little this way and that, licking the air.

'Rashid will tell you whether you can believe me or not,' she said calmly, 'and since you seem to trust him, you'd better listen to him. My name is Leila Pervani. I am not part of the Magisterium, nor am I against it. I am inclined to help my old friend Professor Xenakis, because I used to be fond of him. That's why I came down here. But what are you doing? How did you get in? How do you think you're going to leave?'

'It's obvious what I'm doing. I need my counsellor's help, so I'm setting him free. If you stand back and don't interfere, you won't get hurt. Otherwise—'

'You wouldn't have a chance. Listen to me and stop making idle threats. Upstairs they are in the oratory, and they'll be there for another ten minutes or so. Then the nuncio will come down here and continue his interrogation. If you do as I say, you might be able to get out of the building. Argue with me and waste time, and you will both be dead by the morning. That dæmon is not yours,' she said, indicating Asta.

Lyra said, 'If we ever come face to face again, at a time when we can talk, I'll tell you about it. Now, how do we get out?'

'There is a young woman at the reception desk who will do whatever I tell her. You'll have a minute or so to get through the foyer and out by the street door. Apart from the courtyard that is the only way, and the courtyard is guarded. You'd never get him through. But beware: the oratory is on the ground floor just beyond the reception desk.'

'Was that an Angelus bell we heard?' said Asta.

The woman said, 'Yes. So you haven't got long. Help him up and follow me.'

Lyra tried to lift Ionides from the bed, but she had no strength left.

'Give me the broom, Queen Tatiana,' he said.

Using it as a crutch, he managed to stand and limp after Leila Pervani. Lyra and Asta exchanged a glance as the woman and Ionides left the cell ahead of them, and Lyra saw in the dæmon's eyes something like kinship, affection, fellow-feeling. She felt her heart lift a little as they went out into the corridor together.

Leila Pervani was waiting at the foot of the staircase, under the light. She was wearing a light blue dress, simple enough, but she held herself with such elegance that Lyra couldn't help noticing it, even though the situation was full of peril. The incessant tolling of that bell seemed to make every brick in the walls resonate and remind them of it.

Ionides leaned on the broom for a crutch, and Lyra felt a flare of rage as she saw the twisted way he had to move, a wound in his scalp still bleeding, an ear torn. She took the little stick out of her belt.

The woman said, 'Wait at the top of the stairs while I speak to the girl at the desk. Keep the door shut. When you hear me knock, come out very quickly and follow. Very quickly.'

She ran to the top in silence like a cat, and slipped out before shutting the door without a sound.

'Can you climb the stairs?' Lyra whispered.

'Slowly, Miss Silver.'

Asta darted ahead and listened at the door while Lyra helped Ionides up the steps. It was hard going; he'd lost a sandal, and his bare foot was bloodied. But he climbed steadily and without making a sound. Lyra followed, little Pequeno in hand, Asta watching everything from above.

They reached the top, and a minute went by, and then another, and still they stood without speaking, listening hard. Ionides was breathing harshly; Lyra was trembling with pain and exhaustion, and the bell, still resounding, made her feel on the edge of madness.

Then the door handle turned.

'Come now,' said Leila Pervani, 'at once.'

She stood aside, and as soon as Ionides was out in the corridor, she ran ahead and along to the corner. From there she looked around into the foyer, and then beckoned, and Lyra helped Ionides follow.

The woman lifted a finger before they turned the corner, and when she was sure the way was clear she said, 'Go. Straight out and away.'

Ionides looked at her, and Lyra saw the look she gave him in return, and read all the complexity of affection and sorrow that passed between them. She felt a tension in his arm, but tugged gently and helped him forward. When they were halfway to the main door, the bell stopped.

Lyra stopped too, out of sheer surprise, but hurried forward again as she heard the sound of chairs being moved back on a hard floor, and a voice intoning a prayer, and other voices responding. Then an organ began to play, and then the sound of footsteps and voices talking. Lyra had her hand on the front door and pushed it open, just as the door of the oratory opened behind them.

Leila Pervani saw that and darted towards the first worshippers as they came out. She was calling urgently and pointing back towards the corner that led to the stairs.

'*Quick*,' said Asta, and Lyra urged Ionides out of the door and stumbled after him, letting the door close by itself.

'Better hurry away,' Lyra said. 'They'll be after us.'

'Leila will distract them,' he said hoarsely. 'She will be showing them the door of the cell, and explaining that only diabolical magic could have done that to it, and that I will have changed myself into a lizard with iron teeth, far too dangerous to follow. They have never seen you, and she will not mention you. Queen Tatiana, I owe you—'

'Ssh. Things to do,' she said. 'Later.'

180

Across the road and into the alley to retrieve her rucksack, and then they were in the streets among the early evening crowds, invisible.

Chen the camel-herder, now the master of the ruined research station at Tashbulak, had acquired a companion. Her name was Dilyara. She had worked as a cleaner at the station before it was attacked, and she missed the orderly way of life, the storerooms full of neatly stacked equipment, the process of making things neat and shining. She wasn't a native of the region; she came from further west than most of her fellow workers, and she was used to being alone. A pang of silent nostalgia had brought her to the ruined buildings, and in Chen she found an ideal employer, for that was how she came to think of him. Employer, or thing to clean. She submitted impassively to his embraces, and little by little swept the corridors clear of sand and plaster and broken glass, gathered and tidied away brooms and dustpans and shovels and serviceable rags, watched as he made his oil-fired devils and idols to scare away intruders, cooked whatever edible things she could find, offered responses in her language to the grunts and snarls he uttered in his, and brought him warm water and soap and showed him their functions.

She spent more and more time in the laboratories. The raiding party had smashed things to pieces without any idea of what was valuable, or important, or even offensive to their religious views; it was all equally uninteresting to them, and they enjoyed acting like the clean wind of God, as one of their leaders had said to flatter and encourage them, and just sweeping through and moving on.

Dilyara thought that what went on in these austere and silent chambers had been important and fascinating almost beyond the power of words to tell. She whispered about it with her dæmon, a little fox with large ears and boundless curiosity. The laboratories were a holy place, whose secrets were unknown even to the worshippers who prayed there, where the floors not only needed sweeping but deserved it, where the benches desired to be clean and polished, where what could be repaired longed consciously for the touch of a repairing hand; and there was such a wealth of equipment that a good deal of it didn't need repairing at all. The wind of God had parted around it and vanished.

Dilyara and her dæmon set to work, to clean, to worship, and to learn. They felt blessed. Chen took no notice, but he was cleaner.

The first thing they did was (hastily) to buy Ionides some new sandals and a new shirt and trousers. The second thing was to get to the bus station at Bab al-Faraj, which was not far from the nuncio's residence, and buy tickets for the first bus leaving for a destination anywhere to the east. Baku on the Caspian Sea seemed far enough: a two-day journey, leaving in an hour. While Ionides retired to the washroom to repair what he could of his appearance, Lyra went to the ticket office, where she presented her *laissez-passer* from Mustafa Bey and found herself treated with the profoundest deference: exactly the effect the great merchant had promised.

The bus, she discovered, was one of the new fleet of vehicles Mustafa Bey had told her about, designed for long-distance travel, and fitted out with some luxury. Indeed, it was possible to take a private compartment, as on an international train, and Queen Tatiana felt it would be wrong to do anything less. It was expensive, of course, but Farder Coram's gold would last her a while yet, and after paying for that and a comfortable seat nearby for her personal sorcerer, Lyra just had time to visit the bus-station shop and buy the kind of toiletries that travellers need.

She and Ionides boarded together, saying little until the bus was on its way, with the lights of the city behind them and the darkness of the desert ahead. They sat at the little table in her private compartment sipping the tea an attendant had brought, and Lyra began to relax.

'Now,' she said to him, 'I want to know all about Leila Pervani.'

11

MOUNT DAMĀVAND

Pan lay asleep beside Malcolm on the gryphon's back, but not fast asleep; he was dreaming in a troubled way, and little convulsions shook his limbs from time to time, and quiet cries broke from his throat. Naturally Malcolm couldn't touch him. Instead he whispered: 'Hush, Pan, don't be troubled. She's on her way, just as we are. Somewhere down there on the earth, she'll be moving east like us. She'll be safe. She's strong and brave and clever and she wants you more than anything in the world. And Asta's with her. Who could have thought that that would happen? When you wake up we can talk about everything and decide what we're going to do when we meet the gryphon queen.'

The little dæmon was quieter now. The immense wings of Prince Keshvād rose and fell, beating in the darkness, tireless and regular; and Malcolm would have slept, but for the ache in his hip and the constant unease of being several hundred feet in the air with nothing to hold on to. And it was savagely cold. He watched the stars, and every so often, with the greatest care, he shifted his position to ease the stiffness in all his joints, the gnawing pain in his hip, and felt a little relief; but there was nothing to make it any warmer.

Time passed; he did sleep a little, unwittingly; and he woke with a half-dreaming shock to find Pan curled up against his chest, as if the dæmon had instinctively sought the only warmth there was. So he drew his coat around them both and let his eyes fall shut again.

Then he heard Pan say, 'Malcolm, when you saw the gryphons in that garden . . . had you seen them before?'

'Something like them . . . Pan, can you feel if anything's happened to Lyra?'

'Just generally. Not specifically. We're still one being, obviously, but . . . What was it you saw that was like the gryphons?'

'When Alice and I were travelling down the Thames with you and Lyra, when you were very young, I saw – well, Alice and I both saw – an old river-god. A giant from under the water. He was there in the water close to us. In fact, he held Lyra in the palm of his hand and then he kissed his fingertip and pressed it to her forehead.'

'What did I do?'

'You just lay there with her and watched. And then later we saw a fairy. She wanted to steal Lyra away but we tricked her. She fed Lyra though, she suckled her. Anyway, the point is that the river-god and the fairy were both strange like these gryphons. As if they came from the same order of beings.'

They said nothing for a few minutes, as the gryphons flew steadily onwards, and the stars wheeled slowly round the sky. Then Pan spoke again.

'Malcolm, what do you think the imagination is?'

'I think you probably know more than I do about that. Didn't you set off to find Lyra's imagination? You must have had some idea of what you were looking for.'

'I spoke . . . I wrote that when I was angry, and . . . I thought Lyra had changed. She'd read these books . . . they seemed to be scoffing at everything she used to be. Well, one of them was. Just empty knowing laughter as if nothing mattered at all. And the other one, *The Hyperchorasmians* . . . That was just full of cold hatred for things like the imagination.'

'She didn't take it seriously though, did she?'

'She did. It made her hard and contemptuous.'

'Surely not Lyra!'

'It wasn't anything else. It was that book. I went – when I left Oxford – I went to find the author, and I did.'

'Did you? Gottfried Brande himself?'

'Yes. In Wittenberg. He was just like his book. He had a daughter living with him and she was very unhappy. I don't think he knew how to like anyone, or anything either. It comes through in his book. When Lyra read it, it was as if something left her. Something interested and curious and . . . open-minded. Not intolerant. It was as if the philosopher, Brande, as if he was her father and she was trying to please him. But I was – I was . . . I was so cruel to Lyra. I reminded her of something she'd done – when we separated for the first time – and I accused her of betraying me; I know she didn't really, but it felt . . .'

He was overcome. He couldn't speak, and Malcolm thought he might have been sobbing, but the little dæmon made no sound and lay stiff and still inside the warmth of Malcolm's coat.

'Not long before the old Master died, the Master of Jordan,' Malcolm said, 'he told me something about Lyra that I don't think he'd told anyone else. It was when I was teaching her privately, and I wasn't doing it very well. I told the Master I thought I should stop, he should find a different tutor, and he told me things about when she was younger, when she went away to the Arctic . . . Remember, I'd taken her to Jordan College in the first place, with Alice, so the Master knew I'd been involved in her life, but I knew nothing about that voyage to the north. I didn't know her really at all till I taught her for those few weeks. Anyway, the Master told me about the childhood she'd had at the college, and about how her mother had come to take her away, much against the wishes of the Master himself, and about how he'd given her the alethiometer . . .'

'I remember that. He told us to keep it secret from Mrs Coulter. We used to pore over it for hours trying to understand it.'

'And he told me, the Master told me, that the alethiometer had predicted – remember, this was before she had it, when she was only, what was it, eleven or so – it had predicted that she would be involved in a great betrayal, and that she herself would be the betrayer, and that the experience would be terrible. But of course she must never know about the prediction. And the Master thought that something like that must have happened when she, when you both were away in the north, because you were changed when you came back – sadder, he said, you'd both suffered. He never asked her about it, and he only told me because he thought it might help me understand her and why she was finding things difficult.'

'She . . . It was . . .' Pan was finding it difficult to speak.

'It's all right. You don't have to tell me.'

'No, but . . . It was *foretold*?'

'That's what the Master said. I don't know if the alethiometer can foretell things exactly, but . . .'

'More like a sort of likelihood, or possibility, perhaps . . . Lyra asked Dr Relf that once. But not in connection with . . . We never knew anything about that. About the betrayal prediction.'

'Would it have made a difference, just before you left? When you were quarrelling?'

'Yes, I think . . . I don't know. Oh, probably. But if it was something she had to do, to keep a promise . . .'

'I think if it was like that, it wouldn't count as a betrayal.'

'Did he say anything else? The Master?'

'He told me not to take my failure to teach her – teach you – personally.'

'We both knew she was behaving badly. We were very unhappy about that, and about other things . . . There was a boy we'd come across, in . . . We never told you about other worlds, did we?'

'No,' said Malcolm. 'I'd hoped she might tell me things like that, one day, if . . .'

'If I hadn't gone away.'

'Well, yes.'

'She would. She was getting to like you, a lot. But the boy, Will. Will Parry. He came from a world like ours, but very different. He didn't know he had a dæmon, at first. She and Will, they went somewhere I wasn't allowed to go, into the world of the dead, and it must have been just as painful for him because his dæmon couldn't go there either, and she – I – his dæmon sort of appeared, sort of came to herself on the edge of the world of the dead, and there was only me there . . . I had to teach her everything. We comforted each other. I don't know, I'd have gone mad with fear and loneliness if it hadn't been for . . . But Lyra didn't go there on a whim. She had to. She'd made a promise to rescue someone and she was keeping the promise, and it was just that to do so she had to leave me behind. It was horrible, horrible for us both. But I had Will's dæmon and she had Will himself, so we weren't quite alone. Anyway, at the end, we found that he had to go back to his own world, and we had to say goodbye. For ever. So part of her and me will always be in love with them, and they're out of reach for ever. She didn't tell the Master that, and she hasn't told anyone else ever. You're the only person who knows.'

The little voice was muffled. He didn't finish the sentence. Malcolm was powerfully curious, but nothing would make him pry.

'I think we should have told the Master,' Pan said eventually, 'about what happened, and why. It might have meant that we could talk to each other about it.'

'Didn't you?'

'Not properly. Hardly at all, really. It was just so difficult.'

'Well, when we find her . . .'

'D'you think we will?'

'I'm determined we will.'

A minute went by, and then another. Then Malcolm went on, 'When we find her, we'll talk about everything.'

'Good.'

'The Master told me something else.'

'What was that?'

'About me, actually. Something I didn't know. He said that something I did – something I'd done – when I was young would determine the whole course of my life.'

'What was it? What did you do?'

'It was when Alice and I took Lyra and you away on the river in *La Belle Sauvage*. In my canoe. To keep you safe.'

'Did the Master know that from the alethiometer?'

'He didn't say. But I don't take it very seriously. Every decision we make, anything we do, anything at all, determines what'll happen after it.'

'But some consequences are bigger than others.'

'Well, yes. But I was also sceptical because . . . We don't like to think that things can be foretold. We prefer to think we're free. So I resisted believing what the Master said about that, because it seemed to bind me into a future I hadn't chosen.'

'To bind you to Alice?'

That came as a shock.

'Bind me to Jordan College,' Malcolm said carefully.

They flew on. Malcolm could smell something different in the air, something cold and clean, possibly snow. The night was just at that point when the darkness was full of little momentary swirling points of slightly-less-darkness, not even anything like the first grey of dawn, but perhaps the closest we come to seeing individual photons. The dark was leaching out of the sky; above them, a thousand brilliant points of starlight were being absorbed into the greater background luminosity of the dawn. Malcolm let his mind spread out beyond his senses, and he heard Pan whisper, or thought he did, and he thought he answered, but he had no idea what either of them said. In his semi-dream state he saw a bird high above them: a white bird with sharply angled wings, maybe an Arctic tern, a great traveller on its annual migration.

Then, with a suddenness that was almost audible, the first rays of the sun struck them. They were flying directly towards it, and in the dazzle Malcolm felt as if he were actually inside one of his auroras, as he called them, the spangled ring grown sky-sized and all-enveloping.

The gryphon's wings stopped beating, and the regular tireless up-and-forward muscular thrust stilled to a level glide. Malcolm lifted himself up a little and looked out and down to a wild landscape of mountains and jagged ridges and dark valleys, snow-covered, still in the shadow of night; but as he looked, the sun climbed higher and touched the very topmost peaks, so they blazed like a hundred fires.

From somewhere close in the sky another gryphon cried, in a scream that was nearly a roar, and was answered by several others from further away; and then Prince Keshvād himself uttered a scream that was louder and longer than all the rest, shaking his body so powerfully that Malcolm's hands instinctively gripped the great feathers, and clung even tighter as the gryphon tilted slightly to the left.

'Look!' said Pan. He slipped out of Malcolm's coat and stood upright, staring ahead past the gryphon's head, his face brilliant in the sun.

Directly ahead of them a mountain reared higher than all the rest, entirely covered in snow, majestic and sharp-peaked and symmetrical. Around them in the dawn sky the other gryphons were making their way towards it with them, like a squadron of great ships, an armada, borne on the wind towards the palace of Shahrnavāz.

The battery in the little anbaric truck was fully charged: good for a hundred miles on a decent road, Alice thought. Whether they could make it to a decent road was another matter. Bashing along a footpath in the woods, forcing its way past bushes and through streams, was taking up a lot of energy.

From time to time she stopped, and she and Ben listened hard for the sounds of any pursuit, but heard nothing and moved on.

'We'll have to leave it before long,' said Ben.

'Dunno about *before long*. Best to get as far as the battery'll take us.'

'Yeah, but it's not as if we're going to be very hard to follow. There's only one path, and we're on it. And they'll know where the path leads. They could be waiting at the end for us to turn up.'

'H'mm,' she said. 'What d'you suggest, then?'

'Leave it on the path to block it, then . . .'

She stopped the truck. She'd heard something. He turned his head to catch what it was.

'Voices,' she whispered. 'Two men. Up ahead.'

He could hear them too.

'Out,' she whispered. 'Over that way, quick.'

She indicated left, where the undergrowth was thick. Leaving the key in the ignition, she slipped out of the cab and moved as quietly as she could into the bushes until she was just out of sight of the truck, and then lay down, pulling a low branch across in front of her. Beside her Ben lay down too, and they kept perfectly still while the voices approached.

'Hey, what's that truck doing there?'

'The key's still in it. Look.'

'What's in the back?'

'Spade, rake . . . Bucket, bag of gravel . . .'

'Mending potholes. Why'd they leave it here?'

'Maybe someone nicked it.'

Alice heard the truck door opening.

'Well . . .' said the first voice. 'What d'you reckon?'

'Can't leave it here. Blocking the path, innit?'

'Might as well . . . Go on, jump in.'

More door noises, some scraping of branches, a startled laugh as the little truck lurched forward, the sound of wheels moving away on rough ground, and then silence again.

'Now what?' said Ben.

'Now we find a road and beg a lift.'

Alice lifted herself fastidiously out of the bushes and brushed herself down. Ben was sniffing the air and listening hard.

'That way,' he said, indicating a direction left of the path.

'How far?'

'Twenty minutes if we don't stop.'

'Not much to stop for. Come on then.'

And thirty-five minutes later, they were in a van heading for Oxford.

A palace for the queen of creatures who could fly would not squat heavily on the ground, even when that ground was fifteen thousand feet in the sky. Terraces, colonnades, arches, ledges, balconies, bridges, beacon platforms, dizzying cliff-like rock faces studded with graceful caverns, broad elegant walkways, spires and pinnacles both natural and artificial, all grew like an icy immensity of ancient coral over the peak of the mountain. As Prince Keshvād wheeled and turned in the sky before landing, Malcolm could see the extent of the gryphons' achievement, and two details caught his eye: firstly, every structure was functional, none merely decorative; and secondly, nowhere, in the whole massive complexity towering into the thin air above every other mountain in the range, was there a single guard-rail or protective wall. It was not built for creatures who feared heights.

And it was busy. Work was going on. Gryphons, and other flying creatures too, were coming and going like bees, whether carrying things or not Malcolm couldn't tell; a section of the mountain was being hollowed out, or so it seemed, with the sound of massive hammers beating, though there was nothing to see behind an immense buttress of snow and ice and rock that led down for thousands of feet from the summit. Other gryphons, wearing plumes of scarlet on their eagle-heads, leaped off the palace ledges and soared up high towards the incoming flight, screaming a welcome that sounded like a challenge. Yet more formed themselves into ranks on the broadest terrace on the eastern side of the mountain, in the full blaze of the rising sun, and stood fierce and still.

Down towards them Prince Keshvād glided, and then beat his mighty wings inwards to slow his flight, and extended his lion fore-paws to meet the ground. Malcolm clung firmly to the lion-fur on the gryphon's back as they landed, and with Pan holding on to his coat, he raised himself stiffly as the prince came to a halt.

'Remember,' Pan whispered, 'be *gold*.'

Malcolm's hip was burning with pain, but he managed to step down to the rocky floor without stumbling. The first thing he did then was to move round to face the prince, and then bow as low as he could, hoping the gesture would convey the proper degree of respect and appreciation. The gryphon's face wasn't formed to express any human feeling; Malcolm had to hope that the stiff impassive ferocity glaring back at him would understand his courtesy. It was rather like trying to communicate with a coat of arms. Then the gryphon prince bowed his head in response.

And there was Gulya herself, shaking with fatigue, but eager to explain and mediate.

'Pantalaimon, Mr Malcolm, the official coming out of the mountain now is the vizier to Her Majesty. You address him as Your Honour. He will escort you at once to the Throne Room, where the Queen will—'

Pan said, 'Wait. Too fast. We are not prisoners, nor are we supplicants to be told what to do.'

The vizier, a silver-feathered gryphon with the bearing of a dignified councillor of state, had come close enough to hear. He stood nearby and listened as Pan continued. Malcolm was impressed by the little dæmon's effrontery, but the gryphons were all gazing at him and not at Pan, as the morning sun shone full in his face.

Pan went on, 'We are honoured guests from the realms of gold. Before we meet the Queen we must have time to clean ourselves and rest from the rigours of the journey. We are hungry and thirsty. Once we are refreshed we shall be glad to bring our greetings in person to Her Majesty.'

The vizier bowed his head. 'There is a suite of rooms prepared for you,' he said. 'We do have traffic with the human world, and ambassadors from every realm of any importance are received here. You are most welcome to all the comforts and necessities we can provide. May we know, to begin with, how we are to address you?'

'My name is Malcolm. That will do. My companion and adviser is Pan.'

The vizier inclined his head, and turned to lead the way into the mountain. Gulya hurried to walk alongside Pan, and they both followed Malcolm.

It wasn't possible to see how the gryphons, with their lion-claws, could have carved these tunnels or excavated the great caverns they led to. Malcolm was eager to know – he was eager to ask a thousand questions – but the grave and solemn vizier didn't seem the right person to ask.

A long wide stone passageway, smooth underfoot but with rugged walls, lit at intervals by naphtha lamps on brackets, led to a great gallery open at one side to the sky, its roof supported by pillars carved out of the rock. It might have been a room for ceremonies or great occasions of state, Malcolm thought, because of the splendour of the proportions and the calm austerity of the bare rock walls, the ice-fringed gallery, and the blue sky beyond. Around the walls were half a dozen alcoves cut in the rock, in which fires were burning – fires that seemed to come directly out of the substance of the mountain, and to burn something invisible: not wood, not coal.

Malcolm was intensely curious, and wanted to know more, but the vizier moved on, and led them down a smaller passage set with similar alcoves and smaller fires, to a doorway, and a surprise. A man, a human being wearing a simple white robe and a turban, stood beside the door, bowing. His desert-rat dæmon hid behind his leg.

Gulya said something quickly to the vizier, who inclined his head to Malcolm – still not looking him in the face – and withdrew.

'This man is your servant,' Gulya said. 'His name is Darius. He will supply anything you need. He will not speak, because his tongue was removed, but he can hear and understand your language.'

Darius opened the door, which was made of heavy wood, perfectly jointed and hung, but plain and undecorated.

Malcolm and Pan went in, but Gulya waited on the threshold.

'I shall come back when it is time to escort you to the Queen,' she said. She added something in her own language to Darius, and then left. He bowed and shut the door after she'd gone.

'Darius, do you understand me when I speak like this?' Malcolm said.

The servant nodded. He was about fifty years old, Malcolm thought, lean, scarred, and melancholy. His dæmon was hiding her head away, unwilling to communicate.

'Are you a captive of the gryphons?' Malcolm asked.

Darius shook his head.

'You're a free man, then?'

The servant shook his head again, but more slowly. His situation was too complex for yes-no answers; Malcolm thought he'd return to it later.

He looked around. The room was very simply furnished: a chair, a table, and a neat pile of furs and animal skins on the floor for a bed. Everything was clean, though, and the chair and table were skilfully made from a wood that Malcolm didn't recognise: perhaps a kind of maple. On the table there was an oil lamp, a dish of grapes and apples and a jug of water with two fine glasses.

The air was cold, but a small fire was burning in an alcove – another fire with no fuel.

'Darius, what is burning in there?' Malcolm said.

The servant gestured all around, as if to imply it was the mountain itself that was on fire.

'The rock? The earth?'

Darius nodded, and pointed emphatically to the floor.

'The fire comes from under the earth?'

Another nod.

The one opening in the wall was set with glazed windows, with a heavy curtain that could be pulled across to keep the worst draughts out. The windows gave on to a view over the whole mountain range. Darius beckoned, and Malcolm looked where he pointed, and saw little fires on the flanks of other mountains nearby.

'The whole world's aflame,' said Pan. 'But it's all under control.'

'Is there somewhere I can wash?' Malcolm asked.

Darius turned and gestured for Malcolm to follow. In the next room there was a marble basin, into which a trickle of water was flowing constantly, to drain out into a pipe through the floor.

'Thank you, Darius. Could you come back in fifteen minutes, and then we shall be glad to meet the Queen.'

The servant bowed and left.

'They like their visitors to be cold but clean,' Malcolm said when he came back from the bathroom.

'Look, there's a wooden chest in the corner.'

'So there is – I hadn't noticed that.'

The chest was plainly constructed, and made of cedar. As he lifted the lid Malcolm smelled the fragrance, and inhaled it deeply, transported at once back to the workshop of Mr Taphouse, the handyman at Godstow Priory, when he was helping the old man make a cupboard for the vestments worn at special ceremonies.

I made a coffin out of cedar once, Mr Taphouse had told him. *This old boy wanted to keep the moths out of his grave. Well, the customer's always right, Malcolm, even when he's wrong.*

'What's that?' said Pan, perching on the edge and looking down at the folded cloth inside.

Malcolm held it up, and found a robe, several in fact, of heavy velvets and brocades, as well as shawls of silk. He took the largest robe and put it on. It was deep blue velvet, and only just big enough.

'That's a bit warmer. I wonder who it used to belong to.'

'There's a hat as well.'

It was a cap of astrakhan. Malcolm tried it on, and put it back.

'Later, maybe. We'll have to decide what to do about this man of gold business. Who thought of that? Was that you, or was it Gulya?'

'Not guilty,' said Pan. 'She brought it up first. I just thought it might be useful if they saw you as valuable rather than . . . not.'

'You said she was under a spell.'

'Yes. She's small because a sorcerer put a curse on her – she'd normally be the same size as the others. If she kills him the curse will be lifted.'

'Who is this sorcerer?'

'A man called Sorush.'

'A man, not a gryphon?'

'A man, or . . . something else. A devil, perhaps. He has gryphon slaves, who can't leave because he cuts their wings off when they're young and small. He's hoarded immense quantities of gold, so all gryphons know about him, and they all hate and fear him, but they don't know how to fight him.'

'Does he live among these mountains?'

'I don't know . . . Why do you want to know about him?'

'Thinking ahead.'

'Oh . . . Where is this mountain, Damāvand, anyway? Have you heard of it?'

'I think it's just south of the Caspian Sea,' Malcolm said. 'But I'm sure of very little. I'd like to talk to Gulya, though.'

It was still strange, talking to Pan and not Asta; but it was easy too, as if they both felt the existence of a large body of shared understanding.

There was a knock at the door, and the servant Darius came in without waiting and bowed.

'We are ready,' said Malcolm. 'You can take us to the Queen.'

Darius nodded, and stood aside to let them leave the room first. Outside the great hall they found the vizier waiting, and Gulya, and an attendant group of gryphon guards.

No one spoke. The vizier gave no sign of acknowledgement before stalking away along the corridor. Malcolm and Pan followed, with Gulya, and the guards came behind them. They entered the great hall, where the sunlight striking in through the pillared gallery lit up something that hadn't been there before: a massive carpet covering almost the entire floor, glowing with reds and blues, yellows and greens, browns and blacks and creams in an intricate design that once again, to Malcolm, showed the work of human hands.

Pan was remembering another occasion, long before: when he and Lyra had entered the palace of Iofur Raknison, the usurper king of the armoured bears. It would be something to tell Malcolm about one day. He'd had to hide in Lyra's pocket then, in the shape of a mouse, because she had a plan to trick Iofur, and it was vital that Pan should keep out of sight. But Iofur's palace was grotesque and ugly, covered in meaningless decoration and filthy with the mess of thousands of birds, and it stank of dung and heavy perfume.

By contrast this palace was clean and austere, and it smelled of nothing but snow and mountain air. The only colours they had seen were those on the carpet in the great hall, and the gryphons clearly had more interest in proportion than in the sort of extravagant decorative elaboration that Iofur Raknison was impressed by. The carpet was all the more striking because of the contrast it made with everything else, and because it must have been rolled out and laid in the few minutes Malcolm and Pan had been on their own in the visitors' suite.

They were both expecting some sort of ceremony to announce the Queen – a procession perhaps, or music, or a formal address –

but that was because although neither of them had been in the presence of royalty in England, they were both creatures of Oxford, where little happened without ceremony.

But there was none of that here. One moment the Queen was nowhere in sight, and the next she stepped out of a passageway and into the brilliant sunlight on the carpet.

There was no doubt who she was. She was taller than most of them, and older, with some white feathers among the eagle-brown of her plumage, but it was mainly something in her bearing, a grandeur and confidence, a steady luminous authority that compelled their respect. Malcolm realised at once that they would both have to be very careful indeed. Who had cut out the servant's tongue?

He moved as if to make room for her, but in fact so as to stand fully in the sunlight. Then he bowed and said very clearly:

'Your Majesty, my name is Malcolm, and my companion is Pan. I offer you greetings from my land.'

'You did not come here to do that,' she said. Her voice was harsh, as an eagle's would be, but rich with an almost human expressiveness. Again Malcolm thought: *careful.*

'No, Your Majesty. Your people rescued me and my companion from great danger, for which we are deeply grateful. We are travelling eastwards far from our own country to look for something precious that was lost. I think we shall have much further to travel before we can find it.'

'My attendant Gulya has told me some things I find hard to understand. What is this precious thing that is lost?'

'Imagination,' said Malcolm.

'Explain that to me.'

'May I speak, Your Majesty?' said Pan.

The Queen turned to him. Gulya, standing nearby, was absolutely still, but Malcolm thought he could see in her wide eyes the terror she must have been feeling. Pan stepped forward into the sunlight next to Malcolm.

'Do *you* know what this imagination is, then?' the Queen said.

'I believe you have two kingdoms, Your Majesty, an outer kingdom and an inner one. Is that right?'

'Yes.'

'We human beings – or some of us – believe the same. Some of us don't, but many of us do. The way we move between the outer kingdom and the inner one is the imagination.'

The Queen seemed to be pondering this. Her head moved gently as she looked from Pan to Malcolm, to the courtiers around her, to the great mountains beyond the terrace.

Her gaze came back to Pan.

'You have all lost this thing?'

'No,' he said. 'Just the human girl who is the other part of me. It's her imagination we're going to seek.'

Malcolm remembered the folded pages Ionides had given him under the orange tree of the villa: the speech Marcel Delamare had given, or was going to give, about *The imagination, a false, seductive, and dangerous doctrine.* Did the gryphons really not know anything about the imagination? Or did they have another word for it?

The Queen spoke again. 'And you want to continue this search?'

'More than anything else, Your Majesty.'

Another silence, as she looked at the vizier, and at Gulya, and at Pan, and back to Malcolm again.

'And I hear you are a craftsman,' she said. 'An artificer.'

'In the realms of gold from which I come, the artificer is the highest-ranking person in the kingdom.'

She nodded slowly, seeming to consider the matter.

'That is right,' she said. 'Well, Artificer Malcolm, you may stay here until you have performed a task for me. I have an item in my treasury that is damaged. You will work on it for me. Restore it to its original state, and we shall convey you anywhere in the world you wish to go. Until I am satisfied, you will remain here.'

She nodded, and the vizier stood aside for a man in a jeweller's apron to come forward. He was holding something in a cloth.

He laid it on the carpet and lifted the cloth aside, and both Pan and Malcolm felt a shock of surprise.

The object was about the size of Malcolm's hand. It was made of shining gold, crushed and twisted and torn. There was a dial of ivory, cracked in half, and various wheels and cogs and levers, some loose and hanging out, and it was clear that it would never work again, but there was no doubt. It was – it had been – an alethiometer.

12

RESONATING LODESTONE

Away from the gryphons and back in their quarters, Malcolm said at once, 'It *is* hers, isn't it? I don't know why I'm asking, actually. Of course it's hers. It's the same one I stole from Gerard Bonneville.'

He laid it on the table, next to his lodestone, and lifted back the cloth. Pan peered at it hungrily, trembling, touching it here and there.

'Yes,' he whispered. 'What can have happened?'

'Someone stole it, and then smashed it up. Or dropped it from a height. That's all we can tell.'

'It keeps being stolen,' said Pan. 'A gryphon must have stolen it from Lyra. But we better not say *steal*. They seem to think they have a right to all the gold that exists. But how on earth can you mend it?'

Malcolm was turning it round in his hands, looking at it from every angle. It was crushed and cracked and twisted, and there was no way of knowing what pieces were missing. An expert reader of the instrument would see it with horror, and imagine that it would never work again; a clockmaker would see it as a technical problem, and have the tools to take it apart and put things straight, but might not be able to imagine its function. What could Malcolm do?

'Look! Words,' said Pan, as a line of handwriting appeared on the lodestone.

Malcolm put down the alethiometer and read:

OS to MP

Polstead, where the hell are you? What are you doing? Reply as soon as you've read this.

The Magisterium has discovered something we had not suspected. At various points on the earth there exist anomalous features that seem to function like openings or doorways into spaces not otherwise contiguous. The Barnard-Stokes hypothesis might be applicable here.

There are seventeen of these places known about and listed, and another eight suspected, but not examined. The Magisterium is aware of the implications of this phenomenon for the foundations of their theology. Until recently only three people knew about them: the discoverer, Hugo Beamish, a geographer in the employment of the Magisterium, whose whereabouts are now unknown; the Magisterial President, Marcel Delamare; and a Colonel Wolfgang Schreiber, who is charged by Delamare to find these things and destroy them. So far he has succeeded in doing that with three of them, by thermobaric explosion. The third explosion, in a forested part of eastern Belgium, was fortuitously witnessed by an OS agent, who subsequently investigated and managed to acquire the papers from which Colonel Schreiber was working. It doesn't look good for Schreiber, but they won't be so careless again.

Now tell me where the hell you are and what you're doing.

Godwin

Malcolm said to Pan, 'I'll come back to the alethiometer later. Better answer this.'

Pan crouched down close and peered at the instrument from every angle, while Malcolm wrote:

MP to OS
   Sorry. I was interrupted. I am at the summit of Mount Damāvand, which as far as I remember is near the southern edge of the Caspian Sea. I am a captive, and escape looks very difficult. My captors are the subjects of Queen Shahrnavāz, who rules over a realm extending as far east as Sinkiang, and possibly further. They think I am valuable to them, and will guard me fiercely. By chance they've come into the possession of an alethiometer, broken almost beyond repair. And they want me to repair it. Then, I hope, they will let us leave.
   Please tell me all you know about the Magisterium plan. I think I know a little about these openings.
   Polstead

OS to MP
   Openings listed and verified by Beamish (those marked * destroyed by Schreiber). Precise details of location too long to transcribe now, but available if necessary.

Switzerland*
French Alps
Italian Alps*
Belgium*
Normandy
North Wales
Spanish Pyrenees
Tunisia
Madagascar
Yemen
Azerbaijan
Muscovy, Velikhi Novgorod region

Mongolia, Yolyn Am region
Java, Bandung region
Alaska, Brooks Range region
Brazil, São Paulo region
Australia, Gibson Desert

Listed by Beamish but not verified:
Karelia region
Lop Nor/Karamakan
Morocco/Atlas Mountains
Haiti
Nippon, Hokkaido region
Jordan, Petra region
Sweden, Falun region
Crete

Lot of time on your hands, Polstead? Let me know when you feel like moving on. Oh, and find out about the alkahest.
   Godwin

MP to OS
   Alkahest? Never heard of it. Will enquire when time allows. Captive with me by chance is Pantalaimon, the dæmon of Lyra Silvertongue. You know I can separate from my dæmon: Lyra and Pan have the same faculty. Ten or eleven years ago, he tells me, he and Lyra made a journey to the far north, in the course of which they encountered various 'openings' of the sort you describe (let's call them that). They are formed by human action, though possibly some occur naturally. You are correct about the Barnard-Stokes idea. The openings lead to other worlds, other universes. There seems to be an infinity of such worlds. Naturally the Magisterium would want to close as many openings as it could find. Doubtless Beamish's list is the result of great effort on his part, but I guess there are many more he didn't find.

*Please let me know as much as you can about the Lop Nor one. I
think that is the source of the rose material.*

*Also about Colonel Schreiber's attempts to destroy them.
What effect did thermobaric explosive have? Did they close up
completely?*

*Also about the Magisterium's reaction to the theft of Schreiber's
papers.*

*I shall be able to move on as soon as I have repaired the broken
alethiometer. It is made of gold; the Queen and her subjects are
obsessed by that metal. To be precise, rendered insane by desire for
it. Her palace is built at the very summit of this mountain, and
there is absolutely no access except from the sky. They flew me and
Pan here, and they will have to fly us out, or keep us here for ever.*

*As for Lyra Silvertongue, I last heard of her in Aleppo, but I
know she is travelling east, with the aim of reaching a certain
point in the Karamakan desert, possibly the Lop Nor place on
Beamish's list.*

Polstead

OS to MP

*Thermobaric explosive partially successful at best. Can't destroy
opening entirely – leaves small ragged gaps in the air – but does
make it impossible for human being to pass through. Given that
locations are generally difficult of access, little danger of discovery.
Magisterium now working on improved & more powerful version
of bomb, or better way of directing force of explosion. President
intensely determined to make this work, also set up task force under
Schreiber to work on closing all known openings. You said 'formed
by human action' – more information needed. Also about this
Queen Shahrnavāz.*

All you know, and soon.

*DO NOT LET THIS DISTRACT YOU FROM YOUR
MAIN TASK.*

Godwin

'Later,' said Malcolm, and turned back to the alethiometer. He turned it round and looked at it dispassionately. 'What I'm going to do is take it apart first and see what's missing. The case doesn't actually matter as far as I know – it's the mechanism that's important when it comes to reading it, but since the parts inside aren't made of gold they won't mean much to the gryphons. I could do something with the gold of the case, and make a separate box to hold the workings safe till I can get it back to Lyra.'

'You think we'll find her?'

'Don't you?'

'Well . . . I hope we will.'

'Hold on to that. Now let's see what's missing. The glass, obviously. I don't think it was smashed, though. Someone's unscrewed it, because the frame's just not there, and there are no broken bits of glass. It was crushed like this after the glass was taken out. The frame was screwed to the rim, here . . . Well, that's interesting.'

'What?'

'It screws up anti-clockwise. See the way the thread goes, there?' He pointed, and Pan looked closely. 'The first contact I had with Hannah Relf involved a carved wooden acorn that unscrewed like this, backwards. I saw her unscrew it and I knew it was meant to be for her, because otherwise she'd have tried to do it the other way, anti-clockwise. And this is the same . . . Did Lyra ever open it up to look inside it?'

'No. It would never have occurred to us.'

The golden case was crushed so out of shape that it looked as if it had been held tightly in a mighty claw. Malcolm turned it round and round, looking for any other clues.

'The dial's cracked,' said Pan.

The thirty-six symbols around the outer rim of the dial, whose meanings he and Lyra had pondered for so many hours, had been painted with a brush so small it might as well have been a single hair. Seeing them not through the glass for the first time, but with the naked eye, Pan and Malcolm both wondered at the exquisite precision of the work. Each symbol was painted on a rectangular slip of ivory held in place by a slender golden frame. They were all there, but a great crack had split the entire face in half, and two of the hands were badly bent.

'The needle!' said Pan. 'It's not there.'

'You know it much better than I do. Remind me what the needle looked like.'

'Very slender with a sharp point. Different colour from the hands, and it moved independently. Has it fallen off the axle thing in the middle? The spindle?'

'That's called the arbor. I can't see it anywhere.'

Malcolm lifted the instrument and carefully turned it round, listening for anything loose inside it. There was nothing to hear.

'It must have fallen out when they took the glass off,' said Pan.

'The needle wasn't gold, was it?'

'No. Something different – an alloy of some kind . . . Sort of grey, I think. It moved by itself. You can point the hands where you want, to ask the question, but the needle was the part that gave you the answer.'

Malcolm gently tried to turn one of the three wheels around the edge. It resisted, and he didn't force it. He tried another, and the hand it controlled moved stiffly around the broken dial until it came to one of the bent hands, which stopped it. The third wheel was stuck like the first.

'You've never seen the mechanism, then?' he said.

'No. Can you get the back off?'

'Not without . . . Let me see.'

Malcolm never went anywhere without his boyhood Swiss Army knife, and he opened the long blade now and felt with the tip around the edge of the case.

'I don't think the back unscrews. I think it just clips into place . . . There, you see, if it wasn't crushed I'd just twist here with the knifepoint and it would come open. But it's twisted, and that makes it harder to prise it open. At least I know what tools would help now. Let's see if Gulya's craftsman-prisoner has got some I can borrow.'

The human servants who came and went and worked so silently in the chambers and the stony corridors of Damāvand were not slaves but indentured prisoners, Malcolm learned; not that it seemed to make much difference to them. The man Darius, who had been appointed to look after him and Pantalaimon, had been a minor criminal in Isfahan, tempted like many of the other servants by the thought of the immense riches in the treasury of the gryphons, and (like them) failing miserably to steal some gold and get away with it. The tongue-removal was a standard punishment; the captivity and the labour were to last seven years, of which Darius had served four. The gryphons kept their word: when a captive's time was served, he (almost all were *he*) was flown down to the plains and set free. But silent.

They worked at various tasks. As Malcolm had guessed, the architecture, the carpentry, and the creation of the fire-channels in the walls, all the various services that the Queen and her court and her ministers demanded, were the work of human hands, working under gryphon supervision. All this Malcolm learned in the course of several hours' talk with Darius, Malcolm's rusty Persian combining with the servant's nods and shrugs and grunts and gestures to reach a narrow plateau of understanding. Pan and the servant's desert-rodent dæmon might have done better, except that the dæmon didn't speak at all, and was terrified of everything, especially Gulya. The little gryphon would sit on the table while Malcolm and Pan discussed what Darius had told them, and contributed her knowledge to fill the gaps left by Darius's ignorance or their mutual bafflement.

She was most helpful when it came to the things Malcolm needed.

'Paper and pencils,' he said. 'Not ink and pens – pencils. Then tools. I shall need some small screwdrivers . . .'

And at that point, as at others, he had to explain what he meant. The world of tools and craftsmanship and handiwork was alien to Gulya not only because she didn't have hands, but also because they were human things, and thus degrading for a gryphon to be concerned with. Finally they decided that Malcolm would make a list of the tools he needed, and Gulya would take him to one of the prisoner-craftsmen who might be able to supply them.

OS to MP

Delamare has sent out parties to find and destroy the openings on Beamish's list. Schreiber in overall command. Beamish himself is dead, on the orders of Delamare. A great pity. But clearly Delamare considers these things to be important enough for him to divert resources from his Central Asian project.

That project is now becoming a preparation for war. Apparently he will soon make a 'major speech' on the subject. Word from inside HMG says he's been guaranteed our 'enthusiastic and unbounded' support. Troops already moving.

No one here or in HMG has any idea why he is blowing up these openings. OS has appointed a small team to investigate the nearest openings we know about, but it will take time.

Meanwhile, I've been asking about this Queen Shahrnavāz . . . Gryphons? Really?

Explain.

Godwin

MP to OS

Some realms overlap but don't connect. For example, neutrinos: they take no notice of us, nor we of them. The witches of the north are another. They have their preoccupations, their wars and alliances and interests, but they rarely involve short-lived men and women like us. So it is with the gryphons. Human beings have nothing they want, except gold, for which they have a passion, and manual labour. They consider themselves absolute rulers of two kingdoms: an outer one which comprises most of Asia and Muscovy, and an inner one [sic] whose limits lie beyond the edge of the visible universe. Apart from our ability to mine and work gold, we humans are just not interesting to them. What I discover about them, however, may be of use to OS when I return. I should say if I return.

The alethiometer they want me to repair is the one that used to belong to Lyra Silvertongue, and it's badly damaged. If you have any information about her, I would be glad to hear it.

MP

OS to MP

FOLLOW THE MONEY.

Pan said, 'What does she mean by that?'

'One of the reasons she sent me out here is that money's going bad, and no one knows why. Not just things like inflation, which we kind of understand, but something more fundamental. I'm supposed to be investigating it. And here I am in a place where gold is king, and money means nothing. Well, we have to do what we must do where we are, because we certainly can't do it where we aren't. On with this now for the moment.'

'It might all be connected anyway.'

'It might, yes. Let's hope this craftsman has some decent tools.'

The craftsman-prisoner whom Gulya found was a morose Georgian jeweller called Tamaz Khuroshvili. His principal occupation consisted of prising precious stones, for which the gryphons cared nothing, out of their settings in stolen necklaces and bracelets and so on, and then melting down and refining those settings to purify the gold, for which the gryphons cared everything.

Malcolm had to talk to him through Gulya, and since the jeweller couldn't speak, Malcolm had to put much of what he asked into a form that permitted a yes-no answer. When Khuroshvili realised that Malcolm wanted to borrow some tools, he became agitated, and his magpie-dæmon flew around his head in a frenzy. Pan tried to calm her down, but that was difficult too, because the magpie and the jeweller could both see very well that Pan wasn't Malcolm's dæmon, and that itself was something to be afraid of.

Eventually a sort of fatalism took over. The man shrugged and put his head in his hands and uttered a high hoarse wail, and spread his hands wide, and shook his head, and shrugged again.

'Tell him I am a craftsman too,' said Malcolm. 'I shall look after his tools as if they were mine. And I don't want his job. As soon as I've finished he can have them back, with my compliments and gratitude.'

Gulya explained as much of that as Khuroshvili was willing to understand. With heavy resignation he beckoned to Malcolm to follow him to the bench where he worked, and spread his hands wide over everything there, inviting Malcolm to take his pick.

Malcolm chose a pair of needle-nosed pliers, a heavier pair of pliers with flat jaws, a small but heavy hammer with one flat face and one rounded one, one ordinary screwdriver and another very small one with a swivel head, and a fine-cut file. He also picked out a flat plate of steel about the size of his hand, as a surface to work on. It was very heavy. Khuroshvili sighed helplessly. Malcolm looked up to the shelves behind the bench and noticed half a dozen small bottles with cork stoppers, and gestured towards them. The jeweller nodded. Malcolm sniffed them all, more out of interest than anything else, and then held one up interrogatively.

Khuroshvili shrugged and nodded, as if to say 'What does it matter?' and Malcolm put the bottle carefully in his shirt pocket before pressing his hands together and inclining his head, to say thanks.

Gulya said, 'Is there anything else you need?'

'Not just now. If I find there is, I'll ask you again. Please reassure him that his tools will be looked after.'

She took them back to their apartment and left them.

Pan said, 'What's in the bottle?'

'Linseed oil.'

'What do you need that for?'

'It's just generally useful . . . I think I'll be able to get the back off now. Then we can see what's inside it. I'd like to have taken his vice, but it was too heavy to move.'

'Look, there's more writing coming through.'

OS to MP

Visited the site in North Wales on Beamish's list. Immensely hard to find; almost impossible to see; uncanny. What's on the other side is definitely not this world. Reminded me of Annwn in the Mabinogi; an underworld, a different realm altogether. Tell me everything you know about these things, and do it now.

Godwin

'Well, those are the orders,' said Malcolm. 'While I take this thing to pieces, you do what she says. Tell me everything you and Lyra discovered about places like that, these openings.'

'Everything . . . ? All right. The old man Will met in the Tower of the Angels, in Cittàgazze, said that—'

'Chronologically.'

'Yes. Of course. Well, the first time . . .'

OS to MP

Your information about openings intriguing but unhelpful. The only thing that can make them is in the hands of a young man in another world? Better focus on this one then.

HM gov't passed Corporate Indemnity Act. Building corporations etc. no longer to be held liable for damage caused by products or activities.

News from Geneva: Magisterium holding conference on the regulation of doctrine so Delamare can put his stamp on what we

should all believe. Maybe also his big announcement about war.
HMG to send representative Bishop of Kensington to assure Mag.
of support. Unctuous toadie. Rumour that Gottfried Brande, well-
known novelist and philosopher, will attend and speak.
  Godwin

*

'Monsieur le Président, *why?*'

'Because what he says here in Geneva we can contain. If he says it elsewhere, we cannot.'

Marcel Delamare was walking under the plane trees in a park beside the lake with his private secretary, a Luxembourgeois diplomat and priest called Matthieu Crespin, whose little snake dæmon was listening closely.

'Brande is a menace,' the secretary said flatly. 'He will do us nothing but harm.'

'It's not in his power to do us harm. He has no organisation, his academic standing has dwindled to nothing, he has no followers.'

'No followers! He has thousands – probably hundreds of thousands. Young people everywhere—'

'No,' said Delamare. 'They are not followers. They are fans.'

'If he's so unimportant, why invite him?'

'We didn't invite him. He announced that he was coming, and believe me, Matthieu, it would have caused far more problems to turn him away. You will meet him at the railway station this afternoon and show him every courtesy. The obvious place for him in the programme would be on the discussion panel about doctrine and social responsibility, but he would regard that as an insult and demand an event to himself, so that is what he shall have. He can speak at four o'clock, on Thursday afternoon in the Chapel of the Sacred Presence. Announce it as a rare opportunity to hear one of the most prominent thinkers of the present day, and leave it at that.'

'But Monsieur le Président, what about your speech? The *casus belli* speech?'

'It's not quite time. There are two alliances I want to secure before I announce it. Besides, I think it needs a different context, a single occasion free of distractions.'

'But what's Professor Brande going to speak about? Do we know?'

'It makes very little difference, because, as I say, we shall be able to contain it. You know how a silencer works? Like that.'

'H'mm. As you wish, Monsieur Delamare.'

'Make sure he's comfortably lodged. He will want to see me for a personal interview, which will, with the deepest regrets, be impossible. Ask about his return ticket, and make sure there's a car to take him to the station. Every courtesy, Matthieu.'

'Monsieur Président, of course. But again, may I ask *why*? What possible benefit can his presence . . . ?'

'Oh, we shall learn something from it. There is always something to learn.'

'Leila Pervani,' said Abdel Ionides. 'Well, we were lovers, for too little time. In Alexandria . . . Colleagues also. I was mathematician, she particle physicist. You know the expression *coup de foudre*?'

'Yes,' said Lyra. 'It was like that, was it?'

They were facing each other across the table in the little compartment of the *autobus de luxe*. Asta was crouching sphinx-like beside the window, with Ionides's gecko dæmon on the glass above her. The amber-shaded anbaric lamp on the bulkhead illuminated the damage to Ionides's face, and showed clearly how long it would take him to recover; no doubt, thought Lyra, it wasn't showing her to advantage either.

Ionides said, 'Entirely. Immediately. Intellectually as well as everything else. We speak all night about her research, and then we go to bed, and then we speak about mine. For six months nothing else existed. She was investigating new way of examining the Rusakov field experimentally, I was interested in the mathematics, but I found myself at the limits of that discipline. The only way I could go further was phenomenologically, more or less. Surprising, you see.'

'Er . . . Yes. And Dust?'

'Dust is not the field but the particle associated with the field. Different ways of studying the same thing. Except . . . More complex than that. Everything is more complex, except things that are simpler.'

'Did your research and hers complement each other?'

'Yes, completely. As if it been intended to happen. How could she have been working on the very same thing, so near, in the very same institution?'

'It's forbidden to study Dust in some places. Did that affect the way you worked?'

'Of course. We had to be careful. She was using expensive equipment – she had to make explanations to justify the time for this experiment or that one. As for me, I was already suspicious person. Some papers I wrote were withdrawn by order of the authorities; I had to swear not to touch that subject.'

'So it was dangerous for you both.'

'Yes, and in small society, small institution, like university, full of gossip, full of curiosity . . .'

'I can imagine.'

'But our talks together . . . It was like two people climbing a mountain no one ever climbed before, roped together. We climb so far, so high, no one else could ever understood.'

'What happened?'

'How much detail you want?'

'Lots, later. But now just the main story.'

'All right. The university invent a scandal about her. I defend her, and they dismissed me. The authorities were going to put her in prison, but she escaped from Egypt and went who knows where. She had to leave her work, of course, her team, her research – all finish. As for me, I could see what would happen next: accusations of heresy, trial, lies, prison and maybe worse. So I go to the harbour and find a ship in need of a cook and next day I sail away to Palermo. Easier for me to carry on research than for her. No laboratory, no instruments, no team, just me and pencil and paper. I leave my name behind and become Abdel Ionides, interpreter, guide, beggar, spy, minor criminal, et cetera.'

'What happened to her, though? Why was she in the nuncio's house?'

'You know one time you ask me about the men from the mountains?'

'One time? It was only this morning. But yes, I did.'

'She is with them. At first when I heard this I thought it was impossible, could not be true, a fundamental error. But she is. I had to think: what does she gain from them? Has she gone mad? Remember, she is highly trained, greatly gifted physicist. To do her work she need all the things she left behind in Alexandria. The men from the mountains are the worst kind of fanatics; her research is abominable to them as much as it is to the Magisterium. Also I know her very well; we shared everything. We were lovers. She is passionate about physics, not interested at all in politics and religious argument. If they knew – if the men from the mountains could see into her mind they would kill her at once. Then I thought: maybe she is hiding in the one place they would not look. No university or respectable academic body would ever hire her after Alexandria; she could never do science again. Maybe a rich company like Thuringia Potash with big research department, but maybe not even them. So what does she do? She will want to be close to the matter of Dust, more than anything else. So she gets close to those who want to destroy it.'

'Dangerous.'

'Almost insane. But you see her just now, in that prison cell. She seem insane to you?'

'No. She was shocked to see you, but completely sane and in control.'

Ionides's gecko-dæmon said from the window-glass, 'Darab has not changed.'

'Darab is her dæmon,' Ionides explained.

'And when you saw her, saw Leila – were you glad?' said Lyra.

'What you think, Miss Silver? I was afraid for her.'

'When did you know she was a friend of the men from the mountains?'

'Two years ago. Maybe three. First I think it is impossible, but then I think more, and I know why. Not because she agree with them, but for the same reason I enter your employment, Miss Silver.'

'What on earth do you mean by that?'

'It was the best way to get to Karamakan. Also something we spoke about once – you had a word – alkahest.'

Lyra sat back and closed her eyes. She felt as if the day had been too long, and she'd had enough of it. The comfortable seat that would soon fold out into a bed, the gentle light on the table, the dark night outside through which they were speeding so smoothly – they all urged her almost irresistibly to sleep.

She made herself sit up and take a deep breath.

'Well, you'd better explain,' she said.

But before Ionides could say anything, there was a knock on the compartment door and a voice said, 'Dinner, Your Majesty Queen. With compliments of Mustafa Bey. I enter, please?'

'Yes, come in,' she said, and Ionides moved aside to make room for the attendant to lean past him and place a tray on the table. Shashlik, bread, salad; two plates, two glasses, a bottle of wine and a jug of water. And Lyra realised how hungry she was, as well as how tired.

'Eat first,' she said. 'Then sleep. Explain later.'

But she was too tired to stay awake, and she fell asleep almost as soon as the attendant took the dinner tray away. Ionides spread a blanket over her and went to his seat. Somewhere among mountains the bus stopped to refuel. Lyra heard the driver's voice, footsteps on asphalt, a quiet conversation; one or two passengers got off and gathered their luggage from the attendant. In the state between waking and dreaming, Lyra noticed that Asta was sleeping on the pillow next to her. The bus set off again; Lyra fell back into sleep.

13

A Spy in the House of God

Glenys Godwin knew about what was happening in Geneva because Oakley Street had an agent in the Magisterium. His name was Leenart Karpelin, and he worked in the cathedral archives. He was known to his employers and his few friends as a diligent scholar and a quietly pious individual whose only interest outside his work was choral music; his tenor voice was not powerful, but it was always secure.

The conference on the regulation of doctrine was not exactly held in secret, but it was clearly understood to be a clerical matter, a professional examination of technical and philosophical questions not likely to be of great interest to the simple believer. For example, Marcel Delamare had been working on his notes about the deceptive and baleful nature of the imagination, and was intending to deliver a speech on that subject in a closed symposium. However, there were a few sessions open to the general public, and one of those was the lecture to be given by the celebrated novelist Gottfried Brande. The President's secretariat had arranged it with immaculate skill. It was scheduled at a time of the day and the week when most delegates and other attendees would be tiring somewhat, and more likely to relish a nap than a lecture. It was untitled, because the title Brande had given it (a quotation from the philosopher Hegel) was unfortunately too long to fit in the programme, so no one could tell what it was likely to be about. Furthermore, the speaker's late announcement of his intention to appear had made it difficult to advertise the event with the full effectiveness it no doubt deserved; and finally, in the biographical note, Brande's famous novel *The Hyperchorasmians* was mistitled *The Hyperboreans.*

Leenart Karpelin noted all this, and wrote it down to tell Oakley Street. He turned up in good time for Brande's lecture, and took his seat in the narrow and badly lit Chapel of the Sacred Presence and watched patiently as the twenty or so other audience members arrived. The chapel could hold about a hundred, and the empty seats would, Karpelin knew, carry the Magisterium's message clearly to the speaker.

When it was obvious that no more members of the public were going to turn up, a cleric Karpelin didn't recognise came to the lectern and tapped it for silence.

'Good afternoon, ladies and gentlemen,' he said. His words were almost lost in the lamentable acoustics, and either he didn't realise, or he didn't know how to do anything about it, because he made no effort to adjust his voice. 'We are very privileged today to welcome a most distinguished speaker, a philosopher and, er, novelist known to countless readers in Europe and beyond. Professor Gottfried Brande's work has, ah, been praised for its originality and force both in the academy and in the world of, er, popular fiction . . .'

Karpelin was watching Brande, who was sitting just behind the speaker. At the words 'popular fiction' the philosopher clenched his fists and ground his teeth almost audibly. Karpelin could see the dæmon lying at his feet, a large dog of some kind, try to tuck her head further under a paw than it was already. There was something strange about her, but Karpelin couldn't work out what it was, and meanwhile the speaker was concluding his introduction:

'We are, as I say, deeply privileged in this conference on the regulation of doctrine to hear the thoughts of such an eminent and internationally renowned speaker. Please welcome Professor Gottfried Brande.'

He stood aside as the audience clapped politely. Brande stood up and came to the lectern, tall, gaunt, grim-faced, in a faded black academic robe. Karpelin saw and only just heard him snap his fingers, and saw the German shepherd dæmon slink forward after him, belly to the floor, almost timorous. Karpelin thought that they were the unhappiest creatures he had ever seen.

Brande watched the dæmon lie down again and close her eyes. Then he turned to the audience.

'I have tried all my life to speak and write plainly. I deplore the human tendency, from which I myself have long struggled to break free, to express its thought in metaphor or figurative language generally. To that end I have made a practice of expunging any examples of such loose thinking when I correct the first draft of a piece of writing. I begin by saying this merely because I want you to remember that what I say this afternoon is to be taken literally. It is not an exercise in florid rhetoric. It is far too important to be weakened with imagery. I have come here because a great and convulsive change in human life is about to take place, and I want to describe it with cold and simple accuracy.'

His voice was so much clearer than that of the cleric who had introduced him that Karpelin at first thought that Brande was simply speaking more loudly. But it was more than that; everything about him was intensely present to the senses of sight and hearing. Perhaps because the whites of his eyes were very white, his facial expressions could be read easily even in the poor light of the chapel, and his voice cut through the heavy air like that of a powerful singer; he was simply more *in focus* than anyone Karpelin had seen for a long time.

'There's something wrong,' his mouse-dæmon whispered.

'Ssh. Just listen.'

Brande was standing absolutely still as he spoke. His hands grasped the sides of the lectern, his feet were firmly set on the stone floor. His voice continued steadily, a resonant baritone, clear in every syllable:

'This gathering, we have been told, has been summoned to discuss the regulation of doctrine. Never has there been a time when such a project was both so necessary and so superfluous. Necessary, because we are not brutes, and we cannot live without a common understanding about fact and reason. Superfluous, because all the elements for such a common understanding are already in place, and have been for some – for sunin front of him – have been for—'

He stopped as if he was out of breath. Then he cleared his throat and tried again:

'The elements of common understanding have been in plate – ah – ah – no, not now, no—'

He clutched both hands to his chest and fell down heavily, striking his head on the lectern before hitting the floor.

Karpelin could see everything clearly, because the seat in front of him was empty. He saw the cleric who had introduced the event rise from his chair uncertainly and look around before moving towards the stricken Brande; he saw the hound-dæmon half rise and then stumble away, tail between her legs; he saw some other members of the audience, half a dozen or so, stand up involuntarily, but then pause, because there was clearly nothing anyone could do: Brande was dead, still as marble, eyes wide open.

But his dæmon—

She was loping from one side of the chapel to the other, in abject fear, whining, yelping a little, belly almost on the ground, wild-eyed.

The cleric, bending over Brande with one hand extended as if to stroke his head, became aware of the dæmon with a start of terror and almost leaped over the body to get away from her.

He stumbled off the dais and nearly fell full length himself, but was caught by a man in the front row.

And now everyone was watching the dæmon, who should have vanished, whose continuing existence was contrary to nature, who was as horrifying as a decapitated corpse getting up and stumbling about sightless. Karpelin felt a surge of horror so profound he almost fainted. Everyone was on their feet now, all pressing back and away from her, some uttering cries of fear. Their dæmons were the most fearful of all, clinging to their people, hiding their faces, yelping or whining or shrieking—

And the dæmon herself was running, loping, scuttling, pawing at the door, howling. Karpelin and his dæmon felt a profound compassion mingled with nausea at the utter wrongness of what was happening.

'Open the doors!' someone shouted.

'Let it out – quick—'

It, who a minute before would have been *she*, must have been a creature of the darkness, an evil spirit, a night-ghast. Behind Karpelin someone was being sick. A man more desperate than the rest dashed for the chapel door, but before he reached it the dæmon in her panic and misery sprang up at the handle, and the man cried out and pulled back.

The sounds the dæmon was making were almost like language, but not German or French or indeed any European tongue. Karpelin found himself imagining the survivor of some appalling catastrophe howling in the ruins of her village, her children lying dead around her.

Then the man at the door tried the handle again and this time pulled it open, and at once most of the audience rushed towards it and jostled and shoved to get through. The cleric who had introduced the speaker was among the first of them. The dæmon fled to a dark corner under the communion table and huddled beneath it, thrusting her head down hard as if to bury her face under the stone floor.

Karpelin, curious as a human being as well as a spy, was last to leave the chapel.

His mouse-dæmon whispered, 'Why isn't she looking at him? Why isn't she clinging to him? She's afraid of him more than of anyone.'

Karpelin knew what she meant. 'She was afraid when he was alive,' he murmured in reply.

'There was something wrong with them,' his dæmon whispered back.

Outside they could hear raised voices arguing, explaining, demanding. Any moment now someone in authority would come in. A thought occurred to Karpelin, and he sank to his knees and raised his hands together in an attitude of prayer, just in time; because there were other faces now in the doorway, and uniformed bodies, and weapons.

They might have been police, but they looked more like soldiers. Karpelin could see the shoulder-flash of the Office of Right Duty, which was similar to that of the old and much feared Consistorial Court of Discipline.

The first of the men looked around, noticed Karpelin, but then was shoved aside by another, who was pointing at the trembling dæmon under the table.

'There it is! Look!'

It, again. Four or five men, rifles raised, advanced towards the table, spreading out to cover a wider angle. Their dæmons, dog-formed themselves, were clearly unhappy about the matter. Two of them tried to hang back, unsuccessfully.

'Hey!' called one of the men. 'Come out here!'

The dæmon tried to force her head down even further.

Another man in sergeant's uniform made his way towards Karpelin, casting glances back at the table all the time.

'Sir,' he said. 'Sir. Got to leave the building, please.'

Karpelin opened his eyes and looked up at him, but kept his hands clasped.

'I'm telling you to leave,' the sergeant said more harshly.

'Yes, all right,' said Karpelin. 'I understand. But don't hurt her, will you? She's just terrified.'

'No one's going to get hurt. But you've got to leave. Come on, hurry up.'

Karpelin stood up carefully, and edged his way to the end of the row of chairs. Then something frightened Brande's dæmon. She howled and leaped up, and raced out of the shelter of the communion table, and one of the soldiers was so startled that he fired his rifle, missing the dæmon but smashing a window.

The dæmon was in a passion of fear and misery; she ran with all her force directly into the far wall, as if she thought it was made of paper, and fell back with the bones of her face smashed and splintered, but still alive. Now pain was added to the terror; the poor creature must be nearly mad, thought Karpelin, and his own dæmon was sobbing pitifully; and in came two more men in different uniforms, carrying a long pole with a noose of wire rope at the end.

By now the sergeant had given up with Karpelin, and was more interested in the process of capturing the dæmon. Karpelin could hardly bear to watch, but thought someone ought to witness what was happening, so forced himself to stay, holding his own little dæmon in both hands close to his breast.

The dead man's dæmon was struggling fiercely, but without any sense of where she was or what was happening to her. Her claws kept slipping on the stone floor, and when the men tried to get the wire noose around her neck she screamed and howled and sobbed exactly like a – like a human being, Karpelin thought, but then she was human, of course she was human, and her man was lying dead, and she couldn't die, and Karpelin's own dæmon was pleading with him, begging him to do anything to help, anything at all.

But they had her in the grip of the noose, and there were four of them, big heavy men, dragging her towards the door. It was impossible for her. The doorway was crowded with people shoving and peering and staring wide-eyed, exactly as Karpelin imagined the spectators at a public execution would behave. The soldiers were wielding batons, striking left and right to clear the way to the door for the men hauling the stricken dæmon as she struggled and choked in the noose, and then they were outside and every brutal human face went with them, leaving Karpelin and his own little dæmon to collapse on to the nearest chair and sob with helpless grief.

They brought the news to Marcel Delamare as he enjoyed a glass of wine with some important guests in the garden of *La Maison Juste*.

'Stay here, Matthieu,' he murmured to his private secretary. 'I must see to this.'

Rumours were already flying through the city like sparks from a careless bonfire, ready to ignite any tinder they touched. The grim and lurid personality of Gottfried Brande and the bizarre circumstances of his death combined to produce a sensation that was more than the Magisterium could silence. When Delamare arrived at the headquarters of the Office of Right Duty five minutes after the news reached him he found a small crowd already jostling outside the main entrance.

'Monsieur le Président!' he heard someone call, and recognised the voice of Théophile Engelmann, a journalist who specialised in religious affairs. An instant calculation unreeled in his mind: to talk to him – better or worse?

He stopped and nodded gravely. 'Good afternoon, Théophile,' he said. 'A troubling business.'

'Did you know what Gottfried Brande was going to say in his lecture, Monsieur Delamare?'

'No. We are not in the business of censorship. Good heavens! Professor Brande was of course at perfect liberty to say whatever he wished, and we would have listened with profound attention to the words of such a distinguished scholar.'

'And his dæmon—'

'You'll forgive me, Théophile, but in the present circumstances I can't say anything until I've examined the case myself.'

Other voices: 'Are you going to have it killed?' 'Are you going to put her down?' 'Is it dead or alive?'

Voices were coming at him from every part of the crowd, which was already growing. Delamare held up a hand, shook his head, smiled sorrowfully, and allowed his escort to clear the way through the door and into the building. His owl-dæmon raised her wings and flapped them once or twice in a rare display of annoyance.

'Well?' Delamare snapped at the officer in charge.

'This way, Monsieur le—'

'Still alive?'

'Yes, but in great distress. She can't—'

'There is no doubt that Brande is dead?'

'None whatsoever, monsieur. An apoplexy killed him at once.'

'And the dæmon is injured? Who caused that?'

'My understanding is that she ran so hard into a wall that she caused it herself. Possibly trying to—'

'Take me to her at once.'

Delamare followed the officer down the stairs and into a room designed for the interrogation of prisoners. A table and two chairs were bolted to the tiled floor; there were no windows, just a glaring strip light overhead.

And the dæmon, than whom, or than which, Delamare had never seen any creature more pitiful. He had noticed the 'it' from the voices outside, and recognised the effect it had.

He sat on one of the chairs and watched as the creature tried to hide in a corner, under the table, in another corner, forcing her agonised face against the wall, uttering all the time a choked and stuttering wail.

'Leave me,' Delamare said to the attendant.

'But she might—'

'She can do nothing. Leave, now.'

'I'll be just outside, Monsieur le Président.'

He closed the door carefully as he left.

'Can you understand me?' Delamare asked, speaking very clearly.

No response except a constant quiet note of anguish. Delamare's own dæmon spread her owl-wings and glided from his shoulder to the table, to peer down at the demented being and her poor shattered face.

Delamare tried in German: 'Do you know where you are?'

No response.

'My name is Marcel Delamare. You are in the care of the Magisterium, in Geneva. Do you know what happened to your person, to Gottfried Brande?'

She uttered a groan that was half a growl. She recognised his name, then. Delamare went on: 'We can try to heal your injuries. We can certainly make you more comfortable. Can you speak at all? Can you utter words in any language?'

The dæmon forced a sound out of her throat, and Delamare's owl-dæmon said something in response.

'Persian, I think,' she said to Delamare. And then to the dæmon she uttered a phrase in that language which he recognised as a greeting.

The dæmon did nothing but put a paw over her face, and flinch from the pain, and then take it off. Her eyes were tightly closed. A long soft moan, hardly audible, was the only sound she made.

Delamare tried again in German.

'I think you must have spoken with Professor Brande in this language, but if you would rather speak in a different language and can tell us which, we can arrange for an interpreter. Meanwhile, is there anything we can provide for your comfort? Would you like some water, would you like a rug?'

No response. Apart from the constant quiet moan of pain and misery, she might have been asleep, or dead, he thought – but

228

no, not dead. She would have vanished. Was she perhaps not a dæmon at all?

'Don't,' said his dæmon.

'Don't what?'

'You were going to touch her.'

'Simply to see whether—'

'Don't do it. She would die at once.'

'Die of what?'

'Of shame.'

'That would settle the question.'

'But dishonourably. She's certainly a dæmon. Don't touch her.'

Delamare sat back to watch the stricken creature. She seemed like someone at the very limits of exhaustion and agony, who knows she is alone, and no one will ever help.

'But not *his* dæmon,' Delamare said suddenly.

'Ah!' said the owl-dæmon. 'Then . . . whose?'

He sat forward and said in German, 'Gottfried Brande was not your person, was he?'

The dæmon curled her spine around and tried to put both front feet over her face, but had to stop, because it clearly hurt so much.

'Tell me. How did you come to pose as his dæmon? Why did he pretend you were?'

Delamare regretted, now, that he hadn't attended Brande's lecture, spoken to him beforehand, watched how he was with the dæmon.

She made no attempt to respond, but tears were spilling from her eyes.

He said, 'I think you understand me. You are alone now, and in great pain. I have offered to try and relieve it. We have experts here in the treatment of ailing dæmons. There are medications, there are practitioners of the talking cure, there is even surgery. No dæmon need suffer a moment longer than necessary.'

The tears were pooling on the floor beside the dæmon's broken face. Delamare was convinced now that she understood him.

'If there is anything you'd like to say, perhaps about your original person, perhaps about your homeland—'

The dæmon raised her head and murmured, '*Nichts.*'

And then she vanished as if she'd been made of smoke. All that remained was the pool of tears.

'What did she say? What was that last word?'

'*Nothing.* She had nothing to say and she said it.'

Delamare sat back in his chair. 'So much for that,' he said. 'Well, we shall learn from it. You think it was Persian, whatever it was she said?'

'The last word was German, but yes, the rest was Persian, I think.'

Delamare stood up and opened the door. 'She died,' he told the attendant.

He set off along the corridor, and after a moment his dæmon glided to his shoulder. Delamare gave orders as he left the building, summoning various officials and aides to a meeting at *La Maison Juste,* to begin immediately. A golden idea was already forming in his mind.

*

Leenart Karpelin to Oakley Street:

The sensation caused by the death of Gottfried Brande shows no sign of fading. The official narrative says that Brande was struck down by an apoplexy, the shock of which caused his dæmon to tear herself away from him, mad with fear. She was given refuge in La Maison Juste *while doctors attended to Brande, but despite the best medical care he and the dæmon died within the hour, simultaneously.*

The text of his lecture has been carefully preserved by the Magisterium, and they are said to be considering the possibility of publishing it in his memory.

The dæmon business remains a mystery. Everyone who saw the event knows that Brande died at once; no one believes that his dæmon was in any sense 'normal'. Stories of her behaviour after his death spread and multiply. Some say she still haunts the Chapel of the Sacred Presence. A service of exorcism has been requested by a delegation of the faithful.

A small observation: Marcel Delamare, whose style and bearing are proverbially immaculate, is becoming careless with his dress. A small stain on his lapel, which I noticed yesterday, is still there today, and his fingernails were dirty. I mention this purely because it is so unusual.

*

'*Publishing* it? Really?'

'Oh, not as it is, of course not. But I can see several advantages in a rewritten version, echoing and even anticipating various views of our own.'

Delamare and his dæmon were in his private rooms at *La Maison Juste*, examining the text of the notes Brande had with him when he died. His hotel room had been searched, and other pages of manuscript found in his luggage lay on the desk in front of the President.

'When have we got time to do that?' said his owl-dæmon.

'A young scholar – Maximov, say . . .'

'I don't trust him.'

'Someone else, then. A postdoctoral student would jump at the chance.'

'Same objection applies. Marcel, the only mind that could possibly put this confused and contradictory rant in order is yours. But why would you take time out of—'

'Because there are insights here that are quite new. What he says about language . . .'

'Steal them, then. Simply take them. Then burn the papers.'

'He was going in our direction, that's the point.'

'Put it all in the safe. Lock it away and come back to it when the girl is dealt with.'

Delamare leaned back in his chair and drummed his fingers on the desk. 'Yes,' he said. 'This evening the girl will arrive in Baku, and then that will soon be over.'

14

Dynamic Illustration

When she bought the tickets for the journey, Lyra had picked up a timetable from the ticket office, which gave their time of arrival in Baku as ten-thirty in the evening of the second day of travel. She was inclined to trust the timetable, because every stop they had made so far was precisely at the time advertised. She woke up when the bus stopped to refuel . . . somewhere; there were wooded hills, and she thought she could see a lake; she regretted very much not having a map. And a book to read, or even a magazine or a newspaper.

An attendant brought coffee and pastries, and folded the bed back into a seat. Lyra ate and drank comfortably in the morning light and watched the landscape change as the great bus moved through it, climbing gradually as the road passed woods of oak and poplar and fields of wheat, overtaking donkey carts, once having to wait for a shepherd to move his flock aside.

The road . . . Lyra found herself thinking that all roads led to other roads, which she knew at once was not an original thought, or even a very interesting one, but it put her in mind of the pack of cards the old Turkish gentleman had given her, the Myriorama. There was a road illustrated there, one road that went on for ever.

She took the battered pack from her rucksack and spread the cards out on the table. Where had they come from? Where were they printed? The drawings looked early-nineteenth-century, from a time of romantic poetry and the coming together of landscape and sensibility; the backgrounds were mostly European, German forests, Italian mountains, a Mediterranean coast; the people moving about their business were farmers, soldiers, merchants, brigands perhaps, children at play, a shepherd and his flock holding up the progress of a horse-drawn coach—

Like the shepherd and his flock just then, holding up the bus.

'Well,' she said. 'What does *that* mean?'

She spoke quietly but aloud, astonished into speech by the coincidence, and of course it was a coincidence; but what was a coincidence, anyway? Where did the *meaning* of it come from?

She remembered the process of learning how to read the alethiometer, something she'd done twice: once in her childhood, guided by instinct or guesswork or play, and then again after her return to Oxford from the north, toiling at the long, arduous, painstaking work of bringing the meaning into expressible consciousness.

Was that what the imagination did? See connections between things, connections otherwise invisible, and find a meaning in them? The connection between the shepherd and his flock who held up the coach in the picture and the ones she'd seen a few minutes before on the real road: the meaning of that lay in the fact that she saw the similarity, not in the things themselves, which, unless she saw them, might as well be contingent and meaningless. She had to be part of the process for the meaning to exist at all.

'Is this your new alethiometer?' said Asta.

Malcolm's dæmon had been dozing in the sun on the seat beside her, and Lyra had nearly forgotten she was there. Everything in the past couple of days had happened so quickly, in a frenzy of danger and fear, that just to sit and think, to be still, felt like a sort of beneficent vertigo. Or else it was like being lifted off the earth in a balloon like Lee Scoresby's, and finding an expected companion there; and now she must find a way of talking to Asta that didn't get confused with the connection she used to have with Pan.

'Sort of, I hope,' she said in answer to Asta's question. 'Did Malcolm ever use an alethiometer?'

'No, but we used to watch Hannah Relf use hers. You ask a question by combining three symbols?'

'Yes. Then you have to try and make sense of the answer.'

'Why three? Because there are three hands, I know, but why not two or four? Why did they give it three hands?'

'Because four's too many, and two's not enough,' said Lyra, remembering something she'd heard in a lecture about narrative patterns in folk tales. 'No, I mean it just works perfectly well with three. Combined with the depth of the symbol-ranges, you can say absolutely anything.'

'You might be able to say it, and it might be confirmed by the rest of the system, but you still couldn't be sure it was true.'

'Why not?'

'In any system, like a system of mathematics for example, you can prove a lot of things, but there are always things you can't prove.'

'Is that true?'

'It's not only true, it's been proved. You can prove that there are things you can't prove.'

'True things?'

'Yes. They're true, but you have to look outside that system to prove it.'

Lyra thought about that. 'So three pictures, or four, or ten thousand, it wouldn't make any difference.'

'No. And I suppose it would be hard to fit yet another piece of mechanism in a small case too.'

'There's that, as well.'

Asta stepped up on to the table and looked at the cards. 'But this . . . What's it called?'

'It says "Myriorama" on the box.'

'With this you could have as many cards as you liked. You wouldn't have to stick to three.'

'I don't think it's for the same sort of thing, really . . . The man who gave it to me used it to tell a story to a little boy. Besides, these are pictures of things happening, illustrations, not symbols like the ones on the alethiometer, where they have definite meanings, layers of them.'

'These pictures could have meanings too. But they'd be dynamic and not static.'

'What d'you mean?'

'Well, a symbol like the beehive on the alethiometer, for example, it has many meanings, but each one is fixed . . .'

'Yes, they are. That's right. The beehive means productive work, to start with. Sweetness. Light. Order. Topographical information . . . Yes, they are fixed. That's why there are books with them all laid out in order. There has to be a common understanding of what things mean, or else it wouldn't work at all.'

'But the pictures on the cards here are different, as you said. They show things happening. Illustrations. People moving. Encounters. Events. Things happening in time. That's why the man could use them to tell a story. It would be harder to tell a story with the symbols on the alethiometer.'

'Yes,' Lyra said, thinking about it. 'But then you don't use the alethiometer for that. You use it to see the truth about a situation. The essential elements. That's why it's called a truth measurer.'

'That thing you were using to cut the cell door open,' Asta said. 'That was part of it, wasn't it?'

'Yes, it was.'

'What happened?'

Lyra told her about al-Khan al-Azraq, and the one-eyed Scythian with the captive dæmon in a cage, and about how she'd held the alethiometer to her cheek, loving the beautiful thing before she took it apart. Her eyes brimmed with tears as she spoke. Cutting the cage open, waking the man, seeing him snatch the alethiometer and run away, only to be snatched himself from the top of the staircase by a gryphon; it might have happened years ago, not just a few days.

'That's all you've got left?'

'And the glass. Well, it did keep getting stolen; I was lucky to have it as long as I did.'

She unfolded the little sheet of paper to show Asta the needle. The dæmon leaned down close to look at it and touched it with a delicate claw.

'You need something better than that piece of paper to keep it in.'

'I know, but . . .'

'We'll find something. We'll make something.'

'That's what Malcolm would do, I suppose.'

'Of course.'

'I wonder if he could make another alethiometer . . .'

'If he had the time, and the tools, and the gold, and the – whatever that needle's made of. I'm sure he could.'

Lyra put the needle away. 'Have you ever been away from him for this long before?'

'No, never. It was enough to know that we could if we needed to.'

'Did you ever know anyone else who could separate?'

'No.'

'So you've never seen one of these.'

She found the little black notebook, the *Clavicula Adiumenti*, and laid it on the table. Asta opened it with a claw and scanned it closely.

'Names and addresses . . . All the way to Chorasmia.'

'Names of people who can separate.'

'How did you get this?'

Lyra told her about discovering it in the rucksack of the murdered botanist, and about learning what it was, and about meeting the sorcerer Agrippa in Prague and learning the name of Princess Cantacuzino in Smyrna.

'Is there anyone in Baku?' said Asta.

Lyra turned the pages and found a name and address:

Horace Green, 23 Villa Victor Hugo, Hüseyn Javid Prospekt, Baku.

'English name,' Lyra said. 'Maybe we'll try him.' She closed the book and went on, 'It's odd, though. You'd think we'd still be aware of each other, I mean dæmons and their people, be aware of what each other was thinking, even if we weren't close . . .'

'But a lot of that understanding of each other comes from seeing each other's face and hearing our voices and physical things like that. We think with our bodies, we understand with our bodies, not just with some abstract mind thing. I can guess what Malcolm might be thinking or feeling, and I'd probably be right, but I'd only know for certain if he was nearby and I could see it in his eyes and hear it in his voice.'

'Yes . . . But suppose if there was some awful, I don't know, accident or something, we might feel that. When Pan saw a murder in Oxford I think I felt something then, a shock, something like that. At the same time as he did.'

'Yes, and if it was a big enough shock—'

'Then we'd both die.'

They both fell silent for a moment.

'The worst thing,' Lyra said, 'would be not to be with them, if . . .'

She didn't finish the sentence but she didn't have to. Asta knew what she meant.

There was a knock at the door.

Lyra blinked and sat up and gathered herself. 'Come in,' she said.

It was Ionides. He came in quickly and slid into the other seat.

'There is a Magisterium agent on the bus,' he said quietly. 'One at least. Probably more.'

'Someone you recognised?'

'Yes.'

'Did he see you?'

'No. I don't think so.'

'Who is he? When did you see him before?'

'Two years ago in Bucharest. Then he called himself Dumitriu.'

'Did he know you? D'you think he'll recognise you now?'

He shook his head. 'No reason why he should. We never spoke then.'

'How did you know he was a Magisterium agent?'

'In Bucharest I saw him passing some papers to a man I knew was from the Magisterium. Later I saw them together with a third man. He was not being careful, which is why I noticed him.'

'Perhaps you'd better not go to your seat again. Stay in here.'

'No, Miss Silver. I can watch him from my seat. In about one hour we stop for ten minutes. I shall watch him especially then. You have your little stick?'

'Right here.'

'If you have to use it, strike him very hard.'

He listened at the door and then left and closed it quietly.

'Well,' Lyra said.

'It's a bit strange,' said Asta. 'I'd have thought we were moving out of the reach of the Magisterium. The Angelus bell, for one thing.'

'I didn't really understand that.'

'It was one of the things that Calvin forbade when he became Pope. The last Pope. The Magisterium's control has always been so complete that little flickers of dissent used to be put out at once. And in Pisidia, the murders at the rose growers' meeting . . . Of course, you don't know about that; we're still catching up with each other.'

She told Lyra about the meeting in the theatre and the attack by the men from the mountains, and how Malcolm had killed their leader.

'He just – killed him?'

'The man had already killed an innocent rose-grower, and they would have killed more. It was the best thing to do. The only thing, really. It stopped everything in its tracks.'

'Has Malcolm . . . killed many people?'

'He killed one to keep you alive.'

'Oh . . . Bonneville. Yes.'

Lyra put her hand on the stick, Pequeno, and remembered Farder Coram saying that if good people wanted to defeat evil ones, they would have to be unscrupulous. Perhaps being unscrupulous might include killing people, sometimes. It wasn't easy to think about.

She gathered together the Myriorama cards and then drew one out at random. It showed a young woman walking, as if lost in thought, along the bank of a river where a boy was fishing.

Asta saw what she was looking at. 'Well, what does that mean?' she said.

'I suppose . . . That's me, and the boy is Malcolm, and . . .'

'What's he hoping to catch?'

'Truth. It's the river of time. Truth is elusive, like a fish.'

'You're making it up.'

'It's true enough,' Lyra said.

*

OS to MP

In haste – bad news. I was betrayed, but they won't find this. No more from me though for now. Straighten up and fly right.

    Godwin

15

AN ISLAND IN THE FLOOD

Malcolm and Pan were at the worktable in their quarters. They had an oil light burning on the table because the sky was dark with heavy restless clouds, and gusts of wind made the shutters shake and the lamp flame shiver. Malcolm, a rug around his shoulders for warmth, was making progress with the alethiometer; he had taken the mechanism out, with great difficulty because the case was so distorted, and he was surprised to find it quite uncomplicated. The three wheels were connected to the three hands on the dial with simple gears that were luckily still intact. He could find no mechanism that moved the needle, but since the needle was missing, the matter was irrelevant for the moment.

'When she moved the hands,' he said to Pan, 'did the needle move at all?'

'No. It just sort of hung there. If the glass hadn't been there it looked as if you could just blow on it and it would turn around. It only moved when she thought about the question and when the hands were in the right positions to ask it. Then it looked as if – well, it looked as if it moved all by itself, without any machinery. It didn't wobble or drift or swing loose. It always looked alive to us, the way a clock *doesn't* look alive. Is there no mechanism for it?'

'No. It seems to have swung freely. Maybe there's something missing, but I can't even see a place for any missing mechanism to go. Is there a piece of silk in the cedar chest? A scarf, a shawl, something like that?'

Pan jumped into the chest and rummaged among the things there. 'Here you are. Black too, like the cloth Lyra always used to wrap it in.' He leaped back up to the table.

'I'm going to keep the mechanism aside,' Malcolm explained, wrapping it carefully in the cloth. 'Not mention it to the Queen. It's not gold, so she wouldn't be interested anyway. Later on I'll study it more closely, but for the moment—'

'Look,' said Pan. 'Words again.'

He was looking at the resonating lodestone, which was lying next to the tools on the table. Glenys Godwin's words were appearing as they watched. Malcolm picked it up, and Pan came to perch next to his arm and read it under the lamplight.

'*Betrayed . . .*' Malcolm read aloud. 'That's bad. Damn it! If she had time to write this, she must have got away, but . . . And here I am stuck on a bloody mountain. *Straighten up and fly right?* What's that mean?'

'It's a song about a buzzard and a monkey. She must mean us and the gryphons.'

'She's going to pass her stone on to someone else. I hope to hell she manages to . . .'

Malcolm closed his eyes. His temples were throbbing, and he could sense the kind of tense anbaric crackle and flicker just under the threshold of perception that often announced the appearance of the spangled ring, his migraine aurora, as he'd thought it was called. Perhaps it was because they were so high on the mountain, but the pressure of the atmosphere seemed to have dropped rapidly.

Then Pan said, 'There's a storm coming.'

He'd jumped up on to the parapet, where the wind raised his fur with invisible fingers. Malcolm joined him, wrapping the rug around himself against the bitter cold, and watched as clouds like mountains darkened and loomed over the high horizon, and theatrical beams of sunlight flared and burst free for a few moments to touch this snowy summit or that one so that they glared and vanished like signal lights.

A powerful blast of wind reached their eyrie, shockingly sudden, and threatened to topple Pan from the balustrade. Malcolm's hand reached out at once and held him for a moment, and then he took it away. Neither of them mentioned it.

Lightning, with a thousand forks and rivulets, lashed the black air ahead of them; and three seconds later the thunder exploded, making the mountains ring with echoes and shaking the very substance of the earth. Pan usually loved storms, and Malcolm enjoyed them too, as long as he was not on the water in a boat, and the immense mass of Damāvand should have been a mighty enough shelter. But they both felt the walls of their little room shudder and tremble when the next roll of thunder came, this time simultaneously with the dazzle of the lightning.

'What are they doing?' Pan cried, and he had to cry out or not be heard at all, because a monsoon's worth of rain had begun to pelt the mountain, with the sound of a hundred thousand hooves on hard ground.

'What? Who?' Malcolm shouted back, trying to see where Pan was pointing.

'Gryphons! Flying out into the storm!'

'Where? Oh, yes – five or six of them – surely they can't fly in this—'

But they were, struggling, beating their massive wings, surging up only to drop suddenly as if into an abyss, and then beating their way up again, like swimmers in a stormy sea, fighting with every breath and heartbeat.

'Where are they going?' Pan shouted.

It wasn't unusual to see them flying around the mountain, keeping watch, or bearing messages, or bringing news from the outer kingdom, but it was unexpected to see them risking their lives – as they must have been – in such a storm as this. Malcolm and Pan shaded their eyes from the dashing rain and followed the unsteady flight of the five or so gryphons past the cliffs and chasms of the storm, which had grown from a local darkening of the air to a vast convulsion in a matter of minutes.

Most of the light they saw by came from the frequent explosions of lightning, but from time to time a great rent would appear in the clouds, and as if from another planet a beam of sunlight would strike down into the roiling mass of vapour and darkness. It was in the light of one such beam that Malcolm saw another figure, much smaller than the gryphons, speeding forward through the storm, making for the mountain, dropping down only to be borne up again on a wild current of air, sliding sideways and darting through the turbulence like a minnow in a stream.

'Look!' Malcolm shouted over the screaming of the wind.

In the same moment Pan saw, and cried, 'A witch! A witch!'

Malcolm strained his eyes, frowning, squinting against the wind, dashing the rain away from his eyes.

'Yes – I can see her now – they're going to attack her!'

The five or so gryphons were struggling in the air at least as much as the witch, because their great wings were more easily caught by the savage gusts of wind than the little figure on her cloud-pine branch, who was speeding like a swallow through the gulfs and canyons of the sky.

But they were powerful. She was riding on the storm, but they were smashing through it. And she was in their sights; she was their target.

'One of them . . .' said Pan, and Malcolm held his breath, because the first gryphon had flown close enough to reach out a claw and slash at her; but he had to rear back in the air to do it, and a gust of wind caught him and threw him aside. The witch was reaching for something behind her shoulder – they could only see by the flashes of lightning – and then she had a bow in her hands, and shot an arrow at the next gryphon to rear up close.

He fell back. They could hear his scream of rage and pain, and then he fell, spiralling downwards towards a pinnacle of rock and smashing into it with a force they could almost feel.

Pan was clutching Malcolm's arm, and neither of them knew it. Instead, all the force of their attention was focused on the little figure of the witch, swooping up and diving down again to avoid the slashing claws of the gryphons, who were enraged now. Arrow after arrow she shot, and most of them sailed harmlessly away in the wind; but another one found its target in the throat of a gryphon who tried to dive on her from above. Screaming, he lost control of his flight and just missed her as he fell.

She twisted out of the way but then found the remaining gryphons closing in, and dropped her bow to seize the pine branch in both hands and wrench it up towards the summit – towards their window, with its glowing light – towards the parapet, with the three gryphons straining up after her, buffeted and bowled sideways but always behind her, always surging up, their mighty wings striking at the air and slamming it behind them, their eagle beaks wide to tear the flesh that was so close—

'This way! This way!' Pan cried, and Malcolm reached out over the precipice, clinging to the parapet, calling with Pan, and the witch was nearly close enough to grab his hand. Just below, just behind, those glaring eyes, monstrous and inhuman, and screams and roars of fury—

'Take my hand! Now!' Malcolm shouted, hurling his voice into the wind, and seized her outstretched right hand, pulling her up and over the parapet as the first gryphon reared up and snatched at the balustrade with giant claws, lion claws, but they slipped and lost their grip in the lashing rain, and the massive creature was blown aside by a mass of air as heavy as a tidal wave.

The witch and Malcolm both fell to the floor, and Pan caught her slender pine-branch as the wind lifted it, and dragged it over the parapet and into the quiet of the room.

Malcolm's wound was hurting badly: he had wrenched his hip

as he pulled the witch to safety. He struggled up and turned to help her.

He was thinking: a *witch* . . . Such a strange being. He'd never been so close – never even seen . . .

But he had. Out of the darkness of time, in all this urgency, a memory came: and there it was. All those years ago: the baby Lyra in the canoe asleep in Alice's arms, Pan as a dormouse curled up between the paws of Alice's dog-dæmon Ben, the battered *Belle Sauvage* tied up and rocking softly, Malcolm exhausted but awake on the little island under the moon with the great flood sweeping blackly onwards all around them; and standing only a few feet away, the slender haughty figure of the woman from the far north, the delicate coronet of flowers around her hair, the branch of cloud-pine on the rocks at her feet: Tilda Vasara, queen of the witches in the – what region was it?

'Tilda Vasara? Is it you? Have I got your name right?'

She was drenched with rain, her hair was disordered, her black garments clung to her body and her thighs; and she looked not a day older than the young woman whose beauty had dazed the little boy who'd come through the flood, even to the little coronet of yellow flowers around her head. He struggled up and gave her his hand, and then they both looked at the window, at which the gryphons were still flying and screaming and beating their wings.

He helped her up, and then went to lean out and close the shutters, ignoring the great creatures still scrambling to get a foothold on the wet stone of the parapet. Pan took hold of one heavy curtain in his teeth and pulled it across, and Malcolm closed the other, so the sounds outside faded a little.

'I didn't expect you to forget,' said the witch.

'No, I wouldn't forget. Nor shall I forget this. Why have you come here?'

'To speak with the Queen. Once I knew that you were here, I thought my mission had a chance of success.'

'How did you know we were here?'

'My dæmon saw you on the back of the gryphon prince.'

Another memory: the Arctic tern he'd seen high in the sky above as dawn broke over Mount Damāvand – linked to a different memory: the white bird-dæmon whispering to Alice's Ben as he guarded the baby Lyra in the canoe.

'Where is he now?'

'Above the storm.'

Malcolm pushed back his hair, which was trailing over his forehead and dripping into his eyes. He took a deep breath.

'Will you sit down?' he said. 'We can offer you a chair, or those furs. Are you cold?'

'Never cold, but thank you. The furs will do.'

She sat down, as she seemed to do everything, gracefully. Malcolm the man had a more complicated response to her than Malcolm the boy; even in this time of astonishment and his continuing sense of great danger, he couldn't be unaware of her pale smooth skin, the supple muscles of her arms and shoulders, the way the wet silk clung to her flanks and her thighs. *Put it out of your mind*, he thought, *permanently.*

'Why do you want to talk to the Queen?' said Pantalaimon.

'I want her help for my people, and I want her to accept our help in return. I want to know if they are aware of the danger that faces all the people of the air.'

'They didn't seem very keen to welcome you,' said Malcolm.

'Something is happening to make them fearful. In normal times we take no notice of them, and they of us. Our realms hardly touch. We have different concerns and different interests.'

Malcolm thought that he'd written almost exactly those words to Glenys Godwin only a day or so before. 'But what's happened to change that?' he said.

'The winds are failing. The air is bad. This will affect us all, and we need to talk about it.'

'The air is bad?' said Pan. 'But it seems . . . And the wind outside is as strong as ever, surely?'

246

'Other winds. This will take some time to explain, and by the time—'

A loud knocking thundered at the door, almost drowning the real storm outside.

'Let me speak,' said Malcolm to the witch. 'Don't say a word till we're in the presence of the Queen.'

He opened the door wide, and stood firmly on the threshold. The vizier and three guards made as if to enter, but before they could say a word or move more than a step, Malcolm said firmly, 'Why are you treating Queen Tilda Vasara, my guest, with such discourtesy?'

'She has shot and killed two of my guards!'

'And do you blame her? She came here in peace, to seek an audience with your Queen on a matter of profound importance to all the people of the air, and you send out a squadron of warriors to attack and kill her! Of course she defended herself. Now take us to Queen Shahrnavāz at once, and behave with the proper courtesy.'

The vizier was speechless. He didn't move. Malcolm turned back to the witch and offered his hand to help her up; she got to her feet with that incomparable grace and took the cloud-pine branch that Pan held out for her as if it were a sceptre. She was as much a queen as Shahrnavāz, and the vizier could see it. He stood aside for them to walk ahead of him, and all three followed without any haste into the corridor and along towards the great chamber: the witch in the centre, with Malcolm and Pan on either side of her.

As they went, they could hear voices raised in the chamber and beyond, and the sound of running feet, and the ringing of a deep gong some way off. The storm was still raging outside: even inside the mountain they could hear the howling of the wind and the crash of thunder.

'Where is your realm?' Malcolm said to the witch very quietly, and she replied, 'Lake Onega.'

He nodded. The gryphon-voices were raised in argument or command, as if they were debating something furiously. Malcolm hadn't heard them speaking among themselves, and was curious about their language, but there was no time to think about that, for they had nearly arrived in the great chamber.

One good sign, he thought: the carpet had been laid. This was an occasion of state. They were not likely to be put to death just yet.

There were two wooden stools, ornately carved, set a few feet apart and facing the space where the Queen had stood to receive them before.

The vizier took it all in at once, like the practised courtier he was, and led Malcolm and the witch-queen forward, indicating that Malcolm should take the right-hand stool and Tilda Vasara the left. There was a bustle in the corridor beyond, murmurs and whispers in gryphon-voices, and then all the sounds fell silent as the Queen came in.

The gryphons' eagle-features didn't make for a rich range of expression: ferocity was about all they could project. But something in the Queen's bearing, perhaps the slow cold way she looked from Malcolm to Tilda Vasara and back again, told him that she was on the verge of great anger.

Malcolm bowed calmly. The witch inclined her head. Shahrnavāz settled couchant on the floor, and indicated that they should sit. Tilda Vasara did so with the lightness of a feather: Malcolm, whose hip was troubling him greatly, was much clumsier and almost fell as he felt for the stool.

Don't be embarrassed, he thought. *Just speak with all the dignity you can find.*

'Your Majesty,' he said firmly, 'may I present Queen Tilda Vasara, the ruler of the witch-clans in the region of Lake Onega.'

'And where is that?' the gryphon-queen demanded.

'In the far north-west,' said Tilda Vasara calmly, 'just south of where the ice begins.'

'And why go to my artificer before you spoke to me?'

'He is an artificer?' said the witch, in apparent surprise. 'To my people he is a man of great importance.'

And Pan said, 'In the realms of gold, an artificer *is* a man of great importance.'

Both queens turned to him, and Malcolm marvelled at his impudence.

Shahrnavāz slowly nodded.

Malcolm went on: 'Queen Tilda Vasara sought shelter with me, because she was being attacked by five of your warriors. No doubt they were under orders, but those odds were shameful. She has a message of great importance for all the people of the air, from the most powerful to the least. It needs to be heard. Queen Shahrnavāz, you have been hospitable to me; I ask you to extend that generosity to this gallant queen of the witches, and hear what she has to say.'

'Speak, then,' said the queen of the gryphons.

'Thank you, Queen Shahrnavāz,' Tilda Vasara began. 'For some time, witches of every region of the north have been aware of changes in the sky. Winds are wilder than they used to be, or else they fail altogether. The air is tainted and stale. Freshness has left the atmosphere, by small degrees at first, so small as to be hardly noticeable, but it is getting worse. Sunsets are lurid with colours never seen before; birds migrate at strange seasons, or die in their thousands from diseases unknown to our healers. Tell me, great queen, have your people not noticed the same changes?'

Silence throughout the great hall. The storm continued to shriek and howl and batter the mountain, but not a creature moved. All stood, or like the Queen remained couchant, and watched Tilda Vasara as she spoke with such seriousness.

Shahrnavāz said, 'Tilda Vasara, you speak the truth. The matters you mention have disturbed us too. Now tell me this: do you speak for your clan alone, or are you here to represent all the witches of the north?'

'When the moon was last new, all the clan-queens of the north held a great meeting by the river Lena. We agreed that these changes I describe, and others we have noticed, are beyond the power of witches alone to deal with. They must be affecting all the people of the air. Only a great alliance, more comprehensive than any we have entered before, would have the power to face it and deal with it. Other queens were sent east and west and further north; I was chosen to come south to the great kingdom of the gryphons. It was a lucky chance that here in your palace was residing this man, to whom I had spoken some years ago, when he was young. I know him to be a courageous and truthful representative of his people, and I thought he would be able to do what he has now done, and speak for me to Your Majesty.'

'How did you know he was here?'

'We know many things, Queen Shahrnavāz. We have even been able to discover something about the origin of these troubles.'

The gryphon-courtiers and warriors in the great hall were all still attending with passionate interest. In any other court, Malcolm thought, it would be usual at this point for the principals to retire to a smaller space and discuss the business privately, but clearly Shahrnavāz was happy to continue talking in front of everyone there, and probably the witches, too, were used to open councils. Pan was sitting close by on the floor, turning to each speaker in turn, fierce with interest, and no doubt, Malcolm thought, wondering how all this would affect Lyra. Well, so was he.

'Tell us about the origin, then,' said the gryphon-queen. 'What has happened to bring this about? This is not a recent matter. We have noticed changes in the atmosphere for millennia.'

'And of course so have we. There are many natural things that affect the air: volcanoes, sunspots, meteor strikes, ocean currents. We are familiar with those, as you are. Nature usually rallies, and the atmosphere recovers. But for three centuries now there has been another matter at work. I say three centuries; some of our clan-queens would say two millennia. It's impalpable and silent.

It drifts in invisible clouds and can't be described or fought or destroyed. It's not possible to describe with our language, maybe with any language.'

'Then why are you talking about it?' said Shahrnavāz. 'This kind of chatter is pointless. The phenomenon you describe might as well not exist.'

'May I speak, Your Majesty?' said Pantalaimon.

The gryphon-queen looked down at the dæmon, so small and so confident, and glared but said nothing.

Pan went on, 'I have learned that the wisdom of the gryphons distinguishes between an outer kingdom and an inner kingdom. The outer kingdom is the world we can travel through and measure and make maps of, and gryphons and witches and humans alike can share and understand it. The inner kingdom comprises everything to the distance of the furthest star, and includes the mysteries of the heart and the mind. The witches have a similar understanding. What Queen Tilda Vasara is describing is a matter of the inner kingdom as well as the outer. Unless we realise that, it will be hard to come to an agreement about anything.'

Before Shahrnavāz could speak, Tilda Vasara said, 'The dæmon is right, Your Majesty. I believe that some men and women have another phrase for your inner kingdom: they call it the secret commonwealth. The influence I've been describing affects that part of our world, your inner kingdom, the realm of the understanding.'

Queen Shahrnavāz turned to Pan again. 'When we spoke before you told me about this thing you have been searching for, dæmon, the thing you call the imagination: tell me again what you said.'

'I believe it helps us to move between the inner and the outer kingdoms, Your Majesty. It is very much a matter of the secret commonwealth.'

The gryphon-queen said nothing for almost a minute. She bowed her head to gaze towards the floor, and then turned to look at Tilda Vasara, and Pan, and finally at Malcolm.

Then she raised her eyes to look directly at the vizier.

'Summon Master Ruzbeh,' she said.

The vizier moved to give a quiet order to one of the guards, and then returned to his place. No one spoke or moved. Malcolm tried to estimate how much time was passing; it must have been five minutes, he thought, before there was a stirring among the gryphons, and a murmur of talk, and then the ranks parted to let through a very old man, a human being, not a gryphon. His dæmon was a jerboa, who sat on his shoulder, bright-eyed and curious. The old man was leaning on two sticks, and Malcolm stood to offer his stool, a gesture that pleased the old man and caused the Queen to stare at the vizier again; another few moments passed; and then came a gryphon with a third stool, which Malcolm took gratefully.

Queen Shahrnavāz spoke to Master Ruzbeh in Persian, of which Malcolm could understand enough to know that she was giving a summary of what had been said, and accurately at that. The old man listened closely, his head bent towards her, which made Malcolm think he might be a little deaf; but his eyes turned to Malcolm from time to time, and to Pan, and to Tilda Vasara: ancient eyes that glittered with speculation.

When the Queen had finished her account of the discussion so far, Master Ruzbeh nodded and said a word or two in the same language. Then he turned to the witch.

'I have no northern languages, I regret,' he said, his voice soft and hoarse but clear. 'I hope we shall be able to speak in English.'

'Yes, that would be best,' she replied.

'Is that the case for you too, sir?' he said to Pan, who managed to contain his surprise and say:

'Oh, yes, that would be best for me too.'

Then to Malcolm the old councillor said in Persian, 'You can understand my language, I see, but it would be easier in yours.'

Malcolm nodded, and Master Ruzbeh continued in English.

'If Her Majesty is in agreement, we shall continue like this. You have been speaking about a phenomenon that I have not myself experienced. One reason for that could be that my senses are dull with age. But your people, Your Majesty, have spoken to me about changes like those you have been discussing, changes they have noticed in the skies. Things that would mean less, perhaps, to those of us who are creatures of the ground. I have read much and heard much more in the course of my life, and never has this or anything like it appeared in any history, any poem, any chronicle that I know. Furthermore, reports of it have increased rapidly in the past weeks.'

He stopped to rest for a moment. Malcolm could hear the rattle of the old man's breath in his lungs.

'One witness whose reports are detailed and accurate,' Master Ruzbeh went on, 'has noticed that in the recent past this depletion in the richness of the air sometimes occurs in regions where there has been evidence of sulphurous or fulminating activity at the level of the ground. No cause has been observed for this new effect, though; it seems to be some eruptive or explosive phenomenon, possibly volcanic in origin, though not necessarily occurring in volcanic regions.'

Malcolm felt a jolt at once, and he knew that Pan felt it too: they were both remembering Glenys Godwin's messages on the lodestone. He sensed Tilda Vasara turning to look at him.

Master Ruzbeh continued. 'In the absence of any more information than that, Queen Shahrnavāz, I can only speculate. This activity might be the cause of the decay of the air, or it might be a result of it. It might not be connected with it at all except by coincidence. Without further knowledge, speculation is all I can offer, and I can assure you that my speculation would be more or less valueless.' The old man paused to clear his throat; it took him some time, and his voice was weaker when he spoke. 'There is a word,' he went on, 'which I have heard mentioned in this context, but whose meaning is a mystery to me. It is the word *alkahest*.

Your Majesty, my knowledge is small, and its boundaries firm. I can tell you no more.'

Another jolt. Malcolm looked at Pan, and knew they were both remembering the lodestone message, for the second time.

Queen Shahrnavāz said, 'Humans have been causing explosions for centuries. If they do it to find gold, we let them. These explosions you talk of, Master Ruzbeh: are they in gold-bearing regions? Or are they searching for something else?'

'I have seen it happen,' said Tilda Vasara, before the old man could speak. 'Some uniformed men caused an explosion near a spring that was sacred, and killed a shaman who tried to stop them. We could not understand why anyone would benefit from such an act. There was nothing valuable in the ground. We killed the men, of course. But we've heard of others doing similar things elsewhere.'

Malcolm looked at Pan, who nodded; and then he turned to Shahrnavāz and Tilda Vasara and took a deep breath and said, 'Your Majesties, may I speak?'

Those royal gryphon-eyes, and the green eyes of the witch, might have made anyone quail, but he faced them calmly, and summoned all the clarity he could command.

'From what I have seen,' he began, 'from what I have heard, and from what I can deduce, at various points on the surface of the earth there are places where it is possible to pass out of this world and into another. Places like this are rare and hard to find, and when they are known about they are often revered by the few people who know, and who try to keep them secret. The explosions are the work of the Magisterium, of which you have no doubt heard. Their aim in destroying the openings can only be guessed at, but there are clues in what they have said and other things they have done. The word *alkahest*, which Master Ruzbeh mentioned, has also appeared in connection with this subject, but, like him, I have no information about what it means.

'However, from what Tilda Vasara and others have told me, it seems that the openings have been important to your peoples in, among other things, maintaining the goodness of the air. That being so, the Magisterium is doing evil work in trying to close them, and what we should do – gryphons and witches together, and we few humans who know about it – is to form an alliance to frustrate the work of the Magisterium, and of any other human organisation that shares their aims, such as the group known as the Men from the Mountains, and commercial bodies like Thuringia Potash, who seek only to make money. Our task is to protect the openings between the worlds, whose closure and destruction is causing so much damage. That is our task.'

'One moment, artificer,' said the Queen. 'Let us be as clear as we can. What, precisely, is causing the damage we have been hearing about, this degradation of the air? The explosions? Or simply the fact that these openings are being closed?'

Malcolm nodded deeply, and said, 'I apologise for not speaking more precisely. Master Ruzbeh was correct a few moments ago to point out that it's not always easy to distinguish a result from a cause. Besides, I would add that some phenomena have more causes than one. The degradation of the air, for example, is unlikely to be only the result of the explosions. As Queen Tilda Vasara explained, changes in the air have been troubling witches for centuries, whereas these particular explosions are much more recent in date.

'Because of what I've learned elsewhere, I am inclined to believe that although the explosions and the decay of the air are connected, it is not as cause and effect.

'In the case of the explosions, we know that they are being carried out by agents of the Magisterium. All we can say for certain about their purpose is that they are doing it to close these openings. If all they wanted was to change the composition of the air, there are many things they could have done before now to bring that about. I think, Queen Shahrnavāz, that we have reached the limit of what we all know, and it is time to take action. Our enemy is closing these openings; it is our duty to keep them open. I say we should join together to carry that out. It will take immense work and danger. I ask Your Majesties to consider this question with all the wisdom and experience your people have. Will you form a great alliance to do it?'

Yes, they will, thought Pan. *They will now.*

16

OUT OF BOUNDS

The last stop but one was scheduled an hour before the bus reached the terminus in Baku. Lyra didn't leave the compartment, but sat with Asta watching passengers leave the bus while others joined. She could see Ionides moving inconspicuously here and there on the platform, as if he were merely stretching his legs, but he never went far from the bus and his eyes were scanning everyone in sight.

'We could do with a map of Baku,' said Asta. 'I wonder where the Hüseyn Javid Prospekt is.'

'We could do with a map of the Caspian Sea and everything beyond it. And a timetable of ferry routes, if there is such a thing. And a phrase book. Being on a luxurious bus has made me spoiled, Asta.'

'I expect it'll get difficult again before long. But this Magisterium agent might have nothing to do with us, you know. He might be on some other business altogether.'

'Look,' Lyra said, 'he's seen him.'

Ionides was standing next to a newsstand, against the wall, where the anbaric light from the other side didn't reach him. He was holding a newspaper up, but his eyes and those of his gecko-dæmon were fixed on a man wearing a cloth cap, who was strolling aimlessly, just as Ionides himself had been doing.

Lyra sat back and moved the curtain a little way across the window. Asta crouched lower on the table, and neither of them took their eyes off cloth-cap-man. He'd been called Dumitriu when Ionides had seen him before, and he might well have been Romanian; a nondescript blue suit, hands in his trouser pockets, a small moustache. His dæmon was a sparrow, who sat on his shoulder looking behind as they sauntered along the platform.

'She's seen Mr Ionides,' said Asta.

The sparrow was chirping something into Dumitriu's ear. He inclined his head but didn't look round.

The driver sounded the horn of the bus as a signal that they were about to leave. Dumitriu turned round slowly and waited to let other passengers get on first.

'He's watching without looking at him,' Lyra said.

'If Mr Ionides doesn't move quickly the bus'll leave without him,' said Asta.

Ionides was carefully folding his newspaper. Then he looked all round, and gazed at the announcement board, pretending to check the time against a wristwatch he didn't have.

The last passengers were boarding. Dumitriu wasn't looking at Ionides, but his dæmon was. They moved before Ionides, joining the last two or three people at the steps up to the bus door, and then Dumitriu suddenly looked directly at Lyra, who was too startled to prevent herself from moving back quickly out of sight.

'Stupid, stupid,' she murmured. 'He knows we're here, and I just confirmed it. Fine spy I'd be.'

'He also knows that you know, and you're watching him,' Asta pointed out. 'And Ionides saw what happened, so he'll be aware of everything too.'

'But if I'd had my wits about me . . .'

'Not so easy without Pan. I should have done what he'd have done, and warned you. It was my fault too.'

'At least we know what he looks like,' she said.

Ionides was the last to board, just before the doors closed. Then they could see nothing more outside, for the bus was moving away into the dark.

The bus station in Baku was still being built. Clearly Mustafa Bey's investment was being energetically spent; construction work was going on through the night, and men were clambering over scaffolding and unloading pallets of cement and sand from a line of lorries. A spotlight illuminated the entire height of a crane that was lifting a concrete beam into place. In the middle of it all, buses lined up to embark and disembark their passengers from the four platforms that were already complete underground.

Before the bus came to a halt, while it was still waiting in line on the ramp with the engine throbbing, there was a knock on the door of Lyra's compartment, and an attendant came in with a note. It was written in pencil on a scrap of newspaper, and it said:

'Big clock on Platform One. Go straight there and wait for me. A.I.'

She had never seen an example of Ionides's writing before; this was sharp, spiky, but perfectly legible. She read it with Asta.

'Which platform do we stop at, I wonder?' the dæmon said.

By pressing her head to the window, Lyra was able to see a little way along the length of the platform, but could see no sign of a number. The crowds of people leaving the buses ahead were jostling with those waiting to board; it was going to be hard to force her way through and stay aware of the man who'd be following.

Asta said, 'Maybe wait to leave till we've seen cloth-cap-man get off.'

That startled her a little. Asta was following her thoughts just as Pan did.

'Yes,' she said as the bus moved forward to take the place of the one before. 'Ah, look – there's a sign – this is Platform Two.'

The bus came to a halt. The platform was still thronged. The doors of the bus hissed as the pneumatic mechanism swung them open, and attendants lowered a step.

Lyra peered around the edge of the curtain, ready to move back the moment Dumitriu turned to look for her. But the door was too far along the body of the bus to see fully, and the crowd was pressing; those getting out were crowding around waiting for their luggage, others eager to meet families or friends arriving were pushing forward trying to see them, still others keen to get aboard quickly and find their seats.

'I'm looking for the cloth cap but he might have taken it off,' Lyra said. 'He wasn't very memorable otherwise. And I can't see Mr Ionides at all.'

'Is there only one door?'

'No – we got on at the front, didn't we – or maybe this is the exit and that was the entrance . . .'

The crowd was thinning.

'We'll have to go,' said Asta.

Lyra stood up, made sure her stick was just under the flap of her rucksack, and said, 'Right. Come up to my shoulder. Sit on the rucksack if you like. But we haven't got a choice, really.'

Asta was there in one leap. So unlike the feeling of Pan close to her; strange and disturbing, but reassuring too.

She slid open the door of the compartment, prepared to meet Dumitriu face to face, but of course he wasn't there. A handful of passengers were still lining up to get off – a young man and woman carrying a baby, a middle-aged man in sober clothes and horn-rimmed glasses carrying a briefcase, an elderly woman accompanied by a nurse; and no Dumitriu in sight. Further back along the bus, cleaners were already sweeping the floor and gathering rubbish.

Lyra took her place behind the woman and the nurse, who were slow and careful descending the steps. Asta murmured, 'Can't see them anywhere. Either of them.'

Once they were out of the bus, Lyra looked around for a sign to the other platforms. There was a wide flight of steps going up on the left, and a sign on the platform above it with numbered arrows pointing left and right. Like everywhere else in the station, the platform and the stairs had a not-quite-finished, provisional appearance; wide pillars of raw concrete, anbaric lamps hanging from bare wires, floors without tiling, signs temporarily fixed to the walls. The arrows over the stairs were at least clear to read: they indicated that Platform One was to the left.

Lyra was looking ahead, Asta behind.

'Can you see them?' Lyra said quietly.

'No. Keep going.'

Lyra moved out to get past the woman with the nurse. The young couple were heading for the stairs as well, and the baby was crying. The man had a heavy suitcase in each hand, and the young woman was struggling with a bulging shoulder bag as well as the baby, and looked on the edge of tears herself.

Lyra thought: *If we're with them, Dumitriu's less likely to attack.*

'Yes,' whispered Asta. 'Go on.'

They were at the foot of the flight of steps. She said to the young woman, 'Can I help you? Can I carry that bag for you?'

The woman turned her head, bewildered, helpless, worn out. It was clear that she hadn't understood. Lyra gestured, and the woman's goldfinch-dæmon, perching with the baby, said something to her. She understood, and nodded in gratitude. As she moved to let the shoulder bag slip off, the young man said a few words sharply.

'It's all right, honestly,' said Lyra, and then to her surprise Asta said something in what must have been their language.

The young man said something short in reply, and nodded. The woman let Lyra take her bag, and all three of them climbed the staircase slowly.

At the top Lyra gave back the bag and smiled at the baby, the man's dog-dæmon swung his tail in approval, and the family smiled their thanks and turned away to the right. Lyra began to make her way along the crowded bridge towards the stairs down to Platform One. She watched every one of the passengers ahead of her, confident that Asta was looking behind. Dumitriu was not visible anywhere, and neither was Ionides. Horn-rimmed-glasses man was some way ahead, but she saw no one else she recognised, and she soon lost him.

The stairs gave on to a wide corridor, lit by a harsh fluorescent glare, and most of the passengers moved that way, leaving only a few to continue down to the darker level of Platform One.

'See them anywhere?' she whispered.

'No. But there's the big clock,' Asta replied.

It hung on an iron bracket over the middle of the platform. It said the time was twenty past ten.

Asta jumped down and prowled ahead, looking to left and right. The noise from the rest of the station was muted at this level; there didn't seem to be any buses expected soon, because there were only two or three people sitting on the benches along the wall, or standing reading a timetable on the wall. Lyra had seen none of them before, and certainly Dumitriu wasn't one of them.

'We'd better wait here,' she said. There was an empty bench close to the clock, and she sat down with the rucksack on her lap. Asta jumped up and sat beside her. 'Sorry to make you sit on my shoulder,' Lyra went on.

'No choice. Anyway it was perfectly comfortable.'

'But, you know . . . I don't . . .'

She had no idea what she was going to say. Suddenly it had become awkward between them.

'In an emergency . . .' Asta said.

'Yes, of course.'

'Don't worry about it. But . . . look who's coming.'

They hadn't finished the lighting on Platform One. Fluorescent tubes hung from bare wires at seemingly random intervals, and gave patches of light between wider stretches of darkness. In one of those dark areas, to their right as they sat on the bench, a man was walking slowly towards them. When he came to one of the patches of light, the first thing Lyra saw was a cloth cap. His face was lit for a moment before the peak of the cap shaded it, and then was lost in darkness again, but there was no doubt.

'Dumitriu,' she said.

She loosened the flap of her rucksack and felt for the stick. There it was, the hard cord binding the handle, comfortable to her hand, smooth and heavy. Dumitriu came steadily closer, and he was looking at her; she knew her face was in the light, and she tilted it a little towards him so he could see that she was ready to fight. Asta stood up, her tail waving slowly.

The man was walking in the middle of the platform, but when he came closer he moved out slightly, towards the edge. Was he going to turn in towards her and run up before he attacked? Did he have a gun? How would it happen? And where was Ionides?

Lyra drew the stick slightly out of the rucksack. Dumitriu saw her move, and looked ahead again and carried on walking slowly past, and away down the platform. She realised she'd been holding her breath, and released it.

'He saw what you were doing,' said Asta. 'With the stick.'

'Good. He's turning round.'

But he only made for the timetable on the nearest wall. He ran his finger down a column, presumably of departure times, and then looked at his wristwatch, and then at the clock above the platform, and then took off his watch and adjusted it. He didn't look at Lyra once. Then he sauntered to the nearest bench and sat down.

'Miss Silver,' said Ionides, and Lyra jumped.

He was standing just a yard away, easy and relaxed.

'But – look, he's just over there,' she said, and nodded in the direction of Dumitriu.

'Him? No, that's not him. You see a man with briefcase and big glasses?'

'That wasn't him, was it?'

'It was, but not now.'

'You didn't kill him, did you?'

'No need. When you see bad guy and nearby also policeman and also young woman with open bag, what you do is you take purse out of her bag and drop it in bad guy's pocket and then tell policeman you see him stealing it. They argue for long time, and then policeman's got to arrest him. The evidence is clear. Undeniable.'

'And all the time we thought . . .'

She looked at cloth-cap-man again. He looked entirely innocent.

'Well,' said Asta.

'Thank you!' said Lyra. 'That was very clever.'

'Right, Miss Silver. What we do now? You want to find hotel?'

'It's nearly eleven . . . Too late to call on Mr Green now. Yes, let's find a cheap hotel.'

Ionides had an instinct for that sort of search. Within fifteen minutes they had checked in to a clean but shabby place only a step from the station, and Lyra was falling asleep in a very small bedroom. Asta sat on the windowsill, just watching the street.

Alice Lonsdale's lift took her to St Clement's, just before Magdalen Bridge and the beginning of Oxford High Street. The driver was agreeable enough, but taciturn, and not at all curious about what this young woman was doing on her own; after a few attempts at conversation they sat more or less in silence till the van drew up at the end of the Iffley Road and she said thanks and goodbye.

'Now what should we do, Ben?' she said.

'Find something to eat,' he said.

'Don't be a fathead. Got no money, have we. I mean Jordan or the Trout?'

'Jordan's closer. They'll be serving lunch about now. If we go to Brasenose Lane in about half an hour some of the kitchen staff'll be coming out for a smoke.'

'Worth a try. But we'll have to go to Godstow eventually.'

'To hide, you mean?'

'For a while. Probably not long. Actually,' she added, 'maybe give Jordan a miss.'

'Gossip?'

'Yeah. If they know I'm back it'll be all round the college in five minutes. And I don't trust that place now.'

'Right. Long walk then.'

'Lazy bugger.'

'I wish I was a mouse or a bird sometimes.'

'Bloody mouse wouldn't keep my feet warm, would he?'

'I could sit in your pocket, though.'

She had to try and look as if she was busy, and it would have helped a great deal to have a bag of some sort so she could have pretended to be shopping; she knew she'd never look like a lady of leisure out for a stroll, and even if she was, she'd have something to carry, a shoulder bag or a handbag. *Well, have to do the best we can*, she thought.

They crossed the bridge and turned left down Rose Lane, past the Botanic Garden, and into Cardinal's Meadow. It was a grey, still sort of day, too early in the year for tourists or cricket or punts. There were children playing in their lunch hour in the school ground nearby, but few people on the Broad Walk; an elderly man in tweeds who might have been a Scholar, a couple of young men dressed for football on their way to the Iffley Road sports ground, who gave her an appraising look (one) and a faint smile (the other), both of which she ignored, and further off, just coming into the Broad Walk from St Aldate's, a woman with a basket of groceries.

'Turn left,' said Ben, quiet and urgent. 'To the river.'

'Who is it?' muttered Alice, as she did what he said and turned into the path called the Poplar Walk.

'Hunch your shoulder or something. Limp. Keep your head bowed.'

'Who *is* it?'

'Sheila Murphy.'

'*Shit . . .*'

The woman was still too far off to have recognised Alice, but they were old friends and it would be hard to avoid a conversation if she saw her.

They moved a little faster, with Ben trotting ahead, so it looked as if they were going somewhere for a definite purpose. From time to time Ben stopped and looked around impatiently, but he was really looking to see if the other woman was following.

But she wasn't. She went straight on along the Broad Walk and up towards the High Street.

When she was out of sight Ben said, 'We could just carry on along the river. Not so many people.'

'Yeah . . . Let's do that. Better have some explanation ready just in case, though.'

It would probably be a little quicker too; the river led along the edge of Port Meadow, and then it was only a step to Godstow and the Trout.

'I wonder if there's a search on for us,' said Ben as they skirted the area near the Royal Mail Depot, where Pan had seen the murder of Roderick Hassall earlier in the year.

'Not important enough.'

'We stole a truck, though. Broke a fence.'

'Still not very important.'

'What are we going to say when someone we know sees us?'

'Say they did arrest us, just rounded us up with lots of other people, but they couldn't find anything to charge us with and let us go.'

'That might work, I suppose . . .'

'Thing is, no one knows what they do or why they do it. Don't suppose they know themselves, really, most of 'em. Just following orders they don't understand.'

'He was really trying to frame Malcolm, though, that officer.'

'Bastard.'

'An accusation like that . . . It's impossible to clear it, really.'

Alice thought of Malcolm now, and wondered where he was; and then of Malcolm the boy, and the canoe and the flood, and how cold and scornful she'd been to him at first, and how he'd risked everything to save the baby Lyra, and how much she'd come to realise that and admire him.

'Round by the river or straight across?' said Ben.

They had come to the edge of the great meadow. There was a small group of horses further up, cropping the grass, and a couple of cows nearby drinking from the river. A woman with a toddler was making her slow way towards the bridge at Aristotle Lane off to the right, two girls were walking by the riverbank and talking closely together a few hundred yards away, a couple of men were busy in the boatyard at Medley to the left, but otherwise there was no one else in sight.

'Straight across and keep our heads down,' said Alice.

The meadow was a big place. It would take a good hour to reach the other end, where the Trout stood beside the bridge she and Malcolm had hurried over twenty years ago, just before the flood carried it away.

They set off, walking fast and steadily.

'What are we going to do, anyway?' said Ben.

'Haven't thought of that yet.'

'Can't just go back to work.'

'Brenda'll have something for us to do. Be out of sight in the kitchen.'

'Not for long, though. We could go to London and hide there.'

'Don't be daft. We'll stay at the Trout till we know what the CCD are doing, whatever they call themselves now – Brytsec, was it?'

She felt ignorant, out of touch with the world she used to know. Things had happened in the world, and she'd seen no newspapers, and the women who'd arrived in the camp more recently had brought little knowledge with them.

They'd been walking for five minutes or so when she saw something ahead.

'Is that a man on a horse?' she said.

'Can't see . . . Yes,' Ben said. 'A soldier.'

The rider was certainly in uniform, and he had a rifle sheathed by his saddle, and his horse was moving towards them at a canter. He was close enough already for them to hear clearly when he called:

'Halt! Stop where you are!'

She had to, so she did. She stood still, with Ben close at her side growling softly, and faced the horseman as he pulled his mount up too close, as if he was expecting her to flinch and step back. She didn't, of course, and then immediately remembered that she was a fugitive, an escaped prisoner, and the last thing she should do was challenge any bully in uniform. She took a step back then, and made herself cringe a little.

'You can't go up that way any further,' the soldier said. He was young, only in his early twenties, and easy prey for the dominating Alice; *but not now*, she thought, *not now*.

'Oh. I didn't know. Why? What's happening, sir?'

The *sir* was going it a bit, but she knew the effect it would have.

'That end of the meadow's been requisitioned. Army property. Training ground. There'll be a proper fence up tomorrow. Best thing is get off the meadow over that way—' gesturing behind her and to his left – 'and go round by road. Where you going, anyway?'

'Just up Godstow. See my gran.'

'Where you just come from?'

'Cowley. Been working there but my gran's not well so I thought I'd come and look after her for a bit.'

He looked her over, with all the confidence of someone who'd never been tested at anything. 'Off you go then. The whole meadow'll be out of bounds from next week. Don't forget. Anyone trespassing will be arrested.'

'Thank you,' she said humbly.

She put up with his scrutiny as she walked away towards the path to Jericho. After a minute she heard the jingle of harness and then the sound of hooves as he rode away.

'They'll never be able to shut the whole meadow,' said Ben.

'Want to bet?'

They'd reached the bridge for the footpath that led to Aristotle Lane. She stopped and turned round. There was a lot of movement up at the Godstow end of the meadow, too far away to see in detail: horses, vehicles, a handful of tents being put up.

'The world's changing,' said Ben.

'Better keep our heads down. I hope Brenda and Reg are all right.'

It took another half hour's walking before she turned in to the garden of the Trout and made her way round to the kitchen door. The place was quiet, but it was a chilly sort of day, not the best weather for a drink on the terrace; and there was no smell of roasting joint or frying fish.

'Something's wrong,' she said very quietly to Ben.

She put her hand on the kitchen door, and hesitated. The top half of the door was glass, and from outside she could see that the lights were off.

She turned the handle and went in. The kitchen was cold; there were no voices from the inner rooms, there was no food in preparation.

She was about to go through to the bar and look for Brenda when that door opened and a soldier came in. He was as startled as she was, and his crow-dæmon flapped on his shoulder.

'Who are you?' he demanded. 'What you doing here?'

'I was going to say the same thing to you,' she said mildly. 'I was looking for Brenda or Reg. Are they about anywhere?'

'Alice?' said Brenda's voice from behind the soldier. She sounded unwell. He stood aside to let her through. She was carrying a pile of clean and ironed napkins and tea towels.

'Who's she?' the soldier asked Brenda, jerking his thumb at Alice. He had a sergeant's stripes.

'That's Alice.'

'Alice who?'

'Alice Lonsdale. She's a friend.'

'I came up to see Gran,' Alice explained, as reasonably as she could, 'and I thought I'd look in and say hello. What's going on?'

'We've been requisitioned,' said Brenda. She had gone pale. 'I mean, for billeting, you know.'

'Oh, I see, right,' Alice said, nodding as if it was all clear and obvious. 'Anything I can do?'

'D'you live here, in Wolvercote?' said the soldier, still suspicious.

'No. I live down Cowley way. I come up to see my gran. I used to work here, see, in the bar and that.'

He nodded. 'Carry on then.'

He went out on to the terrace and looked around.

Brenda said quietly, 'Grab those sheets over there and come up to the airing cupboard. Just be normal.'

Alice gathered the freshly washed sheets, which had been drying over the range, and followed Brenda upstairs.

'Is he the only one here?' she asked in a whisper.

'For the moment. Reg is talking to the officer outside. What are you – we thought you were – where've you been?'

'I escaped. They put me in some bloody camp thing down Henley way, I think it was, only the security was so careless I got out and thumbed a ride to Oxford. I tried to get across Port Meadow—'

'Yeah, that's out of bounds. The army's taken over everything up this way.'

'When? Must've been damn quick.'

'Most of 'em arrived just yesterday. But it feels like they've had it planned for months. Listen, are you all right, love?'

'I'm bloody hungry and thirsty, and I haven't got a penny in my pocket. I had to break out of the camp just as I am. Stole a truck, so they might be after me for that too, if they can get their papers in order. They were asking lots of questions about Malcolm, where was he, what did he do, everything. He's lucky to be abroad, if you ask me.'

She wasn't going to tell Brenda about the kind of questions; she wouldn't even tell Malcolm, if she ever saw him again. She helped Brenda fold the sheets, and heard about other people who'd been taken away.

'It's like a different country all of a sudden,' Brenda said. 'There's no one we can ask. Reg tried to talk to old Gordon Rudyard but all he could say was that Parliament had been – what did he say – prorogued for the emergency.'

Gordon Rudyard had been the Member of Parliament for Oxford all Alice's life.

'What emergency?' said Alice.

'It's all been happening so fast . . . Listen, come down to the kitchen and I'll heat up a saucepan of soup and make you a sandwich. We can keep an eye on that sergeant and talk quietly. What about Jordan? You been back there?'

'No. I thought about it but then remembered it was them who had me arrested. That bastard bursar and what's-his-name, Dr Hammond, the new Master. If anyone saw me it'd be all round the college in five minutes, and they'd call the CCD, and I'd be caught. And I bet this time they'd be better at security than that camp they put me in first. Brenda, I can't stay here for long; I can't trust . . .'

She found it hard to speak. They entered the kitchen and found Malcolm's father at the back door, saying goodbye to the billeting officer, who looked past his shoulder and touched his cap to Alice and Brenda before nodding to Reg and leaving.

Reg shut the door and turned to greet Alice, muting his surprise. 'How do, Alice,' he said, sounding hearty but looking around.

'Hello, Reg. Brenda can tell you where I've been and all that. I've got to go soon.'

'You're not going till you've had something to eat,' said Brenda. 'Sit down there and cut yourself some bread and cheese – or there's a nice piece of ham in the larder – and I'll heat up some onion soup.'

Reg, bulky and solid and steadfast, sat at the table and took over the bread knife. Alice could see her own hands trembling, and surrendered it readily.

'All right, I'll wait to hear what Brenda tells me,' he said. 'What's important now is what you're going to do.'

'Have they gone?' Alice said quietly.

Brenda was looking through the glass of the door, and said, 'Yes. I can see 'em both climbing the steps to the road. There was only two.'

She turned to the stove and poured some soup out of a china bowl into a saucepan.

'I just don't know,' said Alice. 'I suppose what I was thinking was just get back home, and I must have thought that Jordan was home till I remembered how I couldn't go back there till . . . till all this was over, so I came up here, and found Port Meadow was out of bounds, and . . . I just don't know what I can do. But if I stay here I'll get you in trouble—'

'Come off it,' Reg began, and Brenda said, 'What rubbish. You'll be safe—'

But Alice said, 'No. I know you won't give me away, but how can I hide here? There's too many people know me round Godstow, and in the city as well. I'd've bumped into Sheila Murphy this morning if I hadn't dodged out the way. I just can't stay here, Reg. I'm not going to sit in a bloody wardrobe not moving all day long. I've got to go on somewhere.'

'Any idea where?' he said.

'Ben said London. But I don't know.'

Reg cut a thick slice of ham and made a sandwich. He put it on a plate for her and then cut some more bread to make another.

'Can't trust London food,' he said. 'Little skinny sandwiches they make there. Eat a plateful and half an hour later you're hungry again. You know anyone there?'

'Not really. It's just there's so many people there it'd be easier not to be seen. I suppose. Shouldn't be too hard to find work.'

Brenda put a bowl of soup in front of her and took a spoon from the drawer. 'Eat that before it gets cold,' she said.

'It *is* cold in here,' said Reg.

Alice had a mouthful of soup and then said, 'Are they going to billet some soldiers here? Is that what you said?'

'He was totting up the rooms, that officer. He reckons we got room for thirty-five. Thirty-five!'

'I'll poison 'em,' said Brenda.

'They *are* going to pay you?' said Alice.

'Yeah, just about. They're not getting my best cooking at those rates.'

'Lucky to get any,' said Reg. 'Listen, Alice, I'm worried about you in London. None of the college servants moved there, nothing like that?'

'Well, actually, Sally Jamieson did, now I think of it. She got a job in the – what was it – big West End hotel . . .'

'Habsburg? Savoy? Claridge's?'

'That was it, yeah. The Savoy. That's what I'll do. I'll go there and see if she can get me a job. Easy.'

She was trying to sound confident, even jaunty. But she could see Reg and Brenda exchange an anxious glance.

'Lovely soup, Brenda,' she said. 'The kind of muck they fed us on in that place, you wouldn't believe it.'

Reg had been cutting more sandwiches. He left the table and went into the office. Brenda's badger-dæmon, Kerin, had been talking together quietly with Ben, and Alice knew that he'd pass on anything important.

'I suppose those clothes are all you've got?' Brenda said.

'Well, course they are. They probably stink. I probably stink. I just had to get out when I saw the chance, and I didn't have nothing to take with me anyway.'

'Well, I'm a lot bigger'n you, but you're welcome to whatever you can find in my wardrobe. There might be a coat that isn't too big. Have a bath too while you're here, if you like. Makes such a difference feeling clean. Don't forget those sandwiches. Or another bowl of soup?'

'Oh, Brenda . . .'

Alice never felt helpless except when she was being helped, which was stupid, but she couldn't help it; and as she thought that, she gave a little snort of laughter which was almost a sob. Brenda pretended not to notice.

Reg came in from the office and sat down again. He put something on the table, and Alice couldn't quite see what it was till she'd dabbed her eyes.

'Pepper in the soup,' she said. 'Reg, what's—'

It was a bundle of pound notes and some change. He pushed it towards her.

'Go on, take it, you goose. That'll do for the train fare to London and to live on for a couple of weeks. Drop us a line to let us know where you are and how you're doing. Don't bloody argue. Take it.'

'Probably would be best, London,' Brenda said. 'Get lost in a crowd, kind of thing.'

Alice nodded and put the money in her pocket. It was hard to speak. Reg went out to sweep the terrace, he said, and Brenda sat down.

'How's Malcolm?' Alice managed to say. 'Where is he now?'

Brenda sighed shakily. 'When we last heard, he was in Constantinople. I wish I knew where he is now. We're not even sure where he was going.'

'Lyra? Did he say anything about her?'

Brenda shook her head. 'She's just vanished off the face of the earth. Not a word.'

Alice finished the soup. Then she said, 'You remember when he was teaching her? About five or six years ago?'

'Yeah, vaguely. Why?'

'Did they quarrel, or something? There was some sort of difficulty, or something . . .'

'He used to grumble about her, about not working and making excuses, but nothing serious. I can't remember, to be honest. He only had a handful of school-age pupils, just to earn a bit extra.'

'Ah. She grumbled to me about him, once or twice. I must say I wouldn't have liked to teach her.'

'It's funny, when she came here, just a few days before she vanished, it was like the two of them had never met before. Like strangers, a bit wary, kind of unnaturally polite. Course, they'd never met as grown-ups before.'

Alice told Brenda about the strange moment in her sitting-room when Lyra had been with her and Malcolm had unexpectedly walked in.

Before she could reply, the terrace door opened and Reg said, 'Here, Alice, I got an idea. I can run you down the canal in the new boat. They got patrols on the river but none on the canal, yet.'

'New boat?'

'It's his pride and joy,' said Brenda. 'Little gas engine. He's too lazy to row.'

'Well, thanks . . .'

'Down to the Castle Mill Stream. Only a step to the station then.'

'You better forget the bath,' said Brenda. 'You don't smell. I'll pack a couple of things for you.'

'That'll be the second time I've escaped from here in a boat,' said Alice. 'I'm making a habit of it. Thank you, Reg. Thanks for everything, both of you.'

17

THE FRENCH TEACHER

The Villa Victor Hugo in Hüseyn Javid Prospekt was a grand building with an ornate marble façade, which might once have housed a government ministry or the embassy of some imperial power, but which had clearly fallen on smaller times; it had been divided into apartments and offices, and it shared its grounds with a nursery school.

'Who is this man Horace Green?' Ionides asked as they stood looking up at the slightly dingy entrance. 'How you know him?'

'I saw his name in someone's address book. We have something in common, and I thought he might help. But I ought to go alone, just me and Asta. Can you wait for us? Look, there's a café over there.'

'You need help, you come running out and I finish my coffee briskly. Or briskish anyway.'

A concierge directed Lyra to the second floor, by way of the oak-panelled lift. Number 23 was one of four doors on that landing. It was ten o'clock, which Lyra thought would be a respectable time to call on anyone.

She rang the bell. Half a minute went by, and then the door opened a little way. A man's face, bespectacled, middle-aged, bald, cautious, looked at her for a few moments, then down at Asta; he looked at Lyra again, and his eyes widened. He took a deep breath and nodded slowly before taking off the security chain and opening the door fully. He had no dæmon.

He said something in Persian, Lyra thought, and she said in English, 'Sorry. You have an English name, and I thought . . .'

He nodded. 'You're English too? Are you looking for French lessons?'

'No. Is that what you do?'

'I teach French, yes. But most of my students are Azerbaijani or Persian. I . . . I think I can guess why you're here. Come in, come in.'

She followed him into the living room, Asta at her heels.

'The *clavicula*, yes,' she said, holding up the little black book. 'Do you remember a man called Roderick Hassall? He would have come this way . . . oh, last year sometime.'

'Yes, indeed. Is that his?'

She let him flick through. He found his own name, and looked at several others.

Then he said, 'Oh, do forgive me. Please. Sit down – let me make you some coffee – or tea?'

'That's kind of you. Coffee, please. My name is Lyra Silvertongue, by the way.'

'Lyra Silvertongue. Interesting name. And . . .' He looked at Asta.

'This is Asta. It's a bit complicated. She's the dæmon of a friend of mine, who's now travelling with my dæmon, Pantalaimon. I . . . Are you busy at the moment? I don't want to interrupt if you have a student coming. But it's not easy to explain quickly.'

'No students today,' he said with what might have been a sigh. 'I've got time.'

He busied himself with water and coffee and cups in the kitchen while Lyra and Asta looked around. It was the apartment of a reading man, probably single; just on the decent side of shabby, just on the friendly side of untidy. Bookshelves overflowed; a table by the window carried papers and dictionaries; a mandolin hung from a peg on a red ribbon. There were some photograms on the mantelpiece, showing a young woman, then the same woman a little older, but there was no sign of her presence elsewhere in the room.

Asta jumped up beside Lyra on the sofa and murmured, 'Nice man. Romantic.'

'The photograms?'

'The mandolin.'

Green came back with a tray and set it down on the low table between the sofa and an armchair.

'Mr – er, Dr Hassall,' he said, 'did he give you that book, his *clavicula*?'

'No. He was murdered. It was with other things in his rucksack.'

'Murdered . . . ?' He was genuinely shocked. 'Where . . . how . . . ?'

'It's probably best if I tell you everything in order,' Lyra said.

'Yes. Yes. How awful . . . My God.'

'I think I ought to begin by explaining how Pan, he's my dæmon, got separated from me in the first place. I had to go somewhere to, to keep a promise, and it was somewhere he couldn't go, so there was nothing I could do but . . . I hated doing it.'

'I understand. Go on.'

And Asta said, 'I was separated in the same kind of way. I mean, my person Malcolm Polstead had rescued Lyra in a flood, when she was a baby, and he had to do something dangerous while I stayed to look after her. And since then we've been separated. It was horrible but we had to.'

Horace Green was a good listener. Lyra took a few moments to sort it out in her mind, and then began with Hassall's death. As the story unfolded she felt like a musician, playing a piece that she knew by heart, knowing both where she was and where she was going, and holding back a little here to make a more effective change in pace there, seeing the span of music to come, taking her time but wasting none, including a detail at this point so it would make its effect more strongly later, cutting out a detail that wouldn't help. It was the first time she'd ever experienced that about herself – except that of course there were all those childish years of tale-telling and lying and making things up that had gone into the making of this new and entirely adult sense of herself as an artist.

It took over an hour, and two refillings of the coffee pot, and Horace Green listened intently to everything.

'Well,' he said when she came to the moment she rang the bell of the Villa Victor Hugo. 'Poor Hassall. I shall have to cross his name out of my *clavicula*. I liked him; he'd clearly been through a lot, though he didn't tell me much.'

'Sebastian Makepeace the alchemist never explained to Pan, to my dæmon, what *clavicula* means, or the other word: *adiumenti*. I just had to find out on the way.'

'It means a little key to help, or to assist, that sort of thing. Every name in here is someone who's lost their dæmon, or is able to separate: someone who understands. You're lucky to have this one,' he said, taking up the little book from the table and flicking through it.

'How did you lose your dæmon? I was told by someone that it's not impolite to ask.'

'My wife and I were walking in the Alps,' he said. 'Our dæmons were both birds. We thought no one had ever been happier. Then one day a hawk – some kind of sparrowhawk, something we'd never seen before – snatched her dæmon out of the air, and my Bellissa flew up to defend him; but my wife died at once from the shock, and her dæmon vanished, and Bellissa was torn out of my heart as the hawk took her instead. She must be alive, because I am, but I've never managed to find her, and my wife is dead.'

'Both gone at once,' Lyra said quietly.

They sat for a few moments without speaking.

Then he said, 'What is it that you came to ask? How can I help you?'

'With anything you know. Anything you've heard about the desert of Karamakan, or about a group called the "men from the mountains". Or . . . Anything about Oakley Street.'

Lyra hadn't mentioned Oakley Street in her story: it was one of the things that would have got in the way. There was no reason why Horace Green would have heard of it, but when she said the name, he raised his head sharply. Asta moved to the arm of the sofa and sat upright.

'Oakley Street?' he said.

'Do you know the name?'

'It rings a bell, but . . .' He shook his head. 'Where is it?'

'In London. Chelsea.'

'Someone spoke of it once, but I only overheard it; he was talking to someone else. But I don't think it had anything to do with Chelsea. Perhaps there's an Oakley Street somewhere else. What's your interest in it?'

'I think . . . It probably means something apart from the address. You know, as if there was a famous oratory or something there, and when people said "Oakley Street" you knew they were referring to "St Benedict's", or whatever it was. Or like "Whitehall" meaning the civil service. But I don't know what it could be. Maybe it's not important at all. I just heard someone mention it once. Like you.'

'Yes,' he said. 'Curious, though. It was someone at an embassy party, not that I get invited to many of those. There was a man who was asking about the Poste Restante, because he was expecting a message from Oakley Street, and the man he was talking to pursed his lips and shook his head, very slightly. I couldn't help noticing. And from what I'd heard about that man, the second one, I think he might have had something to do with intelligence. You know: spying. But I didn't know for certain, and it was all over in a second. But . . .' He shrugged. 'What was the other thing . . . the men in the mountains?'

'From the mountains. Some sort of religious group.'

'No, sorry,' he said, sighing. 'Not much help, I'm afraid. I live a quiet life here. I read the papers, but I seem to read them less and less these days.'

'Oh, and there was one more thing. Have you heard the word *alkahest*?'

'Interesting word . . . Is it Arabic?'

'I don't know. *The destroyer of bonds* . . . That was a phrase that came with it.'

'I'm intrigued. Let me look it up.'

He took down one of a number of large and shabby volumes from an old encyclopaedia.

'Alkahest . . . Here we are. It's a term from alchemy: "The universal solvent imagined by the alchemists . . ." "A material sought by the alchemists, which would dissolve every other . . ." There's more here, but it doesn't add much. Perhaps because they never actually discovered it. That's your *destroyer of bonds*. Atomic bonds, I expect, among others.'

'Thank you,' said Lyra. 'I'm not sure I understand, really, but . . . Anyway, at least I know a bit more.'

'Is it something you're looking for?' he said, replacing the volume on the shelf.

'I suppose I am. But I don't know why.'

'Where are you off to next?'

'East, and further east. But the sea's in the way, so . . .'

'There are regular ferries. Three times a week. To Krasnovodsk, I believe, and further if the captain feels like it, or someone pays him. And then?'

'Oh, then – just further on. Do you know about Mustafa Bey? Have you heard that name?'

'Goodness, yes. He's an important man. Never met him. Mind you, I don't suppose he's interested in learning French. Probably speaks it already. Very rich, very influential. Why do you ask about him?'

'We came here from Aleppo on a bus owned by his company. It was very comfortable. I was wondering if his buses went further east.'

'I don't know,' said Green. 'Sorry.'

'Can I ask you something?' said Asta, from the arm of the sofa. Lyra had noticed her moving there when she mentioned Oakley Street, and she was aware of the dæmon's attention. So was Green.

'Of course,' he said. 'I don't know if I'll know the answer, but I can try.'

'Gryphons. What do you know about them?'

He was surprised by that. He blinked and passed his hand over his head. 'Well . . . Hardly anything. They do exist, I suppose, but they have very little to do with human beings . . . You can see them occasionally in the high mountains, I understand, though I never have. They belong to that class of things in the wild parts of the world that are half myth and half verifiable. But they belong to a different realm really, a different kind of being, different order of things . . . I don't know who would have any knowledge about them. Most people, most educated people, wouldn't talk about them. In the way people don't talk about ghosts or apparitions. You'd be thought a bit odd.'

'Thank you,' said Asta.

'Why do you ask?'

'We saw one.'

'Ah,' he said. He smiled politely.

Lyra said, 'I think it's time we left you to your work. I'm sure you've got lessons to prepare. Are your students young, mostly, or sort of university age?'

'Some schoolchildren being prepared for exams. A few adults with time on their hands taking an interest in French culture. A number of business people eager to trade in French-speaking countries. A mixture.'

She stood up and shook his hand. *A melancholy man,* she thought, and Pan would have agreed.

Green showed them out, and on the way downstairs Asta said, 'A kindly man, haunted by his loss. Courageous. Pity he couldn't tell us very much.'

'Oh, I think he did,' said Lyra.

Outside, they waited to cross the busy road and found Ionides reading a Persian-language newspaper on the café terrace. He saw her coming but didn't look up.

'Take no notice of me,' he said quietly as she came close. 'Go inside. Stay for five minutes and then come out and meet me further down that way.'

A brief nod indicated the direction of the city centre. She made no sign but walked straight past and into the café, which was also a boulangerie and sweet shop. She pretended to take a great deal of time choosing what she wanted, and finally paid for a small pastry and left unhurriedly to stroll down the Hüseyn Javid Prospekt.

'He saw someone watching,' said Asta.

'I couldn't look around though. Did you notice anyone hanging about?'

'From where I am, no. It's too busy to tell.'

Lyra kept looking ahead and across the road to her left, moving her head as little as possible. Once she stopped and looked into a dress shop window, though she was really studying the reflection of people behind her. Then she walked on slowly. About a quarter of a mile down the street, she saw, there was a crossing with traffic lights. The light was green, and the road was busy, so there were four or five people waiting to cross.

One of them was Ionides. Lyra and Asta got to the light just before it changed. He didn't look around, and they followed him across and down the narrow street on the other side.

He stopped outside a bookshop and looked at the display in the window. Lyra did the same.

'Your Green man any good, this French professor?' he said.

'Interesting, but indirectly. Is there someone following us?'

'Yes. Watching the house. When you go in he make a note and waited. A long time, Miss Silver.'

'Was he still there when we came out?'

'Yes. He make another note. But he didn't follow you or me to here. He stay there. Maybe watching your Green man.'

'I hope he's safe . . . Mr Ionides, where should we go for the Poste Restante? Do you think there'd be one main post office?'

'Best place to start. You think there would be something for you?'

'No harm in asking.'

'As Miss Silver, or as Queen Tatiana?'

Lyra looked at him, and laughed. 'I hadn't thought of that. I'd better be both.'

'You need papers, whatever name you say.'

'I've got Mustafa Bey's *laissez-passer* for Queen Tatiana, but I've only been a queen since then.'

'You'll only have one chance,' Asta pointed out. 'You can't go on giving different names till you get the right one. Anyway, who would possibly send you anything here in Baku?'

'H'mm,' she said. 'You never know. Worth a try, though. Let's find the post office. Then we'll get tickets for the ferry.'

'Ferry to where?' said Ionides.

'Wherever it goes. Across the sea, that's the main thing. Krasnovodsk, said Mr Green. What would you advise?'

'Let me think. We go to post office first, then we decide.'

How could anyone have sent her a letter? Lyra thought. It was a silly idea. But the mention of Oakley Street kept coming back to her, and the sense that things were connected in a secret commonwealth way, a way that wasn't simply cause and effect. As they walked through the busy streets on the way to where Ionides thought the post office was, she was simultaneously anxious and excited. It felt as if she'd been working through some complicated problem in mathematics, and sensed that the answer was close, but she wasn't able to see it yet. Or imagine it, she thought; and she wanted very badly to talk to Pan again about imagining things.

But if she let herself dwell on her missing dæmon, and his quest for her imagination, she'd sink into a whirlpool of self-reproach and fear and unhappiness. *Swim clear*, she thought. *Move away from that pull in the water. Trust the world, but swim clear.*

The main post office stood at the edge of a large square where the traffic was heavy. They had to wait for the lights to change before they could cross the street.

'Well?' said Asta as they stood at the entrance. 'Who are you going to be?'

'Actually I'd better be the queen. She's the only one I've got papers for.'

'I wait over there,' said Ionides, and went to a nearby news-stand.

If they had the time, Lyra was sure that Ionides could find someone to forge new papers in whatever name she chose. But for now she had to be the queen and accept all the difficulties that brought, such as the problem now of finding the right counter in the main hall among the welter of signs in three different scripts.

She crouched down and said to Asta, 'I'll have to lift you up again because I can't read the signs . . . I'm sorry.'

Asta leaped up to her shoulder and Lyra stood up. It still felt strange to have another person's dæmon so close, like an intimacy; it made her feel almost shy. But Asta, who had Malcolm's knowledge of languages, simply looked around for a moment or two and then said, 'Over to the left – the counter where the woman in the red coat's waiting.'

'Thanks,' said Lyra, and crouched to let her down again.

She went to stand in line behind the woman, whose dæmon was a greenfinch, staring down curiously at Asta and whispering something into the woman's ear. The woman was about to turn, but the assistant came back to the counter with a handful of letters for her. She took them and signed a receipt and then left, ignoring the chirping of her dæmon, who was plainly agitated by the idea that Lyra and Asta were not one person.

But Lyra moved to take her place and put her *laissez-passer* from Mustafa Bey on the counter. The assistant adjusted his glasses and bent to read it, and then looked up at Lyra, who put a lifetime of effrontery into the calm assurance with which she gazed back.

'Ah,' the assistant said, and inclined his head uncertainly, so she rewarded him with an enquiring smile and spread her hands.

He murmured something she couldn't hear and turned to ask a supervisor. Lyra took the paper and folded it away into her pocket, and then had to take it out again and show it to the older man who came back with him. He spoke to her, but Lyra didn't have to understand; it was clear what he wanted. He read Mustafa Bey's words reverentially and then said something sharp to the assistant, who hurried away.

The supervisor, half bowing, uttered a sentence or two to Lyra, who nodded and smiled with kindly understanding. Then she withdrew her attention from him and gazed around at the architecture, the marble columns, the arched windows, the mosaics on the ceiling illustrating the speed and reliability of the Azerbaijani postal service.

The assistant came back, and he was carrying a small parcel, to Lyra's astonishment. But she showed no expression, and bent to sign the bottom of the form the supervisor laid on the counter, and then took the parcel from him. She checked the name: it was certainly addressed to Her Majesty Queen Tatiana Iorekova, in a clear and practised hand. It was surprisingly heavy, and it had been packaged with professional care and sealed with string and sealing wax.

'*Merci, messieurs,*' she said, and accepted the bows of the assistant and the supervisor. The man behind her in the queue watched curiously. Lyra ignored them all and sauntered elegantly to the big door, where a man was bowing as he held it open.

'Well,' said Asta as they went to join Ionides at the newsstand. 'I'm impressed.'

'Wonderful what you can get away with if you've got a piece of paper from Mustafa Bey.'

'They have something for the queen?' said Ionides quietly. 'Very good. You got a pocket? Put it in without showing anyone what you doing. Now I walk on that side and keep close.'

'Is there someone following us?' Lyra said, and slipped the package unobtrusively, she hoped, into the left pocket of her skirt. She couldn't begin to guess what it was, or who had sent it, or why, but they had to move now, because Ionides said, 'Two men. They watch you go in, they wait for you to come out. Stay close.'

He moved forward at a leisurely pace and she went with him, Asta close by her heels, and Ionides's own gecko-dæmon on his shoulders, facing behind. Lyra could feel the weight of the little package against her thigh.

In the centre of the square was a statue of a warrior on horseback, which seemed to be an established meeting place for the citizens of Baku. There were benches on an area of grass, and flower beds, and a kiosk selling drinks and food. Ionides pointed across the road to it.

'If we sit there we can look all around,' he said. 'You hungry, Miss Silver?'

'I had a pastry, but it was insubstantial. Wispy.'

Lyra stopped at the first traffic light, Ionides close on her left, and waited with half a dozen other pedestrians.

'Are they anywhere near?' she murmured.

The gecko-dæmon said, 'They are close by watching. They will cross with us when the light changes.'

Lyra said, just loudly enough for Ionides and Asta to hear, 'Then we'll walk more slowly than these other people and partway across we'll change our minds and suddenly turn and run back. On my signal. They don't stay red for long.'

'Miss Silver . . .' Ionides began, but the lights changed at that moment, and the small group of pedestrians began to move off the pavement.

Lyra went with them, Ionides close at her side, and the two men came with the rest. When they were three-quarters of the way across she said, 'Now!' and turned and ran back. Asta darted ahead of her. Ionides followed without hesitating.

The two men, though, were caught by surprise. At first they stood still, and made as if to follow Lyra, but then seemed to realise that they'd give themselves away by doing so, and hesitated; and by then the lights had changed, and the traffic was already surging forward, and they had to rush for the nearest pavement – and found themselves cut off from their quarry.

'Very good, Miss Silver,' said Ionides. 'Now we get away before they can cross back.'

They turned down the nearest street out of the square, and then turned right into a smaller street, and then left into another busy shopping street, where a bus was pulling in to a stop.

'Let's get on,' said Lyra.

So they did, together with three other people. Ionides asked the driver something, and paid for them both, and then they found seats near the door.

'Queen Silver, you very lucky,' he said. 'You know where this is going? The Marine Passenger Terminal.'

'Couldn't be better,' she said.

'You still got your package from the post?'

'Of course.'

As the bus pulled away she and Ionides, and Asta, and the gecko-dæmon, all looked around to see if there was anyone who might have been following them; but there was no one who looked in the slightest bit suspicious.

Lyra took out the little package, with its string and sealing wax. She was intensely curious.

'You know who send it?' said Ionides.

'No idea. It's addressed to the queen, so I suppose it can only be Mustafa Bey, really.'

She looked closely at the impression on the sealing-wax, and then compared it with the mark he'd made with his ring on her *laissez-passer*. It was the same: two Arabic letters elegantly entwined.

'Same, huh?'

'Yes. I'll have to break the seal to open it, but that's the point, I suppose. Pity. It's so neatly done.'

The bus was moving through the heavy traffic. Lyra cracked the sealing-wax and peeled it away, and found a complicated knot in the string underneath it. As she prised one strand away from another with her nails, Ionides watched the street, and the passengers who got on, and the buildings nearby, and the progress she was making.

'You want to cut it?' he said.

'No. Might need the string. Nearly got it.'

'Malcolm would keep it too,' said Asta.

The last loop in the knot came undone, and she pulled it apart and tucked the string in her shirt pocket. She unfolded the brown paper and opened it out, and found another package inside, which had been addressed to Miss Lyra Silvertongue, c/o Mustafa Bey, Marletto's Café, Aleppo.

The bus came to a halt. Four passengers got off, and three got on. Lyra found a note with the inner package, marked in red ink with Mustafa Bey's seal:

Your Majesty, Whoever sent this package to you in my care is a person of great ingenuity and faith, which I trust will be rewarded when you open it. I hope your journey to Baku was comfortable. With solemn regards, Mustafa Bey

'I must write him a report,' Lyra said. 'As soon as we're safely on the ferry.'

The inner package was sealed with tape, not sealing wax, and the address was written in heavy black ink. There was no return address. Something about the way it had been wrapped and addressed made Lyra think it had been done in haste. It took her so long to peel back the tape that the bus came to a halt before she had unwrapped the paper, and Ionides said quietly, 'Better put it away. This is the ferry terminal.'

The other passengers were all getting to their feet and gathering their possessions. Several of them seemed to be going to the ferry, because they had suitcases or rucksacks, and there was a mother with two small children who had to edge her way towards the door carrying a folded pushchair as well as a heavy case. A man offered to help carry the case, but she shook her head nervously. One of the children was crying, and the man spoke again, and the mother, anxious and flustered, unwillingly let him carry the pushchair. The passengers behind were jostling impatiently; the driver was looking back to see what the hold-up was; Lyra tucked the package into her rucksack and sat back to wait till they could move.

Two minutes later all the other passengers had left, and Lyra and Asta and Ionides were standing outside the terminal of the Transcaspian Modern Ferry Company, and the unopened package lay safely in her rucksack.

18

NOLI ME TANGERE

Olivier Bonneville, nursing his injured dæmon and his badly injured pride, was still captive in the nuncio's house in Aleppo. Or so he thought: in fact, the nuncio would have been delighted if the wretched boy cleared off altogether. But it suited Bonneville to have a good reason not to risk liberty for a while, so he stayed in his comfortable room and ate his three meals a day and spent most of his time with the alethiometer.

What he learned was intriguing in many ways. Firstly, the girl had left Aleppo and was travelling eastwards. But something was confusing the new method, or else it was proving itself unable to deal with perspective in more than three dimensions, or else he was simply incapable of reading it just then; but the last possibility was so absurd that he put it out of his mind, and remembered the copy of Spiridion Trepka's *Alethiometrica Explicata*, which he'd stolen from the library of the Priory of St Jerome before leaving Geneva.

With its help he was able to read the instrument without feeling sick. Trepka was limited and shallow but accurate as far as he went, and although Bonneville's technique was a little rusty, he was able to follow Lyra's journey with Trepka's aid more comfortably than he could with the new method. Perhaps his sense of balance had been disturbed when the girl kicked him, or perhaps his dæmon's broken wing had a psychological component; yes, that was it. The new method would come into its own when her wing had healed. In the meantime, he knew where Lyra was, though there was something confusing . . . Never mind for now.

Secondly, he turned his attention to Geneva and the Magisterium. He'd followed the politics of the new Supreme Council as much as the new method had let him, and he was glad to have a chance to explore it more fully without having to vomit. Delamare was gathering power to himself with the utmost skill and delicacy; hardly anyone outside the Council had been aware of the way the authority of the President had softly and silently grown, and the Council itself was so pleased with the way things were now done, the efficiency, the smooth and effortless inevitability, that every member was behind him. It helped that he was rewarding each of them tactfully: a new oratory here, funds for a period of study leave in a Mediterranean resort there, silent understanding for a family embarrassment somewhere else. Bonneville couldn't perceive all the details, but he understood very clearly the way things were developing.

It was galling in a way: the circumstances he could see prevailing in Geneva were exactly the sort of setting in which he and his particular talents could have prospered brilliantly. Once he had got the measure of the different personalities who made up the Council, Bonneville put the old *Alethiometrica Explicata* away and set to with the new method.

Just tentatively, just a little at a time, dipping a toe, withdrawing the moment his perception began to waver and disturb his balance, he looked at one after another of the individuals under Delamare's leadership. One or two he had met, a handful more he knew by name, but some were new to him altogether. It seemed that they intended to meet monthly at *La Maison Juste*, that there were twenty-four of them, and that those who lived and worked abroad and couldn't attend every month could appoint deputies to represent them, though the deputies did not have voting rights. Bonneville could follow the intricacies of debate only a little way before the new method failed, and detail was beyond Trepka's reach. Something was blocking him, and he couldn't discover what it was. It can only be a matter of bodily well-being, he told himself. Mentally he was at his peak; he was conscious of a surpassing clarity of thought. But the kick to the kidneys . . . And his dæmon's broken wing . . . They took their toll, these wounds of war.

If he had persisted with the new method he might have found out, but he simply didn't have the physical strength.

So he didn't see what lay behind the blockage in his perception. It was the simple fact that each of the members of the Council had been advised by Marcel Delamare (privately, and confidentially, and in the most kindly way) that it would be better for the Magisterium, and especially for them personally, if they did not speak to one another about Council matters outside minuted Council meetings. The implication was that they themselves of course enjoyed the President's entire confidence, but that other members might not. They could by all means communicate with one another in writing, but it would be better if letters went through the President's office first, so that he could advise on matters of policy or clarify misunderstandings.

It was all new, this Council business, so no one could object on the grounds that they'd never had to behave like that before. Obviously the President knew best. And those members who lived some way from Geneva didn't know one another well in any case, and would have been unlikely to meet in a casual way, or by chance; so no one found anything wrong with the arrangement. And there were no schisms, no little cracks of variance for serious dispute to take root in. At first.

But some Council members did live in or near Geneva, and some of them (in a casual way, or by chance) did sometimes find themselves in one another's company. And inevitably, people being what they are, they would talk about the Council, or the President, or the rules he had imposed, or the rumours of war, or anything else that occupied their attention; and it was natural too that some of them would find themselves chafing under the rule against such conversations.

So it was, one evening in the retiring chamber of the College of Bishops, that three men and two women found themselves in a casual way or by chance together after a fine dinner. They had come there to discuss in a perfectly lawful way something completely unrelated to the business of the Supreme Council, and since that other business had been concluded successfully some hours before, and since all five were Council members, and since the other guests (who weren't) had left, it was not surprising that conversation should turn to the way the new Council was working.

They all knew one another well. It might be said that they were old friends. There was nothing, except the President's warning, to stop them speaking their minds in the company of people they trusted and agreed with about so much. Besides, the food had been excellent and the wine generously poured. The fire was burning brightly; smokeleaf was being enjoyed; the armchairs were comfortable; dæmons were lolling on laps, or knees, or the cushioned backs of chairs.

'I'm very glad,' said their host, the Dean of the College of Bishops, a thin, intense and zealous man, 'to have this chance to talk, in private as it were. In view of what the President is about to announce, it would be a dereliction of our duty not to discuss the matter—'

'What is he about to announce?' said Karl von Landsberg. He was a senior officer of the Court of Common Order, large, red-bearded and soldierly.

'That's very much the point, Karl. We should have been told, and we haven't.'

'Is it Council business, though?' said Mariette Seidel, a professor of philology from Lausanne.

'Do you mean this war declaration?' said Julius Morschach. He was a banker, rich beyond anyone's ability to imagine, plump and sleek and genial.

'Yes, I do,' said the Dean.

'I'm afraid this is completely new to me,' said the fifth member of the group, Georges Parmentier, who had said very little throughout the evening. He was a parish priest from a small town near the eastern end of the lake, who had a reputation for simple piety that was not wholly undeserved. 'War, you say?'

'Our President,' said the Dean, 'is about to announce the start of a "holy campaign" ' – the quotation marks were audible – 'to capture and destroy *something, somewhere*, which he will claim is a source of inspiration and an object of reverence to the enemies of the Authority.'

'A what? A holy campaign? What does that mean?' said von Landsberg.

'A war,' said the banker Morschach. 'I have seen an outline of what he plans to say.'

'But how—'

'Where did you—'

'What on earth—'

'A *war*?'

'Haven't you noticed how he's been scuttling from capital to capital in the past few weeks for talks with governments all over Europe, and beyond?'

'Well, his travels here and there have been announced,' said Professor Seidel, 'but the announcements have been very bland – almost empty of content, in fact – I had been wondering . . .'

'Julius, tell us about this announcement,' said von Landsberg. 'You say you've seen an outline, was it, of what he's going to say. How did you get hold of that?'

'I'd rather not say for the moment. But you can take it that it's genuine. He's going to say that in the name of the Authority and of the entire body of the faithful, it is time to put an end to a source of evil which is corrupting the minds and hearts of countless numbers of people, from innocent children to men and women in positions of power and influence. It must be captured and destroyed.'

'*It*? What is it?' said the professor.

'Drugs, I shouldn't wonder,' said von Landsberg confidently. 'Opium, or worse.'

'The source of it, whatever it is,' said the Dean, 'is concealed in the heart of a desert in Central Asia. One of the most empty and barren wastelands you can imagine. The President has secret information about it. But of course he hasn't told the Council.'

'Well, we should demand that he does!' said von Landsberg. 'This is intolerable.'

'And these treaties and agreements and so on . . .' said Professor Seidel.

'All part of a complicated diplomatic dance. He's gathering support, which means the guarantee of arms and troops.'

'But why are other governments agreeing to this? How do they benefit?'

'By being part of a great movement. By securing the blessing of the greatest religious authority. By giving their populations a cause to cheer for and an enemy to hate,' the Dean said. His eyes were blazing darkly; Professor Seidel found him hard to look at.

'But a war must have an enemy,' said Parmentier. 'A state. A nation makes war on a nation, not a nameless something in the desert. What is the nation in this case?'

'Well, it would be Cathay, or that region known as Sinkiang,' said Morschach. 'But he's not calling it a war, he's calling it a campaign. The object is not to force another nation to surrender, but to destroy this . . . thing.'

'What is this *thing*, though?'

'A place, or a building,' said the Dean. 'That's all anyone knows. But no doubt we shall hear some carefully crafted rumours and exaggerated stories in the press before very long. Agitation and propaganda.'

'What view of this campaign does the empire of Cathay take, do we know?' said the professor. 'It would count as an invasion of their territory, wouldn't it?'

'Cathay is a profound mystery,' said Morschach. 'All we have is rumour, and I doubt whether any nation has more than that. Rumours that the Golden Emperor is in poor health, that he's died, that he's been transported bodily into heaven, that he's been deposed and replaced by a mechanical figure controlled by an evil spirit – in short, what Cathay does or thinks is not predictable. But I daresay they're interested in what might be about to happen in their western regions.'

'But what are *we* going to do about it *now*?' demanded von Landsberg.

'That depends on the precise form of the relationship between the President and the Council,' said the Dean, 'and that is something that's never been made clear. Is it our function to support the President in everything he says and does, with no opportunity to discuss it or veto it? And now without being told anything about this – this *campaign* – we are to be assailed from every side by questions from journalists, politicians, academics, the general public, with no idea what the answers should be? It's intolerable. Really quite intolerable.'

'When is he going to make this announcement?' said Parmentier.

'On Sunday, I've heard,' said Morschach. 'At the Celebration of the Last Supper. He'll preach a sermon calling on all faithful nations to join the campaign.'

'As you say, Jean-Paul,' said Professor Seidel to the Dean, 'this is intolerable. We'll have to stop him.'

'We should call an emergency meeting of the whole Council,' said von Landsberg.

'How?' said Parmentier.

'Well – contact every member and summon them to Geneva!'

'Have you got a list of names and addresses?' said the priest. 'Because I haven't. I suspect the only list is with the President.'

'I know a few, but some of the members I'd never known before,' said Professor Seidel. 'And in any case he directly forbade us to speak to one another. I'm sure this meeting now is against the rules.'

There was a short silence.

'How did we allow ourselves to be put in this absurd position?' said the Dean.

'We'll just have to go and see him ourselves. Do it now,' said von Landsberg, bristling like his badger-dæmon.

'He's in Paris,' said the banker.

'Well, tomorrow then. When he comes back.'

'The structural problem,' said the Dean, 'the basic problem, is one of information. There are things going on that we know about, but only indirectly. Or by rumour. Take this soldier with the explosives.'

'What's that?' said von Landsberg. 'Explosives?'

'Some officer of the Guard, acting on his own, set off a bomb or grenade in the forest above Les Diablerets. Someone died or disappeared. No one seems to know anything about it. Or show any interest, come to that.'

'I think I heard about that,' said von Landsberg. 'Man called Schneider, or Schreiber, maybe. Or Steiner. Might be a simple accident.'

'Has that anything to do with our current preoccupation?' said the banker.

'Only that it's something else we're kept in the dark about,' said the Dean.

'It's not the first time decisions have been made without consulting us,' said von Landsberg. 'There was that odd affair of the dæmon that didn't die when what's-his-name, the German professor, had a heart attack. We weren't informed about the decision to publish the professor's lecture.'

'Which will be redacted almost to the point of incoherence,' said Professor Seidel. 'It was a strange business altogether.'

'Which is exactly why we should know about these things. I think we should confront the President right away. Well? Who's with me?'

'I wonder,' said Morschach, 'whether there's a touch of instability, as you might say, in our President's mental outlook. His mother, I hear, is in a home for the unstable—'

'Oh, gossip, gossip,' said Professor Seidel.

'Nevertheless I think it would be wiser,' said Morschach, 'now that we've aired our concerns to ourselves, not to confront him at once but to spend a few days in discreet investigation, and meet again in a few days' time when we'll all know a little more.'

'And carefully,' said Professor Seidel. 'Caution. Discretion.'

They agreed to meet for dinner at Morschach's bank the following week, cautiously and discreetly, as if in a casual way, or by chance.

Lyra had booked a cabin on the ferry. Ionides said he would rather sleep on deck and keep watch, though there was no sign of the men who'd followed them from the post office, or any other threat. The journey to Krasnovodsk would take forty-eight hours, so there was time for Lyra to wash and change and then sit down at the little table under the porthole and unfasten the package Mustafa Bey had forwarded.

The first thing she found was a card that said:

In great haste. If this ever reaches you, I shall be in prison or dead. Use a pencil. Glenys Godwin, Oakley Street.

Asta read it too while Lyra unwrapped the paper of the inner parcel. Inside it she found a flat piece of stone, darkish green in colour, a little bigger than the palm of her hand. One side was smooth but not shiny, the other rougher, but only slightly.

'I've seen one of these,' Asta said. 'Malcolm had something like it. Someone gave it to him, but I don't know why. He was just beginning to examine it when Mr Ionides came, and I saw Malcolm hide it from him, but I was dozing, so I didn't watch.' She looked at the note again. ' "Use a pencil",' she read aloud. 'Have you got a pencil?'

'In the rucksack somewhere . . .' Lyra fumbled and found it. It was blunt, but it made a mark on the smooth side of the stone. She drew a line and looked at it. 'Now what?' she said.

'She wouldn't send you this if it was just something to make notes on,' Asta pointed out. 'You could use paper for that. It must be—'

'Look! It's fading.'

As they looked, the line seemed to fade into the surface of the stone.

Lyra wrote her name: *Lyra Silvertongue.* The pencil moved well over the surface.

'What were you going to say?' she said.

'Just that it must have some other purpose. Look, it's fading again.'

The letters slowly became fainter until they disappeared. Then something different happened: a mark appeared by itself, and moved over the surface leaving a trail behind it, like writing. It *was* writing.

It said: *Lyra? Is that you?*

Lyra was so startled that she dropped the pencil and Asta leaped down to pick it up, and sprang up again, and Lyra took it with a trembling hand.

As soon as the pencil was out of her mouth Asta said, 'That's Malcolm's writing!'

And Lyra remembered the elegant italic in the letter that had reached her in the Fens. It was the same.

Her heart was beating. She could hardly hold the pencil. But she wrote *Where is Oakley Street?*

And the answer came:

Oakley Street is not in Chelsea.

She wrote: *That's true as far as it goes.*

And it replied *It goes as far as the Embankment. Lyra, is that really you? Where are you?*

On a ferry from Baku to Krasnovodsk. Where are you?

Captive on a great mountain called Damāvand. Pan is with me.

Lyra felt faint. Her fingers loosened and the pencil fell again – she leaned back in the chair – her heart was beating so hard it hurt her throat.

Asta recovered the pencil once more, and Lyra took it, shaking so much she could hardly form the letters:

And Asta is here with me.

A wave of emotion swept up through her body from her feet to the hair on her head. What emotion it was she couldn't have named: it was enough to feel its power and its inexorable authority. It left her limp and helpless.

Are you both well? Both safe?

Yes, yes.

How did you get the stone?

Mustafa Bey sent it – forwarded it – Malcolm, is it really you? Am I dreaming?

Really me.

Captive? You mean a prisoner?

Not exactly. A guest, but under guard. Gryphons.

And where?

Damāvand is at the southern end of the Caspian Sea. Would you like to speak to Pan?

Yes, oh yes, but not like this. It's enough to know he's with you. Is he?

Yes, he's safe and well. He's watching and reading as we talk.

So's Asta. Oh I long to – I don't know what – tell Pan that I'm sorry, sorry, sorry.

He knows. So is he.

She had to stop for a few moments before she could go on.

She wrote: *And – gryphons? Really?*

This is the palace of their queen Shahrnavāz. They desire gold above everything, and I'm working on an alethiometer for her. She won't let me go till I've finished.

Where did that come from? Is it mine?

It might be. Pan thinks it is.

A gryphon stole it from me – is it badly broken?

The dial's broken, but I've taken it out together with the movement and I'm beating the gold case into another shape. The Queen's only interested in the gold. I'll keep the important parts and set it all in another case later.

And I've got the needle and the glass!

As she wrote the words she heard the ferry's whistle sound, and felt a slight motion as the engines began to turn the screw. She looked out through the porthole and saw the quayside and the buildings beyond seem to move slowly away as the ferry steamed out into the open sea.

More words appeared in her stone:

Ionides – is he with you?

Yes. So much to tell you I don't know where to start. Do you know him then?

He came to me in Aleppo and then took me to the embassy garden where you were asleep.

The day the gryphons took you.

Yes.

Was Pan with you then?

No. Already with the gryphons.

He was in al Khan al – can't spell it, just before I was there. When the gryphon snatched up the man holding the alethiometer and flew away. It's been stolen and stolen again and again.

I stole it from Bonneville in the flood.

Of course you did! And then gave it to me!

Asta said, 'Ask him how he's going to get away.'

Lyra wrote: *Asta wants to know how you're going to get away. So do I.*

The answer came. *On the back of a gryphon. Pan knows how to talk to them. Krasno – where?*

Krasnovodsk. Other side of the Caspian. When will you finish the gold beating?

Another day or so. Oh – and a witch is here. She is trying to make an alliance between her people and the gryphons, first time ever. To fight the Magisterium, because their troops are already moving east.

Lyra paused to take that in.

There's just so much she wrote, and stopped. *But I'm holding you up. You must make that gold thing. Isn't it wonderful to talk, though? This stone won't suddenly stop working, will it?*

I don't think so, and yes, it's wonderful. The stones are called resonating lodestones, apparently. Glenys Godwin of Oakley S sent mine to me. No idea where they come from originally.

A bell rang in Lyra's mind. The Gallivespians – the world of the dead – they had devices like this to talk to their commander, who was somewhere else—

I think I know, she wrote. *But later.* She hesitated and then wrote: *Be careful and work well. Love, Lyra.*

Perhaps that was too much. But it was too late; the words were already fading. The ferry gathered speed as it sailed out on to the Caspian Sea.

Georges Parmentier, the parish priest from the eastern end of the lake, was so exceedingly modest that even his shrew-dæmon sometimes found him timid. When she said so, his response was to apologise, which irritated her; but she was too good-natured to reproach him for it. He couldn't help it, and she understood that. The life they lived in the modest parish house in a quiet suburb was orderly, chaste, and simple. He had little idea how much his parishioners liked and valued him, how much his superiors trusted him, how far his reputation reached. He had been profoundly taken aback to find himself first on the High Council, and now in the small faction that seemed to have formed itself almost chemically to oppose whatever the President was doing – if he understood it rightly. His capacity for understanding things was something else he was modest about.

'What should we do, Sylvie?' he said as he sipped his morning tisane in the little garden. It wasn't summer yet, but the day was already sunny and the warmth under the walnut tree was very pleasant.

'Find things out,' said his dæmon. 'Of course.'

'Yes, yes, no doubt about that. But where to start? What to ask about first?'

'What do we dislike most?'

'The Council. I should never have agreed to join.'

'No, you shouldn't. You didn't want to, so you did it in order to feel that you were sacrificing yourself again.'

'Oh, no, no, don't exaggerate. It was something I felt I should do, in spite of the discomfort.'

'I know. But you did have the choice.'

'And now this . . . group.'

'They asked you to join. They wanted you.'

'And already they're plotting against the President.'

'Now you're exaggerating.'

'I don't think so.'

She climbed down his trouser-leg and probed the grass for insects. She snapped up an ant and said, 'You felt uneasy with him, and now you feel uneasy against him?'

'Yes, I did. I do. This business with an explosion – I don't understand it, and I want to know why it's happening. Like the others yesterday.'

'Go and see the General.'

'I was afraid you'd say that.'

She scampered back up his leg and confronted him sternly from his knee. 'No, you hoped I'd say that,' she snapped. 'Finish your tisane – it's cold now anyway – and go and see him at once.'

This must be what living in a marriage must be like, in a small kind of way, he thought for the thousandth time, washing and drying his teacup. Celibacy was not a requirement under the Magisterium, but it was implied very clearly during his training for ordination that marriage was a second-best way of living. Even a humble parish priest would be better able to serve the Authority without the complications and distractions of a wife and children, but it wasn't a natural way of living, he thought very secretly; the stern fondness between him and his dæmon was the most important thing in his life, but a kindly woman, warm and gentle and understanding, soft-fleshed . . . Enough of that. He had to see the General. Sylvie had said so.

'It's about a military matter,' he said to the maidservant who answered his knock.

She had never learned his name. She viewed him with contempt because he had never been a soldier.

'The General's busy,' she said, as she did every time he called.

'I expect he is. I won't take up much of his time.'

She stood aside grudgingly. Her weasel-dæmon scowled at him from her apron pocket.

He wiped his feet and followed her down the unlit corridor to the study door.

'Send him in,' the General called before she knocked.

The maid opened the door and let Parmentier go in, watching him as if he were a vagabond.

'Saw you coming up the drive,' said the old man, standing up to shake hands. 'How are you, Padre?'

He was dressed stiffly, in a thick tweed suit and polished brogues, tight collar and regimental tie. Parmentier was fond of him; General Ravignac was a respecter of traditions and duties and persons. His bulky wheezy spaniel-dæmon opened an eye from her armchair and thumped her tail twice on the cushion before closing the eye again.

'How are your memoirs coming along, General?'

The general waved a vague hand at the confusion of papers on his desk and came to join Parmentier by the fireside. 'Too much of it,' he said. 'Too many memories.'

'Then you're fortunate. Some people have fewer and fewer.'

'Can't decide what's important, you see. Things that made an impression on me, things I managed to do . . . What should go in, what should stay out? I don't know. You know my strongest memory?'

'Tell me.'

'Girl I failed to kiss. Even failed to say a word to her. Struck dumb, you see. Most beautiful girl I ever saw, or ever have seen since . . . I was, oh, eighteen. Dance at some big house – simply didn't have the nerve.'

'Ah, regret. Somebody said it's the things we don't do that we regret most of all.'

'Well, I shall never know, unless there's an afterlife. Maybe we'll be punished more for the things we didn't do than the things we did. Is there a theological view of that, Padre?'

'Almost certainly, but I don't know what it might be. General, I wonder if you've ever come across an officer of the Guard who was seen recently in Les Diablerets. I think his name might be Schreiber, or possibly Schneider.'

The old man's eyes widened very briefly. 'You don't mean the careless fool who killed the forester?'

'I didn't know anyone was killed. Was there an explosion involved?'

The general sat forward. 'Yes, there was. How do you know about it?'

Parmentier had anticipated the question. 'I'm a member of the new Council, you know, the Magisterial President's High Council. The matter came up in a sub-committee. I thought I should find out what's behind it.'

'You couldn't ask the chief?'

'Monsieur Delamare? I really want to save his time. What happened to this forester?'

'Blown to pieces, poor chap. Someone from the nearest village saw a man in a Bataillon Alpin beret coming down shortly afterwards.'

'And this was at Les Diablerets?'

'Somewhere in a steep bit of forest above the village.'

'Did anyone investigate?'

'No. There's what they call an NMT order in place. *Don't touch me*, you know.'

'NMT . . . *Noli me tangere*. Well! I'd never heard of that.'

'Few people have. It's a thing they issue to journalists: don't print anything about this. No one's to speak about it, or write anything. I wouldn't know about it, no one in the general public would, but the village policeman in Les Diablerets is an old chum, and he lets me know what's going on.'

'That's very interesting. Could this soldier have been testing a new kind of bomb?'

'That's what I'd guess.'

'Was anything known about the spot where it went off?'

The general frowned. Parmentier didn't want to tire the old man, who was looking distracted and anxious.

'All very troubling,' said the priest gently.

'Tell you one thing though. A man came to see me a year or two ago – English fellow – Beaming, Beamish maybe – scholar of some sort. He came here because he'd heard I grew up near Les Diablerets, and he was looking for a particular spot – some geological formation, something like that. Or was it the atmosphere? I didn't really understand what he wanted, so I couldn't help. But you know, there always used to be a story when I was a boy – story about a door into fairyland up on the mountain, in the forest. Told him about it. Lot of nonsense, of course – old women's tales – never found it myself, nor met anyone who did.'

'Did you look for it, though, when you were young?'

'Well, might have done once or twice. Never found it. You could hear something, though, on dark nights. Singing, and bells. Not from the village. Nothing like the church or the inn, nothing like the everyday sounds we knew. Infinitely distant, and . . . Excuse me . . .'

He shook out a well-ironed handkerchief and dabbed his eyes. The old soldier was weeping. Parmentier said nothing and waited till the general cleared his throat and put the handkerchief away.

'Damned old fool,' he muttered. 'Sorry, Padre. Caught myself by surprise. The singing was unearthly beautiful. Couldn't speak of it then; other boys would laugh. I only heard it twice, and I longed to hear it again. Like the girl at the ball. Same sort of feeling. Almost as if everything beautiful was in another world, and there was a doorway, and if only I could find it . . .'

Parmentier pictured his friend, the arthritis-crippled old soldier, the hero of the siege of Monterrey, in his campaign tent on the eve of battle with the army sleeping around him; some of his men, no doubt, were praying, and others, no doubt, were drunk; and the young officer sleepless with longing for a girl whose beauty had stunned him into silence, and for singing voices and bells from another world, which had broken his heart.

The general cleared his throat again. 'Sorry, old friend,' he said gruffly. 'Not much help to you this morning.'

Parmentier said nothing for a minute or so, and then said, 'You mentioned the soldier with the beret. Bataillon Alpin, you said?'

'There used to be a regiment called the Chasseurs Alpins. Had a particular kind of beret – unmistakable. Black. This chap was wearing one, apparently. He had a badge – I didn't recognise it when the witness described it to me – a little Roman sort of lamp with a flame at the wick. Probably engineers or something. Army's all mixed up now; I don't understand half of it.'

'Ah, well . . . Do we know anything about the man who was killed? The forester?'

'No. They assume he's dead; no body or anything. Just an explosion, and never seen again.'

'Perhaps he found the doorway into the land of the bells and the singing.'

The general grunted.

'Didn't the police make any enquiries?' Parmentier went on.

'NMT.'

'Ah yes, I see . . . Who issues an NMT order, do you know?'

'It used to be a body called La Maison Juste. But now . . .' The general blew out his cheeks and made an elaborate shrug. 'Better be careful,' he said. 'The public's not supposed to know about that kind of thing.'

La Maison Juste, thought the priest. *Delamare.*

He stood up stiffly and shook hands with the old man.

'Forgive me for not seeing you to the door, my friend,' the general said. 'It's always good to talk to you. Come again soon.'

19

Arctic Healing

'I want to look at your wound,' said Tilda Vasara.

They were in Malcolm's chamber again, and the witch had just arrived from a long private discussion with Queen Shahrnavāz, which he was eager to hear about. It was not exactly at the forefront of his mind, though: he had just put down the lodestone, and the last words that Lyra had written had vanished from the stone, but not from his thoughts.

Night had enveloped the mountain, and the wind was still wild. The heavy curtains stirred in the draughts, the lamplight flared and flickered; the fire in the alcove burned steadily, but did little to warm the room; and Pan, who was normally indifferent to the temperature, sat on the table with a silk shawl around him.

'Why?' said Malcolm, rather stupidly, as he realised at once.

Tilda Vasara said, 'Because I want to see if I can cure it, of course. Show me now.'

He stood up stiffly and unbuckled his belt. The bullet fired by the nurse had hit him in the hip, chipping the bone and lodging painfully in the muscle. When he stayed so briefly at the villa with the orange tree, the Embassy had sent a doctor to look at him, but all he'd done was bandage the wound and give him some painkillers. It was hurting more and more, and was probably infected; Malcolm didn't like to examine it, but he knew that someone should.

'Go on,' said Pan. 'Don't be silly.'

Standing by the table, he lowered his trousers and lifted the edge of his shirt. Tilda Vasara moved the oil lamp closer and unfastened the bandage, crouching to see the damage.

She touched the flesh around the wound, which was swollen and red. Malcolm caught his breath.

'Bad,' was all she said. 'Need to cut it out.'

'Can you do that?'

'Yes. Can you bear it?'

'I'll have to.'

'Yes, you will. I need a bowl of water.'

'I'll call Darius,' said Pan, and jumped down from the table. 'Hot water?'

'Makes no difference to me, but it might to him,' said Tilda Vasara.

Pan leaped up and clung to the bell-pull that was their way of summoning the servant. The bell jangled, and a few seconds later Darius came in from the corridor, a little rumpled from the pile of blankets where he slept.

'Darius, we need a bowl of hot water,' Malcolm said to him, and added to the witch, 'Anything else?'

'I have everything I need.'

Darius bowed and left.

'What are you going to do?' Pan asked her.

'There is something in his flesh that should not be there, so I'm going to cut it out. Then I shall clean the wound with bloodmoss.'

She was unfastening a small pouch at her waist. Malcolm watched as she took out a small iron knife with a wooden handle, its blade as long as his forefinger, and a bundle of dried herbs tied with string.

'Bloodmoss?' he said. 'What is that?'

'You would say antiseptic, analgesic. Other things too. Lie down, please.'

Malcolm lay on the pile of furs, on his left side so that the wound was uppermost. It felt hot, even in the cold air.

'They give you any medicine for this?' she said.

'Some pills to subdue the pain.'

'Any good?'

'Not much.'

'Bloodmoss will work.'

The door opened, and Darius came in with a ceramic bowl. Tilda Vasara indicated that he should put it on the floor beside her, and he did so, looking wide-eyed at Malcolm's wound as he left. The witch moved the lamp to the edge of the table so that it shone on his leg, and sat cross-legged to unfasten the string around the herbs before separating out three or four stems and a dusty bundle of dried moss.

Then she said, 'Take out your belt.'

Malcolm removed the leather belt from his trousers, thinking that she was going to use it as a tourniquet, but she took it and flexed it this way and that before folding it in half and then in half again. Then she handed it back.

'What's this for?'

'You bite it. Stop you squawking.'

'I see.'

Pan, watching closely, said, 'Is there anything I can do?'

'Just keep the lamp good. The wick needs to come up a little.'

Without fingers and hands, Pan had to duck under the glass shade and grasp the knob in his teeth. It was extremely hot, and he knew that if he flinched or moved carelessly and knocked the lamp over, it could set fire to the whole room. He managed to turn up the wick, and withdrew with what he thought was the smell of his own fur burning.

'That's better,' said the witch.

She took the little knife. Malcolm watched with his lifelong curiosity about tools, and said, 'Can I see that?'

She handed it to him, and he turned it round, feeling the weight of it, testing the edge against his thumbnail.

'Sharp,' he said.

'Not enough yet.'

She took it back and rose to her feet before moving to the windowsill, feeling along the stone for a patch that was smoother than the rest. She spat on the blade and sharpened it on the stone, moving it as if she was slicing a layer of atoms off the surface, testing the edge till she was satisfied.

'Now we make it hot,' she said. 'That fire – where does it come from?'

The fire in the alcove was burning steadily, as it always did.

'From inside the mountain,' he said.

'Earth fire. Good. All the conveniences.'

She held the knife blade in the flame, turning it and twisting it until it began to glow. Malcolm could smell the heated iron, and Pan crouched tightly at his side, terrified for him, dreading the prospect of the next minute, but not turning away, because he knew that Lyra wouldn't.

'Belt,' said the witch.

Malcolm lay back and put the folded end of the belt between his teeth, and bit hard.

'*Sisu*,' she said as she sat, and leaned forward to make the first cut.

Malcolm's entire spine flexed upwards as his skull slammed back against the fur-covered floor. He felt a keening in his own throat, and smelled his skin and muscle burning, and heard the sizzle as the hairs on his leg crisped and charred.

'Good. Another cut coming.'

The second time was worse. She seemed to be digging deeper, or cutting further, and twisting and wrenching, or something, and he heard as well as felt it when the knife scraped bone.

'Worst coming now,' she said.

He could barely hear her. There was a drumming of blood in his ears, and his teeth were gripping the belt so hard that his jaw was nearly cracking.

'*Sisu*,' she said again, and the knife twisted deeper, and then something happened in his hip, and a fierce guttural bear-grunt forced its way out of his throat as a sharp bright clink somewhere outside him told of the bullet falling against the bowl.

Malcolm didn't know where his hands were, except that the nails were gouging at the palms, but he felt Pan licking one hand, and didn't know which. His senses were scrambled in a kaleidoscopic synaesthesia, all shot through with blazing blood-red pain.

The witch's hand gently removed the belt from his mouth, and he felt that his teeth had embedded themselves in the tough hide, reluctant to let it go. He breathed deeply and quickly. Tilda Vasara was doing something else now; he heard her hands moving in the bowl of water, stirring it, squeezing water out of a cloth, stirring the liquid, raising water in a cupped hand and letting it fall back.

'Dæmon,' she said. 'Bring me that silk from the table.'

Malcolm dimly saw Pan spring up off the floor, snatch the shawl in his teeth, and dive down again, the silk flowing through the air behind him.

'Lay it flat beside him.'

Pan moved again. Malcolm felt something touch his wound and nearly flinched, but held himself still. Every nerve seemed open to the air, which played on the flesh like a blowlamp.

'What are you doing?' he managed to say.

'Making a poultice of bloodmoss. It will penetrate to every part of the wound and kill the infection and soothe the pain. You can't believe it now, but it will. Just keep still.'

Liquid fell on to the wound, scalding, acid, lacerating. He forced himself to hold still and focused on the calm voice in which she spoke.

'More coming,' she said.

314

This time he was used to it, or he was expecting it, or it was cooler.

'What is bloodmoss?' he said.

'It grows in the tundra. I don't know what other people call it, but that's our name for it: *krovlishaynik*. Bloodmoss. Maybe not moss exactly, but close enough. We know it when we see it. Dæmon, is there another piece of silk in that chest?'

Malcolm realised that his eyes were closed. He opened them and blinked hard, to see Pan springing up and into the cedar chest, and then out again with a silken cloth in his teeth. He propped himself up on an elbow and watched as Tilda Vasara took the cloth and wadded it into a small bundle.

'What are you doing now?' he said.

'Cleaning the wound. Who shot you?'

'A liar.'

'You kill him?'

'Her. She shot herself before I could stop her.'

'Lover, huh?'

'In this case, no.'

'Just crazy then.'

She was dipping the silk into the water and dabbing gently at the wound, which was bleeding freely.

'What do you do with the bloodmoss?'

'Two things. I put some directly into the wound. It dissolves in three days and purifies the blood. The other thing, I make an infusion that you drink. Bad taste but makes you strong boy. Look, see how it works.'

She took a small piece of the sodden moss, about the size of the top joint of her thumb, and laid it on the edge of the wound. In less than a minute the bleeding stopped, and the pain subsided to a warm numbness.

'That hurt still?'

'Much less.'

'All right, now I put some inside. Hold tight.'

She squeezed a little water out of the dark green handful, and then packed it, a pinch at a time, into the wound itself. The numbing helped; he had no doubt about how much it would hurt otherwise, and compared to the knife-point of a few minutes before it was almost blessedly gentle.

'You got a cup? Something to drink from?'

Pan said, 'I'll get it. Do you need some more hot water?'

'Plenty here.'

Malcolm looked at the murky blood-tinged water. 'You want me to drink that?'

'The blood came from inside you anyway, and what is not blood is *krovlishaynik*, which will do you good.'

Pan brought her a horn cup, and she scooped out a little of the water. He sat up as best he could and drank it down at once, and was nearly sick. It was foul, bitter, with a metallic taint.

'Keep still,' she said.

He swallowed and controlled his impulse to vomit, breathing deeply.

'What did you talk about with the Queen?' he said.

'Royal matters. They choose their queens as we do.'

'Always a queen gryphon, not a king?'

'They have kings. This time they chose a queen.'

'But the other matter, the one you came here to talk about . . .'

'Yes. They are angry without knowing more than they do now. They want nothing to change, but the world is changing around them, and they know it and fear it. So we agree, and make alliance.'

'You did? Congratulations.'

'Need to act soon too.'

'Do you know what the Magisterium is doing?'

'Not in detail. Those explosions, for one thing. And separately they are moving large numbers of soldiers eastward, by rail, by road. Not by air. We shall command the sky, witches and gryphons together.'

'Eastward? You know where, exactly?'

'We hear rumours about a desert and a moving lake.'

'Lop Nor. Half swamp, half desert, with streams that change their courses overnight.'

'You been there?'

'Yes, once. Very hard to navigate, and nothing to see on the other side, or so I thought.'

'Other side?'

'An arid desert with a building at the heart of it. I guess that's where the Magisterium forces are heading. Can you tell me more about the places where these explosions happen?'

'Mostly no, because they happen on the ground, in forests or mountains, where witches seldom go. Always wild places.'

'Are they holy places for you? Magic places?'

'For us, not always. For men and women on the ground, maybe.'

'And always in wild places? Never in a city or a village?'

'Maybe. There are many of them, it seems. What you told us – the information from your Oakley commander – brought it all together for me and for Queen Shahrnavāz. I shall speak to her again at sunrise, and you will come with me. Now you sleep.'

Perhaps it was the bloodmoss, perhaps it was the shock his body had undergone during the witch's surgery, but something was weighing heavily on Malcolm's eyelids, and he had no desire to remain awake. He pulled one of the furs over himself and closed his eyes.

Pan watched it all with his heart beating fast. When it was over and the witch was sitting between him and Malcolm on the furs, he said to her, 'Is your dæmon still out in the sky?'

'He's coming to me,' she said quietly. 'He will be here by daybreak.'

'When you're apart, can you think together?'

'No more than you can.'

'I don't know any people who can separate, apart from Malcolm.'

'Neither do I, apart from all the witches.'

'Do you know . . .' He hesitated, because he wasn't sure whether there was a rule of courtesy that forbade such questions, but he went on, 'Do you know a witch called Serafina Pekkala?'

'I did, but she is dead now.'

'*No . . .*' It struck Pan hard. He felt breathless and faint. 'When?' he whispered.

'Seventeen moons ago. She was killed by a missionary.'

'A missionary? In the Arctic?'

'The Magisterium is becoming more aggressive. All their intentions are bad.'

Pan thought: *I must tell Lyra before she hears it from anyone else. And Farder Coram . . .*

'When a witch dies, do you bury her?' he said, and then, 'I'm sorry to be inquisitive. But Lyra and I loved Serafina Pekkala very much. If there's a grave, she'd want to visit and say goodbye.'

'No graves in the far north. The soil is frozen. We leave her in a high place and the birds of the air clean her bones. I loved her too.'

'What happened to the missionary?'

'Her clan killed him and everyone with him.'

'Why did he kill her in the first place?'

'What I heard, and I believe it to be true, is that he knew that witches take human lovers, and proposed such an arrangement between himself and Serafina Pekkala. She refused him in disgust, and told her clan to avoid him and impede his work, and he took the first chance he could and shot her.'

They sat silently for a while. The only sounds were those of the wind buffeting the mountain and rattling the shutters, and the soft hiss of the earth-fire burning in the alcove.

'Does your Lyra love this man?' said Tilda Vasara quietly, looking at the sleeping Malcolm.

'I think she might. But it would be love of a strange kind. When we were young he was her teacher for a short time, and she behaved badly. Even I could see that. He was patient and clever and agreed that he should withdraw and someone else should teach her. But she behaved badly with them too. I could see it and I didn't like it but she didn't listen to me. She was just unhappy. Confused about everything. And then we met Malcolm again in different circumstances. She began to see him differently.'

'And how does he feel?'

'Well, he hasn't talked about it at all, though we've hardly had the chance for that sort of conversation. He might not want to tell me. I think Malcolm might feel . . . very careful. If he loved Lyra, he'd never say it, because she's so much younger.'

'How much younger?'

'Eleven years, I think.'

'Do you know how absurd that sounds, to a witch four hundred years old? Smaller than the clipping of a fingernail. I've been in love many times, and each time with a man centuries younger than myself, who lived no longer than a mayfly; and each time I wished no more than to be a mayfly too, and grow old and die at the same pace as my lover. In the end the sorrow wears us out. This Malcolm and your Lyra are close enough. Why did you say that their love would be of a strange kind?'

'Because neither of them would want to be the first to declare it. They would feel very formal. I think they respect each other a lot.'

'There are no rules. Love can grow even when people respect each other. But they should remember that even if they live for another sixty years, that is not a long time.'

'Are there no men witches, who age as slowly as you do?'

'Not in this world. Now take this.' She reached up to the coronet of little yellow flowers, and took one from the rest, and handed it to him. 'You will meet trouble,' she said. 'Keep this somewhere safe, and when you need help, take it out and hold it up to the sky.'

Pan took it, and immediately an idea came to him, stark and clear and blazing like a comet. And he held up the flower.

'You want my help now?'

'Yes. Could you fly me if I clung to your pine branch?'

'Yes,' she said.

'Can you fly me to Tashbulak?'

'You mean the research station in the desert?'

'Yes, in case Lyra's arrived there. And then on to the red building.'

Tilda said nothing for a minute. Pan thought she was going to ignore him, as if he was a child wanting a sweet.

Then: 'When?' she said.

'Now.'

'You going to tell him?' She looked at the sleeping Malcolm.

'No. He'll guess.'

'You think? Don't betray him. You must leave a message.'

Pan saw that was true, and although his paws weren't formed for holding a pencil, he did his best. He crouched over a piece of paper on the table and wrote:

MALCOLM.
SORRY BUT GONE WITH TILDA VASARA TO
TASHBULAK AND RED BUILDING.
GULYA WILL HELP.
PAN

The witch took up her branch of cloud-pine, torn from the trunk at one end, thick with cones and needles at the other, and held it out. Pan sprang on to it and clung tight, and a few moments later they were in the buffeting air above the mountain, and flying east.

And Lyra was awake. The tempest that was howling around the mountains at the south of the Caspian Sea had a number of offspring further to the north, born from a sudden collapse in the air pressure over the whole region – storms lesser in size but even more intense, which lashed the water and hurled the waves against the shore, against one another, against the rain-filled air, against every vessel whose skipper was reckless enough to take to the water, and in particular, battering the Transcaspian Modern Ferry as it crossed the narrowest part of the sea between Baku and Krasnovodsk. Lyra lay in her bunk, suffering the rolling and plunging of the boat, the constant rumble of the engine, and the smash of the waves as they broke against the porthole of her little cabin. The movement took her back to the first sea voyage she'd ever made, with the gyptians to Trollesund, and to her discomfort in the German Ocean. Pan shared it then, though it didn't seem that Asta did now. Perhaps Pan was suffering elsewhere. She remembered how much better she'd felt on that first journey when she went out on deck, and after a particularly sickly plunge now she thought she'd try the same remedy, so she wrapped herself up as warmly as she could and left Asta to guard the cabin while she went out to let the winds blow her unease away.

Odd, she thought, how she hadn't felt that sort of discomfort on the ferry from King's Lynn. Perhaps the winds were fiercer here in the Caspian. They certainly felt it. At any rate, she was the only passenger on deck, and she found a bench near the lifeboats where she could sit fairly comfortably and watch the white-capped waves and the occasional shudder of lightning in the heavy clouds.

She hadn't sat there long when she felt rather than saw another presence on the bench beside her.

And she wasn't startled, and she felt no fear. The presence wasn't a person, or a night-ghast, or a memory, or a dream: she felt a calm certainty that the presence was benevolent, that it knew who she was, and that she could trust it completely.

'Who are you?' she said.

She tried looking at it, and found nothing to see except a slight thickening of the shadows. There was a bulkhead light further along the deck, but here in this corner by the lifeboats the only light came from the surging phosphorescence of the waves.

The presence moved, but very slightly, and Lyra heard a voice that might have spoken inside her own skull.

'We have not spoken before,' it said. 'But I know who you are. An angel called Xaphania told me about you.'

Lyra remembered with a shiver of fear: Xaphania was the angel who told her and Will that they could not live in the same world, and must separate, and that the only form of travel between worlds must take place in the imagination.

The imagination—

'Xaphania?' Lyra said. 'You've really spoken to Xaphania?'

'Yes.'

'She told me when we last met that there was to be no travelling between worlds. Did you know that?'

'Of course.'

'And she said that we must close every opening between the worlds.'

'That is the truth.'

'But she said that we'd be able to travel in the imagination. What did she mean by the imagination?'

'You understood her then. Now you are grown up, and you've forgotten?'

The voice was perfectly clear inside her head, like those of the angels she'd spoken to at other times. What she couldn't tell was whether it could be heard outside as well.

'I didn't understand, and neither did the boy who was with me,' she said. 'I want to know now more than ever: what is the imagination?'

'The power of making things up. Inventing things. Surely you know that?' said the voice.

'Am I imagining your voice now? Imagining what you're saying to me?'

'No. I'm truly saying it, and you're truly hearing it.'

'I'm hearing it, but I don't believe it. And it wasn't what Xaphania said before.'

'In telling things to children, we have to sweeten the truth. You wouldn't believe the truth when you were young, because you didn't want to, and you would have argued and demanded a truth that you liked instead of one you found unpalatable.'

'I was a child. I couldn't argue with a being like her.'

'You argued with all the authorities of your world. You argued with every law you had ever known. You argued with everyone who told you that Dust was abominable, and had to be feared and rejected. Now you say you couldn't argue with one angel?'

'I couldn't argue then. But I can argue now. And something else: back then, she said the imagination wasn't just making things up – it was a form of seeing. Was that true?'

'As I say, we need to tell children many things to console them. Human parents do that, and it's kind to do so. There are times we need consolation more than accuracy.'

'So she told me a lie?'

'She consoled you.'

'All right then,' Lyra said bitterly, 'I'm grateful for that consolation. But I'm a grown woman now, and it's about time I heard the truth. Because I know that whatever the imagination is, it isn't just *inventing things*. Making things up and pretending they're real *is not enough*.'

'It is enough for the great poets. For the storytellers and the artists of every kind. They take things as they are, things in the world, and play with them and change them about and make something new. Is that an activity to condemn as trivial?'

'That's what you think poets and storytellers do?'

'Why, yes. What else?'

And Lyra didn't know. She knew so little, herself; surely Pan was thinking of something more than that when he went in search of the great thing she had lost.

'But that's what I did when I told lies,' she said. 'I used to be a famous liar. I took things that were partly true and I made up other things out of them. But they were lies. I knew they weren't true as I told them. You can't mean that the imagination is the same thing as telling lies?'

'Where is the difference?'

'The difference . . .' Lyra began, and then thought carefully before going on: 'There is no difference between lies and what *you* said the imagination was. Taking real things and changing them a bit. That's exactly what liars do. That's what I used to do, all the time. I can still do that, if I want to. I'm good at it. Pantalaimon knows that. Why would he go in search of something I still had?'

'Because he wants more. And in following him, you're doing the same. You want more than there is to have.'

'I just want to know the truth.'

'And I've told you the truth.'

Lyra could barely speak. There was a turmoil in her heart at least the equal of the storm on the water, and she was afraid of her own anger even more than she was afraid of the seasickness. She sat still, squeezing her painful left hand to distract herself.

Finally she said, trembling, 'I think you're wrong.'

'Why?'

'I think you're wrong, because I've learned things in the past ten years that I didn't know when I spoke to Xaphania on that beach in another world half my life ago. I thought then that angels must speak the truth, because they know the truth and they wouldn't lie. Well, I knew already that people can lie even if they know the truth, because that's what I did. Lyra the liar. That's what they called me in the world of the dead. I knew that. But I've learned something else too: older people, even people as old as angels, don't know everything. They might give the impression of great wisdom, immense knowledge, the experience of thousands upon thousands of lifetimes, but they can still be wrong. There are still things they don't know. They can speak with great confidence and still be wrong. They can be good and benevolent and kindly and yes, wise too, but they can still get things wrong. There are things I know that you don't – yes, there are. And when you talk like

that about the thing my dæmon has risked his life – and mine –
to go and find, when you describe something so important and
precious in terms of *making things up* and *pretending*, I know you've
got it wrong.'

The angel said nothing. The thickened cluster of shadows that
was all Lyra could see of her didn't move. If she was angry, or
contemptuous, she gave no sign.

Lyra thought: *Am I talking to myself?*

'I'm not sure if you can hear me,' she said, 'so I'll say something
else, just in case you can. Xaphania told me and Will that we had
to stay in our own worlds. That there should be no contact with
other ones. She said every time the subtle knife cut through from
one world to another, it left a gap that Spectres could come out of.
Again, we believed her then. But maybe that was something else
she thought was true, except that it wasn't. Or something she just
said to . . . What was the word? *Console* us.'

Nothing but silence from the shadows.

'Because, you see, there's something I've been thinking about.
The rose oil that's one of the ways people can see Dust – it comes
from the desert of Karamakan, from a building there that the
guards let no one enter. Well, I think there's one of those openings
there. Will and I used to call them windows. Between our world
and the rose world, I mean. I'm going to go there and see if that's
true. Because if it is, and if the rose oil helps people to understand
the truth about things, then I want to keep it open. I want to make
sure other openings like that are protected. I want to make new
ones. Can you hear what I'm saying?'

She felt a kind of shiver, as if she'd just said something she
didn't know, until then, that she believed.

'Yes, and it causes me sorrow,' the shadows whispered.

'Because of the Spectres?'

'Because of a thousand things you know nothing about.'

'But in some ways I do know more than you.'

'You don't know, you dream—'

'When you say *dream*, tell me what you think that means. Truthfully.'

'A dream is your imagination working. A thing of fantasy. Your dreams are empty things, gossamer, fragile, transitory. You have them only to forget them. Wishes, impossible things, horses that fly, clocks that walk about, trees that speak – nothing but fragments of cobweb. Trivial, childish, unimportant. You dream, and I see truly. That's the difference.'

'That's something else you've got wrong,' Lyra said.

'What's that?' The angel's tone was interested, not brusque.

'You think that what matters in a dream is the story, the information, the content, you could say, and that it's meaningless, because it makes no sense and fades and disappears. Of course it does, because the information is not what's important. What matters most in a dream is the emotion that comes with it. Dreams are *soaked* with emotion, with fear, or longing, or love, or excitement, or sadness. They come to give us intense feeling, not information, and it lasts a very long time, long after the information, or the story, is blown away like dry leaves. I know that some angels used to be human beings. Were you ever human?'

'No.'

'Do angels dream?'

'No.'

'Do angels make art? Do you write poetry or compose music or paint pictures?'

'No.'

'Then what do you know about dreams? About the imagination?'

'Let me ask you in return: do *you* write poetry or compose music or paint pictures?'

'I tell stories.'

'By stories, you mean . . .'

'All right, lies, yes. I used to tell lies, till I realised how much other people were hurt when they found I wasn't telling the truth. But I *shaped* them like stories. I timed the telling so that it satisfied something, some taste or other, some aesthetic sense, some sort of need. I prepared the way for a turn in the story, so that it seemed inevitable when it came even though you didn't anticipate it. I gave the characters enough depth to seem real while they were in front of you, and for a while afterwards. I put in just the right amount of detail so the person listening could see what I was describing in their mind's eye without being overwhelmed by things that didn't matter. I was making *art*, you see, a cheap and shoddy sort maybe, for a purpose that might be banal or underhand or greedy, but it was *art*. I was *shaping* things. Making *patterns*. I was just like someone thousands of years ago sitting under a tree carving criss-cross lines on a stick with a sharp bit of flint because they enjoyed looking at it. Or another one cutting holes in a bone and blowing through it and making different notes because they enjoyed hearing it. Or beating a hollow log for people to dance to. Rhythms and patterns and . . . and resemblances. And things that lead from them, like metaphors. Angels were never children, were they?'

'No.'

'You were never children, you never dream, and you don't make art . . . Then I know some things you don't. I understand them from the inside.'

Lyra was aware with all her senses of the lurch and surge and creak of the sea and the ship, the steady thud of the engines below and the howl of the winds through the rigging above, the all-pervasive ship-smell of fuel oil and stale cooking, but she heard not a word from the angel; and when she sheltered her eyes from the rain and peered closely into the shadows beside her on the bench, there was nothing there to see. The angel had gone.

And a little later, as she finally fell asleep in her bunk, the ferry captain made a public announcement: he was turning the ship round, because conditions were worsening and it was not safe to continue. They were returning to Baku.

20

THE SERMON

All the members of the High Council had been summoned to the cathedral to attend the sermon in which Marcel Delamare was to announce the forthcoming holy war. It was made clear to them that this was not an invitation that could be refused. Places were reserved for them at the front of the congregation, where the little parish priest from the eastern end of the lake found himself next to the professor of philology. The other three rebels were seated further along the row, not close to them.

Professor Mariette Seidel greeted Parmentier with a quick guilty little smile, and he responded with a bland 'Good morning.'

On his other side was a lean and ascetic-looking man who, Parmentier remembered, was an expert on classical ethics. He responded stiffly to the priest's greeting, and glared firmly ahead without a word.

The sermon was an addition to the normal liturgy of Celebration, and was to follow the service, so they were in for a long wait, because the cathedral was crowded and every member of the congregation would need to come and receive the bread and wine – except that many of them, as far as Parmentier could see, were diplomatic or political guests, or journalists, or noted scholars; perhaps they would hold back from that part of the ceremonial.

Professor Seidel leaned towards him very slightly and whispered, 'Have you spoken to any other Council members?'

'No,' Parmentier murmured back.

'There are four or five others who agree with us. But they're afraid to become involved in any, you know, activity.'

He nodded. 'I wonder if we'll be able to speak afterwards. Better keep quiet now.'

As he spoke, there was a stir among the congregation and the first notes sounded on the great organ. Everyone got to their feet.

The service began. As usual when he was present at a service being conducted by someone else, Georges Parmentier found himself sinking, or possibly ascending, into a semi-hypnotic state where the words he knew so well, the rhythm of the changes between praying and singing, kneeling and standing up, listening and murmuring responses, all worked together to reassure him that the great virtues were as solid and true as they had been when he was a child. There was a heaven, and its sublime truth was made manifest in these sounds and rhythms and colours and scents. He was a prisoner of the love he felt for it. Once or twice in the hour and a half during which the service unhurriedly extended itself, he noticed that Professor Seidel was trying to whisper something to him, but he couldn't listen, and eventually she stopped.

As the final prayer closed, a new kind of stir became present in the congregation, like the first breeze of the day moving stalks of wheat in a wide field. Wisps of somnolence were carried away; people sat up; an air of expectation, like an anbaric current, seemed to be generated as the figure of Marcel Delamare, elegant in his faultless dark blue suit and snowy shirt with a sober tie, stood up and climbed the steps to the pulpit.

'In the name of the Authority from whom all grace, truth, and goodness proceed,' he said.

Not many of those present had actually heard him speak before. His face was familiar now from the newspaper photograms, but he seldom preached. The eyes that looked up at him now were bright with curiosity. His voice was perfectly pitched, perfectly modulated; like an experienced actor in a familiar auditorium, he knew exactly how to make himself heard without distortion, without shouting, without being muffled or blurred by distance or echo. Parmentier listened with wary admiration.

Delamare grasped the pulpit rail with both hands and leaned slightly forward.

'I had a sister,' he began, 'a sister whom I loved with boundless devotion from the day of my birth. She was three years older than I was, and all through my childhood she played with me, and guided me, and taught me the stories and rhymes that our mother had taught to her. She was the blessed companion of my joys, the kindly consolation in my childish sorrows, the wise teacher and the brave inspiration of my youth and young manhood. If we are very lucky, my friends, we do find someone like that when we are young; it may be a sibling, it may be a more distant relation, it may be a friend or a teacher. We look up to them, we are always glad to see them, we know that our hearts and our minds depend on their truth, their steadfastness, their kindness. So it was with me and my darling sister Marisa.'

No one had been expecting anything like that. The President was a man of intellectual force, no doubt, and of moral probity, of course, but stern and distant, perhaps a little cold and over-formal. But now he was talking not as if to a large and anonymous audience but as if to a small group of close friends, and his voice, so clear and resonant, was warm with emotion.

'I thought that she was the guiding star of my life. I was proud when she had her academic triumphs, because no one was as clever or diligent as my Marisa; I rejoiced when she married a good man, Edward Coulter, and I looked forward to many happy days as a beloved guest in their household in the years to come.

Everyone who knew them said what a happy marriage, what a blessed home they'd make, what a perfect illustration of the union between a man and a woman, both equal in goodness and kindness and swiftness of mind.

'But it did not last. Into her life, from some cruel corner of the darkness, came a temptation I had been sure her nature would hurl aside in contempt.

'A man, an Englishman, a scientist and explorer, a heretic and a sinner who had set himself against the Authority and the agents of his holy doctrine, set out to seduce her. She must have presented a new challenge to this sexual marauder. She was too pure for him to resist. In her mind, so ready to believe in the goodness of anyone who was interested in her, he probably represented something new and intriguing, something radically unlike anything she had experienced before. Something heady and intoxicating. She was a brilliant woman, trained as an experimental theologian; she had written important papers on fundamental physics; she was wise as well as learned; she knew human nature; she was well aware of the lesson of Holy Scripture, the story of the serpent and the woman in the garden, she knew what temptation was, what it looked like and sounded like; but she gave in.

'Yes, she gave in. My sister was no different from innumerable others who have listened to the gentle voice of the serpent, who have felt the gleaming coils encircling them and stroked those jewelled shining scales, that pretty head that wound itself gently along her cheek and under her chin and around her neck. She did not resist, my friends; it was the sorrow of my life that she did not resist. And as is the way of nature, before long she gave birth to a child that was not her husband's.'

He paused a moment and looked around at the wide eyes, the still heads, the silent faces.

'The child was a girl to whom she and the Englishman gave the pagan name Lyra. Conceived in flagrant sin, born with evil joy, this fruit of the serpent and his intoxicated victim was concealed by the wicked pair from the good man who had married Marisa. How could he not know, you may ask: how can a man not know that his wife has borne a child, whether his own or not? Edward Coulter was a diplomat, a diligent and honest man sent abroad to represent his country. His life was one of high politics and grand foreign policy; he was rightly trusted by the King and the government of his nation to travel abroad, to undertake important discussions with national leaders and ministers about great questions of war and peace.

'Imagine a man in such a position, working in a foreign land, trusting in the love of his wife. Imagine him coming home from a diplomatic mission of great delicacy and consequence. Imagine him hearing – perhaps from a servant, perhaps from a friend, perhaps from some scurrilous rumour in the press – imagine him learning about how he has been betrayed.

'This good man did what any man would have done: he rushed to confront the man who had seduced his wife and fathered her illegitimate child. But all his diplomatic skill, all his experience of politics and statecraft, went for nothing when the two of them met. He was betrayed again, this time by his own honour. He could not believe, simply found it impossible to conceive that the villain would wait till his back was turned and then plunge a sword into his heart. Stabbed from behind by a seducer and a coward.

'The law proceeded, but the law found – astonishingly, you might think – in favour of the child's father. A corrupt man saved by a corrupt law. My sister, my dear Marisa, whose brilliant nature had been so cruelly duped, was left alone with the burden of her sin.

'And what of the child? A baby not six months old. A babe in arms. She might – she should – have been put in the care of some good and holy Sisters of Obedience, but the villain snatched her away and placed her instead in the hands of a college of scholars – old men – dusty antiquaries with nothing in their minds but Greek verbs and arcane philosophy – who couldn't possibly know what a child needed or how to care for her, how to bring her up in the ways of virtue and faith, to give her the benefit of a true moral education.

'The father vanished. He ran away, disgraced and out of favour with the society around him. A coward and a renegade.

'As for my sister, she came at last to see the disgrace and the misfortune she had brought to her own life, and with the help of spiritual guidance, she began to make amends, to become the mother she should be. She tried again and again to reach her child, to claim her from the shrivelled and faithless society of the arrogant old scholars the law had appointed as her guardians. Again and again she pleaded with the courts, with officialdom in all its forms, with the stony-hearted judges who listened to her anguished pleas in a cold and hostile silence and dismissed her without a word. Again and again she was refused.

'And what of the child, this lost and lonely little girl, this child born of corruption and weakness, carrying as we all do the stain of original sin but in herself so far innocent?

'She was told all manner of lies about her birth, and of course, as children do, she believed them. When she reached the age of eleven, desperate and unhappy, she ran away from the college she had been placed in, was kidnapped by a band of boat-dwelling criminals and destined for some unspeakable fate in a foreign land. Her mother, my sister Marisa, hearing of this – and imagine the toils of anguish in her heart! – hearing of this, Marisa set off in desperation to rescue her, and bring her home to a mother who could love her with a truly repentant heart, and bring her up in the safety and purity of an Authority-fearing home, and make amends for the sin she had committed.'

He paused a moment, and when he spoke his tone had changed a little: instead of the suffering brother, now he seemed to be standing back a little way, commenting on a common human problem with patient wisdom.

'In a way, of course, this is an old story. It is one of the first stories we learn. The desire to know more, to look closer and closer, to

tear aside the veils of matter and see into the deepest mysteries –
the human impulse to do that, this vile and impertinent curiosity,
was fixed in the human soul as a photogram is fixed on paper,
since the woman gave in to the serpent's temptation in the garden
of Paradise.

'And the results we see in our own lives, the tendency of things
to decay, for clocks to run down, for fires to go out, for the bright
and shining vigour of youth to fade into the distracted anxiety of
the middle years and the exhausted loneliness of old age – these
are part of the consequence of that first fall.

'Because what she did, that mother of us all, was to make a
breach in the perfect surface of the world that the Authority
gave us to live in. Just a little scratch; just a tiny crack. But it was
enough. We all know how once the integrity of a structure is
flawed – the crack in a mirror, the patch of dry rot in the cellar,
the leak in a water pipe – how it grows and spreads, silently,
invisibly, until the whole structure is compromised, until it all
inevitably falls apart. It happens in the physical world, it happens
in the world of politics and business, it happens in the family,
and in the human heart.

'Now, my friends, I am going to tell you something very few
people know. In this world there exist a number of mysterious
places, secret places, that are very like these cracks, these flaws in
the structure, these leaks. Because of that original sin, and because
of the continuing and ineradicable wickedness of mankind, this
beautiful world is vulnerable. Vulnerable to invasion, to poisonous
influences from outside, to alien presences and philosophies, to
ideas that kill, to moral disease and intellectual corruption.

'This is not a metaphor, my friends. Some of you may have been
present at the lecture given here in Geneva not long ago by the
celebrated philosopher and author Professor Gottfried Brande,
the lecture that ended in tragic circumstances with the professor's
sudden death. The lecture, which we are publishing soon in its
entirety, discusses with profound originality the dangers that lie

in the careless and irresponsible use of language, and the need to police our speaking and writing with ceaseless vigilance.

'Professor Brande will be regarded by future ages as a prophet. He had much to teach us before his untimely death. So believe me, my friends, it's in the spirit of Gottfried Brande that I stress this now: my words today are not a metaphor for something else. They are exactly and literally true. There *are* places such as the ones I have referred to. We are indebted to the pioneering work of the geographers who discovered several such places in various isolated corners of the earth, and to the skilful and dangerous work of the engineers of the Magisterial Guard for their continuing attempts to deal with them.

'But the problem is growing. More and more of these places are being discovered; more and more our world, our way of life, the things we love and take for granted, are being invaded and poisoned by alien ideas, wrongful beliefs, and a bestial morality unfitted for the sons and daughters of the Authority.

'And now, my friends, we have found the source of this spiritual evil. The original breach in the surface of the Authority's world lies in a desert in Central Asia, and it is towards that spot that our armies are marching, with our allies and our true-hearted friends at our side. They will reach it; they will destroy it; they will heal the wound in the world for ever.

'And . . . this is the hardest thing for me, my friends. The young girl I spoke to you about – the daughter of my dear sister. And really she is not a girl any more; she is a young woman. Her name is Lyra Belacqua. And to my utmost sorrow, she has thrown in her lot with the enemy. She is working to prevent the great task we are all about to undertake. Like so many young people, unsure of their own minds, she has been persuaded that right is wrong and wickedness is right. Wherever she is now, I hope we can find her before it's too late. In any other circumstances, no doubt there would be a large reward offered for any knowledge of her; but I am not offering that. I simply pray that she is found before . . .'

He shrugged as it were in helpless sorrow. Then he gathered himself again, and stood up tall, and let his voice ring passionately through the great space of the cathedral:

'May the Authority, in all his goodness and wisdom, guide our judgement as we strive to repair the damage done to his world. May he, in all his power and might, guide our arms as we strike a deadly blow at the invader. And finally, in all his love and justice, may the Authority strengthen us for the struggle ahead and bring us safely through to the calm and tranquillity of a world restored.'

He reached out to where his owl-dæmon was sitting on the pulpit rail, and lifted her up to his shoulder as he walked steadily down the steps and out of the nave towards the vestry. The congregation was perfectly still, as if no one wanted to breathe, or dared to. No one looked around, but those whose seats allowed a view of the whole interior were struck by the stillness, the silence, the air of . . . was it fear? Was it awe? Whatever it was, it had thrown a pall of silence and apprehension over the entire crowd.

Even the representatives of the press, and the visiting politicians and diplomats, and the senior clergy, and the civic dignitaries of every kind, were sitting still. Their faces were solemn, or full of fear, or pale determination; some of their dæmons had crept up to their breasts and sought shelter in an embrace.

Professor Seidel leaned slightly towards Parmentier and whispered, 'He is mad.'

It was a very quiet whisper. Parmentier whispered back: 'But he has the congregation.'

He had. The atmosphere was like that of a theatre held in the powerful spell of a great actor's final speech.

After several seconds, gradually, people began to relax, to breathe deeply, to sit up and look around. The silence in the vast cathedral gave way to murmurs and coughs and the shuffling of chairs and feet as people got to their feet and moved into the aisles.

Parmentier glanced at Professor Seidel. Her face was solemn. The man on his other side, the professor of classical ethics, stood up stiffly and fussed with his scarf. A faint smell of cloves came from his overcoat.

'What did you make of that?' Parmentier said quietly.

He stood up too so as to hear him more clearly. More and more people were talking now; there was even a sort of bustle in the atmosphere. Some of the journalists were hurrying towards the vestry, as if they could intercept the President before he left, and claim the first interview; but officials barred the way, and two members of the Magisterial Guard, armed with rifles, stood behind them.

The priest looked closely at the face of his fellow-member of the High Council, and was surprised to see in it such doubt and anxiety. He didn't know the man at all well, and had thought him rigidly conventional in his attitudes; perhaps he'd been wrong. The little priest suddenly remembered the man's name: Duclos.

'Did you believe him?' Parmentier said.

'About the girl? It's plausible. Even likely. Who can tell?'

'About the idea that evil comes from outside the world.'

'It's a startling assertion to make, certainly. Something entirely new, this, how would one describe it – semi-Gnosticism?'

'I agree; it's not something we've heard from this pulpit before.'

'Did it make sense to you?'

Duclos wasn't making superficial conversation. He sounded as if he was asking about the truth.

'No,' said Parmentier carefully. 'I don't think the world is being invaded by the forces of evil.'

He thought of his old friend the General, standing in the forest listening with longing to the bells and the songs of fairyland. The noise from the congregation had risen; everyone seemed to be voicing a strong opinion, or asking an urgent question, or hurrying to get outside and tell this astonishing news to family or friends or a wide readership.

'I wonder if the Council will be summoned to discuss this business,' said Duclos. 'It's a declaration of war, but war against . . . who? What? Are we supposed to support it?'

'We don't need to be summoned,' Parmentier pointed out. 'All of us are here now, as far as I can see. But . . .'

He wasn't sure what he could say next, and in any case the moment was lost. Around them the congregation was alive with voices, and movement, and small groups gathered in fierce discussion or anxious speculation were holding up those who simply wanted to get out. Parmentier tried to look along to the aisle, peering to both sides and standing on tiptoe in order to see what his fellow council members were doing, but it was no good; the press was too great.

'What shall we do?' he whispered to his dæmon as she perched on his shoulder.

'Just go home,' she said. 'Concentrate on getting outside and then go straight to the station.'

He'd already lost sight of Mariette Seidel, and by now the professor of classical ethics was some way off towards the main door, his gaunt bald head visible as he moved steadily through the crowd. He might make a good ally, thought Parmentier, and decided to write to him, if he could remember which university he belonged to.

Slowly and steadily, though with many hold-ups and apologies and a certain amount of jostling, Parmentier reached the main doors and left for the station.

Malcolm read Pan's note with a little shock of disappointment, but no sense of betrayal. He knew Pan had to continue his quest, but he'd grown used to his companionship, the sharp observations he made, the tone of his affectionate half-teasing that was so like the Lyra Malcolm had just begun to know before she left Oxford . . . Of course; because they were one being. And now he was on his own.

He got up and moved around for the sake of exercise. His leg was painful, but less stiff. Before she left, Tilda Vasara had given him her few remaining shreds of bloodmoss and left a note instructing him to keep moving and not stay too long in one position; but he wanted to finish his gold-working, and – well, now he'd have to remind himself to stand up and walk about every half-hour or so.

He had taken the crumpled remains of the alethiometer's case and beaten it flat, and after another visit to the indentured goldsmith and the loan of a few more tools, he had begun to work it into a circlet. The metal was pure and highly malleable; beating it and twisting it was easier than he'd anticipated.

Gulya liked to sit and watch as the gold spread finely under his hammer; she was naturally curious about where Pan and Tilda Vasara had gone, but she was a gryphon, after all, and the sight of the metal held her mesmerised. Malcolm watched her without seeming to, and one day when she was held fast he said, 'Gulya, tell me about the sorcerer and why he put a spell on you.'

The little gryphon said, 'Ah. It is my shame and my sorrow. He has a forge in the mountains – in a cavern – a place where rubies grow. I found my way there when I was young and stupid. I thought I could take his gold, knowing the rumours about the immense hoard he'd gathered, and realising that if he harvested rubies he would also need the gold that is the best setting for them. I thought I could fight him and carry off his gold to present to Queen Shahrnavāz, but I was not strong enough. He defeated me with the aid of a magic mirror and bound me in cords of djinn-fire. Then he asked me about the defences of this mountain and the Queen's palace, but I would say nothing.

'I lay there bound for three days and nights. He drew the cords tighter and tighter, and compressed my body till it was the size you see now. I am still bound. All the fire-spirits in the cavern were laughing at me, mocking, jeering, as my heart burned and my body shrank, and the poor wingless slaves could only watch in pity. They too were bound, or they would have torn him to pieces and set me free.'

'Did you see his gold?' said Malcolm.

'Yes, uncountable numbers of ingots, coins, medallions, chains . . . Gold of the finest quality. It is the richest treasury I have ever seen, apart from our Queen's.'

'Does the Queen know about it?'

'Yes. They are old enemies, but neither can defeat the other. They keep a distance.'

'And where is his cavern?'

'North of Baku, in the Caucasus.'

'Could you find it again?'

Gulya looked at him. It was never easy to make out the play of expression on a gryphon's face: incredulity looked like anger, which looked like scorn, which looked like laughter, which looked like sorrow, which looked like . . .

'Of course,' she said. 'He's not hiding. It's easy to see where his forge is. You can see it blazing from miles around, from the sky, from the ground, from the sea.'

'And you won't be free from this curse till you kill him, is that right?'

'That's right. But what are you thinking?'

'I don't know yet,' he admitted. 'Gathering information, that's all. This magic mirror – tell me about that, Gulya.'

In the little gryphon's mind her own story had already assumed the proportions of a myth.

'He wears it like a shield,' she told him. 'You try to look at him, and all you see is yourself. But he can bend it to make you seem very small and pitiable or very large and . . . also pitiable. Ridiculous. You seem to be fighting yourself. Remember, I was young but I was full-grown. It would have been hard to fight him, and I might not have won, but it was not impossible. I was bewildered by my own reflection, and too inexperienced to overcome it, and so he and his *koruskati* caught me and bound me with djinn-fire.'

'What are these *koruskati*?' Malcolm asked.

'Little imp-things like sparks. They sting and bite and fly too quickly to catch.'

'And the sorcerer, did he ever put down his magic shield?'

'Yes, but there was nothing to see. He is invisible.'

'What was his name?'

'Sorush,' said Gulya.

'Ah,' Malcolm said, sounding satisfied.

He turned to rummage in his rucksack until he found the tattered copy of the poem *Jahan and Rukhsana* and sat down on the pile of furs to look through it.

He was intent on finding a passage in the story where Rukhsana had to defeat a sorcerer, or a fire-god, whose name . . . Yes! There it was: *Sorush*. Malcolm smiled with pleasure, and read on.

In the story, Rukhsana had been abandoned as a baby by her wicked father, who left her on a mountainside because an astrologer had told him falsely that his wife would bear a son. The child would have died, but the great bird the Simurgh, who lived for several thousand years and knew all the wisdom in the world, heard her crying and carried the baby away, intending to feed her chicks on the child's flesh; but when she dropped Rukhsana in her nest, the chicks and the Simurgh herself all cried out in wonder at her beauty. The great bird enfolded the baby in her wings and suckled her, for she was part mammal. Rukhsana grew up with the Simurgh's chicks as her brothers and sisters.

When she was grown, one of her sister chicks was stolen by the sorcerer Sorush. Because Rukhsana had promised to look after her, she went in search of the villain, and found him in his cavernous lair in the Caucasus, which was filled with all manner of gold and precious stones and blazing with the fire of his forge. Sorush was invulnerable to everything on the earth or under it, but the light of the moon would weaken him at once, so he took endless precautions to stay away from it.

Rukhsana, knowing this, had made an amulet out of silver

in the shape of the crescent moon, and engraved it with magic words. Holding this, she managed to overcome the fire-fiend and return her sister-chick to the Simurgh before returning to her quest to find Jahan.

Malcolm looked up.

'Gulya,' he said, 'has your queen got any silver in her treasury?'

She had. The gryphons didn't care for it; it tarnished, it was the wrong colour, it was second-best. But some of the gold they had acquired was in the form of alloys, either naturally occurring or human-made, and one of the commonest was a gold-silver mixture called electrum. The indentured jeweller, Tamaz Khuroshvili, told Malcolm about it.

Speaking through Gulya, and with the extra difficulty caused by the loss of his tongue, Khuroshvili explained that in the time before trade was invented the gryphons threw the silver away, finding it merely ugly. But when they realised that human beings found the silver desirable, they began to exchange it for work or for services that men and women could perform, or for goods they couldn't make themselves. All the building work in the mountain, the tunnelling, the plumbing, the fire-channels, had been paid for with silver. So the metal did have a value for them, and they wouldn't part with it carelessly.

Malcolm explained what he wanted: enough silver to make a small amulet in the form of the crescent moon – small, but big enough to be seen clearly from a fighting distance, and with fixings for a chain or a cord.

Khuroshvili was intrigued, and found a piece of silver about the size and thickness of Malcolm's little finger. He even offered to lend a pair of fine shears to cut the silver, once it was beaten flat, into the best shape. He had a trick, furthermore, to coat the metal with an oil that would keep tarnish at bay for longer than the bare silver would manage by itself. A little clay pot of that sat beside the silver on the bench.

Next Malcolm asked about powder. Did Khuroshvili use any kind of fine powder, perhaps for polishing the gold he retrieved for the Queen? Some kind of abrasive, perhaps, or polishing compound?

By this time, after their several conversations, he and the jeweller had managed to come to a friendly understanding. Khuroshvili didn't ask too closely what Malcolm was planning, no doubt in case it was dangerous to know, and for his part Malcolm held back from the many personal questions he'd have liked to ask. They spoke as one craftsman to another.

So Khuroshvili, saying nothing, merely offered several grades of abrasive powder, which Gulya learned was made from ground pumice. Malcolm chose the very finest grade the jeweller had, as fine as flour, and took as much as Khuroshvili let him, a couple of handfuls in a bag of waxed silk.

Finally Malcolm asked to borrow a small pair of bellows. Khuroshvili laughed and shrugged and handed them over. They shook hands, and Malcolm left with Gulya to take his treasure to their quarters.

'Now,' he said to her when everything was laid on the table so he could look at it and weigh it in his hand and let his muscles and his nerves think about it, 'I want to speak to the Queen. I want to do it privately, out of earshot of anyone else except you. Yes, I know that never happens; but the Queen has never had to deal with a man from the realms of gold before. This is not a request but a command. Gulya, you went to the forge of Sorush alone, and tried to fight him by yourself; you must summon all the courage you have to speak to Queen Shahrnavāz and urge her to listen as I tell her what we're going to do. It's hard, but there's no alternative.'

And he wished Pan had been there, to join them in this venture.

When the ferry returned to Baku the air was still wild, the waves choppy and white-capped. Lyra was looking forward strongly to feeling firm ground underfoot. She found Ionides sheltering from the teeming rain by the gangway, looking anxious.

'You not feeling brisk and easy?' he said.

'I had a bad night. I'll just be glad to get off this boat. What's going on? Have they said anything about starting again?'

'No, Miss Silver. Something else happening.'

The ferry was just tying up. Lyra followed his glance as he looked past the dock gates. There were police cars racing past, their sirens howling, their lights flashing, and their tyres spraying water. The rain was so heavy, the air so dark, that the city was almost invisible, but Lyra thought she could see, beyond the buildings at the dockside, a plume of smoke rising into the morning sky.

'People trying to get the captain to say what's going on, but he say nothing. All the officers like this,' and he pulled an imaginary zip across his closed lips.

'Perhaps this is why they had to turn round,' Lyra said. 'They must be used to storms at sea.'

He shook his head. 'More than that,' he said.

Other passengers joined them at the rail; it was clear that no one knew any more than they did, but everyone was concerned. When eventually the way was opened, the passengers disconsolately or angrily or nervously moved ashore, coats over their heads against the teeming rain, and tried to find somewhere to stay till the voyage could resume.

What had happened was a simple event with a million ramifications.

Mustafa Bey was a man of habit, both by temperament and by necessity. He was at his table in Marletto's Café, for example, at the same time every day; he used a regular team of drivers, secretaries, and messengers; the contracts he made were always rigorously honoured. His clothes, the food and drink he enjoyed, the exercise he took every afternoon, all contributed to the sense he gave of permanence and rightness. His movements were as predictable as those of the planets in the sky, and all the innumerable customers and clients and interests he dealt with had come to rely on this regularity as much as on the clock tower of Bab al-Faraj.

He was perfectly aware, of course, that this predictability was a weakness too. It made him vulnerable. The bodyguards he employed knew it too, and were extremely well paid for their vigilance.

But whatever he paid them wasn't enough. While Lyra and Ionides were arriving in Baku, one of Mustafa Bey's bodyguards approached him on the riverbank, in the middle of his daily walk, signalling as if to say there was danger nearby and he needed to come close; and when he was close enough, he drew out a long knife and plunged it several times into his employer's chest. Mustafa Bey fell dead at once, and a moment later so did the assassin, with three bullets in his head. The other bodyguards were good shots: just not quite good enough to stop the assassin without killing him. No one could make him talk now. A theory emerging very soon afterwards held that the bodyguards had known exactly what they were doing, because they too were in on a plot, and didn't want the killer to reveal why he'd done it, or who'd paid him.

More theories began – theories explaining everything. They proliferated like bacteria in a particularly nourishing solution. The more theories, the less knowledge, it seemed, because in the following hours it became clear to everyone in Aleppo, and in the next few days to everyone who had dealings with Mustafa Bey, from Morocco to Nippon, that the only person who knew everything about the great man's business had been the great man himself. Every detail of his arrangement with such-and-such a farmer in Tunisia to supply dates at such-and-such a price, every clause of his contract with the water authorities of the lower Oxus river to continue their supply of fresh water to the caravanserais east of the Aral Sea, every fluctuation in the price of raw silk in the markets of Urumqi – those and a thousand other matters had been held securely in the living brain of Mustafa Bey, and every single one of them faded to nothing as the blood drained from his body and that brain closed down cell by cell.

The news spread north and south and east and west, as fast as the words could be passed from one person to another. More than any other event for years, the death of Mustafa Bey left the world of the Silk Roads paralysed with fear and shock. Those thousands of contracts and agreements and deals – who would carry them out now? How would suppliers be paid? Who could guarantee that anyone would be paid anything? Lyra was not the only individual with reason to be grateful to the generous merchant; there were widows and orphans, the families of old friends or servants, and not least there was the owner of the Marletto's Café, who foresaw his business losing all its celebrity in a week and dwindling and shrivelling into a faded tea-house no more distinguished than a hundred others in the city.

In Baku, as in many other cities the length of the Silk Roads, people who felt their entire worlds shaking underfoot began to panic, and storm the banks, and loot the markets, and riot. And of course Lyra's precious letter, the *laissez-passer* that had been going to promise her safety and protection and passage with all the authority of the greatest name on the Silk Roads . . . suddenly valueless.

One of the few people unaffected was Lyra, who had heard nothing about the assassination, and was at a table in a hotel courtyard busily writing her first report to send to the great merchant, unaware that he was dead. It was harder than she'd thought it would be; the question was, as always, where to begin? After several false starts, she began with the arrival of the *autobus de luxe* into the unfinished station in Baku. But she couldn't make that work either. In the end she put her paper away and took out the resonating lodestone, and began to write to Malcolm.

21

THE CLEAN WIND OF GOD

Dilyara, the one-time cleaner at Tashbulak and the current companion of Chen the camel-herder, had discovered many curious things among the debris of the raided laboratories.

The clean wind of God, which had swept through the research station with such purity and zeal, had missed many things it might have thought worth destroying if it had known how to think about them. Cylinders of various gases stood untouched; a bank of refrigerating chambers had never been ransacked, because their doors opened in ways unfamiliar to the agents of holiness; the joy of smashing glass for its own sake soon palled, so case upon case of long-dead vegetation slumbered intact on the higher shelves.

Dilyara searched through it all, sweeping, dusting, polishing, looking. The gas cylinders shone; the dead plants were taken out of their cases and thrown away, and the glass washed till it gleamed; the refrigerating chambers opened to a touch once she found the right spot to press. The anbaric power keeping them cold was supplied by photo-receptive panels in the roof that responded even to the pallid twinkle of starlight; the vessels and packages and bottles that stood coated with frost inside them rested just as those who put them there had intended, holding their mysteries from the world and intoxicating Dilyara with the hope of more discoveries to come.

Chen, meanwhile, had subdued a wandering female camel and tethered her close by, and knew from the honks and hoots and snorts in the night that she was already attracting the attention of various wild males. Dreams of a new herd, far larger than the old one, filled his sleep with pleasure. He saw it ranging far over the roads east and west, carrying cargoes that would bring him uncountable wealth and the respect of thousands of people who would utter the name of Chen with reverence.

And the desert slumbered to the south, and the wandering lake of Lop Nor continued in its unpredictable divagations to the east.

*

Lyra to Malcolm:

Mr Ionides and I are at the Hotel Caspari in Baku. The ferry that we thought would take us to Krasnovodsk had to turn back because a fierce storm was making it dangerous to be at sea. No idea what's happening elsewhere – papers are censored. So for the time being we're stuck.

Do you think the alethiometer can be restored?

L

Malcolm to Lyra:

No, I don't think it's restorable. Not to the state it used to be in. There are parts missing, and it needs an expert clockmaker to put it in some kind of working order. But I've kept all the interior parts aside for now and focused only on the case, and I'm beating it into something else.

Pan has left here with the witch Tilda Vasara to go further east to Tashbulak. Captivity made him restless; at least I have something to do. He will be safe with her. I suppose the question should really be whether she'll be safe with him.

*But I'm restless too. I will find you again, and Asta, and you'll
find Pan, and we'll go together into the desert and find this red
building before the Magisterium does.*
   Now back to work. More soon. Please don't take risks.
   M

*

Lyra was sitting at the little iron table in the hotel garden and
sipping a cup of strong coffee, when she read that.

'Pan, you bloody fool . . .' she muttered.

Asta looked up, and Lyra explained.

'He must have gone when Malcolm was asleep,' Asta said.

'Shouldn't have gone at all. Idiot.'

She put the stone away and turned back to her pad of paper.
Lyra's report to Mustafa Bey had turned into a sort of diary-cum-
meditation, starting with her conversation on the ferry with the
angel and ranging back to what Ionides had said to her about the
imagination, and everything she'd ever heard or thought about
that subject, and ranging forward to the very purpose of this journey.
It was becoming important as she wrote more of it and discovered
what she thought, and what else she was able to think, by writing
it, even if it turned out to be not what Mustafa Bey required.

As she sat there in the shade of a cypress tree with a pencil in one
hand and the coffee cup in the other, she heard the sudden howl of
police sirens outside. She and Asta had already been disturbed by
the sound of shouts and people running, but it was the sirens that
made Asta sit up, ears pricked. Lyra put the coffee down carefully,
because the sound had made her hand shake. She stood up warily.

'Careful,' said Asta.

'I want to know what's happening. It might just be a bank
robbery, or . . .'

'Well, we won't be able to help very much whatever it is.'

'No, but Mr Ionides is out there somewhere.'

'I haven't known him as long as you have, but I bet he's capable of looking after himself. What's more, he'll find out about it all much more quickly than we could.'

'I could get a newspaper at least.'

'If it's one you could read, it'll be a fortnight old.'

'I suppose you're right,' she said, and sat down.

'What are you writing?'

'You can read it if you like. It's not private, particularly.'

'Your handwriting's hard to read.'

'Oh, fuss. Just because Malcolm's is all fancy and italic.'

'Fancy is exactly what italic isn't. But listen . . .'

The first blast of the sirens had diminished as the police cars drove off further into the city. Now Asta could hear another sound, and as she listened Lyra could too.

'People shouting,' she said. 'A riot? A demonstration?'

'There's a loudspeaker . . . Can't understand what it's saying. Can't even hear it clearly, but someone's speaking to a crowd.'

Lyra could hear the distorted blare, but it was too far away even to make out what language the speaker was using. Then came shouts, cries, some from quite close to the hotel; and then the first sound of breaking glass.

'I'm going to pack my rucksack,' Lyra said.

Asta jumped down from the table and went with her. Inside the hotel, two waiters were in anxious conversation by the stairs. They stopped as they saw her.

'What's happening?' she said. '*Qu'est-ce qui se passe?*'

One of them shrugged, and then a man in a business suit ran out of an office. He saw her, and stopped short.

'You must – upstairs – quickly – please, into your room,' he said breathlessly.

'What's happening?'

'In the streets – trouble – police—'

'Yes, I can hear, but what's it about?'

'Just please – go your room – lock the door. Now, please.'

He looked over his shoulder at the lobby. Beyond the glass doors, Lyra could see people running in the street.

She nodded, and set off upstairs, with Asta running ahead. The room was safe and clean, with nothing out of place. She dropped her papers on the bed and threw the window open wide. It overlooked the street, and as she leaned out she could see a group of young men come running from the nearby square, pursued by police carrying shields and wearing helmets. The sound of the loudspeaker came from that way too, and then came a volley of gunshots. The loudspeaker-voice stopped abruptly. Someone screamed.

'This is awful,' Lyra said.

More shouts from outside, and the crash of broken glass. Asta sprang up on the windowsill and looked out.

'That was the bookshop across the street,' she said. 'Look, the owner's trying to lock the door but people are pushing him aside. They're pulling books off the shelves and throwing them into the street. And here come some police with shields and guns – and big sticks – they're smashing people aside, hitting them with the sticks – and oh, that's horrible . . .'

Lyra kept to one side as she looked out. The police had surrounded two young men and were smashing their sticks across heads, shoulders, arms, legs – Lyra covered her ears, unable to bear the crack of bones and the cries of pain – then the police were firing bullets into the air, and out of nowhere, it seemed, a mighty blast of water knocked several people, rioters and police alike, off their feet and sent them spinning along the ground. Smoke was drifting through the air.

Lyra found her breath catch suddenly in her throat. Asta fell off the windowsill, but heavily, not like a cat, and struggled on the floor retching and coughing, her chest and belly heaving.

Something acrid was attacking Lyra's eyes and throat. Tear gas . . . She coughed – it made it worse – her throat was blocked by something – her eyes were stinging and streaming, her lungs heaving. She fell to her knees and felt Asta struggling for breath beside her, and fumbled for the window and forced it shut, hoping she wouldn't break the glass in her effort to keep out the gas.

But it shut safely and she slammed the latch down tight before heaving several clearer breaths. Asta – Lyra swung round to see how she was – the dæmon's breathing was fast and irregular, and her mouth was wet, her eyes streaming. The idea came to Lyra that the gas would be worse close to the floor – she had no idea why – she scooped the dæmon up, feeling her heart pound, hearing the rasp of her breath, and held her tight to her heart. Malcolm's dæmon. Too tight! She couldn't breathe like that. She lay Asta on the bed and turned on the tap in the little basin, soaking something – a shirt, anything – and held it to Asta's mouth and nose.

She pressed her own face into it too. It did help a little, and then Asta's chest filled powerfully with a rasping spasm, and she coughed up some saliva and shook her head.

Lyra stood away, soaking the shirt under the tap again and wiping it across her mouth and eyes and nose. The first panic, when she felt she couldn't breathe at all, was subsiding. Her throat was still tight and sore, and the sounds from the street reminded her of everything going on outside the neat little room. Another volley of gunshots sounded very loud in the narrow street, and made her ears ring.

She thought of Ionides. 'Oh, I hope—' she found herself croaking, but Asta interrupted hoarsely: 'He'll be safe.'

She knows what I'm thinking, was what flashed into Lyra's mind, with an odd little flare of warmth.

'It's dangerous though. Those police – guns – they're just shooting at anyone.'

'He'll know that as well as we do. And he'll be better at dealing with it.'

'Yes. I suppose you're right. Oh, that gas . . .'

'Still hurting?'

Lyra felt as if her eyelids had been burned away. Her throat was raw; she knew her voice was thin and harsh and entirely un-Lyra-like. Perhaps it would never recover.

Before she could reply, there was a knock on the door. She stood up and turned round at once. Asta too was standing ready to challenge, ready to defend their space.

'Who is it?' said Lyra in her new voice, but it came out too quietly, so she tried again, as loud as she could bear: 'Who's there?'

'Personal sorcerer. I come in?'

'Oh yes – yes!'

She hurried to unlock the door. Ionides was alone in the corridor, but he looked to left and right before entering the room.

'Better lock it again,' he said.

'Yes – I will . . .'

He sniffed and looked at the window.

'Yes – the tear gas got in, a bit . . .'

'Your eyes all right? Throat?' He was looking serious.

'It's better now I've closed the window. But—'

He held up his hands. 'Sit down, Miss Silver. I got some bad news. This confusion out there – you know why they are all breaking windows and shooting? Sit down,' he said again.

'Why? Tell me!'

'Mustafa Bey. Someone kill him.'

She sat down on the bed, and he took the chair.

'No . . . No!' she said, breathless. 'When?'

'Three days, two days – no one knows. Doesn't matter. Important thing, only thing, is he is not there.'

'My letter . . .'

'Of course your letter. Suddenly, not so useful. Keep it hidden anyway. See how things go.'

'But why are people . . . He wasn't a ruler, a popular king or something, so why are they rioting? And is it happening in other places, or just here in Baku?'

'All along the Silk Roads, so I hear. All the contracts, all the thousand agreements he make. With big companies, with every kind of merchant, large and small, with camel-herders, with factory owners, with shipping lines, every kind of commercial activity – all depending on his memory. All relying on him. This is catastrophe, Miss Silver. There is nothing to take his place. Because of Mustafa Bey, everyone who make business for ten thousand miles know they can rely on money and law and contracts. But now . . . I am surprised they only breaking windows. They will do worse, very soon.'

'He was very kind,' Lyra said.

'He was great man. Not many people I admire, Miss Silver, but Mustafa Bey . . .'

'He would have liked to work with you. He told me.'

'I was honoured to see him even for short while.'

Lyra had never seen him so sombre.

'What's the best thing to do in a riot?' she said.

'Keep still. Don't be visible, don't make noise. This will pass. Then we move away from the city.'

'Yes. I suppose that would be best. What do you think will happen to Mustafa Bey's enterprises?'

'People will fight over them. Strong men, maybe soldiers, maybe politicians, will take them over and steal money out of them and run them badly and then let them collapse.'

'The Magisterium? What about them?'

'You mean, did they kill him?'

'Yes. I think that's what I mean.'

'That is interesting, Miss Silver. Yes, I think maybe they did. They can say, "Look at all this chaos – people need law and order. Governments have failed all over Europe and beyond. The world needs a strong power to govern everything and restore public safety, blah blah. Only the Magisterium, et cetera, et cetera . . . " They have the power. Rumours about this big army gathering to invade Central Asia, maybe they gathered it together for exactly this, and yes, they kill him. It make no difference now, but it might make big difference later.'

She sat back. Her eyes were still streaming; she closed them and held the wet handkerchief there.

'Asta? How are your eyes?' she said.

'Painful. Mr Ionides, did you avoid the gas?'

'I guessed it was coming, so I do like you.' He held up a cotton scarf, wet and dripping. 'I stole it from market. Drop it in a jug of water on café table. The world is full of convenient things, Miss Asta.'

'The siren's stopped,' Lyra said.

There were still a few voices shouting, but the main source of the noise had either moved away or simply calmed down.

'So now we wait,' said Asta.

Lyra was already composing the first sentence of the message she was planning to send on the lodestone, as soon as she could see again.

Malcolm and Gulya were waiting in the carpeted hall for Queen Shahrnavāz. A chair had been set out ready for him; guards waited at the corridor entrance through which the Queen would appear. The vizier stood by, solemn and inscrutable, though Malcolm thought he could detect a suppressed irritation in his manner.

Gulya was more nervous than Malcolm had ever seen her. He wished that Pan hadn't gone; he and Gulya had seemed to reassure each other. In his hands Malcolm held the gold circlet and the confusion of wheels and rods that had been the movement of the alethiometer, and as the guards by the entrance stiffened to their equivalent of attention, and the vizier turned his head to bow to the Queen, Malcolm stood up and gathered the pieces together in his hands. He took care to stand in the full sunlight.

And then Shahrnavāz was in front of them, in all the splendour of her form.

Malcolm stood, but didn't bow; he inclined his head a very little way, like a great leader greeting an equal.

Then, to Gulya's near terror, he said, 'Queen Shahrnavāz, you and I shall talk alone. His Excellency the Vizier and your bodyguards may leave us. Only Gulya will remain.'

The guards shivered with astonishment, and the vizier slowly turned his head from Malcolm to the Queen, and to Gulya, and back to Malcolm. The old courtier must have been affronted, but between the silence of the Queen and the calm certainty of Malcolm he seemed at first uncertain and then stiff with anger and then resigned, for he bowed to the Queen and withdrew, followed by the guards.

Malcolm and the Queen stood facing each other. Gulya withdrew a little way. Queen Shahrnavāz indicated the chair, and Malcolm sat down again.

'Your Majesty,' he began, spinning a yarn as Lyra would have done, 'I have discovered many things about the broken instrument you asked me to repair. The first thing concerns the case, the only gold in it. Gold has a memory, as you know. As soon as I laid hands on it, the metal began to speak to me of the shape it had uncountable centuries ago, when it was torn from the ground and forged into the pure metal. It was made into a circlet for the head of a princess, and only later was it formed into a case for the broken instrument.'

'What became of the princess?' said the Queen. They were the first words she had spoken.

'She is alive now, and waiting for me to join her in the search for something even more valuable than gold.'

Shahrnavāz drew back her head a little, which seemed to signify incredulity, although her expression couldn't change.

'This is the shape the gold remembered,' Malcolm went on, holding out the circlet. 'I restored it according to the desires of the atoms it's made of. Now, in this form, it's almost satisfied, and all it desires is to encircle the head of the princess.'

'I have never heard of the memory of gold.'

'With respect, great Queen, you have heard of it now. It's audible in the wavelengths of the musical tones it emits, and it's visible in the penumbra between the darkness of pure shadow and the brilliance of reflected sunlight.'

'These things are not known to us.'

'When I first spoke to Prince Keshvād, outside Aleppo, I told him and his companions that I was not only gold of flesh but gold of knowledge. I've told you about the memory of gold: that is knowledge you did not have, and now you do. Gold also speaks to those who know how to hear.'

'What does it say?'

'You will learn to hear it, Queen Shahrnavāz, if you persevere. This gold tells me that there is more not very far away, uncountable quantities of gold, simply waiting for you to claim it; and it tells me that that gold wants more than anything else to adorn you and your palace.'

'Where is that gold? Who has it now?'

'A sorcerer called Sorush.'

And suddenly Queen Shahrnavāz threw back her head and screamed more loudly than he thought possible: Malcolm's head rang, and out of the corner of his eye he saw Gulya stagger and flutter her wings in panic.

From where he was standing he could see the darkness of the corridor beyond the entrance to the audience hall, and in it eyes and eyes and more eyes, gryphons pressed together in fear and waiting for a signal to flee or to attack Malcolm and tear him to shreds.

But those eyes could see Malcolm's eyes too. He didn't frown, or narrow them or open them wide, or draw his brows together, but something happened to fill them with a terrifying force.

As they saw him look at them like that, the gryphons in the corridor, those eyes, turned away and vanished into the darkness. The Queen shook her wings and moved her head from side to side, from high to low. She was breathing deeply, but not in order to scream again. She looked at Malcolm, drew her head back, and nodded slowly.

'That gold,' she said, 'is out of reach. The sorcerer whose name you mentioned is beyond our power.'

'But not beyond mine,' said Malcolm. 'The lady Gulya, who has become a stalwart friend to me, has her own reasons for wanting to deal with him, and I intend to help her. We are going to the forge of Sorush, in the Caucasus mountains, where we shall make him lift the curse from Gulya, and transfer all his gold to you. I shall take this circlet to Princess Lyra, and then Gulya will fly us to the desert of Karamakan, where Princess Lyra's imagination lies bound.'

'And where is your companion, the dæmon?'

'He has flown with Queen Tilda Vasara to Karamakan, to prepare the way for us.'

The Queen said nothing for several seconds. As before, she turned her head this way and that, looking into every corner of the great chamber and out over the terrace beyond to the snow-capped mountains and the serene blue sky.

'That seems to me impossible,' she said finally.

'Not to me,' Malcolm replied.

'What power do you have, that you know you can defeat Sorush?'

'I am an artificer from the realms of gold. You should not need to ask what power I have. I summoned the witch-queen Tilda Vasara—'

'She came because you summoned her? You did not say that.'

'Master Ruzbeh, I am sure, will know how we communicate with witches. I can tell you that her sisters are flying here as we speak, and will be here before very long. I have restored the true shape of the gold you asked me to work on, so that its form now expresses its nature instead of being bound against it. I killed the thief and murderer Gerard Bonneville; I carried Princess Lyra safely through the great flood that ravaged our land; I arranged for the jeweller Tamaz Khuroshvili to be one of your servants, because I knew that his skill would be valuable in the struggle we are all engaged in. I have caused all these things to happen, and now I am going to defeat Sorush, with the help of my friend and your devoted subject, Gulya.'

'You know what he does? You know of his prisoners?'

'I have heard that he captured young gryphons and removed their wings so as to make them work as slaves. For that alone he deserves to die.'

'We cannot find a way to kill him,' said Shahrnavāz very quietly. 'As I say, he is beyond our power.'

'But not beyond mine. I am going to make it possible for Gulya to kill him, and release herself from the spell, and free his captives. And in return for that, I want you to give me the gold circlet I made from the broken instrument, and an escort of gryphons to fly me and my companions to the desert of Karamakan.'

The Queen lowered her head in thought. Or perhaps, he thought, in sorrow.

But before she could respond there was a stir from the corridors beyond the audience hall, and murmurs of surprise and alarm. The vizier, trembling, thrust his way past the guards and hurried in to bow to the Queen.

She looked at him impatiently and snapped something in the language of the gryphons, and the vizier tried to reply, but it was Gulya who spoke first.

'Witches! Look! Here they are! Hundreds of them. And more and more – look – clouds of them . . .'

Gulya had flown out to the terrace, and Malcolm and the Queen moved there too, as did the vizier: no one, gryphon or human, could resist a sight like this. Little gliding specks of black against the blue, each with a sort of flutter inside the glide, but all too far away yet to be seen individually; a swarm of bees, a murmuration of starlings – their presence commanded the sky, and more of them appeared every second from the north, making for the mountain-palace of Damāvand, like a current in a great ocean.

And gryphon guards, seemingly caught by surprise, were hastening out to confront them – or escort them; cries and screams and shouts of challenge came from eagle throats and women's throats alike, and might have signalled the start of a bloody war in the air; except that the leading gryphons were drawing themselves up into ranks almost like a guard of honour, vast wings beating to hold themselves stationary in the sky, while the first witches streamed towards them and confidently among them and between them, making for the terrace or parade-ground where Malcolm and Pan had first set foot on Mount Damāvand.

'You have changed the nature of things,' the Queen said.

'Not changed it,' Malcolm replied, 'but seen it differently.'

'Let us go and meet our visitors, then.'

22

CORUSCATING

The impact of Marcel Delamare's sermon was immediate and widespread. The personal element made it irresistible to journalists, who began to search every archive, every reference book, every collection of newspaper and magazine cuttings for pictures of this sister, and found many of Mrs Coulter, and some of her daughter, the renegade. Artists were employed to draw pictures of what Lyra probably looked like now, with the usual implausible results. Business owners and other rich people were swift to take up the hint and offer rewards for her capture.

Alice Lonsdale, reading the *Daily Mirror* during her break from the linen-room of The Savoy hotel in the Strand, gasped and stood up in shock. Sixty miles away, the Bursar of Jordan College read the same story more staidly expressed in a different newspaper, and reached at once for the telephone to call the Master. Hannah Relf, in a coffee shop near Magdalen Bridge, held her cup suspended in the air while she read to the end of the story in the *Guardian*. On a boat in the Fens, Farder Coram's great-niece Rosella saw the story in the *Eastern Daily Press*, and wondered whether to shake the old man's shoulder and tell him;

but he slept so much now, and seemed to need every minute of it. It could wait till he woke up.

Lyra didn't see it at all.

At *La Maison Juste,* an entire floor had been given over to coordinating the search for the mysterious openings and their subsequent destruction. Reports of new discoveries came in daily. Some of them were found to be authentic, though not many: the committee in charge were considering the possibility that there were really fewer of these phenomena than had first been thought.

As for their destruction, Colonel Schreiber's method continued to be the favoured one. A powerful, firmly contained *tonnerre double* explosion left nothing but shreds of emptiness in the air. These gaps were too small for anyone to go through, though possibly small objects or messages might be passed from one side to the other, if there was someone on the other side to receive them. If you put your eye to one of these slits or rents you could see something of what was on the other side, but very little useful, because most of them seemed to be located in barren or waste places, deep in tangled undergrowth or high up among rocky cliffs or scree, and that was true of the world on the other side.

Half a dozen times or so the Schreiber unit met with opposition. Where the opening had been the centre of a local cult or some similar activity, Schreiber's men had to use weapons to deal with the native people who tried to defend it. At one spot in the East Indies, a local university had set up a centre to study the phenomenon, and a large energy corporation was interested in funding it. Diplomacy, not violence, was the answer to that. A word from the President of the Magisterial High Council to the chief executive of the energy company, the award of the Grand Cross of the Order of St Boniface, and opposition faded like dew.

But reports kept coming in, and they all had to be investigated.

*

One of the people most interested in the story of the mysterious renegade (and now possibly terrorist, it was rumoured) niece of President Delamare was Olivier Bonneville. The Magisterial nuncio in Aleppo had turned him out: his room was needed for other visitors. But he'd provided the wretched boy with a small amount of money and a passport to aid his future travel, so Bonneville was able to buy a ticket on an *autobus de luxe* and set off eastwards, in the certain knowledge that with the alethiometer he'd be able to find Lyra before anyone else, and claim a reward as well as regaining his own alethiometer and punishing the girl.

Unfortunately for him, the death of Mustafa Bey brought his journey to a halt in Armenia. The bus driver had stopped to refuel late one afternoon at a small town in the foothills of the lesser Caucasus, and found that the credit attached to the great merchant's name had suddenly evaporated. Cash or nothing, he was told. As soon as the driver learned why, he saw very clearly what the consequences of the assassination would be, told all the passengers to get out because he needed a spare part, and used the little fuel left in the tank to drive to a motor dealer who bought the bus for a decent price, given the circumstances; and then he slipped away.

The passengers, twenty or so in number, sat on the benches of the little bus station, variously bewildered, disconsolate, angry, and resigned. Olivier Bonneville suspected the spare-part story from the beginning, and banged on the door of the station manager's office until the man came out and told everyone that normal service had been suspended for the time being.

'But why?' demanded an angry woman.

'Because of the sad and unexpected disaster in Aleppo.'

'What disaster?'

'The sudden and unexpected death of His Excellency Mustafa Bey.'

That shook them all.

'But what happened?'

'Was he taken ill?'

'When?'

'He was *killed*?'

'Who killed him?'

'What's going to happen to us?'

'When did you know about this?'

'How long will it be before we can leave?'

'Where has the bus driver gone? Can we call him back?'

'What is the name of this place? Is there a police station here?'

'Is there a hotel nearby?'

'Anywhere we can stay?'

'Can we send a message from here?'

And so on. The manager spread his hands, shrugged, shook his head, made expressions of sympathy and helplessness. There was nothing more he could tell them, because there was nothing more he knew.

Olivier Bonneville was frightened, though he took great care not to show it. To be marooned in this wilderness – and with political and social and economic panic soon to follow – was more awkward than he liked. He sat tight, listened to all the voices around him, felt the alarm and despondency growing among his fellow passengers as the daylight lessened.

But no one seemed to be going to do anything or go anywhere, and the manager was helpless. Bonneville swung his rucksack over his shoulder and left the bus station without saying a word.

The town was only just larger than a village. A marketplace, deserted now; a town hall where a flag hung limp, and no lights shone in the windows, and the door was locked; a café of some sort, closed; a few shops, empty. It looked as if the entire population had been spirited away.

So naturally Bonneville made for the oratory. The onion-dome was the second highest building in the town, after the town hall, and it took no more than five minutes to walk there. He had passed all his life among priests and officials of the Magisterium, and knew exactly how to talk to the clergy.

He found the priest in his narrow house right next to the oratory. He had to knock loudly several times before the man came to the door, and when he unlocked it, Bonneville saw it was on a chain. The priest's dark suspicious eyes glared at him through the opening.

'*Père* Katcheres,' said Bonneville warmly, having first checked the notice board in the oratory porch.

'Who are you?' said the priest, taking the hint and speaking in French.

'An emissary from Geneva, on an urgent mission. May I come inside?'

The chain rattled, the door swung wider. The priest was holding something in his right hand, which he tried to conceal behind his back. Bonneville couldn't see it clearly, but he was sure it was a pistol.

He stepped in and removed his cap at once, out of politeness.

'Very kind, Father,' he said. 'I completely understand your precautions,' indicating the door chain. 'Things are a little disturbed right now. I take it you've heard the news?'

'Mustafa Bey?'

'That's right. I imagine that people will be profoundly anxious for a while.'

'What do you want with me?'

'Firstly, Father, somewhere to spend the night. Everywhere in town is closed or empty. I was a passenger on the autobus to Baku, expecting to continue my journey peacefully when the driver had refuelled, but he made all the passengers get out and then drove away without us. I hope you might be able to let me stay with you till the morning, and I'll try to find some other transport then. I was hoping to get to Baku tonight, but . . .' He shrugged, and assumed an expression of regret.

The priest nodded slowly. 'Baku? A long way. Well, come in and sit down. Will you take some tea?' He glanced at the samovar on the table.

'Very kind, very kind.'

Beaming modestly, being a little awkward with his rucksack, not being sure whether to precede his host into the parlour, as invited, or to follow him, Bonneville gave a perfect imitation of a gauche and harmless clerical functionary ill at ease in a foreign land, but doing his best to be polite.

He sat down, pretending to fuss with his scarf, and watched out of the corner of his eye as the priest swiftly put something in a sideboard drawer and closed it again.

'So,' the priest said. 'Mustafa Bey.'

'Indeed. Very shocking.'

'Did you know him?'

In truth, Bonneville had never heard of him, and he didn't want to be drawn into a long discussion about the man. At the same time, he wanted to find out as much as he could.

'I knew his name only,' he said. 'In Geneva we are out of the way of world affairs as much as possible.'

'To be sure. Excuse me a moment.'

Father Katcheres left the parlour and said something to the servant in the kitchen. Bonneville looked around. In the light of the single naphtha lamp and the meagre fire in the stove he saw a small, dingy, poorly furnished room smelling faintly of garlic and strongly of smokeweed. His dæmon settled uneasily on his shoulder, still nursing her broken wing. He stroked her head.

The priest came back. 'So, nothing open in the town?' he said.

'Nothing I saw. But I imagine people are being careful in the temporary circumstances. When did you hear about the unfortunate death of Mustafa Bey?'

'Newspaper this morning. He was very clever man, very important. Many business, charity, hospital, things like that.'

'That was the first time the news came here?'

'This is a small town, Monsieur . . . I don't know your name.'

'Oh. So sorry. I am Benoît Dupont. I work for the secretariat of the Magisterial High Council.'

'Ah,' said the priest, as if he knew what that meant. He put a log in the stove and sat down. Then he nodded to Bonneville, with one suspicious glance at the wounded dæmon.

'So you only heard this morning,' Bonneville prompted.

'Yes. This morning.'

'And what effect did the news have?'

'Oh, big effect. Yes.'

The door opened. An elderly woman came in with a teapot and a cup and saucer. Both men watched as she put the teapot on top of the samovar, which was steaming thinly, and laid the cup and saucer on the table.

'Very kind,' said Bonneville, beaming at the servant, and getting only a sour look in return as she left.

'What do you think will happen next?' Bonneville asked the priest. 'After Mustafa Bey, I mean.'

'More problems.'

'Ah, no doubt. Does your town depend a great deal on commerce and business?'

'No. We are farmers. You know farm, grow food, animals?'

'Ah, yes. I see.'

Father Katcheres nodded. They sat in silence for a minute or more.

'So, tea,' said the priest, and poured some tarry-looking tea into the cup, topping it up with hot water from the samovar. Bonneville had heard of this process but never drunk the result, and when he tasted it he resolved never to do so again.

'Good, no?'

'Yes, very good. Thank you.'

'So what your urgent mission is from Geneva?'

'Ah. Naturally I would love to tell you, but the nature of it is of course secret.'

'To do with new war, perhaps.'

'New war . . .'

'What your president said. New war to destroy bad places. Also to rescue young woman.'

Bonneville sipped his tea critically, burning with impatience. Yes, the young woman: what exactly had Delamare said? The samovar was quietly steaming. Somewhere else in the house, he heard a door shut. The logs settled in the stove.

'I would be interested to know what news you've heard,' Bonneville said. 'Part of my task includes reporting to the President how people are learning about his words. What impression they make, how faithfully they are reported, that sort of thing.'

'So you are spy,' the priest said placidly.

'Oh, no, no, no, I'm not a spy, by no means,' said Bonneville, laughing as it were heartily. 'Simply a humble representative of the High Council, looking into the effectiveness of its work so far from Geneva.'

'Ah.'

Another sip. 'The sermon, the important sermon delivered by the President . . . You saw reports of that?'

'Some. There were some report.'

'What did you think of what he said?'

Father Katcheres smiled and shook his head.

'You didn't see them?'

The priest shrugged, and smiled again. Bonneville understood him to mean *You're not catching me like that.*

Bonneville tried again: 'Did you read what he said about his own family, the sister, the young woman her daughter . . . ?'

Another shake of the head.

'You see,' Bonneville said earnestly, 'this is very interesting from the point of view of the accurate dissemination of news. The young woman, for instance, mentioned by the President. Did her name reach you here in, in . . . in this village?'

'This village name? Madina.'

'Ah, no, I meant the name of the young woman . . . The one mentioned by the President in his sermon.'

'Ah. I don't know. Just *young woman.* No picture.'

Bonneville nodded. Plainly, that was all he was going to get. The priest was hiding behind stupidity, and it made no difference whether that was real or false.

Bonneville tapped his fingers on the table. Father Katcheres watched with a bovine sort of interest. Bonneville thought he ought to reinforce his claim to be an agent of the Magisterium, just in case the stupidity was feigned.

'I've been travelling quickly,' he said, 'and I didn't think I was going to be spending any time in this area, so I know little about it. Tell me, who is your bishop? And where is his seat?'

'Bishop?'

'*Episkop* – something like that?'

'Ah, yes. I know. *Yebisgobos.*'

'What is his name?'

'Nicolai.'

'And . . . do you see him often? Where is his seat?'

'No.'

The holy bastard looked as if he was enjoying this, Bonneville thought.

'Is there a railway station anywhere nearby?' he asked.

The priest shrugged, shook his head, looked bewildered.

'Train – *Eisenbahn. Ferrovia. Chemin de fer,*' Bonneville said tightly.

'Ah. Yes, I have been. Very fast, long way.'

'Is there a station nearby? Railway station – *gare?*'

Another shrug and a blank look. Bonneville took a final sip of the tepid and bitter liquid at the bottom of his cup, and sat back.

The priest said, 'You want more tea? Give me cup.'

Bonneville sat up again hastily. 'No, no thank you, really. That was delicious. But no more.' He put the cup on the table and firmly pushed it away.

Then the door opened. Two men came in, one carrying a rifle, and Bonneville leaped to his feet, nearly overturning the samovar. Behind the men stood the housekeeper. She was beckoning to the priest, who slowly got to his feet and moved out of the way as the first man pointed his rifle at Bonneville.

'No! No! What do you want? *Que voulez-vous?*' Bonneville found himself almost gabbling.

Bonneville's dæmon was flapping her one good wing and digging her claws into his shoulder, and his hands were so high he felt his fingers touch the ceiling. The second man, dressed like the first in a heavy overcoat and an astrakhan cap, reached up and seized one wrist and then the other and snapped handcuffs on them, twisting Bonneville's arms behind his back to do so.

In intense discomfort Bonneville protested in the three languages he knew, without making the slightest impression on the heavy-featured policemen, if that was what they were. The man with the rifle was speaking to the priest, and the housekeeper stood watching with satisfaction as the priest spoke rapidly in answer, frequently pointing to Bonneville and nodding or gesturing as if to imply that yes, this intruder was a villain of the deepest dye, who had threatened to cut his throat and rape the housekeeper and then ransack the poor box in the oratory.

Bonneville spread his shackled hands as wide as the handcuffs would allow, but since they were behind his back, all he got was more discomfort.

'Innocent! Innocent!' he pleaded.

No one took any notice, but the housekeeper shot him a look of triumphant venom. Finally the second policeman raised his hand and snapped a command. The priest fell silent.

'Magisterium! Personal agent of the President!' said Bonneville, his voice shaking helplessly.

The rifleman lowered the barrel of his gun and then suddenly swiped up with the stock, catching Bonneville right on the point of the jaw. He fell and cried out. He would have fainted if he could, but he was too frightened, and he resented it bitterly that unconsciousness was denied him.

The other man dragged him to his feet and shoved him out of the room and out of the house altogether. His companion said a few words to the priest, and followed.

'My rucksack!' cried Bonneville. '*Mon sac!* Rucksack! Back pack!'

He tried to indicate what he meant by shrugging his shoulders and jerking his chin sideways and trying to look at his back. It all hurt. Then they stamped on his feet and pulled his shoes off.

'No, not my shoes, no! Leave me my shoes!'

The soldiers exchanged a word or two and then banged on the door. The housekeeper handed them the rucksack, which, he noticed, had already been opened. One of the men shouldered it and they began to march him away. As he tripped and stumbled painfully over the cobbles, it started to rain.

Lyra was passionately anxious to hear any news, and completely unable to find any. The unrest in the streets had calmed down after gunshots from various directions; a few people were moving carefully about, as she could see from her window, but no shops seemed to be open; the hotel announced that it would be serving basic dishes and drinks only, and during limited hours at that.

Ionides had gone out to see if he could find any source of information. Lyra had written to Malcolm, telling him through the lodestone about the death of Mustafa Bey and the reaction in the streets and everything else she could think of, taking an hour at least with the only pencil she had, which was getting blunter all the time; and there was no reply.

So she and Asta sat together at the window and talked about the people they could see, or wandered through the public rooms of the hotel and into the garden and back again, or speculated about what Malcolm might be doing.

'It doesn't matter about the alethiometer case, after all,' Lyra said as they settled back at the window again. 'It's the works that matter, and if he's got those . . . And I've still got the needle.'

She touched the little paper package in her shirt pocket where the needle was wrapped up.

'Pan's doing something now. He's feeling tense,' she said. 'No – worse than that. Fear without knowing what there is to be afraid of, apart from the obvious. Of being cut off . . . I never realised how important it was to know the news. When we were in the Arctic, me and Pan, it never seemed to matter at all, so we never missed it . . . But now, it's just the feeling of being connected to things that I miss . . . Being part of the world. I suppose it's because we were young then, and we're older now. Maybe.'

'You mean *you* feel anxious, or he does?'

'Both, probably. We're bound to, don't you think? Not knowing anything for certain. And knowing that the best part of me is somewhere else.'

Asta didn't reply. She was crouching, paws folded together below her chin, eyes half open.

'Lyra,' she said after a minute or so, 'you remember the things in that rucksack you found – the one belonging to the man who was killed by the river, Dr Hassall?'

'Yeah. Most of them.'

'There was a battered old book, with a faded red cover.'

'It looked like a poem, but it was in some language I didn't recognise.'

'Malcolm knew it. He could read it. It was in Tajik. A story about two lovers, Jahan and Rukhsana – a kind of Arabian Nights story.'

'Why are you thinking about that?'

'It just came into my mind. So it might be in his mind right now.'

'What was it about?'

'They have to find their way to a garden belonging to her uncle, a sorcerer. They have all kinds of adventures and overcome all kinds of enemies and dangers.'

'Do they get there in the end?'

'I think so. But it's not a prophecy, it's something else.'

'Has he got the book with him? Or does he know it by heart?'

'He has got it. And he does know it, sort of. But if he thinks of something he'd still need to look it up.'

Looking something up . . . Lyra found the pack of cards, the Myriorama, and spread them out on the table at the end of the bed.

'Normally, a time like this is just when I'd look at the alethiometer,' she explained. 'Not so much asking a particular question. Just watching the needle wandering.'

'I thought it only moved when it had a question to answer.'

'Mostly. But sometimes it just wandered. I wonder if . . .' Unconsciously she touched the little paper packet where the needle lay immobile.

Asta noticed. 'If there was a way of balancing the needle so it could move, and you put all the cards around it . . .' she said.

'I wonder.'

Lyra took the needle out and cleared a space for it among the Myriorama cards. But no: it was silly even to try.

'It won't know these pictures, so it won't know where to go. Anyway, remember when we looked at them in the bus? They sort of work differently from the symbols.'

'Yes. That's true. You tell a story with them.'

Lyra put the needle away carefully, and then scooped up all the cards and turned them over so the faces were hidden.

'Pick one,' she said.

Asta reached out a paw and took her time to tap one card. Lyra turned it over to show a picture of rose gardens, the bushes covered in red blooms, with a young woman picking the flowers and putting them in a cart pulled by a donkey.

'So . . .' Lyra began. 'Once upon a time Rosella and Samson were working in the rose garden. They had to pick the roses at exactly the right moment, when the precious oil was at its strongest. This year the oil—'

'Who's Samson?'

'The donkey. He was very strong. He had to pull the cart full of roses to the distillery. This year the blooms were especially heavy, because the oil had never been so . . . so rich.'

'Where was the distillery?'

'Off that way, out of the picture. Rosella's whole family worked there. They took the roses and boiled them in a big copper pot and distilled the vapour. Pick another card.'

Asta moved two or three cards out of the way, very carefully, and put her paw on the card beneath them. Lyra turned it over. It showed two eagles fighting in mid-air, above another section of the same road, the one road that led from card to card joining them all together.

'One day,' Lyra went on, 'Rosella heard a terrible scream in the sky. There were two eagles fighting, tearing feathers out of each other, slashing with their claws and snapping with their beaks. They fought more and more fiercely until one of them fell out of the sky, dead, at Rosella's feet. The other eagle screamed in triumph and flew away, out over the sea until it was just a tiny speck in the sky and then it was nothing.

'But the dead eagle was carrying a message. Rosella could see a little tube tied to its leg, with the letters ROS . . . written on it. She untied the ribbon and yes, there was the rest of her name on the other side.

'She tried to unscrew the lid of the tube, but it wouldn't move. It was stuck tight. Then she remembered a story she'd heard—'

'It screwed the other way!' said Asta.

'That's right. She had to unscrew it clockwise. And inside it there was a piece of paper—'

There was the sound of an explosion outside, as if it came from the square at the end of the street. Both Lyra and Asta jumped. They could hear stones, bricks, tiles, falling on to the cobbled roadway, and then a longer rumbling crash as a building fell down. People were screaming.

And before they could look around, Ionides was with them.

'What's happened?' said Lyra. 'Are you all right?'

'Safe and sound. Miss Silver, Miss Asta, I think time to leave.'

Lyra packed the cards away. 'I wanted to see what happened next,' she said.

'The message on the paper,' said Asta. 'We'll have to wait.'

'It'll give me time to think of it. Where are we going?'

'First we find a boat,' said Ionides. 'Then we go north.'

Lyra was tucking her last shirt into the rucksack. 'What's happening outside? Was that a bomb just now, or what?'

'Big gun. Quick now, Miss Silver.'

There were running footsteps in the corridor outside. Someone was shouting. Lyra made sure the Myriorama was safe, the lodestone was safe, the needle in her breast pocket was safe, and followed Ionides out of the room.

Asta darted ahead to the top of the stairs and looked back to see if Lyra and Ionides were behind her, before racing down and out of sight. They hurried after her and found her standing in the little lobby by the revolving door, her tail swinging quickly. It was easy to read her mood. Lyra felt Ionides's hand on her arm and let him go through first.

He stopped on the pavement outside in the bright sunshine and looked to left and right. As soon as Lyra and Asta had joined him he said, 'Follow me. Don't stop.'

His gecko-dæmon on his shoulder was looking backwards, head flicking this way and that. Lyra followed close behind, with Asta padding swiftly beside her. Ionides led them away from the square and into a succession of side streets, marketplaces, alleyways, shopping districts, past banks and office buildings and warehouses, small factories, wholesale spice merchants, weavers and dyers, until Lyra was almost dizzy. Ionides sure-footedly strode ahead as if he'd known this route since boyhood, pausing only to check that Lyra and Asta were still with him, and to utter a word of encouragement.

'I can smell the open water,' Lyra said.

'Not far now. Keep moving.'

From behind them, they could hear distant shouts and cries and occasional gunshots. There were few people about along the route that Ionides followed, an old woman carrying a bundle in her arms, a drunk man outside a café, a man looting a smokeweed shop.

As they went past three or four children playing on a bit of waste ground, one of the boys picked up a stone and threw it at them. It missed. Ionides picked it up from the gutter and threw it back, hard and accurate, hitting the boy on the ankle and making him hop and curse. His companions yelled obscenities and threw more stones, but all their missiles fell short, and soon they were left behind.

After another five minutes' quick walking, they came out to the waterfront. In the sunny open space, with a light breeze stirring her hair, Lyra felt almost happy, almost free of all her burdens. Life was simple, after all, if you kept moving. If you met trouble you could just walk away from it. Anxiety was a result of keeping still.

She knew that was too simple to be true, but she pretended it was so as to cheer herself up. Ionides was a few paces ahead, looking intently at the boats – pleasure craft mostly, engine-boats or yachts – bobbing on the water, and then he stopped and shaded his eyes against the glitter.

'Miss Silver,' he said. 'Over that way – the fishing boat – red hull.'

It was one of the few fishing boats visible. Lyra supposed that riots or not, people had to catch fish, so most of the working boats were out at sea. But the one Ionides indicated was in the middle of the harbour, smoke coming from its funnel, someone working in the wheelhouse.

'How do we get to it?'

'We steal this dinghy.'

There was a flight of stone steps leading down to the water, and an inflatable rubber dinghy tied up at the foot.

'Miss Silver, come directly after me. Don't wait. Miss Asta, you go ahead and jump in. No claws, please.'

He held the boat steady while Lyra stepped in, careful not to upset the light little craft. Ionides cast off and reached under the seat for a paddle.

'Who is that in the fishing boat?'

'Someone you know. Sit still, Queen Tatiana.'

She did, holding on to the taut rubber sides as he paddled towards the boat. She twisted to look over her shoulder as they got nearer and saw a number painted in white on the rusty red of the hull, but no more, because then they were right up against it, bumping into the side.

'Hold the ladder,' Ionides said.

Lyra grabbed the metal rungs that hung from the deck.

'On my shoulder,' she said to Asta, who leaped there in a moment and settled herself lightly.

Lyra climbed up and on to the deck. Standing at the door of the wheelhouse was Leila Pervani. Lyra stood still at once and then turned to see Ionides just stepping off the ladder. He nodded.

'I thought . . .' Lyra said. 'You . . .'

Asta sprang from her shoulder on to the rail, and stalked along it till she was level with the woman. Leila Pervani held out her arm, and her serpent-dæmon emerged from her sleeve. The two dæmons exchanged a silent and wary greeting.

'Leila,' said Ionides. 'Let's move.'

She nodded and went back into the wheelhouse. There was a man at the stern of the boat, Lyra now saw, and then Leila Pervani did something and the sound of the engine changed to a louder throb, the chimney coughed several gouts of smoke, and the boat began to move forward as the propeller thrashed at the water.

Lyra sat down on a hatch cover. Ionides had joined the woman in the wheelhouse, and the other man was coiling a rope. Ashore life went on; the boat's engine was making too much noise for her to hear any sounds of riot or pursuit, and no one was pointing or gesticulating at them, and no police cars were screeching to a halt by the stone steps. No one seemed to have noticed anything.

Asta jumped up beside her as the little boat passed the harbour wall and sailed out on to the open sea. The air was fresh, the sun threw off little darts of light from the wave tops, and Lyra found herself wanting to caress the fur on Asta's neck as if it were Pan sitting next to her.

Realising, she took her hand away at once. Asta didn't move, but continued to look out at the waves, regal and impassive.

Ionides came out of the wheelhouse and called out a few words to the sailor, who'd finished stowing his rope. The man nodded and went to take over the wheel. Leila Pervani came out, and finding the wind tossing her hair about her face, tied it back behind her neck, and somehow that little change made her faded dungarees look like haute couture. Then she came to join Lyra on the hatch cover.

PART THREE

23

NO, IMPOSSIBLE

Dilyara, the mistress of Tashbulak, had succeeded in reinventing several procedures in basic physics by reconstructing the apparatus to perform them with. She was led by her instinct for play, which had lain dormant for the first part of her life, and about which she felt privately enthralled now; privately, because there was no one to talk to about it. Chen's conversational resources were soon exhausted.

Dilyara regarded the various pieces of equipment that had survived the clean wind of God as the best things ever invented. The little rag doll and the wooden ball she'd had as a child had been lost a long time ago, but the test tubes, the pipettes, the microscopes, the Bunsen burners, the dry ice in the deep freeze, the magnets, the thermometers, the flasks and tanks of various shapes and sizes, the tongs, the balance – it could all keep a person happily busy till they died.

One day, something different happened. She was accustomed to surveying the horizon every morning and evening, just in case, and the binoculars she discovered in the director's office were very useful. She sat on the canvas chair she'd carried up to the roof of the stores with her dæmon on her shoulder and gazed around in every direction, taking note of the flight of birds towards the mountains, of the rise and fall of clouds in the middle sky, of the inconstant light making the far-off sands shiver and coalesce and shimmer like water, of the smoke from the evening fires in the nearby village. And, this particular evening, her dæmon uttered a tiny gasp of surprise: there was a little black wavering figure out on the sands, shaken apart time and again, but always coming together again, stubbornly getting larger, insistently coming closer.

The traveller was coming from the east, from the region of the wandering lake. She knew about Lop Nor from villagers who claimed to know a secret way through the shifting watercourses, and others who scoffed at the very idea, and from Chen, who had once begun to tell her some tall tale, but fell asleep himself part-way through.

Was it one figure or more than one? Was it someone riding a camel?

Impossible to tell at first. Dilyara sat forward on her rickety chair and shaded her eyes against the waver and glitter, adjusting the binoculars this way and that, and presently the shimmering pieces of darkness coalesced into the shape of a man alone on foot. She looked around: where was Chen? At this time of day he was usually on his way to the village, where she was sure he had found another woman to share his new cleanliness with, and where there was drink to be had. With luck, he would know nothing about her new visitor.

The traveller was close enough now for her to see the robe he was wearing: a deep red, with a leather belt around the waist, and part of it thrown up around his head to protect himself from burning and shade his eyes, for he was walking towards the setting sun. His face was only partly visible: a gold-bearded chin, so he was not like Chen or the villagers or her own people, but perhaps a westerner.

The thought suddenly struck her: perhaps he had come to claim ownership of the research station. To demand an account of what had happened to it.

She ran to the ladder and climbed down quickly, and then hastened through the building and out into the dried-up remains of the herb gardens and the rose beds, along the sandy path towards the broken gate at the boundary fence, where the desert began. She brushed her skirt and bodice and pulled back her hair as if she were going to receive some potentate, some ambassador or great leader, and stood waiting beside the broken gate for the traveller to come close enough to speak to. He was limping, she saw, and he leaned on a staff; the battered sandals on his feet were barely holding together, and his hands were deeply sunburnt. The face under the cowl of the robe was gaunt, the beard less golden than it had seemed from a distance.

He stopped a few paces from her and looked around, pushing the cowl back now that he was in the shade of the building. His hair was thin and stiff with sand and sweat. He seemed to be at the very limit of exhaustion. So was his little lemur-dæmon, who lay limply across his shoulders.

He began to speak and then stopped to clear his throat.

'Chen?' he said, looking around.

She explained in her own language that Chen had gone to the village, and that she was Dilyara, and that she had tried to keep the station clean after the destruction by the wind of God.

He couldn't understand everything she said, but replied in Chen's language: 'My name is Brynmor Strauss. I used to work here.'

She told him her name again, and repeated what she'd said a moment before as well as she could in Chen's language.

He nodded, and said, 'What happened here?' He gestured at the broken windows, the shattered fence, the tumbled walls.

'The wind of God,' she said. 'In the form of the men from the mountains.'

'Oh, I see. Did they destroy everything?'

'Much, but not everything.'

'May I come in?'

She stood aside, watching the little face of his dæmon and her huge frightened eyes. Strauss nodded his thanks and painfully moved past and into the ruin.

She felt the sorrow in his slumped shoulders, his painful movements, as he slowly took stock of the place he used to know as a thriving home of work and discovery and companionship. They went all through the building, and he said little, though she knew he was looking at the cleanly swept floors and the way the rubble had been piled together in tidy heaps.

Then they reached the laboratories, her special place. And she began to feel nervous: perhaps he'd disapprove of what she'd done, the alterations, the improvements, the constructions she'd put together. But there was nothing for it. She unlocked the door and let him in.

The sun had set by this time, and it was almost too dark to see, but she knew that the solar-powered batteries would cut in soon so he could see that first, the place had been ransacked like everywhere else, and second, that someone had carefully tidied up and mended things, and arranged what was left intact neatly on the benches, and cleaned and dusted everywhere, and had begun to put together some pieces of apparatus in ways he recognised and other ways he didn't.

He pushed back the cowl over his head and said, 'What is your name?'

He used the respectful form of Chen's language, the one for addressing superiors or equals. Dilyara was nonplussed; she even looked around to see whether someone else had come in behind her.

'No, you,' said the visitor. 'Your name, if you please?'

'Dilyara,' she said very quietly.

'Where did you come from?'

'Not this region. Further west. I used to clean here.'

'The station?'

'Yes. Every day I clean.'

'Did you . . .' He looked at the equipment on the benches.

'Yes, sorry, sorry,' she said, 'not breaking anything. Very careful.'

'I can see.'

He bent over to look at an inverted glass tank resting in a shallow aluminium tray. One of the bench lights stood next to it. In the tank lay a sheet of coal-silk foam.

'You made this?'

'Yes. Sorry. Not break anything.'

He stood up and stretched, as if his back was aching. 'And Chen? Is he still here?'

'In the village. Then he comes here to light his devils.'

'To light . . .'

'To guard. Keep bad things away. See later. Maybe see soon.'

He nodded. She had seldom seen anyone so tired.

'Come,' she said, beckoning him to the door, which she locked as soon as they were through.

'Does Chen know about what you do here?' he said.

'No. Not Chen. Just me.'

'And your name again, sorry?'

'Dilyara. And Samal,' she added, indicating her dæmon.

'Dilyara. I'm Brynmor. And Cariad.'

'Now you want drink and food?'

'Yes. Drink and food. Thank you.'

She led him to the kitchen, on the other side of the building from the laboratories. This was where she and Chen had begun to make a rudimentary home, in which he had shown very little interest, except as a place for sleeping and eating in. It was better than the storerooms he'd slept in at first, but Dilyara was more aware of that than he was. There were rugs on the floor, and cushions piled up for sleeping on, and one of the stove-tops had been used as a fireplace, with a bed of ashes in the middle and split logs piled beside it.

Strauss sat down stiffly and Dilyara brought him a beaker of water. It was cold and fresh and he drank it all at once. She filled it again from a bucket.

'From the well?' he said.

'Yes. It still good.'

She beckoned him to the sink, and then poured more water over his hands, rinsing away the dirt of several days' travel, and gave him a clean rag to dry them on.

He sat down again and leaned back to watch as she kindled a fire and chopped vegetables. Something in this man made her self-conscious, and that made her uncomfortable, but she could do nothing about it. She was used to ignoring her own discomfort.

After a few minutes he said, 'Did Chen ever speak about me and the other man who went into the desert?'

'Sometime. Chen tell me other man come back and speak to him. But then he leave again and then the men from the mountains come.'

'Did he say anything about what we'd seen?'

'I don't know Chen then. I just clean and that's all. He try to tell me sometimes about red building, but then he stop and fall asleep. Is red building there, yes?'

'Yes.'

'You go in?'

'Yes, and come out again. I must tell people important things. But if . . .' He looked around, and gestured to say 'Everything is broken.'

She poured some oil into a wok and held it over the fire, rolling it round and round to spread the oil before settling it between two logs on the stove top. She swept the chopped cabbage and onion off the cutting board and into the wok so that it hissed and flared.

'The thing you were making in the lab,' he said.

'Lab?'

'Where you made that, with the tank and . . .'

'With other things.'

'What were you making?'

At first he thought she hadn't heard him. But their two dæmons, the lemur and the desert fox, were crouching close by with their heads nearly touching. They weren't talking, but they seemed to be communicating somehow. Cariad would tell him later.

Dilyara said, 'I make telvision.'

'Telvision?'

'One time I saw telvision in a rich man house. Big box with glass front, and pictures. Like that.'

'Did your telvision work?'

She looked at him with disappointed contempt, and then turned back to the cooking. She tossed the wok so that the vegetables jumped up and fell back, hissing, several times. Then she pinched up some salt from a box and threw it over the food, and tossed it again once or twice, added some sauce from a bottle, and then tipped it out into two chipped enamel bowls. She took chopsticks from a drawer and gave them to Strauss with one of the bowls, and then sat down herself, her shoulder turned away from him.

'Thank you,' he said. 'Dilyara, I didn't mean to make fun of you. I know it wasn't a real television you were making. I just—'

She spoke swiftly, telling him that she was not a fool, that neither was she a barbarian to put things together without understanding them, that she had tried many times to attract lights and images to her tank, and not without success, after she had found the flasks of hard steam in the cold room, but she would say no more.

'Hard steam?' he said.

'Very cold.'

He tried to find the words for *dry ice*, but they wouldn't come. Hard steam would do. Was she making a cloud chamber? He stole a glance at her as he ate. She was no doubt right to be offended by his silly question, but really he had half meant it: what had she seen? *Lights and images*, she'd said.

'Will you show me?' he said, after a minute.

'Not now. Maybe later.'

'Of course.'

'You stay here?'

'Not for long. Have all the staff gone?'

'Some dead. Others gone.'

'Who died?'

'I don't know names. Chen know.'

He finished the little meal and drank more water.

'Thank you,' he said.

She made no response. He looked at her stocky frame, her hunched shoulders. She finished eating and rose to her feet, taking her bowl and his to the sink. He stood up and did the same.

'No more food,' she said.

'It was very good. Did you grow the vegetables here?'

'Some. Some from village.'

'Is there still a regular bus from the village?'

'Where you want to go?'

'Alma-Ata. Or Urumqi. A big city, anyway.'

'No. Buses all finish. Only camel.'

'I have to get to . . .' he said. He spread his hands helplessly.

She could see that he felt it was impossible.

'Why?' she said.

'I learned some things in the red building and it's very important that I tell the world.'

'Tell whole world?'

Now she was mocking him in payment for his silly question about her television. He nodded; he recognised that.

'Tell as many people as possible.'

'You could tell me,' she said.

That was a test, and he failed it. His expression immediately showed his doubt, and hers in reaction showed her disappointment. Dilyara saw herself with his eyes: an ignorant peasant woman playing with equipment she would never understand, probably illiterate, fooling herself that she was learned and clever like the men and women who had worked here before the wind of God swept them away, whereas in truth she would never be like that no matter how long she lived. Thus, she believed, he saw her.

'I am part of world,' she said.

But her voice was quiet, because some strength had gone out of it.

He took a deep breath, and felt dizzy, and had to lean on the bench for a few moments till his balance returned.

'Dilyara, forgive me. I am more tired than I have ever been. I have seen things I could not have imagined, and I need days, weeks, to think about them and understand what they mean. But I have no time. As soon as possible I must find a way to go back to the people who sent me here, back to Brytain, and tell them what I have seen, and what they must do, what we must all do, as a result. It is desperately important. I thank you for sheltering me, and for giving me food and drink. I am full of gratitude to you, and of wonder at what you have done here at the station, and I would like to talk to you about everything, and to listen as you tell me what you have discovered. But I must sleep before everything else, and then I must go. I apologise for my failure of courtesy. Again, please forgive me.'

That was what he would have liked to say, but he was not sure, as he finished speaking, whether he had really said it. His command of Chen's language was nothing like so extensive. He said as much as he could manage.

But Dilyara was moved by the sincerity of his tone as well as his desperate exhaustion. She stood and bowed, and then beckoned to him to follow her into a small room where there were cushions and blankets, and where he could be private as he probably wanted to. He lay down to sleep at once.

Lyra said, 'No, impossible. No.'

She sat on the hatch cover of the little fishing boat as it bobbed and swayed its way over the water. The sunlight, splintered into a thousand shards, dashed itself against her eyes. Ionides leaned on the rail nearby, and Leila Pervani sat close to her; it wasn't a very large hatch. Lyra could smell her perfume, something rich and faint and subtle.

'Lyra, it's true,' said Leila. 'You are the girl he preached about, the renegade. Marcel Delamare is your uncle.'

Lyra looked desperately at Asta, but the dæmon said, 'I'm sorry, Lyra. It's true. Malcolm and I heard it from Olivier Bonneville.'

'And you didn't think to tell me?'

'It never occurred to either of us that you wouldn't know already.'

'It is true, Miss Silver,' said Ionides.

'You never met him? You never heard of him?' said Leila.

'Never in my life,' said Lyra as firmly as she could manage. 'I thought at one time that my mother had relatives, maybe even a brother, but I was taken away when I was too young to remember anything. And now you tell me he's the . . . The what? President of something?'

'President of the Magisterial High Council. The first single leader the Magisterium has had for several centuries. He is a very clever political operator. I met him once. A man willing to do anything, cheat and lie and betray, and continue to seem mild and courteous and beyond suspicion. Exceptionally dangerous.'

'And this speech . . .'

'A sermon in the cathedral at Geneva. His declaration of war. Everyone knew that was coming, but no one expected the revelation about a family and a niece who is now a terrorist and a fugitive from justice. There are pictures of you in every newspaper in the world.'

'Where did they get those from?'

'Probably they made them up. They don't look like you, not very much.'

'And there is a reward,' said Ionides.

'How much am I worth?'

'Half a million dollars.'

'Only half,' she said shakily. 'Hardly worth the trouble.'

'But the other thing he spoke about,' said Leila – 'you know anything about that?'

'Tell me again. Remember, I haven't been able to follow the news very closely.'

'These holes in the world. Something like that. Openings into other places.'

'Well, I do know a little about those . . . But how did he come to know about them?'

'Didn't say,' said Leila. 'But he's found the ideal thing to scare people with. Secret openings that enemies can come through – or disease, or contamination – or evil spirits, any nonsense. It's ideal for him.'

'Miss Silver, what you know about these things?' said Ionides.

'Well, I'll tell you, but you'll have to believe me. It sounds implausible. No, it sounds impossible. But it's true . . .'

The little boat chugged on, out on to the wide Caspian Sea, and Lyra told them everything she knew about the windows between the worlds. It took longer than she thought it would, and partway through she had to ask for some water, because her throat was dry; and the sun was hotter on her head now, because a lot of time had gone by and it was higher in the sky. Leila and Ionides listened to everything in silence.

'Well, there it is,' she said at last after telling them how Will had closed the last window in the Botanic Garden in Oxford, and with it the way between them for ever.

She had to stop then and swallow hard. Besides, her eyes were brimming over. No doubt it was the sun.

'Anyway,' she said softly.

Leila leaned across and embraced her, and Lyra wept on her shoulder without holding back. Asta too had been listening closely. It was the first time she had heard all this, and Lyra knew the dæmon would tell it all to Malcolm when they were together again, so she had a sense that Malcolm himself was there with them, invisibly, and what she said was partly for him.

Ionides went to the wheelhouse and spoke to the other man. After a moment or two Lyra felt the movement of the boat change as the sailor turned the wheel to port. She pulled away from the woman's embrace and mopped her eyes, breathing deeply, looking around.

'Where are we going?' she said.

'A little further along the coast. It was time to leave Baku, before the riots became organised and word began to spread about the search for you. Best if we stay out of big towns.'

'Yes, I understand, but I want to cross the sea and get to the Karamakan desert. It's urgent . . . Oh, my head is so full of . . .' She pressed her hands to her temples. 'I've got to get to that building in the desert because I think there's one of those openings there. A window to another world, where they grow the special roses that help people see Dust. It's guarded by warriors . . . It's in a red building. And all the time this man, this Delamare – oh! I've just seen how it might be true after all, him being my uncle.'

'Why?'

'Because my mother's name, her maiden name, before she married Edward Coulter, was Van Zee. Or Van der Zee. Same thing as *de la mer.*'

'So it is.'

'All these things to know, all these *facts* lying around me, and I knew none of them. I feel so stupid sometimes.'

'But now you know that fact about him. He *is* your uncle.'

'And he wants to kill me.'

'He doesn't say that. From what he says, he wants to find you and protect you.'

'You believe that, do you?'

'Of course not. He would kill you at once if he could. But he doesn't say that. His talk is all of saving you, rescuing you from the evil powers. But listen, Lyra: what will you do when you find this place in the desert, this opening to the world of the roses?'

'Defend it,' Lyra said. 'Die defending it.'

24

THE DEATH OF SORUSH

Malcolm rode on the back of Prince Keshvād, with Gulya flying on his right and a witch called Tuuli Latvala on his left, a close companion of Tilda Vasara. With her came seven other witches, and Malcolm had spoken to them all before they began the journey.

What he planned to do was land in the mountains to the north of Sorush's cavern, and then approach it under cover of darkness. He had learned everything the gryphons could tell him about the sorcerer, and he had with him all the items he'd borrowed from Khuroshvili the goldsmith. According to Tuuli Latvala, the moon would be full when they reached the sorcerer's cave.

As they flew north along the sea, the witch flew back and forth conferring with her companions, and sometimes soared high above or scouted the air to the horizons east and west. Eventually she flew close to Prince Keshvād, and called out to Malcolm.

'The sky is full of spirits,' she said.

He heard her clearly. 'Spirits of what kind?'

'Many kinds. Some I know and some we have never seen before.'

'I can see nothing but the sky.'

'Then you must believe me. I think they are friendly, or at least neutral. I have spoken to some of them. They know this sorcerer you plan to find.'

'What do they say about him?'

'He is greedy and cunning. Most of these spirits are afraid of him.'

'Are there more spirits than normal in this part of the sky?'

'They've come from elsewhere. From further east. I think they are *apsaras.*'

'I don't know that word. Would they fight for us, if it came to battle?'

'I don't know. This is like no campaign we have fought before. You want to kill this sorcerer, fine, we do that, or the gryphon will do it, that is not difficult. But what then? Back to the mountain?'

'No. Further east, to the desert south of the Tien Shan mountains.'

'And then?'

'Find a red building, and enter it.'

'Just that?'

'Not without Lyra,' he said.

'I have heard of this Lyra. I loved Serafina Pekkala. Where is she now?'

'Somewhere below us,' said Malcolm, 'on the sea, a little north of Baku. Let me read what she says.'

He had been exchanging lodestone messages with Lyra, but the light was failing as the sun sank behind the mountains to their left. It was getting harder to make out the pencilled words.

She wrote: *We are fleeing from riots in Baku. Fishing boat. Heading north. Where are you?*

High above, Malcolm wrote in reply. *Can't see you yet. We can see the lights of Baku though. We are flying to a cave in the mountains north of the city.*

What will you do there?

Kill a sorcerer. Then find you and fly to desert.

Where cave? How far north?

Not sure. Not there yet.

We are maybe a mile from shore. Level with a lighthouse. Three flashes then one.

Malcolm called to Tuuli Latvala, 'Look for a lighthouse a little way north of here. Three flashes and then one. Tell us as soon as you can see it.'

The witch swept up into the night and called to her sisters, and they all streamed away towards the north.

Malcolm was conscious of the smell of burning pitch – just occasional drifts of it in the wind. From various points on the ground outside the city, columns of smoke broke out only to be twisted and torn away by the turbulent air, to be replaced at once by more smoke and occasionally little sparks of fire, and the smell of other fires too – and the glow from buildings on fire, four, five of them, half a dozen or more.

They were flying over the edge of the city itself now, and much of the light down there came from street lights, or the glow from windows and shopfronts, all the normal anbaric illumination they might see above any city in the world. Now the lights of the city were being left behind them, and a different darkness beyond showed the vast mass of the Caucasus mountains. The moon was rising, and soon, no doubt, the sea below and the country beyond the city would be drenched in a colder light than fire. Malcolm couldn't estimate how high they were, but it wasn't easy to look past Prince Keshvād's wings; and all he could see when he tried to look down at the sea was a turbid darkness, with occasional streaks of white where waves were breaking. The smell of burning pitch still whirled past, little ghosts of a smell.

Gulya shouted, 'Great fire below!'

A cluster of industrial buildings was blazing near a wide harbour where a number of ships sat at anchor, and thick smoke billowed up, torn and flung away by the winds. Malcolm could see vessels spraying water and foam through high-pressure hoses, but as he watched, one of the refinery buildings exploded into a fountain of flame, and the sound followed it up through the air: a colossal boom, as long and deep as thunder, reverberating from the mountains and setting the ships rocking on the water.

Prince Keshvād's great voice roared, and Gulya darted forward to speak to him. Malcolm could feel the mighty lungs rumbling below him, and kept very still. Gulya swept up high, swung round, and skimmed down towards him, and landed on Prince Keshvād's back beside him.

'The witches are coming back,' she said, almost breathless. 'Round the headland.'

The city was behind them now, and the headland rose sharp and dark out of the sea ahead. Prince Keshvād beat his wings harder and they rose high above, sweeping around the cliffs and out to sea a little way before tilting to the left and following the shoreline.

'There's the lighthouse!' said Gulya, and through the clouds and the rain and the swirling smoke there it was at the point of the headland, a light flashing one-two-three and then one, one-two-three and then one.

Immediately Malcolm turned his head to look out and down, to the sea directly out from the lighthouse. But if there was a light on the fishing boat it must have been very small, or else they'd dowsed it for safety. Malcolm craned to look out for the quick-darting black-garbed fliers.

'Tuuli!' he cried. 'Here, here!'

Watching them wheel and soar before swooping down close to the great gryphon, he felt his heart gripped, for a moment, by fear. They were so few, and he and Gulya so small, and the task they were facing was so difficult . . .

'Malcolm! Malcolm!'

It was another witch, not Tuuli Latvala, calling to him. 'I can hear you,' he called back. 'Did you find the lighthouse?'

'Yes. And the boat. Tuuli Latvala has gone to speak to Lyra.'

Malcolm imagined the little boat swaying and lurching on the rough sea with Lyra on the deck holding tight to the rail, and the witch landing lightly beside her, and Lyra's astonishment.

'Gulya!' he called. 'Gulya, could you ask Prince Keshvād to fly lower?'

Gulya beat her wings and sped to the great gryphon's eagle head. He turned to listen to her, and said something in return, and Gulya wheeled and came back to report.

'We can land on the ground, but not on the sea. With waves and wind like this, the prince can't risk going low enough to speak to the boat.'

'I understand,' said Malcolm. 'Has the witch spoken to them yet?'

Malcolm looked at the lodestone again. He had only the flickering fire from below to read it by, and he peered closer, conscious that the stone was slippery with rain and that his hands were cold, and held it close to his eyes.

Taking on water, he read. *Can't stay out. Making for shore north side of lighthouse.*

See you soon then, he wrote in response.

'Gulya!' he called, and the little gryphon swooped down to listen. 'Where is the forge of Sorush?'

'It's the cavern that's—' she began, but then cried out with shock.

Malcolm caught his breath.

The entire mass of the mountain range, looming high above the waves crashing on the rocky shore, had suddenly burst into flame. From a thousand and one openings, caves, crevices, cracks, gorges, clefts, caverns, and grottoes a thousand and one orange-red tongues lashed out, licking the stony walls and cliffs above them, flaring this way and that in the tempestuous air buffeting the shore. Malcolm and the gryphons and the witches on their cloud-pine branches could hear the roar of fire even above the howling of the wind. Great swags and banners of flame, sheets

397

and flags of it, tore loose from their caverns and hollows and flew on the wind like blazing vultures eager for flesh to consume.

'Which one is the forge?' Malcolm shouted.

Gulya cried aloud, but her words were lost. Malcolm felt as if a madness had seized him. There was no way back from this now; Sorush would die, or he and Gulya would. As for Lyra—

She was writing again. Now it was the light from the blazing mountain that showed Malcolm what Lyra was saying. He wiped the rain off the stone and held it up so it shone a flaring, glistening orange and yellow. The words came through:

Making for jetty now – white posts—

That was all.

Malcolm read it aloud, shouting the words as clearly as he could. He leaned out and looked down, holding tightly to the great feathers of Prince Keshvād's back. The gryphon was wheeling in the gusty air and scanning the shore below with great sudden sweeps of his head. As for Gulya, she could make no headway against the wind; it was all she could do to stay close.

Then the prince spread his wings wide and plunged downwards in a sickening dive straight towards the little jetty with the white posts. Malcolm's hands were shaking with the effort to hold on, because he had no other purchase than his grip on the thick-shafted feathers. He could hear the roar of the fiery caverns even above the rush of wind, but only for a moment, because Prince Keshvād was beating his wings inward, swinging himself up and back, reaching down with his lion-feet and making ready to land.

But he had only the narrow jetty to aim for. A sheer cliff rose straight up beyond it.

Malcolm could see the boat now, low in the water, still some way out. Then came another mighty sweep of the gryphon's wings, and another, and they hung for a moment suspended in the air before gravity took them the last little way down to the rotting boards and swaying posts of the jetty.

The prince landed securely, and in a moment Malcolm had leaped down from his back. He looked up to speak to the gryphon.

'Prince,' he shouted above the roar of the fires and the howling wind, 'I owe you a great debt. The boat just making for the jetty holds some friends of mine. Please let them ashore.'

Prince Keshvād bent his great eagle-head low to say something in response, and Malcolm heard the words '*If you let Gulya die, I will kill you and all your friends.*'

Malcolm looked him in the eye, and nodded. The little gryphon had managed to land on the jetty, but she was a scrap of paper in the wind compared to the power and size of the prince. Her claws were scrabbling for purchase on the slippery boards. Malcolm bent to scoop her up, and for a moment she fought, twisting to look past his shoulder and up at the prince, but then she fell still, and Malcolm saw something pass between the two gryphons like a charge of anbaric power, and understood at once. She loved Keshvād, but could expect nothing in return; and the prince loved Gulya, but would never be able to express it. It was only the fraction of a single heartbeat, and he saw it all at once. He set her down among the rocks where the wind couldn't catch her.

The remains of a little harbour surrounded the jetty: a fragment of stone wall, a shattered wooden building or two, a path that seemed to lead up towards the mountain in one direction, and across to the lighthouse in the other. Malcolm looked up: flames everywhere, scorching his face.

Then he heard a cry from the sea: 'Malcolm! Malcolm!'

Malcolm turned to see the little boat, low in the water, wallowing clumsily as the engine battled to keep the screw turning. They were only a hundred yards or so from the jetty, and in the light of the flaring mountain behind him Malcolm ran to the end of the shaky platform and clung to the furthest white post, holding on fiercely and calling Lyra's name through the buffeting wind.

Every time the boat thudded down into a trough between the waves, it seemed less able to rise up again. Malcolm could hear the straining engine, and thought they should ease back on the throttle, or risk burning it out; but if they lost headway in the swirling mass of water they'd be swept away from the jetty in a moment. They had to keep going forward, no matter that for half the time the propeller was screaming into the empty air.

Malcolm ran from post to post, shaking them all, feeling for one that was a little more steady than the rest, and peering wide-eyed through the rain and wind. Everything on the sea was lit up by the fires from the mountains; in their lurid glare he could see Lyra, and Asta too; his dæmon was close to her, clinging tightly to the rail and reaching forward for the jetty, but still too far off – and then a man moved her aside and held up a coil of rope, and Malcolm nodded and stood ready to receive it.

The man with the rope was Ionides. He saw Malcolm, and nodded too.

They both knew there'd be only one chance. The boat was tossing and swaying, lurching and falling, and there was no pattern, nothing to guide them except the sense of the right moment; and it came, and Ionides swung his arm hard and the rope flew to Malcolm's hand and he gathered it in.

A few swift movements without the intervention of thought, and a clove hitch secured the boat to the post. Now it wouldn't drift away, and they could work at moving it alongside the jetty and securing the stern.

More screaming from the engine, more thrashing from the propeller, and little by little the boat swung round, battling every heave and surge from the waves. Ionides ran to the stern and took up another rope, and they waited, both of them, watching and judging, while Lyra clung to the rail and someone in the wheelhouse controlled the engine and the rudder.

Then the lurching sea paused again, and up swung the coil, and this time Malcolm braced his feet and hauled on the rope as soon as it was in his hands, straining to pull all the weight of the boat round and bring the side against the jetty. Little by little he got it closer, and then slung the rope over the nearest post and hitched it tight.

The jetty was more or less level with the deck of the boat, but the pitching and plunging made it a hazardous jump. First to try it was Asta, and Malcolm snatched her out of the air and set her down on the slippery planks. 'Go to the rocks,' he said, and she darted away.

Lyra was adjusting the rucksack on her back, trying to find her balance, and then she was ready.

'Ready ... Now!' he shouted, and Lyra sprang with all her strength across the gap. He would have caught her if she'd fallen ten thousand feet; into his arms, as light as a wraith, strong and frail both at once. She clung to him, and he pressed her to his heart and kissed her head without thinking, and then said, 'Run to the shore.'

She ran after Asta. Next came a woman Malcolm didn't know: his own age, it seemed, slender, athletic, possibly Persian or Kurdish; Ionides had to urge her to the rail before she was ready to jump, but she steadied herself and made the leap without difficulty.

Then the last two: first a man who came out of the wheelhouse, a burly fisherman by the look of him, balancing well on the lurching deck, and grasping Malcolm's hand across the gap; and finally Ionides. Malcolm could see that he was not convinced, and in truth the boat was wallowing lower and more sluggishly, and the water was sweeping across the deck. Another few moments and it would be too low for him to reach the jetty.

'Jump, man!' Malcolm roared, and up he sprang, and Malcolm seized his arm and dragged him up off the sinking vessel and over the edge of the jetty.

Seeing that Ionides was safe, Malcolm ran back to the rocks. Asta crouched tensely and as soon as he was close enough, sprang up into his arms, pressing herself hard against his beating heart. Lyra stood close by, soaking wet, shivering, but her face was lively with joy. The fisherman was looking after his own dæmon, a small white bird, and the woman sat calmly, watching everything.

'I'm Malcolm Polstead,' Malcolm said. 'Who are you?'

'Leila Pervani,' she said.

'You a friend of Ionides?'

'Yes. And of Lyra.'

'Good. And you?' he said to the sailor.

'Yusif,' he said uncertainly, looking at the woman. Seeing her nod, he said it again.

The sailor had seen the great form of Prince Keshvād a little further up the rocks, crouching impassively in the light of the flaring mountain, and was clearly apprehensive.

Malcolm looked up. The blazing caverns gave off not only light but sound and heat. A roar blasted their ears that was part subterranean and part tempest, both air and fire, while the heat scorched their faces when they gazed upwards.

He was aware of someone beside him, and turned to see Ionides.

'That gryphon your friend?' he said. 'The big one.'

'For the moment. He is Prince Keshvād. The little one is Gulya. Now we have to find the cave of a sorcerer, but . . .'

'Up there? Which one?'

'Hard to tell.'

'Miss Silver will know.'

His expression, vivid in the glare, was full of mischief and confidence. Malcolm remembered the morning they'd met, under the orange tree at the embassy house in Aleppo, and the impression Ionides had made on him then.

'You came all this way with Lyra?'

'Every step. She save my life, I save hers when necessary.'

'And the woman?'

'You want to find the right cave or not?'

Malcolm smiled briefly. He turned to Lyra. She had gone to sit on a rock, clutching her rucksack. As she looked up at him, Malcolm found he could barely stand for the beating of his heart.

He felt that the two of them might have been the only focus of consciousness in the world, so fiercely were they intent on each other.

He crouched down beside her. 'Lyra, I have to go with the little gryphon to the cave of a sorcerer, who put a spell on her years ago. She will fight him, and she means to kill him. But he's concealed his cave by setting the whole mountain aflame. Ionides says—'

'Whatever he says, it's true. Mostly. He said I'll know the right cave?'

'Yes. Is *that* true?'

'It's true,' said Asta, who'd been listening close by.

Lyra was feeling in her battered rucksack. 'That alethiometer,' she said, 'the one you were mending – it was mine, and here's the glass.'

She passed it to him, making sure his hand was securely around it before letting it go. It wasn't easy to see; the rain was still dashing against his eyes, and the glare of the fires showed him only a disc of glass running with water and glistening with inconstant yellow and orange and red and white flares of brilliance.

'But—' he said.

'There's something special about it, I don't know, the shape or the kind of glass, something. Try and . . .'

He held it up to his eye, unconvinced, and tried to look through it at the mountain. All he saw at first was a blur of flame. He wiped the rain from his eyes and looked again, and saw the flank of the mountain more clearly. He didn't know what he was looking for: the cave and the forge of the sorcerer, of course, but how would he recognise that?

He scanned up and down, left and right, and took the lens away from his eye to look without it: was there any difference?

'I can't—' he began to say, and then all the other things his body was feeling began to remind him of themselves: the bitter cold, the unsteady rocks underfoot, the drenching rain.

He held the glass to his eye again.

Something was different about *that* patch, just below the southern flank—

Yes. It was.

'Seen it?' Lyra said.

Alone among the crevices gushing flame, this one glowed with a steady light. A figure – male – stood in the entrance, looking down—

And at that moment every flame went out, except that one. A few last scraps of fire flew away on the wind, scattering sparks, but otherwise – total darkness.

He had to think: *Don't drop the glass.* In his astonishment he might have let go, and it would have smashed on the rocks at his feet, but he held it securely.

The others were all struck silent. They stood or sat still, looking upwards at the vast bulk of the mountain against the louring sky. Not a speck of light or flame anywhere on it; a great hand seemed to have swept across and put them all out at once.

No one spoke. Malcolm looked again for the little patch where he'd seen the forge – looked with the naked eye, unsuccessfully, and then with the glass.

'What is happening?' asked the woman, Leila Pervani.

'Can you see it?' said Gulya.

'Yes, I can,' he said, and gave the glass back to Lyra. 'Well, Gulya. We have to climb up to it, but I can see where it is.'

'Is it a long way?' said Lyra.

'Yes, and hard. But you're not coming.'

'Yes I bloody am.'

He ran his hands over his head, trying to clear the rain out of his eyes. 'Well, to tell the truth, I shall need some help. Not with the fighting – Gulya has to do that herself – but with the preparation. Handing me various things when I call for them.'

'I can do that!'

'Maybe better with me,' said Ionides. 'Only perhaps. Maybe not, in fact.'

'Thank you, but no.'

'Stay here and guard my rucksack,' said Lyra.

'This Miss Silver or Queen Tatiana?'

'What do you think?'

He nodded cheerfully.

Malcolm turned to him and said, 'When Lyra and I and the gryphon – the little one – come down the mountain, things will have changed. Somewhere in the sky there are witches, under the command of Tuuli Latvala. Remember that name, and watch out for them. They will help us, but I don't know how at the moment.'

'Otherwise we stay here?'

'You stay here till we come down.'

Leila Pervani was looking at him. In the newly fallen dark he could hardly see her, but he had a vivid sense of her expression as he remembered it: fearless, appraising, wary. Ionides stood beside her, his hand on her shoulder. Yusif the boatman sat nearby, stroking his seabird-dæmon.

Malcolm took out the little bag containing the things he needed in order to deal with the sorcerer, and set his rucksack down next to Lyra's and called to Gulya. Prince Keshvād remained where he was, couchant, still, silent. He looked Malcolm straight in the eye, and nodded his head slowly, once.

'When the fires were blazing, I could see a path. We'll aim for that and try to stay on it,' Malcolm said, and set off.

Gulya flew a little, stalked a little, flew again. Asta ran ahead a short way, stopped to look back, moved further on. Malcolm walked steadily: there was a long climb ahead of them.

In the middle airs above the flank of the mountain and below the thickest clouds, Tuuli Latvala and her companions sped to and fro, south to north and back again, weaving a complex pattern that was invisible even to themselves; the weft was their trajectories, and the warp was their knowledge of the behaviour of clouds. This was a curious storm, no doubt about it, but they had seen others like it, and they had its measure.

What they had to do was impose an intention on the mass of clouds directly alongside the mountain and over the sea. Everything had an intention, in the thought-world of the witches, but most things didn't know it, or had intentions that were feeble or contradictory. This storm had been summoned and formed by someone whose knowledge and sky-craft were almost as full as theirs, but who seemed to have a limited mastery of self-contradiction. Tuuli Latvala was able to express this state of things in words, if she needed to, but her companions didn't need words to understand it. They darted back and forth, tightening a thought here, lengthening a thread of influence there, tying together three currents in one greater one, and little by little persuading the clouds to part along a line parallel to the slope of the mountainside.

The flames that had engulfed the mountain so suddenly, and then vanished without warning, had perturbed the witches briefly, but they continued their work unnoticed by the people below; and before very long the vast unwieldy clumsiness of moisture-saturated air found itself wanting to move this way, or that way, and to leave a gulf in the centre of the mass, as if that had been its intention from the beginning.

Tuuli Latvala turned away from the work between the cloud-base and the sea and soared up into the chasm that had been opening above them. The quality of the light up here was quite different from the inky blue-black darkness clinging to the mountain and the rocky shore, because the higher she flew, the thinner were the clouds above her. There was a silveriness that suffused the air, and with it one of the most joyous sensations for a witch, the promise of moonlight on her skin.

Satisfied with their progress, the witch looked back at the mountain. It was completely dark; no moonlight yet came that far through the clouds. Tuuli Latvala flew down to the water's edge, where the waves smashed themselves against the rocks and shook the jetty and moved the wrecked fishing boat this way and that as it lay half submerged. She looked at the rocks where Ionides and the others were waiting, and greeted them briefly before flying up again.

Lyra didn't ask why they had to defeat the sorcerer, though she badly wanted to know. She was content to stumble up the mountain path peering through the dark at Malcolm picking his way faultlessly after Gulya over the rough stones, and feeling all around her a warning heat from the rock itself, as if it could burst into flames again at any second.

Malcolm said nothing; they needed all their breath for the climb and what would follow it. They helped each other when they stumbled, steadied each other when the ascent grew steeper, and climbed more slowly when they needed both hands to move safely. He went ahead and took care to go no faster or slower than she could, always moving forward, always into the darkness, always a little higher with each step.

The rocks underfoot and under their hands were hotter and hotter the higher they climbed. The rain that still fell turned into steam, so they seemed to be climbing among clouds, and Lyra began to fear that they'd lose their way; but the little gryphon Gulya seemed to be sure of the path, and her lion-claws were unaffected by the heat from below.

Asta found it harder to manage, and eventually sprang up with relief to Malcolm's shoulder.

'What's going to happen when we get there?' Lyra managed to say.

'Gulya is going to kill the sorcerer. He put a spell on her so she never grew.'

'And if she doesn't kill him?'

'She'll have to. And she will.'

They fell silent, occasionally whispering a warning about a loose rock or a crevice beside the path.

Not long after that, the rain stopped.

While it was falling, difficult though it made their progress, it had at least kept them cool against the heat of the rocks. Now although the air was saturated with moisture, and steam still rose around them as they struggled upwards, there was nothing to moderate the ferocity of the heat underfoot.

Malcolm was wearing strong boots, but Lyra wasn't. She said nothing, but he could see how painful it was for her, and called to Gulya.

'Where is the forge?' he said.

'Really very close. You can hear the machinery from here. One more effort, and then I shall kill him.'

'You will only kill him if you do exactly as I say.'

'I will, of course I will.'

'But will you remember?'

'You had no fears about my memory before.'

'I know what happens in the middle of a fight. We should have taken time to practise, to train. Me as well as you.'

'I shall kill him, never fear.'

'As you say,' said Malcolm, and then listened. 'I can hear it.'

He stood still, motioning to Lyra to do the same, and they listened.

The sounds came from below their feet as well as from ahead on the path. Hammering, grinding, thudding, smashing sounds, deep in the heart of the mountain, making the rocks shudder all around them, shaking the moisture loose from their surfaces.

'What is it?' said Lyra.

'The forge of Sorush,' said Malcolm. 'He's mining for precious metals and minerals. Harvesting rubies that grow there. Refining the ores. He loves gold as much as the gryphons do.'

'But he loves it for its power,' said Gulya. 'We love it for what it is in itself.'

'I think I see,' said Lyra. 'Is he alone? Does he have any helpers?'

'The *koruskati*, and other beings we don't know about. Malcolm knows how to defeat him. And we shall do it, and I shall kill him, and then you will see my true aspect, at last.'

Something was happening above them. Tuuli Latvala and her witch-companions had gathered in much of the cloud-rack above, and the light that filtered through what was left had a different tone altogether from the black steamy hideous night that had enveloped Lyra and the others as they climbed. The sky was not quite clear above them yet, but it was clearing.

'Let's go on,' said Malcolm. 'He'll see this soon himself, and be alarmed.'

With burning feet they stumbled further on. And soon they came to a buttress in the mountain that obstructed the path. They would have to walk around it with great care, because a fall of several hundred feet lay below.

They stopped behind the buttress and Malcolm beckoned Lyra close, slipping the string of his small bag off his shoulder.

'This is what you have to do,' he said quietly. 'In here there's a flask of water, a bag of dust, a small pair of bellows, and a stone. Put your hand in there now and learn the feel of them.'

She did. The flask was made of some kind of metal, with a top that screwed open in the normal way. She'd need two hands for that. The bag of dust was about the size of Malcolm's two fists together, and held shut with two leather cords. She'd need both hands for that too. She then felt for the stone. It was rough and round, and no bigger than a small apple.

'He's hiding behind a mirror,' Malcolm said. 'When you look into it you'll see yourself, but yourself as he wants to see you. Take no notice of it, and be ready to hand me the flask – take the top off first – and then the bellows, and then open the bag of dust and hold that up too. The stone I'll take now.'

She put it in his hand. And the purpose of all this, she reminded herself, was to get her one step nearer Karamakan and the building in the desert, and to find Pan and the secret of her imagination. That truth lay like a diamond in her heart.

And then they moved around the buttress, and there it was: the cavern, the forge, the stronghold of Sorush. A cleft in the mountainside, and in it a blaze of light and fire, and the sorcerer himself standing in the entrance – invisible behind his mirror.

Lyra had to stop and shake her head. Her eyes were dazzled, not just by the glare of the fires but by the splintering confusion of the images in the mirror.

Malcolm was beside her, and she saw him in the mirror: it showed a strutting popinjay, vain, conceited, but self-pitying, mewling, sneering. She saw herself in the mirror too: a simpering courtesan, painted and half naked, but diseased, with great sores leaking slime and pus. Her form and Malcolm's were iridescent with the light from the forge, glittering like poison beetles. Asta felt sick at the sight of them both.

'Don't look at him,' said Malcolm, and crouched to open his bag. 'Look here instead, and get ready to hand me the flask.'

As Lyra unscrewed the top of the flask, Malcolm stood up and flung the stone directly at his own reflection in Sorush's looking-glass. The mirror shattered and fell to the floor of the cave, and all the reflections vanished. There was nothing behind it.

Nothing there at all. But Malcolm was prepared, and so was Lyra. She held up the flask, and he took it and flung the water at the *nothing*. Then he thrust the spout of the bellows into the bag of ground pumice that Lyra was now holding open, and spread the handles wide, sucking up the dust.

Then he pointed the bellows at the *nothing* and worked the handles in and out so that the dust blew out and stuck to the soaked magician and revealed him standing there, a small man twitching and furtive and naked, and seemingly made of pumice.

And at the same moment the light changed. The glow of the flames seemed to withdraw, just a little way, and into the cave from the night sky above came a ray of moonlight. The witches had moved the clouds aside, and the full moon blazed in the bare sky.

The sorcerer cried out in fear, and tried to cover himself with pieces of the broken mirror, holding up shards of the shattered glass in front of his face, his genitals, his belly.

Gulya had better move quickly, Lyra thought, and so she did: she darted between her and Malcolm and swung her head to fling something out of her beak, and it glittered in the moonlight as it fell at the sorcerer's feet: the silver amulet.

Sorush screamed, and stumbled back. The ground pumice was falling away as the water dried on his body: already only parts of him were visible.

Hurry, Lyra thought, *he'll disappear again—*

And Gulya half leaped, half flew against the sorcerer, claws out, and tore at him and bore him to the ground.

Immediately the pair of them were covered in a cloud of burning, scorching sparks: the *koruskati,* swarming to the defence of their master. Through the flickering confusion Lyra could see them stinging the little gryphon, plunging through her fur and her feathers, and she shook them off again and again – until they seemed to decide all at once to make for her eyes, and she had to pull away and shake her head, but still they clung and burrowed.

Lyra couldn't help it: she ran to her and knocked the little sparks away, stamping them into the rock, never minding how they burned her feet.

Sorush was beginning to scramble away, and Malcolm saw it and sucked the last of the pumice into the bellows before blasting it straight at the sorcerer's face. Lyra heard cries from somewhere further inside the cavern, eagle-screams, and then Sorush was on his feet again and Gulya launched herself at him once more.

This strange contest had rules, Malcolm knew; he could help, but not fight, or the curse on Gulya would never be lifted. Only she could kill him, and only killing him would work.

But Lyra and Malcolm had been joined now by Tuuli Latvala. The witch's companions remained in the sky, holding the clouds back and clearing the way for the moon to shine, but the witch herself was standing beside Malcolm and watching intently as the fight went on.

Sorush was trying to draw Gulya further back into the cavern, and again the little gryphon was surrounded by a cloud of the blazing *koruskati*, biting and stinging and piercing her fur and scorching her feathers. If they did too much damage she'd never fly again, and Asta longed with all her being to plunge in beside her and tear at the sorcerer's flesh with her own claws.

Then Sorush screamed, and in response came a lick of huge flame from inside the cave, breaking against the rocky roof and spreading out and downwards before disappearing. Tuuli Latvala beat at it with her cloud-pine, but Lyra, thinking of the fire-loving pitch in the vessels of the wood, thought, *Don't, don't . . .*

And indeed the cloud-pine caught, and Tuuli Latvala had to attend to that, or lose her own power of flight.

Meanwhile Malcolm too had to hold himself back, because like Lyra he was fearing for Gulya's life now, and they both felt she'd taken on too much, they'd gone too far. Another mighty banner of flame swept out from the depths and enveloped both combatants in its folds.

But there was Lyra.

Malcolm blinked and shook his head, but yes, it was her, standing in the entrance to the cave, and she was holding up the glass from the alethiometer and focusing the moonlight—

Against the incandescent glare of the forge and the angry sparkling of the myriad *koruskati*, the little beam of moonlight was all but invisible. Nevertheless it fell on Sorush's arm, and he twisted away in shock, and Gulya saw her chance and flung herself up again, with wings and claws that must be exhausted, Malcolm thought, and gripped the sorcerer's head in her jaws.

The flames from the forge tried to surge out again as if they were obeying Sorush's will, but they didn't reach as far as they had a few moments before. The volcanic roaring was weaker now, and the thudding of the great hammers was slowing down and sounding uncertain.

Malcolm, and Lyra too, and Tuuli Latvala for that matter, could all see something that had been invisible till then: the cords of djinn-fire binding the body of Gulya tight. She was fighting to loosen them as well as defeat the sorcerer, and Malcolm thought that unless she got them loose, she would never beat him. But unless she beat him, she would never get them loose, he thought at the same time; and he wanted with a passion to leap at the combatants and hold the sorcerer back while Lyra tore at the spell-bindings and freed her.

More and more parts of Sorush were becoming hard to see as the pumice dust dried up and fell away from his flesh, but there was no more water and no more dust, and as for the moonlight, the sorcerer had moved little by little towards the side of the cave, away from the entrance, where the moonlight lay – the only place where Lyra's glass could work.

Sorush was scrabbling, grabbing, losing hold, reaching out to get hold of one of Gulya's wings and break it. And she was writhing and twisting away from his deadly hands, and then she managed to snap her beak shut on his right wrist and wrench it back and forth, working at the bones till they cracked, twisting the tendons, ripping open the arteries till her face and the whole of the sorcerer's arm were covered in his blood.

He was screaming and tearing with his left hand at her wings, her neck, her lion-feet, at whatever he could grasp, but he was weakening, and – Malcolm had to say it to himself before he could believe it – Gulya was stronger, she had shaken off the binding spell-cords. And the clouds of sparking, stinging *koruskati* were falling away too, and then Gulya dug her lion-feet into the sorcerer's belly and surged upwards to his throat, and despite every effort he could make with his one working hand, she plunged her beak

413

in just under his jaw and tore and tore away at the flesh till the *koruskati* were scattered by the blood-spray, till the whole cavern was echoing with the hideous rasping of breath through his open throat, till Sorush fell twisting, writhing, kicking, twitching, flailing and helpless as the life drained out of him.

Finally Gulya struggled to get up and off his body and away, and lay panting and wounded on the rocky floor.

Lyra ran to the little gryphon, caressing her head, cleaning away the sorcerer's blood, whispering words of praise and encouragement. And Tuuli Latvala was kneeling beside her and opening a little horn box of bloodmoss ointment, and Malcolm and Asta were making their way deeper into the cave, where they smashed down the crystal walls holding back the imprisoned gryphons, slaves no more but flightless and wounded still, who came hobbling and limping and crawling out to see the wonder of their delivery, to marvel at the body of Sorush, entirely visible now, ragged and filthy and torn asunder.

'Outside,' said Gulya, and her voice was deeper now, assured and commanding. She was growing larger as they looked: commanding, majestic.

Asta said quietly to Lyra, 'And all that time she was young against her will!'

Tuuli Latvala gave her little box of bloodmoss ointment to Malcolm for safe-keeping, and with a long witch-scream of triumph she flew up to join her companions, still holding back the clouds. The whole mountainside was bathed in moonlight; the twisted rocky path, the great buttress hiding the cavern, all the way down to the shoreline, where the waves still crashed against the jetty and the landing-place.

Lyra could see the little group of figures all the way down there, all standing and peering up, it seemed, though she couldn't distinguish one from another; and then the great form of the gryphon prince moved away from them and raised his head, and she was astonished at the immensity of him, the sail-broad extent of his wings as they beat again and again so that he soared up and over the lighthouse and still upwards, towards the cavern of the dead sorcerer and the gryphon, small no longer, whom he loved.

But while the others were watching Prince Keshvād, Malcolm saw another boat, a little way out still, but making directly for the jetty and the landing-place.

25

High Mountain Cradle

The army of the Magisterium had met the first obstacle that seriously held them back. The desert of Karamakan, and the only-just-reachable red building inside it, lay to the south and east of the high range of mountains known as the Tien Shan, or Celestial Mountains, which extended many hundreds of miles to the east before descending to the level sands where the wandering lake of Lop Nor lay restlessly, protecting the desert from that side.

Delamare and his advisers had considered ordering his army to take the route through the Kazakh steppe north of the mountains, and approach the desert from the Lop Nor side, but decided against it. It would be too long a march, hard to supply, and vulnerable to attack from the unpredictable monarchies of Mongolia and Chingizia, not to mention the Golden Empire of Cathay itself.

The other main route from the west involved using one of the passes through the Hindu Kush, the mountains between the western end of the Tien Shan and the start of the great Himmaleh range, and Marcel Delamare was perfectly conscious of the parallel from ancient history: Alexander of Macedon had conquered everything between Greece and the Hindu Kush, but had never gone further and into Karamakan.

Delamare had moved his headquarters east from Constantinople, moving with his main force across the steppes towards Samarkand, and spent hours at his campaign desk looking at a globe and unfolding his maps of the region and folding them again and re-unfolding them, but whenever he looked at them, nothing had changed: the mountains were still there.

For the first time he began to wonder whether his army might be a little over-extended. There was a reason Alexander had had to turn back; geography was implacable.

Alexander had no flying machines, of course, and the Magisterium had every kind of dirigible and gyrocopter at its disposal. Aircraft made short work of mountains. An airlift, a dirigible, say, moving a large body of troops through one of the high passes that marked the limit of Alexander's reach, could put the Magisterium's army down at the edge of the Karamakan desert in no time, and from there the red building was only a few days' march away.

Except for the *oghâb-gorgs*.

These ferocious and abominable birds haunted the entire range of the Tien Shan, as well as the western part of the Himmaleh. They were fearless lovers of war, man-sized eaters of carrion and makers of it too; nor were they limited to the mountains, but, as Pan had seen, they sometimes ventured a long way west and north, attracted by the scent of shed blood, or the prospect of it. They were cannibals, of course; they were killers and eaters of anything that lived and could move, or had died and moved no more. Biology was implacable too.

In short, the Tien Shan was more or less impassable. A few early travellers had managed to come out alive, but it was only the high prices chargeable in the west for things like silk and spice and rose oil that made the travel worth the risk.

Again and again his advisers said, 'Avoid the mountains,' and again and again he pored over his maps, and read further reports from travellers and geographers and even plain storytellers.

'No aircraft has ever crossed the Tien Shan,' Delamare's owl-dæmon reminded him. 'The birds mob them and bear them to the ground. They are fearless, fanatical, deadly. And then there are the gryphons.'

'Gryphons!' Delamare, who rarely showed any sign of irritation or impatience, swept the map in front of him off the desk and pushed his chair back hard.

'Marcel,' his dæmon warned, 'you'll bring that officious young man in. Move quietly.'

The officious young man was Felix Murad, the assistant secretary Delamare had brought with him from Constantinople. He was competent and efficient, and Delamare liked him, though he did anticipate things a little too eagerly.

'Yes,' Delamare said shortly. 'I know. Perhaps we should send him to the gryphons as an emissary. They have a king, do they? Remind me. Some kind of hereditary ruler?'

'A queen, at the moment. Why not send for Murad in any case? He will know things we don't.'

Delamare nodded reluctantly and rang the little brass bell on his desk.

'I wonder,' he said to his dæmon before the young man came in. 'Gryphons . . .'

A knock at the tent-post, and Felix Murad came in, his sparrow-dæmon alert and bright-eyed.

'Mr President,' he said, inclining his head respectfully.

'Come and sit down, Felix. I want some advice.'

He took a chair and Murad sat upright on the bench nearby. 'Anything I can tell you, sir.'

'Gryphons. I know nothing about them, but they seem to have some kind of authority in the mountains. Firstly, do they exist at all? Or are they travellers' tales?'

'Yes, they do exist, sir, but they have very little to do with human beings. They have their own realms of influence, which hardly overlap with ours. That is why they are often thought of as being entirely mythical.'

'So they are only partly mythical, is that it?'

'Mr President, that sort of distinction is too subtle for a secretary of my rank to understand.'

Part of Delamare's mind automatically sifted out the insolence in the young man's tone, and forgave it; another part admitted the truth of his words. Really, Murad was quite like Olivier Bonneville, in his way.

'When the late beloved Saint Simeon was alive, did the Patriarchy have any dealings with these creatures?' Delamare asked.

'Not in a full diplomatic sense, Mr President. There was a mutual recognition, at a sub-consular level, and occasional exchanges over matters of trade, especially where gold was concerned.'

'Gold?'

'The gryphons are apparently obsessed with it. It's almost a religious thing with them. So if there was a dispute involving ownership, for example, of a sum of gold, the Patriarchy recognised the importance of some kind of diplomatic channel in order to minimise the . . . You understand what I mean.'

'Of course. I would expect nothing else.' Delamare tapped the desk with his fingers, left to right, right to left. Then he looked up and said, 'Schreiber. Where is he now, do we know?'

'With General Bentinck's force in Khorasan, sir. Making adjustments to the *tonnerre double*, I understand.'

'Send to him and order him to join me at once, with all his men and their equipment.'

'Ah. Of course. At once, Monsieur le Président.'

And Murad left, with the slightest possible inclination of the head, and the slightest possible smile in his eyes. He was thinking that the sounds made by Delamare's fingers tapping on the desk were not the same as they usually were, and as he closed the door he saw why: all the President's fingernails were bitten to the quick.

Delamare himself had forgotten Murad already, and was thinking about Bonneville. Where was that boy, anyway?

At that moment, Olivier Bonneville was lying sleeplessly on a hard bunk in a filthy rural prison somewhere in the Lesser Caucasus. He was cold and hungry and frightened. His captors hadn't been able to explain why they had arrested him, but it was clear that they expected to make something out of it; if not loot, then a reward.

They had his rucksack, which worried him most of all. The alethiometer . . . Why hadn't he thought of some way of hiding it, a long time before this?

Well, he had to get it back. And then resume his search, and find the girl, and claim the reward from Delamare. He knew he was on her trail. He didn't know much more than that, because his readings had been scrambled and confusing, and more than usually nauseating, but then he hadn't had somewhere quiet to work in and time to ease his way back into the experience.

And now it was in the hands of these bandits . . . It was intolerable. He said so to his dæmon, who perched painfully on the end of the bunk.

Finally he slept.

He woke up to a bitter morning and the sound of heavy rain outside his cell, which had no window, of course, just bars across an opening too small to crawl through even without the bars.

The hideous glare of a light directly over his eyes, the clattering of a key in the lock, a voice shouting at him in some barbarous tongue spoken by hogs with their throats cut, and a solid kick to his right leg.

'All right! All right! I hear you! Yes, I'll get up! Don't kick me again, you bastards! Oh, God, this is too much . . .'

He struggled up, fending off another kick, and tried to make sense of what was happening.

'Yes – yes – I'm awake – all right, all right! Yes! I'm sorry I did whatever I did to make you arrest me! I won't do it again!

420

Sorry, you lumps of shit! I apologise! What is this? What do you want?'

The guard held out a tin mug, which turned out to be too hot for Bonneville to hold. He put it on the floor quickly. Then the guard threw him a lump of stale bread, and barked a word or two, and left.

Bonneville pulled the blanket up around his shoulders. It was horribly cold, and his head ached abominably, and he was bursting to piss. He stumbled up and made his way to the bucket in the corner, but it hadn't been emptied and the contents had frozen solid, so his urine splashed out over his stockinged feet. His shoes, he remembered too late, were gone.

'Aaacchh – filthy bandits – bastard swine – dogs – tapeworms – dung eaters – oh, look at this – oh, this is intolerable . . .'

He hung his wet socks on the window bars, mopped his feet with the blanket, and slouched back to the bunk. He thought he might as well take a little warmth from the mug of whatever it was, discovered it tasted even worse than the bitter drench he'd had at the priest's house, and simply held it between his palms for the warmth as he gnawed a small mouthful of gritty bread.

When the bread was all gone he lay down and felt sorry for himself. He could do that at the same time as wondering how to get out, and wondering most of all whether these barbarians would steal the alethiometer or just smash it to pieces. But it was too cold to lie still for long, and presently he got up and inspected the door.

It was just a heavy cell door made of some much-scratched and graffitied dark wood. There was no handle on the inside, naturally, but no keyhole either. The open window was too high to look through, and the iron legs of the bed were set directly into the concrete floor.

Bonneville badly wanted the initiative back. He took the tin cup and bashed on the door with it, as hard as he could, over and over.

'*Messieurs!*' he called. '*Soldats! Gentilhommes de la garde! Venez, s'il vous plaît! Au secours!*'

He spoke in French, because everybody understood it. The guards understood the bashing on the door even better, and after a minute or so they opened it suddenly, snatched away the cup, hit Bonneville smartly on the head with it, and went out again.

'*Oh, mais non – messieurs! Venez! Venez! C'est important! Je suis ambassadeur de Genève! Diplomate! Immunité diplomatique!*'

He heard heavy footsteps going away, and distant laughter. He kept on shouting, with no result at all except a sore throat to match his sore head.

Eventually he lay down and slept from pure disgust.

Prince Keshvād and Gulya met joyfully halfway up the mountain path, while Malcolm and Lyra and Asta hurried on down towards the jetty. Sometimes a turn in the path would let them see down to the shore, sometimes that view was hidden from them, but finally they came to a place which gave them a clear view of the jetty and the rocky shore, and there was no doubt about it: a boat, some kind of motor yacht a little larger than the fishing boat that had sunk, arrived from the sea and tied up to the jetty. They could see it happen, but they were much too far away to shout and be heard. Ionides and Leila were making their way towards it.

'What are they *doing*?' said Lyra.

'They're leaving the boatman. Yusif. Look, he's asking to be taken as well, and they're saying no, you can't come, you have to stay.'

'But . . . this is horrible. I can't understand what's happening.'

'Maybe Yusif can tell us.'

'Where are the witches?' Lyra scanned the sky, but saw no sign of them.

'Flown back towards Damāvand to tell them about Gulya killing Sorush. Probably. Though they might be watching the boat, I suppose.'

'I don't think they'd feel that had much to do with them.'

'You're probably right. I don't know witches very well.'

Lyra felt as if her fear and doubt had physical form, like a bruise caused by a stone flung at her heart. She pressed on down the path, with Malcolm watching to see she didn't stumble, because her every limb seemed to be trembling, and soon they found the little rocky cove, with the jetty intact, and the mast of Yusif's sunken boat still protruding from the water nearby.

The boatman was pacing up and down, clearly distraught. He saw them coming and hurried to speak.

Malcolm listened, and then calmly held up his hand. The boatman was speaking in a language Lyra didn't recognise, and he was agitated, gesticulating passionately.

Malcolm said something in reply, and the boatman took a deep breath and rubbed his hands over his head.

Malcolm said something else, in a different language, Lyra thought, and the boatman nodded and replied.

'He says that Ionides and the woman went willingly,' Malcolm explained. 'As if they knew the boat was coming.'

Yusif spoke again, and Malcolm gestured to say, 'More slowly.'

Yusif nodded and said some more, and Malcolm listened closely, holding up his hand from time to time to clarify something, or to ask the boatman to slow down.

He did, and little by little the account became clearer. Lyra understood that the boat had come straight in, as if those aboard knew exactly where to land; that it was larger and more powerful than his own boat, which now lay on the seabed; and that those on board, four men, he said, seemed to know the woman, who greeted them warmly and went on board without hesitation. Furthermore, he said that Ionides didn't seem to be known by them, but that they'd welcomed him as a companion of the woman, and that they all spoke easily together.

Finally, Yusif said that in his own opinion, the crew had some kind of official authority. They wore uniforms, and their boat flew a flag with the emblem of a lamp on it. He told Malcolm that they had pointed their guns at him, Yusif, but that the woman had spoken and persuaded them not to kill him. Then they turned the boat round and made out to sea at full speed. The whole account strained at the edges of Malcolm's linguistic ability, and it took some time before they learned all Yusif could tell them.

'Well,' said Lyra, 'I'm going to give him a bit of money. It wasn't his fault, and now he's lost his boat as well.'

She had nearly come to the end of Farder Coram's store of coins, and the one she gave Yusif might have been more than his boat was worth, or less, she couldn't tell; but he thanked her, and bowed to them both, and set off to walk towards the lighthouse, where, he said, he could stay for the night.

For Lyra, the sight of Ionides calmly leaving with the forces of the Magisterium hit her like a heavy punch to her heart. Leila . . . she hardly knew Leila; but he was a friend. At least he hadn't taken their rucksacks; hers and Malcolm's were still where they'd been put. Lyra felt dizzy, uncertain about her footing on these slippery rocks where the waves were still dashing their spray, uncertain about everything.

And then Gulya glided down to land on the shore. She explained that Prince Keshvād had set off for the south, to tell the Queen and the rest of the gryphons the news that Sorush was dead and his captives were freed, and that untold quantities of gold were waiting to be taken. Meanwhile, Gulya herself would fly Malcolm and Lyra and Asta to a safe place further along the coast, where she could guard them while they slept.

So they climbed on her back, and she took to the air with no effort at all, it seemed; and on a grassy headland a little further north, with the sea below them, and a grove of trees some way inland, and the vast snow-capped range of the Caucasus behind, Lyra and Malcolm climbed down again. Gulya took to the air, to enjoy the power of her new size, they thought.

Lyra stood and looked at everything. Her head was as full as her heart. The night was not cold, and the storm had blown itself out;

the moon shone clearly over the headland, and laid a silver path on the sea. And there was Malcolm, taking off his coat.

'Lie down on this,' he said. 'It'll get cold later on.'

He spread it on the grass near some bushes in the moon-shadow of a rock the size of the fishing boat.

'What about you?'

'It's a big coat.'

Asta had already taken possession of the middle.

'In a minute,' Lyra said, and wandered to the edge of the cliff, and scanned the sea; but there was no sign of the boat, or of the witches.

Her mind was full, and she was overpoweringly tired. She lay down on Malcolm's coat and fell asleep at once.

Olivier Bonneville was dreaming about Leila Pervani, and she was flirting with him, and he was treating her scornfully, which his waking mind approved of; though he enjoyed it when she trailed her fingertips across his head. Half awake he tried to reawaken the feeling, and encountered the lump where the guard had rapped him with the tin mug.

He winced and sat up carefully. Oh, it was cold.

He draped the single blanket around his shoulders and stood up, careful where he put his feet.

'Alethiometer,' said his dæmon, her wounded wing held awkwardly.

'I know, I know. I'm thinking of the best way . . .'

'Use it to tell their fortunes.'

He looked at her. It wasn't a bad idea, at that. 'And tell them . . .'

'Don't think it out in detail,' she said. 'Improvise when you get to it.'

'How's that wing?'

'Bad still.'

'Bitch had some sort of weapon . . .'

'She had a small stick.'

'She kicked me in the kidneys.'

'No, she wasn't fighting fairly at all.'

Bonneville gave her a sour look, and sat down again. 'What we need to know,' he said, 'is what angle these police or whatever they are—'

'Listen. They're coming back.'

He heard voices from the corridor outside, but he couldn't tell what they were saying, or even what language they were speaking. An older man and a younger one, that was all; and then a key rattled in the lock.

He stood up. '*Que voulez-vous?*' he said as they came in, and then, just in case, 'What do you want?'

'We want to give you something to eat and drink, Mr Bonneville,' said the older man, in English.

They were both in uniform, but the older man's was smarter. The younger man was the one who had knocked him on the head with the tin cup. He was only a thug, and Bonneville would have kicked him in the balls at once, if he'd had any shoes, but the older man needed careful handling. Bonneville could manage that too, he told himself.

'May I know why I have been arrested?' he said, in English so as to exclude the younger man from any exchange.

'Of course. You may be aware that an emergency situation has arisen, and the authorities have suspended the civil law for the time being. Our main task is to make sure that the general population is safe. You understand the necessity for that.'

'I don't present any danger to the general population. I am an envoy from the President of the Magisterial Council in Geneva, and as such I have the immunity of any diplomat. I insist that you set me free at once.'

'Let's go somewhere a little more comfortable, and discuss the matter,' said the older man, and held out Bonneville's shoes. 'You might like to put these on first.'

Bonneville took them without a word and sat down to put them on. His socks were still hanging from the window bars, sopping wet. The older man saw them and said, 'I think we can find you a clean pair, Mr Bonneville.'

'I have been scandalously mistreated.'

'These are difficult times,' said the officer, and his soothing voice made Bonneville think that his own tone was peevish and feeble. He resolved to speak more firmly.

'I need my rucksack, and everything that was in it,' he said.

'We shall discuss it all. Follow me, please.'

He lifted his dæmon from the bunk, and the officer led him along the cold corridor to an office that probably wasn't his, because he had to wait for the other guard to unlock the right door for him.

The first thing Bonneville saw was the alethiometer, undamaged, in the middle of the blotter on the desk. His other property was nearby, his clothes folded neatly. Everything that should be there was there. There was also an anbaric heater glowing in the fireplace, and Bonneville sat on the chair in front of the desk and held out his hands to the warmth.

The officer dismissed the guard and sat down behind the desk.

'You claimed to be an envoy of the Presidential Council of the Magisterium. It did not take long to discover that was a lie. You absconded from the custody of the nuncio in Aleppo, and before that, you stole this instrument and two of these books from the *Palais de Justice* in Geneva. You are urgently sought by agents acting directly for Monsieur Marcel Delamare, the President of the General Assembly of the Magisterium. What have you got to say to that?'

'Firstly that I feel reassured, Colonel, to have fallen into the hands of someone who clearly understands the importance of my mission—'

'I am not a colonel. Address me as Brigadier.'

'I beg your pardon. And I understand the purpose of your question, which was to test whether I was truly who I claimed to be. The Magisterial Council is not called the Presidential Council, nor is it called the General Assembly of the Magisterium; and the building in Geneva is not the *Palais de Justice* but *La Maison Juste*. Have I passed the test?'

As soon as he said that, Bonneville imagined a crevasse opening under his feet. Perhaps, since he'd left, they *had* made all these changes, and he'd fallen into a horrible trap.

But the brigadier merely smiled and nodded. 'Good,' he said, and the ground closed up again. 'Now tell me about this instrument.'

'It is an alethiometer—'

'I know that much. What is it doing in your possession?'

'I am the Magisterium's appointed reader. It's in my care, not in my possession. I am travelling east, using it as a guide, in order to find a certain young woman, who has stolen another instrument like this intending to use it to find a great treasure, which rightfully belongs to the Magisterium.'

'A certain young woman? The same one mentioned recently by the President?'

'Of course the same one.'

'Can you prove that the instrument was given into your care? That you are the authorised reader?'

'The proof is that it *is* in my care.'

'You might have stolen it.'

'Another proof is that I can read it, and no one else can.'

'Go on then. Read me what you judge to be the truth about the desert of Karamakan, and about that young woman. Where she is now, for instance.'

'I can't do that here. I need a room away from noise and disturbance. I need something palatable to eat and drink, a table and a comfortable chair, pencils and paper, and access to a bathroom. I also need enough time to formulate the questions and interpret the answers, and the assurance that I shall be free to leave when I've done that, taking with me everything I brought here, including the alethiometer.'

428

'You may have most of that, except the bathroom. Do you think this is a first-class hotel? And you have my assurance that whether your answer is true or not, if it fails to convince me in any detail, I shall hand you over to the civil police. Without the alethiometer, and without shoes.'

'Very well,' said Bonneville, who knew he had no choice.

They locked him in a room with only one window, with frosted glass, and time went by. It was days since he'd engaged with the alethiometer and the new method, and the usual difficulties occurred; but he persevered. This room was noisier than the cell he'd been in, and the sounds of stamping and the slamming of doors and shouted orders might have distracted a less accomplished reader. At one point a gyropter flew down and landed not far away, followed by more shouting, more stamping; he ignored it all.

Sometime later the brigadier threw open the door and said, 'Well?'

Bonneville lifted his eyes languidly and said, 'I haven't finished.'

'You've had an hour.'

'I need longer.'

'That should be long enough.'

'You have no idea of the complexity—'

The brigadier slammed the door hard, staying in the room. Bonneville flinched.

'I'm not interested in your complexities,' the brigadier snapped. 'You claim to be an expert. What have you discovered?'

Bonneville sighed with sympathy, but without contempt. He was pleased with his ability to do that so accurately, but then the brigadier kicked his chair away and sent him sprawling.

'Come on! Get up! You're wasting my time and yours. Tell me what you've found out about Karamakan.'

Luckily Bonneville had not been holding the alethiometer, or it might have fallen and smashed. He got up carefully and sat down, trembling only slightly. His face, the brigadier noticed, was very pale, and he looked nauseous.

'The research station is occupied again,' Bonneville said as steadily as he could.

'Who by?'

'I haven't had time to see. As far as I can make out, one of the former investigators has returned. There is no way of telling his name. He, or they, have been experimenting. That's all I can find out.'

'And the girl? The renegade?'

'She is not far away. I don't know where *we* are, mind you. Where are we?'

'You don't need to know that.'

'It would help.'

The brigadier opened the frosted-glass window, which only disclosed a brick wall an arm's length away. He breathed deeply and turned back.

'Tell me where she is,' he said. 'You can tell that, because you've said she's not far away. Tell me more.'

'As far as I can make out, she's at the edge of – I suppose it's the Caspian Sea. A coast, anyway, in mountainous country. She's not alone.'

'Who else, then?'

'Well, that's what I need more time for.'

The brigadier said, 'Are you feeling unwell?'

'Yes. As I tried to tell you, this process is physically and intellectually demanding in the highest degree. It can't be rushed. There are physical . . . costs.'

'You should have asked to use the bathroom.'

'I completely agree. I asked you about a bathroom, if you remember. Your attitude made it clear that you didn't care whether I used a bathroom or not. As a result, I had to vomit into that waste-paper bin at your feet.'

The brigadier moved away. 'You have to be sick every time you use it?'

'Not always. In cases of exceptional difficulty, I have to cope with nausea.'

The brigadier strode to the door and opened it. 'The bathroom is to the left, along the corridor. Dispose of . . .' He indicated the waste-paper bin. 'That. Then come to my office, and bring the instrument and your notes.'

He left. After a minute Bonneville followed him. He left the waste-paper bin where it was.

He found the brigadier standing outside his door, waiting for him; and as soon as Bonneville was in the room, the brigadier came in and locked the door behind him.

Bonneville couldn't speak, couldn't move. In the chair behind the desk, watching him with an expression of calm indulgence, was Marcel Delamare.

26

THE HARD PROBLEM

Lyra drifted out of a dream in which she was waking up with Pan, and woke to find herself still murmuring to him. They had been talking about Malcolm, and Pan had been telling her that the witch Tilda Vasara had asked him whether Lyra was in love with Malcolm, or maybe it was whether he was in love with her, and the witch was about to say something more; but then she found herself awake.

She didn't move, and she kept her eyes closed. There were voices all around – witch voices, gryphon voices, Malcolm's voice. It sounded like a crowded marketplace or a meeting in a public square. Other sounds went on underneath: gulls, breaking waves on the rocks below the headland, wind in the grass.

She should get up. But Malcolm must have covered her with the rest of his coat, because she was snug and warm, even though the ground was hard under her.

She heard a cat-purr, and opened her eyes to see Asta close by. 'What's happening?' she said.

Asta said, 'Malcolm's talking to Gulya and the prince. There are more gryphons and witches arriving and flying off every minute.'

Lyra looked around. 'Is it private?' she said.

Asta knew what she meant and said, 'I'll keep watch. Those bushes are thick.'

Lyra rolled over and stood up slowly. She was completely hidden. She went into the bushes and made herself comfortable and then joined Asta again, and tried to tidy her hair and brush her skirt clear of leaves and twigs, with Asta picking off the bits she couldn't see.

She didn't want to go and join the others just yet. She was trying to capture some of the essence of the dream before it faded completely. She sat down, and Asta joined her.

'Lyra,' she said, 'how's Pan going to recognise your imagination when he finds it?'

'I don't know. It's a metaphor.'

'Well, I know that. But it worked, didn't it? It made you think he was looking for something that had vanished. So you followed him.'

'Because I thought he might have been right. Something was missing.'

'What did you feel was missing?'

'A . . . certainty about the world. A sort of sense that fundamentally it was true and reliable and just *there*. A sense that we belonged there too. Belonged in the physical world. Whatever that sense was, I'd had it once, and I didn't have it any more.'

'Maybe imagination was the wrong word.'

'No, it was exactly the right word. People who think imagination is just making things up, they're just *wrong*. Even angels are wrong. Imagination is seeing things properly, real things, seeing them fully in all their contexts with all their connections in place, all the things they mean around them . . . The secret commonwealth.'

'I'm still not sure what that is.'

'It's probably the same thing. I'm hungry.'

She stood up, and at the same moment Malcolm appeared.

She felt she was seeing him for the first time. He was happy, and he looked as if he were the centre of a field of energy so intense

433

it could almost be seen. He looked as if this was what he'd wanted to do all his life, that he'd spent a childhood and a youth and a young manhood preparing for this activity and this purpose.

'There's something I have to do before anything else,' he said. 'Don't move.' He reached into his rucksack. 'I'm doing this for three reasons,' he said, and drew out something wrapped in a silk cloth. 'One, for the gryphons; they expect something of the sort. Two, for you. You know they asked me to repair your alethiometer, the one that was stolen from you at the Blue Hotel. I've got what's left of it, and one day we'll repair it properly, but I couldn't repair the case; it was twisted and torn, and I thought the best thing to do was make it into this.'

He folded back the cloth to show the circlet he'd made. It was braided like hazel twigs, or like flower stalks, with little buds along its length. She drew in her breath. He raised it and placed it around her head in the way the witches wore their coronets of wildflowers. It fitted perfectly.

She could hardly speak, but she managed, 'The gryphons expect . . . ?'

'They really believe all the gold in the world belongs to them, but they can make exceptions for other kings and queens. And I told them you were a princess, so it should come back to you. And they agreed. If they see you wearing it, they'll give you the same respect they give me.'

'Do they think you're a prince?'

'Better than a prince. I'm an artificer from the land of gold.'

She touched the delicate circle. 'And what was the third reason you made it?'

'For me. Now let's go and plan our journey to the desert.'

Lyra took a deep breath.

'Malcolm—'

'Yes?'

She reached for his hand, and he took hers gently, knowing it was the left, the wounded one. He raised it to his lips, like a favoured artificer acknowledging a princess, and then she returned the gesture, like a princess acknowledging an equal.

Then they stepped out from the little corner among the rocks, and she found an army gathering.

Olivier Bonneville thought quickly and pointed to the alethiometer, and said, 'You see, Monsieur le Président? I found it, and I was on my way to join your—'

'Enough,' said Delamare. 'Brigadier, would you leave us, please?'

The brigadier, who understood very little of what was happening, saluted and left with a smart click of heels.

When the door was shut Delamare pulled his chair closer to the desk and fixed Bonneville with a look that would have made a basilisk avert its eyes and shift its feet uneasily. Bonneville met it with baffled innocence.

'Boy,' said Delamare, 'you have caused me serious delay. I need that alethiometer in the hands of an honest and competent reader. Doctor Lacroix is with me, and will take charge of that instrument from now on.'

'Lacroix? Seriously? He's—'

'You will be taken to Geneva, under arrest, and kept in custody pending trial until I return.'

'You're not going to return.'

'What d'you mean by that?'

'I mean you're going to die out here, in this barren wilderness. You'll never see Geneva again.'

'If Dr Lacroix discovers that the instrument has been damaged in any way, your punishment will be even more severe. In a moment I shall call the brigadier and have you returned to your—'

'Brigadier! He's a sergeant-major at most. And *damage* – me? The alethiometer? Listen, I'm serious, Monsieur Delamare. This is a dangerous place for you.'

'Where is that girl?'

'In trouble.'

'I said *where.*'

Bonneville felt very tired. He reached out for the alethiometer, but Delamare took it out of his reach.

'I need it,' Bonneville said. 'If you want an answer now, let me have it. Lacroix can give you an answer next week. A vague one. Let me have it.'

'You don't look well, Olivier. I think you need a long period of rest, well away from the strains of theft and flight and refuge and betrayal. Just tell me where she is, and don't pretend you haven't looked for her.'

Bonneville's eyes brimmed with tears. That had worked once before, with Delamare, and it nearly did now.

'Monsieur Delamare, just let me look at the alethiometer, just for five minutes, and I guarantee you I'll find out exactly where she is.'

'Where are the books you stole? Did you bring them with you?'

'The new method—'

'I don't trust it.'

'Please, monsieur, it works. It makes me sick, but it works.'

The boy looked worse than Delamare had ever seen him: ghastly pale, thin, his eyes bloodshot and the lids puffy, his hair filthy and uncombed. His hands were trembling, and he smelled bad. His dæmon, too, looked dishevelled and subdued as she clutched his shoulder.

'You do it here, in front of me, now,' Delamare said.

'Yes. Yes, of course.'

Delamare pushed the instrument across the desk. Bonneville took it with both hands and drew his chair closer. He bent over it, but that put his head directly under the bare anbaric bulb overhead, and threw the dial into shadow.

'I can't see . . . If I could sit there instead . . .'

He spoke humbly, pleading. Delamare pushed against the desk, but it was bolted to the floor. He stood up and changed places with the boy, and his own dæmon, leaning close, whispered, 'You're letting him take charge. Don't give in to anything else.'

Delamare ignored her and sat down in the other chair, realising that yes, this was a place of less power, and it did make him look like a supplicant. But not for long, he assured himself.

Bonneville took a deep breath and gazed closely at the instrument before turning one of the wheels. As he gazed, and before he touched a wheel, the needle crept slowly around the dial, and stopped. Bonneville moved a wheel, and another, and then adjusted them, turning the alethiometer round and comparing that view with the first, and moved one of the hands again, and then moved it back. He looked like someone pretending to consult an alethiometer, having seen it done in a play, perhaps, concerned more with his own performance than with whatever it could tell him; unconvincing, anyway.

'What are you doing?' said Delamare sharply.

Bonneville sighed heavily and closed his eyes. 'Please,' he said.

'Get on.'

The boy opened his eyes and looked around. The office was sparsely furnished, but full of files and papers, and the walls were covered in maps and charts. A large photogram of some kind of politician hung over the desk. In the corner by the window there was a small wash-basin, and that was where Bonneville's eyes rested for a moment before turning back.

'Yes,' he said hoarsely, and then swallowed hard. 'I'm getting on, I'm doing that.'

Delamare couldn't see the symbols on the dial; all he could see was Bonneville staring down, his hands turning one of the wheels forwards, backwards, forwards again. The boy was breathing faster. Suddenly his chest tightened and he strained as if to vomit, only to resist it and sit still. His face was covered in a sheen of sweat, and the pallor beneath was sickly-white.

Bonneville continued his turning and gazing, touching and withdrawing, adjusting and peering, and then a convulsion shook his body and he flung himself away from the desk and stumbled to the wash-basin. Delamare winced as the horrible sounds of retching and vomiting filled the air.

But Bonneville had little in his stomach. He spat, retched again and again, and then sank to the floor weeping. Delamare watched; he genuinely didn't know what to do. After a few moments the boy hauled himself up and turned on the tap to clean the basin and fill his mouth. He rinsed it out and spat several times, and then turned off the tap and went back to his chair, trembling, holding on to the wall to steady himself.

'Well?' said Delamare.

'She's on a cliff overlooking the sea, a lake, something. Maybe the Caspian Sea. Not far from here anyway.'

His voice was rough, as if the stomach acid had damaged his vocal cords. He looked around for something.

'What do you want?' said Delamare.

'Glass of water.'

Ignoring the whisper from his owl-dæmon, Delamare found a glass on a shelf near the basin and filled it. As he took it to Bonneville he admitted, silently, that the boy had won again: getting the President to wait on him was another reminder of who had the power.

Bonneville sipped and lay back in the chair, his eyes closed.

'What else did you see?' said Delamare, resuming his own seat.

'A lighthouse. White with red bands. A small wooden jetty. A man – there is a man with her.'

'Who is he?'

'Never seen him before.'

'Is the girl's dæmon with her?'

'Couldn't see. This is not a telescope, or some kind of photo-film. I can only see what I'm able to force my body to perceive. As you realise, it costs me a great deal.'

'Why do you put yourself through that?' Delamare's tone was sympathetic.

'Because you asked me to.'

'This time, yes. But why did you try that in the first place?'

'Because I'm not Lacroix, or any of the other fakes and cowards. They wouldn't dare. They've tried the new method, some of them, and they've all given up. It's too hard for them. They labour over the old books, looking this up, making a note, putting a slip of paper in the place, looking something else up, making a note – getting nowhere because they haven't got the courage to suffer.'

He groaned involuntarily and clutched his mouth, and ran to the basin to vomit again. Delamare heard a sort of stifled cry, and looked across to see a thick stream of blood falling from the boy's mouth. He uttered a gasp of alarm and hastened to Bonneville's side, but the boy held out a hand to stop him, and Delamare stood still in the middle of the room.

'Olivier? Are you hurt? What's happening?'

Bonneville spat out more blood, rinsed his mouth from the tap, wiped his sleeve across his face. His hawk-dæmon sat calmly on the windowsill nearby, and Delamare realised with a slight shock that she was watching *him*, not Bonneville, and that she had been for some time.

'I just need to lie down,' said Bonneville, and his voice was even hoarser and more strained.

'I'm going to call for a doctor.'

'No, no, I don't need a doctor. This is what always happens. They know nothing about what I have to do, and with the language difficulty it would take all night.'

'It's already morning. You're not moving from here till you've recovered.'

'Here? This office?'

'The building. I'll make sure you have somewhere comfortable to lie down. Meanwhile I'll take this.'

He picked up the alethiometer from the desk before Bonneville could reach it, and then opened the door and called for the brigadier.

The boy sank into a chair and laid his head on the desk. The fake blood capsule was safely rinsed away, but he'd seen that that bitch had somehow destroyed his alethiometer. She would pay, she would suffer, she would know more pain than she could ever dream of.

He let himself be led away to a couch, and closed his eyes.

Pan couldn't talk to Tilda Vasara as he clung to the cloud-pine she was holding. It took all his concentration and strength to hold on to the flimsy branch, which hadn't seemed very flimsy on the ground; and it was bitingly cold.

All he could do as they skimmed through the air above the Caspian Sea was ask himself questions, and try to answer them honestly. Why was he doing this? Impulse. And fear; he was afraid to see Lyra face to face. He was beginning to feel that it had been cruel to leave her in the way he did, and she might not find it easy to forgive him.

What was he hoping to do at Tashbulak? Look around, ask questions, find things out. Why Tashbulak anyway and not the red building itself? Fear, again. He was afraid that if he entered the red building he might not be able to leave. He hadn't shared Lyra's realisation that it might contain a window into another world; all he could think of was a garden of roses, fiercely guarded, with distilleries and bottling plants and ... Whatever else they needed to sell the oil. Workers. Transport facilities ... He noticed his own use of a vacuous word like 'facilities' with scorn.

And that bitter cruel jibe about her imagination? But he was *right*. Perhaps he was wrong to imply that it was her fault, but something had vanished, and they both knew it. And he would give his life to get it back for her – except that of course it would be her life too. Perhaps he should have talked to her and they might have been able to go and search for it together. Or perhaps he should have *been* her imagination. But no: it wasn't just something you could bolt on like a spare part. It was something far more deeply interfused . . . He knew all the poetry that Lyra did, of course, and loved it just as much, and that phrase came to him unbidden and at first unrecognised, from a time when she'd been reading in a whisper and he'd been lying with his head against hers. It was like them: deeply interfused. Something had left her, and it had left him.

He had just reached that conclusion when he felt a change in their movement. Tilda Vasara was gliding downwards. It was still night, but Pan could feel a freshness in the atmosphere, and looking down he could see a shoreline ahead of them. He adjusted his position, feeling stiff and painful.

'I'm going to land,' Tilda Vasara called. 'I'm tired and I want to sleep. Safer during the day anyway.'

'Where are we?' Pan called back.

'The eastern side of the sea. That's all I know.'

She landed lightly in a meadow where three horses were dozing. One of them raised its head, looked at Tilda briefly, and then went back to sleep. The others didn't stir. Tilda's dæmon, the tern, skimmed low over the grass before settling on a wooden fence under some small trees. He said something quietly, and Tilda replied, but Pan was nearly asleep, curled up under a tamarisk shrub, and he heard no more.

The harsh rattle of an air-cooled engine broke into Dilyara's sleep. She hadn't heard that sound for months, and she woke with a start and the thudding of her anxious blood. She was lying next to Strauss, but chastely, for warmth, and now she sat up, careful not to disturb him, and listened keenly. The truck, or whatever it was, was moving round the side of the station and into the space next to the loading bay. That was where the road took them; everything that supplied the station had to go that way.

She sat still, wondering whether to wake Strauss and warn him, or let him sleep. A little snore told her that he was probably better left unconscious.

She pulled the rug over him and stood up, gathering a blanket around herself. On bare cold feet she moved out of the little storeroom where they slept and along the corridor that led to the loading bay. The engine had stopped, and she could hear voices now too. Two men, or possibly three, speaking a language she didn't know, but she recognised the tone of confidence and authority. They would claim they had a right to be here. They would deal with her easily, possibly violently, but certainly more like the clean wind of God than like the botanists and others who had worked here peacefully.

The outer door of the loading bay, a rolling metal shutter closed with a padlock, was rattling as they shook it from outside.

More voices. There was a side door, and they tried the handle. But it was locked as well.

A voice asked a question, and a deeper one replied dismissively. Footsteps moved along the side of the building, without urgency, and then the deep voice called something from further off, and a third voice answered. Dilyara thought she could hear a word or two in Chinese, but nothing she understood. She waited. She wondered if Chen had heard the truck from his comfortable bed in the village; he might be concerned about his camels, or eager to meet a buyer for them; but nothing else happened for five minutes or so, while she got colder and colder and the voices conversed indifferently.

Footsteps returning; an order from the deep voice; the engine wheezing and coughing as it turned over and caught; and after the rapidly diminishing rattle of the truck, silence lay over the station again.

Dilyara went back to bed, where she warmed her feet against Strauss's legs. He didn't wake up.

Lyra stood beside Malcolm for a minute getting a sense of everything: the sky filled with immense gryphon-wings, the grassy ground studded all over with fires that gave off the smell of cooking and the tang of pine-smoke, the swift here-and-there darting of witches taking messages or gathering herbs, voices rising in disputation or giving orders. Malcolm strode to the centre, where Gulya and Prince Keshvād were waiting.

Lyra went with him, and Gulya raised her wings. For Lyra, who had never had time to look fully at a gryphon in daylight, it was a marvel to see her full-grown and beautiful, glowing with power and assurance, stretching out her wings and delighting in their majestic length. She reflected that the gryphons had a strangeness and a presence she had hardly known since her first glimpse of Iorek Byrnison. Prince Keshvād was more reserved than Gulya, dignified, almost haughty, but he saw the circlet around Lyra's brow, and nodded deeply to her. She bowed her head in return.

Malcolm was already deep in conversation with another older gryphon, whose lion-fur was scattered with white hairs and his eagle-feathers deep bronze. They were looking at a map that Malcolm was unfolding. Lyra didn't want to be in the way, so she wandered across the grassy headland, watching all the activity, wondering how an army of such beings provisioned itself, and what they used for weapons, if they needed anything apart from their terrifying beaks and claws, and how they could defend themselves against the forces of the Magisterium; and, all the time, of course, what she would find inside the red building, and what she could do about it.

She sat down at a spot overlooking the sea, and noticed two or three fishing boats already making their way out over the choppy waves. There was hardly any wind, but the sea was still disturbed after the storm; the sun dashed sparks of light from the water, and warmed her face and hands.

Lyra heard a rush of air through pine-needles, and turned to see a witch alighting beside her, as if she were a particle manifesting itself in some great field of the air.

The witch said, 'You are Lyra Silvertongue.'

She was young, and her voice was familiar.

'Have I seen you before?' Lyra said. 'I seem to know your voice.'

'My mother was Serafina Pekkala.'

'Oh! And—'

'She died. She was killed by a missionary.'

She told Lyra the story as Pan had already heard it. Lyra wept.

'And you killed him?' she said when she could control her voice.

'The missionary, and everyone with him.'

'I'm glad to hear it. I loved Serafina more than I can say. Oh, and Farder Coram . . .'

She realised what the news would do to the old man, and found it hard to say any more.

'Coram? He was my father,' said the witch.

'No! Really? Did he know? Did you ever see him?'

'No. I only know what Serafina told me. They had a son, who died, and then I came after, but he had gone back to his people.'

'He never knew about you. This will be joyful news for him, except about Serafina . . . What's your name?'

'Tuuli Latvala. I was the witch who fought the sorcerer with you last night.'

Lyra stood up and embraced her. The meeting would have been joyful; perhaps one day she'd look back and remember it with joy; but her feelings now were too strong for speech.

They wept together, and then felt calmer. Tuuli sat down beside Lyra, and they watched as the army gathered around them.

'When we heard that you were here, we had to come,' said Tuuli.

'Thank you. Thank you. For the first time I feel hopeful.'

'The first time for how long?'

Lyra told her about her unhappiness with Pan, and about the murder of Roderick Hassall, and about her and Malcolm's discoveries in the dead man's rucksack; everything.

'And who is that man, Malcolm?'

'He saved my life when he was a young boy and I was a baby. He . . . he is a very good friend.'

'Not lover?'

Lyra had forgotten how frank the witches could be. 'Not, er . . .' she said carefully. 'He, he made my coronet.'

Tuuli looked at it curiously. Her own, of bright forget-me-nots, was interwoven with her shining black hair. 'He made that?'

'He's an artificer from the realms of gold.'

'And he's commanding this army.'

Tuuli looked around. Lyra thought she had the same commanding eyes as Serafina; and if she was Coram's daughter, she must be some years older than Lyra herself, though she looked so young.

'What do the witches know about this campaign?' Lyra asked.

'Someone is destroying the air and the seasons. The gryphons were going to find out who, and why.'

'Have witches ever fought beside gryphons before?'

'No, never. They are strange, aren't they? The little one, in the cave, who fought the sorcerer . . . So fierce.'

'She killed him because he put a curse on her to make her stay young and small.'

'It's a hard problem. There are some people so bad, all you can do is kill them.'

Lyra wondered if she agreed with that. She remembered Farder Coram – Tuuli's father, after all – saying much the same thing when she last saw him.

They were looking out over the sea. Behind them a voice – a gryphon's voice – shouted orders. They turned to watch, and saw Prince Keshvād spreading his wings and beating them so powerfully that Lyra and Tuuli felt the wind from where they sat. He threw his head back and uttered an eagle-scream, and then leaped into the air, followed by dozens, hundreds of others, their gold-bronze-brown plumage glowing in the sun, their claws extended. They took off in ranks, disciplined and majestic, setting their course towards the east, following the prince and climbing higher and higher over the sea.

Lyra stood up and gathered her rucksack. 'Stay close to me if you can,' she said to Tuuli. 'I'd like to talk to you again.'

'Of course. We are sisters now.'

Malcolm was standing and beckoning to her, and Gulya stood next to him, looking all around at the gryphon warriors as they leaped into the air and sped up and over the sea, joining the great force ahead of them.

Lyra was more than nervous but not quite frightened as Malcolm helped her up on to the broadly-muscled back of Gulya. She had little time to think; Malcolm cried out 'Yes!' to some words from the gryphon, and then the wide wings beat, and all the complex bones and muscles, nerves and blood and life surged up into the air, and Lyra clung to Malcolm as they left the ground behind and set off through the sky to Karamakan.

27

The Bijou of Atlas

As soon as she woke up, Dilyara explained to Brynmor Strauss about the truck and the men in the night. It was hard, because the incident didn't belong in the range of things their common language could manage, but he understood, and tried to reassure her: if they'd gone away, it was because they had no further interest in the station.

But as they were talking, a voice called from outside. It was Chen. Dilyara hadn't told him about Strauss, and she was immediately afraid, for several reasons.

'Is that Chen?' said Strauss.

'I tell him go. He not know you here.'

'It doesn't matter. I remember Chen. I'd like to talk to him.'

'No, no. He not . . .' She couldn't find the words. In her own language she said, 'He change. He is violent and greedy now.'

But she said it quietly and without hope.

Chen called again, impatiently.

'I'm coming,' she called back, in his language, and hurried to open the outside door.

He was wearing new clothes, and looking as if he had important things to do and she was holding him up.

'You get to work,' he snapped. 'There are rich people coming to look at this place. Merchant people. I want it all clean, all tidy. You wash everything, clean everything.'

'Merchant people?' she said timidly.

'Not your business. I talk to rich people now. They want to buy all this, building and land, everything. You make it clean, you understand?'

He was standing on the threshold of the lobby, looking past her and gesturing contemptuously at everything behind her. Then he stopped and blinked with surprise, and took a step or two back. Dilyara looked round and saw Strauss standing behind her, still in the shabby robe and sandals he was wearing when he came out of the desert; after all, there were no other clothes.

Chen's expression changed. It became angry and masterful. 'Who are you?' he shouted. 'What you doing here? Who let you into this building? You have no business here. You beggar, you vagrant! Get out!'

'I suppose you don't recognise me, Chen,' said Strauss calmly. 'I wasn't dressed like this when you guided me and Dr Hassall to the red building. It wasn't all that long ago, either.'

He came forward into the sunlight, and Chen gaped. 'You . . .' he said, searching for Strauss's name.

'Doctor Strauss.'

'Yes, yes. Stauss. I know. You go to red building. You go in?'

'Yes, and came out again, as you see. We've changed places, you and I. I'm a beggar, as you say, and I see that you have become a rich man, Chen.'

'Yes. I make money. Camels.'

Chen was fretting and shaking with anxiety, and Dilyara knew why: he could hardly sell the building to these mysterious rich people if one of the scientists on the staff was still here.

Strauss said, 'Camels, you say? You've got more camels now?'

'Yes, oh yes, plenty camels. You want buy camel? I sell you camel, or two, or three maybe, if you want leave. Right now. You got no money? I know you. I trust you, Doctor Stauss. You take camel, or two, you just go now, wherever you want. You know camels. You good rider, I remember you in the desert, very good. You take best camel, right now, you pay me later, I trust you. Good idea, no? Right now.'

'But I don't want to go right now. I'm exhausted and ill. I need to rest first, and I can do that here.'

'No, no. Not here. Not rest here. You go to village. You go now and they give you food, they let you rest. House with green door, woman there. She give you food. You tell her Chen say. Go now.'

Strauss looked at Dilyara. She was looking down, expressionless. Chen, on the other hand, was fizzing with anxiety and impatience.

'I haven't got the strength to argue with you, Chen. I know this place was raided. I know Dilyara has done a superb job of cleaning it up. What you're planning, why you want me gone – I have no idea. I shall go to the village as you say. House with a green door?'

'Woman there. Tell her Chen say.'

'What is her name?'

Chen shook his head, baffled. Dilyara said, 'Jamila.'

'Thank you. Jamila at the green door. I shall go when I'm ready.'

Chen was going to argue, but said nothing and shrugged.

Dilyara said, 'Who are the rich people?'

Chen saw that Strauss was still looking at him, and said, 'Just merchant people.'

Dilyara, daring, knowing that Strauss was still there, said, 'And you want to sell this place to them?'

Chen replied in a torrent of words in a language Dilyara didn't know. But she and Strauss both saw very clearly that he was angry, and that if Strauss hadn't been there he would have struck her.

'What is this?' said Strauss. 'Wait a minute. Let me understand. You're trying to sell the station? To sell this place? It doesn't belong to you. Who said you could do that?'

Chen was nonplussed for a moment. Then he looked at Strauss's clothing, and at his own, and at Strauss's dæmon, a frightened lemur half starved and thin-furred, and then at his own, a plump and glossy rat; and he drew himself up.

He said, 'What they see when they come here, hey? They see you, beggar, dirty poor ragged homeless tramp, maybe holy man, worth nothing, hey? Then they see me, rich, nice clothes, clean. Man of property. Man of distinction. You think they believe *you*? You *stupid*? Listen, you listen to me. This place not yours. Never yours. You don't own this place. You just work here, they tell you what to do, you do it. Obey orders. Thass all you do. Now I give orders. I tell you—'.

'You know who come last night?' said Dilyara.

Chen was so shocked to be interrupted that he ran out of things to say. She went on: 'Men from the mountains. They come, they look around. You look on the road. You see truck marks. Look.'

She pulled at his sleeve, and Chen, astonished, let himself be tugged out of the lobby and across to the dusty road, where the tyre marks from the truck were still sharp and clear. She led him round to the loading bay. It was as clear as a map: the men's footprints moving from the locked shutter to the other door, the tracks as the truck reversed and drove out.

'When?' said Chen.

'Last night. Dark.'

'You no tell me!'

'I tell you now.'

She didn't say any more; he could see the implications quite easily.

Strauss had come with them, and he was looking at the marks too.

'Three men,' he said. 'Look. Three different shoes. Work boots, combat boots. This is the men from the mountains. They will come back and finish what they started. Destroy this place completely. This is not your rich men, your merchant people. Merchants don't ride in trucks and wear combat boots. What will you tell them when they arrive?'

Chen was gaping. He looked from the footprints to the loading bay, from Strauss's face to the desert horizon, from the tyre marks to the village. Dilyara could see him calculating: sliding every possibility this way and that, adding, subtracting, flicking through the outcomes like beads on an abacus. None of them seemed good.

Suddenly he turned and hurried away, scuttling, half running, half stumbling, making for the village and his camels.

Dilyara looked at Strauss.

'And us?' she said. 'What we do?'

Lyra knew it wasn't going to be a comfortable flight. Gulya was big enough and strong enough to carry both Lyra and Malcolm, and Asta too, but it was something she'd never done before. Prince Keshvād had flown smoothly; no sudden turns or dives disturbed his riders. But Gulya, Lyra kept thinking, was as new to this business as Lyra herself was, and eager, besides, to enjoy the power of her large wings. So they soared, or lurched, or glided, or swung their way over the sea, and Lyra and Malcolm clung together for safety as much as for warmth.

'Do we know anything about the Magisterium's army?' Lyra managed to say during a bumpy passage.

'Not much. Except that they have a new kind of weapon. They've been testing it on various . . . You call them windows?'

'Openings into other worlds? Yes.'

'They can't close them, exactly, but they've found a way of destroying them with a bomb.'

'How do you know that?'

'The witches who came to make a treaty with the gryphons had seen them doing it.'

'So that's what they're going to Karamakan to do . . . They'll shut the opening in there. The one that lets people get the roses.'

'Was that where Pan was going?'

'I hope he still is . . . Oh, what a fool I am. What a fool he is. We both are.'

Malcolm said nothing. He adjusted his coat and pulled it a little tighter around her.

After a few moments, he looked across at her, at the circlet. 'You don't have to wear it all the time, you know,' he said. 'You can take it off occasionally.'

'I don't want to take it off. I love it. Is it *really* the gold from the alethiometer case?'

'Really. It was quite thick; there was more of it than I thought.'

'And you just hammered it out?'

'Well, there was hammering involved.'

'When they asked you to mend it, the gryphons – was it very battered?'

'Battered and twisted and crushed . . . How did it get into that state?'

She told him what had happened in the City of the Moon. 'And you have got the inside? The mechanism?' she said.

'Yes. And I'll mend it, when we get back.'

She was quiet for a moment. 'Do you think we will? Get back, I mean?'

'Certain of it.'

'I wasn't. Wasn't even sure I wanted to.'

They said nothing for a while.

Then Malcolm said, 'Tell me about Mustafa Bey.'

'He was a great merchant. He dealt with every kind of business along the Silk Roads, and he controlled it all from a table in Marletto's Café in Aleppo. It was Bud Schlesinger who told me about him.'

'Bud! Of course.'

'In Smyrna. He said he knew you in Oxford. And he advised me to go and meet Mustafa Bey and ask his advice, so I did. Mr Ionides took me to the café and arranged an introduction, in his own particular style . . . Mustafa Bey was very interested, and very kind too. He gave me a letter – a sort of *laissez-passer* – that would have helped all the way to Tashbulak, if he hadn't been killed. I've still got it, just in case. It was him who told me that Mr Ionides was a professor of mathematics. He seemed to know everything and everyone. I wish I could meet him again and thank him and just talk to him. And someone killed him. And I can't understand why. I can't see who'd gain from it, from his death.'

'Anyone who relishes confusion and disorder and sees a way of profiting from them. What did he say about the roses?'

'He told me how the trade worked, how his agents met the dealers and exchanged, I don't know, gold or carpets or valuable things for them. He sent some people there to find out more, and they came back with rapturous reports about what they'd seen, gardens and lakes and so on, but no real information. Mustafa Bey was interested, but in the way a merchant would be, not like a philosopher or an experimental theologian.'

'Did he say anything about Thuringia Potash?'

'I don't think so. What's that? I've seen the name, but I don't even know what potash is.'

'A big corporation. I think they moved on from just potash a long time ago. They had agents and research facilities in the Levant and further east. They were trying to synthesise the rose oil, but they look as if they've hit a bit of trouble recently. Abandoned buildings and so on . . .'

Lyra thought about it. 'I liked Mustafa Bey, and I wish he was still alive. I'd like to hear from the professor of mathematics. I'd like to know if he's safe.'

'He said something about a third enemy, didn't he?'

'Yes . . .'

'I suppose that sort of enemy could kill Mustafa Bey as well,' said Malcolm.

'On principle, you mean?'

'Or just carelessly. Indifferently.'

'I don't know if that would be worse.'

'Oh, it would be. We can understand the Magisterium; we can work out their motives, even if we don't agree with them. The men from the mountains too. They both think Dust is something evil and dangerous, so they want to destroy it. But if we can't see a motive . . .'

They fell silent again. Not for the first time, Lyra thought how strange this was, lying so close and so comfortable next to Malcolm, to Dr Polstead. The man who had confronted the sorcerer in his cavern, sure and fearless; who had made the circlet that fitted her head so well, of the same gold that had been her companion through the Arctic, through the world of the dead, and that came back to her in this form after its theft by the gryphon in the treasury of al-Khan al-Azraq, thanks to this man, thanks to his daring and his craftsmanship. She thought again how strange it was to feel his arm around her, keeping her warm; to feel his muscular weight so close against her body. And he was a man, after all. Would he want to kiss her? What would it be like if they kissed? She couldn't imagine, but then her imagination was still lost, she remembered.

After a long time she fell asleep.

Pan and Tilda slept through most of the day. He woke as the sun was setting over the sea under a vaporous backcloth of crimson clouds, towering billows and sails of vast extent and baroque extravagance, like a theatrical setting designed by a madman with a bottomless purse.

'Night coming,' said Tilda Vasara. She was cooking a rabbit on a spit over a small fierce fire.

'You prefer to fly at night?'

'Always.'

'Because of the stars?'

'And the moonlight on our skin.'

She turned the rabbit over. It smelled good. 'Want some?' she said.

'One bite, when it's stopped bleeding.'

He looked at the sky again. He wondered if Lyra could see it, from wherever she was now. 'Do you navigate by the stars?' he asked.

'Yes. And by the moon, and the rivers, and the mountains, and the sun, and the winds, and other things you can't feel.'

'How old are you, Tilda Vasara?'

'Four hundred years, maybe a little more.'

'When you saw me – us – me and Lyra, before, whenever it was, during the flood . . .'

'You were asleep. In that little boat.'

'So I can't remember, and I wondered—'

'You wouldn't remember anyway. You were too young.'

'I know. But why had you come there? Were you on your way to somewhere else?'

Tilda lifted the rabbit away from the fire, letting a drop of fat hiss and spit as it fell, and put the carcass down on the grass and cut a leg away with her long knife. It was too hot to put in her mouth so she waved it in the air to cool.

'I was looking for him. The boy.'

'For Malcolm? Why?'

'Because he is remarkable. He was remarkable then. Many of us had heard about him. I wanted to see him.'

'And did he seem remarkable when you did?'

'Oh, yes.'

'How did . . . How was it that . . . How could a young boy from England be known about by witches in the far north?'

She took a big bite of the leg and chewed it noisily. 'Not tender like rabbits of the Arctic,' she said with her mouth full. 'How do *you* know things?'

'We hear about them from people who know. Or people who've been to strange places and come back. We read about them. But you don't read, do you?'

'Some of us can. They are no wiser than the rest of us. Well, we hear things too. In many languages. In the wind. From the animals. From the ice. By loving. By thinking and remembering.'

'By imagining?'

'No doubt.'

'And . . . why was Malcolm remarkable? In what way?'

'You are too young.' She spat out a mouthful of gristle. 'Best thing to do with this rabbit is chew it and spit it out. The blood is good, but the rest – worthless. Tomorrow we kill a sheep.'

The rabbit still smelled good. Pan nibbled off a piece of flesh, and swallowed the gristle anyway.

'Steppes now, then mountains,' said Tilda.

'Do you know about the birds? The *oghâb-gorgs*?'

'The filthy mountain birds. Yes. Like cliff-ghasts, only worse. They come north sometimes, and we kill them. They just rot where they fall. No creatures will eat them. Except maybe others of their kind.'

'How shall we deal with them?'

Tilda shrugged. She cut some more meat off the rabbit and wrapped it up in what looked like greaseproof paper. Pan watched, and she noticed.

'You watch everything,' she said.

'I'm sorry. Just curious.'

'What you curious about now?'

'Greaseproof paper. I didn't think witches would use anything like that.'

'Why not? Very good thing. We trade for all kind of things. If we don't make it but someone else does, we trade. What would you use?'

'I don't know. The rabbit skin?'

'Do other things with that. But not this one. We have to fly a long way tonight. Leave the skin and bones. Maybe someone find it and make soup.'

'Tilda, these openings between the worlds . . .'

'Yes?'

'Have you ever been through one?'

'No. A sister of mine did once, in fact two times. First time, she found a world where each kind of people hated every other kind. War, slavery, murder, jealousy, greed, anger – everyone angry all the time – hate for everything. She came away quickly. Then she went to another world where everyone loved everyone else. Kindness, patience, generosity, affection, tolerance. She came away even quicker. Too dull. Then she came home and fell in love with a Siberian hunter and forgot where the openings were.'

'Did she have any children?'

'No.' She looked at the last colours of the sunset. 'You ready to fly?'

'Do you know how far we have to go?'

'No. We fly till we see it, then we stop. You fall off, I try and catch you, but maybe I can't.'

'I'll hold on,' he said.

Olivier Bonneville lay between sleeping and wakefulness all through the day. Occasionally the door was unlocked, and a guard came through with a tray of food and water. Bonneville tried to speak to him, but they had no common language, and the man was sour-faced and irritable and made no reply.

Bonneville ate the food and drank the water, to keep his strength up, and listened hard at the door, to find out what was happening; but apart from the occasional ringing of a telephone, or the shout of orders being given, or the stamp of heavy boots on the floor outside, there was nothing interesting to hear.

There was a barred window, whose shutters were closed outside, so all he could tell about the surroundings was whether the sun was shining or not. Mostly it was not. There was an open toilet in the corner, whose flush did work, and a sheet on the bed, clean but greatly patched and worn. There was one anbaric bulb overhead, but no switch to turn it off. The room was overheated and stuffy.

So he lay, turning things over with his dæmon. Her wing was healing, but she couldn't fly yet.

'What will he do with us?' she asked. It was the first thing she said when they woke up.

There was only one 'he' that mattered. Bonneville had seen Delamare in this mood before: amused and conscious of his own power, like an executioner wielding a scourge with silky hands.

'He'll keep us with him for the time being. He won't trust Lacroix with the alethiometer, despite what he says. He needs me and he knows it.'

'What's his overall plan though?'

'It can only be to reach that building in the desert where the roses come from.'

'But why?'

'Oh, be quiet.'

'We're just thinking, Olivier.'

Bonneville lay silent for a couple of minutes.

'Because—' the dæmon said.

'I've got a headache,' he snapped. 'Never mind what *he's* going to do. The question is what are *we* going to do.'

That was what she wanted to hear. She groomed her wings, the one with more difficulty than the other, and closed her eyes as she perched on the back of the single chair. Bonneville covered his face with the sheet and strolled through the twilit suburbs of sleep.

Over the fenlands of eastern England the moon shone as brightly as it had done some hours before over the steppes of Central Asia. Farder Coram had wrapped himself in a blanket and taken his chair out on to the roof of his boat to sit and look at the sky, despite the best advice of his niece Rosella, who warned him of dangerous lunar vapours.

'No, gal,' he said, 'if I en't succumbed to lunar vapours in seventy years, I reckon I must be immune. It's the brightest night there's been for months and I want to enjoy it. Tell you what, go down the galley and make us both a mug of chocolatl, why not? Get another blanket and come and sit with me.'

'It's too cold for you,' she said. 'You'll catch your death.'

'No, I reckon my death's a long way off yet. Go on, make us that chocolatl.'

Grumbling, she did as he said, and presently, wrapped in one blanket and sitting on another, she curled up beside him to look at the sky.

After a few minutes she said, 'Does it make you sad, Farder Coram?'

'What, the sky? Sad, no. Well, a bit. Sad when I think of things I won't see no more. But mainly no, not sad. Something else too big for a name, maybe. What about you, gal?'

'Yeah. It's so far away, all them stars, I can't . . . I mean, it's too big. Like you said. Maybe too big to understand.'

'Well, that's what I like, you see.'

'It's frightening.'

'Drink your chocolatl before it gets cold.'

'There *are* such things as lunar vapours, you know.'

'I don't doubt it. But I en't afraid of 'em.'

'Are you afraid of anything, Farder Coram?'

'Plenty of things. The trick is not to let yourself think about them. What are you afraid of, gal?'

'People dying.'

'Sufficient unto the day is the evil thereof. You know what that means? There en't nobody dying here, not yet. Be calm, sweetheart. Look at the moon. Like a jewel, en't she? Imagine her on a silver chain.'

'She en't perfect, though. She's got marks on her.'

'If she was perfect, without any marks, she'd look wrong. She'd look like she was made in a factory.'

'Yeah. New. Untouched.'

'Straight out the box.'

Rosella lay back on the deck and covered herself to the chin. 'If she could see things,' she said, 'she'd see us now, looking at her.'

'What else d'you reckon she could see?'

'Ships on the sea. Horses sleeping in a meadow. A traveller on a lonesome road. People dancing at a wedding. She can't hear the music though, it's too far away. Someone laying eel traps in a river. Lovers . . .'

'Yeah, all that,' said Coram. 'Go on.'

'A poor man and woman with their arms around each other sleeping under a hedge. An owl swooping down on a vole. The tide coming in slow over the mud. A lighthouse flashing. Candlelight in a cottage window. Or in a porthole. A scholar nodding over his books. A cat stalking a mouse through some cabbages. A thief creeping round the back of a house. A witch flying over the ice, all alone in the sky.'

'Where's she going?'

'Somewhere dangerous.'

'And the moon's seeing all that?'

'And more . . . Except shadows.'

'No, she can't see shadows. Nor can the sun.'

'And shadows can't see them neither.'

'That's true.'

'Suppose there was a shadow that wanted to see the sun, and suppose the sun had heard about shadows and wanted to see one of them . . . They'd never be able to. Either of them.'

'That's an allegory of life you got there, Rosella.'

'Is it?'

'No, probably not. There might be a story in it, though, if you could finish it.'

'I'll think about it. Ooh, I'm cold, Farder Coram. I can't stay out here all night. And you ought to go to bed and all.'

'Right like always, gal. You go on down with your blankets and I'll bring the mugs.'

The moon watched mildly as they went below.

28

Double Thunder

In making their unprecedented alliance, both witches and gryphons had borne in mind their particular strengths. For example, witches flew very fast. They weren't part of an army, stratified in ranks and constrained by orders and hamstrung by a strategic plan concocted somewhere far from the battlefield. Each of them was free to act on her own, and they fought fearlessly and without mercy.

And they had the strengths and the weaknesses of that freedom. They could move like spies, alone and unseen in the darkness of the night, and they could range further and faster in the air than a horde of warriors on the ground; and when the power of an army was needed, they could gather like a swarm of hornets and terrify any enemy. The idea of fighting strategically, however, was foreign to them; they threw everything they had into every battle, and never thought of withdrawing *here* to fight better *there*, or holding a force in reserve to take an enemy by surprise.

The gryphons were different in many ways: great predatory monsters, invincible in single combat in the air or on the earth. They could glide on the invisible currents of the atmosphere, and with the twitch of a wingtip they could wheel and circle and then plunge into a dive, lion-claws extended, and destroy any air-creature or flying machine in a single devastating smash. An entire army of gryphons, disciplined, trained, well led, would have been a match for any army on the ground. The gryphons didn't shrink from war, but they didn't provoke it either. At the root of all their activities, all their desires, was gold – gold, and the compulsion to maintain the integrity of their two kingdoms, the outer one from the Black Sea to Kamchatka and from the Himmaleh to the Arctic, and the inner kingdom, the one that included the sun and the moon and the stars.

Prince Keshvād ordered his troops to range wide over the steppes before they reached the mountains of the Tien Shan, and to provision themselves from as many different herds as possible. They were not humans, who robbed and murdered without thought, and cared nothing if they extinguished entire clans. The gryphons needed food: of course they did. Taking a little from many was better for everyone than taking everything from one or two. The nomadic herdspeople regarded it as a form of tax, which they grumbled about but agreed to pay.

The alliance was something new to both sides, intriguing to all of them. They portioned out the various tasks according to mutual agreement, the gryphons ranging high and wide by day, the witches exploring more closely at night. And they all knew that great dangers lay ahead – not least those posed by the murder-birds, the *oghâb-gorgs* of the Tien Shan. With that in mind, one group of witches set about scouting the foothills of the Tien Shan, and agreed to let one witch fly ahead to see what she could discover about the troops of the Magisterium.

Her name was Sala Riikola. This was the sort of task she loved – exploring alone in a wilderness, dark and silent. She was intent on discovery, not violence; that would come later. At first she flew in the middle airs, watching the mountains and valleys below for movement on the ground. As far as she knew, the only danger in the air would be from the birds, and there was little sign of them in this part of the range.

On the ground, she could see the cooking fires of scattered villages and the temporary settlements of nomadic shepherds and goatherds. For many miles those were the only lights she could see, but there was a glow ahead, further up into the foothills, almost like the lights of a town or a city, and she flew towards it to investigate.

She came on it sooner than she expected. It wasn't a town: it was an immense body of soldiers and all their equipment, camping for the night. Tents were ranged in ordered ranks, fires blazed under spitted oxen or camels, the aroma of which rose high into the sky. The smell of roasting meat drifted a long way downwind.

At the edge of the widely spread camp, engineers were making fires too. Sala Riikola saw men using great machinery, repairing axles, hammering iron rims around cartwheels, welding metals for purposes she didn't understand; altogether it signified detailed organisation and great power.

Near the centre of the camp (and she took a risk here by flying low) was a larger tent than the rest, with messengers coming and going, sentries on guard, a flag hanging in the still air from a flagpole above it. She couldn't see any symbol on the flag, but she didn't need to. The fact that it was there told her that this was the command centre. They had some kind of apparatus set up outside it, a series of metal posts linked by wire: all that occurred to her was the word 'anbaric'. It would mean something to the man Malcolm, no doubt, and the woman Lyra.

Sala flew up high and further towards the high mountains, because she could see a light or lights flickering in that direction. As she got closer, the smell of the roasting meat from the camp faded, and another smell took its place – something rank and putrid; faint at first, but unmistakably the smell of death and corruption.

Could it be coming from the small group of men and horses moving steadily up into the mountains? No. They smelled like what they were: men and horses. This was a wilder smell. It could only be the *oghâb-gorgs*. Did they make nests? Did they roost on the bare rocks? She didn't know, but those were things she had to find out. She flew higher, where a cold wind from the heights scattered the stench of decay and carried the freshness of snow instead.

She flew along following the men and watched them at work. Why they were doing this at night, when they could surely see very little beyond their lamps, she had no idea; but she knew that people did things in the dark which they were ashamed to do in daylight, and she flew a little closer, and landed among the rocks outside a little ravine, and settled down to watch.

There were ten or a dozen men, in thick mountain uniform, wearing what looked like gas masks. There was one other man too, in chains, who had no mask. He seemed to be half asleep, or drugged, because he made little effort to struggle or get away. He must have been cold, because he wore nothing but trousers of thin cotton and an open shirt, but perhaps he was near death anyway.

Sala saw the men tie him down to a boulder, under the instructions of an officer. And now he did try to fight back, but he had no strength, and they subdued him easily and made sure he was unable to move.

Then some of the men laid small boxes around the boulder, a couple of steps away from it, and began to join wires between them.

Something was stirring in the air above. Sala heard the sound of beating wings, high up, and an occasional screech almost too high to be heard; but she was a witch, and she heard it. Almost at the same time came the first full thick drift of the stench: rotting flesh, poisoned blood, gangrene – the *oghâb-gorgs*, of course, it could be the smell of nothing else, as if the doors had opened on a feast in a charnel-house.

The men had heard something too. Some of them looked up, to be snapped at by the officer and told to concentrate on their task. They bent over and moved more quickly, and he had to shout at them again and make them take care.

The birds had come much lower now, and their screeching had a note of excitement in it; if they were human, it would have sounded like hysteria. Sala could see them whirling, diving, snatching, snapping – none close enough to threaten any of the men, but showing more and more interest in the prisoner. The lamplight that played on him showed a glimpse of a claw or a wing or a tail when one of them came low enough, and the officer was now running around to check each of the little boxes, and ordering the men to retreat away from the prisoner on the rock.

They needed telling only once. The stink of the birds was enough by itself to make them want to withdraw, despite the gas masks, and Sala felt that she'd stayed too long already. She wanted to fly up and away as fast as she could, but she had come to spy, and—

The first of the birds dared to swoop down and tear at the prisoner. It slashed a deep gash in his exposed chest, and flew off at once, to be followed by another and another – and within seconds she could see the poor man no more: a mass of birds fought over him, tearing and rending and screeching, until he seemed to be merely a mass of blood and black feathers, a heaving pile of murder—

Without any warning all the boxes exploded. First a silent bloom of red fire extending out and up from each box, growing immediately to join all the others until a canopy of scarlet cloud covered the rock, and the prisoner, and the feasting birds, and then came the *tonnerre double* – a rush of air in towards the centre, with a crack so loud it might have been the mountain splitting, and a blaze of light that left a trace in Sala's eyes for minutes afterwards. She watched appalled as white and red and black roiled and tumbled into and beyond and through the space where the poor prisoner had been.

And all around the birds screamed and beat their wings, some hurled upwards, some dashed against the ground, some flung far out from the centre of the explosion.

Sala could hear the officer speaking, giving orders, but none of the men moved except to back away from the victim, now nothing more than a mass of blood and flesh, and the birds that lay dead or dying around him.

In fact, there weren't very many of them – a dozen or so, Sala estimated, still blinking to clear her eyes. The majority of the birds had either been thrown away from the explosion or escaped into the air, and within less than a minute, they returned. Screeching and jeering, they dived downwards right on to the victim's body, and those who couldn't get to it feasted with just as much tearing greed on the bodies of the fallen birds, some of them still alive.

The officer in charge was making notes in a small book. The other soldiers were cautiously trying to get to the boxes that had held the explosives, but the crowd of birds prevented them. Their savage greed had been roused to a state of uncontrollable madness; drunk with blood, they snapped and tore and rent apart every shred of flesh and bone on the rocks around them, more interested at that point in dead flesh and blood than in living, which might fight back.

The soldiers were passing around a bottle. Sala had seen enough; she took her cloud-pine in hand and soared up high, where the air was cleaner. When she could breathe more easily she oriented herself in all the ways witches knew, and set off back to the gryphons.

'He was *bait*?' said Malcolm.

'Exactly what he was,' said Sala.

Prince Keshvād's expression couldn't change, but the way he drew himself up and back was enough to express his disgust.

'What were they trying to do, though?' he said. 'Not just set up an ingenious way to kill some poor prisoner?'

'It was an experiment,' said Malcolm. 'To see if that explosive was any use against the birds.'

'And it wasn't,' said Lyra.

Sala Riikola and some other witches were sitting nearby. She said, 'The officer in charge had precise orders. After the explosion he was beginning to measure how far out the blast had been effective, by counting the dead birds. But the other birds kept attacking him and he had to retreat with the rest of the men.'

'Did they tie the man down inside the ravine, or outside it?' Malcolm asked.

'Just outside.'

'I think they'll try again, and next time do it further in. Exploding a bomb like that in the open air wouldn't hurt a flock of birds as much as doing it in a narrow gully.'

'We don't need to see them do it again,' said Gulya.

'Did the birds have a particular way of attacking?' said Lyra. 'Did they follow particular leaders, or were they just a mob?'

'They were just a mob. They followed the strongest, as in any mob,' said Sala. 'But no regular plan of attack. Biggest and strongest got to the prey first and ate most.'

'But they *did* follow, if they were led?'

'I think they did,' said Sala.

'What are you thinking?' said Malcolm to Lyra.

'I'm thinking of one afternoon on Port Meadow last year, the year before last. The swallows were gathering to fly south. There were hundreds of them in a great flock, and they were excited by the sense of soon flying away, I suppose ... Anyway as we watched them wheeling round and round over the river, Pan saw something odd. I couldn't believe him at first, but then I saw it too. In the middle of the swallows, flying with them, wheeling around just as fast, there was a dragonfly. I couldn't see what sort – it was going too fast – but it was certainly a dragonfly and not a swallow. Normally you'd expect the nearest swallow to snap it up at once, but they were all caught up in the excitement. Pan said it looked as if the dragonfly was leading them, but I thought it just looked as if it had forgotten it was a dragonfly. And . . . that's what I was thinking. That's all. I don't know why.'

The gryphons were silent. They had the habit of remaining absolutely still, like stone carvings; they never seemed under any compulsion to talk. The witches, on the other hand, had listened closely to what Lyra said, and then began to talk among themselves, in their own languages, as busily as swallows in a barn. Her story had clearly described something familiar.

Prince Keshvād said to Lyra, 'You said the explosive didn't work.'

'If they were trying to find a way of dealing with the birds, then that way wasn't it. They could only kill a few at a time, and the rest just flew out of the way and came back.'

'This was the explosive they developed to destroy the openings, the windows into other worlds,' said Malcolm. 'And it does seem to have worked, up to a point.'

Lyra said, 'Is she safe, the director of Oakley Street?'

'I hope so, but I fear not.'

'Further back I saw thousands of soldiers,' said Sala Riikola. 'They must have recruited them from every country. Even if the birds attack them all the way through the mountains, there will be many left.'

'Can we fly high above them?' said Gulya.

But no one knew the answer to that. One by one, gryphons began to withdraw and sleep. Groups of witches still sat together, talking quietly.

Malcolm and Lyra sat where they were for a minute or so.

'Are you cold?' he said.

'Yes, a little.'

'It'll get colder. We'll need to sleep close together.'

'I'd thought of that.'

'How did you manage in the Arctic?'

'I had the best clothing you could get. The gyptians made sure of it, and then Mr Scoresby helped. He was a balloonist. He'd flown all over the Arctic. I think they'd have laughed at what we're wearing here.'

'It can't be helped.'

Asta said, 'Get as close as you can. It's the only thing to do.'

'My coat's big enough to wrap around us both,' said Malcolm.

They moved together. Lyra thought he was thinner than he used to be, but he was still . . . burly? Was that the word? He was warm, anyway, and that was what mattered most. She felt shy, of all things.

'Did you . . .' she began, but then stopped, because she thought he was going to say something, but he didn't.

'Did I what?'

'I don't know. Sorry.'

He shifted position to give her more space, and wrapped the big coat around her. She felt wide awake, but warm. Perhaps the vivid consciousness of his body close to hers would fade a little, and then she'd be able to sleep.

'Where's the strangest place you've ever slept?' he said.

'In a balloon, above the Arctic. I mean in the basket thing underneath it, not in the – you know. What about you?'

'In a grave, in the Gobi desert.'

'A grave? Why?'

'There was a sandstorm and it was there. Not a very deep grave, and the tenant had left long before. Were you nervous in the balloon? Or in the basket thing?'

'No . . . I was perfectly confident. Pan was with me, and the balloonist Mr Scoresby was . . . Well, he just made me confident because he knew what he was doing. And besides, Iorek Byrnison was with us. The armoured bear. I must have told you about him.'

'Sounds like a full load.'

'Well, I was young then. Lighter, I expect.'

'Will you tell me the whole story one day?'

'If you tell me everything about the flood.'

'I thought I had.'

'In that case I want to hear it again, including everything you left out. Like . . . Alice.'

'Alice certainly was in the story. You forgotten already?'

'No. But . . . Were you . . . I mean before this began . . . Were you in love with Alice?'

'What a question, here in the foothills of the Tien Shan! Why do you ask that?'

'I've been wondering it for a while.'

'Have you? Well, since you ask, I was in love with her twice.'

'Twice?'

'Yes. The first time I fell in love with her was in a garden under the ground, when the flood took us into a tunnel and then into the garden of a great palace, or that's what it looked like, with lights in all the trees and people walking about talking and laughing and drinking wine. Alice was on the bank looking after you while I mended the canoe. And she fell asleep, and I looked at her face, because it had changed . . . She always had a little frown, and kept her lips pressed together, looking fierce; but I'd never seen her asleep before, and her expression was relaxed and almost happy, and she was smiling, and she looked so lovely I fell in love with her and I wanted to kiss her but I was afraid she'd wake up, so I didn't.'

'She might not have done.'

'It wouldn't have been right, anyway.'

'Did you stay in love with her?'

'Yes. You have to remember I was only eleven or something. And I'd always sort of hated her because she was a bully and she had a temper. It was just seeing her like that . . . It changed me. I never told her or let her think . . . But we were friends after that. Besides, she was older than me.'

'The difference probably means more at that age, though.'

'Anyway . . . I said nothing about it.'

'But you said *twice.*'

'Yes, I did.'

They were whispering now. The silence around them was full of *fields*, Lyra thought. Cross-currents and different pressures, areas of intensity and of calm; fields of meaning, and whirlpools and vortices weak and strong.

'When was the other time?' Lyra whispered.

'After her husband died. She married when she was eighteen, I think. A lovely man called Roger Lonsdale – a builder. They were exactly right for each other. He was calm and she was fiery, and she was really in love with him, passionately. They were very happy. And then he died. Some scaffolding hadn't been properly fixed and he fell and broke his neck. She changed at once – again – this time back to the old Alice, cynical, hard, cold. All her friends tried to comfort her, but she said nothing, nothing at all to anyone about it. It must have been when I was sixteen. I didn't know how to help her. A year or so went by and then one day she took me to her bed. Without saying a word, just desperate and urgent. I . . . It was seeing her like that, fierce and passionate and generous . . . It happened again. I fell in love with her. Just holding her was enough to make that happen. It was the first time I'd ever kissed anyone like that; the first time for everything. It was wonderful and I loved her.'

'I'd never have imagined . . .' There it was again: her failure of imagination. 'I mean, I must have been quite young.'

'Very young. All I knew was that looking after you was Alice's job, really. I never saw much of you.'

'Did she love you? What happened?'

He thought for a while, and then said, 'I don't think she was in love with me. I think she just needed someone to hold her and make love to her. So that's what I did. And I couldn't help falling in love with her, again. She was so beautiful.'

'Do you still love her?'

'Yes, in a complicated way.'

'Why complicated?'

'I'm not in love with her, not as I used to be. It's unusual, or so I've discovered. Remaining close friends, I mean. Often there are jealousies and betrayals and resentments and unhappinesses . . . One person falls out of love before the other, that's what it amounts to. But with us it was just a gradual gentle sort of change. We stayed fond of each other without jealousy . . . We were lovers for maybe six months. It was a time of enormous growing up for me. I was so grateful to her that, well, it seemed natural for us to be close friends. She's part of my life. I was very lucky.'

Lyra was quiet for a minute. Then she said, 'I think she was too, probably. Thank you for telling me that. I wouldn't ever have guessed . . . Did you notice how astonished I was that time at Jordan when you opened the door and came into her room?'

'Honestly, no, I didn't. I was so struck by Asta's reaction to Pan.'

'Oh yes: she'd seen him alone and thought he'd stolen something. The murdered man's wallet. He realised that in the same moment. He was thrown by that, and I was thrown by the thought of Dr Polstead being close to Mrs Lonsdale . . . and Alice was so embarrassed. You must have thought I was half witted.'

'Never.'

Silence again for half a minute.

'I wonder where she is now,' Lyra said. 'Alice, I mean.'

'I worry about that.'

'When we get back we'll make sure she's safe.'

He moved a little, and pulled the big coat more tightly around them both. Lyra was aware of his body, the boy's body that had learned to make love with Alice, the man's body that lay beside her now, strong and competent and warm. Was that all? Not thrilling and intoxicating and beautiful? *No, not . . . Not like Will,* she thought. That moment in the little wood, in the world of the mulefa, when they kissed for the first time. Nothing like that would ever happen again.

They lay so still that she thought Malcolm must be asleep now. But Asta was purring, so she was still awake; and the grass was awake too, with a light wind moving through and making it whisper in response; and the air, as she'd felt earlier, was full of fields of intention and purpose and memory.

She felt so light that if only she let go of her body, she'd be carried away into the air, among all those fields, as insubstantial as a filament of down. She wanted to let go, but she didn't want to; it was cold up there; she was warm and safe in Malcolm's coat, in Malcolm's arms. She remembered herself sleeping close to Asta, holding her in the same way. What did that mean? Only lovers let that happen. Did she love Malcolm? She was moved by what he'd told her. She thought well of Alice too, because of it. What kindness, and what good sense for them both to know that they were lovers only for a brief time, and to remain friends! And no, she wasn't in love with Malcolm, but . . .

First the red building. Later everything else. She fell asleep.

Pan and Tilda flew along the northern edge of the Tien Shan range, without risking the heights where the *oghâb-gorgs* terrorised every living thing. The effort, for Pan, was extreme; he had to cling to the branch of cloud-pine without resting for a single second. Tilda Vasara said little as they flew. She was intent on covering the vast distance as quickly as possible, because she had caught some impression of anxiety and urgency from her sisters, and she felt bound to these short-lived humans, to Pan and Lyra and to Malcolm and Asta, because of the impulse that had drawn her, twenty years before, to the island in the flood, to the boy and the sleeping baby. To a witch, of course, twenty years were like the blink of an eye, but some things were still more important than others.

They flew down to sleep in the high mountains just north of the desert. Pan was nearly crazy with the desire to sleep, and Tilda was troubled by several thoughts that assailed her as they turned their course south over the heights. Her dæmon, the tern, skimmed alongside them and tried time and again to urge her to land, to sleep, to rest.

'The dæmon will fall,' he said in their language. 'He can't hold on for much longer. Land, Tilda, fly down, find a cave or any shelter at all. You'll kill him, and then the girl will die too.'

She didn't reply; she was exhausted too, and she knew he was right.

'Going down to rest,' she called, and Pan heard her and nodded. He had no strength to call back.

It was towards the end of a murky night; all the peaks ahead of them and to east and west were covered in snow, and the dim light that clung to them was all Tilda had to see by. She flew in a wide circle, heading down towards what looked like a glacier. Mindful of the dæmon's weariness, she didn't spend much time looking for a comfortable valley: there was little chance of that anyway.

She found a narrow gully in a massive rock-face on the western side of the glacier, and made for that. As soon as her feet touched the ice, Pan fell off the pine-branch.

'I told you to hold tight,' she said quietly.

'I did.'

'Come to me.'

She knelt beside him and opened her arms. All the taboos had evaporated; there were no rules in the empire of the *oghâb-gorgs*. He crept painfully to her breast and she embraced him, and she was warm, and like Lyra, he fell asleep.

Olivier Bonneville was awake before the guard kicked him, so he was able to squirm aside and avoid the worst of it.

'What's that for? What are you doing?' he shouted, clutching the thin blanket to himself at the end of the bed.

'Time to get up. We're moving. Don't hang about.'

'What? Where? What's going on?'

The guard spat on the floor and went out, leaving the door open. A sour light leaked in from the corridor; there was no daylight yet, and the cell was thick with cold grey-black stuffy air.

474

Bonneville hauled himself to his feet, shivering, and felt around for his trousers. His socks, still damp from the day before, hung over the bed rail. He grimaced as he pulled them on.

'What next?' he muttered. 'Did you hear what they're doing?'

His dæmon shook her tail and stretched her wings. Bonneville could see that her left wing was not yet healed. She said nothing.

'No, of course you didn't. You heard what he said, though? Moving on?'

A shadow fell through the doorway, and a strong whiff of cologne preceded the brigadier, who stood there tapping a swagger stick against his leg.

'Hurry,' he said.

'Why? What's happening?'

'You're moving on.'

'Where?'

'East. That's all I know. Come on, get dressed. Don't waste time.'

'My clothes are damp. I can't put them on quickly. This is ridiculous.'

'I can call for the sergeant and a couple of men to help you, if you like.'

Bonneville said nothing and went on struggling. *Tap, tap, tap* went the swagger stick. The hawk-dæmon raised her wings again, which only emphasised her weakness. The brigadier looked at his watch.

'Where are you taking me?' said Bonneville, trying to manoeuvre one of the socks over his cold foot.

'Not taking you anywhere. Well, I'm not. I'd leave you to rot here. The President wants you to go with him.'

'But where?' said Bonneville, trying to sound impatient, but inwardly delighting.

Someone called from further down the corridor. The brigadier called back in the same language. Bonneville pulled up the sock and felt the flesh of his leg shrinking away from it.

'Hurry, boy!'

'Where are my possessions? Where is the rucksack you stole from me?'

'You haven't got any possessions. You dressed yet?'

Well, Delamare will have the alethiometer, and I'll soon get that back, Bonneville thought. He stood up. 'Let me have a coat. Or at least a rug. If I die of cold, the President will hold you responsible.'

The brigadier indicated the way out with his swagger stick. Bonneville tried to saunter out, but he was shivering too much to make it look convincing.

The sergeant, or whatever he was, took hold of Bonneville's arm and tugged him forward, nearly dislodging the hawk-dæmon from his shoulder.

'Careful, you ugly fool! Where do they find shitheads like you? Do they breed them in the mountains?'

The sergeant looked at the brigadier and received a nod in response, so he punched Bonneville hard on the side of his head. This time his dæmon did fall. The sergeant's dog-dæmon growled as her wings fluttered in his face, and Bonneville snatched her up before they could fight.

'Enough of that, boy. Keep quiet and do as you're told,' said the brigadier.

'I demand to speak to the President!'

This time the swagger stick came into action. The brigadier lashed at Bonneville's arm, and the boy cried out in pain.

No one said anything else. All Bonneville could do was stumble out of the corridor, out of the lobby, out of the building, and into the back of a motor-van, where he fell clumsily on to the cold metal floor as they slammed and locked the door behind him. The engine was already running, and within seconds the van was moving, and Bonneville was able to cry without anyone seeing his tears. Except his dæmon, and she didn't count.

29

KILKENNY AFLAME

Alice Lonsdale slept in one of the staff bedrooms at The Savoy. She shared it with two other women, who were congenial enough, and they all worked different shifts, so they didn't see much of one another anyway. None of her old friends knew where she was, but she'd managed to let Malcolm's parents have her address, and the name she was passing under: Cathy Hood.

And on the morning when Lyra woke up among the gryphons, after the death of the sorcerer Sorush, Alice found a postcard in her staff locker. It showed a picture of Port Meadow, and before she turned it over she knew it was from Brenda Polstead.

It said:

Dear Cathy, I hope you're well. Our old friend Dr Ralph is going to be in London on Wednesday and would love to see you and say hello. The Egyptian kiosk at one if poss. Love from me and Reg – Brenda.

Wednesday was that very day. Brenda knew how to spell Dr Relf's name as well as Alice did, and the Egyptian kiosk was a coffee stall on the Embankment not far from Cleopatra's Needle; they called it that because Reg had told them about the old man who ran it, saying he was so ancient and wrinkled he might be a mummy himself.

So Alice found her supervisor and made a change to her lunch hour, and at five to one she was sitting on a bench under one of the trees in the Embankment Gardens, from where she could see the river and the obelisk, and a little way along, the coffee stall. The day was grey and damp, and threatening rain.

Hannah Relf arrived only a minute or so after Alice. She was wearing a heavy coat and a dark blue beret, and carrying a Harrods shopping bag. Alice jumped up as soon as she saw her, but then remembered what she was doing, and looked around carefully to see if anyone was watching; she knew she was an amateur at this game, and made herself move slowly and casually.

They exchanged a kiss. Alice was moved by Hannah's warm embrace.

'Let's find somewhere indoors,' said Hannah. 'It's going to rain soon.'

'There's a little café just up that way,' said Alice. 'Oh, I'm so glad to see you.'

'I want to know everything that's happened. But I've got a task for you, and I need to explain . . .'

Alice noticed how Hannah unobtrusively scanned everyone in the street, and how as they approached the café she put her hand in Alice's arm and steered them both firmly past it before suddenly turning back and into the entrance. As she turned, her eyes flicked across the pavement and the roadway, taking everything in.

Once they were sitting at a corner table with bowls of soup in front of them, Alice quietly told Hannah about her arrest, and the prison camp, and her escape.

'Brenda told me you'd been to see them,' Hannah said. 'She knew she'd be safe telling me, but she swore she wouldn't tell anyone else.'

'Oh, I trust them. But it's been like living in a, I don't know, a different country now. Suspecting everyone.'

'We have to.'

'You said you had a task,' she said.

Hannah put the Harrods bag on her lap. 'I want you to take this and give it to someone personally. Don't put it through a letter box or give it to a secretary.'

She handed Alice a package the size of a small book, wrapped in brown paper and securely taped. It bore the name David Ferguson, and an address in Battersea.

'Here's the point,' said Hannah. 'The package is a sort of decoy. If by chance anyone does see you, they'll think that's the important thing. The real message you need to take to David Ferguson is in four sentences I want you to memorise. Say them as you hand the package to him, and make sure you get the wording absolutely right.'

'What are they?'

'I'll tell you in a minute. Now tell me about The Savoy.'

Alice told her what she was doing, and how she'd found the job, and all she could about the way she was living now. Hannah was curious about everything, and particularly interested in the internment camp Alice had escaped from. She listened avidly.

'ORD, and Brytsec,' she said. 'There's a power struggle between those two. The officer who interrogated you was ORD, you say?'

'Very proud of it too. Flaunting his what's-its-names – things on his shoulders.'

'Epaulettes.'

'That's it. He was more proud of being ORD than Brytsec, I could see that.'

'Interesting.'

Hannah was concentrating hard on everything Alice was saying, as if she was making mental notes. Then she said, 'How long have you got? When do they expect you back at work?'

Alice looked at the little clock over the counter and said, 'I'll have to go in about ten minutes. What was it I had to remember?'

'Ready? Don't write it down. Just keep it in your head.'

'I will.'

'Here goes: *Kilkenny aflame is a nine-days'-wonder. Beyond the marshes all the cats are redeemed in flags and banners. Total harvest lies laid out and stripped of circumlocution. Enter the ice-bound belvedere.*'

Alice blinked.

'Don't worry,' said Hannah. 'I'll go through them again till you remember. *Kilkenny aflame . . .*'

They were speaking quietly, under the noise of the coffee machine and the clatter of plates and cutlery and the usual chatter of a busy café. Hannah spoke each phrase separately. Alice's hearing was good; she heard every word clearly, and repeated them several times until she had them accurately. Then she went through them as a whole for Hannah to check.

'*. . . Total harvest is laid out—*'

'*Lies.*'

'Sorry. *Total harvest lies laid out . . .*'

She got to the end with no more mistakes.

Hannah nodded sternly. 'Say it to yourself over and over till you're simply unable to make a mistake.'

'Can I write it down to help?'

'No. Not at all.'

'No point in asking what it means?'

'None whatsoever, my dear. Find David Ferguson, hand him the package, speak those words and then go back to The Savoy and forget all about it.'

Alice looked for her purse, but Hannah shook her head.

'Well, it'll make me feel a bit useful, anyway,' Alice said. 'Give my love to Reg and Brenda. You haven't heard anything from Malcolm, I suppose? Or Lyra?'

'I wish I had. I'm anxious about everything, Alice. All we can do is carry on.'

'Anything else I can do, you know where I am.'

Hannah paid the bill, they left the café, embraced on the pavement, and Alice hurried back to work.

*

She came out of the hotel at half-past five, caught a bus along the embankment as far as Albert Bridge, and crossed over into Battersea. The tide was in and the river was high, and busy with traffic: cargo barges, a couple of river buses, a police launch cruising slowly up towards Westminster. Alice had only been to London once in her life before she was a prisoner on the run, but she was beginning to know her way around now and enjoy the vastness, the anonymity, the busyness. And she loved the river, the same one that flowed through Oxford, though much bigger here, whose waters had carried her and Malcolm and the baby Lyra so many years before. It had been wild then but it was gentle now, the same river, mild and decorous.

The first thing she'd bought when she got there as an adult was a detailed map, and she consulted it now as she stood at the Battersea end of the bridge. Aland Street was tucked away in a maze of small roads south of the park, and it took her the best part of half an hour to find it, a small house in a shabby terrace with nothing to distinguish it from the neighbours except the number in tarnished brass numerals on the door.

She knocked and waited. She waited long enough to knock again. This time she heard a door closing somewhere inside, and then footsteps came to the front door. It was opened by a thin man in shirtsleeves looking as if he'd been busy at something and wanted to get back to it.

'David Ferguson?' said Alice.

'Yes. That's me.'

'I need to know for certain.'

He looked at her coldly, and his eyes flicked to left and right along the street. 'You'd better come in,' he said, and stepped aside.

She followed him in. He shut the door and took a wallet out of his back pocket, opening it to show her a card bearing his picture. It called him Captain Ferguson and said he worked for the Ministry of Agriculture.

'Agriculture?' she said, but then went on, 'Sorry. None of my business. I got this for you.'

She took the package out of her bag and held it out, but didn't let go. He looked expectant.

'*Kilkenny aflame is a nine-days'-wonder*...' she began, concentrating hard. She stumbled over *is* and *lies*, but got it right, and he nodded; and then she released the package. His lips had been moving as she said the words, memorising it too.

'Thank you,' he said. 'You can go now.'

He smiled with unexpected friendliness, and opened the door for her.

'Cheerio then,' she said, and left to make her way back to the river and the bridge, where she caught a bus back to the hotel.

Pan was aching all over, but it was going to be the final part of their journey, Tilda told him.

'Do you get tired too?' he said. 'Does flying use your muscles? All I can see is that you keep hold of the branch.'

'Yes, that's what we do. I don't know how the flying happens.'

'But . . . Do you really not know?'

'I just feel it happening.'

'You really don't make any effort with your muscles, or anything?'

She shrugged. 'Never thought about it,' she said. 'Now you made me think about it, maybe it won't happen. Suddenly I can't fly. What you do then?'

'Apologise.'

'You better. Come on. Last day now.'

'And no birds yet,' he said, finding the least uncomfortable place on the pine branch.

'You trying to look for bad luck?' she said, without expecting an answer, and sprang upwards.

He watched the way she rode the air. There was something birdlike about it, the apparently unconscious leaning this way or dipping down for a moment, raising her shoulders for a brief change of angle that caught the wind and lifted them up; gliding, never straining. The wind did the work. He felt her grip on the branch as well, now twisting a degree or two, now pulling up a little, now pushing it forward and down – not much – just enough to take advantage of a current or an updraught, and all done with as little rational thought, it seemed, as a fish darting through the sea. The witch and the pine together were the flying being, not either separately. She explained to him once that it benefited the pine too, because its seeds were dispersed by the wind, and flying was the best way to make sure it spread widely. Pan remembered Lyra telling him something similar about the world of the mulefa, who rode on wheels that were giant seed-pods which could only germinate if they were shaken out by the hard riding – or something. He'd tell her soon.

Sometime later, as they were flying down into the foothills of the southern edge of the Tien Shan, Pan fell asleep and let go of the branch.

The first he knew about it was a scream from the witch's dæmon, the tern, who was flying beside them. He woke at once with a sense of shame and terror, and cried out himself, but after only a moment he felt himself scooped into the witch's arm.

'Wake up, stupid,' she said.

'Oh, I'm awake now. Did I . . .'

'Just don't sleep in the air.'

'I'm sorry . . .'

'You holding tight?'

'Yes. Thank you, Tilda.'

'You got your eyes open now?'

'Wide open.'

'Look ahead at the mountain with the round top. Not a high mountain – more of a hill. See the little patch of green past the left shoulder?'

'Yes . . . I think so. Yes.'

'That's where we want to go. Soon be there, so stay awake, idiot.'

'I will.'

'Next time, I let you go.'

'Quite right.'

They were already nearly out of the mountains. The view ahead, beyond the hill with the round top, was one of an infinite expanse of sand: brown-yellow-white-buff in waves and ridges and dunes and hollows too far away to make out, but extending to the far-distant horizon; and just before it began, that little area of green, which as they came closer and flew lower resolved itself into a village of wooden huts and beyond it the buildings of the research station of Tashbulak. Pan had never seen a picture of it, but there was no mistake.

'Can we stop on the side of the hill?' he called.

'Down here? Whatever you like.'

She glided downwards. The cluster of once white-painted buildings that had been the research station looked shabby and neglected at first, the planted areas untidy and overgrown, the glasshouses shattered.

'You want to fly closer?'

'No. Just land on the hillside.'

The thin grass was being grazed by a few scrawny sheep, which looked up once and then moved away as Tilda landed. Pan jumped down too quickly and staggered, feeling dizzy, unanchored, almost affected by vertigo. The fall earlier had shaken something loose in his sense of where he was and how his body was related to the earth beneath him, how he could move and balance, how gravity kept him secure; it felt now as if he might have to relearn everything he'd known about movement and stillness, about feeling safe in the world. As for Tilda, she simply lay down on her back under a nearby tamarisk bush and flung an arm over her eyes, asleep at once.

Once he felt less nervous, he examined the research station more carefully. The first impression of desertion and emptiness was wrong, he soon realised. There were half a dozen vehicles parked around it including two large cargo-lorries, and men were moving in and out of the buildings, some in uniform, some looking more like local workmen or villagers. His eye was caught by a plume of dust or sand moving closer, coming out of the desert, which he soon saw was thrown up by an armoured car or something of the sort. It trundled off the sand and on to the paved area behind the buildings.

The cluster of houses closer to where he was watching from was quiet and still. Thin lines of smoke rose from a few of them; some kind of small oxen stood in a corral; a narrow stream came down from the hills to feed a pond; a woman hoed a vegetable patch. The only other human activity he could see was going on at the research station, and it was clearly directed by whatever organisation owned the trucks and the other vehicles parked near the buildings. There was some kind of identifying flag or corporation symbol on the vehicles, but they were too far away for him to make it out. The Magisterium? But it wasn't that. Thuringia Potash? Not that either.

He sat looking down at the place for some time, while endless possibilities revolved in his mind. If only he knew where Lyra was, and what she was doing!

Sooner or later he was going to have to go down to the station and investigate. Better do that after dark, he thought. Better sleep now, in that case, and safely too, on the ground. Tilda was deeply asleep; he joined her in the shade of the tamarisk, and closed his eyes.

During the day after the experiment with the *tonnerre double*, the *oghâb-gorgs* attacked in full force.

The Magisterial army was following one of the trade passes a hundred miles to the north. A small number of witches were shadowing them, to warn the gryphons if they began to move south, but the majority were flying with the gryphons along the southern edge of the mountains. They were talking together closely that morning, which was unusual for witches; their voices were carried clearly on the winds, and although they spoke in their own languages, their excitement was easy to hear.

'Any idea what they're saying?' Malcolm said to Lyra.

'None. I was never in the north for long enough to learn a single word.'

'They sound as if they're looking forward to something.'

'To a fight, perhaps.'

They were flying on Gulya's back, and they could sense that she was excited too, or agitated. It was hard to talk to her when they were flying, but she was calling to Prince Keshvād, and he replied, though the gryphons' own language was impossible to understand. Besides, they were buffeted by strong winds, which sometimes carried their words away.

'You know,' Malcolm said, 'you cried out in your sleep several times. Were you having a dream?'

'Nothing I can remember. Except a general feeling of being anxious about Pan. I thought he was falling at one point and I couldn't catch him.'

'He's safe,' said Asta. 'Safer than we are, probably.'

There was a group of witches, a dozen or so, flying close by. Lyra saw them suddenly move at the same time, a sort of flinching back in the air, and then she realised why. So did Malcolm.

'The birds,' he said.

Lyra smelled it a moment later. Just a waft, but it was enough to make her draw her head back in disgust.

'There they are,' said Asta, standing up on Gulya's back and sweeping her tail from side to side.

Ahead of them a cloud of smoke was rising from a valley between two rocky cliffs. But it wasn't smoke: it was an immense flock of the *oghâb-gorgs*, miles ahead yet but gathering high in the air as if they were being directed and swept up and forward by giant invisible hands. Other smoke-clouds joined them from similar valleys nearby, none of them yet resolvable into individual birds, but all seeming to be impelled by the same will.

'This is real trouble,' Lyra said. 'Have the gryphons got a plan to deal with them?'

'I don't know, but the witches might.'

The birds were closer now – not overhead yet, but within a minute they would be, and already their screaming was painful to the ears. Asta leaped up to Malcolm's shoulder, and Lyra held his arm tightly. It was getting darker: the birds were blotting out the sun, covering the earth with a shrieking twilight. All her senses were confused; it seemed as if it was the sound of their thousands of wings making the sky dark, and the darkness that was stinking – because the carrion-stench of the *oghâb-gorgs* filled the air around them and ahead of them, thick and foul and rotten.

The leading line of gryphons had climbed high to face them. In close formation they hung still, and seemed about to dive, but 'Look!' cried Malcolm, pointing at the last remaining patch of clear sky.

A witch – it was Sala Riikola – was speeding across the narrowing stretch of clear sky towards the great dark wave of the oncoming birds. Behind her came another two witches, and three, and then a dozen, and more. Beside the massive power of the gryphons they seemed frail, like cut-out shapes of paper.

'What can they do?' said Malcolm.

'I don't know, but they'll manage,' said Lyra.

Sala and her companions were flying directly at the *oghâb-gorgs*, and that seemed to disconcert the leading birds, some of which parted to let the witches through, while others turned in confusion and started tearing at one another.

'I wish we could see it from above,' Lyra said. 'They've got a plan, but it's hard to make out from underneath.'

And as Lyra watched the shrieking, flapping, screaming darkness that was now overhead, she could make out the shapes of Sala Riikola and her sisters racing through the mass in a wide anti-clockwise curve that took them from one side of the sky to the other and back again in half a minute.

They were screaming themselves, human voices lashing the flock with commands and encouragement: faster! Faster! Round and round!

'It's working!' cried Malcolm. 'Your dragonfly story – the swallows over Port Meadow—'

Lyra and Asta were trembling with excitement as they watched, cheering on the witches as they led, and urged, and whipped the flock on, faster, tighter – and then it was fully under their control, every single bird seized with the passion of belonging and the desire to do more, fly faster, fly closer, fly as one entity.

And little by little the half-dozen or so witches moved to the edge of the great wheeling flock and detached themselves from it, commanding it from outside, making it tighter and tighter and lower and lower. They rode the racing air like the army of Genghis Khan riding their powerful little horses; they had a complete mastery of the elements.

'What are they doing?' said Asta.

A moment later, they all saw. The huge vortex of birds, helpless to resist, was spinning downwards and further down and then – Lyra gasped – driving down like a screw into the mountains below. In the course of less than half a minute the entire flock smashed into the rocks, conscious of nothing except the desire to fly faster and faster; it wasn't separate birds any more, it was one entity, and air, water, earth, fire – it would have forced itself into any of them, crazed with longing, insane with desire.

And the witches circled above, watching as the ground heaved and seethed with blood and screaming and madness. Those birds who hadn't died at once saw nothing but carrion in the broken bodies of their kin, and fell on them with shrieks of savage greed. The gryphons screamed their approval in long eagle-cries that resounded from the mountains.

But, 'Witches!' Lyra cried: 'No! Oh no!' For she had seen two – three of them, engulfed by birds in the hideous melee and borne down into the rocks. It was only when the tumult began to clear that she could see what had happened, and Malcolm and Asta, and Gulya and Keshvād too, cried out in dismay as the remaining birds tore into the black-clad bodies, soon to be displaced and torn apart themselves in the frenzy of madness and blood.

Prince Keshvād screamed and soared high, and then flew down in a long glide towards a flat-topped ridge ahead of them, sloping down towards the treeline. The gryphons followed, and the main body of the witches came after them. By the time they reached the ridge, most of the noise was far behind them. Looking back, Lyra could see only a few black specks wheeling above the death-spot, and then one by one they too plunged down to take part in the feast, and left the sky clear and clean.

Keshvād landed first, and called his gryphons to come to order, rank upon rank of them in their strength and pride. Gulya landed too, and Lyra and Malcolm, together with Asta, slipped down from her back to stand beside her as the witches came to join them. Some were weeping; they had all seen their sisters borne down into the ground.

'Witches!' cried Prince Keshvād. 'That was a noble action, daring, skilful, victorious. We salute you. Apart from your three gallant sisters, are you all safe?'

'Some wounds, Prince,' said Sala Riikola, 'which we shall need to treat, because the birds will have been carrying pestilence and disease. We have herbs for that, but we need water and fire.'

'Can you get what you need from the trees below?'

One or two of the witches had been scouting along the treeline, and one spoke up: 'Yes, Prince. There is a spring a little way further down, and dead wood among the trees.'

'Then we shall rest here till sunset while you do that. You have done us all a great service. That was the greatest flock of those foul birds in the whole of the Tien Shan mountains.'

'Destroyed by the memory of a dragonfly,' said Sala Riikola. 'But look – is that Tilda Vasara?'

She was pointing to the south-east. Malcolm, looking that way, saw the tiniest movement in the sky, and at once felt his private aurora spring to life in response. Nothing changed in what he saw: a barely perceptible shiver in the air, no bigger than a photon, it seemed at first, but there it was.

The attention of everyone else was focused on the approaching witch. She saw what had happened, and swooped down low over the carnage before flying up again to join her companions.

Malcolm sat down to keep himself from falling.

'What is it?' said Lyra quietly.

Malcolm's eyes were closed. He said, 'It's a thing I see. I call it the spangled ring. My private aurora. Something sets it going, a tiny flash of light in the outside world or a jagged pattern in a carpet and slowly it gets bigger. It closes me down for a few minutes until it gets so big it just passes out of the visual field.'

'Sort of migraine thing?'

'Yes.'

'Do you want to lie down?'

'No need for that. I just keep still.'

Lyra was desperate to ask Tilda Vasara about Pan, but the witches were eager to talk together, sorrowfully about their dead companions, excitedly about the dragonfly-manoeuvre suggested by Lyra's story, proudly about the enormous flock that they forced to destroy itself. And they were anxious to hear from Tilda, so in return she began talking to them, urgently, passionately, angrily; Lyra watched and listened as her eyes flashed, her voice rang.

Asta calmly stepped up on to Malcolm's lap and purred. He stroked her back. Lyra sat down beside him.

'Does it happen often, the spangled thing?'

'Not very often. Not regularly. Something outside me, out in the world, triggers it and then I'm captive till it's over.'

'Why *spangled*?'

'It sort of sparkles. Like the moon and her spangled sisters bright. Usually just in black and white, but I'm seeing colours now. First time for that. A deep blue under everything and bands of pearl-white and maroon, I think . . . Hard to see it clearly . . . It moves, it flashes.'

His eyes were still closed. His face was flushed; Asta had stopped purring and just touched her face to his chin. He looked mesmerised; he looked both focused and dreaming.

'Creamy-yellow,' he murmured. 'Not pearl-white.'

'Lie down,' Lyra said, because he looked as if he was about to topple over.

He did as she said and lay back on the rocks, putting one arm over his eyes. She took his other hand and he gripped it firmly. It was curious, this feeling that she was protecting him, so strange that she thought about it closely. They stayed quiet and still. Asta lay soft between them.

30

HE IS YOUNGER THAN YOU ARE

The gryphons were holding some sort of council: Prince Keshvād and Gulya were listening intently to three of the commanders, who were speaking in turn, arguing courteously but firmly.

Lyra saw the witches move. They were turning towards her, and Tilda and Sala Riikola were coming. Some of the others set off back towards where the fallen witches lay, no doubt to deal with their remains with honour.

The two witches came to sit next to Lyra, looking at Malcolm curiously. Tilda was curious about Lyra too, and their eyes met with a flash of mutual recognition.

'He's watching something,' said Tilda, meaning Malcolm.

Lyra remembered that Tilda had spent time with him and Pan in the gryphons' palace. She didn't seem concerned about him, Lyra thought: simply respectful. Asta stirred, but didn't wake.

'You're Tilda Vasara,' said Lyra.

'And you are Lyra Silvertongue.'

'You took my dæmon with you,' Lyra said. 'Why?'

'He asked me to.'

'Where is he now?'

'A day's flight away, no more.'

'Was he safe when you left him?'

'Alive, yes. Safe, no. He has been in danger ever since he left you. So have you.'

'What is he doing?'

'Spying.'

'Spying – for what? What's he looking for? Didn't he tell you anything?'

Sala Riikola was surprised to hear any short-life woman speak to a witch-queen quite so fiercely as Lyra was doing.

Tilda was calm in response. 'There's a village on the hill just above the research station. We stopped there. We could see from the hill that the station buildings had been smashed up, windows broken, a wall or two knocked down, that sort of damage. Not destroyed completely. In fact, it seemed as if someone had already begun to repair it. The rubble was laid out neatly – bricks placed in tidy heaps, lengths of timber set together. Pan wanted to search properly, but he was going to wait till nightfall. We saw no one there except a couple of village people working on their land, but people had been and gone from the research station, because there were tracks of their wheels.'

'Pan didn't want to go on to the red building?'

'Not then, but he talked about it. He said he'd go there with you.'

'We'd have to go separately . . . That was the rule. To keep out people who couldn't separate from their dæmons, I suppose. But why, I don't know.'

'I know nothing about that. He said you and he would go there together. I guessed he knew what he was talking about.'

'Yes . . .'

She fell quiet. Both of them looked at Malcolm, who was sleeping peacefully.

'You know,' said Tilda, 'this man is younger than you are.'

Lyra looked at her. 'I don't understand,' she said.

'I said exactly what I mean. You are older, he is younger.'

'I still don't understand. And I thought time didn't matter for witches as it does for us.'

'A witch can be four hundred years old, but still seventeen. And I have seen human children seven years of age, who seem to have lived through centuries. Numbers have little to do with it. This man is younger than you are. I can see this, and you can't, so I tell you, and if you listen, you'll know.'

Lyra looked down at the sleeping Malcolm again. The sun gilded his face and his hair.

'He told me you cured a wound he had,' she said.

'That's right. Someone shot him in the leg. I had some bloodmoss, so I made a decoction and cleaned the wound.'

'Who shot him?'

'I don't know. What will you do at Tashbulak?'

'Find Pan, first, and then go to the red building. After that . . .' She shrugged, and looked at Malcolm.

'Will he come with you?'

'I hope so,' said Lyra carefully.

'Did you come all this way alone?'

Lyra had to think. 'Well, until Seleukeia I was alone. But there I found a guide, a man called Abdel Ionides. He was very helpful on the next part of the journey. But he . . . I don't know where he is now. He just left me unexpectedly.'

'I've heard of that man. Did he steal anything from you?'

'No. He was honest in that way, at least. I came to trust him completely, and I really thought he was truthful, in spite of . . . in spite of everything he said and did, really. He pretended to be a sort of vagabond, a rogue, but he'd been a professor of mathematics and he knew a lot about all kinds of unexpected things.'

'When did he leave?'

'On the night when Malcolm and Gulya killed the sorcerer. He just went off in a boat that belonged to the Magisterium. Actually now I think of him, he never claimed to be honest, except in a sort of ironic way, for mischief. I was very sorry to see him go.'

Tilda nodded. 'Stay with him,' she said, looking at Malcolm. 'Remember what I said about him.'

'I'll remember. Even though I don't understand it.'

'He is courageous and clever and honest and faithful. But he is younger than you.'

Tilda leaned across to kiss Lyra, and left without another word.

Lyra sat still, a little dizzy with the witch's words, because they rang true. Was the witch warning her about something? Or was it just nonsense?

It troubled her, and she pulled her rucksack to herself and hugged it, as if for warmth. Asta yawned and stretched and sat up to look at Malcolm, who was still asleep.

'Lazy,' she said. 'Lyra, can we look at your cards? The Myriorama?'

'Of course.'

Lyra opened the rucksack and felt inside. There was the little box, but her fingers also met the smooth surface of the lodestone resonator, and she brought that out first.

'That too. I want to know how it works,' said Asta.

'I think it must be something to do with entanglement. The particles of this one are connected with the ones in the stone that Malcolm's got, and they respond when—'

'It's responding now.'

'*What?*'

'There are words on it. But Malcolm's asleep! They can't be from him.'

'It can't be . . .'

But Asta was right. As it lay in Lyra's palm, the flat surface of the resonator was revealing, letter by letter, words that seemed to float into focus from deep inside the stone. Once she had read them, they disappeared to make room for more, as if it knew what her eyes were looking at.

Dear Miss Silver!

Yes, it is I, your 'sorcier particulier', Abdel Ionides, also known as Professor Rashid Xenakis, and more briefly as 'Master Parathanasius'. When we waited for you and Mr Malcolm on the beach under the mountain I took advantage of his absence to borrow from his rucksack the stone that is in my hand as I write these words.

I am aware that you will be feeling certain 'misgivings' about my actions, and possibly even a little mistrust in consequence. Let me clarify for you and Mr Malcolm the reasons behind what Dr Pervani and I did when we left with the Magisterium vessel.

Dr Pervani has been acting a 'double role', very dangerous, I assure you, in seeming to act for the Magisterium while secretly working as an agent for the group known sometimes as the 'men from the mountains'. Both sides, she assures me, are despicable. She would like to see the destruction of both. Everything she has done has been done with that purpose in mind.

Before the Magisterium vessel arrived so unexpectedly we had every intention of continuing with you on your journey to the red building in the desert. Dr Pervani is convinced, as you are, that the secret of the 'Rusakov field' is to be found there. Myself, I am, as you know, a sceptic about many things, but I trust her reasoning about this. The red building is of central importance.

When the vessel came into view on that stormy sea we had no more than a few seconds to decide what to do. That was the point at which I borrowed the lodestone. Dr Pervani intended to continue her pretence to be on their side, and I went with her, claiming that I would throw all the resources of my intelligence and experience into the struggle alongside her. Fortunately I was able to convince her colleagues of my 'bona fides'.

Now we are bound for Karamakan, as you are. When we arrive there we expect to find the Tashbulak station in the hands of an enemy both to the Magisterium and to you, and an enemy also to the 'men from the mountains'. This enemy is very insidious, very deadly, and unless we can think strategically it will be the death

*of us all. These are complex currents. I shall write before long and
tell you exactly what we discover, and we can formulate a 'plan of
action' together.*

*Please respond to me, my dear Miss Silver, Queen Tatiana. I
hope with all the heart of a vagabond that you are safe, and that
you will find your beloved dæmon, if you have not done so already.*

Abdel Ionides

Asta sat and read it with her, and then they looked at each other
without a word. Lyra blew out her cheeks.

'Well,' she managed to say.

'You trust him?'

'Yes. Well, no. Of course not. He's a thief and a liar and God
knows what else. But . . . Yes, I trust him. Naturally. He helped me
such a lot . . .' She ran her fingers through her hair. It felt stiff and
dirty, but that was too bad.

'Who are you talking about?' said Malcolm.

Lyra turned to look as he sat up carefully, blinking at the light,
shading his eyes with his hand. 'Can you see all right now?' she
asked him. 'Has your spangled thing gone?'

Asta butted his chin softly, and he stroked her back. 'Yes. It's
gone, it's clear. It just leaves me feeling a bit washed-out. What are
you looking at?'

She showed him the lodestone. He screwed up his eyes to look
at it, puzzled at first, and then realised what had happened.

'You mean this isn't mine? It's yours? Then who . . .' He screwed
up his eyes to read it fully, and laughed. ' "*Took advantage of his
absence*" . . . Very good. He doesn't say anything about who he's
travelling with. They must have crossed the Caspian by now.'

'Who d'you think this other enemy is?'

'I think he's loquacious enough to tell us if he has the chance.
Are you going to reply?'

'Of course. As soon as I find my pencil.'

The point had broken. Malcolm offered her his knife.

'Can you do it?' she said.

He took it and she watched his deft movements as the shavings of cedarwood and grains of graphite fell away. The pencil was perfectly sharp in seconds.

'Don't you like using a knife?' he said.

'My hand hurts. Thank you.'

She began to write:

Dear Mr Ionides, thank you for this message. I think you are very dishonest for stealing the lodestone, but I'm glad you did. You don't say where you are now. We are on the southern edge – she checked with Malcolm – *of the Tien Shan mountains. Where are you? How are you travelling?*

We want to know more about this other enemy. Who are they? What do they want? Tell us all you know.

She stopped there. She wanted to tell him more about that other thing, the alkahest, the universal solvent: was that the third enemy, in some way? But it was hard to sum up. Instead she went on:

Today we survived an attack from the ogabgorgs – don't know how to spell it – the witches tricked them into destroying themselves. The main army of the Magisterium is further north. We are safe but need more information now.

  With my greetings,
  Tatiana R

She thought that was how queens signed themselves.

'Tatiana?' said Malcolm.

'I was Tatiana Iorekova, the queen of . . . I forget where. Novaya Zemlya, that's it. He was my personal magician, my *sorcier particulier*. That was to get the audience with Mustafa Bey. I still can't understand who'd gain by killing him, though.'

'This third enemy, perhaps,' said Asta. 'What do you know of them?'

'Nothing.'

'Ionides thinks they might already be in control of the research station,' said Malcolm. 'But look, Gulya's coming. Perhaps it's time to leave.'

The gryphon landed close by. The beating of her wings set up powerful eddies in the air and blew Lyra's hair across her face as well as ruffling Asta's fur. Gulya was still not used to managing her new size and power, but she clearly delighted in it.

'If we leave now,' she said, 'we could arrive at the Tashbulak station by sunset.'

An idea occurred to Lyra. It came out of nowhere, but it had been generated by the report from Tilda as well as the message from Ionides.

'Gulya,' she said, 'you know that my dæmon, Pan, went ahead with Tilda Vasara?'

'Indeed. And she has come back without him.'

'Well, I want to do the same thing. Go ahead. But I want to go directly to the red building.'

'Lyra, why?' said Malcolm. It sounded like a genuine enquiry, not like the beginning of a reproof.

'Because Pan's in danger. I don't want him to go into the red building before I do. Just a feeling I have. Will you fly us there, Gulya?'

'Yes. But only if Prince Keshvād agrees.'

'Of course.'

Without hesitation Gulya stretched out her wings and sprang into the air, wheeling high and then gliding down swiftly towards the prince.

'Lyra,' said Malcolm again. 'Why?'

'This third enemy. I'm frightened by what he says – Ionides, I mean. Frightened for Pan, and frightened for all of us. You will come, won't you?'

'As if I'd ever do anything else.'

She looked at him. His eyes were clear again and as blue as the sky, and he seemed to be made of sky-things altogether: air and sunlight. She felt a little burst of joyful laughter, to think that someone like this was on her side, and then she saw Gulya spring up from the ground and sweep through the air back towards them. Malcolm stood up and gathered his coat and rucksack, and Lyra stood beside him. Gulya landed with such a beating of her wings that Lyra was nearly buffeted off balance, and knocked into Malcolm. He caught her deftly.

'Gulya,' Lyra said, 'who are the enemies the gryphons think are the most dangerous?'

Gulya said, 'We fear no enemies.'

'I know you are fearless. But which enemy could do the most damage to the world?'

'One we can't even see. One we don't suspect for a moment. One we ignore. I can't tell you who they are, because it's in their nature to be invisible and unsuspected.'

'Do gryphons have stories about the end of the world?'

'We have stories about everything, but not that.'

Lyra nodded and put back the things she'd taken out of her rucksack, with the lodestone on top. Malcolm put on his big coat, and with Asta on his shoulders, he climbed up on Gulya's back and helped Lyra up after him.

'Ready?' said the gryphon, and raised her wings. A few moments later they were in the air on the last leg of the journey to the red building.

As twilight fell, Pan moved down the hillside towards the village and the research station beyond it, moving quickly, keeping close to the ground. Twilight was better than full darkness for hiding in, but the trouble was that it didn't last.

He stopped several times to listen and to smell the air. He heard all the sounds he would have expected from a small village at dusk;

voices, the crackle of flames, goat-bells ringing occasionally as the animals moved around in their enclosure. Someone was intoning a prayer inside one of the houses; children were squabbling; men were laughing. He caught the smells of wood-smoke, of grilling meat, of dung, of grass, and beyond them all, the bare and empty scent of the desert. A dog barked, and another took it up. Pan knew they had smelled him, but ignored them and moved on through the tough grass towards the ruined station.

The moon would help when it rose, but it was now almost fully dark. Pan's night vision was good, though, and the shattered buildings and broken windows of the station lay fully open and clear.

He moved all around the buildings, noticing every slight glow from inside, counting the seven vehicles parked behind, listening to every faint sound that reached him. From the village side there was little sign of occupation, but from the desert side half a dozen windows – or the spaces where windows had been – were lit, and three or four people were moving about inside the place.

The vehicles parked outside were mainly the kind used for moving cargo or building materials. One had the brand-mark of Thuringia Potash on the side; the others had different symbols, and names in languages that Pan didn't recognise. They were all covered in the dust of hundreds of miles' travel.

Oh, Lyra, he thought. *I can't go much longer without you to talk to. And to fall asleep with. I'm weaker than I used to be and this is all frightening and I'm so tired of being alone . . .*

He couldn't even think much more than that. He stood still under one of the trucks and listened. If he concentrated, he could hear the sound of small burrowing creatures under the sand; and some kind of insect like a cricket was scraping away monotonously nearby; and there was the sound of an anbaric generator, no doubt the one that was powering the lights in the building, running on a naphtha engine; and the human voices that came from the nearest rooms in the building as people went past the broken windows. A woman, or two women, and maybe three or four men.

They spoke in different languages, but also in English, as if that was the one they had in common. He couldn't hear enough of that to be sure what they were talking about, though he recognised some words like generator, logistics, hydrocarbon. These people must be experts from somewhere planning to restore the research station, but that wasn't hard to guess. Lyra could have imagined that herself.

He caught himself thinking that, and felt a pang of guilt. He'd set off full of self-importance to find the imagination he said she lacked, and now here he was, remarking to himself that she—

His skin bristled. A little shape was creeping out of an open window. It might have been a monkey, but it was moving too slowly; or a reptile, but there was something simian about it; but the main point was simpler than either of those. It was a dæmon. It was impossible to mistake.

Alone too. So a separated dæmon, whose person might be anyone, anywhere.

The dæmon stayed for a moment, silhouetted against the light from the room behind, and Pan saw that she (no doubt about that either) was a lemur, and small, and emaciated. She looked unwell.

Moving very carefully, she climbed down a drainpipe to the ground, and at once almost disappeared into the shadows. But Pan could see her movements as she crept along the base of the wall, her claws not well adapted to walking on the ground, and began to follow her. She was intent on something, and he was intent on finding out what it was.

He slipped out from under the truck. There was a luminous quality in the air already, as well as the light from the building. He padded swiftly across the sandy ground and stopped under the shadow of a large metal tank. He could still see her a little way ahead, but then she reached the corner of the building and turned out of sight.

He darted forward, hoping the voices from the open window would cover the slight sound of his feet. Two men talking freely now, in Chinese, possibly; not arguing, but discussing something energetically. A glass clinked on a bottle. Pan slowed down as he reached the corner, and stopped, and listened hard.

No sound of dæmon-feet on sand, and he'd see nothing unless he looked round the corner; so he very carefully did.

Instantly something slashed at his face. He sprang back and found his balance, and then darted out past the corner and turned to see her. She hissed and snarled and leaped at him, furious and terrified, and in a moment they were tumbling over, biting, shaking, scratching, but he was stronger than she was; and in little more than a moment he had her pinned beneath him with his teeth in her throat. They both fell still.

She *was* thin, as he'd seen, and not strong, and her fur was threadbare like an old carpet; but she wasn't old. She lay trembling and silent. Little by little he loosened his jaw, but as soon as she felt that, she began to struggle again. He gripped her throat with his paws, and she tried to speak, and couldn't; so he whispered, 'English? You speak English?'

There was no reason why she should, of course; any one of a hundred different Asian languages would have been more likely. But she nodded faintly, and he went on, 'I won't hurt you. My name is Pan. I'm separated, like you, and my person is on her way here. What's your name?'

He loosened his grip a little, and she murmured, 'My name is Cariad.'

'I'm going to let go. But don't run away. I want to talk to you.'

Another slight nod. He let go of her throat and sat back to let her roll over and sit up.

'Where's your person?' he said.

'He is asleep in there.'

'You don't sleep when he does?'

'Not since we were separated.'

'How did that happen?'

She suddenly writhed away, and tried to run, but he was too quick for her, and caught her before she reached the corner of the building.

'Don't do that,' he said. 'I'll always catch you. I want to know things, and only you can tell me. What's his name, your person?'

She was trembling. He thought she was trying not to sob.

'I won't hurt you,' he insisted. 'Promise. But you must tell me these things. What's your person called?'

'Brynmor Strauss.'

'Strauss . . .' Something plucked at his memory. A rucksack . . . violence, the murder by the river . . . pages of handwriting on cheap lined paper . . .

This was the dæmon of the man who'd written the journal he and Lyra had found in the dead man's rucksack.

'Cariad,' he repeated unbelievingly. 'Your person wrote a diary, about your journey to the red building in the desert – and his colleague Dr Hassall brought it back to England with him—'

'What happened? How do you know that?'

He told her briefly some of what had happened: the murder of Hassall, the discovery of the diary, his parting from Lyra and the journey to Tashbulak.

'You *left* her? Why?' She was astonished.

'I thought it was the right thing to do, but I was wrong.'

'But why come here?'

'We both think there's something we want and it's in the red building in the desert. But you went into that building, didn't you? You and Dr Strauss?'

'Yes.'

'And what did you find?'

'No, no, no . . . Terrible things.'

He still held her firmly, though every part of her was straining to get away.

'What d'you mean? What sort of terrible things?'

'It's abominable . . . No, no. The worst thing . . .'

'Why can't you tell me?'

'It . . . I can't find the words . . . You should speak to Brynmor. Or Dilyara. She knows some of it.'

'Who's Dilyara?'

'A cleaner. She helped Brynmor.'

'All right, I will. But give me some idea.'

She struggled again, and then fell limp as if she'd fainted; but he knew she hadn't, and kept his hold on her.

'Tell me,' he said again. 'What did you find in the red building?'

'Come with me then. I'll show you.'

She sounded resigned, and sullen, but very frightened. He followed her inside.

Some miles to the north, Olivier Bonneville was trying to sleep in a tent on frozen ground on the eastern flank of a spur of the Tien Shan mountains. He had been travelling as a semi-prisoner, semi-indentured labourer of the Magisterial army, his labour consisting of attending every meeting called by Marcel Delamare and writing detailed minutes, as well as obeying every order, however trivial, of the President himself. He cursed the job. He cursed the cold. He cursed his luck, he cursed Delamare, he cursed Lyra, he cursed the series of absurdities and blunders that had placed him in this situation, and he cursed the fact that the alethiometer was in the hands of that tortoise-witted reactionary Lacroix.

So he turned from side to side, he tried sleeping on his front, on his back, on his side again, and he seemed to be getting colder and colder. He pulled the rough blankets up around his neck, and then his feet got cold; he pulled his knees up so as to cover his feet, and then he got cramp and had to straighten them again; there was a separate draught from every direction; the camp bed was rickety and creaked whenever he moved; the guard stamping up and down outside had a habit of groaning under his breath.

So when he finally did fall asleep, he was not pleased to feel a hand on his shoulder almost at once, and to hear a whispered voice saying, 'Olivier, wake up. Wake up!'

He tried to sweep the visitor aside with an arm flung outwards, but his wrist was caught at once and the voice said again, 'Olivier, wake up. Look and see who I am.'

There was something familiar . . . Was he still dreaming? The voice . . .

He blinked hard and peered up. The faint light of an anbaric torch lit a face he'd seen before, outside the city of ruins, the city of lost dæmons, where this man had persuaded him not to shoot . . .

'You!' he said.

The visitor pressed a finger to his lips, and shut off the torch.

'Not so loud,' he whispered. 'Yes, Olivier, it's me, your old friend Abdel Ionides, come to help you.'

'Last time your help was no good.'

'It was very useful, my boy, and I will help you more now. But first listen carefully. I come with a message for your leader, Marcel Delamare, the President himself. I can't go to him directly, because I would be shot before I reached him.'

Bonneville blinked again and tried to shake the sleep out of his head. 'But why—'

'I'll tell you if you listen. I represent the group known to some people as the men from the mountains. For various reasons, we want to reach that red building before the Silvertongue girl does. You understand me?'

'Yes. So what? I knew that already.'

'I want you to go to Delamare and tell him we are ready to discuss a joint campaign. We want to avoid being caught up in needless distractions such as fighting one another. Tell him we shall meet whenever he is ready, and he can send a signal with that new bomb he has, the *tonnerre double*. Yes, we know about that. He must combine the charge with graphite to make black smoke, and fire it into the sky.'

'He won't believe me. D'you think I'm a fool? D'you think *he's* a fool?'

'Give him this. Tell him you stole it from me.'

Ionides felt inside his fur-lined cloak and handed something to Bonneville: a small slim document with a stiff cover.

'What is it?'

Ionides switched on his torch again, long enough for Bonneville to see that he was holding something like a passport, and that it belonged to Leila Pervani.

'*Her?*'

'Ssh.'

'I thought she was part of the ...' Bonneville thought he couldn't be awake yet. He wasn't thinking clearly. But there was her photogram, her unmistakably, the beautiful bitch. 'But why give it to him?'

'Go to him now, and tell him I came to you. He is a sceptical man. Give him this document. Let him examine it closely. It is perfectly genuine.'

The faint light shining up from the torch gave Ionides's face the air of a painted devil in a puppet play.

Bonneville said uncertainly, 'I could have stolen it . . .'

'No, you could not. She is more cunning than that. It will carry conviction, which your words alone, my dear Olivier, will not. She made a powerful impression on M. Delamare when they met. Give him the message: we can join forces. We are very close.'

'I don't believe you. How could you be close without alerting the sentries?'

'There was a sentry right outside this tent, Olivier, and yet here I am.'

'Did you kill him?'

'He is unable to take any further part in the campaign. Go now, Olivier. Wake up M. Delamare, and don't forget the signal. We shall be watching.'

With a warm smile and a friendly pat on the shoulder, Ionides stood up silently and switched off the torch.

'Oh,' he said: 'one more thing. All this time, you track Miss Silver to exact some revenge for your father. But dig deeper, my friend. Ask your alethiometer who sent your father to prison. Ask why. There is much you don't know.'

He dropped something into Bonneville's lap. It was small and heavy . . . He felt it: a clasp knife.

'Hide it carefully. It is very sharp,' said Ionides, and he vanished into the dark.

The icy draught made Bonneville shudder. He longed to be asleep again, but the perfect face of the woman and the devilish face of Ionides gave him no choice. He found himself uttering a little sob, and swallowed it at once. No choice.

The wording of the message Hannah Relf had given Alice to pass on to the young man in Battersea concealed the key to a set of complex instructions that led, after several days, to a knock on Hannah's door.

Rain was falling in the darkness. The figure who stood on the doorstep was wrapped in a hooded cloak, and carrying a heavy bundle. Hannah hastened to let her in, and looked both ways along the quiet road of terraced houses before closing the door.

'Glenys!' she said, but quietly.

Glenys Godwin threw back the hood and then put her bundle down before shaking the rain off her cloak and all over the carpet and the walls. 'Sorry,' she said.

Her bundle spoke in a ghostlike whisper. 'Can you let me out?' it said.

'Sorry, Meurig.'

Glenys unwrapped the bundle and lifted out her dæmon, the paralysed civet cat.

'Never mind the rain,' said Hannah, taking the cloak and putting it on a hanger on the hatstand. 'Come in, come in. Are you cold?'

'Yes. Cold and tired and hungry.'

'I'll make you some coffee and scrambled eggs. Sit by the fire and get warm. Then I want to know everything. Oh, there's some whisky on the sideboard.'

She looks ill, Hannah thought as she beat some eggs in a saucepan. Her own dæmon sat beside Glenys's as he lay on the hearthrug, and they murmured together. The kitchen opened directly into the sitting room, so the women weren't far from their dæmons; Glenys brought the whisky bottle and her glass and came to talk as Hannah put on the kettle.

'Did you come on the train?'

'No. I think they're watching all the stations. I took the auto-coach to Basingstoke and then another coach from there.'

'Long journey.'

'Nevertheless. Thank you for Kilkenny. My Battersea man was impressed by your messenger.'

'She's a bright young woman. She escaped from a transit camp, if that's what they call it, somewhere in the Thames Valley.'

'Why did they put her there?'

'It was the general round-up in the first flurry of suspicion, remember? Lots of people were swept up quite unnecessarily. She managed to get away, came back to her home in Oxford, and then thought she'd be safer in London. She was probably right. She's working as a chambermaid at The Savoy.'

'Anyway, she did well. Going to use her again?'

'Oh, I think so. How do you like your eggs?'

'Not very dry.'

'They're ready then. Could you put the water in the coffee?'

They sat down at the little kitchen table. They'd known each other for a long time, but hadn't been close friends; their different fields of activity meant that they seldom saw each other.

'I didn't hear any news in prison, and I've only seen one paper since they let me out. What's happening?' Glenys said.

Hannah gave her a summary of political events since her arrest. As she went through the changes of government, the reorganisation of the civil service, the assumption of emergency powers, the violent crushing of strikes and protests, Hannah realised herself the extent of the turbulence that had overtaken the country.

'The monetisation—' she said, but Glenys interrupted at once: 'The *what?*'

'The way some of the poorer colleges have already started making approaches to corporations of one sort or another. They're even talking about naming rights, like football teams.'

'What, the Anglo-Oil Balliol?'

'Not quite that yet, but it'll come. Just a creeping corruption.'

'That's one of the things I sent Polstead out to look at.'

'But the worst thing,' Hannah said, 'is just the failure of every kind of newspaper, magazine, regular gazette . . . We hear rumours, and we can't check them; we hear at third hand about riots in big cities, but no one knows why or what they're about; we don't even know whether the government is still in place. There was a rumour only yesterday that the whole Cabinet had resigned and appointed a Protector, and that the King was under arrest, but I've heard nothing since then. What did your newspaper say?'

'Absolutely nothing worthwhile or true. Nothing but guessing games with big prizes and lottery news and pictures of celebrated actresses. Certainly nothing about the Cabinet resigning.'

'How did they treat you in prison?'

'Did you know they had special suites reserved for those who could pay?'

'Certainly not! How long's that been going on?'

'Not very long. You get a two-cell apartment, with decent food and comfortable furniture and privileged access to visitors and mail.'

'Did they offer one to you?'

'No. I came in a different category. Enemy of the state, that's what they call it. We had to share cells with prisoners guilty of violent offences. Thank God for combat training. Now, I haven't been able to talk to anyone, obviously, and I need to know everything you've heard about what the Magisterium army is doing in Central Asia. I know some intelligence services abroad are still active and effective. Does anyone in Oxford hear what's going on outside Europe?'

'Yes, but slowly and partially. Most of the usual traffic has been stalled and disrupted – there was an assassination, a Syrian merchant, I believe, who sat at the middle of a very big network of intelligence as well as commercial business. That made everything shrink back a bit. The last I heard of Delamare and his expedition to conquer the East—'

'Is that how people talk about it?'

'Historians are more taken with that phrase than political analysts. Anyway, the last I heard, he'd led his army out of the Tien Shan mountains and south towards Lop Nor.'

'Right through the famous wandering lake. Asinine! What the hell's he playing at?'

'Don't know. But the main news from Central Asia is the extraordinary speed of the development plans from Cathay and elsewhere. Muscovy's involved – so are corporations from Europe and New Denmark. The man I talk to is an economist. He says it's the most important thing that's happening anywhere; Delamare and his ten thousand men are nothing in comparison.'

Hannah refilled her glass and another for Glenys. 'That *is* interesting,' she said. 'I remember picking up traces of that before I was arrested. What exactly are they developing?'

'Roads, canals, railway lines, landing grounds for air travel . . . And my economist friend believes they have some form of instantaneous long-range communication.'

'Bugger,' said Glenys. 'I could be *doing* something about this if I wasn't in danger of arrest. Have you heard anything from Polstead, or the young woman?'

'No, and I'm worried. I thought you had a way of communicating with Malcolm, with him directly?'

'Not any more. I knew I was going to be arrested; I managed to send my half of the system to the Silvertongue girl, care of the merchant who was killed. Whether she received it or not I don't know, but it was no use to me any more.'

Hannah sipped her whisky and said, 'Well, you can't go anywhere else for a while. You're welcome to stay here. Or I know a place a little way out of the city where you'd be safe: Malcolm Polstead's parents' pub. Absolutely solid and reliable. Though no – wait – the army's occupied Port Meadow, and they're requisitioning everywhere nearby . . . Better keep away from there.'

'In fact, I'm legally free, thanks to Kilkenny, but still on a wanted list. They'll have thought of some other charges by now, and concocted the evidence. I know the Trout; I went there once a long time ago with Tom Nugent. I'll find somewhere safe. A bed for tonight, though, and a hot bath . . . I spent last night in a wood near Hounslow.'

'You look remarkably well on it. Do you need any more clothes? I can easily slip out in the morning . . .'

'Yes, I do. Thank you. I'm very glad you were in this evening, Hannah.'

'I'll go and make up your bed, and then we can have another drink.'

'Good. I want to hear more about what your economist says.'

31

MERCHANT PEOPLE

Cariad led Pan into the station at a point where a wall had
fallen. Dilyara had begun to clear it, but much of the masonry
was too heavy for her to move. The two dæmons climbed lightly
over the twisted steel beams, the crumbling plaster, the broken
glass, and Pan followed her down a swept and tidied corridor
until they came to a door open on a lighted room.

'We'll wait here,' Cariad whispered. 'Just listen and see if
Brynmor's in there. Or Dilyara. She looks after the place.
Brynmor trusts her.'

They crouched next to the wall beside the door. People were
talking in the room, not urgently, nor in a carefree relaxed way
like friends after a good dinner, but with a businesslike seriousness
that was nevertheless informal. Pan could tell that, even though he
didn't recognise the language they were speaking. But suddenly
they switched and continued in English: three men's voices and
two women's.

'The lake is the biggest obstacle,' said a young man.

'Lop Nor? No,' said a woman. 'Look at what's happening at the
Aral Sea. A simple matter of drainage will remove it altogether.
And think of the Suez Canal. How they built that.'

'I don't see the similarity. For one thing—'

'Getting the supply chain for fuel and so forth in place first,' said another man. 'Is that what you mean, Petra?'

'Exactly.'

'But you can't plan any infrastructure if the ground itself shifts about.'

'I think that's largely mythical, that moving business,' said a younger woman.

'Even so, we'd need to stabilise the soil—'

'Which we can do. More important to my mind is the need for refuelling stations on the main link.'

Pan turned to Cariad. 'Are these people . . . ? Where do they come from?' he whispered.

'Cathay, maybe . . . Different places.'

'Do they come from the red building?'

But she was moving away. She stalked slowly past the open door, stopping to look in before moving on. No one seemed to notice her, so Pan stopped there as well, and saw the three men – in their twenties or thirties – and one older woman, and a young woman seemingly about Lyra's age, sitting casually around or leaning against the counter where a coffee machine was steaming. All their attention was focused on one another, and none on the open door. He could see their dæmons, small and unobtrusive, perching or sitting silently.

He turned to Cariad, but she had vanished. He cursed himself, and moved on past the door. There was something odd about those dæmons, and he wanted very much to ask her about it. It was as if they were asleep, or drugged.

He moved very carefully back into the open doorway. No one looked at him. It was as if he was invisible.

'. . . But thinking more boldly,' said one of the men, 'I know our concern should be with the Great Road project, but there's no reason why a canal shouldn't solve a lot of the major problems.

I mean, there's no shortage of water running off the mountains before it all soaks into the sand.'

'If it was all directed—' said the young woman.

The other woman said something in Arabic. The conversation continued in that language, and Pan carefully moved further into the room. One of the men moved his head a little to look at him, and Pan froze; but then the man turned back to the conversation and took no more notice.

Pan looked around. This room looked like a sort of small common room or recreation area, a space where people would go to drink coffee or eat sandwiches or play cards during a break. It was untidy, but clean enough: perhaps it was one of the spaces Dilyara looked after. He noticed an anbaric clock fixed to the wall, and others; five altogether, showing the time in different places. He guessed that here in Tashbulak it was perhaps nine or ten in the evening, an odd time for people to take a break from work, unless they were working to the time in – he calculated roughly – western Europe, as one of the clocks showed.

Pan looked at the dæmons of the people speaking. A sparrow, a small dog, a wren, a lizard, and a small rodent of some sort, perhaps a mouse. They perched or lay apparently asleep. Their people never spoke to them, and the dæmons never offered a comment or asked a question: it was quite unlike any such gathering Pan had seen. Normally he'd expect the dæmons to be awake, interested, responsive, to be included in the talk and the interactions. That's what things were like. That happened everywhere and always.

Except – and he remembered it with a sickening lurch – at the hideous place at Bolvangar, in the high Arctic, where he and Lyra had made their way in order to rescue her friend Roger, half a lifetime ago. The nurses there who looked after the stolen children had dæmons who behaved not like the people they were part of but like little trotting mechanical dogs or dolls, or *pets*.

He and Lyra had only just escaped being separated under the silver guillotine, which cut children away from their dæmons: it had been almost the worst moment of their lives. The nurses, they thought, must have undergone the same sort of operation for their dæmons to be so compliant, so much less *real* than they should be.

Had these people been separated by force like those at Bolvangar?

But that wren was looking at him with what might have been a faint curiosity, and that dog, at the feet of the young man by the counter, had cocked his ear when Pan came in, though he didn't open his eye. They were taking notice of the people, though unobtrusively, or even surreptitiously. It was just that the people didn't seem to be aware of *them*.

The mouse-dæmon was sitting in the pocket of the blue cardigan that the young woman had thrown over the back of her chair. He looked out, and his eyes met Pan's, and immediately closed, like a child who thinks that if he can't see, he can't be seen either.

Pan wondered if the dæmons could talk to one another, or whether they were mutually invisible: whether he was the only being there who could see them.

He moved slowly further into the room, closer to the mouse-dæmon in the blue cardigan. The people went on talking, switching languages whenever someone else contributed a remark or a question. They were fluent and seemingly at home in whichever language they were using. Pan paused beneath the cardigan, which was hung casually over the back of the owner's chair, and looked at the dæmon again. The bright mouse-eyes were still closed.

'My name is Pan,' he whispered. 'Can you hear me?'

'I don't know,' came a whisper in return.

'What do you mean? You answered the question. You *can* hear me. What's your name?'

'I don't know. I had one, but it was lost.'

'Doesn't *she* talk to you?'

He looked up. The young woman was talking about financial something or other; Pan couldn't follow it. The mouse-dæmon tried to tuck himself further down into the pocket.

'I know you can hear me,' Pan whispered. 'But I'm not sure *she* can. Am I right?'

'I don't know. It's hard.'

The little dæmon sounded as if he was frightened of everything, and wanted nothing more than to be invisible.

'She doesn't seem to hear me,' Pan said. 'None of them do. Or see me.'

'They do, but they don't notice.'

'Do you? I mean, do you see the other dæmons here?'

'It's difficult.'

'You can see me, though, can't you? Or you could if you looked. Why don't you want to talk?'

'We just don't.'

'You mean *we dæmons*, or *me and my person*?'

'Both, I think.'

'You never talk to another dæmon?'

'It's wrong.'

'Who told you it's wrong?'

'We just don't do it.'

'Where do you come from? Do you come from the red building?'

The mouse-dæmon shrank away. He seemed crushed by fear and misery.

Then Pan thought of something else, and said, 'Are you separated?'

'I don't know.'

'You don't *know*? Do you . . . d'you know what I mean by separated?'

'No, no, no, I don't want to . . .'

'Or do you come from a different world?'

'Please go away. Please. This is frightening.'

'Well . . . I don't mean to frighten you. I'm sorry. If I see you again, I'll pretend not to notice you.'

He felt a little frightened himself. There was something repellent as well as pitiful about the abject state of this dæmon, and he wondered whether to approach another of them, but before he could move, the young woman's chair scraped on the floor and she stood up, as if her break was over. Two of the others began to move away with her, leaving the older woman and the man by the counter.

Pan looked for the mouse-dæmon to acknowledge him, but he never lifted his head from the cardigan pocket as the woman slung it around her shoulders, and then they were gone.

The young man at the counter shifted a little and poured himself another mug of coffee. His dæmon, some sort of small terrier, lay curled up at his feet, apparently asleep. The other people continued their conversation, mostly in Italian now, which Pan could understand a little, and they were talking about money or banking, and how some new form of money was making it easier to trade.

Pan looked up at the arm of the chair, where the older woman's lizard-dæmon was lying, also asleep. He waited for a flicker of movement from the dæmon, and saw none. But the conversation was coming to an end, and then he saw something he'd never seen before: the woman gathered a bag from the floor, picked up the dæmon as if he were nothing but a handkerchief, and dropped him casually inside the bag before snapping it shut and standing up. Pan felt sick: the dæmon looked boneless, as limp as a dead worm.

The woman got to her feet, said 'Ciao' to the man, and left.

Pan had seen enough. He wanted to find Cariad, and he wanted to talk to Strauss, and he wanted to think about what he'd seen and heard; and most of all he wanted to talk to Lyra. No, not just that: he wanted to press himself against her, to feel her heart beating, to cherish the warmth of her blood beneath her skin.

Above all, he feared seeing her like the woman with the cardigan, completely indifferent to her dæmon, to him. How could he bear it? How could she? He wanted to warn her. Something was wrong here.

He crept away from the lighted room. Cariad was nowhere to be seen. Pan was too disturbed to look for her; all he wanted to do was hide. He curled up to sleep under a staircase.

Pan woke up to the thunder of banging on doors and of stamping feet. His hiding place under the stairs was safe for the moment, but probably not for long; he crept as far as he could into the shadows and watched as the feet came closer.

Soldiers' feet, in boots, sand-coloured camouflage uniforms. Shouts in French and German, and in Tajik, and in English too: 'Come out! Show yourselves! Armed military!'

A door opened cautiously. From where Pan was crouching he could see a woman who might have been the cleaner Dilyara looking out, full of fear; then she withdrew and closed the door silently. He cursed: if he'd had his wits about him, he would have darted in. Cariad must be in there with her and Strauss. They could have discussed what to do. Now the soldiers were moving along the corridor, banging on all the doors with the butts of their rifles and shouting.

Another of the doors opened, but not cautiously, nor in anger. The woman who came out was the older of the two women he'd heard talking during the night, the one who'd picked up her dæmon so casually. She was dressed in a khaki shirt and slacks, and her hair was neatly styled.

'Who are you?' she said in French to the soldier who'd been about to slam his rifle into her door.

'Magisterium. Come out.'

'No, I don't want to. I shall stay here till I'm ready. Who is your commanding officer?'

'Not your business. Do as we tell you.'

Pan was impressed by her calm confidence. The soldiers seemed unable to speak in less than a shout; her voice was just as it had been in the coffee room, the tone conversational, the manner formal.

'No. I need an explanation of who you are and why you're here. But you are a sergeant, and I want to speak to an officer.'

She stood with arms folded and without a flicker of doubt in her expression. The sergeant had been joined by two others, who were clearly expecting him to dominate her, and now seemed a little disconcerted to find that he couldn't. One of them looked at him enquiringly.

'I'm not going to stand here arguing with you,' the sergeant said in a tone that tried to be menacing.

'Good. As soon as you move out of the way I can go about my work.'

'What work?'

'Business. Development banking.'

He was disconcerted. 'Where's your boss?' he demanded, after a pause that was a little too long.

'I'm the boss.'

'Go and report to Captain Schalken. He's the officer in charge.'

'Report to him? I think he will report to me.'

The sergeant's dæmon, a terrier with docked ears and tail, had been growling almost silently, crouching behind his legs; now she uttered a short angry bark. He put down a hand to calm her. The woman took no notice, but continued to look the sergeant directly in the eyes. Pan thought of her dæmon, limp in the bag she held over her shoulder, perhaps asleep, or paralysed, or dead . . . No, this woman was afraid of nothing, and the sergeant knew it. He moved aside without a word, and let her pass calmly down the corridor.

He turned to the other two soldiers and snapped, 'Come on, get on with it.'

The other two moved stolidly along the corridor, knocking on doors, shouting for their occupants to come out and identify themselves. No one did, and soon the soldiers had gone round the corner and out of sight.

Pan ran out from the shelter of the stairs and scratched hard at Dilyara's door. He heard voices, and after a moment the door opened cautiously. He darted through before the woman could shut it.

'Cariad?' he said softly.

'No! Go away!' came her reply.

Dilyara stood holding the door, puzzled. Cariad lay on the heap of blankets in the corner, next to a man who seemed almost dead from exhaustion and hunger. Cariad was clinging to his neck. Dilyara shut the door and came to stand next to the man, protectively. Her own dæmon was sitting by her ankles, trembling.

'Cariad,' whispered the man. 'Don't be frightened, now.'

'Who is this dæmon?' said Dilyara.

'My name is Pan,' he said, keeping his voice as calm and quiet as he could. 'My person is on her way here. Cariad, tell them what I told you last night. I want to know what's inside the red building.'

'Where have you come from?' said the man. His voice was dry and faint.

'Brytain. Oxford. Cariad will tell you. You've been inside the red building, and I want to know what you found there.'

Dilyara sat down on the floor and helped the man to sit up a little. She took his hand and he clung to it tightly.

'Don't go there,' he said. 'It's a terrible place. There's a sickness there, a plague of some kind. Everyone who goes there gets infected. We shall die soon. I came out so I could tell the world about it. But now I think I shall never leave Tashbulak.'

'It wasn't always like that, was it, that other world?' said Pan.

'Didn't know *then*. Just know *now*. It's a different place from anything I . . . Tell your person she must never go there and she must tell this world, here, our world, about the plague. The only safe thing is to stay away.'

'The plague – is it just in the red building, or everywhere?'

'You wouldn't under—'

His voice gave out, and he started to cough, a dry rasping cough that seemed to tear the surface from his lungs. Cariad was weeping. Dilyara brushed the damp hair away from his face.

'Don't strain . . .' Pan said helplessly. He felt there was nothing he could do; the woman's little fox-dæmon was already comforting Cariad. 'But anything you can tell me . . .'

Dilyara said, 'Dr Bryn too tired. You leave him now.'

'How long has Dr . . . Bryn been here? When did he come back?'

'Three days.'

She turned back to Strauss, whose cough had diminished into a shallow scraping breath, and stroked his forehead. His eyes were closed. She murmured something in her own language, and he managed to nod.

Pan said, 'Cariad . . . Can I speak to you?'

The dæmon said, 'Leave us! Go away! It's not good, it's not good at all – you're making everything worse – please just go away!'

'I want to protect my person. She's coming to meet me. If she goes into the red building—'

'Don't let her!'

'What will happen?'

'She will be like Brynmor.'

'So the disease – whatever it is – affects people but not dæmons?'

'Both. Differently, maybe. You think *I'm* not affected?'

'No,' he said, 'no, no – I'm just confused. I'm sorry. I beg your pardon, all of you. I'm just trying to understand. But I'll leave you now.'

Cariad went to Strauss's head and began to stroke his damp hair, glaring at Pan all the time.

Dilyara watched him inscrutably. Then she said. 'You. Dæmon. What your name?'

'Pan.'

'Pan, you come with me. I show you true thing.'

Brynmor nodded faintly. Cariad was as surprised as Pan, but then Dilyara got to her feet. There was a steady kind of dignity in all her movements, and Pan found himself admiring her as he followed out of the room and along a corridor.

She ran a little way, on the balls of her feet, in total silence, listening when she came to a corner. Pan darted after her and, along with Dilyara's fox-daemon, slipped through the door she opened into a room with heavy blinds on all the windows. When she shut the door, they were almost in total darkness.

Dilyara struck a match. This was clearly one of the ruined laboratories, but he could see in the little flame that the benches had been cleared, and some kind of apparatus stood under a sheet. She pulled the sheet off and he leaped up to see better.

'No speak,' she said. 'I show you true thing.'

She removed a tray of some substance from a thickly insulated cupboard, working quickly and silently. She adjusted the position of various stands and sheets of glass and then switched on a small anbaric torch before beckoning him to come close.

He crouched in front of it and saw the little darts of light she'd discovered.

'What are—' he whispered, but she shook her head fiercely.

'Dr Bryn say this cloud chamber. But these little spirits. They come out of space. Now look. Be strong now.'

She reached over to the next bench and picked up something about the length of her thumb, wrapped in a torn curtain. Uncovering it, she showed Pan something that made him shrink back and feel sick: the body of a creature something like a guinea pig. He knew at once it was a dæmon. *A dæmon's body?* How could there be such a thing? It was impossible. But there it was, and she was holding it with care, almost with reverence, he thought; certainly with respect.

He was about to speak, but held his tongue. She placed the dead dæmon next to the cloud chamber, and at once the little sparks, which had been moving in every direction either in straight lines or in smooth curves, suddenly swerved away and careered back across the glass, as if reacting to the dead dæmon with fear or revulsion. New sparks shot into the space and immediately seemed to rebound or even make a conscious choice not to go near that side of the tray.

'What does that mean?' he whispered.

Dilyara moved the dæmon, and little by little, as if cautiously, the sparks resumed their random criss-crossing.

'Whose . . .' Pan said, indicating the dæmon's body.

Dilyara shrugged and wrapped it up again. 'Merchant person. Dr Bryn don' know. Now you go, unnerstan? You leave now.'

Pan said, 'Yes, I will. Thank you. I hope Dr Bryn gets well soon.'

She began to put her apparatus away, and pointed at the corner of the laboratory, saying, 'You go that way. No one see you.'

He found a fallen section of wall behind a cabinet, and slipped out into the corridor. Moving quickly and silently, listening first before turning a corner, Pan crept through the building looking for a way out. He saw no soldiers, but once he found a group of the merchant people blocking his way. They were talking in what he thought was Russian, in a way that made him think they were preparing for a meeting; they carried papers and files and briefcases, and they were standing outside a large double door. As he came close to them he moved more cautiously, but it was like his experience the evening before: no one seemed to see him. And their dæmons were passive, in pockets or on shoulders or at their feet, looking at him with sly eyes before looking away in silence.

One of the merchant people opened the door, and they went in and left the corridor empty. Pan moved on and found a broken wall, and climbed over the smashed bricks and twisted girders into the open air of the morning.

He took several breaths of the desert-scented air. High in the glaring blue sky a gryphon was flying steadily towards the east.

*

In the morning sunlight coming through the open flap of his tent, Marcel Delamare sat at the mahogany campaign chest that had accompanied him all the way from Geneva. It was a handsome piece of furniture that contained, as well as drawers for his clothes, an escritoire whose writing slope was backed by a mirror that acted as a shaving-glass, and various small drawers for pens, or ink, or documents, or cufflinks, or medicines, or money, or eau-de-cologne. It was transported in a packing case that needed two strong men to lift.

Olivier Bonneville stood nearby. He would have been sitting, but the only other chair was occupied by Abdel Ionides. Delamare looked cautious, but otherwise inscrutable; Bonneville looked haggard. He kept shifting his weight from foot to foot.

'And what are you offering?' said Delamare.

'Collaboration,' said Ionides. 'You asked us for this before, if you remember, with my colleagues in Constantinople. We listened, but heard no more from you. Now circumstances have changed, and so might your view of them. If we pool our knowledge and our resources, we shall have a better chance of dealing with this phenomenon.'

'I don't need your knowledge, or your help,' said Delamare, 'and as for resources – all you seem to have is a rabble of semi-savage fighters and some weaponry that is out of date and poorly maintained. What do you mean by this *phenomenon*, anyway? Which phenomenon are you talking about?'

'Dust. The Rusakov particle and its field.'

'Well, you see, we're ahead of you there too. We already understand it, and what we are going to do is destroy it.'

'What do you understand about it?' said Ionides.

Delamare was intrigued by this man: he looked like a beggar, but spoke like a scholar, and his confidence was unshakeable. It was easy enough to believe that he was speaking for the men from the mountains, and only a pity that the woman Pervani had not come instead of him.

'We understand enough,' said Delamare, 'to know more than we once did. We thought the trade might be controlled, but circumstances have developed, and we know now that everything about it must be destroyed, for the safety of humankind .'

'I see,' said Ionides.

'And you, I believe, have similar – shall we say doctrinal misgivings about the matter.'

'You propose to begin, I understand, by blowing up the opening through which the rose trade has been carried on for so many years. And you have a new kind of bomb with which to do it. Correct so far?'

Delamare made no response, audible or visible.

'Correct, then,' said Ionides. 'One might wonder, if that is your sole aim, why you have gathered an entire army and invaded a continent. One might think you had something other in mind than merely closing a hole.'

Delamare was conscious that Olivier Bonneville was still standing nearby, listening to them. The boy's cheeks were red; he was either tired or embarrassed by something, though Delamare could not think what.

'Olivier,' said the President, 'go and wait for General Pollock to finish the report he is writing. Then go to your tent and make a precis of it on one side of a piece of paper and bring that, and the full report, to me.'

Bonneville swallowed hard and left without a word. Delamare turned back to Ionides. 'How do you know that young man?' he said.

'We met near Aleppo. There was a slight misunderstanding, which we solved to our mutual satisfaction. I haven't seen him since. Again, M. Président, may I ask the question: why have you gathered an army large enough to invade another world?'

'For the glory of the Authority. Why do you talk about "another world"?'

'Shall we talk plainly? You know as well as we do that these openings reveal other worlds. You want to close them permanently, because you have – in your phrase – doctrinal misgivings about such things. So far, I can understand you. What I don't understand is taking an army to do what one platoon of soldiers could do in five minutes with a single bomb. The only possible reason for your expedition is to invade the other world through that particular opening. I mean the world, for the sake of completeness and clarity, where the roses come from.'

'How does that concern you?' Delamare asked.

'I have a colleague, Dr Leila Pervani, with whom I conducted research into the roses and the oil extracted from them. We are interested in the roses for reasons of experimental theology, or science, as they are now calling it. We have taken the chance of talking to you frankly, and you will respect that, because our friends the men from the mountains have a different view. They want, for reasons that seem good to them, to close the opening to that world permanently, as you say you do. They are not interested in exploration and discovery, in speculation, in science at all. We are.'

Delamare sat back. Of all the things he might have expected this man to say, this was the last. He watched Ionides with narrowed eyes, but said nothing.

Ionides went on. 'I have come to you, Monsieur Président, with a simple request. My colleague and I want to enter that other world without being prevented by you. That's all. Once we have gone through the opening, we shall stay out of your way and pursue our own interests entirely.'

'But why should I let you do that?'

'Simple,' replied Ionides. 'I can show you the only safe path through the wandering lake of Lop Nor.'

'The wandering lake . . . Do people still believe in that?'

'They do. With good reason. When the Tarim river changes course, the lake changes with it, since the Tarim is its only source. Varying rainfall from season to season, earth movements, irrigation and other human activity – all these things shake the course of the river like a whip. The old lake drains into a new one as new channels are cut by the changing currents. The result is a region of salt flats and marshes, unexpected deep water, invisible and fathomless bogs. Any traveller who tries to cross the lake region had better have a reliable guide. It seems to me, M. Delamare, that by coming this way round the Tien Shan mountains, you have committed your army to a death march. You need a guide.'

Before he was sent away, Olivier Bonneville had noticed a strange expression on Delamare's face. He did something with his eyes; Bonneville had seen it more than once in recent days, and it had appeared as soon as the visitor began talking. Without frowning or raising his eyelids, he seemed to make his eyes larger. The pupils seemed darker, the whites almost glowed. He looked scarcely human, more like a mask or a picture drawn by a clinical specialist to illustrate an extremity of obsessional madness. Bonneville marvelled at how Delamare could look like that and yet remain in control of his smooth and courteous voice. Did he know, and do it on purpose to frighten and dominate? Or did he have no idea what his face was giving away? At any rate, he was looking at his visitor with just that expression.

Ionides was interested to see it, but he remained calm, cool, at ease. A few seconds passed. Delamare looked away; he turned to his desk and shifted through some papers. He picked one up and studied it, before turning back.

Finally he said, 'You have painted a dramatic picture, Professor Xenakis. Oh, yes, I know who you are. Why should I believe that a failed mathematician and would-be expert on the cultivation of roses would be able to guide anyone across dangerous territory? Even with the dangers clearly exaggerated to impress the credulous?'

'We have to take some things on trust in this world,' said Ionides, 'and perhaps in every other. Dr Pervani and I have been through the Lop Nor region several times. I have charts of each journey, and extensive notes on the geomorphology of the changing watercourses. Your alternative to a march guided by us is a journey into constant peril on unstable pathways, laced through by a hundred streams that can change in a moment from a trickle in a dry riverbed to a raging torrent that bursts its banks and carries rocks and trees away with it – all depending on rainfall days before in the mountains a thousand miles behind us. Haven't you heard about the great army of the Cimmerian warrior Skandar, who tried to invade the Golden Empire through Lop Nor? Ten thousand men perished without a blow being exchanged. Or the fifteenth Golden Emperor himself, who led a vast body of soldiers through the region as he tried to annex the whole of Dzungaria, with the same result? No doubt you were told before you entered the Tien Shan mountains of the dangers from the abominable *oghâb-gorgs*, and no doubt you listened, because you had prepared a defence against them. A wise general does listen to advice. Will you not listen now, as we warn you about Lop Nor?'

Delamare's mind was uncomfortably disturbed. His leadership of the High Council had been marked by success after success; his feat of gathering an army and moving it to this wild region, without any significant losses, had made his generals proud and his soldiers confident and eager to conquer; in his own mind, the President was conscious of a calm mastery of events and a deep clarity of purpose. So why was he disturbed? Worse than disturbed: something large, something meteorological in scale, was playing havoc in his head.

Lop Nor was the reason.

He had chosen this route because he was sure it would take them safely to Karamakan and the red building. The account Ionides had given him of the wild variability of the Lop Nor region had woken a number of fears that he had tucked away out of sight, mesmerised by his own successes. Yes, he knew the stories about armies destroyed by the swamps and quicksands, but they were examples of poor generalship. He prided himself on his ability to tell the difference between information and imagination: these stories had the taint of invention about them; he could smell it.

There was only one flaw in the visitor's account, one thing missing from his proposition.

'Why?' he said. 'Why would you help us through Lop Nor? *What* would you gain by it?'

'Access to the red building,' said Ionides simply. 'If we go with you, we shall get there. On our own, we shall not, because you will destroy us.'

'You say "we", and "our". Is your companion nearby?'

Ionides merely smiled.

'So you've formally parted company with the men from the mountains.'

Ionides said, 'But we have told you this: they are committed to destruction, and we are committed to discovery. If, as it seems, you want to conquer rather than merely destroy, there is a small hope that my colleague and I might have a short time to enter the other world and investigate the things we want to know about, without getting in your way. And I hope that you might find our discoveries valuable, or at least interesting.'

'So you accompany me and my army through Lop Nor, in return for our allowing you into the red building to carry on your research without impeding our project?'

'That's correct,' said Ionides.

'And what about coming back?'

'Oh, that we can manage for ourselves.'

A little patch of clarity and stillness appeared in the sandstorm of Delamare's thoughts. He could always kill this man and the woman whenever he needed to, after all. And no one would offer to guide an army into a region where they would face their own deaths.

'I think you could do with some refreshment,' he said. 'We can discuss this further over a glass of Tokay. Will you join me?'

'Very kind,' said Ionides, and Delamare poured a glass of the golden liquid from a decanter in the campaign chest.

They toasted each other's health.

'That young man,' said Ionides, 'your secretary or whatever he is.'

'Olivier Bonneville. You said you'd met him?'

'It was a misunderstanding on both sides. No harm done. How did he come to be in your employment?'

'He was the son of a cousin of mine. She died a widow when he was young, and naturally I took him into my household. I am fond of him. I may say I love him like a son of my own.'

'It does you both credit,' said Ionides. 'He is clever and enterprising. You know he was sheltering in the house of the nuncio at Aleppo?'

Delamare merely looked at him, his eyes a little narrower.

'And you know that Leila Pervani was staying there at the same time?'

Delamare smiled, but with curiosity.

'If you search his property,' Ionides went on, 'you will find a passport belonging to Dr Pervani in his possession. He stole it from her. She told me she was impressed.' He set his wine glass down and stood up. 'Now I must go, my dear Monsieur le Président. I look forward to our joint enterprise.'

He bowed ironically, though it was hard for Delamare to tell, and left. In truth, the President was feeling as though he'd been wound in a cobweb while he wasn't looking, and it wasn't a feeling he was used to.

32

The Pieces Gather on the Board

Among the servants, clerks, secretaries, and emissaries who helped Mustafa Bey control his multifarious enterprises was a young woman called Tamar Sharadze. She was a graduate of the University of Tblisi, a statistician and expert on complex systems, and Mustafa Bey had admired and profited by her clarity of thought and singleness of purpose. Her dæmon was a small butterfly of intense blue, who spoke little. In the turmoil that followed the assassination, she was the best-placed person to make sense of the confusion, and showed a determination and authority no one had seen in her before. She made decisions and gave orders as if the great man himself were speaking through her. She saw without having to think about it where the most urgent matters were occurring, and how to deal with them; and before a week had passed, she might as well have been Mustafa Bey himself, reincarnated and purposeful.

Securing the safety of the roads was what preoccupied her most to begin with. She had travelled herself, as far as Tangier to the west and Kyoto to the east, and her powerful memory as well as her efficient manner had ensured that the assassination had provoked less disturbance and anxiety than anyone expected among the agents, the dealers, the brokers, and the carriers who together made up the Mustafa Bey trading empire. A week's alarm, and then calm descended again.

She made sure that the assassin's background was thoroughly investigated, and any associates found and arrested. She contacted the representatives of the Magisterium, including some who had refused all dealings with Mustafa Bey, and made sure they knew that a new management was in charge now; and found out all that could be known about the progress of the army under Marcel Delamare.

She had been closely watching some changes that had failed to attract the attention of Mustafa Bey, in particular the road- and rail-building and the other transport developments in the western provinces of the Golden Empire. Her late chief had taken a strong interest in his own new bus routes west of the Caspian Sea, but had overlooked, she thought, the great prizes to be won in Central Asia for whoever found the best solution to the problems of desert travel in the modern age.

She also gave considerable thought to the question of what sort of organisation she was in charge of. Under Mustafa Bey it had a thousand different faces and ten thousand different interests in a hundred thousand different towns and villages and caravanserais, with a thousand thousand small deals being made every day. It was beyond the capacity of a single human memory to take in, even that of Dr Sharadze, and it had only worked because Mustafa Bey, by some perhaps supernatural means, transfused through every branch of this complex tree the life-giving sap of trust associated with his name. Dr Sharadze realised that she could not supply that precious liquid herself, so she would have to act very quickly to replace it with something else: a structure that was not only immensely robust, but above all, with a line of authority that was easy to understand at any point, and with the means to enforce it. And that would involve a profound reformation of the medium of exchange.

So the Mustafa Bey Company came into legally attested being, with as its brand-mark a picture of the late chief, drawn 457 times before the artist got the proper balance of wisdom, kindness, shrewdness, decisiveness, and visionary optimism into the image, which was to be reproduced on every document and piece of packaging the company generated.

Dr Sharadze also set about modernising the communications inside the company. Marletto's Café was all very well in an age of camel-paced transport and personal interaction, but times were changing. Soon a splendid new building was being planned, one that would unfortunately require the construction of a wide new circulatory traffic system and the demolition of the block containing Marletto's. Dr Sharadze became intensely interested in this scheme, in its size and scope, and she made arrangements to visit other urban centres on both sides of the Caspian Sea, where she wanted to speak to architects, engineers, and geologists about their plans for developing what she was already calling the Mustafa Bey Freeway. It was while she was examining some drawings for this and other projects, in the new office in Samarkand, that Dr Sharadze was interrupted by a visitor.

'Thank you,' she said to the architect. 'I shall be in touch very soon.'

The man gathered his papers and left.

Tamar Sharadze turned to the visitor. 'Pervani? Leila Pervani? How do you do. You'll realise that our dear late chairman had an immense capacity for detail; you'll forgive me for not yet being on top of it all. Your business concerns what, in fact?'

'I was Mustafa Bey's agent in Sinkiang,' said Leila. 'I sent him regular reports about the progress of different enterprises between Urumqi and the Aral Sea. I heard, of course, about the awful murder, and I wanted to express my condolences as well as make sure that his successors were fully informed about conditions west of the Golden Empire . . . I was so sorry to hear about his death.'

Tamar Sharadze had seldom been in the presence of someone quite so much more beautiful than she was. She watched impassively as Leila Pervani artlessly dabbed her eyes, she noticed how Leila glanced at the royal blue butterfly dæmon on her lapel, and she waited for the visitor to compose herself.

'I'm extremely busy,' she said finally, without any tone of regret. 'Thank you for your sympathy. I'm sure you understand. Did you have a particular message for Mustafa Bey?'

'I thought it would interest him to know that the army of the Magisterium, under the command of the President Marcel Delamare, has advanced to the eastern end of the Tien Shan range.'

'So far, already?'

'It seems as if they intend to cross Lop Nor on their progress to the south.'

Tamar Sharadze narrowed her eyes and nodded. She said nothing.

Leila Pervani went on. 'The way is clear now, you understand, for the Karamakan project to go ahead.'

'You spoke to Mustafa Bey about this?'

'Oh, yes. It was something he was particularly keen on promoting.'

'He discussed it with you?'

'At length. You'll understand, I don't know who you are, exactly, and how much I need to explain . . .'

'Of course. I was Mustafa Bey's chief of staff in Aleppo and further west. Now I am acting Chief Executive Officer. Whatever you have been used to saying to him, you may safely say to me.'

All Tamar Sharadze in fact knew about Karamakan was that Mustafa Bey had some small dealings with suppliers in that region. She knew nothing about a 'project'. But she had studied with experts the art of extracting information, and this Pervani was clearly emotionally affected by the events of the past days.

'The Thuringia Potash Company is deeply involved,' the visitor began. 'As you know, they're no longer exclusively concerned with mining . . .'

Tamar Sharadze reached for a pencil. The office they were sitting in was rented, and she didn't know where everything was, but she could find a pencil and paper. She wrote as Leila Pervani continued to explain, and a long, complicated, intriguing story began to unfold: rich with possibility, laced through and through with the implication of inexhaustible profit, studded with gem-like particles of recognisable likelihood, and fictitious in every sentence. Soon Tamar Sharadze sent for some more paper.

'Oh, and one more thing,' said Leila Pervani as she got up to leave.

'Yes?'

'I wondered where these came from.' She laid a freshly printed banknote on the desk.

'Where did you get that?' said Tamar Sharadze, as if interested. She turned it over. It was for a small denomination, and the picture of Mustafa Bey, as recently approved for use throughout his business, was prominent amid the decorative and calligraphic flourishes.

'I was given it among the change when I bought some shoes. It's new, isn't it? I hadn't seen one like it before.'

Tamar Sharadze nodded and pushed the note back across the desk. She said, 'We felt that the system of exchange used across Mustafa Bey's wide range of businesses could be simplified and standardised, as it were. A thousand different transactions made by barter every day – increasingly difficult to keep track, no standard rate of exchange – it simply doesn't work these days. When Mustafa Bey himself was in charge, things were different, of course. But now the world is moving in a modern direction, and money must move with it.'

'And all so swiftly done.'

'It had been felt for some time that a project of this kind would be necessary. Preparations were in place already before Mustafa Bey's unfortunate death.'

'I understand,' said Leila Pervani, folding the note into her purse. 'So I expect I'll see many more of these.'

'I hope you will.'

Tamar Sharadze's smile was final and dismissive. During the whole of their interview, Leila Pervani's serpent-dæmon had been watching the small sapphire-coloured butterfly on the lapel of Sharadze's midnight-blue jacket, and was interested to see that he did not move a millimetre.

Olivier Bonneville was not used to horses; he had been taught to ride during his military service, but hadn't taken to it. The horse he stole from the camp above Tashbulak, however, was docile and willing, and he remembered enough about harnessing it to get the saddle on the right way and loosen and tighten the right straps. With his wounded dæmon safely inside his coat, he mounted, after three attempts, and urged the horse to move forward and out on to the grassy slopes of the foothills.

The bulk of the army was some way off to the east, under the command of one of Delamare's senior officers, and guided by Abdel Ionides. Delamare remained with a small body of guards and engineers, led by Colonel Schreiber; they would move straight towards the red building once they had a signal that Lop Nor had been successfully crossed.

So no one saw Olivier Bonneville set off on his stolen horse. No one, that is, except Pantalaimon, together with Dilyara and her dæmon. They had gathered on the roof of the storage area, around the canvas chair from which Dilyara had seen Brynmor Strauss emerge from the desert some days before. Strauss was asleep down below, with Cariad close at hand; Dilyara wasn't sure if they'd ever wake up. Pan had come to like her very much, for her quick intelligence and solid kindness, and he joined her on the roof to watch the sunrise, and just to talk.

He was telling her about Lyra and his search. She listened carefully, asking only occasionally if she didn't understand. He found himself imitating the way Lyra would explain something, getting things in the best order, leaving out everything irrelevant.

She was watching him as he stood on the rim of a skylight, but after a few minutes he noticed a very slight movement on the horizon behind her. It was so small and so far away that at first he didn't think anything of it, but then he found himself trying to focus on it, and losing concentration on his story.

'Dilyara, can you see something moving over there? On the horizon?'

She turned, shading her eyes against the rising sun. 'Little thing,' she said. She reached down for the binoculars she kept under the chair. 'Ah,' she said. 'Horse. I think it was camel but no, it is horse. Young man riding.'

She held the binoculars for Pan to look through. He put his face close to one of the eye-pieces and tried, but the focus wasn't right, and then he lost his balance on the skylight, and then they tried again, this time with Pan standing on the wooden arm of her chair; and finally the image swam into clarity.

'Bonneville!' he said, startling himself.

'What you say?'

'I know him. He's the man who's hunting Lyra! He must be going towards the red building – the place Dr Strauss came back from . . . I can't let him get too far ahead. Dilyara, I've got to follow him. Thank you – thank you for everything—'

'You going now?'

'Yes. I must go after him.'

'I want to hear the end of story.'

'When I come back. Promise. I swear. Thank you! But I've got to go after him . . .'

He ran to the edge of the roof, checked again that the little silhouette was still there on the horizon, and leaped down and scrambled after it over the sand.

*

Lyra lay awake, wrapped in Malcolm's coat. He murmured occasionally in his sleep: names mostly, including hers, but nothing coherent. Gulya's tireless flight lulled them both at first, but Lyra hadn't slept for long. She was wide awake, and her eyes were wide too, gazing past Malcolm out to the gryphon's wing, steadily beating, and past that to the stars beyond.

Her heart was yearning as never before – yearning for Pan, for that lost rebellious part of her, that woodland-smelling self who'd set off in anger to find the priceless thing she'd lost so carelessly. She was also yearning for something simpler: for human contact. She was pressed close against Malcolm, but he was asleep, and anyway . . . Would that ever work? Oh, it was too hard to think about.

She made herself think of other things. The Rusakov field, and how it related to Dust, or if it *was* Dust. The rose oil made Dust visible, but only rose oil from the other world would do. No doubt something in its chemical composition resembled the wheel-tree oil that Mary Malone used in her amber spyglass; perhaps there was something in every world that had a similar property. She remembered the moment in the Jordan College retiring room when Lord Asriel, telling the scholars about the special emulsion he'd used (which of course, she saw now, must have been based on the rose oil) to make the lantern slides he was showing them, and saying of the picture on the screen 'But it isn't light – it's Dust', and the sudden silence that fell. She thought of herself now, explaining to him everything they'd found out since, and where she was going, on the back of a gryphon, and she thought of his eyes when he smiled, as he did so rarely – but he would smile now, he'd smile at her now.

Or rather than the field making the Dust visible . . . suppose it was the other way round. Maybe it was Dust that made the field visible. Could it work like that? Maybe Ionides would know. She hoped very much that he was safe, that he was nearby, that he and Leila Pervani could continue their work . . . She thought of them together, a duet so ill-sorted and so perfectly harmonious. Working together at something important; Lyra thought now that that must be the most perfect endeavour for two individuals. She felt a kind of gratitude to them, for showing her that possibility.

The stars were fading. From somewhere to her left a faint light was diffusing into the sky. It brought cold with it, as if she hadn't been cold enough already. She pulled Malcolm's coat more tightly around her, and he stirred.

'Sorry,' she murmured. 'Didn't mean to wake you.'

'Not asleep.'

'Yes you were! You were snoring.'

'I don't snore. It was Asta purring.'

'You snore,' said Asta sleepily.

'All right, I give in. Why did you wake me up?'

'I want to know about the alkahest.'

'The what?'

He sat up, startling her, but it was only to stretch and yawn.

'The alkahest. Something to do with alchemy,' she said.

'Why are you asking about that? Where did you hear the term before?'

'In the dead city. Why do you ask?'

'The Director of Oakley Street referred to it on the lodestone resonator. Who spoke about it in the dead city?'

'I heard some voices . . . They sounded as if they were warning me. *The alkahest, the destroyer of bonds* . . . But I couldn't hear any more, and I've been asking people if they know about it, and no one does except a French teacher in Baku, who looked it up in his encyclopaedia. The universal solvent, apparently.'

'H'mm . . . A universal solvent. Impossible.'

'Why?'

'Well, what would you put it in?'

'A . . . I don't know. A crucible, whatever that is. An alembic? One of those round flasks with a long spout pointing down.'

540

'A retort. But that wouldn't work, you see. Nothing would work. If it dissolves everything, nothing could contain it. Here's a jar of alkahest – oh dear, it's gone. And now there's a hole in the floor. The alkahest in a jar is a paradox. Like a square circle.'

'*The destroyer of bonds . . .*'

'They said that too, did they?'

'Yes, they did. The French teacher thought it might mean atomic bonds. The forces that hold them together.'

'It *would* be a universal solvent, if it could do that,' Malcolm said. 'Did the other things your voices said make sense?'

'Yes. I think I could trust them. As if they came from the secret commonwealth.'

'And they were—' Malcolm pulled himself up a little. 'They were warning you?'

'A mixture of things. Warnings, and . . . I can't remember them all.'

'Who first told you about the secret commonwealth?'

'A gyptian man who helped me to get to the Fens when I first set off after Pan. I told Asta about it. It's a way of seeing things, really.'

'I want to know more about it.'

'Mr Ionides had the idea that it could be a field.'

'Ah. Yes, I see. That's good.'

'Like the Rusakov field. It might *be* the Rusakov field.'

'What's Dust, then?' he said. 'How are they connected? Or are they the same thing?'

He wasn't testing her on her knowledge: it was a genuine question, asked by someone who genuinely wanted to know.

'It's . . . I don't know. It's the Rusakov particle, isn't it? The particle associated with the field? Somehow?'

'What does that *mean*, though? What's happening when we see it? What's physically going on?'

'Maybe Dust has to be there because . . . Maybe like with a rainbow, the atmosphere has to be saturated with water vapour, doesn't it? We don't see rainbows on dry days. Maybe we can't see this without Dust.'

The first tiny part of the sun's disc emerged from behind a mountaintop. It was like a trumpet call; the whole sky seemed to ring with it, and the world was still waiting for an answer to a question neither Lyra nor Malcolm had quite articulated, which hung like an overtone in the intense azure.

'Anyway, it wasn't actually Rusakov who discovered it,' Malcolm said.

'Really?'

'He wasn't a genuine scientist – he was a lackey for the Muscovite government. It was discovered by a colleague of his, and Rusakov claimed the credit.'

'Cheat! Then he shouldn't have a field named after him. It should be called the Rose Field.'

'All right, the Rose Field it is. From now on.'

'But we still need to know about Dust.'

'What did your Ionides say about it?'

She shifted her position and sat up. 'He's not *my* Ionides. He's a scholar as well as a servant and a vagabond. He'll have his own answer . . . I can't guess what it would be, but it would clarify things a bit. Like he did with the *field* idea for the secret commonwealth.'

'Come to think of it . . . He did tell me something. Under an orange tree in Aleppo. He said the Rusakov field was . . . How did he put it? Associated with consciousness. We'll ask him to tell us more, if we ever see him again.'

'Oh, we'll see him again. He's immortal.'

Malcolm ran his hand through his hair. The sunlight lay across his face, and lit up the golden bristles on his chin and cheeks.

'D'you want a bit more coat?' Lyra said.

'No, I'm fine, thanks.'

His eyelashes were golden too, she noticed. He turned his face away from the blazing sun, and saw her watching him, and smiled.

'Lyra,' he said, 'why did Pan say he was going to look for your imagination, d'you think? Why was it that in particular that was missing?'

'Perhaps he was right. Perhaps I had lost it. I was reading a couple of books that he hated . . . They both disparaged it in different ways.'

'Simon Talbot? *The Something Pretender*?'

'*The Constant Deceiver.* Yes, he was one. He made me feel sick, as if there was nothing solid underfoot.'

'And you say that, while flying through the air on the back of a gryphon!'

'I know. I can't think what he'd make of this. He'd have to deny his own senses. The other book was by Gottfried Brande.'

'*The Hyperchorasmians.* I couldn't read it.'

'*The Hypercolonics*, as Pan called it.' She smiled. 'He was right about those books, and I just didn't listen to him. They were both . . . iniquitous.'

She looked down. She was sitting cross-legged, with her hands entwined in her lap. She opened them and looked at her left hand, the palm and the back, still swollen, still bruised, and then at her right. That was just grubby. She put them together again.

'I wonder what he thinks now,' said Malcolm.

'Pan? I'm not sure,' she said. 'But it must have something to do with those openings. Maybe the imagination is a sort of wind that blows through all the worlds.'

Malcolm looked out to left and right. 'It's a good image,' he said.

'It sometimes feels like that. As if it's true. It shows us true things.'

Lyra looked at her hands again. There was something she wanted to say, and it would only come if she tried hard and honestly to find it.

'We haven't been in the same place, me and you, with enough time, before now,' she said after a moment. 'There's so much

I haven't told you. These openings . . . For me they have a complicated meaning. I've seen them being opened. You had to cut them with a special knife. I met a boy from another world, a boy called Will, and he and I found ourselves in the city where the subtle knife was made. He had to fight someone who'd stolen it . . . He didn't want to; the whole story is too long to tell, even here, even now. But he had to, and he became the knife-bearer, and the old man who had been a previous knife-bearer told him how to cut through the air and open another world, and how to close it again. So in order to escape from danger we did that, and I've been in I don't know how many different worlds, all right here, as close as this' – and she swept her hand through the air, like Serafina Pekkala's goose-dæmon sweeping his wing to illustrate the same thing ten years before – 'and we can't reach them except with the subtle knife.'

'Where's the knife now?'

'With Will, in his own world. Unreachable. But we were warned by an angel, when it was all nearly over, that it was dangerous to open other worlds, because bad things came out of the gaps between one world and another. She said we had to close all the windows we knew about and any others we found, and live only in our own worlds, because we could only be strong and healthy in our own worlds. We had to be content where we were. We couldn't travel to other worlds, except in our imagination. We didn't know what she meant by that, but we believed everything she said, and went back to our own worlds, and . . . Years went by. And then a few months ago Pan and I quarrelled and that made him think my imagination had left me, or I'd lost it, or something. So he went to look for it. And I was left to wonder whether he was right, or whether he was mistaken, and what the imagination was anyway, and what the angel had meant . . . And that's why I set off to follow him, wherever he went.'

Malcolm was silent, sitting still, listening closely.

'And just a few nights ago,' she went on, 'on the ferry from Baku, I saw an angel again. I thought she was the same one as before, till she spoke. And I asked her what she thought the imagination meant, and the answer she gave showed me that she knew nothing about it either, nothing at all.'

'What did she say?' said Malcolm.

'She said that the imagination was just our minds making things up, bits of fantasy jumbled together, like a dream. But she was wrong. You see, angels . . . They don't know what dreams are. They don't make poetry or art. They don't *play*. What Pan said, the thing he said I'd lost – he was right. It's something *fundamental*. And I *had* lost it. So on that ferry from Baku I saw a bit more about what it was. It's not something to do with good and evil, or good and bad, either. Angels might be good, and the Magisterium might do evil things, but they're both wrong about this. Just . . . *wrong*. Like in the Arctic, when Pan and I saw that Dust must be good in spite of everyone saying it was bad. Here it was again, the same idea in a different form. It's a sort of . . .' She clenched her hands, trying to find the right words. 'They think that things can only be true or not true. But what you learn when you play, or tell stories, or in a dream, is that things can be both true and not true.'

'If it's not X, it's got to be Y?' said Malcolm. 'If you're not with us, you're against us.'

'Yes, just like that. There's no room for any other answer.'

'It's a sort of binary absolutism.'

'Exactly. But some things are both X *and* Y. Or like when someone says "Art is nothing more than pretty patterns." But the truth is that it's pretty patterns *as well as* lots of other things. And what that means . . . Well, what it means is that we must keep the windows open. Dust, or rose oil, or the imagination, or the Rose Field, or whatever we call it – we *need* it.'

'Good so far. Go on.'

'Well . . .' She felt unsure, and also that she was trembling on the edge of a discovery. 'I think the Rose Field, the truth about things, isn't just *out there*, it's *in here* as well. And the imagination isn't just *in here*, it's *out there* too . . . The Rose Field needs what we have as much as we need what it has. What matters is that it must be free to flow through all the worlds. There was something Asta said once – incompleteness or something . . . A theorem . . . Someone's theorem. In any system, there are things you know are true, but you can't prove that they are if you only use arguments from inside the system. Something like that.'

'Gödel's theorem. How does that fit in?'

'Well if that's true, then it means that if you find a system that seems perfect and complete, where you *can* prove everything – then you're wrong. You're not looking properly. Because we *need* the gaps, you see? We need the holes where one world opens up to another. A system isn't complete unless there's a hole in it. We need the things we can't explain, things we can't prove, or else we die of suffocation. The secret commonwealth. The Rose Field. They're *necessary*, and so are all the windows and doors and openings, to let the wind blow through all the worlds . . . I can see it at last, Malcolm, I can see what it all means. That's why all the authorities want to block up the openings, and that's why we must fight to the death to stop them.'

'I think I always believed that,' he said. 'I hadn't thought of it like that though. I just felt it was true.'

'Were you ever troubled about it? About that sort of thing?'

'No. About that sort of thing, as you put it, I never had any doubts. You're much more complicated than I am, Lyra. I'm lucky to be plain and straightforward. When I see how much it troubles people, I mean when they feel that something's wrong with the world they live in – I feel sorry for them, but I can't do much to help. I had a friend when I was an undergraduate who worried himself to death, literally; he killed himself. He was tormented by the question of whether he was real, and where his responsibility lay if he was unreal, and why he felt responsible if the world was empty of meaning, and what he could do about it . . . His dæmon stopped talking and just lay down, and then he did the same, and within a week he was dead. I felt so sorry for him, but I couldn't understand anything about it. I was simple, and he was complicated, and I saw that that was a fundamental difference between us. I accepted the world as it was, and he didn't. He was unhappy and I was happy.'

After a few moments she said, 'Are you still happy?'

'Yes. If that means do I feel at home in the world, then yes, I do, and I am happy.'

'I am too sometimes. And you're not simple at all. You can't be an artificer from the realms of gold if you're simple.'

Lyra's mind was full of that edge-of-possibility feeling. There was *something* that lay just out of sight, and the prospect of it thrilled her . . . No, nothing so definite as a prospect. You could *see* prospects, but she felt this with a different sense: she felt it tremor like a mirage with delight.

She lay back and covered her eyes with the sleeve of Malcolm's coat, holding the thought close to her like a happy dream. The gryphon flew on towards the east.

Pan could tell, even from a distance, that Olivier Bonneville was no great horseman. In fact, it looked as though he would very much rather get off and walk. It didn't take long for Pan to find him, even with the disadvantage of having to look through the grass, but there were occasional shrubs of juniper or tamarisk he could climb up and spy from, and the ground wasn't completely flat. He followed throughout the day, stopping whenever Bonneville did and being careful not to doze off and lose him.

Despite his uncertain progress (stopping to adjust the saddle or to tighten the girth or to sit down and rest or to fill his water bottle or to look at one of the horse's hooves or to look slowly all around the horizon) it was obvious that Bonneville had a clear idea of where he was going. Late in the afternoon he stopped again, and this time he looked intently in one direction ahead of him, persuading the horse to stand still, rising up uncertainly in the stirrups to see a little further through some binoculars, and unfolding a map to peer at it closely.

Pan watched from a small willow a couple of hundred yards behind him as the sun was going down, and saw the boy dismount stiffly before stretching and bending and then taking off the saddle and hitching the horse to a broken tree. His dæmon, the hawk with the broken wing, was still clutching the saddle; Bonneville lifted her off and settled her tenderly on the tree.

There must have been a stream or a pond nearby. Bonneville loosened the rein and the horse bent to drink. Was he going to camp for the night? It was getting dark quickly; so yes, he was. Pan moved down from his willow and padded silently through the grass till he was near enough to hear the conversation between Bonneville and the dæmon.

At first he thought they were speaking a language he didn't know at all, but as he lay still he began to recognise a word here, a phrase there, and almost make sense of complete sentences now and then. It seemed to be a dialect of Italian, and then he thought it was mainly German, and then possibly a little French. However, what they said wasn't very interesting; Bonneville mainly seemed to be grumbling, and the dæmon seemed to be agreeing.

Bonneville broke a branch off the tree and gathered a few sticks to make a fire, but without much success at first. He got through a lot of matches before it caught properly, and by that time the flames provided the only light, because the sun was fully set. Pan watched as he carried the dæmon to a lower branch and settled himself down to cook a piece of meat. The fire wasn't hot enough, and the meat kept falling off his stick and into the ash. Pan remembered the deft and effortless way Tilda Vasara had cooked that rabbit in the mountains, and felt almost sorry for this urban boy, so clumsy and helpless; but he couldn't help being impressed by his determination.

He waited till Bonneville and his dæmon were asleep. Then with great care he moved towards the dead tree and climbed up towards the dæmon, testing each claw-hold before putting his weight on it, making no noise at all.

He made his way very slowly along the branch, and stopped when he came close enough to reach out and touch her.

'Dæmon,' he whispered. 'Dæmon of Olivier Bonneville.'

He'd done this before. It was sometimes possible to wake someone gently by waking their dæmon, but that wasn't his intention now.

'Dæmon, what is your name?' he whispered.

'Arethusa,' she murmured, still asleep.

'Arethusa, I don't want to wake Olivier. I just want to talk to you. Don't wake him up.'

'No.' Her voice was low and tender.

Pan went on: 'What does he want?'

'He wants his father.'

Pan was startled, but only for a moment. 'His father the physicist?'

She stirred a little, but said nothing.

'And what does he want with Lyra?' said Pan.

'Sister.'

That shook Pan even more.

'Arethusa, I don't know what you mean. Is Lyra his sister?'

'Yes. Half-sister. Same mother.'

'Mrs Coulter was *his mother*?'

'Of course.'

'Does he . . . Has he, have you always known that?'

'No. He realised it only recently. It shocked him to realise that Marcel Delamare was his uncle.'

'Marcel Delamare . . .'

'The President of the High Council of the Magisterium. Olivier's mother was Delamare's sister.'

Pan trembled. The connection with Lyra fired his curiosity. 'So if Lyra's his sister, Delamare is her uncle too,' he said.

'Yes.'

Pan was taken aback. 'I don't think she knows it,' he said slowly.

'Delamare does.'

'And what does *he* want?'

'To capture her for her grandmother to play with.'

That made Pan feel chilled at once, colder than he'd ever felt flying through the night sky. 'Mrs Coulter's mother is still alive?'

'Only her malice keeps her alive. Death is afraid to come near her.' The hawk-dæmon shifted on her perch. Olivier Bonneville turned over in his sleeping bag.

'Don't wake up,' Pan whispered.

Bonneville murmured something that might have been a name.

Pan said quietly, 'Does he know what happened to his father?'

'Undone by Delamare. Framed. All lies. So many lies.'

Well, Pan thought, *what did that mean?* But both boy and dæmon were restive now; it was time to leave. Without another word he turned away and climbed silently down into the grass again, and set off in the direction he remembered Bonneville heading, towards the red building. His mind was racing.

The witch Tilda Vasara flew on a long loop to the east. She was interested in the progress of the army Delamare had sent that way, knowing the unpredictable ways of the wandering lake. The only safe way to cross Lop Nor was through the air above it, and surely they knew that?

But evidently they didn't. With the valour of fanaticism and the armour of righteousness, the soldiers of the Authority forced their way forwards into the marshes, into the innumerable torrents and the new waterways and the old riverbeds, the mires and the quicksands.

Tilda Vasara flew above, watching it all with sorrow. Some of these men were brave and handsome, some of them were foolish or cowardly; some hoped for salvation, some hoped only for treasure; some were kindly and some were corrupt, but the lakes and the fens and the shades of death gave every one of them the same welcome. And the witch saw it all, with wonderment and pity.

33

INTO THE RED BUILDING

The diary of Roderick Hassall, which Lyra had read so long ago, it seemed to her now, had spoken of a bare sandy desert which he and Brynmor Strauss had had to cross to reach the red building. And Gulya had flown above long stretches of sand, it was true, but as they flew on it seemed that the empty desert was losing ground to vegetation. When Lyra woke up in the very early morning, what lay below them was more like a forest.

Among the green-grey treetops that stretched ahead in the early light as far as they could see, Lyra made out a single spot of red. She pointed it out to Malcolm, and over the next few minutes they watched it resolve from a point of scarlet light in the glow of the rising sun to a roof of red tiles with turned-up eaves in the Chinese manner over a long rectangular building of brick, with a row of small windows under the eaves, but no windows at ground level. As Gulya flew around above, looking for somewhere to land, they saw a clear space at one end of the building, where a flagstoned floor surrounded a flight of seven wide steps up to a portico.

Two guards, soldiers in simple uniforms of dark red cotton, stood in front of the portico, blocking the way to the door behind the massive red-painted wooden columns. They carried spears. They looked up as Gulya flew above them, and watched with subdued alarm as she landed and Lyra and Malcolm stepped down off her back.

'This is where Strauss had to speak Latin, isn't it?' said Malcolm.

Lyra watched. The guards didn't move. They held their spears pointing forward, and stood with one foot ahead of the other, as still as the columns behind them, as if this was something they had long trained for.

Malcolm stretched to loosen his limbs, and Lyra did the same, finding it strange to feel firm ground underfoot. Malcolm asked Gulya to pass on a message of gratitude to Queen Shahrnavāz, saying that never had an artificer from the realms of gold worked for a wiser or more generous sovereign. Lyra thanked her too, and Gulya would have said several things in return, but her friendship had been first and always with Pan, and she was clearly anxious about him; and besides, she needed to be going back to Prince Keshvād and her people. So their farewells were heartfelt, but brief.

Lyra and Malcolm shaded their eyes to watch the gryphon fly up and away, and then turned back to the guards. They hadn't moved an inch.

All the time Lyra was conscious of the immense bulk of the red building. She didn't have to look at it directly; it pervaded her vision even when she looked away from it, because the sun just rising struck the bricks and tiles like a gong and brought out their deep and sonorous crimson to colour the air all around. The sky was clear; it was going to be a hot day, in this world at least.

'Well,' Malcolm said, 'let's try.'

Together they climbed the seven steps till they were on a level with the guards, who kept the spears pointing at them. The soldiers looked more Persian than Chinese: Lyra remembered Strauss saying something like that in his journal. She saw, too, that if they had dæmons, they were well hidden; and that they seemed healthy and fit, though their faces were lined and their eyes were tired. Their uniforms were old and worn at the seams.

'May we enter this building?' she said in English, slowly and clearly.

They looked at her and said nothing.

Then the taller guard said, '*Akterrakeh.*'

Malcolm turned to Lyra. She realised that she hadn't told him her discovery of what it meant, and said, 'They're asking if we came by water and by land. Because . . . I'll tell you why later.'

'*Akterrakeh* – Oh, I see. *Aqua terraque.* Latin it is.' He thought for a moment, his eyes half closed, and then said to the guards, '*Neque per aquam, neque per terram, sed per alas.*'

Lyra looked at him and raised her eyebrows, and he murmured, 'Not by water nor by land, but by wings.'

The guards were nonplussed: this man was clearly speaking the truth, because they had seen the gryphon land and fly away again; but how could they reconcile that with the clear instructions they were bound to obey?

Lyra wanted to say more, but she sensed Malcolm's silent confidence and said nothing. After a minute's urgent discussion, the tall guard raised his spear vertically and stood aside. The other guard did the same, leaving the way clear to the door.

Malcolm nodded his head and put his hand to his breast in a gesture he hoped would convey respect and thanks. Lyra remembered from the diary that the guards Hassall and Strauss had faced had asked for money, but these two, she thought, looked too weary to make any further challenge. Their responsibility weighed heavily on them; they looked like the last soldiers left to guard a civilisation, their uniforms thin and ragged in places, but clean and pressed; and she found herself admiring them if only for that.

The door was heavy, but it opened easily, swinging silently on oiled hinges. The sunlight fell through on to the wooden floor.

Lyra went in first, with Asta at her heels and Malcolm following. Her first impression was of the enormous size of the place. They had seen that from outside, of course, but whereas from outside they could only see part of the whole building, inside they could see all of it. It was one great hall, and its proportions were somehow perfect; if the ceiling were any higher, or the breadth of the place any less, it would have felt uncomfortable. Lyra had no idea why, but she was certain of it.

The floor was made of oak boards, worn and a little bowed in places, but it felt solid to walk on. The only light in the space came through the door behind them, and from the row of windows high up in the walls – too high for them to see anything outside but the sky. The sunlight lay in bright parallelograms on the floor and made the swirling particles of dust in the beams glow like specks of gold. But it was what lay all around that made Lyra and Malcolm gasp and clutch each other's hand in wonder.

Every inch of the walls from end to end and from floor to ceiling was covered with an immense picture of a landscape.

It surrounded them completely. The door they'd come in through was at one end of the building, and a long way off at the other end there was another door, and both had a plaster surround that made them look like part of a classical painting. The door ahead was depicted as if it stood in a small marble folly, a temple or belvedere perhaps, in some immense garden where lawns ran down past it to a broad lake in the distance, and the one they'd just come through seemed to be the entrance to a grotto, among rough massive rocks overhung with ferns and mosses.

'I've never seen anything like this, anywhere,' Lyra said quietly. 'Have you?'

Malcolm shook his head. He seemed to be struck silent, and stood gazing all around, slowly, attentively, taking it all in.

'I can't find the words,' Malcolm said after a minute. 'It's just overwhelming. Whoever painted this has seen pictures from everywhere – seventeenth-century France, eighteenth-century England, ancient Rome, ancient Greece . . .'

'Cathay too – see the pagoda over there?'

'And the New Danish transcendentalists – look at those cliffs over the river . . .'

'That little bridge is pure Nipponese. Isn't it? And the lady with her umbrella in the puff of wind . . .'

'And her dæmon snapping at a butterfly.'

As well as the scenes that reminded them of their own world, there were buildings and landscapes that were unfamiliar. But every part of the picture showed human activity in one form or another: men and women were walking to and fro, carrying parasols to keep the sun at bay or working in gardens where roses grew, watering the beds or gathering the blooms or planting new bushes, or unloading carts full of the flower heads into a barge drawn up at the shore of the lake. Wherever they looked, some productive or enjoyable human activity was being carried on. Here some musicians were playing to an audience seated on a lawn, there some carpenters were putting up the framework of a graceful little temple under the direction of an architect consulting a paper in his hand, somewhere else children were dancing in a ring, in another corner gardeners were tending to espaliered orange trees against a brick wall.

Lyra and Malcolm wandered from place to place, taking in only a fraction of the hundreds of details, marvelling at the harmony of the whole panorama, moved by the vision of happiness and prosperity embodied in wood and plaster and paint.

Lyra felt her breath catch in her chest. Something – one of the scenes – reminded her powerfully of something, and she saw that Asta was looking at it too.

Suddenly Asta said, 'That's a scene from the Myriorama – look! That girl reading a book with her fingers – and here's another one – the people loading the carts with roses!'

'Yes! So it is! And there's another – the little café at night . . . They're probably all here, if we looked. I just can't believe it.'

Malcolm saw a corner of the wall that looked as if it was

556

illustrating the poem of Jahan and Rukhsana: two lovers hand in hand entering a garden.

'Is it a picture of the rose world, d'you think?' he said. 'Of what's outside here, I mean?'

'We'll see in a minute. Oh, Malcolm, it's lovely . . .'

'And they have dæmons in that world,' said Asta.

And Lyra could see the dæmons everywhere, helping with the work, talking to their people, playing with children.

Then Malcolm pointed out something that Lyra hadn't noticed. In the corner least lit by the light from the high windows, chairs and tables had been neatly stacked. Going over to look more closely, Malcolm the artificer was intrigued by the design of the chairs, which folded by means of a joint he'd never seen before so as to take up little room. He picked one chair up and moved it this way and that, delighted by the cleverness of the craftsmanship and determined to make something like it himself if ever he returned to his own bench and his own tools.

'Oh, and look!' said Lyra. 'This is what the tables and chairs are for!'

And there, above the stacked furniture, the painting showed a view of the very interior they were standing in. The tables and chairs had all been laid out, and a hundred or more figures were sitting, or standing, or moving from one place to another, and two or three or four people were sitting around each table, and . . .

'Bargaining? Trading?' said Lyra.

'Looks very like it. Buying and selling. This is an exchange, like a wool exchange or a corn exchange . . . This is where people come from our world to buy the oil.'

'But this picture . . .'

'It's extraordinary. I know nothing like it, anywhere. Not just the size but the scope of it . . . If people in our world knew about it, they'd make pilgrimages to see it. I mean, this, where we are now, is still our world, isn't it?'

'Yes,' she said with certainty. 'But the picture shows the rose world, I'm sure. The way there must be through the door at the other end. But I don't think artists from our world made this . . . Malcolm, we've got to go on. But I want to spend hours here, days, looking at everything. Copying parts of it. It's got all their life in it, everything they ever do . . . And they look happy, you know? As if everything is right and it all fits together and it all works . . . It's how things ought to be, don't you think?'

But she hadn't got it quite right, she thought. Everything she said about the picture was true, and it made her happy to look at it, but she wasn't happy because the people in the picture were happy; she was happy because it looked as if the painter had been happy with the work, and loved it, and was happy to know that other people would love it too. And she was conscious that her attention to the painting was part of its effect, as if her gaze that was speeding here and there, resting for a moment to look at a detail, then darting elsewhere, and hovering, and soaring up again, and seeing how this young couple by the lake here were forming the same shape with their arms that a pair of swans were forming with their necks over there, and marvelled at how the artist had seen it so clearly – as her attention did that, it seemed to her that her attention itself, her consciousness, was a bird flying through the landscape, in a place where it was completely at home.

Malcolm, watching her, saw how her involuntary smile dissolved the hard wariness that had been her natural expression since they had found themselves together again. Her eyes brightened among tiny creases that one day would be laughter lines, and her lips moved silently, and he realised that she was talking to the Pantalaimon who'd left her. The impression was so strong that he even found himself looking for the dæmon in the painting, and in the patterns of sunlight and shade on the floor and the walls.

They moved along the length of the building towards the far door in its painted setting of a little marble temple or folly, with a copper dome surrounded by a balustrade. A man and a woman, elegantly dressed, were painted there pointing at a little town on the lakeshore to the right, with an oratory and a campanile, a market square, a town hall, and a stone bridge.

'Ready?' Malcolm said.

'No, course not. I want to stay here for weeks. But yes, let's go through. We've got to . . . No guards here, unless they're outside.'

'Well, here goes,' he said.

He reached for the iron handle and turned it, and the door opened smoothly and silently, like the first one.

Light flooded in, bright daylight. They blinked and shaded their eyes. Asta ran through at once and stood still suddenly, her tail waving tensely. Malcolm followed and abruptly halted, as she'd done.

'Well,' he said. 'You were right. It's a different world.'

Lyra came to stand beside him.

The door opened on to a little mound, so they were able to see for some distance. The air, the atmosphere of a different world, was spring-like and warm; the sun shone brightly in the clear sky, showing a million details on the ground.

But this was not like the world in the picture.

Wherever they looked the soil had been disturbed, and was being disturbed even more: great earth-moving machines were at work, digging, lifting, flattening, carrying, dumping, scooping out rocks and soil and the plants that had been growing there, tearing huge ragged wounds in the ground and rolling back and forth along a wide road of crushed stone. Most of the plants that were now being carried through the air, their roots still embedded in great masses of soil, were rose bushes with blooms as red as blood.

There was enough of the landscape left for them to see what had been there before the earth-moving began. The painting had shown the landscape exactly, and the bones of it were there still – the mountains on the horizon, the lake at the foot of the slope in front of them, the little town on the lakeshore – but how completely it was being changed!

'What are they *doing*?' said Lyra.

Asta heard her and turned to them, and then she stopped: she seemed to see something, and turned away at once and ran to Malcolm, springing up into his arms. Lyra felt a little lurch in her heart: she wanted Pan more than ever, she wanted him to run to her and leap up just like that – but something was badly wrong here.

Malcolm was listening closely as Asta whispered something. He looked at Lyra and said, 'Be careful where you look.'

'Why? What . . . ?'

Then she saw what Asta had seen: the body of a jackdaw. Of course Lyra had seen dead birds before, but the sight of this one hit her in the pit of the stomach. It was the body of a dæmon. It was a dæmon, dead.

She gripped Malcolm's hand.

No one had ever seen the body of a dæmon. A dæmon was alive, or it was nowhere – or rather everywhere: when the person died, the dæmon dissolved into the air. Lyra had seen death; she had travelled through the world of the dead; but she had never seen a dæmon that was no longer alive.

'Oh, Malcolm,' she whispered.

Asta was pressing her face into Malcolm's neck. Lyra longed for that sort of closeness, and for Pan – Oh! And a chill as she thought: if Pan came here by himself, and had to see things like that, and she wasn't there for him . . .

All the different implications of the word *betrayal* came clustering around her, again.

'But what is this place? What are they doing?' Malcolm said.

'They're tearing up the roses . . .'

'They're changing everything. Look at the river over there.'

In the middle distance a river had been flowing in a series of short curves towards the lake. Excavating machines were tearing into the banks and swinging their bucketloads of soil high in the air before dumping them in a waiting line of trucks, which drove a little way and tipped their loads on the bare earth where a field had been. Other machines built the soil up into a straight embankment.

'They're changing the course of it . . .' Lyra said, and then, 'But why? For irrigation? What would be the point, with the river already there?'

The more they looked, the more evidence they saw of wholesale change. If the new embankment showed the future course of the river, then it would run directly towards the place where a bridge was being built to span it: two steel towers where suspension cables would carry a wide roadway. Machines whose details were too far away to see were in place at each end of the bridge. The noise they made was loud enough for Malcolm and Lyra to hear it clearly in the morning air.

'Cable-spinning machines,' said Malcolm. 'Machines and engineering and people building great structures . . . I used to love that sort of thing. But this is all wrong, somehow.'

'Is the dead dæmon . . .' Lyra began, and went on, 'I don't know what I was going to ask. That's part of it. Obviously. Is that a town over there?'

The air was shimmering a little now, as the sun rose higher.

'It looks like the town in the picture. We'll have to go there if we want to know any more.'

There was no one nearby to ask, apart from the workers operating the machines, and they were busy. Lyra looked back at the door they'd come through, and found that the great red building had vanished (of course: it was in their world, not this one). In its place was a much smaller wooden structure, with the tall black door and its decorated frame set into it like a piece of stage scenery. Behind it stood a little copse, green leaves against the bright blue sky.

Turning round again, she saw that the hill where they were standing swept down to the lake, just as the painting had shown, but now workers with their machines were busy constructing a road leading up towards the building.

'Look,' Malcolm said. 'All this activity – it's all going on because of the opening, the window, the doorway, whatever we call it. It's all centred on here. Look, see what they're doing to this road – it's going to lead right up to where we're standing, and then from the junction down there it'll go away to the east and west.'

'How can you tell? It's just a jumble to me.'

'No, they know exactly what they're doing. Get the road clear in your mind, and then it all makes more sense. There's something to admire about the scale of it; changing the whole shape of the landscape . . .'

'But . . . They're destroying everything. Not making it better.'

'They'd probably say "developing". But I agree. Let's see if we can get to the town.'

This land had supported other crops as well as roses; as they made their way across the overturned earth, Malcolm and Lyra saw torn-up orchards of apples and apricots, and a wide meadow that had been growing some kind of oil plant, Malcolm thought, and was now being cleared for the foundations of what might have been a factory or a warehouse. The air was filled with the sound of machinery; the occasional shouts of query or command were the only evidence of human life. There must be people controlling the machines, Lyra thought, but she could hardly see them. A face behind a windscreen, a man in overalls climbing down from a cab to adjust a lever, a supervisor with a hard hat and a clipboard pointing something out to a crane operator; all of them busy, no one just looking on or wandering by.

'Can you see any dæmons?' she asked.

'Yes, but not many . . . I'm not sure.'

'This might be a world where they just don't have them. Though they did in the picture.'

'What about the dead one?'

She shuddered. 'I can't take that in, can you?'

'No,' he said. 'I didn't see if she had a wound or anything. It was just as if she'd died of . . .'

'No, I don't think she was wounded. She *was* dead, though, wasn't she? Not just asleep?'

'Yes. I'm afraid so. Some disease?'

'A disease that only affects dæmons? Have you ever heard of one?'

'No. But you've seen more worlds than I have.'

'In some worlds, people don't have dæmons at all. Asta, what are *you* thinking about this place?'

'I'm thinking the same as you. I wish Pan was here.'

'Yes, but do you feel . . . I don't know: do you feel ill, or anything? Any sort of unease or weakness or something like that?'

'Not so far,' she said carefully. 'I was shaken by that poor dæmon back there . . . But look at those men laying pipes. Can you see their dæmons?'

A hundred yards or so to their left, four men were taking a break from their task of laying heavy pipes in a newly dug trench. Their crane was still and silent; the sun was reflected brightly from the smooth black material of the pipes waiting to be lifted from the back of a large truck next to the trench. The men were sitting in the shade of the crane machinery, eating from bowls with chopsticks, drinking from bottles. Nothing different from anything Lyra and Malcolm could have seen in their own world, except for the way the men's dæmons were behaving. One was a small terrier-like dog, who tried to distract his man by scratching at his knee, and kept being slapped away. Another was a thrush, who perched on a stone nearby, her head drooping, unmoving and ignored; the third was a small lizard-like creature, tucked into the man's shirt pocket, her head hanging loosely outside. The fourth was somewhere out of sight.

The men looked up as they came near, but gave them only a quick glance before going back to their food. The terrier tried again to get her man's attention; this time he punched her hard on the side of the head and she fell down and lay there whimpering. Lyra flinched. None of the others paid the least attention.

'Remember Gerard Bonneville?' said Asta.

Malcolm looked at Lyra. 'The man I stole the alethiometer from. His dæmon was a hyena. We saw him beating her with a stick. I think he'd broken her leg at some point.'

'The man who . . .'

'Yes. The man I killed.'

'I'm glad you did. D'you think he came from here?'

'No. He was just abominably cruel. People are cruel in our world too.'

'Yes, but it's uncommon. That's why we notice it. But here it seems to be just the way things are done. Automatic.'

They walked on further over the turned-up earth, making for the town in the distance. The day was getting warmer, and the sound of machinery tearing and grinding added to the oppression both Lyra and Malcolm were feeling. They came to what had been a curve in the river, where tons of mud and soil had been dumped to make a new embankment. Willows lay with their broken branches trailing in the water and their naked roots in the air; excavators dragged them whole and entire out of the mud and dropped them in the buckets of giant dump trucks, while further along another machine was dredging a new channel for the river. The air was full of the smell of exhaust fumes.

And no one seemed to see them, or shouted to them to move out of the way, or showed any interest in their presence.

'It's as if we were invisible,' Lyra said. 'D'you think if we actually spoke to someone . . .'

'We'd have to shout over the noise of the machines. And they're all too occupied with what they're doing. I'm surprised we haven't been told to clear off, though. On a site back home someone would have chased us away a long time ago.'

'And they all seem to know what to do. No foremen or supervisors giving orders.'

'Wait, there's someone. I'll ask him.'

A man with a theodolite was checking the elevation of the wooden building that housed the opening they'd come through, nearly a mile behind them now; clearly that spot was being used as a sort of reference point. The ground the theodolite stood on was being cleared for the foundations of a big building that might be an office block or a factory.

Malcolm waited till the man had taken a measurement and made a note, and then said, 'Excuse me, can I talk to you for a moment?'

The man looked round, saw Malcolm, and shrugged.

'Can you tell me what you're doing?' Malcolm said.

The man shook his head. Malcolm said it again, in French, and German, and Latin, and Tajik. Each time the man just shrugged and spread his hands. Lyra thought he looked as if he might be Persian, or Persian in her world, at least. His dæmon was a pigeon, perching unsteadily on the wooden case of the theodolite. She looked bedraggled. When Asta approached to try and befriend her, she cowered away.

Malcolm tried once more. Lyra thought he might have been speaking Greek this time, but it made no difference; the man shook his head, clearly growing impatient, and made a go-away gesture before turning back to his theodolite. The dæmon raised her wings, though, and uttered a timid coo. The man ignored it and turned back to his theodolite.

'Well, let's keep on,' said Lyra.

There was a track where the earth was slightly flatter than elsewhere, and easier to walk on. There was a bulldozer moving along from the town towards them, crawling on its caterpillar tracks. They moved to one side to give it room to pass; the driver took no notice of them.

'They're just not interested,' said Malcolm. 'Not hostile. Just indifferent.'

'Is it them, or us, though? Maybe it's us being invisible.'

'I don't think so. They can see us and hear us if they choose to, like the theodolite man. It's an attention thing.'

'And all this building . . .'

'If these were rose gardens – or fields – there must be some sort of factory fairly close. A distillery. Do you know anything about how they make the oil?'

'No, but thinking about it . . . I suppose they'd gather just the flower heads, because they wouldn't want the prickles. One of the Myriorama cards shows some young women picking rose heads and carrying them in big baskets . . . Actually, there was the same scene painted on the wall of the red building, Asta pointed it out. Then, I suppose, they'd boil them in a big vat and . . . I don't know what next. Or maybe crush them.'

'No, I think boiling would be the start.'

'And distilling, that comes into it somewhere, probably. I don't know what that means, though. Did you ever see the rosewater dishes in Jordan?'

'Enormous things.'

'I used to polish them for Mr Cawson. He said they were running out of rosewater, and it was hard to get. I think that was the first I heard of the rose business . . . I wonder how Mr Cawson is now, under the new regime.'

'I wonder how Alice is. But yes, rosewater – you'd make that, if you had lots of roses. You'd boil the petals in a big vat and distil the steam and that would be the rosewater. And the oil would be floating on the surface of the boiling water in the vat – not much of it – just drops. Intensely concentrated.'

'Would you need a big building? Like the one being built near the theodolite man?'

'Not if you did it on a local sort of scale. You could set the equipment up in an ordinary barn.'

'Mr Cawson gave me a little bottle of the rosewater, because I wouldn't be allowed to attend the Feast and that was the last of what he had . . . That was very concentrated, I remember.'

566

'I wonder where it came from. But you can see why they trade in the oil and not the rosewater.'

'Smaller quantities. Easier to carry . . .'

'Much easier. Most people who bought it might never suspect what else it could do.'

'Look,' said Lyra, pointing to an excavator tearing up the ground at the edge of a meadow. 'The sign.'

Most of the earth-moving machines they'd seen until then had borne the signs or painted names of the companies that owned them, and both Lyra and Malcolm had noticed that they were not owned by one firm alone: many different colours of paintwork, many different styles of design, proclaimed that they were owned by many different companies. Some of the names used Roman lettering, while others were painted in scripts Lyra had never seen before.

But the excavator she was pointing at now had the letters TP painted on the cabin door, together with the red-and-white rampant lion of Thuringia Potash.

'Well,' said Malcolm. 'And I thought they were failing.'

'Why?'

'I met a man in Aleppo who used to be an accountant with Thuringia Potash. The place they had there – like a factory or a research place – was neglected, paint peeling, plants not watered and so on, and I wondered why, and he said they'd closed down because TP had a big new project further east. But he didn't know what it was.'

'Well, this is further east. But . . . they couldn't get one of those machines through the opening in the red building, could they?'

'There must be others. More openings I mean, bigger ones. Or else . . .'

'Or else just the *idea* of a machine like this. I mean the plans, the blueprints, the technical knowledge. Then they could make . . . Except for all the things they'd need in place to do that.

But maybe time passes at different speeds in different worlds. I don't know. There *must* be other ways in.'

If Pan had found one of those, though, he might be anywhere. Her heart felt heavy in her breast.

'Nothing would surprise me now,' Malcolm said. 'Shall we try this man?'

The man he meant was driving towards them in a small truck with some machinery in the back of it. Malcolm stood in the way and waved him down.

As he came to a halt Lyra could see that he was some kind of supervisor: he wore office clothing, not overalls and heavy boots. He waited for them to come close, but he left the engine running. His expression was busy, patient, focused somewhere else, but polite.

Malcolm said, 'English?'

'I speak English, yes.'

'What are you building here?'

'A communications hub.'

Malcolm and Lyra exchanged a look. It was an expression neither of them had heard.

'Communications . . . Roads, railway? A canal?'

'All of that, yes.'

'What's the name of this place?'

'It will have a name when it's ready. At the moment it's just called the expressway.'

Lyra was looking for the man's dæmon, and then she saw her, lying on the floor on the passenger side. She was a mongoose, and she lay limp and still. Her eyes were open and blank.

'Is your dæmon all right?' Lyra said.

'Yes. Who are you and why are you here?'

'Travellers. We were caught in a storm and lost our way,' Malcolm said.

'Well, you can't stay here. You'd better move somewhere else. Building sites are dangerous places.'

Before they could ask anything else he put the truck into gear and drove away.

'I wasn't sure what to ask next anyway,' said Malcolm. 'This is all impossible.'

'She wasn't all right. I think she was dead, his dæmon.'

'So do I.'

They looked ahead. They were nearly at the first buildings at the edge of the town, a nondescript group of small buildings dominated by a tall chimney. There was no one around.

'Distillery?' said Malcolm.

A paved road led towards it from the churned-up edge of the nearest meadow. Rose bushes were still growing there, the first they'd seen since the ones being torn up further back.

A stone building like an open barn lay next to the road. As they passed they could see some kind of machinery inside it, still and silent. They went inside to look: a brick furnace under a large copper vessel, various tubes above it leading to another vessel, obviously a condenser, Lyra thought knowledgeably. Shelves on the barn wall carried rank upon rank of empty bottles. The air in the place smelt very faintly of wood-smoke and fuel oil and, under everything else, roses.

'As you said. Pretty simple,' said Lyra. 'No dials and pressure gauges and so on.'

'It's a simple process. They'd have used something like this hundreds of years ago.'

A wooden crate part-filled with bottles stood near a pile of other crates, all empty.

'They stopped in the middle,' she said. 'Something must have interrupted—Oh!' She'd seen the body of a desert fox, another dæmon, in a wooden bin against the wall, half smothered in decaying rose petals.

'Let's go out,' said Asta. She was still in Malcolm's arms.

'Good idea,' he said.

Outside the barn they found a woman who seemed to be waiting for them. She was old and thin, dressed in what they guessed were the clothes of a peasant, and with wild grey hair. Her expression spoke of suspicion, hope, and curiosity. In her arms she held a dæmon, a ferret, whose eyes had the same look as hers.

'Well, who are you?' she said at once, and in English. Both Lyra and Malcolm were familiar with that kind of voice: upper class, confident, brusque.

'Malcolm Polstead,' he said, 'and Lyra Silvertongue.'

'What are you doing here?'

'I'm looking for my dæmon, Pantalaimon,' Lyra said.

'He came here without you?'

'I hope he didn't. But I haven't found him yet. May we know your name?'

'I am Silvina Policastro. This is all the property I have left. My family used to own all this land, including the door into the desert. Now it is the property of a company of . . . I don't know what they are. They seem to have many names. Merchants. Development people.'

'And you grew roses?' said Malcolm.

'This soil grows the most beautiful roses in the world. Or it used to, and it would still, if they left it alone.'

'The people who are digging up the land back there?'

'Yes, those people.'

'Did they buy it from you?'

'Buy? I had no choice. I had to sell it. Choice means nothing any more.'

'May I ask about your dæmon?' said Lyra.

The old woman held him closer, and he bent his head and rested it on her breast. Her glittering eyes were fixed on Lyra's.

'We don't want to pry,' Malcolm explained, 'but this seems like a world where dæmons are not safe. Is there some sickness they catch?'

Lady Silvina looked at Asta, still in Malcolm's arms, and her wary expression melted into a tender longing. Lyra saw tears in her eyes.

'I want to lie down,' the old woman said. 'I am very tired. I don't understand much any more.'

'These development people,' said Malcolm, 'did they give you a fair price?'

'How could anyone tell what was fair? We used to be able to judge that sort of thing. We lived by trading. But they brought in this new money and everything has to be bought and sold with that now, and I can't understand it. I'm not the only one. And I'm not stupid. Value . . . We used to know about value and fairness. But now I have to pay rent to live in my own house. Who can judge things they don't understand?'

'Thank you,' Lyra said, not wanting to tire her any more.

The woman stood and watched as they left, and finally turned back to the house that wasn't her home any more.

Malcolm and Lyra walked away towards the main road. They were both thinking about the dæmon bending his head to lean on the old woman's breast.

'They're not well, either of them,' said Malcolm.

'Could it be that they're separated?'

'No. I don't think it looked like that.'

They had to step aside; a truck filled with gravel was heading towards them, making for the construction site. The driver didn't look at them as he passed.

They walked on half a mile or so, talking together. It would have been so pleasant if things were different, Lyra began to think; but it was hot, and getting hotter, and the noise of the machinery was never-ending, and their rucksacks were not getting lighter. They passed a farm, and then another with a small distillery like the one they'd just seen, deserted and empty. Before long they came to the edge of the little town, like those Lyra had seen in pictures of Alpine countries, or the Balkans, with an onion-domed oratory and a campanile and narrow streets leading to a marketplace in front of a town hall.

It was like any market in their own world; stall-holders were selling vegetables, fruit, cheese, meat, and one or two stalls offered shabby-looking household items like brushes, dusters, buckets. The awnings over the stalls were striped in colours that a long time ago had been bright, and the town hall, for all its Gothic-looking crockets and finials and spires, looked forlorn. Perhaps it was being repaired; men were erecting scaffolding around it.

'Are you hungry?' said Malcolm.

'I think I am. I'm not sure. We haven't got any local money, though. Local? What am I saying? This is a different *world*. The old lady spoke about a new kind of money, didn't she? I've got two gold coins left that Farder Coram gave me, but that's all, and I don't suppose they'd be able to give any change even if they took them. We'll manage somehow.'

That illusion held till they tried to buy a loaf of bread. Lyra proffered one of her two coins, and the woman's expression changed so quickly, and in so many ways, that Lyra was bewildered. The woman looked shocked, then embarrassed, then cautious, then furtive, and finally, with a little shake of the head, cold and unfriendly.

'Let me try,' said Malcolm.

Lyra moved back and watched as he spoke to her, easily, calmly, in what sounded like Persian. The stall-holder responded carefully at first, glancing around as if looking for some figure of authority who might stop her, but then agreed to swap the loaf for a small bottle he took from his rucksack.

'Impressive,' said Lyra. 'What did you give her for it?'

'The last of my *brantwijn*. Let's see if we can swap something for some cheese.'

A propelling pencil bought them a piece of some hard cheese like cheddar, and then a little pair of nail scissors from Lyra paid for half a dozen apples. Each stallholder was unwilling at first, and the apple-merchant took out a handful of banknotes from a wooden box and shook them angrily in Lyra's face, tapping them hard with her forefinger. It was clear what she meant: she wanted proper money, bank money. But the delicacy of the pretty scissors won her over, and she put the apples in a paper bag and thrust them at Lyra, gesturing *Go, go somewhere else, don't stay here,* looking around cautiously as the bread-woman had done.

'There we are,' said Malcolm as they left the marketplace and turned down a little street towards the lake, whose water they could see shining ahead of them.

They were looking for somewhere to sit and eat. It was getting hotter; a comfortable bench beneath a shady tree would have been ideal, but all they could see along the length of the lakeshore was work being done to build up an embankment. Excavating machines, trucks carrying away soil and other trucks bringing blocks of concrete, men working with shovels or boiling pitch: the noise was incessant, the smell of tar inescapable.

They moved on further to the right, towards a little bridge that spanned a stream flowing into the lake. The work on the new embankment hadn't reached this far, but beyond the bridge they could see more activity with machines and trucks. There was a shady tree, but although there was a stone base beneath it that had supported a bench, the bench itself was gone.

'Well, we can sit on the grass,' said Malcolm.

His coat was uncomfortable. He took it off and spread it out beneath the tree, and they sat down to share the bread and cheese.

'I can't understand . . .' Lyra began, but stopped as she realised that there were so many things about this place that she couldn't understand, it would be hard to choose what to say first.

'Neither do I. Anything.'

'Have you ever seen a place with so much building going on?'

'No, but . . .'

'But what? Anywhere like it?'

'Some parts of our world. Parts of London. Parts of Oxford, even. Paradise Square . . .'

'Oh yes. All those old terraced houses near the Royal Mail place.'

'Did you see – as we came into the marketplace here – did you see that old building covered in scaffolding?'

'I thought it was a town hall.'

'It might have been, once. There was a sign above the door, and it said it was going to be a brand-new shopping centre, developed by Thuringia Potash.'

'But there are lots of shops in the town. Isn't it already a shopping centre?'

'The old shops don't pay rent to Thuringia Potash, and the new ones will.'

'Is that how it works?'

'Always, everywhere. It's only just beginning in our world; it looks as if it's more advanced here.'

Lyra thought of Jordan College, and its new Master Dr Hammond, once of Thuringia Potash himself, and probably still involved with it. How long before it would be Thuringia Potash College?

Something was troubling her memory, but she couldn't see what it was. She thought of Malcolm describing his private aurora, the spangled ring; this was similar, she thought, but with memory. The idea was still there, at the heart of a shimmering tangle of ideas and images, but she couldn't work out what it had been.

Malcolm said something. He was looking over his shoulder at the houses across the bridge. A terrace of small brick-built houses followed the line of the stream and turned right to follow the main road along the lake shore. They looked as if they'd once been neat and well kept and comfortable, but now most of them seemed to be empty, with paint-peeling front doors and uncurtained windows. The exception was the house on the corner. There every window box was filled with scarlet geraniums, the white paint on the front door was fresh and clean, the brass fittings brightly polished.

Three men were standing outside the front door, and one of them was knocking loudly. That was what had drawn Malcolm's attention.

'They look like police or something,' said Lyra.

They wore black uniforms, and two of them had guns. They knocked again, even more loudly, so that no one inside could have failed to hear.

Malcolm slowly stood up. 'Someone's answering,' he said. 'Stay behind the tree.'

The door opened a little way and an old man looked out. His raven-dæmon sat on his shoulder. He said something; the chief of the three men listened courteously, even taking off his cap, and then began to speak himself. One of the other two stood back into the road and looked up at the windows; a curtain inside twitched across.

The old man listened to the policeman, and then said, not loudly but very clearly, 'No, I'm sorry, I'm not going to let you in. There was a general alert yesterday – didn't you hear that? We're not supposed to let anyone into our houses, uniforms or guns or nothing. You're strangers to me. I can't tell who you are nor where you come from, nor what authority you're answering to.'

The policeman replaced his cap and said something in a low voice. Lyra couldn't hear the words, but his tone sounded steady and implacable. Clearly they'd reached an impasse.

The old man replied in a couple of short sentences. There was no need to hear them: he was saying no. Then he shut the door and the policemen spoke together briefly before turning away. The chief wrote briefly in a notebook, looked at the upstairs window, and turned and led the other two away.

'Did you see their dæmons?' said Lyra.

'There was one in a pocket, half dead, by the look of her. Otherwise, no.'

'They'll be coming back pretty soon. Let's talk to the old man before they do.'

'But—'

She had already gathered her rucksack. 'We're reporters,' she told him. 'Just follow me and take notes.'

He bundled the scraps of their meal into his rucksack and did as she said, looking back along the lakefront road to see if the policemen had gone. They were nowhere in sight; all the other activity continued, untidy but purposeful.

Lyra knocked on the door. The old man was still close by, and he opened it at once.

'I told you—' he said, and then halted. He looked along the road, in both directions, and then back to her, puzzled.

'I'm sorry to bother you,' she said. 'My name is Lyra Silvertongue. I'm a journalist, and my colleague and I are interested in the way this town is changing. Have you got a moment to answer some questions?'

He looked doubtful. 'You see them policemen a minute ago? They'll be back before long.'

'Henry?' called a woman's nervous voice. 'Who is it?'

''S all right, Ethel,' he called back. And then to Lyra and Malcolm, 'Come in, then, you might as well.'

He stood aside, and Lyra saw his raven-dæmon watch her with bright eyes, and then turn to look at Malcolm. She noticed how neat and clear everything was; the only thing out of place was a bag of knitting on the hall table. The old man shut the door.

'Come into the parlour,' he said. 'We can see 'em before they get here.'

The parlour was a neat little room with a bay window from which they could see along the lakefront in both directions. There was just room for a small sofa and two chairs.

'Sit down,' said the old man. 'Have the chairs. This old sofa sags terrible. Ethel, these two people are journalists. Not police. Oh, our names are Mr and Mrs Butler.'

The old man's wife had been busy in the kitchen; the smell of baking came into the parlour with her, and she was wiping her floury hands on her apron. She was grey-haired and plump, and her dæmon was a turtle dove nestling on her shoulder.

'You from the papers?' she said.

'Yes,' said Lyra. 'Well, a news agency really. We're based in Baku, but we're travelling this way to look at conditions throughout the region.'

'What sort of conditions?' said Mr Butler. 'What d'you mean?'

'Economic conditions, among other things,' said Malcolm. 'How is your work being affected, for example?'

The old man scratched his chin. 'This new money . . .' he said uncertainly. 'Can't easily say.'

'We used to be the toll-keepers here,' explained his wife. 'Every-one coming into the town from the east, from that way –' gesturing out of the window towards the right – 'they had to pay a toll for the upkeep of the bridge. It was only a penny per traveller, double for a loaded cart or lorry. Had been for years. Paid us a wage and a living, and made sure there was enough to keep the bridge in good repair. Then this new money come in.'

'When did that first appear?' said Lyra.

She shook her head. 'Can you remember, Henry?'

'Four years ago. Everything had to be charged in tokens and roubles. They tried to call them roubles, but that didn't last. Just tokens and credits now. A hundred tokens makes one credit.'

'We didn't understand what they meant, you know, what they were really worth.'

'Roubles?' said Malcolm. 'Did it come from Muscovy?'

They looked puzzled.

'No,' said the woman. 'Just everybody seemed to be using tokens all of a sudden. No one knew where it came from. Sit down, do . . .'

Lyra and Malcolm took the chairs. Malcolm fished a notebook and pencil out of his pocket and began to make notes.

'We was told there was something called an exchange rate,' said Henry, sitting down beside his wife on the sofa. 'Never heard of that before. All the traders, the rose growers, they had to use it as well. It seemed easy when they told us about it, simple and straightforward to understand, kind of thing. But for us, you see, charging money wasn't easy when you had no change to give them. We needed change back then, coins like, for using the bridge. Everyone knew what a penny was. But tokens and credits . . . What were they supposed to look like? What did they mean? We didn't know.'

'Messed it all up,' said Ethel. 'Everyone knew the old system. Travellers all had a penny in their pockets for the bridge. It sort of held us all together, all knowing things like that. Just the habits of our lives.'

'We tried to buy some bread in the market,' said Lyra. 'Does every trader have to use the money now?'

'By law, yes. It's changed everything.'

Malcolm was writing it all down.

Lyra went on, 'Can I ask about something else? We noticed it as soon as we came into this world. Is there a sickness that affects dæmons here? Both your dæmons seem to be well. But some others we've seen even seem to have died—'

The toll-keeper's raven-dæmon suddenly uttered a shriek loud enough to hurt their ears. The old man stood up, trembling, and his wife held on with one hand to her dove-dæmon, who was uttering soft moans of fear. She reached out to her husband's hand with the other, and he took it tightly.

'What you talking like that for?' the toll-keeper said, and his eyes were blazing with anger. 'How dare you come into decent people's houses and frighten them with thoughtless things like that, lies, terrible things? En't you got any decent manners?'

His anger was directed at Lyra, and she felt shocked and frightened and guilty, though she didn't know why. She also saw that the old man was as much frightened as angry.

Malcolm turned to face him. 'My colleague meant no offence,' he said. 'Please excuse us. We've only been in your world for an hour or so. Things are still very strange to us. But if there is a condition that affects the well-being of your dæmons, we want to tell the world about it. Our world.'

'So we can help safeguard people who aren't affected yet, and maybe help cure those who are,' Lyra added.

'Where's your dæmon then?' the old man demanded. 'You might be the source of all this trouble yourself. You thought of that?'

'My dæmon left me a few months ago. He said he was going to look for my imagination, and I've been following him ever since. I'm still looking now.'

'Sit down, Henry,' said his wife. 'This maid can't be to blame any more than we are.'

'I won't have bad talk in my house,' the old man grumbled.

'No, you shouldn't,' said Lyra. 'I wouldn't either. I apologise for upsetting you. It really wasn't bad manners though. It was ignorance, but I know better now. There's another thing we need to ask about. Who's in charge of all this building work? How long has it been going on? Who's paying for it? What are they hoping to do?'

'It's all them companies,' said Ethel. Her dæmon was calmer now; he settled on her shoulder, but still hid his head in her hair. 'They make up what they call a conglomerate, but they never said what that meant. They called a meeting in the town hall, things to eat and drink, little booklet things they gave out, pictures on a screen, and speeches, and it sounded like heaven. Everything thought about. Schools for the children, parks, hospitals . . .'

'What we didn't know then was that they counted everybody there as voting in favour,' said the toll-keeper. He was less angry now, but Lyra and Malcolm could see he was still trembling underneath. And so could his wife, who was looking at him fondly and anxiously and patiently. They were still holding hands. 'So we were voting in favour without knowing it. They said later there'd been no need to take a vote officially because everyone was already in favour of the idea. Clearing old buildings out the way, setting up new roads, a new market, new systems. Knocking things down . . . This house is going, the whole terrace is going. There's going to be flats here. Small apartments for business people, and machines to take the toll automatically. And we thought we'd be here all our lives. No pension, you see, just taking the toll like we'd always done. It was like a wind was coming, a hurricane, to sweep all the old things out and replace them with new ones.'

'It was around then that the dæmons started getting sick,' said Ethel. 'People seemed to have a different feeling about them, I don't know why. Ever since I was a baby everyone had their dæmon, it was like part of you.'

'What we couldn't understand,' said Henry, 'was how people came to forget those old ways, kind of thing. As if everything they used to know had suddenly become just unwanted.'

'It was fashionable,' said his wife. 'Young people started to pretend they weren't interested in their dæmons, like it was out of date to take any notice of them. Then they just became a nuisance for some people.'

'An embarrassment,' her husband put in.

At that point, like a spark on a little trail of gunpowder, a thought in Lyra's mind caught light and raced away, and she saw herself before Pan had left her, deep in the works of Brande and Talbot and their followers, fashionably ignoring her dæmon entirely until he began to fade and weaken. It could have happened so easily.

'That's it,' said Ethel. 'Not just dæmons, either. Other things we used to rely on. You know, like the idea of helping your neighbour. Or having laws that companies have to obey, like about not building on public land. That road along the lakeshore, you seen that?'

'They're widening it. Building up the embankment,' said Lyra.

'They never got permission to do that,' said Ethel. 'That's public land. Builders used to have to apply for permission to alter public roadways, but now they just do as they want. It'll change everything.'

'And the town hall in the market square. We don't need a town hall no more, they say, because decisions about public affairs are going to be made by company boards, to save a lot of townspeople's money, apparently. So they're going to pull the town hall down and put up a hotel or a big shop or something. But it's no use talking to 'em. It's like arguing with fog. They got lawyers who—'

'There's someone coming,' said Malcolm, who could see out of the bay window. 'Police, or soldiers.'

Ethel gave a little gasp and shrank back into the sofa. Henry sat up and put his arm around her, and she turned her head into his neck.

''S all right, my old love,' he murmured. 'They won't part us. Whatever happens, I won't let 'em put us apart.'

Their dæmons, raven and turtle-dove, were whispering to each other on the back of the sofa. The old man was holding his wife closely to himself.

There was a rap at the door, very loud and very sudden.

Lyra stood up. 'I'll go,' she said.

'Lyra—' said Malcolm.

'No. I know what to say.' She left the little parlour as there came another knock at the door, louder and more impatient than before.

More knocking at the door. Lyra took off her circlet and smoothed her hair down before she opened the door.

'Good morning,' she said. 'Can I help you?'

The man was taken aback. He even stood down to the step below. 'Who are you?' he said.

'My name is Tatiana Iorekova. I am a queen of the witches of Novaya Zemlya. Who are you?'

His expression was puzzled and cautious. She could see he'd been prepared to be angry, and now didn't know what to do with the expression he'd been practising.

'I'm a security officer. Are you the . . . Is this your house?'

'No. Is it yours?'

'Where's the . . . What did you say you were?'

'The queen of the witches of Novaya Zemlya.'

He looked her up and down. 'That's not true,' he said. 'You got any identification to prove what you just said?'

'Of course I have. Here you are.'

She took out Mustafa Bey's letter. He scanned it quickly and gave it back.

'Anyone could have made that. You've got to leave here now. I want to speak to the occupiers.'

'But you didn't read the paper I gave you. You're going to claim you didn't obey the law because you couldn't read?' Lyra said. 'Will the courts be impressed by that defence?'

'No, because it won't reach the courts. Gather your belongings and go, now.'

Then Malcolm said, 'What's going to happen to Mr and Mrs Butler?' He had appeared beside Lyra without a sound.

The officer blinked and sighed. 'Did you hear what I said to your . . . friend here?'

'My colleague. Yes.'

'And did you hear me say one word about the future of Mr and Mrs Butler?'

'No.'

'That's because I don't know what's going to happen to them. And I don't know because I haven't asked, because it's none of my business. We'll take them to a transit camp, and then they can go or they can stay. They've had fair warning. If they stay here, we won't be answerable for the consequences.'

'You'd pull the house down around them?'

The officer shrugged.

'Where's your dæmon?' said Lyra.

'Dunno. Now I've told you to move out the way, because you're impeding an officer in the course of his duty.'

Lyra saw his subordinates move forward a step or so, a dozen men, all uniformed and armed. Malcolm remembered something from a very long time before, something in his childhood: an old lady addressing a crowd of soldiers, and forcing them to leave – it was the Priory at Wolvercote, of course! Sister Benedicta speaking to the officers of the court of Child Protection, who had come to take the baby Lyra away from the nuns who were looking after her – and he, Malcolm, and old Mr Taphouse the handyman, were listening as she chastised them. And now as Lyra stood on the doorstep facing the officers it was like seeing a dream about that memory, because Lyra was standing firmly, her chin high, her eyes glinting, just as Sister Benedicta had been twenty years before. *Of course*, thought Malcolm, *she wouldn't remember: she'd been a baby asleep in her cot.* But it looked for a moment as if she were consciously modelling herself on the brave old nun.

Only for a moment, though. And Malcolm thought that if Pan had been with her, she would have challenged the men, and outfaced them, but he wasn't, and she was incomplete. It was the wrong moment. He saw her flush with mortification. One or two passers-by stopped and watched in mild curiosity, but without anything dramatic to see, they soon moved on again.

'I told you to move,' said the officer in charge. 'Mr and Mrs Butler have had plenty of time to take their belongings elsewhere. You can help them, or you can leave, but you can't stand in the way.'

He stepped up to stand on a level with her. Lyra felt Malcolm's hands on her arms, and realised that she'd been trembling with passion, a dead-end passion, fruitless and empty. The officer snapped an order and the men raised their rifles. Behind her, the parlour door opened and Mr and Mrs Butler came through, slowly, arm in arm, a soldier behind them holding a rifle. They had nothing. Lyra gathered up the knitting bag from the hall table and thrust it into Mrs Butler's arms, and she held it like a baby.

At the same moment Lyra saw something clearly for the first time. It was as if a blocked channel in her mind had suddenly opened, and a rush of understanding poured through clear and free.

'Malcolm,' she said, 'I know what the alkahest is.'

34

THE ALKAHEST AT WORK

After a day's travel over sand and gravel, Pan was following Olivier Bonneville and his horse through some rough grassland that led gradually down towards the trees where the red building stood. He could see the distant scarlet roof quite clearly, and whenever he passed a shrub or a small tree he scrambled up to get a better view; but the roof was still the only part he could see.

A path through the grass was gradually becoming easier to follow. People and animals had trodden this way, maybe for many years, maybe for centuries. Bonneville seemed easier in his mind now their goal was visible, or so it seemed to Pan; he even tried to encourage the horse into a trot, though the horse would have nothing to do with it. When they stopped for a drink, just before the trees really began, Pan decided to make himself known.

He ran through the branches to the tree nearest to where Bonneville had stopped, and called out, 'Hey! You! Bonneville! I want to talk to you.'

Bonneville started with surprise and looked all around.

'Up here,' said Pan.

'You!'

'Yes, it is.'

'You fucking polecat. Where is she?'

'No idea. If she's ahead, she'll have gone into the building. If she's behind us, she won't. That's all I can tell you.'

'What do you want?'

'Well, I want to stop you killing her, for one thing.'

'I'm not going to kill her,' Bonneville muttered.

'Speak up!'

'I said I'm not going to kill her. But Delamare might, and he's not far behind us.'

'The Magisterium man. Your uncle.'

Bonneville's head snapped up again. His face was pale and angry. 'Better not get close to me,' he said.

'Oh, I won't hurt you.'

'I wasn't thinking about that.'

He shook the reins, and the horse trudged on. Pan followed through the branches. The trees were close enough now to make that easy enough.

'What does Delamare want?' he called to Bonneville.

'He wants to kill her, and he wants to blow something up. Both at the same time would suit him very well.'

'And if you don't want to kill Lyra, what *do* you want?'

'She's got my father's alethiometer. I want it back. Then I'll leave her alone and forget about her.'

'No, you won't. Her alethiometer is broken. And she's your sister.'

Bonneville slumped a little in the saddle. 'How do you know that?' he said quietly.

'I thought it was common knowledge. What I'd like to know is how *you* heard of it.'

Bonneville rode on, saying nothing for over a minute. Then he said, 'What's in the red building?'

'I don't know. I think Lyra might think . . .'

'What? What might she think?'

'It's a doorway to another world. We've seen them before.'

He scoffed. 'Think I'm stupid?'

'Well, no, but you do stupid things. Impulsive things. You should stop and think. Didn't you read your uncle's sermon? I don't suppose you were there to hear it. He certainly believes in doorways to other worlds. He thinks they're the way evil comes into this one.'

'Well, you weren't there either. How d'you know that?'

'Must have read it in some newspaper.'

Bonneville rode on. The horse was finding the going harder now; branches hung low over the path, and Bonneville sometimes had to lift them out of the way before they could pass.

After a minute or so he said, 'Common knowledge, is it? About Lyra?'

'No. She certainly doesn't know. If you want the truth, I heard it from your dæmon when you were asleep.'

'Bastard.'

His dæmon was perching as still as stone behind him.

'Do you remember your mother? Mrs Coulter?' Pan said.

'No. She was probably in it with her brother. Inventing lies . . .'

Pan, whose memories of the woman were bright and terrifying still, was tempted to tell Bonneville everything he knew; but he held back.

The horse stopped suddenly. Bonneville, who wasn't expecting that, almost fell from the saddle. 'Can you hear that?' he said.

Pan turned his head one way and then the other to locate whatever sound Bonneville had heard. There was a light wind rustling the leaves, and some sort of small bird was singing not far away, but it was a different sound that Bonneville had heard, and after a few moments Pan heard it too.

'An engine,' he said. 'From back there, the way we came.'

'Delamare and his bomb. Fuck. Can you see the red roof? How far is it?'

Pan leaped higher up the willow tree and called down 'Close. Another few minutes, no more.'

'Right. We'll push on as quick as we can. That engine's labouring – he's finding it hard going. We'll get there before he does.'

He shook the reins. The horse slouched forward.

Bonneville was urging it hard, but the horse was stubbornly unwilling to be urged. Pan leaped from tree to tree – easy now they were closer – and thought of telling Bonneville to leave the horse and go forward on foot, because they were only a matter of minutes away from the building. The trees grew too thickly for them to see anything below the scarlet roof, but Pan had the impression of immensity, and of silence too, a silence in which the air-cooled engine of whatever sort of truck or armoured car was following them kept snarling closer and closer.

Finally he leaped down as the horse passed below, and clung to Bonneville's jacket for safety.

'What you *doing*?' cried Bonneville, squirming in the saddle.

'Shut up and get down. Leave the horse to block the path and do the rest on foot. We're nearly there.'

Bonneville's dæmon raised her one useful wing in protest, but said nothing as she clung to his shoulder. He clambered down awkwardly, the horse moving a step or two as he set his foot on the ground, but he recovered and lurched forward, hitching his rucksack over his shoulder. The horse had already discovered some palatable grass beside the path and didn't seem inclined to move away from it; Bonneville gave it a pat on the neck as he followed Pan towards the red glow through the trees ahead.

Less than a minute later they came to the flagstoned area in front of the flight of steps up to the portico. Pan had had the idea that there would be guards, but his memory of Strauss's journal was hazy, and there was no one there now.

Again they stopped to listen for Delamare's engine.

'It's closer,' said Bonneville.

'Hurry up then. Open the door.'

Pan sprang to the top of the steps and looked at the twin columns, whose red paint was peeling, and at the edge of the tiled roof above as Bonneville ran up after him. The sound of the engine came clearly through the trees now: Pan expected to see it at any moment. Bonneville turned the handle, and was as surprised as Malcolm had been when it turned so easily.

'Quick,' he said, and Pan darted past his legs and into the great hall.

They closed the door at once and looked around. Pan was looking for a way out: Bonneville was just amazed. Pan saw the door at the other end of the great dim hall and ran towards it, the scratching of his claws on the wooden floor loud in the enormous silence. Halfway across, he stopped and turned. Bonneville hadn't moved; he stood looking all around and above as if struck by a revelation. There was a painting of some sort on the walls, and perhaps Bonneville was looking at that.

'Come *on*!' Pan said, as loud as he dared. The vehicle following them had arrived on the flagstoned forecourt: the driver gave a little burst of the throttle, and then the engine cut out and fell silent. Bonneville came to his senses and began to run, following Pan towards the other door.

And when Pan was nearly there, with Bonneville close behind, the door opened behind them. Light fell in, and the figure of Marcel Delamare stood silhouetted in the entrance.

Lyra and Malcolm stood and watched as the old couple came out of the front door. Malcolm was eager to fight in their defence – she could tell by the tension in his stance – but she squeezed his hand and knew he wouldn't be foolish; he'd be cut down in a moment.

Old Mr Butler leaned towards her and said quietly, 'You will tell them, won't you?'

'Everything,' she said. 'Everything we've seen.'

Mrs Butler smiled nervously and clutched her bag of knitting as they left. They couldn't march, so the soldiers had to adapt themselves to their pace as they moved away from the lakeshore and out of sight round a corner.

Malcolm was looking at Lyra. 'What next?' he said.

'I don't want to go too far away from the doorway. You know, the opening. If Pan had come through, I know he'd wait for me somewhere nearby. I just don't want to be somewhere else when he does come.'

'Good idea. Let's go back. And what were you going to say about the alkahest? You'd just seen what it was?'

'Yes! It *is* the universal solvent, just as it says in the encyclopaedia. The destroyer of bonds. Look at what's happening here – all the old ways and habits that brought people together, like bartering and trading – just dissolved. Wiped away by new ways people don't fully understand. The new roads that go who knows where but just tear up the rose gardens and knock down perfectly good houses. And—'

'What about the dæmon sickness? Is it responsible for that too?'

'That most of all! What's the closest bond there is? It's between people and their dæmons. Somehow when you're separated, like we are, the bond is still there, but this isn't the same at all. With the sickness here, people just seem indifferent. They're not interested any more. But it's not just happening here. It's every kind of bond, in our world as well. Like the new Master of Jordan, breaking the old connection between me and the college, because I was costing them too much. It sounded so reasonable when he said it. Money. They had to save money, because . . . Everything about the alkahest is *reasonable*. It's reasonable to make money, to save money . . . It's so *powerful*. Why have I never seen it before? It gets everywhere. Didn't you tell me something about Thuringia Potash – they had a branch or a laboratory or something in Aleppo?'

'That's right. They'd just abandoned it because it was losing money. And that meant that all the things that depended on it had to go too. Jobs, businesses . . . There was a café where the TP staff used to eat. Going bankrupt.'

'All being dissolved. The more I see, the more obvious it seems . . . I really think I'm beginning to see it at last. Everything having to give way to money.'

'How does Mustafa Bey fit into this idea? You trusted him, didn't you? But he was a trader above everything else. And he was building a new road, wasn't he? And running buses on it?'

Lyra rubbed her head. It was true, and it was a fine and comfortable bus, and no doubt various carriers and small traders and couriers and camel-train owners would go out of business because of it. It wasn't simple.

'I don't know,' she admitted. 'Yes, it's true, of course it is. And of course people have always knocked things down and built other things in their place. But money's different somehow. It swallows everything . . . Even the Magisterium, and the men from the mountains, even the people who wanted to destroy the roses took them seriously. They were wrong about them, but they felt they were important in themselves. But Thuringia Potash and all these other companies are only interested in the rose oil as a unit of value. If an acre of roses makes money, fine, but because the roses and the oil *themselves* aren't important, they'll tear them up in a moment. All those fields being dug up: it isn't because the developers hate the roses, it's because they can make more per acre by growing peanuts, or by building a factory.'

She was thinking this out as she said it, and she remembered Silvina Policastro, and her dæmon laying his weary head on her shoulder.

'The thing that troubles me most,' she went on, 'or one of the things . . . I'm so tired, Malcolm, I can't think straight . . . It's something like this. In making rose oil each part of the process is an end in itself. The roses are beautiful as they grow. Distilling the rosewater and making the oil are crafts worth knowing, things worth doing in themselves, things you can get better at and take a pride in. So people who did them used to have a *connection* with the soil and the seasons and the light and the weather, and they felt the sun and the wind and the rain on their skins – the alkahest will change all that. They'll soon be sitting in offices under artificial light entering figures into ledgers and account books and their dæmons will be dying beside them, and no one will care, and no one will know why.'

They were walking through the town as she spoke. Malcolm said little, but they both knew that if he did, he'd say that she was being absurdly romantic, that tending plants was hard physical work, that ledgers and account books had to be attended to as closely as rose gardens if civilisation was to work at all. Lyra felt a wide still melancholy, not anguish, not misery, but the endless grey light of a still day on a motionless sea, as she thought about what she was saying and saw more implications. It was like watching the sand darken slowly as a tide came in, along the whole length of the shore, as far as she could see, the water seeping through under everything there was, dissolving every bond.

They moved on through the town and out along the road towards the little wooden building that led to the rose exchange. Work was continuing all around; the noise of engines, of the grinding of metal on stone, of heavy soil falling into a line of trucks, was constant and all-pervasive.

Then Malcolm stopped and said, 'Your circlet . . . You were wearing it in their parlour, and you took it off as you left the room to go to the front door . . . You didn't leave it there, did you?'

After a couple of steps Lyra stopped too. She had her back to him, so Malcolm couldn't see the range of expressions that crossed her face.

'I put it in her bag of knitting,' she said after what felt like a long minute. He didn't move. 'They had nothing,' she went on. 'I couldn't do anything else.'

Malcolm walked up and embraced her and kissed her forehead. It felt to them both as if he wanted to speak, but couldn't find the words.

In fact he had all the words he needed, but now he knew he'd never say them.

Finally he lowered his arms and they stood away. She looked up to see how much further they still had to go, and settled her rucksack more comfortably, and took another step. He walked beside her.

They would be there in about five minutes, she thought.

Delamare's dæmon, the white owl, spread her wings and plunged forward off his shoulder and swept silently up into the dim open space of the great hall. Naturally she would see better than he would, and naturally both Pan and Bonneville froze in fear.

She circled high above the floor, disturbing the dust particles in the beams coming through the high windows, and Pan thought that if he tucked himself into the very corner of the hall, she wouldn't be able to reach him. Bonneville, meanwhile, knew that she was already at the limit of the distance she could reach from Delamare, and would have to return to him soon; and as she turned in a wide circle she glided lower and lower towards the man as he strode in through the doorway and out on to the empty floor.

Bonneville turned and ran as hard as he could for the far door, the one to the rose world. Pan watched the soldiers begin to drag their bomb on its wheeled sled up the last steps and through the entrance. It was too wide to come in, but under the direction of a grey-haired officer with an Emperor Franz Joseph beard, the men took out some crowbars and an axe and began to hack and tear at the door-frame.

The white owl-dæmon was back with Delamare, but she looked all around, her head turning in a moment from this way to that, her wide eyes gleaming in the dimness. When she looked at Bonneville, who had almost reached the door, Pan darted away from his corner and after him across the wide stretch of floorboards between them. Even as he ran he could see the owl's head turn again, back to him, and then with a high scream she launched herself into the air again, but not high this time: she kept low over the floor, her wings beating the dusty air in complete silence, heading directly for him.

Could he turn on the floor more quickly than she could in the air? That appalling *silence* meant that he had to keep watching her even as he ran. Bonneville had almost made it to the door. There was some sort of curious architectural decoration there, red-painted pillars, painted dragons – but the owl-dæmon ignored that and made straight for the figure with the rucksack, as he ran fast and straight, reaching towards the handle; but then the dæmon uttered a strangled cry and brought herself up sharply as she came to the furthest extent she could separate from Delamare.

Pan heard a coughing shout from behind him: Delamare himself, reacting to the dæmon's pain with his own. As the owl fluttered helplessly away from the door and back towards him, Delamare stumbled forward towards her, urging the soldiers to follow. Colonel Schreiber was uttering commands, hard and loud and clipped, and the men dragged their sled across the floor and into position hard against the door, between the red pillars – and where was Bonneville?

Pan hadn't seen him go through. Delamare was yelling in fury – because suddenly, out of the darkness at the edge of the hall, there was Bonneville.

Pan gasped and stopped still. Bonneville was fumbling with something – his rucksack lay on the floor, and his sparrowhawk-dæmon perched on it, her injured wing hanging low, while Bonneville seemed to be plucking at something in his hands. Pan was mesmerised – and then he nearly died with fear; because Delamare had come close enough for his dæmon to fly freely, and she had swooped unheard and plucked Pan up into the air. He could feel her claws in his ribs.

35

DUST AND ROSES

Malcolm and Lyra came to the door at the same moment, and she reached for the handle; but it wouldn't turn.

'It's locked!' she said.

'It can't be – there's no keyhole. Let me try.'

She moved aside and he twisted it firmly, with no result.

'You can usually feel what's going on inside a lock,' he said, 'but this doesn't feel like a lock at all. It's absolutely rigid. Can you hear anything?'

She put her head to the door. She was conscious of the warmth in the wood from the sunlight that had been shining on it, and of the slightly rough surface where a layer of varnish was beginning to peel off, and of the utter stillness beyond it.

'Nothing,' she said. 'Can you remember – when we came through a couple of hours ago, or whenever it was – was this actual door the thing that opened the way? I mean, was the door on this side or on the other side, our side?'

'All I can remember was the complete shock I had when it opened. Let me try again – perhaps there's a trick.'

He pulled the handle this way and that, trying to hear any tell-tale clicks or catches.

Asta, who'd been listening too, said, 'People who came here with oil to trade would have to be able to open the door. Unless there's a guild of doorkeepers or something who know the secret.'

'Let's try knocking,' said Lyra, and did.

But it sounded solid, as if the wood of the door was cemented fast to a wall of brick. Perhaps it was, on this side; but everything on the other side was in a different world—

'I can hear something,' said Asta.

She was standing very close to the door, absolutely still. Lyra strained to hear, but heard only the constant grinding of earth-moving machines behind her and a heavy silence through the door.

Malcolm looked up at the roof of the little wooden structure. He could reach the edge of the cedar shingles on the roof, and worked them back and forth trying to dislodge one, but they were fastened securely.

'There!' said Lyra. 'I heard it too. A man shouting.'

She pressed her head against the door again; *something* was happening through there, but nothing was clear.

Malcolm heard something too. He seized Lyra's arm and pulled her clear, and then the door exploded.

Inside, Colonel Schreiber and three of his men were killed at once. Two others stumbled away in time. Pan lay stunned on the floor: the owl-dæmon dropped him in a fit of terror because not far away Olivier Bonneville was stabbing a clasp knife deep into the throat of Marcel Delamare. The man writhed and kicked and tore at his killer's hands, and as Pan came to his senses and saw what was happening, a fountain of blood shot high into the air. Bonneville was sawing hard at Delamare's neck, his own face now a scarlet mask of hatred and terror. Then he let go of the knife and turned away sobbing as the life continued to spray out of the President of the High Council of the Magisterium.

Eventually the kicking stopped and the fountain became a trickle. In the same instant the owl-dæmon, who had been tearing at the sparrowhawk with the broken wing, vanished into a cloud of minute particles which themselves faded rapidly into nothing.

Pan gathered his strength. There wasn't much left. The fall had stunned him, and the explosion a moment later had thrown him some way across the floor, to come to rest gazing helplessly up at the distant rafters of the roof.

He rolled over and sat up trembling. 'Olivier,' he called. His voice was a thin croak. 'Olivier!'

The boy was crouching on the bloodied floor, weeping and clutching his wounded dæmon, sobbing like a little child, orphaned and desperate.

He didn't respond. Pan wanted to go to him, but the floor was a lake of blood. Where the red pillars and the ornamental dragons had been there was a mass of shattered wood and billowing smoke. The bomb had smashed everything nearby into shreds and splinters, and the opening into the rose world was crushed, obliterated, shredded to a cloud of shining fragments in mid-air.

Outside, Malcolm and Lyra lay where the explosion had thrown them, on the bare soil partway down the slope.

Their ears rang. Every sound was muffled, every sensation felt as though it was swathed in heavy cloth. Lyra's mouth had grit or sand or ash in it; she had to spit before she could make a sound, and even that was hard, because she could summon no saliva. Malcolm had fallen heavily on the hip where he'd been shot, and despite the healing of Tilda Vasara and her bloodmoss, the wound was painful.

He could speak, though. He said, 'Anything broken?'

Lyra could hardly hear him. She sat up with difficulty and shook her head, but her ears were still not functioning properly.

Her eyes were dazzled too, or else the air was filled with dazzlement. She was reminded of the *koruskati* swarming around the cavern of the sorcerer, but these particles were smaller than the ones of fire. Whatever light they had came from inside them; they weren't lit by the sun of the rose world, and some were darkened by the elsewhere they came from. Little by little Lyra realised what they must be: splinters and shards and tiny broken pieces of what was once visible through the opening – in other words, her own world. The way through was shattered.

'Oh,' she cried, 'no, no, no!'

Malcolm was struggling to get up, but his leg looked as if he couldn't move it at all.

'Lyra! What is it? Are you hurt?'

Now she was sobbing too, crying with anguish. 'Malcolm – the opening – they've blown it all up . . .'

She was trembling, trying to clear her mouth and her eyes and her ears, as close to despair as she had been under the silver guillotine at Bolvangar. Then she felt a touch on her leg. She reached out and felt the rich fur of Asta, and thought for a moment it was Pan, though she knew it wasn't; this touch was strange even though it was familiar, after her days with Malcolm's dæmon.

And Asta was speaking to her, but her words were too faint to hear.

'Asta? I can't hear you – Asta, are you safe? Are you all right?'

She climbed on to Lyra's lap and up into her arms.

Malcolm called, 'Tell her what you told me!'

'What? What?' said Lyra.

Asta pressed her face against Lyra's cheek and spoke again. Lyra felt the vibration through her bones, but the words weren't clear. Realising that, Asta pressed her paw against Lyra's breast pocket.

'What is it? What do you mean?' Lyra managed to say.

As she felt for the same place, Lyra had a vivid memory of crouching in the dim corridor of the nuncio's house, carving tiny pieces of steel away from the lock with the point of the needle, while Asta watched out for it when it fell.

'I . . .' Lyra's head swam. 'Yes. I remember. With the . . .'

And now she had to do something even harder. Her shaking hand felt through the cotton of the shirt pocket, and found the little paper bundle still in place.

'Careful,' Asta said.

Lyra heard that a little more clearly, and coughed and tried to clear her throat.

'You don't have to tell me,' she whispered hoarsely. 'Watch if it falls.'

'What are you doing?' called Malcolm.

'Cutting through. What's happening down there?'

She meant the road-building. Some of the great machines had stopped, or had throttled back their engines, but her eyes weren't focusing properly, and there still seemed to be clouds inside her vision.

Asta spoke for Malcolm: 'Some of the workers are coming up here to see what happened. About five or six men. Apart from them, it's all carrying on like before.'

'Was it very loud, the explosion? I couldn't tell.'

'Yes, very.'

'And the building . . .'

'It must have all gone.'

'Everything? All the pictures? The painting?'

'It sounded like everything falling. Everything.'

Lyra, unfolding the paper, tried to look back at where the door had been, the door and the little wooden building behind it; but there was nothing of it left. Perhaps it was just her eyes, she thought, with a wild hope. Then her fingers found the needle.

'Here. Look, I'm just going to wipe my fingers – they're covered in grit.'

She pushed the needle into the seam of her coat to keep it safe and rubbed her fingers hard on her skirt. She could hear a little better now; Malcolm was explaining something to the workmen, and then a supervisor called them back to work, and they went without any more curiosity.

'I've got to find . . . a place to start cutting,' Lyra said, removing the needle. 'Oh please . . . Don't let there be nothing at all . . . But it's so hard to see . . .'

She was talking half to herself, and Asta saw that and didn't reply. Lyra tried to stand up, only to find every limb weak and trembling, and a horrible dizziness engulfing her. Asta saw that too.

'Lyra, listen. About an arm's length away to your left there's a broken tree trunk. If you reach out you could hold on to it.'

'Don't take your eyes off—'

'The needle. I'm not.'

Lyra kept her eyes closed so as not to be overcome by the dizziness and felt out till her hand met the slender trunk.

'Right,' she said. 'Here I am. Now let's have a look.'

She steadied herself and opened her eyes. The air seemed to be full of swirling particles that might have been water vapour or motes of dust. The place where the door had stood in its frame, and where the building stood behind it, had become just another empty little piece of land, where rough grass grew between stones.

Malcolm called, 'Lyra? What can you see?'

'Not very much. Just let me concentrate.'

She tried to focus on what was close. She could see the shattered tree trunk; she could even see that it had been a willow. But the particles in the air – if only they'd keep still . . .

'Asta,' she said. 'Can you see these floating specks in the air?'

'Yes, millions of them.'

'Are they all moving? Or are some of them still? I can't tell.'

It would have been hard to see even if she had her full sight. But it did seem to her that among the myriad drifting tiny shadows and glints, there were some that didn't move.

'Not very many,' said Asta, 'but yes, some.'

'I think they might be little fragments of the thing I want.'

The bomb Colonel Schreiber and his team had been working on so assiduously had done almost everything they wanted. The opening between Lyra's world and the rose world had been smashed and scattered over an area about the size, Lyra guessed, of – well, what? Of the front quad of Jordan College, perhaps. Or bigger; she couldn't possibly tell. Or smaller; she couldn't see.

But each of those fragments, the ones that kept still in mid-air, was a tiny opening into her own world, big enough, perhaps, if she was lucky, if everything worked as she hoped, if she could keep her hand from trembling, if she didn't lose her grip – just big enough for the point of the needle.

She felt for balance and settled her hand on the tree. It was only a slender trunk, splintered at the top with the upper part trailing on the ground, but it could take her weight and keep her steady.

She let her eyes rest on the air in front of her, focusing on nothing yet, just letting the little specks drift and float. When she saw one that definitely didn't move, but simply hung there, she blinked – and lost it.

'Don't hurry,' said Malcolm's voice.

'Oh! Where are you?'

'Behind you. Don't look round. Keep your head still.'

'You know what I'm looking for?'

'Asta told me. I'm looking for these things that keep still. I can see a few of them, but one blink and they're gone. What's the best thing I can do?'

'Just stay close and catch me if I fall. I'm very dizzy.'

'I will.'

'Are *you* all right?'

'Fine.'

She let her awareness drift together. Remembering what Giorgio Brabandt had told her about seeing the secret commonwealth, she relaxed her attention as much as she could and just watched the air.

And part of her mind knew that it all might be a fool's errand. She'd cut through wood and steel with the needle, but those things were in her world, and stayed there. She'd never actually cut through into another, as Will had learned to do. And the holes, the tears and the gashes left by the explosion were so small – maybe she wouldn't be able to put the needle into one even if she could see it – and perhaps the bomb had torn open the way into another world entirely—

No, that was her mind wandering.

Just find one speck that doesn't move in the air. That's all for now.

So she tried again. She could never have thought how hard it was, because concentrating on just one thing was impossible, but she mustn't think of anything else.

Except . . .

If Pan was there, close by in the other world, their own world, perhaps he'd be able to hear her.

So she said, 'Pan? Are you there?'

Only the ordinary sounds of the morning went on, the noise of the machinery above everything else. But there was still birdsong: she could hear that too. And voices? Were those voices, talking? Perhaps it was just the workmen further down the slope.

She tried again, more loudly, and Malcolm joined in: 'Pan! Pan!'

She closed her eyes to hear better and called again.

Was that a responding voice? That faint distant cry?

'Pan! Pan!' She gestured to Malcolm not to call: she needed to hear Pan, as faint as he was, and he needed to hear her voice clearly, above every other sound. 'Pan!'

And then, the one thing she wanted above everything else in the world, her dæmon's voice: 'Lyra! Here, Lyra!'

'Stay there! Pan, don't go away! Stay where you are!'

Every nerve in her body was shivering. She peered through streaming eyes at the place in the air where his voice seemed to be coming from. Everything shimmered, nothing kept still. But there was his voice again: 'Lyra, Lyra, I'm here!'

'I'm coming, Pan! Promise! I'm right here! Just looking for the right place . . . Don't go away, whatever you do!'

There was one of the little torn gaps – a bit larger than most of them – and light was moving behind it, but such a small thing, no wider than the tip of a fingernail before it was filed. And no, she'd lost it again; but yes, there it was . . . She tried to line it up with things behind it, the edge of a group of trees, the windscreen of that red bulldozer further down, the corner of a stone wall around a distant field across the lake . . .

Yes, there it was, and it hadn't moved, and she could find it again.

'Nearly there, Pan . . . Can you still hear me? Are you there?'

'Still here.'

'I'll try again . . .'

Bracing herself against the trunk of the toppled willow, she reached out, supporting her wrist with the other hand, and placed the needle point precisely into the tiny gap. It slipped away – but that was because her other hand, still hurting from the assault by the soldiers in the train, was painful to keep in that position. She let it hang before lifting it up again, and she heard herself uttering a long low moan of weariness and pain, but shut it down and gritted her teeth and lifted the needle once again, found the spot at once, and cut down as far as she could reach.

And the air opened, and there was her own world, and Pantalaimon tumbled through and into her arms.

36

An Incident by the Lake
at the Moon Festival

S he fell backwards, and he fell with her, and then they were
kissing and kissing, just as Nur Huda had told her they must
do. Asta was somewhere close, and so was Malcolm, but for her
there was only Pan, and she loved him, the dæmon of her heart,
the missing part of her she'd crossed the world to find.

She tried to say the words clearly, but couldn't. 'Are you
hurt?'

'No – just knocked sideways – are you safe?'

'Yes – and is that still our world in there?'

'Yes. But the red building – it's in pieces. So much has changed,
Lyra—'

'It's changing here too. It's all . . . I must make that opening
bigger. So we can get back, and all kinds of reasons—'

'Is that Malcolm? Is he here?'

'Pan,' said Malcolm from close by, 'what's happening now?
Who's there?'

'The soldiers are dead. Delamare is dead. Olivier . . .'

'Bonneville?' said Lyra. 'Was *he* there?'

'Yes, but he's gone, I think. Lyra, I don't know how to begin. I found out so much that's surprising – things we never suspected – it's hard to believe now, some of it. What are they doing here? Building roads? What is this place?'

'It's all changing. Everything's changing, Pan. I can't think clearly.'

'There's so much to say. Who's that? Do you know them?'

He was looking down the slope towards two figures, a man and a woman, who were walking up towards them: Abdel Ionides and Leila Pervani.

Lyra cried his name with pleasure and tried to run towards them, but found all her limbs so weak it was hard to balance. Ionides caught her before she fell.

Olivier Bonneville had been dazed by the explosion, but not knocked unconscious. His senses came back to him, mostly, as he held his wounded dæmon to his heart and felt along the bloodied floor trying to work out which way was upright. His dæmon shrieked with all her power and alerted him to the great landscape that was about to fall on his head. He looked up and scrambled away to a bare space somewhere in the middle of where the building had been, where the sun shone in through the bare rafters on his bloodied hands and his gasping throat.

He coughed and spat and wiped his mouth and then saw the blood. He must have wiped it all over his face. Where was Delamare? Dead, dead, gone. Everything was over.

His dæmon was crying somewhere behind him.

'All right, sweetheart, all right, my love, I'm here . . . I'm coming . . .'

The explosion had hurt her too, and she was already wounded. He tried to stand up, and found more blood trickling down his face: his own, it must be. What was hurting? Was he cut somewhere? Yes, his scalp was torn, and now he realised it, the pain redoubled. So the blood – was it his after all? He wiped it out of his eyes with a wrist.

He reached out a trembling arm and the hawk-dæmon clawed her way up to his shoulder. It was enough to feel her there; they didn't need to talk.

He listened . . . For what? For any sign of life. Voices, he thought, there would be voices if anyone was alive, but he couldn't hear any. The tumbled wooden walls creaked and settled here and there. There was even some kind of bird singing outside.

He tried to remember exactly what had happened. He had cut Delamare's throat. The man had looked him full in the face, but his power had flowed away with the blood; it was just a mask that watched him, and Bonneville had laughed. Meanwhile that preposterous colonel figure with his absurd imperial beard had blown himself and his clockwork soldiers to smithereens, and good riddance.

But the girl . . . Was she inside the building when it blew up, or outside? There was a moment – maybe he'd dreamed it in a temporary coma – when he seemed to see her and that polecat-dæmon hugging and kissing. The sun was shining on them: so outside, probably. And the dæmon had been in the building a minute earlier. Damn it, they'd come part of the way together. So he must have got out, and therefore Colonel Puffgutz's bomb must have worked, and blown a hole between the worlds.

Carefully, so as not to fall over, and to avoid setting off a minor avalanche in the shattered walls, Bonneville picked his way towards where he thought the door had been.

Lyra's head was still ringing. Everything she tried to hear was muffled; the air was still thick with the dust from the explosion. She held Pan close as explanations flew back and forth between Malcolm and Ionides and Leila; it was easier not to listen, so she and Pan whispered murmurs of love and relief and silly happiness. Maybe everything would still be difficult and dangerous, but for the moment she was content to rejoice in her dæmon again.

The others were speculating about whether it would be safe to go through back to their own world; perhaps they should prepare for danger there, and stay away from the opening till it was clear what was on the other side.

And here in the rose world the sun was shining and the machines were silent. A few workmen or supervisors were moving here and there, taking measurements, making calculations, writing notes. But citizens of the place were out as well, children clambering over the heaps of earth and gravel, parents keeping them away from the still machines, pointing to this or that mountain or boat on the lake or meadow that had changed since they last saw it. Down in the town itself, preparations were being made for a carnival or a festival of some kind: flags flown from the public buildings, chairs and tables set out on the pavements where there had been none the day before, strings of lights laced through the branches of the trees growing by the roadsides. At the harbour, people were building some temporary structure, but it was too soon to see what it was going to be.

As the land heated under the warm sun, cool air from the lake began to move gently up the slope of the hill and bring with it something of the festival atmosphere of the town. Lyra and Pan felt it clearly, and so did Leila; Malcolm and Ionides were deep in conversation about politics, possibly, or maybe they were talking about physics. They all wandered downwards, drawn by the sounds of voices and hammering and laughter.

Olivier Bonneville looked around, curious and careful. They were tearing up the ground everywhere he looked. Somebody was making money from this, and no mistake.

But there wasn't much he could tell from earth-moving machines: they were the same everywhere. The only problem here was why they'd stopped. He needed to look at people, and walk around among them, if he wanted to find things out. He was good at reading faces and characters. He could get information from people without their knowing it – as in the Café Cosmopolitain in Geneva, where he'd first discovered the close family connection between Delamare, and Lyra, and – he now realised – himself. He thought about the skilful way he'd questioned those three journalists drinking after the Magisterial Congress, and smiled with pleasure. He'd be able to find out a great deal about this place, and with very little trouble.

Down there in the town, people were building a low platform by the harbour, with seats around it and chairs and some other things being set out. He took a few minutes before he recognised the 'other things': music stands. It was a dance floor. And strings of flags were being hung up, and cables with coloured lights. From up here on the hill, Bonneville couldn't tell very much: he needed to go and mingle, talk, find something to eat and drink.

Nobody seemed particularly interested in the wooden building, or in the explosion that had destroyed it. A few individuals had made their way up to look at it, or were making their way now, but with a desultory sort of air, as if it had never been all that interesting even before it was blown up.

'He never said anything about this place to us,' said the sparrowhawk-dæmon. 'I suppose he didn't know much, mind you. If no one was allowed through.'

'Anybody'd think we were invisible here,' said Bonneville. 'No one's looking at us, even.'

'They might be afraid of us. You've got blood all over your face.'

'Shit! You should have told me.' He felt his face with hands that were bloody too.

'Don't do that! You're making it worse. Look, there's a stream . . .'

A little trickle of more-or-less clear water ran under the road through a culvert. Bonneville scrambled down and splashed his face and cleaned all the blood he could see off his hands.

'Is that better?'

'Under your jaw, there . . . That's better.'

It would dry soon. They moved on and passed an inn, or some kind of drinking-place, with a bench outside where two old men were smoking and talking.

'Good day,' Bonneville said. 'Bonjour. Guten Tag.'

'Good day to you, my boy!' one of the old men replied. The other raised his beer glass in greeting.

'Excuse my ignorance, but I'm a traveller who's come a long way, and I'm interested to see what's going on. People seem to be preparing for some kind of celebration, is that right?'

'Absolutely correct!'

'Don't they celebrate the full moon where you come from?' said a man with a long clay pipe.

'The full moon . . . I see. Well, no, as a matter of fact. This is new to me. Music and dancing, by the look of things.'

'Where are you from, then?' said the other man.

'Basel. Switzerland.'

'Come to buy rose oil? You're out of luck, if you are.'

'No, just travelling, looking at things, writing a bit.'

He looked at the dæmons of the two old men. One was an aged poodle, grey and bony, asleep on the bench. She raised an eyelid to look at Bonneville and then closed it again. Another was a starling, head drooping on the man's shoulder.

'All this earth-clearing going on,' Bonneville said, 'what are they building here?'

The smoker shrugged. The other shook his head slowly. 'Doesn't concern us, really,' he said. 'Won't make no difference.'

Bonneville nodded, as if agreeing with this shrewd assessment.

'Cheerio, then,' he said, and walked on.

The smoker waved his pipe, and they fell silent until Bonneville was out of hearing range. His dæmon, looking back, saw the smoker say something, and the other man laugh.

Lyra and Malcolm and Ionides and Leila Pervani felt strangely awkward, like people invited to meet together for the sole purpose of – meeting together. But the sun was warm, and the machines were silent, and human conversation was pleasant to hear. By mutual agreement they didn't go back at once through the opening

Lyra had cut and into the ruins of the red building, though Malcolm privately took care to mark in his mind exactly where the opening was, lining up this rock and that bush and a high point in the hills across the lake. Ionides saw what he was doing.

'Miss Silver cut that opening?'

'Yes. Did you ever see her doing something like that?'

'She cut me out of a prison cell. But not into another world. Good idea to fix in your memory where it is.'

'You were doing the same,' said Malcolm.

Ionides said, 'Course! I am her personal sorcerer. Have to look after her. She won't remember where it is, that opening, not exactly. Very hard to see.'

They looked back. It was almost invisible.

'Are you and your friend intending to stay in this world, or to go back?' Malcolm asked after they'd moved on, following Lyra and Leila Pervani.

Ionides held back for a minute or so before answering. Malcolm watched: he was genuinely thinking it over.

'We used to work together, me and her,' Ionides said eventually, 'at the University of Alexandria. Physics. Different approaches, but all the time Rusakov and his field and his particles. We found some things that made it dangerous for us, and eventually we had to escape.'

'What sort of things?'

'We were treading on the edge of many-worlds theory, and also consciousness. It began to be inevitable that we would discover something forbidden, never mind that it was true. We had seen samples of the rose oil, we had seen some of what it revealed, we had heard of this rose trade and the strange place it was carried on. We were eager to get to this place and the red building you had to pass through to get here. But the university authorities fixed a scandal and forced us out. We went separate ways, so now here we are, and I earned the honour of becoming personal sorcerer to Miss Silver on the way. And now we shall stay and work. But all this construction . . .'

He gestured around. His expression was doubtful and anxious.

'I don't think the developers are interested in roses, or consciousness, or the Rusakov discoveries,' said Malcolm. 'What they want is money. It makes everything dissolve. If they think they can make money out of your work, nothing will stop them. Incidentally, Lyra has decided that the Rusakov field is now going to be called the Rose Field.'

'That right? Well, she is a queen of the witches. Whatever she says must be.'

For the rest of the day Bonneville thought and acted like a shadow. It was another thing he was good at, he thought: silence and obscurity. He stole some salami and an apple and sat to eat them at the harbour, at the end of a little alley, watching every face he saw. If he had a table and a chair he would have consulted the alethiometer, which lay in his knapsack silent and still, and full of information. He thought more than once of taking it out anyway and just holding it, turning the wheels, watching the needle swing on its own path, stopping and returning and moving on. It was beautiful to watch even if you didn't understand it.

But he would have been too conspicuous. People liked to look at it; they were curious, they asked questions, they wanted him to tell their fortunes. It would draw attention without giving him a chance to read it properly. It would make them remember him. It had to stay out of sight.

And all the time he scanned faces, not staring, not keeping his gaze on one particular girl, not letting himself be noticed. Just looking lightly, glancing, resting a moment, looking away; and sometimes back again, if he thought those eyes had a similar brightness, or that hair a tint of hers, even under that dark dye; or those light movements a touch of her supple strength; or anything about her at all that brought the name *Lyra* to his mind.

Why was she called that anyway? Whose idea was it? What did it mean?

Never mind. Didn't matter. She was here. He'd see her eventually. And that hefty red-haired bastard, and the beggar with the scar who'd fooled him so completely, and the woman from the nuncio's house in Aleppo who'd seen him humiliated. All around him people were hanging up lamps, bringing more chairs and tables for the dance floor, setting up booths and stalls around the edge of the harbour, even decorating boats with garlands of flowers and coloured flags.

The little alley was all very well for a few minutes, but Olivier couldn't sit there all day. Beyond some brimming dustbins opposite him there was a door, which he guessed opened out of the back of a cheap café, because at one point the door opened and a girl in an apron tipped a basin full of potato peelings over the nearest bin before slamming the door as she went back inside.

But the door bounced, and didn't catch. It hung open a little way, and Olivier could see a flight of wooden stairs inside, so he stood up quickly and darted in without pausing to think.

The kitchen was straight ahead; the stairs were on the right. He ran up the flight with light feet, and found a dirty store room cluttered with broken chairs, sacks of rice and potatoes, a rack of apples, and best of all a window overlooking the busy harbour.

He'd eaten, he was hurt, and he was tired. He found a spot near the window, found a chair that worked, propped himself up more-or-less firmly, and watched the activity outside. She'd go past eventually, and then he'd follow her.

Pan and Lyra said little during the day, because much of what each had to say was only for the other, and it wasn't until much later, after they had all eaten together, that the girl and her dæmon could talk as they needed to, together and alone.

They sat on a grassy bank at the edge of the lake, with the town at their right and a ridge of mountains some way off to their left. Ahead of them across the water, the tops of the tree-robed hills were already turning silver as the moon rose from behind the little hill where the rose exchange, and the opening into Lyra's world, had stood.

They could hear snatches of music and bursts of laughter and the murmur of conversation from the town

'Tell me again about Olivier Bonneville,' Lyra said. 'I just can't get it clear. It's too strange altogether.'

'He said Mrs Coulter was his mother – he just found out. And something about Delamare and lies.'

'Our brother . . .'

'Half-brother.'

'Well . . . same thing, almost. Who was his father? Oh – wait a minute – of course, Malcolm knew him: the man Gerard Bonneville, in Wolvercote. Apparently he used to beat his dæmon. Then later on Malcolm killed him. When we were too young to understand anything.'

'Remember what a shock it was to learn who *our* parents were . . . '

'Finding out from the gyptians . . . People ought not to do that. To keep children from knowing things, I mean. They should tell the truth.'

They sat quiet for a minute. Along the shore to their right, coloured lights were coming on, and short snatches of music, like three or four bands tuning up, came to them over the water.

'Where did you look for my imagination?' she asked.

He looked at the moon, just clear of the hills. She followed his eyes.

'Like Orlando looking for his lost wits?' she said. 'Was that what gave you the idea?'

'Well . . . It began as a figure of speech. I was exasperated. I didn't mean it literally at first. But then I was committed to it and I didn't want to stop. And it might have been true.'

'What, that my imagination was . . .'

'Missing. Or you didn't trust it. Or you tried not to believe in it. And *that* was true.'

'Yes. I think it was. Pan, if we hadn't been able to separate, we'd have been joined together hating each other for ever.'

'Well, how wise you were to abandon me in the world of the dead.'

'It was the worst thing I ever did.'

'But you had to. I can see that now. You know the old Master knew you were going to do it? Malcolm told me.'

'How could the Master know that?'

'The alethiometer. It said you were going to be involved in a great betrayal.'

Lyra felt something fall across her face, something small and light: a leaf. She caught it and sat holding it. 'Well, I'm glad I didn't know,' she said.

'It would have been impossible for us to know something like that. Impossible to live with the weight of it. He was clever, the old Master.'

'Remember that dinner with the new one?'

'The pharmaceutical executive. What a smooth diplomat he was.'

Lyra shredded the leaf and let the pieces fall on the grass.

'This is the wrong time of the year for leaves to behave like metaphors,' Pan said.

'But they do. Everything does, all the time.'

'Was the gold circlet Malcolm made for you a metaphor, then? Where is it, by the way? I haven't seen it on yet.'

'It was lovely,' she said. 'As beautiful as the alethiometer itself, almost. But . . .' She told him about the old couple who'd kept the bridge, and what she'd done with the circlet. 'I had to,' she said. 'It was just fair. And the way they . . .' She had to swallow hard. 'Just the way they sat there, on their old sofa, side by side and holding hands, and I could see how much they loved each other and how completely he relied on her and she relied on him, and how they . . .' She sobbed, suddenly, surprising herself, and finding it hard to carry on. 'So then I thought if I hid the circlet in her bag of knitting, they'd at least have something to sell and a bit of money to live on for a while. But I had to tell Malcolm and I don't think he was . . . I don't know.'

'I watched him making it. He told the gryphons he was an artificer from the realms of gold, and he proved it.'

'One day I'll explain to him . . .'

'But you have done.'

'I mean . . . . I don't know what I mean.'

'You know when he saved us in the flood – I mean, you know *about* it – well, apparently a witch came to the Thames, in the flood, to look at him. We were asleep, but she looked at us too. He told me. And just recently, when Malcolm and I were imprisoned by the gryphons, she came again, because he was there.'

'The same witch?'

'Yes, the same one. She cured the wound in his leg. She asked me if you and Malcolm were in love.'

'What? What did you say?'

'I said I couldn't imagine it, and in any case he was in love with Alice. He should marry Alice, really. Ideal. We'll have to put the idea into his head.'

'How did you know that?'

'Just thought of it.'

'You know, he was in love with her twice, when he was younger. He told me how it happened.'

'Well, there you are. He knows how to do it.'

Olivier dozed for some of the time in the little storeroom, and woke in the late afternoon to see her in the road below. She was with the red-haired man, Polstead; they'd stopped to buy ice-creams. It was a shock to see her, but there she was, no doubt about it.

He ran down the stairs silently, and watched them from the alley, and followed when they moved on. The town was busy, like any waterside town during a holiday in good weather. The streets were crowded; anyone who'd only seen the place when the construction was going on would have had no idea how cheerful the place could be during a festival. It wasn't hard to keep Lyra and Polstead in sight while not being seen himself. As the sun set and darkness gradually filled the streets, it became even easier.

The first coordinated piece of music sounded from the town, where all the lights were glowing and people were now dancing at the harbour's edge. Lyra swayed, just a little, in time with the tango from the band – or bands, for soon another one joined in with a faster dance, and the two groups played quite happily together, if not at all in tune. It seemed to Lyra that the dancers were expressing something about the night and the town and the moon as they swayed and swung around the little dance floor in the harbour, and about more things too.

Pan took up her thought. 'As if they're saying yes, strangers are digging up the roads and knocking down the buildings, and things are changing everywhere, but still a tango is a tango . . .'

'And that swing the strings do as they climb the scale, and the trumpet above them holding on to the long note and then all plunging together down when the bass changes the rhythm . . . They love that. You can hear they do.'

'The band loves it too. Look at the conductor. Can you see him? Never seen such a show-off!'

'But listen to how he holds the beat back just a tiny bit and then releases it again – he's really good. I don't care how much he shows off.'

They listened, and Lyra swayed. She felt her whole being inhabiting the rhythm.

After another chorus she said, 'I wonder if we can hear Dust as well as see it. It's just another sense, after all.'

'We haven't worked out what Dust is yet.'

'We have, almost. Mr Ionides used to study it. The Rusakov field – the Rose Field – he was explaining about fields and particles and how each one is an aspect of the other, sort of—'

'Look at it one way and it's a field, look at it another way and it's a particle, you mean?'

'I did say *sort of.* But he began to say something else, about consciousness. Then he stopped and asked about Karamakan. I wonder, though . . .'

The tango came to an end, and the dancers clapped and cheered, and Lyra could hear that the other band had been playing a waltz, but they worked quite amicably together. And soon they were both playing again, and more people had joined the dancing.

'Is Dust there if we're not there to see it?' said Pan.

Lyra had to think. 'I don't know,' she said finally. 'If there'd been a way to discover that, I think they would have done it. But I think we might have been confusing things.'

'Why? What things?'

'The Rose Field and Dust.'

'Now *I'm* confused.'

'Well, a few minutes ago I thought that the dancers were expressing something about the night and the town and the moon, that they were sort of saying what those things would say if they could dance. But perhaps the night and the town and the moon *were* saying things, and using the dancers to say it.'

'And us? Are we just looking at it and . . . being conscious of it?'

'But no, wait . . . I saw something then about imagination too.'

'What?'

'Maybe it doesn't come out of the Rose Field, it comes out of us. It happens when we see it. The Rose Field needs it in order to be seen.'

'You mean it's Dust?'

'Yes, I think it is. It's our response to the Rose Field.'

'And the Rose Field needs it . . . Well, what's the Rose Field then?'

'It's really there, around everything. It's everything being conscious. We're all bathed in it, everything conscious, and everything *is* conscious. It's . . . it's what metaphors do, when they show us connections between things. And the way we see them is Dust. Dust is what happens when our imagination touches the Rose Field.'

'So it wasn't a wild goose chase.'

'Doesn't seem like one now. We've got it, Pan, we've got it.'

Another round of applause came from the dancers, and Lyra and Pan laughed.

'It works both ways,' said Pan. 'Betcha.'

'What d'you mean?'

'Suppose the Rose Field depends on Dust as well. Without Dust it just sort of lies there, sort of inert. But we think about it, and that's our imagination, and the Dust flows through it and fertilises it, like pollen, and it all comes to life.'

She said, 'Yes!' and clapped her hands.

He rolled over on the grass and yawned and stretched. 'And the Myriorama,' he said. 'You were going to tell me about that.'

'So I was. But it's dark.'

'There's plenty of light.'

'Well, all right . . .'

She found the cards and began to spread them out. Pan watched closely.

Behind her, Olivier Bonneville said quietly, 'Sister.'

All her nerves seemed to jolt at once. She dropped a card and swung round to look at him. Pantalaimon bristled and sprang into her lap. The light from the festival, the coloured lamps and the spotlights and the mirror ball, was all coming from behind her now, and her expression would have been hard to see if it weren't for the rising moon, whose plain silver light shone over his shoulder and full into her eyes. Her face was brimful of emotion.

'Well, brother, then,' she said shakily.

'All right if I join you?'

'Go ahead.'

The first time she'd ever seen him, in an alethiometer reading using the new method he'd invented, she had thought he was Will. A similar build – similar hair – but then he'd turned round, and it was obviously not the Will she'd loved, but someone else, defensive, sullen, threatening. The second time had been during the brief but ferocious struggle they'd had in the Brazilian Embassy garden in Aleppo. Those were the only glimpses she'd had of this shadowy figure, this secretary or agent or whatever he was, this son of the abominable Gerard Bonneville, the man whose dæmon was a three-legged hyena: the man whom Malcolm had killed to protect her and Alice.

And now here he was, picking up the card she'd dropped and handing it back before sitting down cross-legged and comfortable close by. He was thin and his clothes were dusty and ragged, but he had the sort of clear-cut good looks which would go well with expensive tailoring and a fashionable setting. That was how she put it to herself at first, but – perhaps because the moon was behind him, and the light illuminating his face came from the town, multi-coloured and inconstant – she saw layer upon layer of expression and subtlety, sorrow and pity, hope and understanding, in the eyes that looked back at her.

'When did you find out?' she said.

'Not long ago. The alethiometer would never tell me when I was younger. It kept still and didn't move when I asked about that, or about her, our – mother . . . Did you know her?'

'Mrs Coulter? Yes, briefly, when I was younger.'

'Is she dead?'

'Yes.'

'And you called her Mrs Coulter.'

'What did you call her?'

'I didn't call her anything. I didn't know the woman I thought was my mother wasn't. But I have an early memory, of a woman singing to me, and I wonder now . . .'

Lyra thought of the night on the Smyrna ferry, singing nursery rhymes to the child who'd been saved from the wreck.

'My real mother – I mean the person who mattered most – was a barmaid called Alice,' she said.

Pantalaimon had been braced for attack, or defence, all the time he'd been on her lap; now he relaxed his muscles and flowed down on to the grass. Olivier's hawk-dæmon watched from where he'd set her, on his knee. She inclined her head, and Pan moved cautiously towards her. Lyra and Olivier both watched as their dæmons touched, nose and beak, and then Bonneville lifted her gently down on to the grass.

'What are you playing?' he said, indicating the cards.

'Oh, it's not a game. It's a story. But you have to fill in the words.'

'And the alethiometer? I know it's broken.'

'It was stolen by a gryphon. We've got a few bits, and the movement is all there. Malcolm's going to mend it.'

'Malcolm. Oh yes. I came across him in a bazaar somewhere. D'you think it can be mended?'

'If anyone can do it, he can.'

He nodded. He watched the two dæmons, talking together very quietly a yard or two away. Then he turned back to Lyra.

'What's the story then?' he said. 'The one on the cards.'

She handed it back to him. It showed a man in a long cape, riding a horse through a forest, clutching a small bundle against his breast.

'*Erlkönig*,' he said. 'I know this story.'

'What story?'

'*Wer reitet so spät durch Nacht und Wind, Es ist der Vater mit seinem Kind.*'

'I still don't understand.'

'It's a poem. And a song. It's a father with his child and the father wants to keep him safe, but the Erlking whispers to the boy promising all kinds of things, and by the time the father gets home, the boy is dead.'

'I think I've heard the song.'

'I used to think I was the boy.'

'Oh . . . How old were you?'

'I suppose young enough to be frightened.'

'And your father . . .'

'No, I didn't think it was him. It was someone else. Have you got the rest of the story there?'

Lyra held out the pack. 'Take a card.'

He took one and held it up in the moonlight so they could both see it. It showed a girl on the bank of a river, or a lake, reaching out to take a letter from the hand of a boy in a boat.

'You have to carry on the story using what's in this picture,' she told him.

'Oh. Well, she's the Erlking's daughter. The boy isn't the one from the poem, because he's dead.'

'Who is he then?'

'He learned the poem at school. He always wanted to see the Erlking's daughter, but he only half believed it was true.'

'What's in the letter?'

'We won't know till she does.'

Lyra put the card back in the pack.

'Well, that's how it works,' she said.

He stood up and took something out of his pocket. In the multi-coloured fairground light, Lyra saw that it was a heavy clasp knife. The dæmons stopped whispering together and raised their heads to watch as he stretched out his arm behind him and then hurled the knife as far as he could into the lake.

'That's over,' he said, and sat down again.

'What are you going to do when you get back?' she said.

'Get a job. All I know is the alethiometer. Someone'll pay me to read it for them. I want to find out more about the new method. There's a lot to discover.'

'I want to ask you about that . . .'

'And what are you going to do?'

'Go on telling stories, I expect,' said Lyra.

THE END

Like as a ship, that through the Ocean wide
Directs her course vnto one certain cost,
Is met of many a counter winde and tyde,
With which her winged speed is let and crost,
And she herself in stormy surges tost;
Yet making many a bord, and many a bay,
Still winneth way, ne had her compasse lost:
Right so it fares with me in this long way,
Whose course is often stayd, yet neuer is astray.

Edmund Spenser, *The Faerie Queene*, Book IX, Canto xii, 1

Acknowledgements

The debts I owe to these people, and to many more who will have to remain unnamed till I find their names in my notes and files, are uncountable and in some cases lifelong. To list them all and express my gratitude in full would take up more paper than the story does. I was going to note which of these friends is no longer alive, but as that list grew longer I changed my mind about it: they are still alive in my memory, all of them, and their influence remains.

Andrew Parker, Anthony Hinton, Bill Laar, Brian Mountford, Caradoc King, Carlo Rovelli, Caro Fickling, Chiara Marletto, Chris Wormell, Christine Baker, David Deutsch, David Fickling, David Sturgeon, Dinah Birch, Enid Jones, Eryl Williams, Glyn Williams, Gordon Dennis, Graham Chainey, Heidi Lightfoot, Helen Cooper, Iain McGilchrist, Ian Beck, James Hawes, Jonathan Kingdon, Jude Pullman, Julia Bruce, Kristen Poole, Laurie Frost, Liz Cross, Merfyn Jones, Millie Hoskins, Nancy Siscoe, Neil Philip, Peter Bailey, Philip Goff, Richard Eeles, Ronald Arnold, Rosie Fickling, Rowan Williams, Ruth Knowles, Sue Cook, Suzie Sheehy, Tim Brighouse, Tony Merrifield.

At the beginning of this book we meet briefly the character Nur Huda el-Wahabi, whom we met in *The Secret Commonwealth* and whose name I borrowed, at the request of those close to her, to commemorate one of the victims of the appalling fire at Grenfell Tower in 2017.